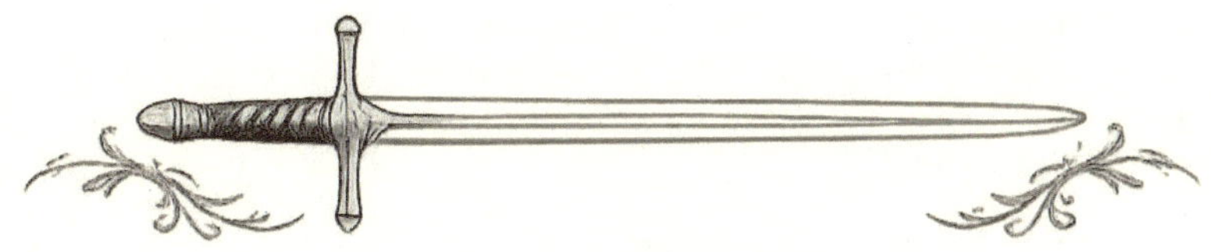

# THE FORGED HEART

First edition.

Cover design by the author.

Map illustration by the author.

*For vedrānos.*

## The Western Continent of Veridion

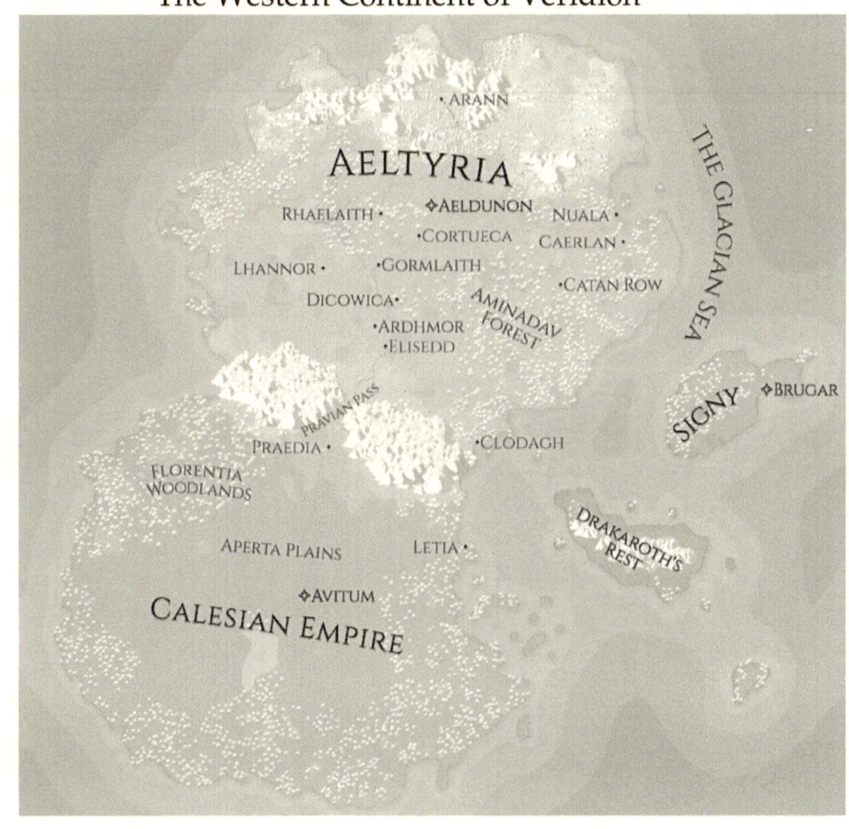

# CHAPTER ONE
## *Omens*

*"Omens do not lie. It is the heart that refuses to hear them."*
—Aeltyrian proverb

Mētanos 20, 1223
*Aleaia*

*I have to save him.*

The thought rang like a bell in my skull, bright and unrelenting. My fingers locked around the hilt of my sword. I gripped it until my hand throbbed, and its weight dragged behind me, heavy as guilt, carving a line through the blood slicking the stone.

Pain tore through me, searing until my vision was a haze of flickering light. The air reeked of blood. Metallic. It coated my tongue, slid over my teeth, dripped into my eye until I wiped it away with a trembling hand. My legs nearly gave out, but I forced them forward.

One step. Another.

Only one thought remained—

*I have to save him.*

I jerked awake, my breath catching in my throat as I sat up too fast. My heart pounded. Sweat chilled on my skin.

The loft was dark and still. The wool blankets lay hot and heavy across my legs. I shoved them aside and drew in a long, shaking breath—then another, slower. My shift clung to my chest. I tugged it away with one hand, then lifted my tangled, sweat-damp hair off the back of my neck with the other, the strands sticking lightly to my skin.

I heard Papa's voice, steady in my memory.

*In through your nose. Out through your mouth.*

I obeyed, drawing deep breaths until my pulse slowed, until the rhythm took hold. I told myself it wasn't real. That I was home, and Papa was there. Grandma and Grandpa too.

The dream clung like smoke, curling into every corner of my mind, impossible to hold, impossible to forget. I'd lost count of how many times I'd dreamt it. Always the same struggle, the same unseen figure, just beyond reach, the same terrible certainty I wouldn't reach him in time.

As a child, I'd run to my father sobbing. By the time I was sixteen, I kept it to myself. The fear had dulled with the years, though the desperation had etched itself into me like a scar.

I rubbed my arms, the kind of motion you repeat just to feel like you're still real, still here, still yourself after that kind of dream. Motion helped—chores, chickens and goats, the gentle, predictable rhythm of the farm.

That's how I'd soothe myself. How I'd always done it.

I cracked the shutter next to my bed just enough to peer outside. No snow yet, though it felt cold enough that it might start soon. The horizon had begun to blush with the soft hues of dawn—rose, gold, the faintest breath of blue. The sight should have brought comfort. Most mornings it did, but this morning, the light only reminded me I hadn't slept.

Papa's snores rumbled behind the curtain that separated his bed from mine. I'd try my best not to wake him.

I rose from the straw-stuffed mattress and dressed in silence, every movement practiced and efficient. I gathered my doeskin boots in my arms and crept barefoot across the warped floorboards, avoiding the ones that creaked loudest. At the ladder, I gripped the sides and descended with careful, balanced steps, silent from the years of slipping by unnoticed.

On the packed earthen floor, I eased on my boots and pulled my cloak from its peg. The wool was coarse and worn thin in places, but it was warm enough as I stepped outside.

The world was cold and quiet under the dawn sky. My breath left me in pale clouds. Frost rimed the fence posts and silvered the brittle grass. I crossed to the barn, tugging my cloak tighter against the gust. Early Mētanos had no business being so bitter.

Our farm wasn't large. Under Calesian law, we Aeltyrians owned nothing. We were permitted a single fieldmark, just enough to till, to scrape by, never enough to dream, but just enough to keep us quiet. To keep us small.

It paid the tributes. Most years, it fed us too.

We kept a few goats for milk, a handful of pigs behind the house, and one old horse—Bran, a gray gelding who had once been strong and spirited. He'd brought us here from Aeldunon, when I was a babe. I learned to ride on him when I was little. Now, though, he mostly shuffled through the pasture, shaggy and speckled with white. This morning, he stood near the fence, head lowered, breath misting as he nosed the grass.

"Morning, old man," I murmured.

I reached through the slats and scratched behind his ears. He leaned into it, then resumed his slow, half-hearted search for something edible. I'd take him out later, let him stretch his legs if the weather held.

The goats noticed me as soon as I stepped into the barn, their soft bleats rising in expectation. Mira, the oldest, let out a long, grumpy sound and stamped for good measure.

"I'm going, I'm going," I muttered.

I tossed hay into the trough and brushed stray stalks from my sleeve as they crowded in, jostling, their bodies warm around me. I fetched the milk pail and dropped onto the stool beside Mira. She turned her head to eye me, then stood still as I began to work.

The barn was quiet, save for the shuffle of hooves and rustle of hay. Warm milk struck the tin in a steady beat. Our two barn cats prowled about, tails twitching as they waited. The scent of straw, dung, and old wood filled the air, comforting in a way I could never quite explain.

Snow would come early. I felt it in the hush clinging to the trees, in the wind's edge, in the way the birds had gone silent. When it came, it wouldn't creep. It would fall all at once, heavy and unrelenting. For most, that meant rest.

Not for me. Not with Papa.

We'd disappear into the woods like always, far from wagging tongues and watchful eyes. Even as Succamos buried the land in snow, he'd put me through drills until my arms shook and my legs gave out.

Sword work. Form. Footwork. Again and again.

I sighed. I didn't ask why anymore. I already knew the answer.

I'd live, marry, and die in Rhaelaith like everyone else. The village didn't need warriors. It needed hands in the soil. Teaching me, though, that was the only piece of the old world he had left. The man I knew had farmer's hands and a furrowed brow, but he'd once been a soldier. Posted in Aeldunon, he'd been there when it fell.

My mother died in battle. He returned to Rhaelaith to raise me.

*Deserter. Coward.*

The words came from the mouths of men who had never marched, never fought, never watched the world crumble to ash. I still remember the first time I heard them hissed behind our backs, sharp as flint, soft as rot. They clung to me like mud I couldn't scrub off, echoed in the silence when others turned away.

Sixteen years later, the shame still clung to him. My grandparents bore it too, unless someone needed my grandmother's healing or a birth seen through.

I shook the thoughts loose before they could fester. Nothing good came from following that path.

By the time I finished in the barn, the world had begun to stir. Sparrows—the few that remained at that time of year—called from the eaves, and a breath of warmth touched the air. I carried the milk inside and set the pail on the table near the hearth. Then I took up the empty water buckets from beside the door and stepped back out.

The path to the river was worn smooth by years of footsteps. Here and there, old roots twisted across it like bones. At the water's edge, I crouched low and dipped the first bucket. Cold bit into my hands. I filled the second, my fingers aching by the time I tied them off and started back to the house. Halfway up the hill, I adjusted the ropes biting into my palms, swore softly, and plodded on.

As I crested the rise, I saw Papa standing on the porch, leaning against the rail, a steaming cup in hand. Probably chicory root. He raised it in greeting.

"You're up early for a change," he said, voice still rough with sleep. His brown eyes glinted over the rim of his cup.

"Someone has to work around here," I replied, breath still catching from the climb.

He reached out as I passed, plucking hay from my hair. "Since you've done it all, we might have time for hunting. Go say goodbye to your grandmother."

"Yes, Papa." I shouldered the door open and carried the buckets inside, setting them near the hearth with a thud. My palms were red, the skin raw where the ropes had rubbed.

Grandma glanced up from the pot she was stirring. "About time. I thought we might die of thirst waiting on you."

I smiled as I crossed the room. "I'm off to hunt with Papa." With a kiss on her cheek, I gently tucked a stray strand of her dark, silver-streaked hair behind her ear. "Where's Grandpa?" I asked, voice lower.

She clucked her tongue. "Still abed. Being lazy."

That wasn't like him. He rose with the sun every day.

"Don't worry yourself," she said. "Bring back a fat hare and he'll perk up."

"I'll try," I said, and slipped back out.

I skipped down the steps to join Papa at the gate. The sun had begun its slow climb, casting long shadows across the frost-laced fields. We set off down the path toward the woods, boots soft against hard-packed earth. Rhaelaith should have been waking. Vendors should have been setting up, children dashing between carts, the smell of bread in the air.

Instead, the village was still. Windows were shuttered against the cold, the lane empty.

"Where is everyone?" I asked, tightness settling beneath my ribs.

"Sweating sickness," Papa said. "Keeping to their homes."

We passed the village edge and entered the trees, leaves crunching underfoot, wind whispering through bare branches, and I breathed deep the scent of damp earth. His words had left me uneasy. Sickness meant the Empire would stay away, which wasn't always a bad thing, but it meant we'd be bereft of news and trade.

I started to speak, hesitated, then tried again. "The dream came again."

He grunted in acknowledgement. I looked at him. His jaw was tight. He never liked it when I mentioned the dream.

"I wish I knew what it meant," I said, quieter this time.

"It means you've been listening to too many stories," he said. "Dreams come and go. You give them too much weight."

"It's the same dream I've had since I was little." I flexed my hands. "This time it felt… worse."

He stopped and turned to me as I came to a halt next to him. There was no anger in his face, just caution.

"Aleaia," he said, voice gentler, "I don't have answers. Let it go."

"Maybe Grandma would know. It can't hurt to—"

"It can," he said, mouth tightening. "Keep it between us."

There was no room left to argue.

I nodded, though the tightness in my chest didn't ease. I didn't like keeping things from her, but I knew the danger. One whisper in the wrong ear, and the Inquisition would come with chains, not questions.

There was no one else I could tell. No sibling. No friend. Even as a child, I'd been set apart. Other children sensed it. A few tried to be kind. Kindness faded. Maybe something was wrong with me, I thought, or maybe Papa's distance had become mine, too. I'd learned to live with it. It hurt less when I stopped expecting anything else.

I let go of the memory of the stares. The weight. The whispers. In the forest, everything was simpler. The air was rich with the scent of wet leaves and moss, and I breathed it deep, let it cleanse me, releasing my worries to the winds of Tauranis.

Papa passed me a quiver and my bow without a word, then nodded toward a patch of tall grass. "Hares love these spots," he said. "There's a den just past the bramble."

I crept forward, placing each step with care. The trail led to a small hollow where the grass dipped and flattened into a nest, just as he'd said, though it was empty, for now. I looked back and caught his eye. He nodded once.

I nocked an arrow but didn't pull yet as I moved with him through the brush, breath slow and measured. We worked without speaking, splitting around the thickets, circling the likely ground.

When I spotted the hare, my pulse quickened. Large as one of our barn cats, its ears twitched as it sniffed the air. I raised my bow to pull, held my breath, and loosed. The arrow struck true, and the hare fell without a sound. I stepped forward, crouched beside it, and touched its still-warm fur.

"Thank you," I whispered, as I always did. A prayer to Lithau out of respect for her creation.

When I returned to Papa's side, he was crouched beside another hare, inspecting its size. He glanced up at mine as he stood.

"Well done," he said, placing a hand on my shoulder.

It was a simple thing, but it warmed me. Praise from him never came as flattery. It was earned.

We hunted for another hour, shadows in the thinning brush. The hares had been busy, so our bags were heavier than expected. By the time the steady rush of a waterfall reached our ears, we had enough to trade and plenty to eat.

"We'll stop here for a rest before heading back," Papa said, easing onto a moss-covered log near the pool.

I sat beside him and pulled a pouch of blueberries from my belt, dumping a few into my palm. I offered him some. For a few heartbeats, we ate in silence.

"Jory Rhosan came by again," Papa said.

I knew where this was going. "No."

"Why not?" he asked.

"Because he's annoying." I ate another berry, eyes fixed on the pool.

He waited a breath before trying again, a trace of amusement in his voice. "That's it? He's just annoying?"

I turned to look at him fully. "Because he's a self-righteous, rude, arrogant arsehole who likes the sound of his own voice more than he likes me."

"He wants to marry you," Papa said. "I'd say that means he likes you well enough."

I didn't have words for it yet, only the certainty that *well enough* wasn't enough for me.

I made a low, unimpressed sound and held out the rest of the berries. "I'm not marrying him. And I've lost my appetite just thinking about it."

"All right. All right." He took the berries with a sigh. "I'll tell his da the answer's no."

"And why," I said.

His mouth twitched. "And why."

I could tell, by the way he looked at me, that he was testing me.

"This is the thanks I get," Papa said. "Tried to raise a daughter with manners, ended up with a menace."

"I'll tell him myself if it's easier." I shrugged. "And you didn't raise me with manners. You raised me with a blade and a foul mouth."

"Look how well you turned out anyway."

I bumped my shoulder against his. "You did all right, old man."

He grunted. "I did, didn't I?" Then, more quietly, "Still. I want to know you'll be looked after when I'm gone."

I snorted. "Grandma and Grandpa are ancient and still do plenty."

He exhaled through his nose. "The war aged me. Like a dog."

I tilted my head. "What do you think my mother would say, hearing you complain like that?"

He didn't answer right away. Just looked up at me, eyes narrowing, not with anger, but with something older. Sadder. "You've got her eyes," he said. "Gray as pewter. Sharp as flint."

He looked away again, turning the berry in his palm. I said nothing, because this was the only way he'd talk about my mother: caught off guard and uninterrupted.

"She'd be proud of you," he said finally. "Proud of who you're becoming. And she'd tease me for being long-winded, say I'm turning into my father."

"She'd be right. You do sound like Grandpa."

He groaned. "That's what I get. A daughter with her mother's tongue and my temper. Lucky me."

I raised my waterskin to hide a smile. Something pricked at the edge of my vision. I looked up. Perched in the highest boughs above the falls, nearly hidden in the dark green, sat a raven. White as snow. Still as stone.

"Papa." I touched his arm. "Look."

He followed my gaze. His shoulders stiffened.

"An omen," he said. The word landed with weight. Final.

The raven watched us in silence. Its feathers shimmered in the morning light. The air shifted, too quiet now. Too still. Something twisted low in my belly.

"I don't…" My voice faltered. "I don't feel well."

The cold crept through me, slow and certain, like frost moving beneath my skin.

My breath hitched.

The light dimmed.

Papa's voice cut through the haze, sharp with fear. "Aleaia!"

My body gave way.

The last thing I saw was the raven spreading its wings.

Then, nothing.

# CHAPTER TWO
## *Valediction*

*"When stillness falls where breath should stir,*
*And silence walks with wings of white,*
*The soul may drift where none yet dwell,*
*To drink the dark before the light."*
—The Song of the Stars, Cycle VII: The Cycle of Spirit

Mētanos 21, 1223
*Aleaia*

"Come on, girl. We have to go." Strong hands pulled me upright.

"Papa?" I blinked against the late morning light. "What—?"

"I'm here," Papa said, steady as ever. "But we've no time to linger."

My body sagged, too heavy to hold. Everything in me ached to lie back down. "I'm so hungry… and thirsty. Can't we eat first?"

"We'll eat on the road."

I drank from the water cup he pressed into my hands, gulping until it was dry. "How long was I…?"

"You slept longer than usual. Through the night and into late morning. Your grandmother found no cause for it."

"I don't remember anything," I murmured. My hand brushed the quilt—too thick, too soft. This wasn't my bed, wasn't the loft. It was my grandparents'. "Where is she? Where's Grandpa?"

"They took our place upstairs," Papa said. "They're still there, but they're not well."

Tears pricked my eyes as I turned my face to the wall. "The sickness?"

"Aye," he said softly. He knelt to shove my feet into my boots the way he used to, back when I was small. Then came the cloak around my shoulders, the pack thrust into my hands. "I've gathered what we'll need. You can piss when we get on the road. No time to waste."

I understood, even if I didn't like it. The longer we stayed, the more we breathed the illness in the air. "Can I at least say goodbye?" My voice trembled.

"Only from down here," he said. Harsh. Final.

"All right, Papa."

"I've said mine. I'll be outside."

He paused at the threshold. "Leave the windows open."

He stepped out without waiting for my reply.

I gripped the ladder for steadiness, heart thudding.

"Grandma? Grandpa?" My voice was small.

"She's resting," Grandpa said, his words rough, ragged. "Do as your father says, girl. I'll tell her you were thinking of her."

I lingered at the bottom rung, the silence pressing close. The kind of rest he meant was the kind no one woke from.

The memory of the white raven returned, sudden, like icy water through the ribs. I knew I would never see them again.

"I… I love you, Grandpa."

"And we've loved you more than words can tell—"

Whatever came next vanished into the coughing that took him.

I stepped into the morning light and closed the door behind me on the only home I had ever known.

# CHAPTER THREE
## *Gone Before Rudamos*

*"No child of Aeltyria was born to die on her knees. Let them come, and let the stones drink deep."*
—Queen Eavan, before the Siege of Aeldunon

Mētanos 27, 1223
*Aleaia*

I hated riding double. I shifted for the hundredth time since mounting up behind Papa, legs half-asleep, spine jostling with every step.

"We've never come this way before."

"We have," Papa said. "You were too small to remember. We came from the other direction then. You were bundled tight and strapped to me like a sack of turnips."

I laughed. "Did you make a habit of traveling with turnips tied to your chest?"

He glanced back at me with a hint of a smile. "Not usually. Truth is, the horse bore your weight, tied to the *saddle* like turnips."

A snort escaped me. "Much more dignified. Have you decided where we're going?"

"Aeldunon."

The thought of so many people, sick and clustered together, made me wrinkle my nose.

"We're not going *into* the city, are we? The sickness must be worse there than it is in the village."

"Not yet. We'll head into the wilds for a time. Gods willing, just a couple of decadia."

"You sound relieved," I said.

"There's a kind of freedom out here. Traveling." He drew a long breath, as if savoring it. "When things settle, we'll go on to the city."

He always had a distaste for cities, said they were too crowded. Aeldunon would be the hardest of all, I knew. He hadn't been back since the war. Whatever thoughts he wasn't saying, he'd chosen to keep to himself.

"My legs are going to fall off," I said. "May I walk for a while?"

"That's no bad idea. I'll walk with you."

I was already off the horse before he'd finished, boots striking the packed earth with a dull thud. After I groaned and stretched, I fell into step beside Papa.

He lifted his hand to measure the sun, squinting at its angle. "We've maybe two hours of light left. Time to look for a place to camp and get something in our bellies. I'd hoped to lay a few traps before dusk."

"Yes, Papa." I couldn't stop thinking about my grandparents, about leaving them helpless in our little home. How would they manage, if they were sick? If they even lived. I waited a few paces before speaking again, my voice low. "Do you think we were right to leave Grandma and Grandpa like that?"

He didn't answer at once. When he did, it was blunt as a fieldstone. "It's not always a choice between right and wrong. Sometimes all you've got is bad and worse. What else could we have done?"

I nodded, though my throat tightened. Staying would've risked catching the sickness. Maybe brought it with us.

"Do you think we'll get it anyway?"

He grunted. "You've never been sick a day in your life."

That was no answer. I frowned and pressed on with the bravery of youth. "There's never been anything like this before. And when I collapsed—"

"Your grandmother didn't think it was the plague."

It had been six days since I had seen the stupid bird and fainted in the forest. Grandma had found nothing wrong with me, and if she found nothing, there was nothing to find.

"What did she think it was?"

"She didn't know." He looked at me then, just for a moment. "I told her about the dreams."

"As I had wanted to do for years?" My voice was flat. "And?"

"She scolded me. For waiting. For silencing you. I'm sorry, Aleaia. You were right."

He rarely apologized. I could count the times he had on one hand, and I'd never expected him to yield on this. I might have pressed him, demanded more, but something in his tone told me it wasn't easy for him to say. That was enough.

"Let's veer off the road here," he said. "Remember, when choosing a campsite, stay hidden from the road to avoid being seen by anyone passing by. Safer that way."

He led Bran into the woods, weaving between narrow trees as the path vanished behind us. We camped in a clearing within a stand of elderwood, the ground dry and layered with needles. Once the camp was set, I sat cross-legged beside the fire, holding my cup of warmed ale in both hands.

Our travels had fallen into a rhythm. We'd walk by day, camp by dusk, eat whatever we had, and then my father would talk, tell stories of old Aeltyria. Not the kind sung in taverns when the Imperials weren't around, not with rhymes or flourishes. His were lean and measured, worn smooth by time and repetition.

"We're near Drenn's Crossing. Five miles west. Was a chokepoint," Papa said, handing me a strip of dried meat. "Four Calesian cohorts came through—that's a thousand soldiers a piece—trying to reach Aeldunon. Queen Eavan stopped them. No army, no siege engines. Just her guard, a handful of battle-mages, and her stubbornness."

He leaned forward, elbows on his knees. "Bastards spent days building bridges of standard timber planks, lashed and braced. Didn't matter. She waited until the middle of the night, rode down. No warning."

He gestured with the meat. "She stepped out onto the riverbank. Thick ice, fog across the field. According to the reports, the air went strange. Hot even if it was Mētanos, and prickly. Then she raised her hands and called lightning. First bridge split right down the middle."

I shifted, eager to hear what came next, but I needed to understand. "Without a storm?"

Papa hesitated. "Yes. She didn't need one. There were clouds and that was enough."

I hadn't grown up with magic. Didn't understand a bit of it. How could something come from nothing? For a long moment, the fire cracked between us.

"But how?" I asked.

"I don't know exactly how she could call lightning, because I only possessed a little earth magic," he said at last.

"And she was a lightning mage? I thought last time, you said she was a fire mage."

He took a deep breath, probably for patience. "She was the Daughter of Aelan. And the Daughter of Aelan could do many things others couldn't. Like her foremothers, she could command all the elements and then some." He waved a hand. "Anyway, it works on instinct. The way a swordsman moves without thinking."

I stared into my cup. "I don't understand how that's even possible."

His mouth pressed into a line. "I know."

It had to be hard for him, I thought, to raise a child without the thing that connected our people to the land.

He ate the last bit of his meat and sat back, arms crossed loosely over his chest. "She brought down the rest of the storm next. Flooded the river before the Calesians could regroup. First wave drowned outright. The ones behind tried to charge, but she turned the bank into a killing field. Focused strikes. Fire and lightning hot enough to melt iron."

I looked up at him. "And she lived through that?"

"She led the charge. Bought the capital a decadium. Kept the south from falling. The Fellglow Blade never left her hand."

I blinked. "That's not a myth?"

"It's real," he said. "Or was. Beautiful blade."

The silence that followed was the kind that carried weight. When his eyes met mine, they held grief, worn and quiet. It made me want to squirm. I looked away. "I wish I could've seen it."

He smiled, but it didn't reach his eyes. "I'm glad you didn't."

I hesitated, then bit my lip. A question weighed on my tongue. "How..." my voice dropped. "How did Aeltyria lose, with such power at our disposal?"

Papa let out a long breath and rubbed the back of his neck, head shaking slowly.

I regretted the question. "I'm sorry," I said. "I shouldn't have—"

"No. It's past time I told you. You need to know these things." He swirled the last of his drink in his tin cup, scowling into it. "Queen Eavan's strength wasn't common. A handful of mages came close, but most of us weren't mages. We were soldiers. Archers. Swordsmen. Fighters who'd trained our whole lives with a sword and shield and still couldn't stop what came."

He tossed a bit of bark into the fire and watched it blacken. "Calesians learned fast. First, they figured out how to spot the mages. Then they started killing them first in battle. That worked for a while, until we gave the mages galvarium plate. And then the Calesians found something better. Incolumium."

I was familiar with galvarium—a metal they said was harder than iron, nearly indestructible except with spirit fire—but the other, I'd never heard of. I repeated the word. "In-columium?"

"A metal," he confirmed. "Rare. Hard to forge, but the Empire spared no cost once they learned it suppresses magic. Makes chains the gifted can't break, no matter how strong. They clapped them on nobles, scholars, anyone they wanted to keep alive. The rest, the ones who weren't worth the cost, were culled."

I stared into the fire, the crackle and hiss of sap the only sound for a few breaths.

"They didn't stop at shackles," he added. "Started making weapons out of it. Blades that cut through enchanted armor. Shields that soaked up spells like rain in sand. You'd think you were safe behind three layers of warded steel, then you'd watch a ballista split your brigan in two."

"Brigan?"

"Commander."

My stomach turned. I had seen plenty of animals butchered but never anything like what he described.

"At Aeldunon," he went on, voice low, "they loaded trebuchets with clay spheres filled with powdered incolumium. Smashed on impact. The dust coated everything. Mages couldn't cast. Couldn't breathe without choking on it. That was bad enough. Then they learned to mix the powder with oil. Set it alight. Couldn't be doused by water or magic. Anyone caught in it burned."

I shook my head. "That's monstrous."

"It was," Papa said simply. "And effective. That's war. Nothing makes you feel more alive than nearly dying. It's a twisted thing. One I hope you never understand." He gave a grunt and stood. "That's enough for one night. Don't stay up too late."

He tossed a few more branches onto the coals, banking them low, then turned toward his bedroll without another word.

Later that night, as the whispers of a wintry wind drifted through the trees, I lay wrapped in my bedroll, weary to the bone. The grief I carried for my grandparents struck sharp as it returned.

I stared up at the night sky, a dark canvas pricked with stars and wondered what Aetheria might be like for them. Surely they must be there, waiting for us, waiting for Papa. A land of golden twilight, where rivers sang, and the wind carried the voices of those long passed. A place where the earth never tired, the sky never darkened, and the souls of the dead wandered free, held not by flesh or time.

That was the way Papa had always described it.

Papa had taught me the old ways in secret, even as the Empire demanded loyalty to Anvallus. To the Calesians, he was god of all things. We knew him differently. To us, he was the Great Unmaker, the one who loosed Drakaroth upon the world. In secret, we gave our prayers to Lithau, the Mother of Creation. Still, I couldn't help but wonder if Anvallus was stronger than we'd ever feared. What else could explain the reach and might of the Empire?

I exhaled slowly, my breath turning to mist. All of it—faith, history, grief—was distant and inconsequential in that moment.

This journey had already taken me farther than I had ever gone from the bounds of Rhaelaith. We wouldn't last long in the wild. Aeltyrian winters were lethal. They claimed the unprepared without mercy, their icy grip swift and silent.

I looked over at Papa, oiling one of two swords he'd hidden these long years. The second lay beside my bedroll, entrusted to me. In Calesian-ruled Aeltyria, the law forbade weapons unless one served the auxiliaries. Even after swearing allegiance at adulthood, an Aeltyrian caught with a blade faced death. Papa had hidden both blades since the war.

I thought, then, how dangerous that had been for him. And again, I wondered why he'd done it. There had to be some purpose, to justify the risk.

He paused then, head tilted, listening. A moment later, he turned toward me and held up a finger, pressing it to his lips in a command for silence. A slight nod toward my blade said the rest.

My heart kicked. I slipped from the bedroll, pulled my boots on with practiced speed. My sword was already in my hand by the time I reached the fire and smothered the coals with a scoop of dirt, careful not to make a sound.

The underbrush stirred. Bran stamped and snorted, eyes wide.

I drew my sword slowly, the way Papa had taught me, quiet and controlled. I laid the sheath on the bedroll.

My fingers ached from how tight I gripped the cold hilt.

My stance was too stiff. My breath too loud in my ears.

A voice cut through the dark, thick and graveled and speaking Calesian. "Seems the old man has the hearing of a hound."

He stepped into the clearing, broad as a stone gate. His cloak was stiff with blood and dirt, his leathers patched with years of wear. On his cheek, glaring red beneath old scars, was an 'M,' burned deep.

Murderer.

He'd survived the fustuarium. Only monsters came out the other side of that.

Papa moved in front of me. I stood just behind his left shoulder, sword at the ready. The blade trembled, so I shifted my grip until it steadied.

Three more men emerged from the trees.

Four against two.

My stomach twisted, but I breathed in slow. Held it. Let it go. Papa had trained me for this, but I'd never killed a man. I'd never even fought one outside the practice ring.

The branded one took his time looking me over. When he smiled, it made my skin crawl.

"I'm feeling generous," he said. "The plan, old man, was to kill you and take the girl. But since you caught us…" His grin widened. "Three silver. She's skinny, but we don't mind."

Papa's voice came low and cold. "Here's my offer: walk away while you still can."

The outlaw laughed. Not because he was amused, but because he'd already decided to kill us. "Ah, maybe I won't be generous after all." He nodded to one of the others. "Grab the girl. Kill him."

Steel rang out as Papa met one of them halfway. I locked eyes with the one rushing me. The smallest of the four, he was wiry. Fast. Wild. His blade flashed in the firelight, swinging too wide.

He lunged. I stepped aside, caught his weapon with mine, and shoved. The clash jolted up my arms. He stumbled, hissed through his teeth, then came again, sloppier this time.

Papa's voice echoed in my head. Hold your ground. Let them show you their rhythm. Find the space between the strikes.

So I held.

The man raised his sword high, foolish. I slipped inside his guard and drove my blade into his side. It struck with a jolt, solid and wet. His knees buckled. I felt the weight of him go slack around the sword. I shoved my boot against his stomach and yanked the blade free.

Then came the blow, like a hammer to the side of my head.

Pain exploded behind my eyes. The world tipped. I dropped to one knee. My hand didn't let go of the sword only because my fingers had locked around it.

I swung blindly at the attacker's legs. Steel met something hard. Not flesh. My wrist jarred. Laughter followed, low and close.

He wore iron strips in his boots. Papa warned me once.

He grabbed my braid and hauled me upright. I gritted my teeth as his hand caught my wrist and twisted it behind me.

Too close to strike. No room. No air.

I kicked. Useless. Tried to jerk free. He was stronger.

*My knife,* I thought.

I reached across my body, fingers fumbling. The blade came free. I stabbed his thigh.

Once.

Twice. He grunted, staggered, but held tight.

A third strike.

Then a fourth.

Something tore inside him. He howled and dropped me.

I clung to the dagger in his groin, dragged it down as I turned. His scream choked off as I tore the blade free and blood poured in heavy bursts. He fell to his knees, then face first. He twitched, then stilled.

I turned, looking for Papa.

He stood a dozen paces off, his arm slick with blood, hanging limp. He still held his sword, though, still warded off the branded one and one other.

I ran.

The last outlaw turned to meet me, swinging wide with an axe. I ducked, felt its wind in my hair, and came up behind him.

I spun, brought my blade down on the back of his neck, just above the shoulder. It struck deep and stuck fast.

I braced a foot against his back and pulled. The sword tore free with a crack. He pitched forward. Blood steamed in the cold. He didn't move.

I turned just in time to see Papa fall.

His knees hit the earth. One hand clutched his belly, blood gushing between his fingers. His sword was gone. He looked up at the branded man looming over him, then past him. To me.

His lips moved. *"I love you."*

The blade swung.

Took his head clean.

I don't remember drawing breath. I just remember the sound that ripped out of me as I charged, screaming and wild, my blade up and swinging.

The murderer turned in time to catch my strike. Sparks flew.

He didn't flinch. Just shoved me back with a single sweep.

"You cost me three good men," he said, as if listing coin lost in a game. "You're going to pay for it."

My hands shook. Rage and grief burned behind my eyes. "Fuck you and your men."

He chuckled. "Oh? Offering, are you?"

Then he came at me.

Too fast. Too heavy.

Slammed into me like a wall. I flew backward and hit the ground hard enough to drive the breath from my lungs. My sword skidded away. The knife I'd had in my hand flew from my grip and vanished into the dark.

Then his hand cracked across my face. Light burst behind my eyes. Blood filled my mouth.

I tried to crawl. He climbed on top of me, pinned my legs down with his body.

His hands closed around my throat.

I thrashed. Clawed. Found nothing. My feet kicked uselessly.

"Stop fighting," he snarled, and struck me again.

My head rang. My jaw throbbed. I was going to die.

On my back.

In the dirt.

Eyes open.

Body cooling.

Bones for the foxes.

Gone before Rudamos.

I flailed again. Weak now. Slower.

My hand hit something at his hip. *A hilt?*

I grabbed it and stabbed blindly. He roared.

Again. Fingers tightened at my throat.

The third strike slid deep. He screamed and reeled back, blood gushing from his side. His grip released. I rolled free, coughing, choking, vision swimming.

I crawled. Found my sword. Turned.

"You bitch!" he roared.

He tore the knife from his ribs and lunged.

I brought my sword up—badly, clumsily.

He stopped mid-stride. No clash. No scream. He just jolted, then dropped.

Behind him stood a stranger—tall, armored, and calm.

The man wrenched a blade free from the base of the outlaw's skull with a brutal twist. Blood dripped from the steel.

I could only stare.

Red plumed helmet. Silver plate. Legion.

Someone important to the Empire.

I recoiled on instinct, hand clutched to my bruised throat, still choking on air that didn't want to come.

Others moved behind him. Imperial soldiers, torches in hand, helmets crested with red horsehair.

The man in silver pulled off his helm, and a tumble of ash-brown hair fell free around his face, damp with sweat.

Not a man but a boy, no older than I was. He stepped forward, crouched in front of me.

His green eyes met mine. Not cold or cruel. Soft. I thought he pitied me, like a wounded animal.

I hated it.

"Apologies, my lady," he said quietly, voice rough with dust and smoke. "That you suffered such violence in my father's lands."

He offered me a waterskin, and I, not realizing what he had at first, flinched. A raised Calesian hand often landed hard on Aeltyrian flesh, after all.

But the strike never came.

"I am Valerius di Calesia," he went on. "And you are now under the protection of the Second Army."

# CHAPTER FOUR
## *Preparation*

*"From chaos, order. From rebellion, peace. From conquest, glory."*
—Carved into the arch of Avitum's Northern Gate

Mētanos 43, 1223
*Aleaia*

In my first days with the Calesian Army, grief clung to me like a second skin. I tried to remind myself that I was lucky. Lucky that Lord Valerius had found me, that I'd lived through the blood and smoke in the clearing. If he hadn't, and I'd somehow survived on my own, my life might have unraveled into something far worse.

Better the sword than the whip.

Better to march than to bear the slaver's yoke.

Better to make stew in a tent than coin on my back.

When I arrived in camp, my duties were those of a camp follower, my days consumed with the backbreaking work of keeping pace with the First Cohort of the Second Army's First Legion on their long march south to Avitum.

My first assignment was in the mess tent, preparing meat for the evening stew. I glanced down at my hands. New blisters rose beside healing cuts, raw and red from labor and cold. The older wounds, scabbed and rough-edged, still stung when I flexed my fingers. The skirmish had left its marks. My face bore them, too, though I hadn't yet seen the worst of it. The healer had told me the swelling was going down, though, and the bruises had already begun to fade. That didn't stop the ache when I moved, or lighten the iron that had settled in my bones.

My body was healing. My mind hadn't even started.

Nights were the worst. The old dream—the one that had followed me since childhood—was gone. In its place stood the memory of my father's death. I woke from it with my breath caught in my ribs, as if a blade had lodged there and twisted while I slept. Sometimes I thrashed. Sometimes I cried out. On the worst nights, I did both.

The other girls never shamed me for it. They brought me water, whispered comfort, laid a hand on my back until the trembling stopped. I hadn't expected such kindness.

Daylight helped. Most days, I buried myself in the rhythm of work, trading grief for tasks. I scrubbed, fetched, cooked, served—whatever the cook needed. So long as my hands stayed busy, I could keep my memories caged.

But grief is patient. It creeps in through cracks, clings to smells and sounds, and waits for your guard to slip.

And I carried so much heartache, not just for my father, but for my home, my grandparents. I wondered what would become of the goats, and the chickens, and where Bran was. I couldn't remember burying my father.

The first time grief found me in daylight, I was preparing the meat for dinner. The scent of broth was thick with marrow and herbs, but beneath it, sharp and sour, was blood. I reached for a slab of meat. The flesh was slick beneath my fingers, the fat pale and glistening. I set the knife to it, expecting the usual drag of sinew and gristle. The blade slipped through like nothing.

Too clean.

Too much like—

My stomach turned.

The wet feeling of steel through flesh hit something in my chest. It shouldn't have mattered, and once, it wouldn't have. I had helped butcher game before, back home. I'd dressed rabbits, and helped with deer when the snows came early and patrols were lax. This was different, because it wasn't the meat, really.

It was the likeness to a different kind of meat.

My grip faltered. A cold sweat broke across my back. I blinked, but the mess tent was already fading. The clatter of pots vanished, replaced by the hush of pine needles underfoot. The indistinct murmur of soldiers became the chaos of shouting men, steel on steel, the wet gurgle of someone dying.

I was back in the clearing.

Only paces away, I was too far to stop it, but close enough to smell the copper in the air as blood arced from my father's throat.

One heartbeat he was my father, breathing and alive.

The next, he was only a body on the ground. His eyes—so familiar, so constant—stared up at nothing, the light gone from them.

Something clattered nearby. The noise jolted me back. The mess tent rushed back around me—the simmering pot, the fire's heat against my legs, the soft glow of hanging lanterns overhead.

My breath was ragged in my throat. Had there been anything in my belly, I'm sure it would have come up. My hands trembled, damp with sweat. I wiped them on my apron, glancing sideways. I took a deep breath, down into my gut, and prayed no one had seen.

I told myself it was just meat.

Just food.

Just another task.

"Dieter?" the cook asked.

I turned, stiff, and found him watching me.

He was a thickset Calesian man, weathered from years beside the cookfire, with arms of braided rope. His apron bore the stains of long labor, sleeves rolled to the elbow. He frowned, not with impatience, but with the quiet measure of a man who noticed more than he said.

"You all right, girl?" His voice was coarse, but not without kindness.

I swallowed, forced the air back into my lungs.

*"Esam bau—"* The words slipped out before I could stop them. I caught myself, found the Calesian. "I'm… fine."

He nodded once and gestured toward the stew pot. "Best get to it, then."

"Aye—yes, sir."

I had to be careful. I could speak both Calesian and Aeltyrian equally well, but the latter would earn me a beating if I wasn't careful. There was no room for mistakes like that here. No space for weakness.

There was no time to fall apart. The legionaries would file in soon. I exhaled slowly, straightened the kerchief over my hair, and bent to my task. My fingers still shook, but I gripped the knife all the tighter. I finished cutting the meat and scraped it into the pot, stirring more vigorously than I needed to. The heat flushed my cheeks, gave me something to focus on.

When the soldiers arrived, the mess tent filled with life—bowls clattering, voices rising and falling in conversation, bursts of laughter here and there from the far tables. I ladled stew into bowl after bowl, hands moving with practiced rhythm.

And for a little while, I was too busy to think of anything at all.

I filled bowl after bowl before the tent flaps parted with a sharp snap, and the air shifted like a held breath. Conversation faltered. Spoons stilled mid-motion. I glanced up and saw why a hush had rippled through the room.

Lord Valerius had entered.

"As you were," he commanded.

A few soldiers offered greetings before returning to their bowls, quieter than before.

He moved as someone who never questioned his right to be seen, the weight of his presence unmistakable. The deep blue fabric of his cloak and the tunic he wore under it were plain but fine, the kind of cloth I'd only heard of. At his side, the hilt of his sword caught the firelight.

*A fine display of power and wealth,* I thought, and immediately hated myself for it.

I was only alive because of him.

Lucius Tutela followed close behind, the kind of man who looked carved rather than born, every glance measuring threat and weakness. His blue eyes swept the tent, catching everything. He looked years beyond his liege lord. From what I'd heard, the gap between them wasn't so wide, but battle did that to people. Aged them.

*Like a dog*, Papa had said.

*Not now*, I thought, pushing the grief back down.

Beside him walked Marcus Frugi. He studied the room as if it were a game already half-played, his dark gaze flicking from face to face, noting pieces and gauging odds. The other girls said he'd given up the sword recently, though he didn't look much like he'd ever touched it.

"Despite all that, we need to quicken our pace if we want to outrun the worst of the winter," Valerius said over his shoulder. His tone was low but firm, the voice of someone used to being obeyed.

*Typical. Spoiled Calesian noble.* I turned back to my tasks, and this time I didn't feel bad about it.

Lucius gave a brief nod. "As you command, my lord. But the men are near spent."

"I know. But—" Valerius stopped speaking.

I didn't move, but my skin prickled. I wasn't looking at him, not directly, but I felt it. Like the sun on bare skin, I could feel him watching, even with my eyes closed. Even turned away.

And when I dared to look up, I saw that I wasn't wrong. His eyes weren't sweeping the line, weren't taking stock. They were on me. It wasn't how commanders looked at soldiers, or how men looked at women. As if I were a riddle he hadn't realized he was trying to solve.

My hand tightened around the ladle before I realized it. There was no reason for him to notice me. No cause for his gaze to hold mine. And still it didn't shift.

I hated the heat that crept up my neck.

The moment stretched until Marcus bumped Valerius with his elbow. "I doubt we'll get anything useful out of you now," he said, voice light and needling. "Perhaps we should continue this discussion in private. After a hot meal."

My throat went dry. I'd hoped no one would notice, but Marcus had. Worse yet, Lucius followed his gaze. All three of them were looking at me.

If only I had some of that magic my father talked about so I could command the earth to swallow me whole.

Valerius showed no sign of embarrassment. No indulgent smirk. No apology. He stepped forward without a word, approaching the long table where I stood behind the stew pot.

It was solid, if splattered and stained with the afternoon's labor, but even that felt thin as parchment with him on the other side. There was no danger in him for me, or so every instinct insisted. My heart beat harder as I remembered the way he'd spoken to me in the skirmish's aftermath: gentle, careful, as if I were broken and he feared to press too hard.

I dipped the ladle into the stew with hands that were steadier than I felt and filled his bowl with care, choosing the best cuts of tender meat, thick slices of potato, and rich broth.

As was expected. I wasn't doing it because I *wanted* to. At least, that's what I told myself.

I felt the weight of his attention settle on me again, heavier now that he stood so near. "Aleaia, was it?"

He pronounced it cleanly—*Ah-LEE-ah*—even if it carried an accent on his Calesian tongue.

Like he'd practiced it.

"Aye—yes, my lord."

"You seem to be on the mend," he said.

I swallowed. My mouth felt like it was full of sand. Seeing him up close in the lantern light made my first impression burn back to life: handsome, strong features, keen eyes the color of rain-washed pine. Sharp, but not cold. Like one of the old knights, the kind who haunted the songs of my childhood—honorable, doomed, and far too noble for a place like this.

Gods, where had *that* come from?

"Yes," I managed, though it came out tight. I cleared my throat and tried again. "Yes, my lord."

Behind him, Lucius coughed, unmistakably pointed. Valerius ignored it.

"I'm glad to hear it," he said. "How are you finding camp life?"

"I want for nothing here, my lord." The words were formal, reflexive, spoken without thinking. "Thank you for your kindness."

He reached for the bowl. His fingers brushed mine. It was only a flicker, but enough to send a jolt through me. I didn't pull away, but my grip shifted, unsure whether to hold on or let go.

"Thank you," he said quietly.

I let go. My cheeks burned. I dropped my gaze to the ladle, to the grain of the table, to anything that wasn't him. I wanted the moment to pass unnoticed, for the heat in my face to fade, for the world to keep moving.

"I understand you have some skill with the blade."

The words landed like a miscast stone in calm water. I stiffened. Why did he mention it?

Before I could answer, Valerius added, "You're not in trouble. Once you've recovered, I'd like to place you among the ranks, if you've no objection."

The breath I let out was shaky but silent, as if my body had been holding it too long. I would be a slave, but being an auxiliary, if I managed it, would come with small dignities. A full belly, warm clothes, the shelter of canvas overhead. Meager things, but they would be mine. I would have a place.

Not freedom like I had before, but something like it. Close enough. The unease bled from my shoulders, replaced by something steadier: purpose.

"I've recovered enough, my lord," I said. "When should I present myself tomorrow?"

From behind Valerius, Marcus chuckled. "You judged her right, Val. She would have been ill-suited to a life in domestic servitude. She might even be a proper replacement for Liora."

I froze. They had spoken of me, beyond my hearing, weighed my future without my knowing. I knew I had no say in such things, but it stuck in me like an arrow to the gut. And who was Liora? Why did she need replacing?

Valerius turned, his glare toward Marcus swift and sharp. When he looked back at me, his expression softened.

"I apologize for my crude companion," he said, voice pitched lower, meant for me alone. "After we reach Avitum, report to the training yard. The morning following our arrival."

I dipped my head. "Thank you, my lord."

He lingered a breath longer, then stepped aside so I might serve the others.

The exchange should have meant nothing. Just a passing concern for a girl dragged half-dead from the woods. A scrap of kindness, nothing more. And yet the weight of it lingered, unresolved. It stayed with me long after he had gone to sit and eat his meal.

I added a log to the fire, stirred the pot, wiped my hands on my apron. Told myself to focus. To move on. I didn't mean to glance toward his table.

Or maybe I did but didn't realize.

Either way, I found his gaze already waiting.

The air changed, just slightly, as though something brushed against me that wasn't wind or heat or smoke.

He looked away a heartbeat later, a ghost of a smile on his lips as he turned back to his bowl. I lowered my eyes, pulse thrumming, and said nothing. Just stirred the pot and pretended I hadn't noticed.

But I had. And so had he.

We never had time to figure out what any of it meant, though. The journey southward to Avitum, deep in the heart of Calesia, took five more decadia of hard marching. Winter pressed close behind us as we left Aeltyria.

At home, people had spoken of Calesians with venom in their voices, and at first, I wondered why, when all I saw was the mercy. In every village we passed, the cohort's healers erected tents to treat the sick. Legionaries passed out bread and dried apples to plague-starved children.

But the same soldiers who offered care one day enforced cruelty the next. It was still Calesian-occupied Aeltyria, after all. Still the empire that had bled my people with impossible tributes, outlawed our language, and traded us like chattel. In every town square, slave auctions followed trials..

Yet when Valerius presided, no one was sold, I noticed. Traders left with empty ledgers and tight mouths. Sentences were handed down, but no chains were clasped. A minor rebellion, perhaps, but one I noticed. How could I not?

I thought about it as I walked beside the baggage train, the clatter of wheels and the slow rhythm of hooves my only companions. I didn't want to talk to anyone, kept to myself out of fear that they might ask me something that made me feel something.

"You're deep in thought."

His voice startled me, and I turned to find him beside me, as if thinking of him had summoned him, walking beside me as if it were the most natural thing in the world. As if he wasn't a son of the Empire and I wasn't the lowest creature under its boot.

"My lord," I began, voice tight with surprise. "What are you—"

"Shhh." He lifted a finger to his lips, eyes bright with mischief. "I'm marching. Guarding the baggage train. What does it look like?"

He wore the plain kit of a foot soldier—no cloak, no visible rank save for the way he carried himself.

For a moment, I could only blink at him. Then, cautiously, I replied, "I suppose it does look that way, my lord."

Valerius laughed, a warm and unguarded sound that caught me by surprise. "It's been days since I last saw you. I've been meaning to check in, but it's no easy task to slip away without my wardens dogging my every step."

"I've no complaints, my lord," I said, careful with my words.

"You've all you need? No trouble with your kit? Is your bedding sufficient?"

I felt my brow arch before I could stop it. What sort of lord asks a slave that? Did he mean to offer me a better place to sleep?

Surely not his bed.

"I have more than I arrived with, my lord. More than I had when you and I first met."

He nodded, as though weighing the answer. "I'm glad to hear it. Where's home?"

The knot in my chest eased. "A village south of where you found me. Rhaelaith."

His gaze sharpened. "The sickness hit them hard."

I wanted to ask if he'd been there, if he'd seen my grandparents, and if they were alive, but I didn't dare. Truth be told, I was afraid to hear his answer.

Still, I answered, my voice thin. "It did. Most were dead before my father and I left." The words came, but my throat closed around the last of them. I had to swallow before I could speak again. "My grandparents among them."

For a time, neither of us said anything. The only sounds were the steady creak of the baggage wagons, the crunch of boots on frost-hardened ground, and the distant noise of a thousand soldiers trudging southward.

Valerius spoke again, softer this time. "I'm sorry. Leaving must have been difficult. And then you lost your father, too."

I turned my face away, blinking hard. My breath hitched once before I caught it.

"It's in the past now, my lord. There's no undoing it." I glanced sideways, gave the faintest shrug. "It's the way of things for my people. We endure."

I saw little of him after that, and so much more of the world than I had imagined when I lived in sleepy little Rhaelaith.

We marched through green country first. Rolling hills veiled in mist, stone fences half-swallowed by moss, streams that ran cold and clear over dark rock. Sheep scattered at our passing. Smoke curled from low cottages tucked into folds of land, their roofs weighted with sod and age. The air smelled of rain and peat and growing things. Even in grief, it felt familiar. Like home stretched wider than I had known.

The climb into the Pravian Pass stole that softness away. The land rose sharp and bare, wind-scoured and pale, where nothing grew without fighting for it. Snow clung in the shadows even as the days lengthened. The cold there was dry and biting, stripping the breath from your lungs and sound from your thoughts. We marched in silence, wrapped tight against a sky that felt too close, too empty.

On the far side, the world changed again.

The air warmed. The light shifted, turning brighter and harder. Hills gave way to open plains and ordered fields cut into the land with measured lines. Olive trees replaced pine. Stone buildings rose square and pale, their walls clean and sharp-edged, untouched by moss or time. Roads ran straight as spear shafts, paved and measured, indifferent to the land beneath them.

By the time Avitum appeared on the horizon, white and gleaming against the sky, I felt as though I had crossed not just distance, but into another way of being altogether.

I drew a breath as the city came into view.

It was beautiful. White stone towers rose above the city walls like spears pointed at the sky, gleaming in the sunlight, precise and cold. The symmetry of the buildings, the clean lines and polished faces, made me feel as though I'd walked into something not made for people, but for gods.

Or tyrants.

I stared as we passed under the gates, unsure if the prickling down my spine was admiration or warning.

I hated the way it made me feel small and misplaced. Buildings loomed too tall, blotting out the sun. The ground beneath my boots felt unnatural. The streets were cobbled evenly. No wagon ruts. No mud. No wild roots pushing up through stone. These weren't the worn paths of Rhaelaith, shaped by time and feet.

Crowds lined the roads as the main body of the legion, which we'd joined just before the Pravian Pass, marched in, their cheers rising like the tide. Flower petals rained down from the balconies above—red, yellow, violet. Sweet-smelling things that stuck to my clothes and hair. People shouted and waved, leaning over rails to catch sight of the soldiers. Men clapped and cheered. Women blew kisses. Some cried out names, others just threw themselves at the noise. A few of the city's whores called down with practiced voices, offering beds, baths, or both, hitching their skirts like they were airing out laundry.

The city adored its army, and the legion, to their credit, didn't falter. They marched shoulder to shoulder, eyes forward.

Even Valerius, at the head of the column, ignored the attention.

I kept my head down near the rear of the formation, grateful to be overlooked. The petal-covered streets blurred beneath my steps.

I said nothing. Met no one's gaze.

I was a simple country girl, after all.

# CHAPTER FIVE
## *The Standard*

*"Any legionary who raises a hand in violence against a fellow soldier shall be stripped of rank, pay, and honor and is no longer fit to wear the dragon."*
—Imperial Code of Conduct, Article 4.2.1

Rudamos 75, 1230
*Aleaia*

I fixed my gaze on the registrar, jaw clenched. I drew a slow breath. Just looking at that miserable piece of shit made my blood boil.

"The notice states registration remains open through tomorrow," I growled. "I'm within the limit."

The registrar drummed his fingers against the desk, chin resting on his other hand. He squinted at me, as though deciding whether I was worth the trouble of a full sentence.

"For *you*, it's closed," he said at last, dry as dust.

I let out a short, bitter breath. The audacity. The tournament notice sat in front of him, creased but legible, and still he lied. I looked out the tent flap, around the courtyard, not in search of help, but witnesses. Was no one else seeing this? Just the usual downturned faces and polite avoidance. The guard nearby snorted, his smirk landing like spit on a wound.

"Specifically for me? And why is that?" I asked, straightening as I spoke each syllable clear and sharp as flint.

The registrar leaned back and shrugged. "The directive comes straight from His Majesty—"

"Oh, bullshit," I said, scoffing. I clenched my fists to keep from striking him.

"Slaves aren't eligible. Now, I believe there's a privy in need of cleaning somewhere. Off you go." He waved me away, already turning back to his parchments. He'd dismissed me as a slave with his soft hands, like I hadn't bled and made the Empire's enemies bleed for seven years. It would have been laughable if it wasn't so damned insulting.

I stepped forward and slammed my hand on the desk. He jolted upright, nearly knocking over the inkwell. "You will not dismiss me like some common servant," I grated out.

A firm hand clamped down on my shoulder and pulled, turning me. The registrar's guard leaned in, breath sour with ale. "Maybe if you could read, girl, you'd understand."

I stiffened, my hand twitching toward the hilt at my hip. The only thing that stopped me from running him through was the prospect of being hanged or flogged. I met the guard's gaze without flinching, lifting my chin. I wouldn't let him look down on me.

"I am no one's *slave*. I've served this Empire for seven years. Honorably. Faithfully. I earned my citizenship." My hands clenched at my sides, nails biting into my palms. "And you, soaked in drink and stinking of piss, think to insult me?"

The guard gave a lazy shrug. "You're still a northerner. An ashborn nothing. If your betters tell you to go, you go. Like he said. Out of his sight."

*Ashborn*. An insult, a reminder that I was born of the ashes of a country razed to the ground in Claudius's conquest.

I drew a slow breath through my nose, held it for a moment before releasing. I had to think. Words wouldn't change their minds, but a report to their superiors might shut them up. Without another glance, I turned on my heel.

I made it three steps before the guard called after me. "Wait. Maybe I spoke too soon."

I halted, praying silently. Lithau, grant me patience enough not to end up in a hangman's noose today.

The words were a trap, I knew, but still I turned. "What?"

He stepped in, too close, and the smirk returned. "Why don't you explain it to me in private?" His hand slid over my hip, fingers pressing hard against my waist.

The touch landed like rot, filth pressed deep. Fury rose in me, cold and clean. The sort that didn't shout but killed. Or wanted to.

I lunged.

He caught my arm and swung. His knuckles cracked across my cheek, the blow whipping my head to the side. My vision blurred. The ringing in my ears was almost a relief—one more thing I didn't have to listen to.

I drove my knee into his groin. He wheezed and folded. I seized his collar and slammed him into the desk. Oak met flesh with a hollow crack. A satisfying sound, that one.

I didn't stop.

Shoved him down again, face-first this time. Parchments flew.

The registrar let out a shrill squawk and bolted, knocking over the stool in his scramble to escape.

The guard clawed at me, fingers tangling in my braid as it fell over my shoulder.

I saw the inkstand, grabbed it and smashed it into his skull.

The sound it made was dull.

He collapsed against the desk's edge, then slipped and dropped like a sack of grain. The corner of the stool caught the back of his head on the way down.

He didn't move again.

I stood there, ink black on my knuckles, panting, heart thudding. I stared down at the guard sprawled beneath me, his face slack, blood darkening his temple.

If he was dead, my life was forfeit.

If he wasn't, it'd still be a night in a cell.

Again.

Third time this season.

I closed my eyes, took a deep breath.

Boots pounded outside. Shouts rose beyond the canvas.

The tent flap burst open and three legionaries stormed inside. One dropped to his knees beside the fallen man, fingers pressed to the side of his neck. "He's alive," he said after a moment. "Eyes are dull, though."

"Shit," muttered another, turning on his heel. "Get a healer. Now."

The third stepped toward me, hand resting on the hilt of his sword, though he didn't draw. "Don't move."

I wasn't fool enough to provoke them further. I dropped the inkstand and held my hands up in surrender.

Voices barked orders outside. Then the flap rustled again and a healer ducked inside. An older man in a sweat-stained tunic, his satchel was already open as he knelt by the guard. He checked the wound, pried open an eyelid, passed a bitter draught beneath the man's nose.

Nothing.

The healer let out a breath. "We'll need a stretcher. Skull took a nasty knock. He might not wake."

Silence followed.

Then the senior guard turned to me, voice low but firm. "You're coming with us. Tribune said straight to him the next time you caused trouble."

One of the others stepped forward, holding his hand palm up toward me. "Hand over your weapons."

*Fuck.*

There was no point in resisting. I reached for my belt and unbuckled my sword, fingers numb around the leather strap. The knife from my boot followed, hilt first. The guard snatched both.

Then they took me by the arms to lead me from the tent and through the barracks courtyard in silence. I kept my chin high. My lip was split, and my cheek throbbed with every heartbeat, but I'd done worse damage than I'd taken. That wasn't victory. It wasn't anything. Just another mistake I couldn't take back.

They shoved open the door and brought me inside.

Lucius Tutela—now Tribune of the Second Army's First Legion, my tribune for the past year—sat behind a battered desk. Half-buried in scrolls, quill in hand, he didn't look up at first.

One of the guards cleared his throat. "Sir. You said to bring her straight to you."

His quill scratched once, twice, before he set it aside with a sigh as his eyes passed over me—swollen cheek, dried blood, the smear of ink on my sleeve. He looked as unimpressed as I had ever seen him. And I had seen him like this more often than I'd have liked to.

He leaned back in his chair. "Well," he said. "Let's hear it."

I looked away, at anything and anywhere but him. I knew how this went. They'd tell the Tribune what they saw, but never what led to it. I was already guilty. It was already all my fault.

The guard to my left spoke first. "We found her in the registrar's tent. Varus was down, ink all over him, looks like a hit to his left temple. She was standing over him, holding the inkstand."

He said it like I just walked in and decided today was the day I would clobber a man over the head with an ink pot.

Tutela said nothing. The pause was heavy as stone.

The second guard shifted his weight. "Top of the desk was cracked. Blood on the edge of the stool. He's breathing, but he hasn't woken. Or hadn't, when the healers took him."

Tutela gave a curt nod. "Thank you. That'll be all."

The guard to my left hesitated. "But lord, what if she—"

"I'm not afraid of her. That will be all," Tutela said again.

They gave quick salutes and left, the door shutting behind them. I clasped my hands behind my back and didn't move.

Tutela folded his hands on the desk. "What do you have to say for yourself this time?"

"I didn't... I didn't mean to," I ground out.

"Can't hear you," Tutela said.

I drew a breath, and when I spoke again, it was louder. "I didn't mean to cause him that degree of harm, my lord. I went to register for the tournament. The registrar said it was closed to me. Said I was a slave. Told me to go scrub a privy. I got a bit loud with the registrar. Drew the guard's attention. He called me 'ashborn.'"

Tutela gave a low grunt.

"I turned to leave, to come speak to you, but the guard made indecent comments. He was drunk. Then he put his hands on me, and I... may have been a bit too rough in the lesson I meant to teach him."

Tutela stood, brow furrowed. "Your behavior is unacceptable, Dieter."

"I understand, my lord, but—"

"But nothing." His voice cracked like a whip.

I straightened, took a sharp breath through my nose.

"You cannot strike every man who offends you. You're a soldier of the Second Army, not a brawling tavern wench. You must show restraint."

I lifted my chin. "He dishonored the uniform of His Majesty's forces, my lord. He was drunk on duty, insolent, and grossly inappropriate. Where was his restraint? He required discipline. I gave it to him."

Tutela drew a hand down his face, slow and deliberate, as though rubbing at a headache that had taken root and wouldn't leave. His gaze sharpened and his voice dropped to something colder. "It was not your place to discipline him. You are the optio of the Tenth Century. Entrusted with our newest auxiliary recruits. You know better. I *expect* better."

I preferred anger to the disappointment in his voice.

"As optio, I'm owed a certain degree of respect. Especially from a common guard."

I bit the inside of my cheek, hard enough to taste copper.

"My lord," I added after a breath, "*he laid hands on me first.*"

"You should've broken away and come straight to me," Tutela snapped. "Do you think I tolerate that kind of conduct? Even from First Army?"

My hands clenched and unclenched behind my back. "No, my lord," I said, the words tight behind my teeth.

"I would have told—not asked, told—his Tribune that *his* punishment would be a flogging in front of this legion and his own. I know Varus. This wasn't his first offense. It would have been justified."

"Even for someone like me, my lord?" The law did not favor foreigners, especially not former slaves.

Tutela waved off the question with a flick of his hand. "I would have left that out. But in this instance, it looks like you attacked a natural-born citizen of the Empire. If he dies, you'll stand trial for his murder. Do you understand the weight of what you've done?"

The silence stretched. My tongue stuck to the roof of my mouth. I swallowed against the dryness, trying to clear the knot that had gathered behind my breastbone.

I drew a breath, steadied it. "My lord… he'll wake. Once he sleeps off the ale."

"For your sake, I hope so." Tutela sighed. "You're a valued soldier, Dieter. But there's a line. And you're standing on it."

I said nothing at first. Then, after a few heartbeats, I decided that if I was going to get in trouble, at least I'd be heard first. "With respect, my lord, the Imperial Army has a deeper problem with discipline."

Tutela's expression flickered, just enough for me to see it. A hairline crack in the stone. He glanced away, then back as his hand dropped to his side. "You're not wrong," he said, quieter now, tired, almost. "This isn't the first time. But even so, you'll reflect on your actions in the confines of a cell, at least for tonight. Once he wakes, we'll find something suitable to appease his Tribune."

"Yes, sir."

He met my eyes. "Pray to the Creator that he does."

"Yes, sir," I said once more.

His voice hardened again. "You'll be fortunate to keep your rank. And if he dies, even that won't matter."

That landed. No blow, no bruise, but my insides clenched all the same. Years of labor, gone with a single misstep. I felt the press of it like a blade laid flat against my ribs, heavy and cold.

There was nothing else to say. "Understood, my lord."

Tutela moved to the door and opened it. Two guards entered without a word, armor clinking against itself as they moved to flank me again. They didn't even look at me.

The descent into the bowels of the castle was long and winding. Stone corridors twisted inward, coiling tighter the farther we went. The air turned damp, thick with mildew and the sour tang of decay. Somewhere far off, water dripped.

When we reached the cell, the guards shoved me in without ceremony. I stumbled, caught myself, and turned. "That wasn't necessary," I snapped.

They didn't answer. The door clanged shut behind them, the lock scraping as it was turned.

I turned, eyeing the cell in the dim light. It was as glorious as I expected: bare stone, piss-stained straw probably infested with lice or fleas, and a chamber pot in the corner that might last have been emptied during the war.

I sat down against the least wet wall, cold stone biting through my trousers. Damp crept into my shoulders, my spine, my knees. Better than the stench of piss-soaked wool and mold I'd find on the pile that was meant for sleeping. I leaned my head back and stared up at the ceiling, at the dark lines running through the mortar.

I'd spent seven years in the Imperial Army.

Seven years of holding my tongue. Of eating every slight, every insult. Of enduring the way the men looked at me as if I were meat one day and nothing the next. And still, they expected me to kneel for their praise.

Seven years of doing every godsdamned horrible thing they required of me.

And then I'd landed myself in here three times in one season. Three fights. Always the same kind of man. Always the same kind of silence after.

Some of the other women had found ways to survive it. They giggled through it, bartered favors, turned a blind eye. I couldn't. Wouldn't. I hadn't joined the legion to make friends or find glory. I'd joined because it gave me food. A roof. A blade. A horse, once, though that was gone now. Somewhere to sleep that usually wasn't wet or burning or torn apart by war.

And maybe, if I made it to the end of my service, I could go back to something quieter. Goats. Chickens. An old gray horse. Soil that didn't bleed when you turned it over. Something like the home I'd lost.

I looked down at my hands. Blood flaked from the crease between thumb and forefinger, dry now, but still visible. They'd say I lost control again. They'd be right.

I just didn't care anymore.

The darkness pressed in, thick as wool, smothering the edges of thought. The silence was so loud. It always was. I'd spent years chasing motion, keeping my hands full so my mind couldn't wander. Solitude and stillness stripped that shield away, left me exposed and raw, remembering.

I'd thought the Second's colors might protect me. In exchange, I'd let them spend a season stripping away the things that made me myself.

I was sixteen when they replaced it all with discipline, endurance, and obedience. Days started before dawn, and they were long and brutal and filled with marching. Gods, we marched until our feet bled.

When we weren't marching, we trained with heavy equipment. Wooden swords that weighed more than the real thing. Heavier shields. Heavier armor than we would ever wear in battle. When we finally carried the real thing, it felt almost light. And we were always in motion—swimming fully clothed with weapons, climbing things that didn't need to be climbed, digging trenches, building roads, raising camps at the end of exhaustion.

Optios didn't nurture. They tested who would break and who would endure. Some of us died. Most of us wished we would, but none of us ever laid down and let it happen.

That would have been disobedience.

We were cut loose from our old lives and bound together in one built on suffering and the absence of privacy. Over time, the legion became the only stable thing in my life. That suited me. The people and places that had made up my old life were already gone.

After the ambush in Tuath Forest, a centurion noticed the way I spoke Calesian. Hardly any accent, he said. I was fluent in both tongues, tested enough to be trusted, so the Empire made me a bridge. They sent me when the rebels held fast. The voice of peace at the edge of a blade.

I could convince them. And I did.

"No harm will come to your families. I give you my word," I'd said to an elder bracing the longhouse door with his own body.

Then came the betrayals. Promises unkept. Surrenders turned to executions. A village razed days after parley. Children taken. Killed.

"They'll be safe. I swear it," I'd said to a mother clutching her daughter's hand, like I believed it. Sometimes, I did. Each time, the lie was mine to carry.

Would my father have understood? Would he have spat in my face?

I rubbed at the blood crusted in the crease of my thumb, then let my hand fall again.

Despite it all, I was still grateful to him, if not the Empire. To Lord Valerius. If he ever asked, I'd follow him, because he'd seen me when

I was nothing and handed me a sword and a future. Grim as it was, it was better than anything I could have made for myself. He wasn't like the others, the handful of times I'd seen him since we met. Didn't sneer at dirt under my nails or talk down to me in that clipped patrician drawl. He listened. Fought beside us. I'd seen him drag wounded men from the mud with his own hands. Maybe he was born in silk, but he wore the command like armor, not ornament.

The Praesidium Regalis—the personal guard of the royal family—was the one thing left that still might be clean. Better wages, better housing, but most of all, it would never ask me to hurt anyone but those who tried to hurt him first. It was safer.

That was my dream. Safety.

A dream gone up in smoke or smashed with an inkstand. I shifted against the wall, let my head fall back against the wall. They'd put me on scribe duty, if I made it out of this, no doubt. Quills, ledgers, and some basement-dwelling clerk barking orders like he hadn't pissed himself the last time a blade came near him. It would be punishment dressed as necessity.

The weight of it all—my ambition, my temper, my damnable honesty—settled on me.

I folded my arms, more to hold myself still than for warmth, and I shut my eyes. Not to sleep—just to stop seeing.

# CHAPTER SIX
## *Duty*

*"What is bravery, if not standing where another should have died?"*
—Caedmon, First Sword of Aeltyria

Rudamos 85, 1230
*Aleaia*

I'd picked a stupid fucking season to get into trouble.

Sweat ran down my spine, soaking through my tunic as the late sun beat down from a cloudless sky. Every breath dragged heat into my lungs, parching my throat no matter how much water I drank. I swiped my forehead with the back of my sleeve, salt stinging my eyes. My arms ached from the day's labor, but the real torment lay beneath.

Shame, coiled and riding close to the skin.

The man I'd struck had lived, but I was still paying for it. Relegated to hauling timber and iron fittings for the repair of the Anvallan Temple while the legion drilled, I felt the weight of consequence in every splinter, every sun-scorched hour.

Everything I'd worked for, gone up in the flames of my temper.

The work was done, the last of the tools loaded in the wagon. I thumped the side. The driver snapped the reins. The aurochs groaned, trudging forward, and I stood in their wake as the wheels creaked across the stone.

Peeling off my gloves, I wiped my palms on my tunic and let out a breath. A warm gust stirred my damp hair, bringing the scent of sawdust, sweat, and freshly hewn pine. The temple loomed before me, pristine white columns gleaming like sunlight on snow. I traced the carved reliefs with my eyes: gods locked in battle, creation springing from the wound of Lithau's heart.

I'd hauled stones for this place like any good penitent.

I was too tired and thirsty to even think about what that meant. I took the waterskin from my belt and drank.

A flicker of movement above caught my eye. Perched on the highest eave was the white raven. It tilted its head at me, feathers bright as new snow, beak dark as pitch. Watching. Always watching.

My grip tightened on the gloves in my hand. If I had a bow, I'd skewer the damn thing and eat it for dinner.

The raven spread its wings and launched into the air, vanishing with a soft rush of wind. My breath caught. A prickle crept down my spine. I turned, looked around the square—face to face, wagon to gate—searching for what had set my nerves on edge.

Nothing. No shouting. No horns. No smoke. Just the sun, the dust, and a whisper of wind.

I drank again, longer this time, thinking the heat had addled my mind. The cool water helped, but the unease sat in my gut like unbaked dough.

A rider emerged through the temple gates. No crested helm or cloak of authority. Just plain riding leathers. Quiet authority. He rode with the easy confidence of a man born to the saddle, his shoulders relaxed, spine straight, one hand loose on the reins. The breeze teased strands of ash-brown hair across his brow, sunlight catching the gold threaded through the darker waves.

I recognized him at once.

Valerius di Calesia.

A single guard followed behind, armor polished to a gleam. I watched them dismount. Their movements were unhurried but precise. Soldiers to the bone. I meant to look away, but Valerius turned, his gaze catching mine like a tether pulled taut. Then he smiled, small but real, and that slight betrayal of formality sent my pulse skittering.

My fingers clenched around the waterskin before I replaced it on my belt. I straightened, brushing a hand over my tunic, too aware of the sweat clinging to it. Of course he showed up when I looked like this. Couldn't have arrived first thing, when I resembled something halfway decent, before I smelled like an old boot.

Why did that matter to me?

As he approached, I dropped to one knee, eyes on the cobblestones. Black riding boots halted before me, polished and spotless.

"Aleaia Dieter?"

His voice still held the same warmth it had when we first met, but gods, that voice. Naturally, it had aged too well, like everything else about him. Smooth as velvet, it cut straight down to—

I stiffened, shoved the feeling down with the rest, and kept my gaze low.

"Please, stand," he said.

"Yes, my lord." I stood.

"No need for that, either," he said, waving off the deference. "Just Val will do."

I blinked. What sort of commander—a Legate, a prince—told a subordinate to call him something so familiar?

"It's been a long time, hasn't it?" he asked.

"Has it? I've been under your command for all of it."

He smiled, a glint in his eyes, like he knew how to slip past my defenses without trying. "I know," he said. "How are you?"

"Well enough, my lord. And you?"

"Better, now."

My pulse skipped once, hard enough to annoy me.

The last time I'd seen him up close, he'd been only a little taller than me—close enough that we'd met as equals, both of us still growing into our limbs. Now he stood taller by a head, broader in the shoulders.

And his face was sharper now, honed like everything else about him. High cheekbones, a strong jaw that looked like it stayed clenched even in sleep, a mouth made for command, barely gentled by the warmth in his eyes. His eyes were the same green I remembered, though I didn't remember them being so bright. Or maybe I'd just never let myself look this long.

The boy I remembered was gone.

I'd stared too long. I blinked and dropped my eyes.

"What brings you here?" he asked.

"Oh." I twisted the gloves in my hands. There was no dignified way to dress up a punishment detail. "I'm... part of the work crew, my lord."

"The work crew?" His brow lifted. "I thought these crews were—"

"My lord!" The foreman's voice sliced across the square. For once, I was glad to hear it. He arrived at a brisk trot, tunic damp with sweat, face red from the effort. He looked between us, his gaze narrowing on me before settling on Valerius. "Is she bothering you?"

And just like that, my gratitude vanished.

Valerius turned, expression cool. "Quite the opposite. I approached her. Are you ready for the inspection?"

"Yes, my lord. Right this way." The foreman bowed and stepped aside.

Valerius turned back to me. "I'm afraid I must go. Duty calls."

"It does that. Often and loudly, I find," I said.

He laughed and I held onto the sound like warmth between my fingers, allowing myself a smile.

"Would you mind if I stopped by again after I've answered it?"

"No, my lord. Of course not." I dipped my head.

"I will, then." He hesitated, then inclined his head and turned away.

I watched him cross the temple yard, his gaze flicking back once before he rejoined his guard. The foreman puffed behind, struggling to keep pace.

I didn't know what it was about him that lingered. Only that it always did.

I sank onto the curb, arms draped across my knees. Sweat was drying in itchy patches along my back. Across the square, Valerius gestured toward the temple frontage while the foreman flailed through some excuse or another. I couldn't hear the words, but his hands told the story, as Calesians' hands always did.

I didn't need to hear him to know the foreman was being politely flayed alive.

The temple looked flawless to me. Then again, a royal wedding demanded divine perfection.

My eyes drifted to the guard beside him. Straight-backed, motionless, one hand near the pommel of his sword.

Alert. Too alert, maybe. Something was off.

He wasn't watching Valerius. He was watching the rooftops, which wasn't inherently odd, except for how he did it. You see, I had been a scout, so I knew what it was to look without expectation. His gaze swept the skyline again and again, sharp and deliberate.

Waiting.

I stood, slow and quiet, followed his line of sight. The surrounding balconies were empty. Shutters drawn. Rooftops bare. A knot formed in my chest. He was anticipating something, but what?

The third time his eyes darted upward, I caught it.

A glint.

Faint. Metallic. Hidden in a shadowed alcove.

An arrowhead.

The bow behind it, drawn.

I didn't breathe. Couldn't.

My gaze snapped to the guard and what I saw gutted me. He wasn't moving to shield Valerius. He'd seen it, too, and he was stepping aside.

Clearing the path.

The gloves slipped from my hands.

I didn't shout a warning. If I called out, the archer would loose before I got there. My focus narrowed. My heart thundered, drowning everything else. My vision tunneled to where Valerius stood.

I had to reach him.

I ran.

No time to think. Only to move.

He turned at the sounds people made when I shoved them out of the way, brow knitting. His hand dropped to the hilt of his sword, body shifting into a fighter's stance. He didn't know what I meant to do.

The guard moved to intercept.

Too slow.

I ducked, light on my feet, and slipped past. He stumbled, off balance. I was already through.

Between Valerius and the arrow.

I crashed into him, arms flung around his neck by instinct, not thought. My body struck his with enough force to stagger him a step.

He caught me. Arms locked around my waist as I sagged against him. For a heartbeat, it felt like an embrace.

Then came the pain. A blinding burn tore beneath my left shoulder—white-hot, like steel driven through flesh.

Blood spilled down my back, hot and thick.

"Aleaia!"

"An archer..." I gasped. "My lord..."

Each word scraped me raw. My head dropped against his chest, hair sticking wetly to his tunic.

The world receded. His voice still reached me—low, urgent—but I couldn't follow it.

I was drowning.

The warmth slipped away. Everything went dark.

# CHAPTER SEVEN
## *Near the Veil*

*"I came near the Veil once. I did not sleep—I dreamt.*
*And in those dreams, I saw things not yet done.*
*I think the end remembers the beginning."*
—Queen Eavan, before the Battle of Aeldunon

Rudamos 85, 1230
*Aleaia*

Where am I?

Consciousness flickered, threadbare, drifting at the edges of my body, but not far enough gone to dull the pain. It raged through my back.

Molten.

Merciless.

I couldn't move. My eyes wouldn't open. Sound pressed in—raised voices, the thud of boots on stone, the jangle of metal.

"Get the surgeon!" Valerius's voice, stripped of the calm he wore like armor.

More footsteps. A door flung wide. Someone running. Orders shouted down corridors.

Then a hand at my back. Shaking. "I'm sorry," Valerius said.

Pressure followed.

The pain. Gods, the pain. It flared like white-hot fire.

Blinding.

Brutal.

Unrelenting.

A cry tore free, raw and involuntary, before everything slipped loose.

*I have to save him.*

The thought rang out like a bell, familiar and inevitable.

My hand gripped the sword hard enough to whiten my knuckles, to carve the hilt's pattern into my palm. Blood coated the blade, warm and fresh, running in thin rivulets over my skin. I hoped it was theirs.

Much of it might've been mine.

With each step, it dripped to the stone in a slow rhythm.

The pain pulsed, sharp and blinding. My vision wavered, smearing into light and shadow. The air stank of iron and fire, thick enough to choke. Blood pooled in my mouth. I spat. Wiped my face with a shaking hand and kept moving.

One step.

Another.

Because all I could think was—

*I have to save him.*

# CHAPTER EIGHT
## *The Vigil*

*She watched as stars forgot the sky, and whispered breath to one who lay*
*Not for love, but so the soul would choose again to stay.*
—The Song of the Stars, Cycle VII: The Cycle of Spirit

Rudamos 87, 1230
*Aleaia*

My senses returned slowly, before my body would listen.

The dull throb in my back, under my shoulder, pulsed with each beat of my heart. My lips were cracked and my eyes, swollen. But I couldn't complain about where they'd put me. Sheets, warm and clean, wrapped around me. Someone had tried to keep me comfortable and done a damn good job of it.

Soft, golden light flickered behind my eyelids and from somewhere beyond the window, crickets sang to the night wind.

Footsteps crossed the floor. Slow. Measured. I followed the sound, straining toward the faint rustle of parchment. A sigh. The pacing picked up for a few strides.

A door creaked open.

"Fetch Tutela," Valerius said. The door shut again with a click.

His steps came back slower. I felt the shift as he neared, the slight lift of the blanket's edge, then its careful return. The mattress dipped as he sat beside me.

"I am so sorry." His voice was rough, uncertain. "I'm sorry that the treachery and pain that follow in my wake have found their way to you."

Fingers brushed my cheek, tucked a lock of hair behind my ear. The touch lingered, then withdrew.

Silence stretched.

Then the door groaned open again.

"My lord?" Tutela's voice.

"Come in." Valerius stood, footsteps retreating.

A chair scraped stone. Then another.

"Good to see you alive and in one piece," Tutela said. His voice was steady, though tension edged beneath it. "I heard there was trouble near the Temple. Tell me what—fucking Hel, is that Dieter?"

"It is. There was an attempt on my life," Valerius replied. "And I suspect my own guards were behind it. One of them tried to put an arrow in my heart. She took it instead. I was with Amatus when it happened. Had to fight him off in the street after it missed its mark."

Tutela's breath came sharp. Angry. "Anvallus's balls."

"I'll need to replace them," Valerius said. "I want you at my side, as part of my personal guard."

Tutela hesitated. "Shouldn't we wait for your father's sanction?"

"Not the Praesidium Regalis," Valerius said. "*My* household guard. I'm taking up the governorship in Aeldunon. And when she's healed, I want her to serve in it as well."

Silence settled between them, thick with calculation. From the farther chair came the soft rhythm of fingers tapping wood—Tutela weighing implications, if I had to guess. At last, he spoke. "Your father's approved the formation of a personal guard?"

"I'm not asking," Valerius said. "It's done. I'm informing you, and I'd like your agreement. I won't compel you."

Tutela sighed. "You have it, of course." He paused. "What else do you know?"

"What I told you is all I know," Valerius replied. His voice had tightened. "Marcus is investigating the depth of the conspiracy."

"All of them, you think? Even Liora?"

"Yes," Valerius grated out.

Lucius let out a short breath through his nose.

"Dieter served with us," Valerius added.

Tutela's answer came slow. "She did. But she's drawn some, ah, attention lately. That might bring resistance, if His Majesty looks too closely."

"Attention?" Valerius asked.

"Trouble."

"For?"

"Fighting."

Valerius scoffed.

"Most recently," Tutela went on, "she actually tried to join the Praesidium Regalis. She was denied entry into the tournament. The registrar's guard made certain remarks about her lineage. Used a vile name. When she tried to leave the tent, he escalated. Unwelcome hands. Inappropriate words."

"She struck him?"

"Several times," Tutela said, with the edge of approval. "He deserved it."

Valerius hummed in agreement.

"I didn't want to discipline her. But it was the third time this season, the man was laid up for a while, and his tribune demanded something be done. I confined her for a day and put her on labor for a decadium. She was on that detail at the temple when this happened."

"He one of ours?"

"No. I would have told you if he was. First Army."

"Cassius's man, then," Valerius said, as if it didn't surprise him.

Tutela grunted.

"If she agrees, she'll get better than she asked for. And she gets to go home."

A few heartbeats passed. Lucius's chair creaked. "My lord," he said. "Do you mean to reward her with a position that might again require her to take a blade for you?"

*No, no, don't dissuade him,* I thought. I tried to move. To speak, to object. Nothing came.

Valerius took a breath. Let it out slow. "I can trust no one more than someone who's already stood between me and death. She's free to refuse, as are you."

Tutela sighed. "I wanted a change anyway. I'll do almost anything to get out from behind a desk buried in parchment. I accept."

Valerius chuckled. "No paperwork. No administrative duties. Take care of each other, watch my back, and swing a sword when needed."

I wanted to accept. I had to tell him. A low and broken sound escaped me. My hand lifted.

Tutela straightened. "Was that her?"

"Get the healer," Valerius said.

A chair scraped back. Footsteps retreated.

Valerius leaned close. "Aleaia?"

My eyes finally obeyed when I commanded them to open. The world swam for a moment. He was inches away, kneeling beside the bed. His green eyes found mine—searching, steady. Gentler than I'd ever seen them.

"Welcome back."

"Water," I rasped. "Please."

He moved at once. As I tried to sit up, my body protested, my limbs slow to obey and pain sharp in my back. Still, I tried.

I leaned on my right arm. When he offered the cup, I reached for it.

Pain lanced through me. My arm gave out. The cup slipped, water sloshing over the rim.

"No, no. Allow me," Valerius said.

He cupped one hand under my chin, brought the cup to my lips with the other. Tilted it carefully. The cool water soothed the rawness in my throat, cleared some of the fog from my mind.

Then I felt the closeness.

The way his eyes never left my face, focused entirely on something as simple as helping me drink. That he was the one tending me—

I became suddenly, painfully aware of how little I wore. Bandages wrapped me from underarm to waist but Aelan's mercy, I was indecent. My cheeks flushed hot.

"Ah, so you do have enough blood left to blush," he said,. "I was beginning to wonder, given how much you left between the Temple and here."

"Where are we? How long?" It came out more gruffly than I intended.

"The castle infirmary. We brought you to the temple first, but they couldn't manage your wounds." His jaw tensed. "One of the priests thought it best to remove the arrow. He was wrong. The bleeding wouldn't stop. I put you on my horse and brought you here myself. That was two days ago."

I blinked, trying to make sense of it. One detail pushed through the haze.

"You carried me?" Why that stuck, I didn't know.

"I had to. You couldn't walk." He leaned back, arms folded, mock-stern. "You bled everywhere. The cobbles, my saddle, my horse. Very inconsiderate."

A breath escaped me—half laugh, half sigh. "My apologies, my lord."

"Accepted. Just this once. But on one condition."

"What?"

"No more 'my lord.' Call me Val. Please."

I'd never but now was not the time to say so. I shifted, wincing. "Have you been here the whole time?"

"Yes." Quiet. Stripped of command. "Where else would I be?"

"You must be needed. You didn't have to stay."

"I needed to be here. Nowhere else."

I didn't know what to say to that.

He shrugged. "You lost a lot of blood. Someone had to make sure you didn't try to rise and do something foolish. The healer was needed elsewhere."

I looked down at my hands. "Thank you."

"You've saved my life, Aleaia Dieter. Should be me thanking you."

"As you saved mine. Years ago," I said.

"I remember." His voice gentled. "Seems that's the nature of us. Saving each other."

"I think I got the worse end of the deal." I lay back down, on my right side this time.

"Then maybe I owe you another." He leaned forward, tugging the sheet up over my shoulder. "Though you've only just awakened, I must ask something of you."

"Anything within my power."

Something in his expression shifted so quickly I might have imagined it.

"I'd be honored if you would be my sword and shield. Professionally, rather than recreationally."

I laughed, then gasped and grimaced as pain lanced through me.

Valerius reached out instinctively, his hand resting lightly on my shoulder, concern flickering across his face.

I knew what he intended. I'd heard everything. And yet, hearing him ask struck deeper than I expected. This was what I had wanted. So why did it feel like a trick?

My voice came quiet. "Why?"

"I find it difficult to come by trusted companions of late."

I nodded slowly. "I would say yes, if not for the fear of reassignment."

Valerius shook his head. "No need to worry. Your duty would be to me alone. Not the Praesidium Regalis. That breaks convention, but I intend to break a few."

The thought of the Praesidium Regalis attending him chilled me. Splintered loyalties. Blades pointed both ways. "Will they be with you? The Praesidium Regalis?"

"No. I don't plan to linger in Avitum while my father takes his time replacing what failed. We'll leave as soon as the investigation and trials are done. Could be a few days. Could be a couple decadia. Hard to tell."

I nodded.

"The post is yours for life, if you want it," he said. "You're free to resign whenever you like. But for as long as you stay, my path is yours."

It felt impossible.

Too clean.

Too irresistible.

Too close to freedom.

My chest tightened. Heat prickled behind my eyes. I blinked hard.

"My lord," I said thickly, "you're teasing me. Or I'm dreaming."

He smiled. "No."

"That's just what a dream *would* say."

A quiet huff of breath left him.

"Your offer is more generous than I deserve," I murmured. "I accept with all my heart."

He reached out, his hand closing gently over mine. "Thank you," he said.

The warmth steadied me, and I held it tighter.

Footsteps echoed in the corridor. His fingers lingered a moment longer before slipping free.

The healer entered, her assistant close behind, arms full of baskets.

"Well, it's about time you decided to join us," the healer said, sweeping to the bedside. "My lord, we're grateful for your vigil, but we'll need the room."

"Of course." Valerius rose. He looked at me once more. "I'm not going anywhere. I'll be in the hall if you need me."

He stepped out, and the healer set to work.

# CHAPTER NINE
## *What is Owed*

*"What is freely given binds tighter than any chain.*
*The hand that offers becomes the hand we trust again."*
—Common Aeltyrian Proverb

Dēwamos 17, 1230
*Aleaia*

Navigating the upper ranks of Calesian society would've been tiresome at the best of times. Doing it with my arm in a sling made it worse. Eyes followed me wherever I went, not because I was impressive, but because I was a spectacle. I looked like I'd lost a fight and survived it badly.

I'd tried going without the sling a few times. Every time earned me a reminder—a jolt across the ribs, breath held until the sting passed, and the arm dangling useless again. The healer's reprimand had left little room for pride. Wear the sling or tear open something important. Simple enough.

The surgeon said the arrow had gone in low, skimmed bone, clipped something that bled far too well, and lodged in my lung. Another inch and I'd have drowned where I fell. A good shot, if killing me had been the point.

That thought still crept in at odd hours, uninvited.

I sat with my back to the sparring ring's wall, watching Lucius—as I'd come to call him—and Valerius within. Blades met with a rhythm I knew by heart. I'd been raised in the Aeltyrian style, which was fluid, like dancing with steel. Those two fought like the Calesians they were: precision, no wasted energy, and a two-handed sword if you were big enough to wield it.

I hadn't held a sword in three decadia. Gods, I missed it.

"What has you so troubled?"

Marcus Frugi's voice cut across my thoughts. He sat beside me without asking, watching the pair in the ring.

I didn't look at him right away. Something about him was off. Too polished, too smooth, like a blade that had never drawn blood. Eyes that watched too much and saw too little.

"Not troubled," I said. "Just enjoying the blessing of being right-handed."

His brows rose. The corner of his mouth twitched. Smug bastard was trying not to smirk and failing. "A stroke of luck indeed," he said, wincing as Lucius slammed his shield into Valerius hard enough to stagger him.

Valerius caught himself, quick and sure, the way men moved when the sword had been part of them longer than not. He didn't just fight. He moved like the fight belonged to him.

I watched longer than I meant to, eyes snagged on the lean cut of him.

I blinked and turned away, annoyed that my heart had noticed before my pride.

"Are your preparations for Aeldunon complete?" Marcus asked.

"Yes. I don't need much." I didn't ask if he had. Didn't care. He answered anyway.

"It took nearly a decadium to pack my household. Creator know when we'll be back." He glanced sidelong, brown eyes direct when nothing else about him was. "You must be pleased, though. To return home."

That word, *home*, landed hilt-first in my ribs.

"I suppose," I said, and left it at that.

Marcus didn't catch the warning. He kept on like a man too fond of his own voice. "Aeldunon's a marvel, in its way. Moss, smoke, dirt that clings no matter how much gold you slap over it. You'd know better than I, being from there."

"I'm from a village southwest of it," I said as if scraping the words from the bottom of a boot. "Never had reason to go."

He hummed, as if that meant something. Then, too casual, "You might stop there on the way. I imagine the ashborn would like to see one of their own dressed in bronze."

I turned my head, slow and deliberate. Let him feel it. My pulse thudded. "The. What."

*I could probably slide a blade right between his ribs,* I thought. *He's soft as a babe. I could do it one-handed and not break a sweat.*

"The ashborn," he said again, as if it were nothing. "What the legion calls the locals. Ash in the blood, ash all around. It stuck."

I just stared, stunned that the arsehole had said that to me. Long enough for him to realize he'd misstepped badly.

Then I laughed. Dry. Sharp, like steel on bone.

"I'm sorry, is that funny?" he asked.

"If you ever say that word in my hearing again," I said, voice low and even, "I'll pin your tongue to the ground with my knife."

He offered a thin, brittle smile. "No offense meant, of course."

I said nothing as I held his gaze, hoping he felt how close he was to Vespera's touch in that moment.

"No need for dramatics," he said lightly.

He left without haste, as if he were the one dismissing me.

Only when he was gone did my hands unclench. The taste in my mouth was sharp, old anger—iron and ash.

I'd fought for the Empire. Killed for them. Lied and betrayed my own people for them. And still, that name stuck like soot to my skin. *Ashborn*, as if my blood itself had been burned. Even now, with new rank and new orders and a post most legionaries would kill for, I was still the outsider. The northerner. Lesser.

I breathed deep into my lungs, so I felt it in my belly, then out, like coaxing a campfire from a spark. I did it again, then once more. By the third time, the anger was back in its cage, where it belonged.

I looked back at the ring just in time to see Lucius slip—bad footing, or bad luck. He went down like a sack of oats, sword flying wide, swearing as he hit the ground.

Laughter, sudden and real, burst out of me before I could stop it. I slapped a hand over my mouth, but it was already out.

Lucius, sprawled in the dirt, looked over like I'd stabbed him. "Wait until you're allowed to pick up a sword again, Dieter," he called. "We'll see who's laughing then."

I smirked. "Remind me why I was detained?"

Valerius looked over at me, grinned, and tapped Lucius on the back of the head with the flat of his blade. Lucius stood, ready for another round.

A servant approached the edge of the ring. "My lord, a message for you," he called out to Valerius.

He handed his sword off to a nearby attendant and motioned the boy closer, then accepted the message he offered. After skimming the contents, he said something to Lucius, who nodded and handed his sword to the attendant as well.

Valerius splashed water over his face from a barrel, then straightened, wiped off with a cloth and caught my eye. He waved me over.

I slid down from the wall and crossed to him. "Yes, my lord?"

"I have something to show you," he said. "Come."

I fell in beside him. Lucius trailed behind, whistling off-key.

"What happened?" Valerius asked.

"Nothing worth repeating."

"Something is wrong," he said, eyeing me. "The arm? Your back? Lucius's face?"

The corner of my mouth twitched. "Aye."

Lucius grumbled. "Sorry, it's the only one I've got."

Valerius glanced back. "Lucius. Give us a moment."

With a sigh, Lucius moved ahead of us.

We walked in silence a while longer. I glanced at Valerius. He didn't press. Just walked beside me, steady and quiet. I weighed that quiet like a blade in my hand.

"Lord Frugi called me ashborn," I said, letting the words go like a confession.

Valerius's face didn't change, but his pace slowed. "Did he, now?"

"He suggested I take leave to visit family." I hesitated. "That was bearable. He doesn't know about them. It was what came after. Said he 'imagined the ashborn would be eager to see one of their own dressed in bronze.'"

He didn't respond right away.

"I threatened him," I said. "Told him if he said it again, I'd pin his tongue to the ground."

Valerius blinked. "That's vivid."

Heat rose in my face. "I'm sorry."

"Don't be. I didn't say it was unwarranted." He leaned closer, voice dropping. "Did it help? Saying it?"

The scent of leather, sword oil and saddle soap lingered between us. Distracting.

"He looked afraid. I felt better."

"So yes. Good." His eyes met mine. "I'm sorry about him."

"You didn't say it. He did."

"No, but I'm the reason you were both there." His voice went flat. Final. Like a blade laid on the table. "He'll leave you alone when I'm done with him."

*When I'm done with him.* He said it like it was a fact, not a threat. I wasn't used to that, to being defended without condition. It tugged something loose in my chest.

The scent of hay and leather thickened as we neared the stables, warm, earthy and familiar. Hooves shuffled behind wooden slats. Birds nested in the rafters overhead. The stable master—a wizened Calesian man with bowed legs—looked up from the feed trough as we entered. At Valerius's wave, he set down his bucket and shuffled toward a far stall.

"Mornin', milord," he greeted, voice rough. "I'll fetch him for you."

Moments later, he returned, leading a tall dapple-gray courser, coat catching the light like smoke on water. The stable master handed over the reins with a bow.

"He's a fine one. My boy says he's got more stamina than patience."

Valerius nodded, turned to me, and without any ceremony at all, extended the reins to me. "And now, he's yours."

I stiffened, staring at the horse, then at Valerius, and back again. My feet edged backward of their own accord, as though the reins were a serpent instead of a gift.

"No," I said quickly. My hands lifted, palms open, as if to ward him off. "My lord, I can't—"

Lucius, of course, snorted. I shot him a glare sharp enough to flay hide.

He lifted one brow, made a noise halfway between a cough and a laugh, and turned to walk away. "Right. I'll go fetch the tack."

Valerius remained still, brow arched in something just shy of amusement. "You're refusing me?" he asked mildly.

"I can't accept this, my lord," I said again.

"You do realize it's a fifty-five-day march to Aeldunon," he said flatly.

"I've marched it before," I said. "Seven years in the legions."

And in that moment, I would rather have marched to my grave than owe him more.

"Hmm." He studied me. "Maybe once, but I know you rode before you earned your staff. And you were good."

I had been. There had never been anything like the freedom of ripping across the moor at full gallop, wind on my face and in my hair, the world falling away beneath the pounding of hooves.

He tilted his head. "Oh, have you forgotten how to sit a saddle?"

That struck. "Of course not," I snapped.

He didn't smile, but the shadow of one lingered on his lips. "You'd shame yourself walking beside a train of mounted officers. And you'd shame me, too, because it would appear I gave you no better."

I was being outmaneuvered into gratitude and I hated it.

"This isn't a gift," he added, voice quiet. "It's a tool. Same as your sword. I take care of my own."

I said nothing at first, then stepped forward and took the reins. The courser snorted softly and leaned into my hand, warm breath huffing against my sleeve. Gods, I wanted him. Not just the horse. The ride. To be myself again, if only for a little while. Wind and speed and the open field.

But what would it cost? Would this be something that could be taken from me later?

"Why?" I asked. The word was quiet, unsure.

Valerius shifted, hooked his thumb through his belt, looking down at his boot, propped against the trough like he had all the time in the world. "Because you've earned it," he said, as if that settled everything.

Behind us, Lucius muttered loud enough to be heard, "He's never bought me a horse."

I raised a brow and turned just as he sauntered back toward us, entirely unrepentant.

Valerius didn't even glance at him. "Get shot with an arrow meant for me and we'll talk."

Lucius wrinkled his nose. "Expensive."

Valerius waved him off without looking.

"Understood." Lucius gave me a wink and wandered off toward the tack posts again, feigning interest.

I frowned. "Then let me repay you. I will."

"No. This isn't a favor." He met my gaze. "It's what's owed."

My fingers closed more tightly around the reins. I met his gaze and held it, just long enough to feel the weight behind his words.

He broke away first, turning back to the horse.

"What will you name him?" he asked.

After a moment, I said, "Argenti."

Valerius repeated it, the name rolling from his tongue with a trace of approval. "Argenti. A fitting name for a silver steed."

He stepped closer, unhurried. The warmth of him slid into my awareness, a heat I hadn't braced for. It was too much, but I didn't know how to stop him.

I swallowed. "Thank you, my lord."

"Call me Val," he said gently. "I keep asking, hoping you will. Please."

"Thank you… Val." The name felt strange on my tongue, like I'd bitten into something unexpectedly sweet.

I turned back to the horse, offering my hand. Argenti huffed, sniffed, then allowed me to stroke his muzzle.

The stable master grunted. "Well, I'll be. Likes you already. Mean bastard bit the last one who tried that."

I glanced over my shoulder. "Did he?"

Valerius cleared his throat. "Yes. The last one was me."

I tried not to laugh. "What happened?"

"He was sizing me up. Decided I didn't pass." Valerius gestured toward the horse. "That's why you don't have to worry about how much he cost. Either you take him, or he's off to the butcher to become sausage."

I turned back, brushing my fingers down Argenti's neck. I started to speak, then stopped just long enough to steady my voice. "No one's ever given me something like this."

I didn't mean the coin. It wasn't about gold. It was the gesture. The thought. The idea that someone looked at me and saw worth. I wasn't sure what to do with something that didn't come with chains or scars.

Valerius tilted his head. "Didn't you have a horse when you were cavalry?"

I huffed a faint breath. "We didn't own the horses. Not as light auxiliaries. They belonged to the Empire, just like we did." My hand moved again along Argenti's neck. Slower now. "You ride what they give you. Feed it, fight on it, watch it die under you, or die with it. If you live, you get another." I stilled. "But they're never yours."

He stepped in close, shoulders nearly brushing. Solid. Steady. The heat of him stirred something deep and low inside me. "Well, for better or worse, this one is all yours."

"Thank you." I hesitated. Then, softer, "Not just… for him. For what it means."

*Freedom,* I thought.

"You're welcome."

I looked up into his eyes and stilled. Whatever he saw in me, it held him there for just a breath too long.

"I've preparations to finalize for tomorrow," he said, looking away and settling back into that composed rhythm. "I'll take Lucius with me, give you time to get acquainted with your man-eating warhorse."

I looked toward the gates, to the hills beyond. The city's heat pressed close, thick and stifling. "I thought we might…"

"Might what?"

I let the hint of a smile tug at my mouth. "Go for a ride. A real one. Away from here. Just for a while."

He smiled back. "As much as I'd like to, duty wins today. But soon. I promise."

I nodded. "I'll see the healer, then. One last time."

"Of course. Meet me in the courtyard afterward, dressed for a public appearance. We're due one last round of formalities." He stepped back. The space between us stretched wider. Colder.

I moved to Argenti's left and reached for his mane, only to pause when Valerius spoke again.

"Wait. Let me have the stable master saddle him for you."

I placed my left foot against the courser's foreleg and vaulted up in one smooth motion. Settled onto his back like I was born for it. Looking down at Valerius, I let a faint smirk tug at my mouth. "No need."

He shook his head, laughing under his breath. "Very well. You'll use the saddle for the journey though, won't you?"

"I will." I nudged Argenti forward, guiding him out with a shift of weight.

"Aleaia."

I drew up and turned back toward him.

"Yes?"

His expression had softened. "Please be careful."

The smile came easier this time. "When have I ever been anything else?"

# CHAPTER TEN
## *Auctoritas*

*"True authority is not taken—it is borne.*
*In silence, in suffering, in the strength it takes to rise and choose restraint."*
—commonly cited in healer's texts and military manuals

Dēwamos 17, 1230
*Aleaia*

I pushed open the infirmary door, boots scuffing stone. "Hesta, are you here?"

"Coming!" Her voice floated from the rear, quick steps following. No doubt expecting another crisis to steal what little peace she'd managed. That was usually how it went.

She appeared in the doorway, eyes searching me for blood. Her face eased when she saw me standing whole. She tucked a strand of flaxen hair beneath her cap and sighed.

"What's happened now?" she asked. "You don't look any worse for wear."

"I'm not." I raised both hands. "Just stopping in before we leave for Aeldunon. As instructed. And to give the new girl her orders."

The tension eased from her shoulders. "Thank the Creator. On the table, then."

"You didn't really think I'd gotten into more trouble, did you?" I climbed up with practiced ease.

"With you? It's never if. Only when." A twitch at her mouth betrayed her. She pulled the partition shut behind us. "Arms up."

The right obeyed. The left made it halfway before pain gripped my back. Tremors took over. It dropped into my lap like it didn't belong to me. "Damn thing still doesn't work."

"It works. Just not how your pride wants it to." She stepped closer. "Grip my hands."

We moved through the usual tests of resistance, pressure, and strength. I did better than five days prior. Not by much, but enough that she gave a curt nod of satisfaction. Then came the part I hated.

"Lift your tunic and left breast for me," Hesta said.

I did, then felt her fingers touching near the incision along my ribs, where the surgeon had repaired the damage.

"It's healing well," she said, then stepped behind me to check the others.

I held still.

"Good," she said. "No signs of corruption. And it's healing remarkably fast. I've never seen the like."

She never commented on the other scars—the ones I hadn't earned honestly. I never asked what they looked like. Just thought about them in the dark when sleep wouldn't come.

"Doesn't feel that way."

"It's only been two decadia. What did you expect? A miracle?"

"Only two," I scoffed. Two decadia. Twenty days of clumsiness and silent dread I'd never wield a blade again.

"Have you needed papaver?" she asked.

"No."

Her eyebrow lifted. "Not once?"

"It binds me up so bad I'd rather be gutted. Last time, I spent three days in the privy fighting for my life."

That earned a proper laugh. "Well, suit yourself. Keep the arm out of the sling when you can. Move it gently. No sudden strain."

"How gentle?" Gods, being restricted like this had to be one of the deepest layers of Hel.

"No shield. No sword. No saddlebags. I'd rather you didn't ride but I know you must, so don't you dare mount using that arm."

I narrowed my eyes at her. "Oddly specific."

"You've done each of those. Lord Tutela told me before you tore something."

"I'm sorry." I meant it. "I don't wield a sword with my left arm."

"It's about balance, and you're too stiff right now. The more you use it *within limits*, the more it'll return. Rush it, and you'll undo everything." Her voice softened. "I know patience isn't your strength, but don't risk what you've gained."

I nodded. "Understood."

"Don't get comfortable yet." Hesta turned toward the stairwell and called, "Mariana! Get down here!"

"Coming, mistress!" came the distant reply.

"The new healer?" I asked.

"Not so new. Been with me two years. Took to fieldwork better than most. She's had plenty of practice, thanks to you lot." There was pride in her voice. Subtle, but there. That alone earned the girl some respect from me.

"We've certainly given her enough wounds to work on."

"I'm surprised you haven't met. You're here often enough."

"You said I needed 'a firm hand' and didn't want to 'inflict me on her,'" I said flatly.

Hesta sniffed. "Couldn't keep her from you forever. She's capable. I'd go myself if she weren't."

Footsteps approached. A woman's voice came from the other side of the partition. "May I come in?"

"I called you, didn't I?" Hesta said.

The curtain rustled, and the woman stepped inside. Plain gray robes, green sash tied at the waist, hair pinned in the Calesian style—efficient, proper—but it was her face that caught me. Skin only a shade lighter than mine. About my age. High cheekbones. Dark eyes. Black hair.

She was Aeltyrian, or at least in part. Enough to notice.

"Yes, mistress. Oh!" She dipped into a quick curtsy. "My lady, Mariana Gallo, at your service."

I waved. "Look at me. I'm no lady. Just Aleaia."

She nodded. "Of course."

Hesta snapped her fingers. "Look here. Check the sutures every day. Sweat's no friend to healing. They can come out in another decadium, if she behaves."

Mariana leaned closer. Her hands were soft, careful. They'd harden. "Yes, mistress."

"She can go without the sling," Hesta went on, "but nothing heavier than a waterskin for now."

"So no armor?" I asked. How was I meant to perform my duty without it?

Hesta helped me pull my tunic back down. "No plate. Maybe mail. You'll need help either way."

I slid off the table, adjusting my clothes. The stitches pulled, and it felt strange to use my arm again, but not enough to stop me. "You're the one coming with us to Aeldunon?" I asked Mariana.

"Back to Aeldunon, actually. I grew up there."

That made sense. The accent was right, but someone had taught her how to speak and stand, and had gotten her to university.

Hesta waved us off. "Out, both of you. I've sick to tend and no patience for loitering."

Outside, sunlight spilled across the stone steps, catching dust in a lazy shimmer. I squinted, more aware of the pull in my back than the warmth. I rolled my left shoulder.

"If you grew up in the city," I said, "you'll have to show me around. I've never seen it."

Mariana brightened. "I'd be glad to. Where are you from?"

"Rhaelaith."

She blinked. "Never heard of it."

I chuckled. "Most people haven't. Small village. Southwest of the city. About fifty families, before the plague."

"It must've been lovely."

The memories washed over me.

Goats on the ridge.

My father's hands in the soil.

River cold enough to sting.

Hearth smoke curling from the chimney.

Just for a moment, I had it. Then it was gone.

"It was," I said softly.

"Anyway," I said, clearing my throat. "We leave at dawn. Travel's slow with the legion. Eight to ten miles a day if we're lucky."

"I've never seen one all at once."

"Usually we just swap out cohorts but all the ones up there are overdue to come back south. It'll be less grand than it sounds. Too many to move quickly. The smell in summer…" I wrinkled my nose in memory. "The animals reek. So do the men. And if they stay too long in one place, they strip it bare."

Mariana laughed. "You talk like you're not one of them."

"I'm not," I said with pride. "Not anymore. Even when I was, I knew what we looked like. And smelled like."

She twisted her fingers in her sleeve. "I'm not the only healer, am I?"

I shook my head. "Each cohort has one for the legionaries."

She still looked worried. "A thousand is still a lot for one healer."

"It is. But they all know the basics, and with luck, they won't all get sick or hurt at once. And legionaries avoid the infirmary like…" I smirked. "Well. Like the plague."

She smiled. "Indeed."

"It's true. I knew a man once who took an arrow to the calf and thought he'd walk it off."

Mariana stared. "You jest."

"I wish. Snapped the shaft, tied a filthy scrap of cloth around it, and kept marching. By the time anyone checked, the wound stank so bad the horses wouldn't go near him."

She clapped a hand over her mouth, snorting. "By the Creator, what happened?"

"He refused treatment until we dragged him in. Hesta had to cut it open. I sat on his chest while three others held him. He screamed loud enough to rattle Astralis. Lucky he kept the leg."

Mariana groaned. "You're all impossible."

I laughed. "I'm surprised Hesta never told you."

"She probably thought it'd scare me off."

"Ah. Did it?"

"No," she said. "I want to go home. I'll do almost anything to get there."

I nodded. That, I understood. "I'm also supposed to make sure you know that you're to serve as Lord Valerius's household healer."

"I know that much."

I nodded. "On the road you'll see to just him, Lord Tutela, Lord Frugi, a few staff, and me. If something big happens, you'll be expected to help the cohort healers. Once we reach Aeldunon, the castle infirmary's yours."

"I hope I don't have to lance any abscesses upon arrival," she muttered.

I smiled. "Any questions?"

"No. I've a few things to finish inside. See you tomorrow?"

I nodded. "I'll come fetch you before we leave. You'll have time to load your things."

"Thank you, my la—Aleaia." She corrected herself, dipped a curtsy, and disappeared inside.

I turned to Argenti, giving his reins a tug as we made for the inner bailey. The stables there held the royal mounts and steeds of the Imperial Guard—creatures with bloodlines older than most noble houses.

"Careful," I warned, handing him off to a stable hand. "I'm told he bites."

"Yes, mistress."

The boy reached out. The moment his fingers touched the reins, Argenti pinned his ears, lunged, and snagged the edge of his sleeve.

The boy yelped and staggered back. "Oi! Mean bastard, ain't he?"

I smirked, patting Argenti's neck. "I did warn you."

The glare I earned was sharp, but he took the reins again—more cautiously. Argenti tossed his head, tail swishing like a banner in triumph.

I turned toward the keep.

Behind me, the boy muttered, "Better manners on a rabid dog."

"Watch yourself," I called back. "He understands insults too."

Silence followed. I let it hang and climbed the servants' stair, smiling to myself.

The smile faded as I realized I had no idea what one wore to a public appearance with the second son of the Empire?

My room offered no answers. Just bare stone walls, a narrow bed shoved in the corner with a worn chest at its foot, and armor that leaned where a servant had left it. The brazier sat cold in the summer heat. The breeze through the arrow-slit window wasn't enough. The room felt close. Thick.

Inside the chest were two spare tunics, a pair of threadbare trousers, and my father's copy of our scripture, *The Song of the Stars*. Certainly nothing nice enough to stand next to a prince.

I brushed dust from the tunic I wore. This was my good one. My boots were scuffed, but I could clean them, and then I might be presentable if no one looked too closely.

I looked over at the armor. I supposed I could wear that, instead, though the idea sent a dull throb through my shoulder and along my side. I missed its weight and its purpose, but if I put it on alone, pain would surely follow. And it was only standard issue. Would it be enough?

I knew, then, who I could ask.

My feet carried me to Valerius's chamber. I knocked twice. It was still strange, having my old tribune this accessible, being his equal now. *Maybe I'll get used to it in time,* I thought.

"Come in," Lucius called.

I cracked the door and leaned in. "Everyone decent?"

"Yes, of course."

I stepped inside. Lucius sat alone at the table. A bowl of fruit rested between two chairs, beside an amphora and two cups.

"Why wouldn't we be?" he asked, raising a brow as he poured wine.

I shrugged. "I've lived around men long enough to know to ask first. Where's his lordship?"

"Next room. Buried in correspondence. Let him be."

I hesitated. Then drew in a breath. "I'm not here for him. I need your advice… if you're willing."

Lucius looked up, amusement flickering in his eyes. "Did it hurt?"

"What?"

"The asking."

The man was so different from the tribune, I almost laughed.

He poured a second cup and slid it across the table. "Here, before you choke on it."

I took it with a huff, the corner of my lips twitching despite myself. "Thank you."

I took a sip. The wine was smooth, dark as blood, and did nothing to quiet the unease churning in my chest. I lowered the cup, tracing its rim.

"I don't know what I'm supposed to wear to wherever we're going. Armor?"

Lucius plucked a grape, rolled it between his fingers, then popped it in his mouth. After a moment, he answered, "Not always. But this time? Yes."

I frowned. "This time?"

He gestured to the chair across from him. "Sit. You need to eat."

I sat carefully, set the cup on the table before me. I reached for a fig and found it too soft, already splitting. Its sweetness clung to my fingers. I set the ruined thing back on the plate and wiped my hand on my trousers.

Lucius exhaled. "It's an execution. Our predecessors."

"Already sentenced?"

He nodded. "Tribunal found them guilty. Long list of charges, but treason's the worst."

I sat still. I'd hoped for those words. They deserved worse. Still, only two decadia? That was fast for nobles.

"The tribunal never asked for my testimony," I said.

Lucius arched a brow. "What would you have added? You took an arrow to the back."

"I could've spoken to what I saw. Why I went to—"

"They confessed," he said, cutting me off with a flick of his hand. "Everything. Nothing you could've said would've mattered more and there's no harsher sentence."

I exhaled through my nose.

Lucius leaned back, eyes piercing but not unkind. "You don't have to be the hero of every story."

Gods damn him. He was right.

He straightened. "So. Wear your armor."

"All I have is legion kit."

He shrugged. "Same as me."

I frowned. "Yours is better."

The words came out sulky and I regretted them immediately.

Lucius chuckled. "Nobody's looking at us. We're the only ones in the household guard. We'll be underdressed together." He wiped his hands, gestured at my arm. "Where's your sling?"

"Hesta told me to go without. No lifting anything heavier than a water skin."

"How big a water skin?"

My lips twitched. "As big as the one on my belt."

"Hm." He glanced out the window at the afternoon sun. "We should head to the courtyard soon."

I rose. "All right. I'll see you down there."

# CHAPTER ELEVEN
## *Blood & Gold*

*"The lion wears no crown, yet all kneel before its hunger."*
—Emperor Tiberius di Calesia, First Book of Sovereignty

Dēwamos 17, 1230
*Aleaia*

The sun was merciless.

My armor—tightened by Lucius—held the heat like a forge, baking me from collar to greaves. Sweat crawled down my spine, stinging over half-healed flesh. The humid air clung like damp wool. What had once meant safety was now a prison of steel.

Below, thousands packed the stands shoulder to shoulder, their hunger as thick as smoke. They hadn't come for justice, but for blood.

The stench of earlier executions lingered: blood, churned dust, the ripe press of unwashed bodies. My stomach turned. Anvallan law offered no clean death to traitors. Not when the High Priest could distill worship from suffering. Pain was spectacle. And Anvallus, apparently, loved a show.

Sunlight flared off Valerius's armor, catching gold trim and polished edges. He stood iron-straight, shoulders locked. His helm, crowned in crimson plume, cast his face in shadow. Only the smallest tells gave him away. His fingers tapped—once, twice—on his sword hilt before falling still. His pacing was too measured to be calm.

Valerius came to stand beside me, gaze sweeping the pit, jaw tight. The muscle beneath his skin twitched once, but I saw it.

"This is…" he began, the words pulled thin. "More difficult than I expected."

His words caught me off guard—not the meaning, but the honesty. "I'm sorry, my lord."

He exhaled slowly. "I pursued this. I thought I wanted to see them suffer." The pause was thick as tar. "But there's nothing. I just feel... nothing."

My fingers twitched halfway toward him before I stopped myself. I might've offered a hand to a fellow soldier, but I couldn't offer even that, then. Not to a prince. Not unless I fancied joining the spectacle below. Any words of consolation I might have spoken died on my tongue. What did you say to a man who felt nothing for those who tried to kill him?

"Perhaps it's better that way," I said quietly. "Better to feel nothing."

He shook his head. "No."

I didn't know what to do with that.

He stepped to my right, positioning himself between Lucius and me as the balcony braced for the Emperor's arrival. The two men bent their heads together, speaking low. That was good. Lucius was Valerius's closest confidante and friend, and could offer more than I.

I turned back to the pit. The condemned were being led out—four of them, silent and shackled, chains dragging behind them. They didn't struggle. Didn't plead. Just walked, as if they'd already left their souls behind. I'd never met them up close but I'd heard of them: Amatus Arvina, Alexus Procillus, Naevia Crus, and Liora Alcaeus. Children of the elite nobility of Calesia, they'd brought shame and dishonor upon their houses and now they'd suffer for it.

Amatus looked the worst. Bloated and broken, his face was a purpled mess. He moved like his bones were glass, one misstep from collapse.

Lucius let out a low whistle. "By the Creator. You said you fought him, but it doesn't look like he got a hit in."

Valerius didn't answer. Just kept his eyes on the procession below.

Alexus clutched Naevia's hand, and she wept openly, without shame. They edged toward the center of the arena, eyes darting to the arena walls, searching for escape.

Liora didn't flinch. She looked composed—chin lifted, pale eyes swept the balcony, calm and calculating. Sunlight caught the wild tangle of her golden hair. She found Valerius and dipped into a mocking curtsy, slow and unhurried.

"The gall of that one." Lucius shook his head.

She'd been Valerius's betrothed once, but more recently betrothed to his brother. My people were open-minded when it came to love and romance but even I found that disgusting.

Love was a burden. I'd seen what it made of people. Fools, mostly. I was glad to be spared it.

The herald's voice cut through the din. "His Majesty, Emperor Claudius di Calesia."

Silence fell over the arena like an executioner's blade. The great iron doors groaned open behind us, and the Emperor entered.

He wore crimson and gold, the mantle heavy enough to bury a lesser man. Black embroidery coiled down its length in the shape of Drakaroth the Devourer, wrath of Anvallus. A golden circlet rested on his iron-gray hair, crusted with enough jewels to ransom a province. Time had hollowed his cheeks and thinned his frame, but none of it softened him.

Valerius was his father's son. If not for age, the mirror would have been near perfect. They bore the same carved jaw, same proud brow, same rigid bearing forged under armor and pressure. Their eyes set them apart. Claudius's were near black, a void.

Around me, the others knelt.

I dropped to one knee

Too late.

I felt his gaze settle on me like a blade.

"You," he said, and I knew without looking that he spoke to me. "There is something familiar about you." He stepped forward until his shadow spilled across my feet.

*Fuck.*

My lungs tightened. The heat, the armor, the ache beneath the wrappings, all of it vanished under his scrutiny.

"Get up," he commanded.

I stood, kept my head bowed.

He reached out, gloved fingers lifting my chin. "Look at me."

I obeyed. Met his eyes. Focused on breathing through my nose.

The balcony's height became strange comfort. If I jumped, if I landed just right, maybe I'd die before I could be punished. Better than standing here, spine locked, blood pounding, under the stare of a man who crushed kingdoms without blinking.

Claudius turned my head to study my profile. His frown deepened. He looked at me like something half-remembered, eyes narrowed.

I didn't move, stayed still as stone in a breaking storm. I'd seen slaves at auction inspected the same way—turned like livestock, picked over with cold disinterest. The familiarity made my blood run cold.

Valerius leaned in, not enough to block the view, but enough to draw the Emperor's attention. "She's one of my new household guards, Your Majesty. You may have seen her in the keep."

"Perhaps." Claudius didn't sound convinced, but he let go of my chin. The weight of fear eased from my shoulders.

"Strange that you would choose a northerner to stand beside you. You know they can't be trusted, Valerius."

"I must respectfully disagree, sire," Valerius said. "All of the condemned today came from the noblest houses in the realm, and this soldier nearly gave her life for mine."

Claudius made a thoughtful sound. His gaze lingered on his son, unreadable, then slid to Lucius. A flicker of something like approval touched the old man's face.

"Ah. Lucius Tutela. I suppose you make up for the other one." His voice curled dry as dust. "Sword of Calesia. I trust you've not grown dull."

Lucius lifted his chin. "Not yet, Your Majesty."

Claudius gave a mirthless chuckle. "Of course not. You secured what was once thought unconquerable. The south would still be a mire of squabbling tribes if not for you."

Lucius didn't preen. "I did my duty, sire, as the Empire required."

Claudius nodded. "Yes. And now you stand here, watching the consequences for those who failed to do theirs."

A stooped retainer stepped forward, hands like withered branches. He bowed low. "If it pleases Your Majesty," he said, "all preparations are in place. His Excellency awaits your signal."

Claudius raised one hand toward the opposite balcony, and his brother, the High Priest, stepped forward.

There was no softness about Renatus di Calesia, only austerity, wrapped in gold-threaded robes. His face was sharp, half-lost beneath a towering ceremonial headdress. The sigil of Anvallus, a gold sunburst, gleamed at his chest, swaying on a thick chain.

Even from across the arena, I saw the sweat glistening at his temples. His crimson robes were dark beneath the arms. Devotion, it seemed, offered no shield from the heat.

A trumpet cried out, long and loud. Then Renatus spoke, his voice like iron striking stone. "Citizens of Calesia! Before you stand traitors! Oath-breakers who conspired against the throne! Who sought to murder the Emperor's own son!"

The crowd rippled with a mix of gasps and rising outrage.

"They swore to protect him, and instead raised steel against Valerius di Calesia, Prince of the Empire, Legate of the Second Army! For such treason, there is no clemency. Not even for the sons and daughters of noble houses."

The murmurs cracked into shouts of rage, approval, and bloodlust. It surged like a tide.

Below, guards moved with precision, freeing the condemned and stepping back. They tossed weapons at the prisoners' feet: rusted blades, splintered shields. Probably castoffs from a graveyard of forgotten drills.

The portcullis slammed shut behind the guards, and the prisoners moved to choose the weapons they'd die with.

Renatus lifted his arms. "Our Creator, Lord Anvallus, shall have their blood spilled this day!"

Another larger portcullis under the balcony groaned on its tracks as it lifted.

The first lion stepped into the light.

He moved with slow purpose, bone and sinew rippling beneath his golden hide, each step a reminder that we humans were but prey to them. His yellow eyes swept the arena, tail twitching.

Then the second. The third. And the fourth.

The Empire favored such executions. These were beasts from Calesia's southern reaches—massive, golden-maned predators, untouched by domestication. Not trained, but starved until hunger became a weapon.

Cruel as it was, I felt no pity. Not for them. Not here.

The crowd erupted not in horror, but rapture. Voices rolled like thunder, a storm of bloodlust, and I could taste bile at the back of my throat. People who had never done violence often called for it the loudest, I found.

I glanced at the arena walls. They were high and iron-ringed. There would be no escape for man nor beast. Only spectacle.

Beside me, Valerius exhaled and slid a finger beneath his chinstrap, then under his collar.

"Reached your limits already, boy?" Claudius asked.

"No." Valerius didn't look at him. "I only wonder if this should be such an exhibition. A simple execution would have sufficed."

Claudius kept his eyes on the pit. "Our people must see the consequences of treason."

Below, the lions moved with unhurried menace, circling the sand. The largest—a brute with a bronze mane—lowered its head, nostrils flaring as it tasted blood in the air.

I'd never seen such things before, not outside of a book, but I knew they were symbols of conquest. Brought from jungle and desert to remind the Empire's enemies—and its people—what waited in defiance.

Claudius turned to Valerius. "A fitting display, don't you think?"

"They're strong," Valerius said. "Beautiful, too. Meant to be wild, in the land where they were born."

"They are meant to do as Anvallus wills," Claudius replied. "And your uncle divined the traitors should die by the beast on your standard."

The lion on his standard—gold on blue—stood for House Alvareti. His mother's house. A house that ended with him.

Below, the beasts' chains dropped.

The Aeltyrian handlers ran, but they were too slow. One vanished under a blur of muscle, his scream cut short as blood sprayed the sand. The second made it two steps before a lion caught his arm and yanked him back. A single thrash ended the sound.

The arena filled with the sound of killing: flesh rending, bone cracking, the wet thud of bodies torn apart.

Claudius didn't flinch. He watched in silence. "We used to take them young," he said. "Barely weaned cubs, raised in our menageries."

My eyes remained on the lion that feasted, muzzle dark with gore.

"We thought they'd learn to kill on command. Learn their place."

A cry rang out. *"Domavira Lithau, gavel melior en em!"*

A prayer. *Lady Lithau, have mercy on me,* he pleaded, his words lost in the roar and the sound of death.

There would be no mercy. Only blood.

My stomach twisted. Watching soldiers die in combat was one thing. This wasn't war. There was no honor in this. The slaves had done nothing but hold chains.

"Something was always missing," Claudius said, unfazed by the screams. "They grew large. Hungry. But when the time came, they hesitated. They'd lost something. Their nature."

The lions, now blooded, turned toward the condemned.

Amatus braced, his shield raised, feet set. The lion moved like lightning. Paws hit him square, drove him back. His shield shattered. Sword spun free. Claws ripped into his ribs. Jaws clamped on his throat. There was a wet crack.

The crowd roared.

Claudius didn't blink.

"These are different," he said. "Raised in the wild. Brought here only after they learned what they were."

Naevia still wept, clinging to Alexus. Her hands shook as she guided his sword to her belly.

Begging him.

Alexus nodded. Kissed her once. Then drove the blade beneath her ribs.

She sagged in his arms, blood soaking the sand. He laid her down gently, his face stone-still.

Claudius turned to Valerius. "You see the difference?"

Valerius didn't look away. "A lion raised in captivity doesn't forget how to kill when starved."

Something flickered in Claudius's eyes. Not pride. Something colder. "No. They hesitate," he said. "That makes them weak."

Alexus rose. Dropped the sword. Ran.

A lion struck him at the knee. Claws raked his legs. He hit the ground hard, shouting. Teeth closed over his shoulder. The sound vanished into the crowd's thunder. He thrashed once. Then stilled.

Only one remained.

The Sun of House Alcaeus stood alone, gripping her sword in both hands. Golden hair clung to Liora's face. Her eyes locked on the bronze-maned brute pacing the far wall. Its breath hissed, low and rhythmic.

Then it lunged.

She moved. Sidestepped. Pivoted. Blade up.

The strike landed. Not clean, but deep. The lion roared and staggered, blood pouring into the sand.

The crowd gasped.

I didn't want to admire her. I did anyway.

Claudius tilted his head, almost wistful. "Pity about Liora. She would have made a worthy empress."

Liora turned her head.

Not to the Emperor or Renatus.

She looked at Valerius, lifted her chin. Eyes bright in the sun.

Her voice rang clear. "For the Empire!"

She turned. Blade raised and ready.

The lion struck.

The blow slammed her down. Its jaws closed on her throat. Blood surged, soaking her tunic. Her sword slipped.

She didn't scream. She didn't struggle.

The lion held her until she stopped moving. Then it let go, staggered a few steps, and collapsed. It lay still.

Silence.

Only the sound of tearing flesh remained.

Then the crowd roared again.

Claudius didn't move. His voice came quiet. Cold.

"You are strong, Valerius. Disciplined. But you were raised far from the shadows and whispers of court. You think yourself above it."

He gestured to the pit. "This is what it means to rule. And you are not above it. Cassius understands this. You must as well, in the north."

"Yes, sire," Valerius said, his voice flat. Lifeless.

Claudius nodded, eyes still on the carnage.

"You'll leave for Aeltyria soon. Remember this lesson. The land festers. The people forget. They need more than punishment. They need to be governed. Ruled. Taught what it means to kneel."

Valerius turned.

And found me.

Over his shoulder, his eyes met mine, and for a breath, the noise vanished. No lions. No blood. Just him and me.

Then he looked away.

Claudius met his son's eyes at last. "You will not disappoint me."

# CHAPTER TWELVE
## *Ghosts*

*"They do not haunt with blood or bone,*
*But with the silence left alone.*
*The dead lie still. The living mourn,*
*And bear the hauntings they have borne."*
—The Song of the Stars, Cycle VII: The Cycle of Spirit

Dēwamos 28, 1230
*Aleaia*

I pulled my cloak tighter, hunching against the downpour. The wool clung to me, heavy with rain. The road had dissolved into muck, Argenti's hooves squelching with each step.

The first days had been clear, the sunlight warm on my face as Avitum faded behind us, its towers shrinking in the blue-gold haze. I'd ridden with wind in my hair, the world stretched wide before me, and Valerius never stopped me. Never brought me to heel.

I'd felt almost free.

We headed toward the Pravian Pass. Beyond it lay home. Not the ruin I remembered or the fields and burnt villages of my childhood. Something new waited, governed by Valerius, guarded by me. For the first time, it felt like a future I could claim. One that could claim me.

That had been a decadium ago.

Now everything was soaked from cloak to smallclothes. Even my armor chafed where damp padding pressed into raw skin. The thought of scrubbing and oiling metal again made my shoulders ache worse than the march.

"I'll need to check your wounds the next time we stop!" Mariana called from the infirmary wagon.

"Fine," I yelled back over the downpour.

She vanished back into the canvas. She was dry in there. Maybe warm.

I wasn't sure which I envied more.

I shifted in the saddle and reminded myself I wasn't a court girl. I was a soldier and I'd survived worse.

Ahead, Valerius rode alone. Since the executions, he'd withdrawn. He slipped off alone whenever he could, as if silence was the only thing he could bear. I felt for him, of course, but I wouldn't press. Whatever grief he carried, it was his.

A scout's voice carried through the rain. "My lord, the bridge ahead is underwater."

"We'll have to stop and wait out the storm," Lucius said. "If we go too far off-road, we'll bog down in clay, and the river's too deep to ford."

Valerius gave a short nod. A horn blast followed. The line slowed.

We made camp there, in the Aperta Plains, halfway to the mouth of the Pravian Pass that would take us into Aeltyria. The Florentia Woodlands loomed, dense and close, too tight to maneuver cleanly. Once we crossed into the trees, the forest would offer little room to maneuver, much less rest. For now, the open hills gave us room to breathe.

The Second Army's First Legion made camp quickly, efficiently. Tents rose in rows, cookfires blazed, and in a short while, the legionaries had settled into the familiar domestic rhythm of an evening after a march.

By dusk, I'd finished laying out my bedroll in the command tent. The canvas muffled some of the storm. Lanterns flickered through the rain. Lucius's voice carried as he gave orders, but the words were lost to the wind. He'd join us soon, along with Mariana and Marcus.

Valerius sat at his desk, hunched over damp pages. The light was too dim to read by, but he hadn't moved. He'd sooner go blind than ask for a candle.

I sighed. No one told me I'd have to protect him from himself.

I crossed the tent. Kneeling beside a crate, I reached for a stub of tallow candle.

His voice cut through the quiet. "Are you angry with me?"

I stilled. "Me, my lord?"

"Yes, you," he said, glancing at me.

I blinked. "No?" Even to me, it sounded unsure. I turned to the brazier, lit the wick, and set the candle in a pewter holder. "I apologize if I've seemed so. May I ask why you think that?"

"You've been distant since we left Avitum," he said, gesturing to the chair across from him. "Please. Sit."

I obeyed, posture stiff. He thought *I* was distant? "I thought you wanted space. You seemed upset. I thought it best, after..."

"After I learned my guards—including my former betrothed—plotted to kill me? And I watched them die horrifically in the arena?" His voice was bitter steel. "Or after my father told me to rule a backwater with an iron fist?"

Backwater. The word cut deeper than it should have. Still, foolishly, I felt as if it was my place to apologize. "I'm sorry, my lord."

His expression shifted. The tightness in his mouth eased. "No. That's mine to carry. I knew about this assignment and my father's expectations long before the tribunal. It's not Aeltyria that weighs on me."

I hesitated. "Is it the other part, then?"

"Liora?"

I didn't understand why he mourned her. They hadn't parted well as far as I knew.

Liora Alcaeus had been the jewel of her house—eldest twin, beautiful, with a family richer than half the nobles of Calesia combined. Every noble son with sense had wanted her. Only Valerius matched her, and only Cassius might have outdone him, but he was already betrothed to the Princess of Darabon.

Valerius and Liora had been fast friends, by all accounts. She'd even joined the Imperial Guard to stay close to him. Or so they said.

But when the Crown Prince's engagement ended, everything shifted. Liora didn't hesitate. Within a decadium, she cast Valerius aside and accepted Cassius's proposal. Too quick. Too clean. Like she'd been waiting for it.

The thought settled low in my chest. Heavy. Solid. Like iron hammered into place.

"It's not that she left me," Valerius said, breaking into my thoughts. "That was years ago. By the end, she wasn't the woman I'd pledged myself to." His voice had dropped, quiet and worn. "It's the betrayal. From all of them. I don't understand it. I trusted them. Trusted her. And now I don't know if I ever really knew any of them."

His pain wasn't for show. It cut clean and lay bare between us.

"Their lack of honor is beyond reason," I said carefully. "Though I do wonder…"

He looked at me. "Wonder what?"

"Why the Crown Prince allowed her to be executed. She was to be his wife."

He paused, eyes narrowing in thought before he shook his head. "I don't think he cared for her," he said at last. "Not really. She was useful. Her name. Her fortune. That house controls vast holdings in the east. Or they did. I think Cassius took her to fund his wars. He already lives in luxury, but once he wears the crown, he'll bleed the Empire dry."

I frowned. "All the more reason to keep her alive. Wed her. Profit from her."

Valerius stood without a word and crossed to the table near the brazier. He uncorked an amphora and poured two cups, the wine catching dark in the candlelight. He returned and offered one to me before settling back into his chair.

"Why would my father have him take a bride when he could take a fortune?" he said. "Treason gave him an excuse. It made him look like a loyal son of the Empire while he stripped her house to the bone."

I accepted the cup and took a slow sip. The warmth settled in my gut.

"Do you think he was behind the attack?" I asked. "Maybe that's why the executions happened so quickly. He was afraid they'd lose their nerve and talk."

Valerius swirled the wine, the surface catching light in slow spirals. "The thought crossed my mind. But no, I don't think so. My father needs me to hold Aeltyria for him."

"Lucius said the tribunal convicted them without evidence."

"They confessed under torture," he said flatly. "That was enough for my father. He wanted it done and buried. In Avitum, that's justice." He looked down into his cup. "He's growing weaker, and everyone knows it."

I gave a slight nod. "The Emperor seemed formidable when I met him."

"He was, in that moment. But not always. He loses time. Forgets things. It's worse than he lets on." Valerius's jaw flexed as he hesitated. Then, with a bitterness that rang more tired than sharp, added, "And if I were to guess who benefits most from that..."

He didn't say the name. He didn't have to. *Cassius.*

I studied him. This wasn't the battlefield I knew. This was his world. The one of whispers, of poisoned cups and knives that came after dusk. I had no right to ask.

But if I meant to keep him alive, I needed to see what he saw. I chose my words carefully.

"Cassius has always struck me as the kind of man who prefers a throne without a shadow over it," I said.

Valerius's gaze lifted, a brow arched.

I held it. "If he's moving pieces, I need to see the board. I can't protect you from a game I don't understand."

He didn't answer at once. Something flickered behind his eyes. Not surprise at the thought, but at the fact I'd spoken it aloud. That I wanted to know. Then he nodded, slow and thoughtful.

"Then I'll show you the board. As much as I can." He paused. "I didn't think you'd want any part of this."

"It's not about want. It's necessity."

He set the wine aside, fingers tapping once against the table before stilling.

"You already know about Cassius. But there are others. Titus Severian commands the First Army, loyal to the crown but easily swayed. He favors Cassius, of course. So does Renatus."

"Why aren't you Legate of the First Army?"

"So the Crown has teeth," he said. "First Army belongs to the firstborn. Second Army to the second. The Third was raised in our lifetime to protect the Temple's interests. It's commanded by the High Priest."

"If they ever turned on you, you'd be outnumbered two to one."

"Yes. But Cassius would need ironclad justification. The cost of a civil war would be astronomical, in both lives and coin."

"Why would he want to hurt you that way?" I asked.

He shifted in his chair, the candlelight playing along the edge of his profile. "I'm not the heir. I was never meant to rule. But I have soldiers. Land. A name people trust. That's enough for Cassius to want me gone. He always has."

He didn't look at me when he said it. Just kept his eyes on the wine in his hand.

"We don't share a mother," he said after a moment. "His was a Caedmon. My father's first wife."

"Orlaith Caedmon," I said quietly. "My father taught me about her."

"She… suffered. Cassius worshipped her. Still does, in his way." He ran his thumb along the rim of the cup. "My mother came later. From House Alvareti. A political match. I think Cassius hated her for it."

He drew a breath, long and deliberate.

His voice turned quiet. "I was born early. Decadia too early. I came small, fighting for breath. She didn't survive the birth. Some days… I wonder if that was the plan. If he *made sure* I came too soon. If he's been trying to erase me since before I ever drew breath."

"Then he's not just dangerous," I said, holding his gaze. "He's patient. And he's been playing this game since he was a child."

Valerius nodded but didn't speak.

When I finally looked away, I felt the pain in my back, taut as a bowstring. I stretched slow and careful, lifting my arms and rolling the stiffness from my spine with a low sigh before letting one fall over the back of the chair. The movement was instinct, nothing more—a release after too many hours in armor.

"Good thing you've got me," I said with a soft smile.

He didn't answer. Didn't move anything but his eyes. His gaze dropped—not far, just a flicker downward—and lingered. I caught it. Saw the way his attention snagged and held, the faint tightening at the corner of his mouth before he reached for his cup and drained it in one pull.

*Did he just—no. He wouldn't.*

I raised a brow. "Are you all right, Val?"

He opened his mouth, then closed it again.

The tent flap snapped open. Mariana swept in, brisk and damp. Lucius followed, her medicine chest balanced on one shoulder.

Valerius let out a breath like someone had thrown open a door in a room gone too hot.

I let the silence stretch a beat longer. My heart pounded, not from fear or caution, but from something quieter. Something warmer.

No one had ever looked at me like that before. Not with equal parts want and hesitation. Not like I was a woman instead of a weapon.

I smiled. Small. Honest.

I caught his, too—the faintest curve of his mouth, a quiet upturn at the corner.

"Where do you want it?" Lucius asked, shoving back his hood and wiping his face with a sleeve.

"Just there on the right, please," Mariana said, nodding toward the space beside my bedroll. "Thank you. Aleaia, may I examine your wounds?"

Lucius glanced between us, then arched a brow at Valerius. "Oh, Mariana, you ought to check his lordship first. He looks a bit unwell."

Valerius didn't take the bait—at least, not right away. He reached for the amphora and poured another cup of wine with every ounce of poise he could summon. "Is this what passes for a field report now?"

"You told me no parchment pushing. I'm managing camp stability," Lucius said, dropping the chest with a thud. "Seems the command tent was getting a bit unstable."

"You're welcome to take first watch tonight. Since you're feeling so energetic."

"Excellent," Lucius said. "Gives me time to work on a ballad. I'm thinking something about a moonstruck legate and his northern guard."

Valerius coughed and set his cup aside.

Mariana crossed the tent, dropped her satchel beside my bedroll, and shot me a look sharp enough to pierce chainmail. "Come here so we can get this over with," she said, already rolling up her sleeves.

I rose, sighing heavily as I crossed the tent.

Valerius set his cup down and stood, reaching for his cloak. "Lucius, let's see what the mess tent has to offer."

Lucius didn't move. "You mean besides stale bread and boiled disappointment?"

Valerius didn't look back. "I'm willing to risk it."

Lucius sighed and followed. "One day, I'd like to see you encounter a woman with a satchel and not try to flee."

"It's not the one with the satchel," Valerius said.

I watched the tent flap sway shut behind him, one brow arched. He was running.

Interesting.

I sat on my bedroll and stripped off my tunic, tugging it over my head in one motion. The undershirt stuck beneath my arm, catching on the half-healed sutures. I hissed and yanked it free, tossing it aside.

"*Es maron*," she admonished in Aeltyrian.

I blinked. The language hit like cold water. I hadn't heard it spoken like that—freely—in years.

"You speak Aeltyrian," I said in kind. "Aren't you worried?"

"There are only the two of us here," Mariana said gently. "I won't tell if you won't."

She reached into the medicine chest and pulled out a small pair of hooked scissors. With practiced ease, she uncorked a vial and poured saltwater over a folded cloth.

I hesitated. "It's just... I haven't spoken it in a long time. Not like this."

Not for comfort.

Not without orders.

Not without hurting someone else.

Mariana didn't ask. She only nodded, positioned me the way she needed—with my left arm up, holding myself out of the way—and went on with her work. "This next part might pinch, but it won't hurt."

I still flinched at the first snip from reflex, more than pain.

"Sorry," I muttered.

Mariana chuckled. "Reflexes like that, it's a wonder you made it through training."

She worked in silence, snipping and plucking with deft fingers. After a time, she said lightly, "You both looked strange when we came in. Did we interrupt something?"

I kept my face still. "No."

Mariana hummed, unconvinced.

I shifted, then said more firmly, "Absolutely not."

"If you say so," she said.

"Are you from the city proper?" I asked, shifting the topic with all the subtlety of a warhorse.

"I am. Castle-born and raised. My mother runs the kitchens there." Her tone softened. "It's been six years since I last saw her."

I nodded, unsure what to say.

"Will you visit your family while we're there?" she asked.

"No." I kept my gaze on the tent wall. "There's no one left."

For a while, the only sound in the tent was the soft rasp of linen and steel.

"I'm sorry," Mariana said.

"No need," I answered, voice worn thin. "It was a long time ago."

The silence that followed wasn't uncomfortable.

After a breath, I added, quietly, "Still. Thank you."

"My mother has a habit of adopting strays," Mariana said, her voice light but sincere. "If you ever need someone fussing over you with soup and too many questions, she'd love you."

"Thank you." And I meant it—the gratitude. Mariana didn't know what she was offering. But the warmth in it was real.

Even so, I wouldn't take it. I never would.

Everyone who'd ever loved me had died for it.

And that was all it took to let the darkness in: a few words of Aeltyrian, and a reminder that I was an accursed thing.

"All done," Mariana said. "I took out every other stitch. We'll see how you fare before I remove the rest. You still need to be careful."

"I will."

Mariana began cleaning and packing away her instruments, her movements brisk and methodical. Then, more lightly, she asked, "Shall we join the others at the mess tent?"

I pulled a clean, dry tunic from my pack over my head, slow and careful. "I think I'll stay. Rest a bit."

Mariana paused, watching me. But she didn't press. "I'm not hungry either. After all the rain, all I want is to sleep."

I didn't answer. Couldn't. The pressure behind my eyes had started to build, sharp and sudden. My throat was tight. If Mariana said one more kind thing, I was going to fall apart.

*Please, just go.*

"I'll send something back with Lucius in case you change your mind," she said softly.

I managed a nod.

When the tent flap closed behind her, the silence returned.

Heavy.

Unforgiving.

I sat on the bedroll and stared at the corner where the brazier flickered.

Rest. Right.

I lay down after a time, but sleep didn't come. There would be no rest. Not tonight. I knew that.

Not with the memories creeping in—jagged-edged and unwelcome. The things they'd said to me. The ones who'd trusted me because I wore their face. Because I spoke their language. Because I'd sworn the Empire would keep its word.

And then stood there when it didn't.

*"Lay down your arms. You will be safe, I swear."*

I'd stood in the village square, mud to my ankles, hope thick in the air. They'd listened. Elders, children, warriors with rusted spears—all of them trusted me. Believed me.

That night, the soldiers came.

They didn't bother with questions. Just lit the homes and strung the ealdorman up from the granary. The screaming didn't last long. But the quiet afterward did. I remembered that silence more than anything—the hush of a place that had lost every voice worth hearing.

*"Give them the names. Your family will be spared."*

A boy. Seventeen, maybe. Bright-eyed, shaking, but eager to help. He handed over a list of passing riders, thinking his family would be spared.

They nailed his tongue to the longhouse door.

Burned the others alive in the storehouse meant for grain.

I found him still breathing. Just barely.

He'd hanged himself in the barn as soon as he found rope.

The third lie was the one I had wanted most to believe.

*"Pay the tribute. Do what you can. When the Empire comes, they'll see you've given everything, and it will be enough."*

It was a ruinous sum, but they tried. Melted jewelry. Bartered livestock. Pulled rings from the fingers of the dead.

I rode with the cohort when they returned.

Watched the prefect call their effort an insult. Watched him laugh at the lightness of the bag.

Then watched as the soldiers began their work.

I didn't throw the torch.

But I stood there when the doors were kicked in, when the screaming started, when they hung children from the Elder Tree like offerings.

I'd had a sword.

I didn't draw it.

Not once.

Because how could I? I was one woman.

He asked me directly if I had told them what he demanded. I recounted my words.

Got ten lashes for insubordination.

For offering comfort.

Then I was reassigned.

Sent to the First Legion as an optio.

They called it a promotion.

But they took my horse.

I squeezed my eyes shut, but the voices stayed. The words echoed—brittle, merciless.

I turned onto my side and pulled the blanket tight around my shoulders, up over my ears as if I could smother them out.

Tears came slowly at first. Then faster. Soaked into the rough wool, muffled and unseen.

Aeltyrian lived only in my prayers then: spoken low, and only when no one could be hurt by the words.

*"Domnaviraos, gavel melior en em. Salel te uluse taengeí am gavrein thravan. Ganan. Voram gavamin naet, et am naeroa sethel enen reveu nū. Ta es darilos. Ta es thelmiros."*

*My lady, have mercy on me. Forgive the grievous things I have done to survive. To endure. I wish I hadn't, and I can't take them back now. It is my sorrow. It is my regret.*

No one heard.

And when the ghosts let me be, sleep finally took me.

Like Vespera's touch—

slow,

quiet,

and cold.

# CHAPTER THIRTEEN
## *Hunger*

*"The Second Son never beds the same girl twice—
unless she's guarding his door."*
—Scratched into the privy wall behind the mess, Avitum barracks

Dēwamos 29, 1230
*Aleaia*

The morning meal was thin—salted oats in dented tin bowls, a wedge of hardtack tough enough to crack teeth.

I sat across from Valerius in the mess tent, canvas seams dripping steadily above. Around us, legionaries murmured in low clusters. No laughter. Just spoons scraping tin and shoulders hunched against the damp. The quiet wasn't discipline. It was hunger, gnawing at patience, tightening throats. Rations held, but not for long. The land had been bled dry within a day's ride.

No game. No grain. Nothing.

Soon they'd start trading favors. Or stealing. Or worse.

I broke the hardtack, dipped half into the oats to soften it enough to chew. Barely.

"We've three days left," I said, watching steam coil from my bowl.

"If the river drops another hand-span, we could move in two," Valerius replied without looking up.

I nodded. A clatter echoed down the tent, followed by a muttered curse. Valerius tore his bread slowly.

After a heartbeat of silence, his voice dropped. "How did you sleep?"

"Well enough." I dipped the bread again. "Why? Did I snore? Thrash?"

He shook his head. "No."

"Sometimes I do. If I dream." I wondered why he'd asked. In all the mornings I'd woken to stand beside him, he'd never asked before.

He didn't answer right away.

"I have them too," he said finally. "Sometimes I wake with my heart racing, like I've been running from something I can't see."

I stilled. He wasn't looking at me. Just the oats in his bowl.

I stirred mine once, slow.

He hadn't offered comfort. Just truth, his own. And for a moment, I wondered if I could give him one of mine. If it would help. If it would matter.

I said nothing, but something in me eased.

"I was thinking we might go hunting," he said.

I nodded. "Good idea. The forest floor should still be damp. Rain'll help mask our steps. Anything holed up will be hungry."

"Are you allowed to pull a bowstring?"

"I haven't been told not to." I shrugged. "I'll bring a light bow and let you get most of the game."

He chuckled. "Let me?"

"Yes," I said, smiling. "But only this once."

He laughed, warm and honest, and something inside me softened in answer.

"Should we invite Lucius?" I asked.

Valerius shook his head. "He's not much for archery."

"If we're going, better soon. Morning's slipping."

"Agreed." Valerius rose.

We left the mess tent, boots sucking at the wet earth. At the command tent, I swapped my stiff legion boots for soft deerskin. Strung my bow. The grip was familiar, worn smooth.

The last time I'd done this with anyone had been seven years ago. My father beside me, proud of every strike. Grief never waited for a proper moment. It struck in tasks like this, drawn up by memory. Worse yet were the quiet hours, when nothing held it at bay. Like last night.

I stood by the tent flap while Valerius gathered his gear. When he finished, we crossed camp again. He stopped at the quartermaster's tent and lifted the flap to tell Lucius where we were going.

"If you're not back by sundown, I'm coming after you," Lucius called from inside. "Is Dieter out there?"

"Yes, sir, and I heard your warning," I called back, rolling my eyes.

Valerius chuckled as we walked on.

We passed a knot of legionaries crammed under a sagging tarp, slurping stew and gossip with equal appetite.

"Three times in one day," one said, shaking his head like he'd heard a ballad worth repeating. "Afternoon in the command tent, bathhouse wench before dinner, then back in the tent again last night? That's a triumph."

Another gave a low whistle. "Heard one of them needed the healer afterward."

A snort from the first. "Doesn't surprise me. Ashborn girls are all fire and no staying power. Don't get enough to eat."

"Still," one said, "his lordship's got stamina."

"Well, he hasn't had anyone more than once since the Alcaeus girl. Gods, she was—"

The laughter died when one of them looked up and saw Valerius and me. "Fuck, they're *right* there."

"To the latrine trench," Lucius said dryly, stepping out from behind a tent like he'd been waiting for the cue. "All of you. Full kit. Now."

The men scrambled to their feet without a word.

Valerius shifted beside me, jaw tight as he looked to Lucius. "Thank you."

Lucius didn't look at him. "Wasn't for you."

Shame twisted in my gut, mean and bitter, as we moved on toward the camp gate. They thought I'd bedded Valerius.

Thought I wasn't enough to satisfy him.

That I was a novelty. A warm body to replace the last one.

Ashborn. Cheap. Disposable.

Valerius spoke again, voice low, maddeningly calm. "Really, they didn't say you were unsatisfying. Just that I was… remarkably vigorous."

I turned and looked at him. Slowly. If I'd had the authority, I'd have put him in the trench with the others Lucius was working to death.

He cleared his throat. "Which is, you know. A compliment."

I stared for a long moment, unable to believe he'd just said that to me with a straight face, then shook my head and turned away.

We passed through the gate and headed toward the woods. My boots sank into the soaked ground, each step louder than it needed to be. I walked like I wanted a fight. Maybe I did.

Valerius tried again, more gently this time. "None of it happened. Not with the girl. Not with anyone."

I snorted. "I know. I was there," I said flatly.

"What?" His head snapped toward me.

"In the tent," I said slowly. Where did he think I meant?

Something in his expression eased.

"Only part they got right was that I… attempted to visit the baths. It went poorly. Deeply unsatisfying," he muttered. "For everyone involved."

I exhaled and shook my head again. I didn't want to hear this.

"I wouldn't care if you had, you know." The words escaped me before I could stop them.

Valerius glanced over. "What?"

"If you'd gone to the baths and had a great old time while I was…" I trailed off.

What could I say? While I was curled up in a blanket, crying over dead villages and boys with nailed tongues?

"While I was too exhausted to move," I finished.

A lie. To him. To myself.

It did bother me. I hated that it did. I hated more that I didn't know why.

We moved deeper into the trees, leaving the camp behind. The moment the last tent slipped out of sight, I stopped. Turned on him.

"The truth is, I don't like being compared to a traitor. To someone who used her closeness to you to try and kill you. Who, it seems, got close just for that."

Valerius opened his mouth. "We were betrothed as children, Aleaia—"

I held his gaze. "Let me talk. Correct me later."

He nodded. Quiet.

"They forget how I got this position. What I bled for. I still can't draw a full bowstring, but they think I'm here because I'm fucking you? That I'm your—your what? Concubine?" The word cracked on my tongue. "They don't remember the years I spent in the legion. The wounds I carry. But they know where I sleep. Who I guard. Every hour of the day."

I looked away, jaw clenched until it ached.

"I didn't think I cared what they said. But I do. And I hate that I do."

Rain pattered soft around us—on leather, bark, skin. Gentler than I felt.

Valerius stepped closer—close enough to touch, though he didn't.

"I remember the truth," he said. "The girl who stood her ground when others ran. The woman who stepped between me and death. Who ran into the fire when she could've walked away."

I held his gaze a breath too long.

Then I turned, walked away. My boots squelched in the wet grass. The trees whispered ahead, rain brushing the leaves like breath.

Valerius didn't follow right away. A dozen paces passed in silence before I spoke again. "You smell like rosewater, by the way."

He caught up beside me. "Do I?"

"It stinks. You're going to scare off all the game." I was being petty and I knew it.

He cleared his throat. "Would you prefer I join those other three on the Shit Run instead?"

It was sharper than I expected. Well-aimed, even. I wasn't about to let him see it land. I bit back a smile.

"She was kind," he said. "Did all the right things. It just… didn't help. Wasn't the right person, I guess."

I had no answer to that. Something shifted in my chest. Unwelcome. Uninvited. He hadn't said it *for* me. He'd just said it, and somehow, that made it worse.

We reached the tree line, where grass gave way to brambles and shadow. I stepped over a slick root, meaning to keep walking, when his hand brushed my arm, light and careful. I stopped again. Turned toward him.

"I want to apologize," Valerius said. "For something I said yesterday. I never had the chance."

My brow furrowed.

"For what I said about your homeland. Calling it a backwater." His voice was soft, shaped with something heavier than regret. "I've spent more years in Aeltyria than Calesia. I do know better. I'm sorry."

His eyes didn't waver. Neither did mine.

It wasn't the apology that rattled me. It was that he meant it. I could feel it, like warmth in my hands. I turned without answering and walked into the woods.

Without looking back, I said, "Thank you."

Rain whispered through the canopy above.

We said nothing else.

And the forest took us in.

# CHAPTER FOURTEEN
## *Unarmored*

*"The Fifth Flame waits in silence.*
*Not for permission, but for presence.*
*For the soul that sees and does not recoil."*
—The Doctrines of the Fifth Flame

Dēwamos 29, 1230
*Aleaia*

By late afternoon, the storm had abated, leaving behind the hush of dripping leaves and sodden earth. Mist clung to the forest floor. My boots squelched with every step, water pressing from the seams with a pitiful little squish.

We hadn't seen so much as a hare.

I brushed wet foliage aside and squinted at the faint, overgrown line that might once have been a game trail. "It seems I've greatly misjudged our direction."

Behind me, Valerius made a sound—a low hum that might've meant agreement, amusement, or both. "I thought you were an outdoorswoman."

"I said I *prefer* the outdoors," I replied, pushing another branch out of the way. It snapped back and slapped damp needles across my shoulder. "I've spent the last seven years with some thundering arsehole shouting where to march. I haven't had to think about it much."

"Fair." He ducked beneath a drooping bough.

"If you've got a secret knack for finding the way, now would be the time to speak up."

"It was only a suggestion. I don't mean to be a thundering arsehole."

I glanced back at him and caught the edge of a smile he wasn't bothering to hide.

"But perhaps we should find shelter before we end up soaked again."

I huffed a laugh and stepped over a moss-slick root. "Lucius is going to have my hide for this."

"He wouldn't really strike you," Valerius said mildly.

"He hasn't yet." I shrugged. "But I've never lost a prince before."

We passed beneath gnarled spruce. Water clung to the branches, dropping in lazy beads onto my cloak. Overhead, the light had shifted again, gray and thin, bleeding toward dusk.

"The longer we're out here," I muttered, "the worse the hiding will be."

"He won't lay a hand on you."

For a moment, that almost sounded protective.

"You're his relief. Without you, he'd be stuck at my side every moment," Valerius said.

I laughed softly. "That's almost flattering."

He glanced my way, brow arched. "From Lucius, that's practically affection."

"You're generous with your definition of affection."

The hush stretched between us again, broken only by the sigh of wind in the branches and the slow drip of runoff from the trees.

I exhaled. "You might be right. About shelter."

Valerius cast me a sidelong look, one brow lifting, mouth curving. "Let this go down in history as the day a woman admitted I was right."

"A truly memorable occasion," I said, dry as bark.

I could feel his eyes on me. Warm as the grin in his voice.

"I'll treasure this moment," he said. "It may never happen again."

I shook my head, the corner of my mouth tugging despite myself. "You're insufferable."

I was struck again—something that happened more often now—by the impertinence in me. Not too long ago, I'd been afraid to speak to him at all, but now I was familiar with him. Too familiar, maybe.

The trail narrowed, swallowed by underbrush, slick with rain. He moved ahead, ducking beneath a hanging bough. I followed, branches tugging at my cloak as I tried to keep my footing.

And then he glanced back.

Just a tilt of the head.

Just enough to meet my eyes over his shoulder.

A shaft of light caught him then—rain-damp hair, cheekbone lined in gold. His mouth curled, just a little. Smug. Unbothered. Unfairly attractive. Gods, he knew. He knew I was watching him.

My pulse jumped. I looked away.

Then stepped wrong.

My foot slid on moss.

"Fuck!" I swore as I went down.

Of course it was the left side that hit first. My bad hand shot out and caught the edge of a trunk. The right flailed, useless, and pain lit my side and shoulder like a brand as I slammed flat on my back.

The world spun. A burst of white behind my eyes. I clenched my jaw hard and swallowed the sharp sound rising in my throat.

*Don't do anything embarrassing. More embarrassing anyway.*

Valerius was beside me in an instant, kneeling close. His gaze swept over me—shoulder, elbow, face. Just enough to read the damage.

He didn't speak right away, but his mouth twitched, just once. Like he knew exactly what had happened and regretted almost none of it.

Then he spoke, gently. "Did you hurt anything?"

"Just my pride, I think." A lie, if I ever told one.

He extended his hand then, palm up. An offering.

I stared at it. Then placed mine in his.

His grip was warm and steady. He pulled me upright carefully, eyes flicking to my shoulder like he thought it might splinter under his hands.

I winced. Pain flared, sharp enough to drag a hiss through my teeth. My fingers lingered in his longer than I meant them to—partly for balance, partly because I hadn't quite decided to let go.

He covered my hand with his other palm, firm and quiet. "Are you sure?"

"My last shred of dignity's in tatters." I cradled my elbow as I tested the arm. "But otherwise, I'm fine."

He didn't argue. Just watched me like he was waiting for the truth I hadn't said.

I looked past him toward the slope. "There's a rise ahead," I said. "Might be dry under the pines."

We pressed forward, each step muffled by the soft decay of the forest floor. The hill lifted us into a stand of old red pines, their boughs low and dense enough to shelter.

"This'll do," Valerius said, dropping his pack beside a fallen log.

I lowered myself onto it with care. My back and side throbbed, sharp and deep, and my left arm pulled tight against my ribs. I didn't need to check. The bandages were soaked. I could feel it, tugging with every breath.

Valerius knelt in front of me, brows drawing together. "Let me see."

Let him see?

See the scars? The bruising? No. Too many questions.

"No." The word came out too fast. Too harsh. I tugged the edge of my cloak across my chest like armor.

"Aleaia." Just my name. No pressure. No command. Only stillness. Quiet and steady. Like he would wait as long as I needed.

"You'll just shout at me."

"When have I ever shouted at you?"

My mouth twitched. Almost a smile. "There's a first time for everything."

"Well, it won't be today," he said gently.

"I just…" My voice thinned. I kept my eyes on the ground. "There are a lot of… scars."

I swallowed hard. Why did it matter? He'd seen worse, hadn't he? Wounds that festered. Limbs taken clean. But those had been earned.

Most of mine weren't.

"It's all right. Nothing could make me think you're less—" He paused. Just a breath. "Less."

I felt it settle low and heavy, though it wasn't suffocating. Not pity. Not a lie. Just something reined in for my sake.

I didn't answer, and I couldn't look at him.

I couldn't just bleed to death out here in the woods. And he didn't keep me around for my looks anyway.

My fingers touched the clasp of my cloak.

I exhaled and worked it loose. The cloak slipped from my shoulder. My fingers found the hem of my tunic and eased it up carefully, exposing the damp linen beneath.

He reached to help, lifting the wool gently. It clung at first, then peeled away with a soft, wet sound. I shivered, though the air was warm.

I heard the sharp intake of his breath behind me. A shift of weight. The faint rustle of cloth as his hand stilled mid-reach. At first, he said nothing.

Then, softly, "Oh."

Just the sound of someone realizing they hadn't known what they were about to see.

My scars. The ones that never healed right. I kept my gaze fixed forward. It felt worse than I'd feared, not because he recoiled, but because he didn't. Because he was quiet.

Shame welled, dark and familiar. Not just for the marks, but for what they meant. For what I hadn't stopped. For what I'd said to make them happen. For everything that came after.

Please don't ask.

He had to know. There was no mistaking lashes.

I wanted to explain. Gods, I wanted to say something. To tell him it hadn't been weakness. That I'd tried.

But the words lodged behind my ribs. Saying them would mean opening something I wasn't ready to bleed.

And if he pitied me—

*No.*

I couldn't bear that.

My eyes found the roots near my boots, the dark smear of rot along the log.

"I deserved them," I said.

And gods, I hated the way my voice sounded. Like a confession hardened into fact.

The silence that followed wasn't judgmental. It was worse. It was the unbearable weight of being seen. And I didn't want comfort. I just wanted it done.

I shifted, dragging the tunic higher, baring the soaked bandages beneath. "Just wrap it," I said. "Please."

There was the muted creak of leather as he opened his satchel. The whisper of linen. No questions.

My ears burned from shame. What was he thinking? That I was weak? That I'd earned it? Or worse, that I hadn't? Did he pity me for it?

Valerius knelt behind me, close enough I could feel his warmth through the humid air. The moment stretched, suspended. He worked slowly. Gently. Like someone who'd seen a thousand scars like mine and understood what silence was worth.

The cloth met my skin, clean and soft. He anchored one end low across my ribs, over my shift, and began winding it upward in slow, careful spirals. His hand steadied my waist—just his palm, braced there, a single point of contact to keep me still.

I had to remind myself to breathe.

Halfway through, his voice came quiet enough it barely reached me. "You didn't deserve it."

Just that.

Just a truth he needed me to hear, whether I believed it or not.

I didn't answer at first. Didn't breathe. Just let the cloth circle once more, drawn snug across my ribs.

"I know you're wondering... how. I'll tell you about it one day," I said quietly. "Not today. Probably not tomorrow. But one day. When I can find the right words."

When it didn't feel like failure.

When I'd earned the right to tell him.

My voice stayed even but thin at the edges. "I'm sorry."

His hands stilled for a heartbeat, just long enough to be felt, then resumed, unhurried. He tied the bandage off with practiced fingers. He didn't press. Didn't offer the kind of comfort I hadn't asked for. Only said softly, "I'll be here."

It landed like warmth through steel.

I felt something shift. It wasn't trust, not yet, but the start of something that might hold it.

He turned away, giving me space to fix my tunic and cloak without feeling watched. When I was done, he sat beside me and passed a waterskin into my hand.

I took it without speaking. Drank. Handed it back.

I wasn't sure what else to say.

A twig cracked nearby.

We stilled, then saw it at the same time: movement in the trees.

A buck stepped into view, steam curling from its nostrils. Its antlers caught what little light there was, crowning it in soft gold.

I moved on instinct, reaching for my bow, but stopped when pain flared, white-hot and sudden. My shoulder screamed. I hissed, breath sharp through my teeth.

Valerius turned at once.

"You'll have to," I whispered. "I can't draw."

"You sure?" he murmured.

"No. But I'm hungry."

He rose and offered his hand. This time, I didn't hesitate. I took it. Let him pull me to my feet.

He checked his bow, thumb brushing the string, then took an arrow from his quiver.

I stepped in behind him close enough to feel the warmth coming off him in the damp air.

"Watch the shoulder." I kept my voice low near his ear. "Just behind the foreleg."

He nodded, but he was too tense. My hand slid to the edge of his ribs, fingers light. "Breathe from here. Not your chest."

He drew a breath in deep, then held it.

I frowned. "I said breathe."

He let it out, slow and uneven.

I didn't question it. Just brushed my fingertips along his knuckles where they'd tightened too much around the string. I leaned in, breath brushing his ear. "Loosen your grip. You're choking the shot."

He loosened, then pulled the bowstring taut.

The buck lifted its head. Then stepped.

"Now," I whispered.

The arrow flew clean and straight, striking deep just behind the foreleg.

The buck jerked once, then dropped. No cry. No thrashing. Just silence.

Valerius let out a breath, still staring toward the trees.

I caught his arm, a smile breaking loose. "Dead center. That was clean."

"That was your shot," he said. "I just let it fly."

"I didn't do that much," I said. Before I could think better of it, I caught his hand in mine, tugging him forward.

And he didn't let go, his hand tightening around mine.

At the deer's side, I knelt. Steam still curled faintly from its nostrils. Its eye had gone glassy, half-lidded. I checked the wound first. Straight through the heart. No waste. No suffering. I laid a hand against its neck, feeling the last trace of warmth ebb from the skin, and exhaled.

"Well," I said. "You'll do."

Valerius chuckled. "Was that praise?"

"Something like that." I shot him a look. "Don't get used to it."

I hesitated. I owed this animal thanks, but I only knew one way to offer it. How much would that seed of trust bloom then, I wondered?

I'd say the words anyway, I decided. If he called it heresy, turned his back, so be it.

"My people…" I started. The words felt strange in my mouth. I cleared my throat. "We pray for the animal's sacrifice."

But Valerius didn't even blink. "You never need ask with me."

I let my fingers rest on the hide as I bowed my head.

*"Laeth tóa alureth velael te talen nadrovin. Sola te anathar ebres tóa draeth et theil bravau."*

*Let your spirit return to the earth unburdened. May the forest drink your blood and grow strong.*

The words slipped into the hush beneath the trees, soft as breath, as I made the first cut, guiding the blade with practiced ease. The air turned sharp with blood as the hide was opened. Few words passed between us while we worked, but the rhythm held—knife, weight, cloth, breath.

We quartered the meat, wrapping what we could carry. The rest we tucked beneath dry brush and stone, far enough from the rise to keep scavengers away from us while we slept. The bones, we left behind. Nothing was wasted.

By the time we made it back to the clearing beneath the pines, my arms ached and my shoulder throbbed. The sun bled gold through the branches. Dampness still clung to bark and stone.

I didn't complain. Just crouched and gathered kindling while Valerius cleared space beside the log, laying the stones for a fire. I struck the flint, spark catching on the second try, and I fed it dry moss first, then brittle twigs, then thicker wood that cracked loud and smoked as the flames took hold.

We rigged a spit from two forked branches and a straight shaft, balanced easily over the fire like I'd done hundreds of times. The scent of meat curled into the clearing, rich and heavy. Fat popped and hissed as it hit the coals.

I rolled my shoulder to keep it loose and sat on the log, arms folded across my knees. The ache in my limbs was the good kind. The earned kind. Somewhere behind the tree line, the first stars began to show. I watched them blink to life, one by one.

"Lucius is going to kill us," I blurted out.

Valerius huffed a laugh beside me. "Not if he gets lost trying to find us."

"He won't," I said. "He's infuriatingly competent."

"So are you," he said. "And here we are."

My stomach growled loud enough that I knew he heard it.

"Was that you?" he asked, surprised.

I laughed. Real. Unchecked. "Yes! I'm starving, I told you. Gods, I can't remember the last time I looked forward to dinner."

Valerius stared. "You eat with me nearly every night."

"Aye," I said, slipping into familiarity. "The company's tolerable. But this—" I nodded toward the spit, "this is a *real* dinner."

He was still looking at me.

I felt it, so I glanced at him. "What?"

He smiled. "I was going to say you're—"

I held his gaze then.

He laughed softly, glanced away and back at me again. "You're radiant when you're happy."

My breath caught at the way he'd said it—earnestly. There was no jest in it.

I looked away. "I am happy. About dinner," I said. As if that explained everything.

It sat between us for a few heartbeats before he spoke again.

"Is it common in your village, to master the bow like that?"

I leaned forward to turn the spit, watching the juices sizzle as the meat shifted. My mouth watered.

"No," I said. "My father was good, and he had me pulling a bowstring from the time I could walk. Most people don't bother. Hunting bigger game's illegal for us. Traps are easier. Less risk, less time."

"You're a good teacher," he said. "I couldn't have made that shot without you."

I smirked, eyes still on the spit. "I've seen you at the archery range. You're not that bad."

"I'm not that good either." He nudged a loose pebble near his boot. "Not like someone who could hit a moving target at sixty paces on horseback."

That had been an archery contest, and the prize was supposed to have been dinner with the Legate—with Valerius. I'd won, but he had been called away.

"That's mostly true," I replied. "It was fifty-eight paces when I measured it out later, but I suppose sixty sounds cleaner when telling the story. Where did you hear it?"

"Lucius told me," he said. "He informed me of your progress from time to time. Over the years."

I paused. "Over the years," I echoed.

He didn't flinch, but he didn't elaborate either.

"That's a lot of years," I said, poking at the coals with a stick. "That's a lot of interest on *Lucius's* part."

Still nothing, though he was very deliberately and very obviously not looking at me.

I glanced sideways, biting back a smile. I was teasing him, and I knew it. I liked that I could. "Maybe I should be sitting at this fire with him instead."

Valerius turned to look at me. Sharp. Sudden.

"No," he said, too fast.

I tilted my head, studying him.

He looked away just as quickly. "I asked him about you. Wondered how you did after you joined. If you'd made it through training."

That wasn't a deflection. It was an admission. An opening. I took it.

"That shot was in Ostala. So that was... four years in." I glanced at him. "Took four years for you to ask?"

Valerius didn't look at me. "*I* asked about you," he said. "Several times. Over the years."

The fire popped. Fat hissed in the coals.

I gave a wry exhale. "Good to know someone gave a shit whether I was alive or dead."

Valerius turned his head, just enough to be heard, and when he spoke, there was no trace of teasing in his voice. "I did."

I leaned toward him, bumped his shoulder with mine, light and brief. Meant to be nothing.

He leaned back just enough to keep the contact. I didn't pull away. I just felt the warmth between us.

And for a little while, that was enough.

# CHAPTER FIFTEEN
## *Fallow*

*"You don't leave a field fallow because it's useless.*
*You do it so it stays useful."*
—Jurian Dieter

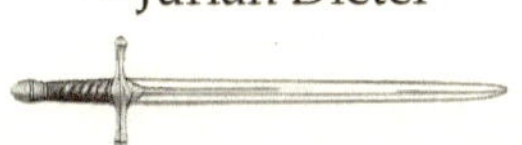

Dēwamos 30, 1230
*Aleaia*

By the time we reached the command tent, Lucius was waiting outside, arms folded.

"Back before breakfast," he said. "Impressive."

Val almost smiled at that.

I caught the slip only after it happened—*Val,* not *Valerius.* Somewhere between firelight and silence, his name had shifted, become something closer. I didn't correct myself. It felt right.

He shifted the bundle under his arm and held it out.

Lucius raised a brow.

"Venison," Val said.

Lucius peeked inside and let out a low, appreciative hum. "Oh, darling, you spoil me."

"Don't share it," Val said. "You'll never be rid of them."

"What happened to coming after us if we weren't back before dark?" I asked.

Lucius didn't blink. "I never said how long after dark. Just that I would."

I pressed my lips together as I looked at him. This could not be the same man who was once my tribune. The man they called the Sword of Calesia.

"It's 'after dark' now, isn't it?" Lucius asked.

I looked him over: breeches, undershirt, no shoes. "You don't look like you were about to leave."

He shrugged. "You've seen me fight barefoot."

Val shot him a look. Lucius only grinned.

Then Val turned to me, warmth still lingering behind his eyes. "You should check in with Mariana."

"If I don't go, will you order me to?"

"I'd rather not," he said.

I exhaled through my nose and turned to head toward the healer's tent.

He called after me. "Come find me after."

"Gods forbid I go a single morning without making someone's life harder," I muttered, waving him off without looking back.

Behind me, Lucius's voice cracked through the morning haze. "Anyone still standing around staring will be running laps to the privies by midmorning. Move!"

A few soldiers scattered at the edge of my vision.

Had they been staring? I wondered. I was sure it wouldn't help the rumors, the two of us walking into camp after having been out alone all night. I'd be lucky if some priest didn't call for me to be flogged for indecency.

Not Val. Just me. Because I was the woman *and* Aeltyrian.

The canvas flap of the infirmary tent fell closed behind me, muting the stir of the waking camp. Inside, the air clung thick with boiled nettle, stale sweat, and something sour beneath it. Bile, maybe. Or gut-rot. I didn't know how Mariana could stand working in a place like that.

I blinked, adjusting to the dim.

She stood near the center cot, sleeves shoved to her elbows, hair twisted into a mess of pins and tension. A pale, trembling legionary knelt beside a half-full basin, retching hard enough to rattle the frame.

I recognized him as one of the bastards from yesterday.

"Ah. The leader of the little Shit Run. Should've kept your mouth shut, eh?"

He looked up, eyes glassy and bloodshot, then groaned and slumped forward, arms locked around the basin like it might keep him from falling apart.

"Keeping his mouth shut would, in fact, have prevented this from happening. In both senses. Second one this morning," she added, voice stretched thin. "And if it's like yesterday's, he'll be lucky if he can keep water down by dusk."

She handed him a damp cloth and turned to her satchel—stuffed with bundled herbs, twisted roots, and stained linen.

"If it's not fevers, it's gut flux. If not that, it's boils or torn stitches or some fool trying to walk on a leg I told him not to use. I swear, some of these men would march with both arms hacked off if you promised them stew at the end."

"Just the men? No one needs arms to march, really," I said.

"There aren't as many women—"

She straightened.

Turned.

Her eyes locked on me, narrowed. "Why are *you* here?"

"I can't visit my friend?"

"In the daylight, it's not a friendly visit."

I shrugged. "I only brought *one* of the problems you listed."

She pinched the bridge of her nose and sighed. "That's what they all say. We'll see. Strip."

I glanced at the legionary still hunched over the basin. He sagged like a wrung-out rag, arms wrapped tight around the basin like its weight was the only thing keeping him upright.

"Does he look like he cares?" she asked. She snapped a rag over her shoulder and pointed to the side cot.

I unfastened my cloak and let it fall away as I sat down on the cot, then eased my tunic up past my ribs. The fabric stuck where the bandage had bled through. It peeled away with a soft, wet sound.

Mariana clicked her tongue. "Oh look. Another wound ripe for corruption. How'd you manage this?"

"Slipped. Landed flat on my back. I was... distracted."

She raised a brow. "By?"

The memory of Val—the light filtering through the leaves, catching his profile just right—flitted through my mind and left me feeling like I'd lost my footing again.

"A large... stag," I said, keeping my gaze on the tent wall. "I don't want to talk about it. Just stitch me up and send me on my way. It'll hurt less."

She didn't sigh or argue. Just reached for her needle and a thread of catgut, then sat behind me on the cot.

"Fine," she said. "But next time you're distracted, try not to land on my work."

Her hands moved with practiced certainty. She cleaned the wound in silence, wiping away the fresh blood, inspecting the skin beneath with a sharp eye.

"You're lucky it didn't tear deeper." Mariana threaded the needle.

"I'm not lucky."

"Hold still," she said.

The first stitch burned less than the last time, but worse in its familiarity. A biting pull. A thread dragging through skin I couldn't quite call numb. Still, I said nothing. Just clenched my jaw and stayed still.

She was three stitches in when I asked, "How bad are the... the other scars? I've never seen them."

Mariana was quiet long enough that I wasn't sure she heard me.

"They're scars," she said at last. "Not pretty. But not shameful either."

I kept my eyes on the canvas wall. The pull of the needle dragged raw through skin already bruised.

"I didn't ask if they were shameful."

"No," she said. "You didn't."

She reached for the shears—small ones with the iron handles—and snipped the thread.

"Mostly flat," she said. "Clean healing. You're young and ate well. You probably had muscle even then. Like now."

She rinsed her fingers in the basin beside the cot. The water had gone cloudy with blood, herbs, and whatever dirt the bandage hadn't kept out. "I've seen worse. Like I said, you're lucky."

"Will they... fade? In time?" I asked.

"They might. But Aleaia, they're not anything to be ashamed of," she said gently.

I clutched my hands together, bit my lip. Easy for her to say, when she was free of the kinds of scars and marks I bore. No man would ever look at her and say, *'oh.'*

When the last knot was set, Mariana sat back. "There. You open this again, and I'm pinning your arm to your tunic."

I let the breath out slow through my nose. My shoulder throbbed in time with my pulse. "Understood."

Mariana stood and dusted her hands on a cloth already stiff with dried blood.

"I'm putting you on restricted duty until it's healed. You ride in the infirmary wagon when we march. Sleep in the infirmary tent with the others."

I sat up straighter. Something flared beneath my ribs, sharp and sudden, enough to send a cold rush to my temples.

"No," I said anyway. "No, I won't."

"You will," Mariana replied, already reaching for a fresh roll of bandages. "And I'll tell his lordship myself if you don't comply."

"Who's going to relieve Lucius?"

"That's not your concern. Or mine."

"Son of a—" I swore under my breath.

"I'll send one of the aides with you to collect your things," she said, still maddeningly unfazed. "They'll carry them. And you come straight back."

She didn't wait for a response. Just turned away and knelt beside the still-trembling legionary in the center cot.

I'd come to her for help and she'd stripped me of duty and purpose. I bit back the impulse to say something rude, and instead muttered, "Fine."

I pushed to my feet, bracing against the throb in my side, and looked around the tent. One aide was grinding herbs like the mortar had insulted his lineage. The other was pretending not to see me, folding and refolding a stack of linen that had no business being touched again.

"You," I said, pointing at the linen folder. "With me."

The boy flinched, then snapped upright, stiff as a pike. He looked like he'd rather be sent to scrape privies.

I didn't wait for a reply. Just pushed through the canvas flap into the gray morning light. My boots splashed in the mud as I strode toward the command tent.

Lucius looked up from his chair outside, arms folded and legs stretched out before him, eyes still heavy with sleep. When he saw me coming, his brows lifted.

"Shit," he said. "Val, fire inbound."

The flap cracked as I shoved through.

Val rose from his seat, brow furrowed. "What's wrong?"

I didn't answer. Just turned to look at the aide panting behind me. I pointed to the pile at the tent's edge—my bedroll, pack, armor, sword. "There. Go on. Gather it up."

Val just watched me and the way I moved—tight through the shoulders, my left arm tucked closer than before.

I couldn't look him in the eye. Gods, I was so angry I couldn't even give him a proper recounting of what had happened. "I have to... leave. Here."

Lucius raised his brows, but to his credit, he held his tongue.

Val's gaze shifted to the aide, who was now fumbling with my breastplate and sweating like mishandling it might get him flogged.

"You could've asked someone stronger," he said. "Lucius makes a decent pack mule."

"I took the one who was available."

The aide managed my bedroll and most of the pack before nearly dropping the sword.

Val stepped in without a word. He gathered the rest—pauldrons, greaves, gauntlets—bundling them under one arm, scabbard in the other. It wasn't graceful. He didn't seem to care.

I bristled. "I didn't ask for help."

"You didn't have to."

I grunted in frustration and turned to leave the tent.

We walked in silence. Around us, the camp stirred with soldiers hauling gear, fire pits coughing smoke, hooves clattering as scouts mounted up. The aide lagged, staggering beneath the load.

Val adjusted the plates in his arms, the greaves tapping with each step. "So, where are we going?"

"Infirmary tent."

After a moment, his voice came quieter. "Why are you moving out of the command tent?"

"Mariana's orders. I'm on restricted duty."

"Oh." He sounded relieved. "Why?"

"Not healing properly, she says. I told her it was an accident. She didn't care."

"And where exactly am I supposed to find you, if I need you?"

It was too careful to be only concern or duty.

I cleared my throat. "She said I ride in the infirmary wagon. Sleep in the infirmary tent."

He frowned. "That seems—"

"Excessive?" I snapped. "Aye. You can take it up with her if you want to argue."

"I wasn't going to argue."

"I wish you would," I said.

It came out too fast. Too raw.

Val's brow lifted. "Oh, do you? And what would I be arguing?"

I threw up my hands. "I don't know. That it's absurd. That I've fought through worse. I'm not going to fall apart walking across a godsdamned camp."

"You're not," he said, calm as ever. "But you're also not healing."

I clenched my jaw.

He adjusted the weight in his arms. "Besides, if I argued, she'd win."

"Can't you just order her not to..." I trailed off, then forced it out. "Not do this to me?"

Val looked at me. Steady. Quiet.

"What is she doing to you?"

"She's taking me away from—" *You.* My voice caught. "From my duty. That's all."

It wasn't entirely true, but it was close enough and sharp enough to end the conversation. Or so I hoped.

The infirmary tent's edges snapped in the breeze. Mariana stood in front of it already, arms folded.

She didn't speak at first. Just looked at the three of us: Val with my armor still in his arms, at the aide trailing behind, and me standing between them like a conscript who'd mouthed off.

She eyed the armor and sword. "You didn't need to bring those."

Val's breath left him slowly. "Her things?"

"She'll need the bedroll and her pack, but no armor or sword," Mariana said. "She won't be allowed to carry either. May as well have left them in the command tent with the rest of the restricted gear."

My spine went rigid. "Could've said that before we hauled it halfway across camp."

Val shifted the weight he carried a little higher. "Is she allowed to eat dinner in the command tent, provided Lucius and I supervise?"

I looked between them, mouth opening and closing once in disbelief. "I am *not* a godsdamned prisoner."

Mariana's mouth twitched. "No. But you are a patient. Sit still, heal properly, and you can eat wherever you like."

Val nodded once. "Thank you."

Then he turned and walked back the way we'd come, still carrying my armor.

I watched him go. My chest ached with something heavy and nameless

With nothing else to do, I turned and ducked into the tent, the canvas flap whispering shut behind me, and waited to heal.

# CHAPTER SIXTEEN
## *The Weight*

*"Even the stars must bear what cannot be burned away."*
—The Song of the Stars, Cycle VII: The Cycle of Spirit

Dēwamos 39, 1230
*Aleaia*

By the time we left the Aperta Plains, I'd spent a decadium confined to the infirmary wagon during the day and to the healer's tent at night. Always under someone's watch, every rut and stone rattling through me. The pain in my shoulder and side had dulled to something manageable, lingered like a coal left to smolder, aggravated by the stillness and bumping in equal measure. Everything ached—my back, my legs, my pride.

They could've let me ride. *Walk*. Gods, I'd have taken marching barefoot through clay before enduring one more mile like freight. All the time I had to think led me to the conclusion that this was inhumane and it was time to speak up.

"If you don't allow me to walk," I called toward the front, "I might just set this wagon alight."

Mariana sat beside the driver, enjoying what little breeze the road afforded while I stewed like cargo. She didn't even turn to answer me.

"No."

"You keep spirits in here," I taunted. "The blaze would be spectacular."

"The answer is still no."

"I thought we were friends. You wound me."

"For someone so mortally offended by hindrances to duty," she said, glancing back, "you certainly don't make mine easy."

I changed tack. "Perhaps you could accompany me. Take my hand. Lead me like a child."

"Lead you like an ass, more like," Mariana said.

Val had drifted back through the column, trailing just behind the wagon. I caught the twitch in his shoulders, laughter barely restrained.

I glared, though there was no heat behind it. "What if sitting here gives me a sore? A sore on the arse of his lordship's household guard!"

Mariana sighed. "You're a sore on my arse, Aleaia."

"Maybe, but I am also a legionary. I require movement. Purpose. Dignity."

Val edged closer on his horse, a smile tugging at his mouth. The shift revealed what was behind him.

Marcus.

On a donkey.

Lean and shaggy, it looked thoroughly unimpressed with the man on its back. Marcus tried to sit tall, but the beast lurched with the grace of a drunken goat.

Val lifted a hand, motioned subtly to Marcus, then glanced at me. The gesture said it all:

*There. Enjoy the fruits of my labor.*

I stared.

Then burst out laughing loud enough to startle the wagon's driver.

It was just starting to fade when Val drew alongside the wagon and leaned in just a little, voice low and rich with mischief. "Seems you're in need of a rescue."

I looked up at him, eyes narrowing in suspicion. "Are you teasing me, too?"

He didn't answer. Just held out a hand.

*Gods bless him,* I thought.

I stood, hunched in the back of the wagon, then braced a foot on the rail and grabbed him. Val shifted in the stirrups and hauled me up hard. A moment later, I was in the saddle, settled in front of him, the heat of his chest at my back, his arm around my waist to steady us both.

"Aleaia Dieter!" Mariana's shout rang out from the driver's seat. "Valerius di Calesia, my lord, don't you dare!"

He pressed the reins into my hands and leaned close, his voice hot at my ear. "Get us out of here. Straight down the road."

"What?" I blinked at the leather reins now resting in my palm.

"You said you needed movement." He hesitated. Then, warily, he asked, "You have ridden double before... right?"

I didn't answer.

Just kicked the horse into a canter.

Val swore under his breath, both arms wrapping tighter around me to stay mounted. "You absolute menace."

I smiled into the wind, my braid whipping loose behind me. "You *gave me* the reins."

The destrier surged forward. He was bigger than Argenti, heavier through the gait, but not unmanageable. Not to me. I shifted my seat, nudged with my knees, and the beast responded like it had known me all along.

"They weren't kidding," Val said, his breath brushing my ear. "You really are that good. You don't fight him. You listen."

"Who are 'they'?"

"Everyone," he said, a chuckle threaded through the word.

I laughed. "What, did you think I got my rank because I looked good in armor?"

"I hoped that wasn't the only reason."

Sunlight spilled across the road, dust dancing in the hush of wind through tall summer grass. I loosened the reins and angled off the trail, down the slope toward the river valley. Wildflowers bowed beneath the horse's hooves. The army behind us blurred into distant hoofbeats and the occasional groan of a wheel swallowed by wind and distance.

Val shifted again, relaxing into the rhythm.

"Turn left at the next rise," he murmured, lips brushing too close to my ear.

I glanced back at him. "Why?"

"You'll see."

I guided the destrier up the rise, his voice still warm behind me. The trail narrowed as we climbed, flanked by thistle and grass tall enough to brush against our boots. I squinted toward the crest.

And then the world opened.

Open fields stretched to the horizon in a patchwork of green and gold and amber, threaded with deep wine-red where firegrass had taken root. Beyond it all, the eastern range of the Egon Mountains stood like sentinels, their jagged peaks still tipped with snow.

But it was the lake that stopped me.

Tucked between the hills, still as breath, it mirrored the sky, flawless and endless, the blue so clear it looked like silvered glass. A flock of birds wheeled above it, wings flashing silver. The warm southern wind picked up, dry and clean, and carried the scent of pine.

I eased back on the reins, bringing the destrier to a halt.

I didn't speak at first. I couldn't.

Behind me, Val was quiet, too.

After a few heartbeats, I murmured, "This doesn't feel like the Empire."

He didn't answer, and at first I thought I had offended him and committed treason. He must have felt me stiffen.

"It doesn't," he said softly.

And those two simple words bled the tension out of me.

I tilted my head, turning just enough to catch his expression. "It feels like something older. Like something they haven't touched."

His eyes lingered on the lake. "They haven't."

I drew a deep breath and let it settle in my chest. Like something fragile. Like something I couldn't keep.

I don't know why it came to mind, or why I needed to say what I did next, but it was out of my mouth before I could stop it.

"The last time I rode double," I said, "was with my father. The day he was killed."

I didn't look back.

Val hesitated. "Does it get harder, as we get closer?"

"Not harder. Just..." I swallowed. "Sharper."

The breeze lifted strands of hair from my neck. I let it.

"He was patient with me. Everyone else saw him as hard, unmoving. But with me…" I breathed out. "He let it soften. Just a little."

I felt his arm tighten around my waist. I didn't mind.

"He taught me to listen. To wait. To speak when it mattered." A faint smile touched my lips. "So much of who I am started with him."

*Stop.* The thought came sudden. *What are you doing?*

It was already too late. The ache rose—not the sharp edge of grief, but its weight, familiar and suffocating.

"I never let myself mourn him. There was always something else to do. Another road. Another duty." I turned my head slightly. "I think you'd have liked him."

His answer was quiet. "If he raised you, then yes. I would have."

I looked away. "They called him a deserter. But he only left Aeldunon because of me. Because my mother fell."

Because of me.

The first life unraveled by my birth.

The tears came fast and hot and uninvited, but at least they were silent. My breath shuddered, and something in my chest gave way. I wiped at my face once. Twice. Gave up. There was too much.

"He would be…" I choked on the words I never meant to say. "He would be so ashamed of me, Val."

He leaned forward, pressing his cheek lightly against my shoulder, both arms wrapping tight around me. He didn't say a word.

"I'm sorry," I whispered. "Gods, I'm sorry."

He lifted his head, breath stirring the hair at my temple. "For what?"

"For the terrible things I've done. For this. We don't even know each other that well. How embarrassing." My fingers knotted in the fabric of my tunic at my thighs. I couldn't meet his eyes. "I've hurt so many people, Val. You'd hate me if you knew."

The silence that followed was neither judgment nor comfort.

Then he spoke. "I wouldn't. I know you."

"It's only been, what, forty days?" I asked softly. "How could you?"

"Doesn't matter," he said. "I know who you are."

I went still.

"I don't know what you've done, and I don't need to. You're not the sum of your worst days." He shifted slightly with the destrier beneath us, arms still holding me firm. "I see you now. That's enough."

After a few heartbeats, I found the breath and the gall to ask, "Do you ever feel like this? Like the past is always right behind you? Like you're dragging it?"

"I do," he said. "Eventually, you learn to carry it. You walk with it."

I nodded, slow. "Some days it's heavier than others."

"Maybe it's because you've carried it alone for too long."

I looked down.

Then I laid my hand over his.

"Thank you," I said. "For listening. For everything."

We stayed like that a while, with his arms around me, my hand on his, the destrier shifting beneath us, the sunlight warming everything it touched.

"We should get back," he murmured against my hair. "Before they think we've deserted."

I tilted my head up, just enough to meet his eyes. "Tell me I don't look like I've been crying."

What I found in his gaze stole the breath from my lungs—steadiness, warmth, and something deeper that stirred through me like wings beating against bone.

"You do. The wind will fix it, though. Doesn't change anything." Then, softer still, "You're still beautiful."

I didn't want to feel it. Gods, I didn't, but the way he looked at me when he said it—like I was already something worth holding, even cracked and tired and sore—made me feel safe. Like if I let go, even for a moment, he'd catch me.

I turned my face away. Not to hide. Just to breathe. The silence that followed wasn't empty. The wind moved through the grass. The horse shifted under us, content. The moment held.

When I finally gathered myself and took up the reins, I guided us back toward the road. As the sound of the column reached us again, I cleared my throat.

"So…" I said. "Marcus. On a donkey. How and why did that happen?"

"Because of what he said to you in Avitum," he said simply. Calm. Even.

I twisted slightly in the saddle to look at him. "So you put him on a donkey?"

"I gave him a mount," he said. "And it would be an insult for him not to ride it all the way to Aeldunon. It was a gift, after all."

I don't know how he said it with a straight face. I laughed, low and sharp, the kind that caught at the edges of delight. "It's the ugliest donkey I've ever seen. That's what he gets for thinking he's better than everyone."

Val chuckled. "He's not."

"I thought he was your friend."

"He was. Is, sometimes. It's… complicated," he said.

We reached the edge of the column just as Mariana stepped out from beside one of the wagons, hands on her hips, fire in her eyes.

"Aleaia Dieter," she called, her voice like thunder on the march. "If you don't get back in that wagon right now—"

Val raised one hand, calm and composed, and turned toward the nearest tesserarius.

"Set camp," he said.

The order rolled down the line like a ripple across still water. Soldiers moved. Wagons slowed. Everything shifted around us.

I blinked. "Did you just…"

Val leaned in, a smile brushing his lips.

"Oh, look at that," he said. "You don't have to get back in."

I didn't answer.

I looked ahead as the army settled around us.

The weight was still there. But it no longer pressed quite so hard.

# CHAPTER SEVENTEEN
## *Arrival*

*"Elisedd stands as a testament to the Empire's civilizing hand— quiet now, and loyal by law."*
—Imperial Survey of the Territories, compiled by Emperor Claudius

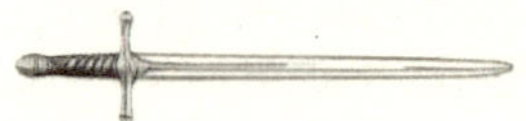

Dēwamos 50, 1230
*Aleaia*

Carved like a wound through the Egon Mountains, the Pravian Pass still bore the memory of the war, and the monsters that came after it. It was thirty miles of high desert, which made it freezing, wind-scoured, and barren.

When it lay behind us, the city of Elisedd sprawled in the valley below, tucked into the green-shouldered foothills of southern Aeltyria. It was the Empire's jewel, and its strongest grip in the region.

The encampment spread across the lower slope like a floodwater of neat rows of tents, stacks of crates, smoke spiraling from cookfires. The First Legion would rest just long enough to rotate cohorts. The Fourth cohort would remain. The rest would march again soon, bound for Aeldunon.

I rode beside Val and Lucius, the three of us dressed in plain travel garb instead of armor. The sun felt better that way, warm against my back and clean on my face. The wind carried pine, trampled grass, and the faint scent of far-off smoke. I breathed it in, slow and deep, then sat up straighter in the saddle and glanced ahead. The trail curved down through golden pasture and wheat-stubbled fields, across a bridge over a stream, and right up to the gate.

Perfect for a little mischief.

"First one to the stream gets the last of the honey bread," I said.

Lucius arched a brow. "You're still on restricted duty."

"Mariana's not here," I said.

Argenti tossed his head beneath me.

"Scared you'll lose?" I asked.

Val shifted beside me. "Sure you want to test that shoulder?"

"I'm not doing a handstand in the saddle. This time." I grinned, turning away. "You're welcome to keep pace. If you can."

Then I kicked.

Argenti surged beneath me, all muscle and stamina, tearing down the path like he'd been waiting all his life to fly, to be free like that. Wind whipped my braid behind me. I didn't look back.

Lucius cursed. Val gave chase.

Gods, it felt good to be out of that fucking wagon.

The wind howled past my ears. Pine and sun-warm grass flew past. I leaned forward, my body moving with Argenti's stride, fluid and easy. And then, because I could—

I stood in the stirrups, let go of the reins, and spread my arms wide, all balance and instinct.

For a few breaths, I was air.

Speed.

No wounds.

No duty.

No ghosts.

Just me and my horse.

Free.

My mouth opened with a wild whoop, fierce and unrepentant.

Val's voice snapped behind me. "Aleaia!"

I caught the reins again, twisted in the saddle, and smiled at him like the sun had come up just for me, soft at the corners and unguarded with joy.

The stream flashed ahead, glinting like silver thread across the grass. I leaned into Argenti's neck. "*Tarron*!"

He leapt, clean and sure, landing with a splash on the far bank. I reined him in, heart hammering and breath quick, and turned to wait.

Val came next, reins pulled tight. His jaw could've been carved from granite. "What in Hel was that?" he demanded.

"Victory. And stretching." I let the words hang. "You told me to be careful with my shoulder. I was."

Lucius came to a stop behind him, laughing so hard he nearly slid from the saddle. "You're going to kill poor Val. I don't know whether to commend your form or report you to Mariana."

Val gave me a look that might've passed for stern, if not for the glint in his eyes.

I raised a brow. "You can breathe now."

"That was reckless," Val said.

"I trust him," I replied, patting Argenti's neck. The courser snorted and tossed his head, ever my loyal accomplice. "He's a good boy, no matter what anyone says."

Val exhaled, slow and shaky, and looked away, but not before I caught it.

That smile.

Small. Helpless. Real.

We kept on down the path toward the town. Slower now. I wasn't of a mind to catch any more arrows.

"Glad to be back home?" Lucius asked.

"It's where I was born. Not sure I'd call it home. Everyone I knew is gone." I hesitated, then added, "I grew up farther north, anyway, in a little village in Lascebar. Only time I've ever been down this way is with the army."

The ache stirred, dull and recognizable. I pressed it down.

"I grew up near Letia, in Alvaretia, on the coast of Calesia, but I was fostered here in Elisedd," Lucius said. "Val too. Haven't been back in ages."

"So which is home?" I asked.

"Alvaretia," he said simply. "My family's still there."

Val glanced over. "You should visit them, once we're settled in Aeldunon."

Lucius shook his head. "I've no desire to take the Pass alone."

"Could you take the Drustan to the sea and travel by ship?" I asked.

He shrugged. "Suppose I could. We'll see. You'll need more guards before I could even consider it, so probably not until next year."

"We'll take on more once we're there," Val said. "A few from the First Cohort show promise."

As we neared the gates, one of the town guards stepped forward. *"Drast! Vo ancales derē?"*

I turned to Val, my voice shifting with it. "He's asking who we are, my lord. Do I have your permission to respond in Aeltyrian?"

Val nodded without hesitation. "Always. You needn't fear reprisal from me."

I raised my voice and said in Aeltyrian, *"Aro usaunes, Archir Valerius Calesii. Taron in Calesii."*

*His Highness Prince Valerius di Calesia. Speak in Calesian.*

"Yes, my lady," the guard replied in Calesian, stepping aside and motioning his companion to do the same. "You may enter, my lord."

As we passed through, Lucius leaned closer. "Were you chastising him?"

I laughed. "Sounded that way, didn't it? I told him their lord had arrived and to speak in Calesian, since he doesn't understand Aeltyrian."

"It's remarkable how many here speak both tongues with ease," Val said, his tone easing. "Would you teach me? If I'm to govern well, I should understand more than a few phrases."

I glanced at him. "I will, but first, you'll need to make it legal."

He smiled. "Then I'll start the moment we reach Aeldunon."

"The fact that they spoke Aeltyrian so openly means their lord must have approved it," I added. "Which is a direct break from Imperial law. I can't think of another reason they'd be so brazen."

"You give her a little rank, and suddenly she thinks she's a scholar on provincial law," Lucius muttered, clucking his tongue.

I smirked. "I'm just a woman trying to keep her tongue, sir."

"How many times do I have to tell you to stop calling me that?" Lucius sighed. "We're equals now."

"It's out of respect for your age, not your position," I said.

Lucius sputtered. "I'm only five years older!"

I shrugged, shameless. "Could've fooled me."

That earned a bark of laughter from Lucius, and a full, real laugh from Val.

We reached the inner gatehouse, where a fresh set of guards stood at attention. This time, I addressed them first and in Calesian. "Good morning. Kindly inform Lord Triarius of Prince Valerius's arrival."

One of the guards stepped forward, brow furrowed. "Where is your standard?"

I frowned. Could they truly not recognize their own Legate without his banner?

Val answered before I could, impersonal, but firm. "I left it in camp, by design. A small party flying the lion through this territory invites more trouble than honor. Lord Triarius will vouch for me."

A voice rang out from just beyond the gate. "Val, my boy!"

A silver-haired man in a scarlet tunic strode toward us with the kind of confidence that didn't need announcing, the kind lords wore like a mantle when command has become natural.

"Stand down, you aurochs!" he bellowed.

The guards obeyed at once, stepping aside.

Val and Lucius dismounted, handing their reins to a waiting slave. Val's face had shifted into that polished mask he wore so well. No smile. No warmth. Just the courtesy demanded of a prince.

I swung down from Argenti, passed the reins to another slave, and stepped forward with my own mask firmly in place. Mine was different though. It said *I belong here,* even when I thought I didn't.

Lord Triarius clapped a firm hand on Val's shoulder, then Lucius's. "And Lucius, visiting your old mentor at last."

"Not by choice, I swear," Lucius said, clasping Lord Triarius's arm.

Then the lord's gaze landed on me. "And who's this? A new slave?"

I bit the inside of my cheek. Prayed the mask wouldn't crack.

Val's voice came cool and controlled, "Gavius, allow me to introduce Aleaia Dieter, one of my guards. Aleaia, this is Lord Gavius Triarius, Prefect of Elisedd. Before that, he had the distinct misfortune of squiring both Lucius and me."

I bowed my head with just the right amount of deference. "A pleasure, my lord."

Triarius looked me over, slow and deliberate. Measuring. His eyes narrowed slightly, as though weighing something unspoken.

"Well met," he said at last. Then, to Val, "They do make fierce warriors, once you win them over."

Val didn't blink. Just offered a single nod. "Unfortunately, I'm not here for a social visit. I've been tasked with inspecting the fortifications on the way to Aeldunon."

"My lord, it would be an honor to show you the stronghold the Emperor has built and graciously entrusted to my care. This way, please."

He turned on his heel and we followed him deeper into the fortress.

We passed through layers of defense—outer gatehouses, inner gates, stone towers crowned with watch platforms and rows of archers above. Every angle calculated to intimidate. I barely noticed the stone. I watched the man.

Triarius carried himself with a commander's balance—straight spine, smooth stride, that well-honed edge of politeness that could just as easily cut if you weren't careful. He was the Empire's man and I trusted him little.

He led us to the smithy, where the prefect was keen to show us a new forging method.

Lucius fell in beside me, crossed his arms, and leaned closer. "He takes his time with new people," he said, voice muted enough to go unheard under the clang of hammer and hiss of bellows. "Eyed me the same way when I first arrived. He'll warm up."

I gave a small nod. Maybe he did eye people, maybe he was wary, but I doubted he'd asked if Lucius was a slave.

The prefect launched into some ramble about airflow, bellows design, and heat retention. I listened with one ear. My gaze drifted to Val.

He met my eyes and offered the barest shrug of apology.

When Triarius was done, we moved on. I stepped into the great hall with Lucius at my side, a half-step behind Val and Triarius.

The contrast hit me. Cold stone columns and thick timber beams above, heavy with history and weight. Yet flowers sat in arrangements on the windowsills and hung in long garlands from the rafters, bright and fragrant against the stark backdrop. The long table was set for a meal and decorated with floral and beribboned centerpieces.

We approached the seats laid out for us. Out of my element, I matched Val's pace and followed his lead, sitting beside him.

Triarius settled across from us and Lucius beside him. "I'm not usually one to indulge in such extravagance as you see all around you now," he said, waving a hand.

A slave approached on cue, balancing a tray with four goblets, an amphora heavy with wine, and a plate of sliced meats, cheeses, and ripe fruit. She moved with the grace of someone long practiced—pouring without spilling, eyes lowered, posture flawless. Then she slipped back into the shadows.

Seated at Val's left hand, with the least seniority, it should've been my task to taste his wine, as was custom. I reached for the goblet.

Val caught my hand—gentle, but firm—and set it aside. He said nothing. Just slid the cup across the table and set it before Lucius.

Lucius gave him a look, dry as old leather. Then, with theatrical resignation, he lifted the cup and drank.

I folded my hands in my lap and stared down into my own wine. He wouldn't let me do it.

"Tomorrow marks a momentous occasion," Triarius said. "My son is to be wed to the ealdorman's daughter. He's insisted on including a few Aeltyrian customs to ensure her happiness. Her family's been here since dawn hanging flowers."

My thoughts churned. The guards here spoke Aeltyrian without fear. Triarius's son was marrying an Aeltyrian girl, a union outlawed under imperial law. Yet this was the same man who assumed I was a slave. Who owned them. Who smiled now, unbothered by the contradiction. Who said nothing when Val had passed the tasting to Lucius.

I wondered how he squared it with himself. Maybe he'd never bothered to try.

It was assumed the wine was safe, since it hadn't killed Lucius, so Val reached for his goblet and took a measured sip, unhurried.

"Marrying for love and political advantage?" he said, the edge of a smile in his voice. "He's a lucky man."

Only once he drank did I allow myself to select something from the tray. A bit of everything, taken with care. I chewed slowly.

*I have a great deal left to learn about statecraft,* I thought. I couldn't see how this match was anything but a liability. From a Calesian perspective, at least. An Aeltyrian ealdorman's daughter would never be seen as a proper match for a prefect's heir. Shouldn't he have chosen a southern girl with wealth, land, or influence?

"Don't know about that," Triarius said. "It's more to her advantage than his. This sort of marriage would be impossible back home. But here, it lifts her to the edge of Calesian nobility, and that's as likely as not to get me in trouble with your father. It's good for local relations, though, and that might save my skin."

Val raised his goblet. "I doubt you'll face much in the way of consequence. The worst he would do is force you to retire."

*What about the girl?* I wanted to ask. She would be blamed as a seductress.

Triarius scoffed, but the sound rang hollow. "He wouldn't have to use much force. But speaking of fortunes, it's no small thing to have a prince of the Empire—our soon-to-be governor—grace us for such an occasion. Will you join us tomorrow evening?"

My breath caught. If he said yes, I'd be expected to attend.

Aelan help me. What would I wear? A dress would strip me of command. Armor would be unsuitable. Either way, I'd be on display and judged for it.

"It would be an honor to do so, old friend," Val said without hesitation.

*Fuck.*

I took a long drink from my goblet.

Triarius pressed on, light in tone but not in scrutiny. "And where is Marcus? Don't tell me he prefers the company of the camp to the comfort of my hall."

Val didn't miss a beat. "He found his bed too warm to leave at such an hour. But he'll join us before the wedding, I'm sure."

Triarius chuckled, shaking his head. "Some things never change."

To my right, Val lifted his goblet and drank again, unbothered by it all. At ease. As if this place, this world of polished stone and measured words, belonged to him.

And I—

I wasn't sure where that left me.

# CHAPTER EIGHTEEN
## *Starlight*

*"Love does not come with gentle hands.*
*It breaks like waves on bitter sands.*
*It burns, it scars, and still we yearn—*
*For ash to fall, for flame to turn."*
—The Song of the Stars, Cycle VII: The Cycle of Spirit

Dēwamos 51, 1230
*Aleaia*

I didn't even own a gown.

Lady Eliana, however, made sure I understood that I'd be an embarrassment if I didn't wear one. Her silks came with steam, servants, and a smile sharpened with scorn. I was sure she thought she said it kindly—that she knew I wouldn't have anything suitable—and that it was her duty to ensure I looked presentable.

*Presentable.* Like a soldier scrubbed clean for parade.

Or a slave at auction.

I did consider wearing a grain sack out of spite.

But refusing would've proved her right. So I let them dress me. Let them twist my hair into something courtly, cinch the bodice tight enough to keep my pride inside it.

And then I was off to the wedding.

The gray-blue silk clung like a second skin and felt too soft, too light. Each step down the ribbon-marked path felt uncertain. The kid-leather soles weren't made for stone or slope, and the breeze kept teasing the skirt around my knees. It pulled where it shouldn't, bared me in ways armor never had.

How did anyone walk in this? I wondered.

The faint note of a harp reached me on the wind, low and beckoning. I lifted my head. Ribbons and silver charms danced from the boughs ahead, catching the last of the sun like shaken stars. The music pulled me toward it, beckoned me with equal parts softness and persistence. The ceremony had already begun. Val would be waiting. Lucius too. And Marcus.

Which meant I'd have to translate.

It had been easy at the gate. Standing beside Val, I hadn't stumbled. My voice had held steady. No memories clawed at me there.

But Marcus was different. Nothing about him felt safe.

I stepped into the grove.

Torchlight spilled through the clearing, flickering against garlands strung through the trees. The ancient oak at the center stood dressed in broad silver ribbons, its branches arched overhead like a crown. On one side stood the Aeltyrians. On the other, the Calesians.

It didn't take long to find Val where he stood near the front, flanked by Lucius and Marcus. He was mid-sentence when he saw me. Something crossed his face, brief and unguarded, before Lucius leaned in, spoke in his ear, and Val recovered.

But not fast enough to hide it.

I took my place beside Val, keeping my expression still despite the heat blooming high on my cheeks.

"Apologies," I said, quiet but even. "It took longer than I anticipated to…"

I wasn't sure how to describe it, the process of getting ready.

"Well, look at that," Marcus drawled, already drunk. "Didn't know they bothered tailoring silk for ashborn. Tell me, Dieter, was the dress a gift, or payment?"

The air snapped tight.

Lucius blinked. "Gods, Marcus, what in the fuck is wrong with you?"

I didn't move, except that my fingers twitched for a hilt I wasn't wearing.

Val stepped forward, eyes hard as flint, cold, and focused. Without a word, he reached out and caught Marcus by the back of the neck. Like a handler with a dog that had bared its teeth. "Walk with me."

Marcus stiffened. "Val—"

"I said *walk*."

He turned him bodily, hand locked at the base of his skull. Not tight enough to bruise, just tight enough to control. They vanished into the trees.

I just stood there, heart thudding behind my ribs.

Lucius exhaled beside me. "That was out of line."

"He's drunk."

"No." Sharper now. "It was unacceptable. No man should speak to a woman like that. You've earned every godsdamned thing you have."

I kept my voice flat. "He wanted to humiliate me."

"He wanted to remind you what he thinks you are. Thought that made you easy to corner." Lucius's gaze flicked toward the trees. "He's lucky it was Val."

I turned to him. "I can hold my own."

He gave me a look. Then gestured at the gown. "Not tonight. Not in that."

I arched a brow.

"You look nice. Can't let you ruin the one time you wear a dress."

I wasn't sure what to say, so I simply said, "Thank you."

Lucius waved it off. "I have sisters. I'd say the same to them."

I stared at him for a long moment. I wasn't sure what that meant.

When Val returned, he looked composed, adjusting the cuff of his sleeve. His knuckles were red.

Lucius didn't miss it. "Well?"

Val didn't glance his way. "Alive. Probably wishes he wasn't. He won't be a problem again."

I started to speak, to thank him, then stopped when I caught the look in his eyes. Calm, but not the kind that comes from peace. The kind that follows blood.

He shook his head once and looked at me. "Are you all right?"

"I'm fine," I said.

His gaze held, hot and expectant.

I shook my head, looked away. "It's not the first time."

"Look at me," he said softly.

I did.

"If anyone speaks to you that way when I'm present, I'll make sure they leave wishing they hadn't. And if I'm not, you tell me. I'll handle it."

I didn't answer. Couldn't.

Then a horn cut through the clearing, sharp and bright. The harpist struck a new chord.

I stood beside Val, the silk whispering against my legs.

The bride emerged in a gown of vivid blue, a crown of wildflowers woven into her dark hair. She looked beautiful, but it was the way she looked at her groom that caught me off guard. She was unflinching, steady. Certain with the quiet resolve of someone who had chosen and would not be moved.

Love gave people that kind of light.

My gaze shifted to the young man beneath the oak—the prefect's son. He stood tall, proud, his eyes fixed on no one but her. Val had joked Triarius might face little more than retirement, but everyone at that table knew better. The Empire didn't take defiance lightly. They'd strip his family bare—his father's post, their land, their influence.

And still, the boy smiled. As if none of it mattered.

His siblings stood near him, bright with happiness. Even Triarius had taken his place beside them. Only Eliana stood stiff in her finery, spine straight as a sword. She watched the Aeltyrian bride with that particular kind of cold I knew too well. Calculated. Patient. Measured in seasons, not seconds.

I only hoped the girl wouldn't bleed for it.

Love might burn bright.

But it never came without consequence.

The music swelled, then stopped.

*"Folamí harē..."* the shaman began.

I blinked. The words washed over me for a beat before I remembered my role. I reached out and gave Val's sleeve a small tug. He leaned down at once.

"Should I translate for you?" I murmured.

He nodded. "Please."

I whispered the words in Calesian as the officiant continued in Aeltyrian.

"We gather here today to witness the joining not only of Attius and Ceri, but of their two peoples," the shaman said. "In this sacred grove, before kin and kindred, I ask you to speak the vows from your hearts. Attius, what do you vow to Ceri?"

Attius's hands shook slightly as he took hers. "I vow to love you fully, with all that I am, in plenty and in want, in this life and beyond. The gods were merciful the day they led me to you, and more so still to let me love you."

A faint flush crept up Val's neck. I tried not to stare.

"And Ceri, what do you vow to Attius?" the shaman asked.

Her voice rang clear through the grove. "Though my love for you is boundless, I remain my own. You cannot possess me, for I am free. Yet every day, I choose you. And if you choose me, I will offer you all that I have, all that I am. In joy and sorrow, in strength and frailty, I am yours."

Beside me, Val straightened.

I kept my hand on his sleeve. "I'd rather not shout in front of a hundred people."

That earned his cooperation. He bent closer again.

"Perhaps I should've brought a stool," I added under my breath. "You've a long way to bend."

His smile softened.

"Do you both embrace this union freely, without fear?" the shaman asked.

"I do," they said in unison.

"Let the wind bear witness, carrying this vow from mountain to sea. May the sun warm your hearts and stoke your passion. May the waters nourish you and quiet your grief. May the earth lend you its strength, and the fire within never falter. From this moment, Attius and Ceri, you are bound."

Attius stepped forward and cupped her face.

The kiss began soft and slow, then deepened with boldness. Her fingers found his jaw, anchoring him. For a moment, it was as if all the fear, all the risk, had burned away. Only certainty remained. Something in the way they kissed slipped past my guard. It wasn't show or desperation. It was trust.

Not in gods or nations, but in each other.

And for a breath, I believed it too.

That maybe love wasn't always ruin.

Maybe it could survive, even in a world like this.

The cheer that rose was thunderous. Earned. I smiled and joined the applause.

*"Sethon arai an lega!"* someone shouted from the back, loud and gleeful.

Laughter rippled through the crowd. Another cheer followed.

"What are they saying?" Val leaned in.

I laughed breathlessly. "He said, 'Take her to bed.'"

Val chuckled, but when I looked up at him, something had shifted. The smile stayed. But behind it, something quieter had settled.

"What?" I asked, still smiling.

His voice was soft. "When you smile... it's like starlight. Bright. Beautiful."

The words hung between us, soft and impossible to ignore, tugging low and warm beneath my ribs. For the briefest flicker, he looked like he expected me to laugh.

I looked away, the smile still tugging at my mouth. The truth in his voice had struck something too tender to deflect. "Careful. Someone might think you mean that."

"I do," he said.

My smile deepened. Small. Reluctant. Impossible to hide.

Without another word, he offered his arm. "Walk with me?"

I slid my hand into the crook of his elbow. The muscle there was warm and solid beneath the silk. I ignored the small, traitorous flutter low in my chest.

We walked on in silence. The torchlit path, strewn with petals, opened into the wider field beyond. A great bonfire blazed at its center, casting sparks into the dusk. Behind it, the flower-adorned dais shimmered in lamplight. Tables bowed under the weight of food and wine. Flutes and drums beckoned the guests to dance.

"They look so happy." I glanced toward the bonfire where Attius and Ceri now walked hand in hand. "Like the whole world narrowed to just the two of them."

"They do," Val said, watching them with that quiet sort of admiration he rarely showed.

It took me a few steps to find my voice again. "Still. This was a risk. For both of them."

He didn't answer right away. When he did, his voice held the kind of gentleness that always caught me off guard. "Some things are worth the risk."

My fingers tightened slightly on his arm. To let go now would've said too much about how badly I wanted to believe him.

"Aleaia!" I turned at the sound of Mariana's voice. "You're a vision!"

I let go of Val's arm, grateful for the interruption. "Thank you. I didn't expect you to come."

"Mariana," Val greeted, inclining his head. "Good to see you."

"Evening, my lord." She dipped a brief curtsy to Val but spoke to me. "I managed to slip away. I only meant to observe the castle healer's clinic, but they put me to work."

"I'm glad you came," I said, and I meant it.

She looked between me and Val. "Am I interrupting?"

"Not at all," I said quickly. "Stay at the castle tonight. You can share my room. It's too dark to go back to camp."

"I'd planned on it. Come on." Mariana grinned, grabbed my hand, and dipped her head toward Val. "Sorry, I'm dancing with her first."

Val's gaze found mine. "Enjoy yourself," he said quietly. "I'll be near the newlyweds' table."

Before I could object, she pulled me into the ring of dancers. I glanced back over my shoulder, offering Val an apologetic smile.

We joined the circle hand-in-hand. The rhythm was steady, the steps easy. I moved as if I'd never forgotten how. Because I hadn't.

Dancing isn't so different from swordplay. You just do it without the steel, but it's still balance, breath, instinct. I didn't have to think. Just move.

The warmth of the fire, the steady thrum of the lute, the wild hush of pipe and drum threaded through the smoke-sweet air. We turned with the circle, skirts swaying in time, passing torchlit faces and bright laughter. Beneath my boots, crushed herbs released their scent: basil, rue, and something sharper I couldn't name.

Lucius cut in, half-drunk and graceless as he swept Mariana away. She went with him, grinning like she'd just won a bet.

The steps were more than familiar. They were freeing, loosening something in me with every turn, every breath. It was remembering, like my body had been waiting to feel light again. The music tugged at something buried, something I hadn't let rise in years.

Eventually, I slipped away from the dancers, back toward the tables, and poured myself some wine. I knew better but I'd slake my thirst first, then see to food. I'd be glad for fruit or meat or anything solid to keep myself steady.

I stood near the edge of the firelight, cup in hand, the beat of the drums still pulsing through me.

When Val looked up from the dais, where he'd been speaking with the newlyweds, his eyes found mine like they always did. He excused himself and crossed the clearing in a few long strides.

He stopped in front of me, and for once, he didn't look entirely sure of himself.

"Aleaia," he said. "I've had more than a bit of wine tonight, so forgive me if this comes out clumsy, but if I don't ask now, I won't." He extended a hand. "Would you dance with me?"

I doubted he was as drunk as he claimed, but I set my cup aside and placed my hand in his without hesitation.

"I could use a lesson or two," he said, smiling. "I've never tried an Aeltyrian dance."

"This one's simple," I told him. "Most are. Just let the music guide you."

I took his hand and placed it lightly at my waist, his fingers tentative and careful, and rested my own on his shoulder. When I placed my other hand in his, I looked up and asked, "Ready?"

At first, I led. His steps were cautious, a little too precise, like he was memorizing rather than moving. He watched me closely as he tried to match my rhythm.

"You're thinking too hard," I said.

He chuckled. "I'm not used to stumbling through these things."

"You're not terrible."

That earned me another smile. It reached his eyes first, warming them, softening the line of his mouth, easing the tension there. For a breath, he looked… lighter. Like the weight he always carried had let go of him, just for a moment.

And something in me caught—a flicker under the skin, like a missed step or a shift in the wind.

He adjusted again, more relaxed now, easing into the pace.

"See?" I said, letting him guide me. "Not so difficult."

And it wasn't. Our steps aligned without effort, the movement fluid and natural.

My pulse quickened—maybe a little from exertion, but more from the warmth of his hand, the closeness, the way his eyes flicked down to mine and lingered just a moment too long.

Surrounded by laughter, torchlight, and the hum of song, the flicker caught, then bloomed.

It wasn't duty, or fear.

It was joy.

# CHAPTER NINETEEN
## *The Cursed Oath*

*"But ash will cling where flame has fed—*
*It stains the skin, it marks the dead.*
*And those who love through curse and cost*
*Will find what's taken is never lost."*
—The Song of the Stars, Cycle VII: The Cycle of Spirit

Dēwamos 51, 1230
*Aleaia*

The music slowed. So did our steps. Around us, the revelers drifted away, movements heavy with wine and weariness. A few dozed in the grass. Others slumped beneath tables. The bride and groom had disappeared.

"Weddings back home aren't nearly this much fun," Val said.

I looked up.

Regretted it instantly.

He was so close that the heat of him pressed into my thoughts, muddling them. I could feel it coiling through me, tightening with every breath. Wine and woodsmoke clung to his skin.

I cleared my throat. "Anvallan priests are forbidden to marry, aren't they? Maybe that's why they make weddings so dreadful."

He laughed, low and warm. "Out of jealousy?"

"That, or spite."

"Probably both," he said.

His smile faded, but the warmth in his eyes stayed. His hand rested lightly at my back, too steady for someone claiming to be drunk.

I let my head rest against his chest.

The rhythm of his heart, solid and warm, unraveled something in me I hadn't realized was knotted, something I'd buried deep.

Gods.

How long had it been since I'd felt safe?

I felt his cheek against the top of my head.

I didn't move. Didn't trust myself to.

And then the doubt crept in.

*What will others think? What about duty?*

*This is dangerous for him.*

*I'm cursed.*

*Tainted.*

*Lethal.*

I shut my eyes. Forced it down. Wondered why I couldn't have one moment—just one—without a cost. Just one breath that didn't bleed.

"Aleaia," he murmured.

I pulled back slightly and met his gaze.

His hand rose, brushing the edge of my jaw. Then tilted my chin gently, like I might vanish if he moved too fast.

His eyes held mine for a heartbeat. "May I—"

A table tipped behind us. A cask struck the ground with a hollow thud.

Val's hand fell from my face, his arm tightening around me, shielding.

I blinked, dazed.

The moment cracked.

Shouts followed startled laughter and half-sober noise from the far side of the clearing.

Lucius's voice rang out. A clipped curse in Calesian followed.

We turned to find him near the fallen cask, squared off with another legionary. A small knot of men had formed around them, their postures too loose. Too careful. That stillness soldiers wear when a line's about to be crossed.

Val's expression shifted, flickering, just for a moment.

"Excuse me," he said quietly, laced with regret. "I should stop Lucius from ruining a wedding."

I nodded as he stepped away. His stride was calm, but the intent behind it was clear.

I watched him cross the clearing. Lucius stood in the center, jaw clenched, every movement taut. The other man—older, slurring—said something sharp and taunting, though I couldn't make it out.

Shoulders tensed. A few men edged back. The way soldiers do when they sense the edge and want no part of what waits beyond it.

Val stepped between them, one hand lifted, not to strike, but to hold, to draw a boundary.

I felt it in my throat first. The catch in my breath. The tight pull in my chest. Admiration, maybe.

Even when he wasn't near, he filled the space he left behind.

I looked away, over the edge of the field. If Lucius was picking fights, where was Mariana?

An arm locked around my waist.

I stiffened, twisted, my hand flying to the hilt that wasn't there, fingers closing on nothing.

A gasp tore loose as I struggled, eyes wide with realization. "Marcus, what are—"

He silenced me with his mouth on mine, rough and punishing.

His lip was split. Swollen. Blood mixed with the stink of wine as his mouth ground against mine. His breath was foul. His stubble scraped like sandpaper. He held tightly with all the greasy intent of a man who thought he had the right.

I shoved him back with both hands.

Spat to rid myself of the taste of him.

I wiped my mouth with the back of my wrist. "What in the fuck do you think you're doing?"

My eyes swept the clearing. The music still played. No heads turned.

Marcus swayed, grinning so wide his lip bled. His eyes gleamed with drunken delight and something uglier beneath it.

"His lordship isn't around now, is he?" he slurred. "I've seen how he watches you. Like you're some prize worth chasing. Thought if I said it in front of everyone, he might remember what you are."

"You're drunk," I said flatly. "Get out of my sight. Now, before I lose my temper."

He stepped in again. Closer. His voice thickened.

"Ashborn refuse in a legionary's cloak. Pretending you're one of us. Pretending you belong. You don't. You never will."

I didn't flinch. "You're not half the man you think you are, Marcus. And if you ever had the spine to face a real fight, you'd know I don't need to pretend."

He leaned in so close that his breath hit my face, hot and sour. "He's had whores and noble girls both, but never one with dirt in her blood. Never one who smelled of sweat and smoke and the ruins of a dead country."

I'd disliked him before, loathed him now, but never had any idea he despised me so. It struck me silent, the depth of his hatred for me.

His grin widened. "But if he's so eager to bed a beast, I thought I'd get my turn first."

*Ashborn.*

*Beast.*

*Dirt in my blood.*

Worst of all, he spoke Val's name as if they were equals. As if loyalty and brotherhood meant nothing. As if Val's name belonged in the same breath as filth like this.

How dare he?

It made me want to break something.

To break *him.*

He reached for me again. "He's gone soft. Weak. Letting filth like you play soldier while our empire—"

My fist cracked against his jawbone. A clean hit. Hard and final.

Marcus reeled, legs tangling beneath him. He went down hard, the cloak twisting as he hit the ground, face-first, the fabric spilling over his head like a shroud.

I stood over him, breath shallow, hand throbbing from the impact.

Flexed my fingers once, then turned and walked away.

At the table, I poured myself another cup of wine. My hands still trembled.

The copper of blood sat thick on my tongue, mixed with ash and bile.

*How dare he?* I thought again.

The rage had come fast, hot, and sharp, but beneath it, something colder stirred.

Not fear of him.

Fear of what came next, borne on the wings of memory.

Things I'd felt mixed with things I'd seen.

*A flagrum, biting into my back again and again.*

*The gallows.*

*Ravens pecking out my eyes.*

*My body strung up on the gates of Elisedd, limbs pale against black stone, bones picked clean.*

*A warning.*

I brought the cup to my lips and drank.

Sweat prickled along my scalp and spine.

Val stepped beside me. "Someone made a slight against the First Legion. Said they were soft. Lucius took—"

He stopped, eyes sweeping my face. "What's wrong?"

I flinched. "Please… don't be angry."

He didn't look away. "What happened?"

"I hit… someone. Over there." I gestured toward the fire. Marcus still lay where he'd fallen, his face half-hidden beneath the fold of his cloak.

Val gave a short laugh, but it rang hollow. "Dropped him like a sack of meal. Do you know him?"

I hesitated. My pulse surged.

"I do," I said softly. "And so do you."

The world pressed in too loud, too close.

"I'm in so much trouble, Val. I hit him—I didn't think. He kissed me. Forced it. There was blood in my mouth, and I couldn't—and he wouldn't stop, he wouldn't go away, and I—"

"Aleaia." His voice cut clean through the spiral. He stepped in and took my hands, not to stop me, but to steady me. To bring me back.

"But he's a nobleman, and I'm—" My voice cracked. "The things they'll do to me—I'd rather die."

"Look at me."

I met his eyes, bracing for the blow.

For the shame.

For the cold, merciless consequence.

"You are not in trouble," he said. "You defended yourself. That's all. And I'd have done far worse than knock him unconscious."

My mouth parted. No sound came.

"You're safe," he said again, slower now, his thumbs stroking the backs of my fingers. "No one saw. No one's coming for you."

Still I waited, stiff as stone. Waiting for the sting. The judgment. The hands dragging me away.

"Please don't let them—"

I couldn't speak. My breath came fast. Shallow.

"Breathe, Aleaia," he murmured. "In through your nose. Out through your mouth."

*In.*

*Out.*

"There you go. Again."

*In… and out.*

Only once the pounding in my chest began to ease did he speak again, calm and even.

"I'm going to take care of it."

I held his hands tighter when he moved to pull away. "I'm so sorry."

He stilled. Didn't even blink.

"It was Marcus."

The name hit like a dropped blade.

"I'm sorry," I said again, quieter this time. "I tried to walk away. He wouldn't let go."

His jaw shifted. My pulse jumped at the sight, but not from fear. Whatever he was holding back wasn't for me.

"Thank you. For telling me." He released my hands, then reached up, tucking a loose strand of hair behind my ear. His fingers lingered just long enough to cup my cheek. "I'll be right back."

Then he turned.

He didn't raise his voice, didn't bark a command. Just a word passed to the nearest guard, then the next.

Moments later, two men crossed the clearing. They hauled Marcus up from the ground and dragged him off like something spoiled. As I watched them go, the knot inside me loosened.

Val returned and folded me into his arms. "Nothing will happen to you," he said. "You did nothing wrong."

His words cut straight through the noise of shame and fury and the echo of too many nights spent too afraid to speak.

"No one will touch you while I draw breath," he murmured. "I swear it."

The words landed like stone in my chest, rang in my bones like a vow too dangerous to make and impossible to forget.

I looked up at him. "What if he tells his father that I—"

"I've known Marcus a long time," Val said. "He wouldn't confess to losing a fight, not even under torture. And besides…" His smile tilted, wry. "I already hit him once tonight. More than once. You've nothing to worry about."

I drew a breath, willing my heart to slow.

"We should find Lucius and Mariana," he said. "Head back to the castle before someone does something truly regrettable. And so help me, Lucius had better be where I left him."

We moved through the thinning crowd. The fire still burned, but most of the guests had wandered off. Only a few lingered near the musicians, swaying or slumped in pairs.

It didn't take long to find them. Lucius sat near one of the benches, elbows on his knees, a goblet dangling loosely from one hand. Mariana stood in front of him, hands on her hips, delivering what looked like a thorough scolding, though the sway in her stance and the pitch of her voice betrayed her own share of wine.

"You are not sleeping out here," she was saying. "You're his lordship's guard. You shouldn't even be this drunk. There are only two of you! Who's going to relieve Aleaia later?"

Lucius blinked up at her. "You're moving around too much. And talking too much."

"You're slurring and you can't stand straight," she shot back.

I exchanged a look with Val. He sighed and stepped in, taking the goblet from Lucius's hand to set it aside. "Enough of that. Let's go."

Lucius groaned. "M'tired."

"I know. You can sleep once we get back." Val gripped his arm and hauled him upright. "Gods, you're heavy."

It took effort and a string of low curses, but Val managed to keep Lucius on his feet and sling one of his arms across his shoulders. Lucius stumbled, barely conscious, kept upright only by Val's stubbornness. Mariana fell in beside me as we made the slow, awkward shuffle back toward the castle.

We'd made it halfway when Val gave a frustrated huff, shifted his stance, and hoisted Lucius over his shoulders in one clean, practiced motion. "Anvallus's balls, Lucius, what've we been feeding you?"

I let out a tired laugh. "And here I thought you were the one we'd be carrying back."

"Me? I'd never drink this much. He shouldn't either." Val adjusted the weight again. "He should be reduced to half rations for a season."

A while later, we entered the great hall to find it quiet in dim torchlight.

Val eased Lucius down beside the hearth, wrapped his cloak around him, and said, "Good night, brother. I don't envy the head you'll have tomorrow."

We climbed the stairs together, slow and steady. At the landing, I gestured left down the hall. "Mariana, my room's just there. I'll be along in a moment."

"Mm-hmm." She yawned and slipped inside, already half-asleep.

I turned to Val. "I'll check your room before you turn in."

He nodded and opened the door, stepping aside to let me pass.

I entered ahead of him. Eyes swept the corners. Window latched. Nothing disturbed. Everything where it should be.

I stepped back into the corridor. "All clear."

He lingered in the doorway, one shoulder against the wood, watching me. "Are you sure you're all right?"

I nodded once. "I've been through worse."

"If you'd rather keep watch from inside tonight, I wouldn't mind. If it feels safer."

I hesitated. Then shook my head. "If I do, someone will talk. They'll say things that'll follow us both."

He held my gaze a moment longer, then gave a slow nod. "I'll leave the door unlatched. Just in case."

"Thank you," I said. The words came out quieter than I meant them to.

His smile lingered a second longer before he closed the door.

I crossed the corridor, changed into more practical clothes, and returned to my post. I told myself it didn't matter, that he'd only meant to be kind, but the words stuck like a sliver beneath the skin.

My chest still ached from the way his eyes had lingered.

Like he saw something worth protecting.

And damn me, I wanted to believe it.

I shut my eyes.

It had to end.

Not because I didn't feel it, but because I *did*.

I was starting to want something I could never keep.

I pulled my cloak tighter around my shoulders and leaned against the stone.

I didn't deserve the joy I'd felt.

Not after what I'd done. Not when everyone who'd ever loved me had paid for it in blood.

Letting him in wouldn't be brave.

It would be like stepping barefoot into broken glass: painful, and impossible to take back.

It would be his death sentence.

And I couldn't let him be next.

# CHAPTER TWENTY
## *Folklore*

*"Stories aren't for scaring children, girl. They're for reminding them—what waits in the woods, and what comes when we forget."*
—Elder Naedyn of Rhaelaith, to a young Aleaia

Dēwamos 58, 1230
*Aleaia*

It took us six days of marching to cross over Elisedd's northern border into Lascebar. The province was thick with pine and smelled of wet moss and smoke. It was Dēwamos—the hottest season of the year—but the night air had teeth. When I was little, I'd have been barefoot, shrieking with laughter as I ran to the riverbank in nothing but a shift.

Now I only wanted to sit by the fire and burn the chill out of my bones. I'd spent too long in the south. I pulled my cloak tighter.

Behind us, the camp had quieted. Tents stood in neat rows. Watch fires crackled. The usual din of men settling in had faded into wind and dark.

Val and I walked northeast, beyond the outer palisade, toward a weathered old wooden road marker. A patrol had found something carved into it. The legionary hadn't recognized the script and passed word up the chain.

Val had gotten a translation from one of the auxiliaries, but he wanted me to see it, to read it myself, as if my voice gave the words weight. I hadn't missed what that meant.

Just like I hadn't missed how often he adjusted the rotation schedule to keep me near during the softer hours of evening.

"Think we'll have time for a round of Talon tonight?" I asked, glancing up at him.

Val shot me a sidelong look, his mouth tugging into a grin. "I always have time to be humbled at a game I taught you a decadium ago."

I laughed. "You let me win."

"I still think you already knew how to play and let me believe I was teaching you," he said with mock severity. The mischief in his eyes lingered.

I pressed a hand to my chest. "So now I'm a liar and a cheat? Gods, you wound me. I thought you were meant to be noble."

"Noble? Here I thought you admired my humility." Then he leaned in just slightly, voice dropping to that register that always curled low in my stomach. "You disarm me with a smile and finish me with strategy. I never stand a chance."

"Then you shouldn't let me that close," I said, more seriously than before. "You'll lose every time."

His gaze held mine. "If it makes you happy, it feels like I've won anyway."

I shoved his shoulder. "Oh, stop."

He didn't stumble. Just looked at me and laughed, unguarded, as if nothing had changed.

Around us, though, everything had. The nearest legionaries had gone still.

The silence dropped like a cloak.

Soft. Sudden. Heavy.

My stomach turned. What had I done?

I stepped back and did the only thing I could think of. The only thing I knew would fix this, at least in part.

I dropped to a knee and bowed my head. "My apologies, my lord."

He swore sharply under his breath.

"Don't," he said, the word sharp as steel. "Get up."

I stayed where I was. "I forgot myself. I humbly beg your forgiveness."

"I doubt you've done a thing humbly in your life," he said. His voice stayed low, but the edge left no room for disobedience. "I said get up. You don't kneel to me."

Slowly and stiffly, I rose. It wasn't the reprimand that stung. It was the conviction behind it. That he meant it. That he saw me as his equal or near to it.

And that was the danger, lying in wait like an ambush I should've seen coming.

We kept walking, but the ease was gone, replaced by something tighter. I'd let myself get too familiar. Too close. I'd started to mistake games and glances and fireside laughter for something warm and safe.

He was a royal. The Legate of the Second Army. He'd forgotten that, and I'd overlooked it. And he'd be the one to bleed for it, if he didn't remember.

He leaned in. "If we were alone, it wouldn't have mattered."

Time to remind him.

"But we weren't," I said, eyes forward. "So it does."

We didn't speak again. The path curved toward the marker.

The wind turned colder, scraping across the rise and hissing through the grass. We came to the board—splintered, staked into the earth, streaked with dark strokes.

Val stood behind me. "That's it?"

There was nothing impressive about it. The markings looked like they'd had blood rubbed into them, thick and rust-dark, still tacky in some places, flaking in others. The script was Aeltyrian.

It was also sloppy. Erratic. Jagged. Written in fear.

Val leaned in. "Can you read it?"

"Aye." My voice came quiet. "It's a warning. Just like you were told." I traced the first line with my eyes. "It's a Lascebaran dialect," I said. "Half of Rhaelaith spoke that way. My father used to correct me when I slipped into it. It says, 'Beware the Children of Asena.'"

A gust swept through the tall grass, sharp with the scent of iron.

Val frowned. "Who wrote it? And why now?"

"Someone local. They were frightened, or angry. Probably both."

"What's Asena? And why beware her children?"

"It's just an old Aeltyrian tale," I said. "Meant to frighten children out of the woods."

"Hmm." He glanced over at me, tone casual. "We're overdue for a good tale around the fire. This one fits, if you're willing."

He knew I liked to tell a good story. He was being indulgent.

"If that's your wish," I replied coolly.

He narrowed his eyes slightly.

"We should return, my lord." I turned and lengthened my stride, the wind tugging at my cloak. He caught up easily.

"We danced together in Elisedd," he said, loud enough for anyone nearby to hear.

He was persistent. I'd give him that. And he knew he wasn't reminding me of the dance, but of what almost happened. I refused to answer.

"You didn't complain when I got you out of the infirmary wagon, either."

We both knew exactly what he meant by that, too. It was a reminder that I'd shared a saddle with him, pressed together from shoulder to seat. *That* memory was sharp. I had to answer.

"*You* asked *me*," I said, walking faster. "Both times. *I* must have *your* permission to touch *you*."

"I give it now and for the rest of my life." He threw up his hands. "There. It's fixed."

I stopped and turned, hands on my hips. "Do you intend to announce that to the camp?"

He stepped in, a breath away, and mirrored the pose, too close.

Then came the thought, loud and uninvited—

*If he leaned just a little farther, he could kiss me.*

"Would you like me to? I will, if that's what stops—" He gestured between us, a tight sweep of his hand. "Whatever this is."

His gaze didn't waver. Firelight picked out the lines in his face, the hard set of his mouth.

I didn't flinch.

"You're right about that, at least. Whatever *this* is, it needs to stop," I said.

The echo was intentional. He'd meant the conflict, the tension. I meant the closeness. The softness. And he knew it right away.

"And what is it, Aleaia?" His voice softened. "What needs to stop?"

I wanted to say it. To tell him I had to protect him from me.

The words wouldn't come.

"You're infuriating sometimes, *my lord,*" I said instead, and turned away. I was a coward.

"Aleaia," he called. Then, louder, "Aleaia, stop."

I had no choice when commanded so publicly. I stopped, turned.

"Stop what, my lord?" My voice rang clean and hard. "Stop walking? Stop insisting we keep the order of things?"

Heads turned. Conversations dulled.

Val stepped forward, arms crossed. "You were ashamed. I tried to comfort you. Reminded you of your place. Your importance. What is infuriating about that?"

"I don't need comfort," I said sharply. "I need *you* to accept the way things are. My *place* is beneath you. I am as important as your shield. What I did was wrong. An apology was required. It would've been better if you'd let it stand."

His brow furrowed. "You *want* to be wrong? Or you're hoping someone punishes you for it?"

"No." I exhaled, sharp and unsteady. "I'm wrong whether I want to be or not. Everyone saw me touch you like we were equals."

"We are—"

"We *aren't,* my lord." I held his gaze. "And you know it."

The hush that followed was subtle, but I felt it. That low ripple when too many eyes and ears turn toward one place.

Let them.

Val looked past me, something tightening in his expression. Then his voice dropped. "This isn't the time or place."

He turned and walked away. I followed, each step heavier than the last.

*Doing the right thing isn't supposed to feel like this,* I thought. *But it has to be this way, because being close to me is as dangerous as any battlefield.*

"Good evening, Mariana. Lucius," Val said as we approached the fire near the command tent. His tone was even, like nothing had happened.

"There you are," Lucius said, rising from his stump. "The quaestor was looking for you."

"No, sit," Val said too quickly. "What did he want?"

"Something about ration records?" Lucius returned to his seat.

Val grimaced as he lowered himself to the log. "Pity I missed him."

"Right." Lucius scoffed. "Nothing like balancing the quantities of dried lentils to send a man off to sleep."

Val's gaze found mine. Drifted to the space beside him. Back again.

I didn't move at first, but appearances mattered.

Crossing to the log, I accepted a mug of ale from Mariana. "Thank you, Mari."

"You're welcome," Mariana said, settling beside Lucius.

I sat, careful to leave a couple hand-spans of space between Val and me. He exhaled beside me. Quiet. A little unsteady.

I took a sip before speaking. "We just came from one of the signs near the perimeter. Something about the 'Children of Asena.'"

Lucius raised a brow. "What do you make of it?"

"Don't know yet. But I've been asked to tell the tale, to give it some context," I said, glancing at Mariana. "Mari, you've heard it before? It might be a local one."

"I heard it once or twice growing up," she said. "But it's been a long time."

"It's a spoken tale," I said. "There were written versions once, but little survived the war. What remains lives in memory."

I adjusted my grip on the mug, looked down into it. The fire snapped in front of us, throwing light and shadow across the circle. I thought, for a moment, about how I'd always wanted to be a storyteller, a keeper of the old tales, when I was a girl. Close enough, I supposed.

"I'll do my best to honor it," I said.

I took one last sip and cleared my throat.

"Long ago, when the continent was still broken, there were two old nations, Ostala and Lascebar. Bitter rivals. They fought over rivers, over rocks. Land that belonged to no one, and everyone. The kind of land men die on, and gods forget.

"One day, in one of those battles, a young warrior named Cian was struck down. He didn't die, not then. But he fled the field, wounded and half-mad. Blood in his eyes. Voices in his head. He staggered into the woods and left the war behind him.

"The wolves found him. He should've died. Should've been torn apart and left for the crows. But one of them, Asena, wasn't like the others.

"Some say her coat shone like moonlight on water. Others say her eyes were silver, and she could see straight through a man's soul. Some say she was once a woman, cursed by Lithau for breaking an oath. Others claim she *was* a goddess herself, in another shape.

"Whatever the truth, she took him in. And for a time, he lived among them. Ran with them. Slept beside Asena. And in time… she bore him children.

"Not wolves. Not men. Something else. They were fast. Strong. Clever. Harder to track than smoke on the wind. And hungrier than anything the old world had known.

"By day, they walk as men. By night, they hunt as beasts. Some swear they shift at will. Skin to fur, tooth to fang, smile to snarl. But every tale agrees on one thing: they are dangerous. Cunning. Blood-bound and blood-starved. And they never forget a slight.

"Some say the line died out long ago. Others insist they still live among us, wearing borrowed faces and waiting for the right time to strike. But in Lascebar, when someone goes missing, when a hunting party doesn't return, when the wind howls and doesn't stop—

"They say it's Asena's bloodline, come back to claim what was taken."

I leaned back, looking at each of them.

"They are the Children of Asena. And the message by the road wasn't just a tale. It was a warning."

"People here really believe that?" Marcus said mildly. "No wonder they lost the war. Poor savage things."

The fire popped. No one spoke.

Not Lucius. Not Mariana, half-Aeltyrian herself.

Silence settled like consent.

Not mine.

I turned toward him. My voice stayed calm, but it carried. "Care to test how savage I am, Marcus? We can settle it in the square, *tuchlus*."

"Aleaia." Val's voice was low. Tired. Not sharp, but not backing me, either. "Enough."

I didn't look at him. Didn't blink. My eyes stayed on Marcus.

Val wasn't wrong, but he wasn't with me, and the difference mattered more than I wanted it to.

I took a long drink.

*Good,* I thought. *We need a little distance.*

Boots approached. A sentry stepped into the circle of firelight and saluted. "My lord. A patrol from the northern edge hasn't returned. They're late by nearly half a watch."

Val stood. "Who was leading?"

"Decanus Beran, sir."

Something prickled along my spine. Ten legionaries couldn't just vanish.

Val's face was hard as flint. "Send a runner. I want their last known position confirmed. Double the watch. Updates every hour."

The sentry nodded and slipped away.

The fire crackled. A horse snorted in the dark. The cold pressed close.

I looked at Marcus. "Still think it's just a tale for children?"

# CHAPTER TWENTY-ONE
## *The Task*

*"Some don't wait for death to find them. They go out and meet it with their boots on."*
—Gallus Tutela

Dēwamos 59, 1230
*Aleaia*

We found no trace of the missing patrol. Their tracks vanished northeast of camp, swallowed by brush and silence. No blood. No broken branches. Just absence.

By morning, another sentry had vanished, last seen before heading off to take a shit just beyond the torchlight of his post.

Val didn't wait for a third. He ordered the legion inside the old, weathered stone walls of Gormlaith. They needed repair but were better than anything we could raise in haste.

We sat at the worn table in Gormlaith's longhouse, the air stale with smoke. Across from us, the ealdorman leaned forward, his face carved by time, voice thick with a Lascebaran accent.

"They take or kill one in ten, lord," he said in slow, careful Calesian. "Calesian, Aeltyrian, men, women, children—they have no care. We learn this. They take Lord Varro."

"The elder or the younger?" Val asked.

"The elder, lord. The young one refuses to come out of the castle until the she-wolf is gone."

*Coward,* I wanted to say. But I held my tongue.

"Why haven't you sent word to Aeldunon, or Elisedd, or Avitum?" Marcus asked. "Or tried to assemble a search party?"

He asked it mildly, with what might have passed for genuine curiosity.

Still, I wanted to gut him.

"We try, lord," the ealdorman said, spreading his hands. "Some of them are good with a bow. They shoot down birds. Lord Varro forbids a search party. I think he is afraid we run away. We sent a messenger, but they took him, and his horse. Nothing returns. It is like a siege."

"Any idea where their lair is?" Lucius asked.

"No, lord. We sent our best scout. She did not return." He exhaled. "I am glad you came, my lords. And lady." He nodded toward me.

I met his eyes, leaning back slightly. There had to be a shaman here, a keeper of not just stories, but *histories*. The ealdorman hadn't mentioned one.

Not yet. We'd have to ask, and he might be too frightened to admit the truth.

I could ask in our shared language.

It stirred something tight and knotted in my chest.

Using Aeltyrian to dig into old blood, old stories, old wounds, to get what we needed was too close to what they used me for. What I *let them* use me for.

Only this time, no one would pay the price for my voice.

Right?

That's what I thought before.

And look what happened.

Ash coated my tongue.

I lifted my cup. My hand didn't shake. Thank the gods for that.

I drank deep. The taste lingered. Bitter. Stale.

Time to get to it.

I spoke in Aeltyrian, voice soft. *"Es derē ó druvir harē?"*

Is there a shaman here?

The ealdorman's eyes widened. I'd asked it in Aeltyrian and in front of a Calesian prince.

Then he looked to Val. The approving nod Val gave settled whatever tension remained.

The old man replied in kind, *"Nirau te celmabreath. Cear esmirau te vathia. Ara es ó siltha, sena."*

*Near the elder tree. Just beyond the path. She is a seer too.*

It felt like stepping back into one of those old rooms where secrets were extracted at blade point. I had to get out.

I rose. My joints ached. Breath pulled tight in my ribs.

I dipped my head. *"Dearel tó, ser."*

*Thank you, sir.*

I walked out into the sunlight.

The noon heat struck like a slap. Stone walls burned with it, throwing it back in waves. My pulse hammered. I couldn't feel my feet. My skin was too tight.

Then came the smoke.

Not wood smoke.

*That smoke.*

*Burnt linen. The greasy stench of skin blistering in flame. It filled my throat, clawed at the back of my nose, coated my tongue until I could taste nothing else.*

*And then the light shifted.*

*Just enough to make my stomach clench.*

*The air shimmered—firelight.*

*Echoes of screams.*

*"How could you? You're one of us!"*

*The voice wasn't there, but it was in me.*

I blinked. Hard.

Stone. Sun. Not fire. Not now.

A shape moved beside me.

Lucius.

He didn't speak. Didn't touch me. Just stood close enough that I could feel him, solid and real.

Then, low and steady, he asked, "You here with us, Dieter?"

A rope to grab.

I took it. Gave a short nod.

He grunted. "Don't wait too long to speak up. I'll drag your sorry arse back if I have to."

He knew. He understood.

I let out a breath I hadn't known I was holding. "I won't."

The door creaked open behind us. Boots crunched on sunbaked stone. I straightened. Fixed my eyes on the rooftops across the way.

"Care to share with the rest of us, Dieter?" Marcus asked.

That wasn't curiosity in his voice. It was a blade wrapped in silk.

I'd already hit him once and walked away clean. Much as I wanted to do it again, I couldn't. Not there, not then. My hand found my sword hilt. I wouldn't draw, but it steadied me. Gave me control.

Before I could answer, Val cut in. "Marcus, could you check in with the quaestor for me?"

Marcus blinked, then inclined his head. "Of course, my lord."

He swung up onto his donkey and rode off without another word.

Lucius watched him go. "What was that about?"

"Nothing," I said, turning toward him. I knew he meant Marcus's comment, but I answered as if I'd misunderstood. "Poor man was struggling in Calesian. I thought it easier to speak a more familiar tongue."

Lucius didn't press. Just watched me like he wasn't sure.

"If you wanted a translation," I added, steadier now, "I asked if there was a shaman—a lore-keeper. Figured she might know something about Asena. He said yes. She lives just beyond the path to the elder tree. I thanked him. That's all."

Val exhaled. Ran a hand through his hair. "If you think she can help, we should pay her a visit."

We walked down the narrow main road of hard-packed dirt, cookfires guttering in the dust, clotheslines sagging between beams. The air reeked of sweat, leather, and piss, thickened with smoke and wet dogs. Noise swelled like a living thing: muddy boots, barked orders, dishes clattering behind a curtain. Four thousand soldiers and camp followers were crammed into the space meant for five hundred.

We'd taken the town to protect it.

We'd probably destroy it ourselves.

The cottage sat against the wall, the lintel smoke-stained and the northern wall covered in moss. Bird bones hung from the awning, clicking in the breeze.

I stopped and turned to Lucius and Val. "You should wait here."

I'd said it sharper than I meant. My jaw hadn't unclenched since the longhouse. Since Marcus. Since the smell of burning flesh clawed out of memory. I was on edge because of it and felt a pant of guilt. I looked at Lucius, who didn't deserve the bite, and softened.

"She won't trust Calesians," I said. "We're not supposed to follow the old ways. She'll fear punishment."

Would she be wrong? I didn't know how far Val would go. Or what Emperor Claudius would do when he heard of it.

"Very well," Val said quietly. "We'll wait."

I felt his eyes on me as I took the path to the door. It stood ajar. Incense curled in the warm air. Amber, maybe. Or juniper. I knocked once.

"Grandmother?" I called out.

A bent woman stepped into view, stiff with age, hands lifting as if to ward me off. "Gods above. Why does your ghost trouble me?"

Perhaps age had blurred her sight. I hoped she could still answer my questions with some clarity.

"My name is Aleaia Dieter," I said gently. "I came seeking your help."

Her hands lowered, slow and wary. "I am Senona. I suppose I'll help, if I'm able. What is it you need?"

I stepped inside. "What can you tell me about the Children of Asena?"

"Why do Calesian soldiers care for forest stories?" Her gaze sharpened.

"We were tasked with stopping the kidnappings, but if you're happy to let them continue—"

I moved to leave.

"Wait."

I turned back to her.

"As you said, they take our people," she said. "Some killed on the moor. Some dragged into the trees. Their matriarch commands them." She eased into a chair at her table, motioned for me to sit across from her. "It's always been this way. Once each year. Lately, more often."

"The matriarch?" I sat. "Asena?"

She nodded.

"She still lives?"

"She is immortal, child. But immortal is not the same as untouchable."

I took a deep, slow breath. My patience was wearing thin already. "Speak more plainly, grandmother. Lives are at stake."

"If her heart is taken, it might end them all."

"Might." That didn't sound promising. "There has to be more to it than that. She's one woman. Surely someone could have done that before me."

"Could they?" she asked. "We don't know their numbers."

She was right about that.

"That's how it worked with other curses, isn't it?" I asked. "Before the Fade."

"I dislike calling it that." Senona poured hot water over loose leaves, handed me a cup.

I took a sip. It burnt my tongue, and the heat clawed its way down to my gut like fire with teeth. I pressed my tongue against the roof of my mouth.

"The magic didn't fade away. It didn't leave, either," she said. "It's still there. Just out of reach, where it was last touched."

Cryptic or no, she was still the best source of information I'd find to help these people, so I plodded on. "What would someone need to know to find her?"

"She's older than memory. A sorceress. Illusion is her weapon. That's how she bound the warrior who fathered her children. They've lived in the forest for centuries. This violence? It's new, and unlike them. Something's changed."

When I nearly drained the cup, she took it, poured the dregs into a shallow saucer, and leaned close, her brow furrowed. Her hand trembled, and she swore softly under her breath.

"What is it?" I asked.

She was silent for a long moment, drawing a breath deep before she spoke again.

"Her magic will deceive you," she said softly. "But if you go into the woods, you will end her reign. Help will come from an unexpected, perhaps unwelcome place."

Her fingers tightened around the saucer. She'd seen something else but held back.

"And?" I prompted.

"The year ahead will be filled with trials. I wish I could see more. That's all Avani will let me take from the River of Time."

Pressing her wouldn't work. Not with women like her.

I shifted the footing. "How can you see anything, if magic's out of reach?"

Senona met my gaze and held it. The longer I looked, the more it felt like she was peeling me apart grain by grain, measuring something she wasn't saying.

"It isn't gone," she said. "As I said. It's just on the other side of the door. But you..." Her voice dropped. "You've touched it, too, haven't you?"

The image of the white raven flashed in my mind, as I'd first seen it, and as I'd seen it in Tuath, and Avitum.

I stood too fast. The chair scraped, nearly toppled. I caught it with one hand, set it upright. "I must go. Thank you, grandmother. May Aelan's blessings be upon you."

"And upon you, child," she murmured.

Her eyes lingered, soft with pity.

The walls felt closer now. The air thick with herbs and old stone. Smoke. Earth. I crossed to the door, each step heavier than the last. Shoved it open and stepped into the light.

Fool. You gave yourself away.

My heart raced as her words clung to me. That look—she'd seen something I hadn't meant to show.

Val sat on the edge of the garden wall, Lucius beside him, arms crossed.

"How did it go?" Val asked.

I walked to them, each step deliberate. When I spoke, my voice was flatter than I wanted. "Well enough. I'll explain in the longhouse, if that pleases your lordship."

He didn't respond, but that silence said plenty. I turned toward the path and they followed.

They talked in hushed voices, doubtless trying to avoid my hearing. My ears were keen, though. Better than they planned.

"What happened?" Lucius asked.

"Nothing," Val said.

Lucius snorted. "Doesn't look like nothing."

Then they went quiet.

Once we were back in the longhouse, I relayed what I'd learned, carefully. No mention of magic, or the tea leaves. No sense handing Marcus a reason to summon the Inquisition.

"Our options are limited," he said, far too pleased with himself. "We could attempt a sweep of the forest, but the risks are considerable. Unfamiliar ground. Scouts might not return."

Val leaned forward. "The alternative?"

Marcus folded his hands. "We could send someone to eliminate their leader directly. That would leave them disorganized long enough that we could pick the rest off."

"Varro tried that already, didn't he? Sending a scout?" Lucius asked.

"He did. But they didn't send the right person. This would require someone… stealthy. And lethal," Marcus said, his eyes landing on me.

The others turned to me, then, to lay the obligation at my feet.

"So it's me," I said. No need to disguise the resignation.

"You *are* the most suited for the task," Marcus said, as if assigning kitchen duty.

He didn't bother to hide the satisfaction. It was neat, lawful, and mostly bloodless. And worst of all, it was correct.

A single death in the woods—mine—was cleaner than risking a hundred.

Maybe this was the answer I'd been circling all along.

Kill the monster. Die doing it.

No more danger to him.

No more pain.

No more me.

"Definitely stealthier than I am," Lucius offered, trying to lighten the mood.

It didn't land.

Val looked troubled. "I don't like the idea of you going alone, Aleaia. Are there any from the First Cohort who could accompany you? One of the new guard candidates?"

I heard the concern. It hurt more than if he'd ordered me.

"No," I said. "I move faster alone. Quieter."

Val said, "I'll go with you."

The room went still and silent.

I sighed. He said it like it was nothing, but I could see it already: him refusing to stay behind me, stepping into danger meant for me, both of us bleeding in the dark.

Brave. Loyal. Well-meaning.

And a liability. And too important to sacrifice.

Lucius and Marcus both spoke at once—protests, objections.

I didn't listen. I looked at Val. I wanted to ask why he was making this harder. Why he was making it hurt.

"I'll manage," I said as I stood. Dipped my head. "And I'll leave tonight. Please excuse me, my lord."

I had preparations to make.

# CHAPTER TWENTY-TWO
## *Valediction II*

*"I had waited seven years to touch her. I was not about to lose her now."*
—Valerius di Calesia

Dēwamos 59, 1230
*Valerius*

I lit the lamp low. Lucius was asleep or pretending to be. I sat at the edge of the bed and pulled out my journal. Set the inkpot beside me. Unstoppered it. Dipped the quill.

And I stopped.

Something was off in the journal's binding. A page near the middle, creased. I hadn't marked anything there.

I flipped back. Saw the handwriting.

Not mine. Hers.

And I knew.

She chose this, here.

Not a letter left on the table.

Not a farewell tucked in with my gear.

A note, left in the one place I might've missed it until it was too late, unless something told me to look.

*Val,*
*I told you I'd done terrible things.*
*That one day you'd see me for what I am.*
*Now you'll never see me that way. Thank the gods.*
*I have a way to make it count.*
*To trade my life for all the ones lost in Gormlaith.*
*To keep you safe.*
*It's not a noble end, but it's cleaner than most.*
*For me, that's enough.*
*Please don't waste your anger on this. Don't waste your grief.*
*Tell Lucius I'm sorry he has to trail after you like a nursemaid now.*
*Tell Mariana not to cry.*
*And tell yourself you didn't fail me.*

*You were the best thing that ever happened to me.*
*I'm sorry I didn't know how to be yours.*
*—A*

My breath hitched halfway through the last line.

The pressure in my chest locked tight. One hard beat, like a hammer against the ribs. My throat was dry. Eyes burned.

She wasn't supposed to leave until near midnight.

That's what she'd told me, and I was going to go with her, whether she wanted me to or not. But she was already gone.

Hours ahead, alone. Marching straight into death with that cursed steadiness I admired and hated with every bone in my body.

I stood before I realized I'd moved, journal still clutched in one hand, her words echoing in my mind.

*To keep you safe.*

*I'm sorry I didn't know how to be yours.*

"Fuck," I muttered. "*Fuck.*"

She never meant to come back. Never told me because she knew I'd try to stop her. And she was right.

I opened the chest at the foot of the bed, as hastily as I could without waking Lucius. No crest. No gold. Just leathers. Blade. Rations.

I moved like I was being hunted. Like if I didn't get there fast enough, she'd vanish into the trees and never come out.

At the edge of the firelight, I stopped only once. Tore a blank page from the back of the journal. Scribbled a few lines for Lucius. Just in case.

Then I strapped on my sword and slipped into the dark.

# CHAPTER TWENTY-THREE
## *A Moth to a Flame*

*"She said the flame would make me shine—*
*But all it left was ash and spine."*
—Aeltyrian skipping rhyme

Dēwamos 59, 1230
*Aleaia*

I moved through the forest beneath the full moon. Light spilled across the path where shadows should've hidden me. I couldn't wait for it to wane, much as I wanted to. If the missing men were still alive, they wouldn't be for long.

In pitch dark, the wolves would have owned this place. This way, the odds weren't good, but they were better.

Branches clawed at my arms as I followed the signs I could find, faint though they were. I'd foregone armor. It would have been too loud, too bright.

Torchlight flickered ahead, finally. I moved toward it.

A lone sentry stood at the mouth of the cave. I'd need to take him quietly. No blood. If these things had even half a wolf's instinct, one scent could summon the pack.

I moved like smoke, keeping my steps silent. Hooked my arm beneath his chin and yanked him back, letting my weight do the work. No panic. No sound. No blood. Just pressure.

He went still. I lowered him to the ground and slipped inside.

Lantern light wavered along the stone walls, dim and uneven, leaving shadows deep enough to hide in. The farther down the corridor I moved, the tighter the dark pressed around me.

The first chamber opened like a mouth, wide and low, lined with rough-hewn tables. Enough seating for a hundred. The air hit harder here.

I'd smelled it before. It was, after all, the stuff my nightmares were made of. Flesh. Cooked. Rich and greasy, with a sweetness that didn't belong. It crawled down my throat.

I pushed it down. Didn't have time for it.

I glanced around the space. The hall had fed many. Maybe it still did.

Farther in, the stench worsened. The reek of ash and rendered fat hit like a hammer. It was thick, acrid, and burned down to memory. My stomach turned. I swallowed it back. Kept moving. Steps silent on the stone.

A chill dragged down my spine. My hand went to my blade—

A shadow tore from the wall beside me. An arm locked around my throat, dragging me into the dark.

I twisted, slammed my elbow into his ribs, but his grip held, iron-strong. My fingers scrabbled for the knife in my boot, just out of reach.

He caught my wrist, wrenched it behind me. Pain snapped through my shoulder.

I snarled. Bucked. Drove my weight into the fight.

He didn't budge. Worse, he laughed as he swept my legs from under me and slammed me to the stone.

I kicked, writhed, but another shape dropped onto me. Pinned my arms. Snapped iron around my wrists.

My breath hissed out, not from pain.

From fury.

From the sheer audacity of it.

From the shame of being caught unawares.

I hadn't seen them. Hadn't heard them.

Chains jerked me upright. Fingers gripped my jaw, forced my head up.

"Pretty, as promised. Our brother will be pleased."

"You piece of shit," I spat and lunged, sinking my teeth deep into his forearm. Blood flooded my mouth, hot and thick.

His scream echoed through the cavern. That, at least, I enjoyed.

"Not the living!" his partner chastised.

Something slammed into the back of my skull. White burst behind my eyes.

I spat the flesh onto the floor. "You're already dead, arsehole."

The unbitten one shoved me, stumbling, down a corridor—a different one than I'd come in by. I fought every step. Chains cut into my wrists as I twisted, heels dragging against stone. My curses came low and relentless. My muscles burned. The manacles didn't give.

I dropped down, made myself deadweight. They pulled me, hard, into the next chamber, rife with the tang of rusted iron and the sweetness of rot. The stench closed around me. Every footfall landed with a wet squelch. The ground sucked at my boots. I couldn't see it, but I felt it, and that was worse.

Torchlight flickered, then revealed the truth.

Worse than any battlefield.

Bodies hung by their feet from the ceiling. Human. Throats slit. Blood still dripping in slow, rhythmic splatters.

Butchered like game.

They weren't just killing. They were eating them.

My eyes swept the room, fast. Desperate.

All men. Every single one.

Beran among them.

No women.

My stomach heaved.

Sweat chilled on my palms.

Where were the women? Death was a certainty I had prepared for, but whatever they were doing to the women—what they'd do to me—was sure to be worse than this.

The next chamber opened, vast and circular. The ceiling vanished into shadow. The walls were lined with bone.

A woman sat near the back on a throne of antlers and skulls. Her eyes gleamed like polished obsidian. Firelight danced through her silver hair, and the faintest curl of satisfaction touched her mouth. A massive black wolf sprawled at her feet, rising as I was dragged forward, a growl rumbling deep in its chest.

I realized two things.

First, that I should have believed the shaman.

Second, that this was Asena.

Men stepped from the edges of the chamber, robes bloodied and faces half-lost to soot and shadow. They hauled me toward the altar at the center.

Asena descended from the dais, the wolf trailing at her heels. Her eyes fixed on me, bright with hunger and awe.

"You'll do," she said, voice smooth. "Strong bones. Good hips. I was beginning to worry."

I met her stare without flinching. "You should be worried."

She stopped before me, head tilted, appraising me like some rare beast brought in from the wild. Her fingers brushed my chin, light as breath. A claim.

"Still full of fire. Good. That makes them last longer." Her smile widened. "The child you'll carry, Daughter of Aelan, he'll burn just as brightly. A king for the empty throne."

I jerked my head back. "I'll gut you before I carry your filth."

She laughed. Wide. Tooth-bared. Amused. "Oh, child. You don't get a choice."

One of the ash-marked followers stepped forward, fingers reaching for the laces at my collar.

I recoiled hard. "Don't fucking touch me!"

The blow to my stomach came fast. Hard. I folded around it, the breath torn from my lungs. Before I could recover, they grabbed my tunic and yanked. The seams split with a sound like bone snapping, loud enough to silence the chant mid-phrase.

"Easy, brother," another said. "These are good clothes. We can use them for the children."

They stripped me, yanking my boots off, dragging my trousers past my knees while I kicked, twisted, and cursed. They left me in my shift, torn at the shoulder, damp with sweat.

Two of the bastards hauled me forward, up the dais stairs, and slammed me chest-down onto the altar.

The stone was slick, cold, and sticky beneath my cheek. My arms were wrenched forward and shackled above my head. My legs followed, spread and locked in iron rings bolted to the base.

Not this.

Not like this.

My skin crawled. Breath flared through my nose. Fear beat hard beneath my ribs, but defiance rooted deeper still. I hadn't begged, and I wouldn't.

Beyond the altar, Asena's men gathered in a wide circle. Their chanting rose in low, guttural waves, rhythmic and pulsing, moving through stone, through chains, through my bones.

I gritted my teeth. Thought I might piss myself or vomit. Maybe both.

The wolf stalked into view again, massive and silent, yellow eyes fixed on me as it circled the altar like a beast awaiting command.

Something rose in me. Hot. Bitter.

The only weapon I had left.

Born of fury and fear and too many dead.

It ripped from my throat before I could stop it, sharp and bright as a blade drawn in the dark. "In Galdorin's name, I curse your line!"

A man approached with a shallow bronze bowl in both hands. A thick paste filled it—dark, ruddy, pungent with blood and crushed herbs. Another knelt beside me and dipped his fingers into the mixture.

"May your sons die screaming, with steel in their throats!" I shouted.

The first touch was cold as ice as they pulled my shift up, painting slow across the small of my back. Another followed higher, between my shoulder blades, just above the torn edge of my shift.

Still, I cursed them. "May your daughters be barren as salted earth! Let them birth nothing but ash! Let no kin mourn you, and no grave remember you!"

The Children of Asena whispered their rites in a tongue I couldn't recognize. It was older than Calesia, older than Aeltyria.

My stomach twisted as the wolf crept closer. Its breath came in thick bursts across the backs of my legs, mingling with the cold of altar stone beneath my chest.

They meant to use me. Break me. Seed me with another beast to strengthen their kind.

Me, who'd trained with a sword since I was a child.

Who rode like the wind and danced with steel.

Who guarded a prince.

Commanded.

Survived.

They'd reduce me to a womb.

Asena's voice rose from the circle, rich and heavy with power. She stood at the head of the altar, arms outstretched. "My son, come forth. Flesh of my flesh, born of power. Take your bride. Bring forth new blood."

Every muscle in my body coiled. Ready to fight. To kill. To die.

I twisted hard, chains biting. Breath ragged. Fury boiling in my throat.

I spat on the altar stone. "You think you'll make a son? A king? You'll make a monster that'll tear out your heart and shit on your corpse."

Asena's gaze slid to mine, cool and untouched. Dismissive.

The wolf pressed closer. Its breath hot against my skin.

Then came the sound—distant. Sharp. Unmistakable.

Steel on flesh.

The rhythm of killing drawing near.

Around me, the nearest sons of Asena stilled. Heads tilted. Nostrils flared.

They smelled it too, the fresh blood and iron.

Heat surged through my chest. Relief, laced with fear, because I knew who it was.

And fear let my mind betray me, just for a breath.

The image hit like a blow, clear as a memory.

I saw it—

*Val falling.*

*His body on the stone, blood pooling beneath him.*

And then it was gone with a blink.

Not here. Not now.

He shouldn't have come.

Everyone who stood too close to me bled for it.

Around me, the ritual faltered. They turned toward the sound of steel while they drew their own.

I raised my voice once more. "Galdorin sees me," I said, sharp and steady. "He sees you too! And he's coming with a blade!"

Steel on bone near the entrance.

A scream, wet and choked off mid-breath.

Panic and chaos bloomed around me.

And through the haze, I saw him.

# CHAPTER TWENTY-FOUR
## *Galdorin*

*"He does not shield the weak. He steadies the hand that strikes."*
—The Song of the Stars, Cycle VI: The Cycle of Stone

Dēwamos 60, 1230
*Valerius*

The first died before he knew I was there.

One clean stroke to the neck. No sound but the wet snap of tendon and bone.

Second one turned too slow. I split him at the collar, cut to the spine. He dropped screaming, then silent. Better than he deserved.

Third came fast, slashing wide. I ducked under it, stepped in, and rammed my sword through his gut. Buried it deep, to the hilt. He went slack and hit the ground.

I turned to kick a fourth away from me.

I hadn't seen her yet, and I had to know if she was alive.

Then I heard her, sharp and clear. A godsdamned war cry. *"Galdorin silest em. Ar silest tó sena! Et ares calinge sen ó valer!"*

I saw her.

Chains around her wrists. Blood on her shift, pulled up around her waist. Bruises darkening her skin, those cursed runes smeared across her back like filth. They'd bound her to an altar like a fucking offering.

Fury flared like fire poured down my throat.

Another bastard rushed the altar, sword raised. I moved—three strides, fast. Caught him by the shoulder and drove the sword straight through his back. Blood sprayed, hot and fast.

One came from the left, wild, swinging high. I caught the blade, twisted. My knee hit his gut, hard. He doubled over. I drove my fist into his face and dropped him.

Every muscle screamed to rip the world apart.

No questions. No words. Just get her free.

I turned back to her.

I pulled the dagger from my boot, jammed it beneath the hinge of the right manacle, and brought the pommel of my sword down. The bolt snapped. Her wrist was free.

I couldn't think.

Couldn't speak.

Could barely breathe.

I pressed the dagger into her hand.

More were coming, charging the steps.

I'd kill them all. Every last one of them.

For touching her.

For chaining her.

For even thinking they'd break her.

*Aleaia*

"Aleaia!" he called. "Catch!"

I moved the dagger to my left hand, twisted on the altar, and caught the sword in my right, barely. My grip almost slipped, blood-slick and shaking.

He'd seen the man rushing the slab from the other side.

The man's blade came down. I pulled back, jerking the chain on my left wrist taut across the stone. He missed me, hit the chain instead.

And I drove the sword up beneath his ribs.

He crumpled in a tangle of limbs and blood.

My hands were free now, but my ankles still bound.

I wedged the dagger into the joint of one cuff and struck with the sword's pommel, as Val had done. Took me two tries, then the hinge cracked.

I did the same to the other. A blow, a snap, then freedom.

I had blood in my mouth, steel in my hand, and wrath in my chest.

Barefoot and breathless and nearly naked, I slid off the altar. The stone beneath my feet was slick and cold.

Val held the foot of the dais, bloodied and relentless, fending off two men. Another was circling behind him, blade raised.

I pivoted and threw the dagger from my off-hand. It struck the man in the collarbone. Not blade first. Not the throat. But it slowed him enough for Val to turn and finish him.

Beyond his shoulder, in the firelit haze, Asena stood watching, that same maddening calm on her face. Smoke coiled between us. Beside her, the great black wolf let out a deep, guttural growl.

She had to pay for what she'd done.

I surged past Val, ducking through his foes with the single-minded purpose of ending her burning behind my ribs. As I passed the man I'd hit with the dagger, I caught sight of it on the ground.

I didn't stop. Dropped low. Snatched it and rose in one motion.

Then stopped.

She was gone. The wolf too. As if by magic.

The tapestry behind the throne swayed slightly. A hidden corridor.

For the span of a heartbeat, I was torn. My gut screamed to chase her—for the ones she'd killed, for what they'd tried to do to me—but Val was still fighting. I couldn't leave him.

"Fuck." I turned back, held fast by heart and duty, my anger tempering into something sharper.

Grit.

Enough to move, to kill, to drag myself through whatever came next.

To finish it.

A spear thrust from the right. I slipped left, caught the shaft beneath my arm, and drove my blade into his throat. Let the spear fall with the body.

Another lunged, sword high. I caught the blade on my crossguard, twisted hard, and slammed my foot into his chest. He crashed backward, weapon clattering across stone.

Two more closed in. I ducked beneath a wide slash from one, drove the dagger up beneath the ribs of the other. As he dropped, I turned back to his partner.

Three times, I gave ground, dodging his furious strikes.

On the fourth, I caught his blade on the dagger and countered with my sword. He slipped away, light on his feet, blood slicking his arm.

We circled, panting and bloodied.

He held his weapon low now. Cautious.

I rolled my shoulders, shook the ache from my arms, and beckoned him forward with my dagger.

Val appeared behind him and drove a boot into his spine.

The man stumbled.

I stepped in and brought my blade down across his neck.

And that was the last of them.

I stood still. Breathing hard. Eyes sweeping the carnage.

The braziers' light crawled across blood-slick stone, casting long, uneasy shadows. The scent of gore and char clung to every breath. No more chanting. No clash of steel. Just silence.

Val cleaned his blade, then turned to me as he sheathed it, still breathing hard. "What—the fuck—were you thinking?" he ground out.

I couldn't bring myself to look at him. "Someone had to stop them."

"You almost died!" He stepped closer, gestured broadly to the room. "You knew there were too many!"

"No. I thought—"

He grabbed my shoulders, firm enough that I thought he'd shake me. "Don't fucking lie to me!"

My breath shuddered. I went still.

I wanted to tell him the truth.

That if someone had to die, I thought it may as well be me.

That in so doing, I'd solve a few problems.

"I found your note, Aleaia," he growled. "You didn't plan to come back."

My heart sank. He wasn't supposed to find that until I was already gone. Beyond the Veil.

"You left it like it was nothing. Like I was *nothing*." His grip softened, just slightly. "Did you think I wouldn't follow?"

"I didn't—" My voice caught, the words stuck in my throat like thorns.

"Didn't what? Didn't want to live anymore? Didn't want anyone to stop you?"

"Yes." The answer was true for both questions.

He let go as if the contact burned, then stepped back, hand raking through his hair. The silence that followed felt thick. He stared at me like he didn't know whether to hold me or walk away.

"Why?" he asked. "Why would you want that?"

I swallowed hard. "I think—"

I couldn't say it. Not the whole of it. Not that death was the only way out. The nightmares. The memories. The danger I posed to him.

If I said that, he would only come closer.

He'd already followed me into the dark.

I was supposed to shield him, but I hadn't done that. I'd hurt him. Put him in danger just by standing beside him. He wanted more than I could give. I'd felt it in Elisedd. I'd felt it since then, too.

What he wanted was forbidden. Dangerous. More so because of what I was: a curse.

"You scared me. Don't—" His voice cracked. "Don't do that again. Please."

He reached for me. Hesitated. His hand hovered, fingers curling back before they touched.

Then it dropped to his side, not quite steady.

My chest tightened.

Part of me wanted to lean into it.

Part of me knew neither of us would survive if I did.

His mouth tightened, like holding himself back hurt more than any wound. "Are you—are you hurt?" he asked, softer than before but only just.

My shift stuck to me, damp with sweat and blood. My back throbbed. My shoulder ached. Nothing was broken. Nothing that counted, anyway.

"No," I said.

His eyes lingered on my wrist, the blood, the bruises. He didn't press. Just nodded.

"She's not gone," he said.

I turned toward the darkened corridor. "No. She ran."

I looked at him again. Bloodied. Furious. Here, because he came for me. I owed him my life. Again. And maybe he'd have been safer if I'd left without saying goodbye.

That note had been my own selfish need and almost gotten him killed. This wasn't the moment for that truth, though.

"We have to finish this," I said. "Before she tries to finish us."

Val nodded. "And once we do, we finish this," he said, motioning between us.

I didn't answer.

While he checked the fallen, I crossed to where they'd left my things, and set my weapons down to take inventory. My boots were scuffed and bloodstained, but intact. My trousers were torn at the knee but still serviceable. I pulled them on in silence.

The tunic was worse. I held it up by the shoulders. Ruined. I let it fall again.

Val's footsteps came up behind me. His tunic appeared over my shoulder. "Here," he said.

I turned. He didn't look at me. Just ground his teeth, like he always did when he was serious or angry or both. His eyes stared into the dark.

"Take it," he commanded, giving it a small shake.

I hesitated for a heartbeat before I took it and pulled it over my head. It hung loose, sleeves nearly to my knuckles, and smelled of smoke, steel, and him. I rolled up the sleeves of his tunic, buckled my sword belt, checked the edge of my blade. Still clean.

His shirt clung to him while he finished checking the pockets of those we'd slain, damp with sweat and blood. Warmth crept up my neck. I looked away.

He stood, stepped closer, and held up a small iron key. "Found this."

I still had one manacle on my wrist—the left one. I held out my hand to take the key, but he shook his head.

"Give it here," he said gruffly.

I'd never seen him so angry. I didn't dare argue, just lifted my wrist. He took my hand in his, turned the manacle over, and fit the key into the lock. The cuff opened with a squeak, and he tossed it away.

He didn't let go, though. He kept hold of my hand, rubbing the raw, bruised skin with his thumb. Gentle. Thoughtful.

I pulled back. There was no time for that kind of tenderness.

I bent and picked up the dagger. Elegant. Balanced. Too fine for me. I held it out, hilt first. "This is yours."

He glanced at the blade, then at me. "Keep it."

"I don't need—"

"I said keep it." His voice was quiet. Final.

I sighed. I wasn't sure what to say, so I just slid it into my boot, where my own knife should've been. A tight fit, but it held.

He started to speak. "Aleaia, I—"

"We're wasting time," I interrupted. "She's still ahead of us. Nine are here. The wolf's likely with her."

He wasn't looking at me. His face unreadable. Shoulders taut.

If I faltered now, I'd drag him under with me.

I drew my sword, took a torch from beside the throne, and crossed to the tapestry at the back of the chamber. With the tip of my sword, I pushed it aside. A narrow corridor, cut into stone.

"This is where they went," I said.

I stepped into the gap, torch held high to keep out of the smoke. The passage narrowed, forcing us to go single file. When we reached the threshold of the next chamber, I tossed the torch forward. It bounced across the floor, casting long shadows on the walls.

I took a deep breath and stepped into the dark.

# CHAPTER TWENTY-FIVE
## *The Darkness*

*"The past is not dead. It walks beside us. Sometimes it wears our face."*
—The Song of the Stars, Cycle IX: The Cycle of the End

Dēwamos 60, 1230
*Aleaia*

I wasn't in the cave anymore. It was the clearing.

Where this all began.

Four of them circled. Two with longswords. One, a broadsword. The last was the branded man.

I knew this moment.

Every grim step of it.

At sixteen, I'd charged in without thinking. Seven years later, I saw my mistake for what it was. I should've flanked. Called out. Gone for the leader.

The smaller one turned. Swung high.

I slipped inside his guard, sank my blade into his side.

Flesh gave. The blade stuck fast. I braced my foot against his belly and yanked. It tore free with a wet sound. He collapsed into the mud, limbs twitching once before they stilled.

I felt the one behind me—instinct.

I ducked, swept his legs out from under him with my blade. Let him fall.

And for a moment, it felt so real that I wondered if all my life since then had been the vision. If this was real. If I was getting one more chance to get it right. I turned, looked for Papa.

He stood ten paces off, blood slicking his left arm from shoulder to wrist, running down his fingers. His grip slipped on the hilt, but he was still fighting. I ran toward him.

The last outlaw came at me with an axe, swung wide. I ducked low. My boots slipped in the damp earth as I rose behind him, sword already raised.

I brought it down where neck met shoulder. Bone cracked. Flesh gave. The impact jarred through my arms like striking stone. The blade bit deep. I braced my foot against his back and yanked.

It tore free with a wet sound, dragging sinew with it. Blood sprayed my face, hot and thick. He collapsed into the mud, limbs twitching once before they stilled.

I turned and saw Papa on his knees, trying to stand. One hand pressed to the gash beneath his ribs, trying to keep his insides in. Blood gushed between his fingers in ribbons. His other hand reached for his sword.

It was just too far. Just like last time.

The branded man stood over him.

I hadn't seen him move. Hadn't seen how he got there.

Papa looked up. First at the man. Then past him, right at me.

His eyes locked on mine and everything else fell away. The clash, the cries, the ache in my ribs.

His mouth shaped the words, *"I love you."*

Then the blade came down.

Clean. Silent.

No sound but wind, steel, and the dull thump of Papa's head hitting the earth beside his knees. His body stayed upright for half a breath before folding.

I didn't move.

My legs shook. My teeth ground together. A scream rose in my throat.

Something inside me split.

The scream tore free, scraped raw across my ribs as it left me. There was only the Mētanos cold and the sword in my hand and the earth beneath my feet.

With a flicker, the trees vanished. The branded man. Papa's body. The sword.

Just a moment before, I'd been sprinting across the clearing. Now I stood in the mud, but it wasn't the forest anymore. It was a village square.

Not the place where he died.

The place where I lied.

Lhannor. A hill village north of Gormlaith, more pine than people. It hadn't meant anything to the Empire until it sheltered rebels. Three of them. Wounded. Starving. Already gone by the time the Empire arrived. That didn't matter.

Smoke from hearth fires stung my eyes. Taran Caerwyn, the ealdorman, faced me with his hand on his son's shoulder, posture stiff with unspoken fear.

"Lay down your arms," I said. "You'll be safe. I swear it."

And they did, because they believed me.

A girl handed me a bundle of dried flowers. Her trust settled in my chest, sweet and cloying.

That night, the Empire came with fire and steel.

"What are you waiting for?" my centurion said, roughly shoving a torch into my hand.

My hand shook. I threw it on the nearest eaves and prayed no one was inside. Flame ripped across rooftops. I hated myself for it.

Taran fought back with a pitchfork. He never stood a chance.

They ran a sword through his back. His eyes locked on mine, wide and disbelieving as blood bubbled at the corner of his mouth. "But you're one of us," he gasped as he died.

They strung him up on the village's northern gate. His feet dangled. His breeches darkened as his body emptied itself. He twitched once. Then nothing.

The smoke choked me. The air stank of fat and burned hair.

Lira, the girl who gave me the flowers, died in the cellar with her family.

By morning, the square was quiet but for the crows.

I closed my eyes against it, and when I reopened them, the village had vanished.

The smoke still clung to my clothes. Blood crusted beneath my fingernails. Only the world had changed.

Catan Row. A poor little town in Ostala.

Stone walls loomed around me, damp and cold. Rain trickled through the temple's broken roof above and landed on my skin. The stink of mildew and rot soaked the air.

A boy sat cross-legged in the dirt, shoulders hunched as he wrote. His fingers trembled. Ink smeared beneath his palm. He was seventeen, too brave, and too trusting.

Emrys Danwyn. I'd talked him into giving us the names we wanted.

"It's the only way," I told him. "They'll show mercy to you and yours, if you cooperate."

He looked up at me, quill trembling between his fingers. "You're a good soldier," he said. "That means they'll listen to you, doesn't it?"

I nodded. I believed it. I had to.

He smiled, uncertain but hopeful. I'd given him something worth clinging to. "They say you're skilled with a blade. When this is over," he said, "maybe... maybe you could teach me?"

"Aye," I'd said. "Maybe. You'd have to join first, though."

He nodded. Believed me.

I took the ledger from his hands. Clapped his shoulder in thanks and took it to my centurion. He said I'd get to help.

"That's the reward," he'd told me, smiling.

Smiling. Gods.

We lit the storehouse. Smoke poured through the seams in the timber. Inside, people clawed at the walls. One woman pressed her face between the slats, eyes bulging, skin splitting.

"Help me! Please!" she screamed before she disappeared into the flame.

I found Emrys in the barn an hour later. One end of a rope around a rafter, the other around his neck. Stool kicked aside. He was still twitching.

I ran. Blade in hand. Ready to cut him down.

"Don't," my centurion told me.

I stopped. I *was* a good soldier.

Emrys's eyes were still open.

Still wet with tears.

I took a step back, the weight of what I'd done pressing into my chest like a stone too deep to shift. The barn dissolved around me and when the world reformed, I was standing in another square.

Caerlan. Another village, deeper in Ostala. The grief there was older and quieter.

They didn't scream or beg. They just gave.

Caerlan's tribute came in fragments: wedding rings pried from the fingers of the dead, melted trinkets, the last Calesian coins they had. The shaman handed me the sack with both hands.

"Will it be enough?" she asked. "It's all we have."

"Aye," I said. "It has to be." I convinced them, and myself. If people gave everything they had, the Empire would see that as enough.

I rode to present it to Centurion Varenius. He sneered and spat on the sack. Dropped it in the dirt.

"Not enough tribute to justify this many children," Varenius said. "Too skinny to even be slaves. Dieter, take care of it."

I sobbed openly. I couldn't stop myself.

My sword never left its sheath.

Because I couldn't be a good soldier anymore.

The soldiers didn't wait.

They started with the youngest. Made the parents watch as they strung them up on the Elder Tree. Inside the temple, I heard screaming, then weeping.

Later, they tied me to a post. The leather bit deep, lash after lash splitting skin until my legs gave way. They threw salt in the wounds before sending me on to Avitum.

They took my horse and called it a promotion.

That was last year, wasn't it? I suddenly couldn't remember what year it was.

The sky darkened, black clouds rolling across to blot out the sun. The ground beneath my boots dried. The air went still. No fire. No ash. No blood.

Only silence.

Aeltyrian rebels knelt in the dirt, bound and broken. One clutched his brother's hand, whispering prayers through shattered teeth.

I stood beside the tribune. Helmet tucked beneath my arm. Posture perfect. I was older. Much older. I ached the way I would if I spent twenty years in the legion.

"These are the last," he said. "You're sure?"

I nodded. "Yes, sir."

He raised a hand. When he dropped it, the killing began.

One by one, the soldiers stepped forward, and I with them, even as I tried to stop myself. Everything in me screamed that this was wrong.

And still my blade pressed to throats.

Again.

And again.

No one forced me.

I did it myself.

Because it was easier.

Because it made me useful.

Because now, I was one of *them*.

I was the sword.

The promise.

The lie.

A sound cut through the haze.

A voice, low and ragged. Familiar.

"Aleaia!" Hands gripped my shoulders, real this time. His voice cracked, strained at the edges. "Aleaia, wake up. Come back. Now."

I was flat on my back. The stone was cold.

The cave. I remembered.

Val knelt beside me, blood streaking his face, his eyes searching mine. His hands didn't shake, but he held me like I might disappear if he let go.

The memories came back in a surge, like a knife in my skull. I clutched my head, nails digging into my scalp, trying to claw them out. The visions had shattered, but the pain remained. It wasn't imagined. It wasn't some phantom spell.

It was real.

Blood. Smoke. Screaming.

And my voice, speaking every godsdamned lie.

"Fight it, Aleaia," Val said.

So I did. I forced my eyes open, dragged a breath into my lungs like someone pulled from deep water. Everything hurt. My ribs. My throat. Whatever was left of my soul.

Despite everything, despite the part of me that had begged to stay lost, I was still breathing. And I had to get myself together. The pain didn't disappear, but it ebbed, like mist giving way to morning sun.

My voice rasped, cracking. "Val... are you hurt?"

A blinding light flashed in my head. Pain lanced through my skull. I winced.

"I killed the wolf," he said. "Or what I thought was a wolf. But—"

Asena's voice answered before he could finish, ringing through the cave like judgment long delayed. "Why do you pretend to be anything but the Empire's dog, girl?"

I groped nearby until my hand found the blade in the dark—cold, familiar. Val helped me sit up, then to stand. Pain pierced behind my eyes. I staggered, caught myself on his arm, teeth clenched hard enough to hurt.

"You've been murdering innocents," I said. "You'll answer for it."

She stepped from the shadows, into the light of the single torch. Tall. Regal. Her voice slid like steel drawn slow.

"Innocents? You gave the orders. You fed their names to your Calesian masters. You lit the roofs and gave the promises. And now you speak of justice?" Her hollow laugh echoed off the stone. "You wear no crown. You command no magic. You failed the man who raised you, and you betrayed every village that ever trusted your voice. The daughter of Aelan, turned to a dog in foreign armor."

Magic sparked to life at her fingertips, silver and searing, curling into a shape like a blade made of light.

She moved.

Not toward Val. Toward me.

Val saw it.

He didn't shout. Didn't hesitate.

He threw himself into my path, his shoulder slamming into mine just as the spell struck. I hit the ground hard. Stunned.

The impact caught him full across the side of the head.

He hit the cavern wall with a sickening thud and collapsed in a heap. Blood trailed from his temple, his nose. He tried to rise once, one arm braced beneath him, shaking. He made it halfway to his elbow before his body gave out, head dropping back to the stone.

And then he was still.

I scrambled to my feet, blade already in hand and turned on Asena. My first strike missed.

The torch sputtered once, then died. Blackness swallowed the cavern whole.

I drew a breath through my nose. Let it out through my mouth, slow and steady.

I had to stay calm. Had to protect him.

I'd sworn an oath to him and this one I meant to keep.

Nothing else mattered.

Asena's cold laughter echoed through the dark. "Is your will strong enough, daughter of Aelan?" Her voice lingered, then slipped into silence.

A heartbeat.

Another.

*Click.*

Claws on stone. Off to my left.

I turned toward the sound.

Closed my eyes.

Slowed my breath.

Listened.

Another click. Then another.

Claws scraping.

Lifting.

I moved on instinct.

My blade swung toward the belly of the thing that leapt.

The sword flew from my grip as we crashed to the stone in a tangle of limbs and blood and raw violence.

The weight of the creature crushed me. Forelegs pinned my chest. Jaws snapped inches from my throat, breath hot and rancid. Slaver hit my collarbone, thick, warm and slick as bile.

I reached down into my boot.

Grabbed the hilt of Val's dagger.

Slid it into her side.

I twisted the blade.

I shifted. Rolled. Wrenched the beast off balance and moved to straddle it.

Except it wasn't a beast anymore.

Just the woman.

I ripped the dagger free of her belly and drove it toward her throat, aiming for the hollow. She caught it between her hands, holding me at bay.

When I was younger, I always thought, that when things like this happened, I'd say something clever. A curse in return. A denial. A vow.

But nothing ever comes.

It's always just me and the blade and the strength it takes to kill.

Only breath. The burn in the arms.

Asena rasped the words through clenched teeth. "I name you accursed. May every life you touch wither. May every—"

The rasp in my throat as I bore down. Inch by inch, the blade slipped past her hands and found the space beneath her chin. The dagger slid in clean.

A single thrust to the hollow of her throat. No more. No less.

Just what needed doing.

And then it was over.

I realized that none of it had been real.

Not the wolves. Not the pack.

It was all just shadow. Illusion.

Drawn from fear. Fed by belief and memory.

I yanked the blade free, wiped it once on my sleeve, and stood. Shoved it into my boot.

I didn't spare the body another glance. Stepped over her and toward the wall. Val had hit it and would be close to it still.

"Val?" I called, small and quiet, caught on something raw inside my throat.

No answer.

I moved forward, one hand on the wall. I slipped once in blood. Not his. I kept going.

My foot struck something soft. I dropped to my knees and reached for him in the darkness. Tried to turn him over and couldn't. My hands were slick. I wiped them on my trousers, smearing blood from hip to thigh. Then tried again.

Once I got him on his back, I touched his face, his damp hair. His head was still in one piece, thanks be to Aelan.

"Val?" I lowered my head to his chest, heard a strong, steady heartbeat and felt breath move beneath it.

A sound tore free, half sob and half laugh.

He was alive.

"You stupid, stubborn bastard," I whispered. "You're not done. You hear me? You don't get to leave me here."

My hands searched for blood, broken bones, anything worse than what I already felt. I found nothing. I sat back on my heels, stared into the dark. My jaw clenched so tight it ached.

Val was breathing.

Asena was dead.

And there was nothing left to fight, just then.

The thoughts had barely formed before the weight came crashing down again.

The tears followed.

Ugly. Unstoppable.

My pulse thundered in my ears. Sweat slid along my temple, stinging the cut above my brow. I pressed my hands to my eyes, willing it to stop.

I tried to breathe.

Each draw caught halfway, chest tight, lungs burning.

I needed something to hold onto.

I reached for the one thing that hadn't slipped away.

Val.

I lay on the floor beside him, draped my arm over his chest. I focused on him, the rise and fall of his breath. I pressed my face into the side of his neck. The silence wrapped around us, thick and still, while I waited for Val to wake.

I stayed like that for a long time. Listening. Breathing. Making sure he was still alive.

This was my fault.

I'd come alone. I hadn't expected him to follow.

I should have.

I couldn't even die properly, and I was so godsdamned tired of surviving.

I couldn't try again—not with this stubborn, maddening, beautiful fool willing to throw himself in front of some kind of magic like I was worth dying for.

Because he lived. Because I did, too.

# CHAPTER TWENTY-SIX
## *The Storm*

*"They called her storm, not for the ruin she left behind—*
*but for the way the sky opened to let her pass."*
—The Song of the Stars, Cycle V: The Cycle of Storms

Dēwamos 60, 1230
*Aleaia*

Val groaned in the dark. I sat up and moved away, leaving no sign of how close I'd been.

"My fucking head," he muttered, voice thick with pain. "Please tell me you killed her."

"Of course I did," I said. "Do you think I'd be here tending to you if I hadn't?"

"I can't think anything right now," he said with a breath of a laugh.

I eased him upright, careful to support his weight as he sagged into me. "Easy now."

"If being hurled into walls earns me such tender care," he murmured, "I might just make it a habit."

I stood and retrieved my sword. Wiped it on the hem of my tunic, though I couldn't see if I'd cleaned it well, and slid it into the sheath. Then I turned and offered a hand and hauled him to his feet.

I put my arm around his waist and told myself he needed the stability.

"Dizzy?" I asked.

"A bit," he admitted, quieter now.

I couldn't see his face, but I felt the damp chill of his skin. His steps were sluggish, uneven. His was the kind of unsteadiness that spoke of deeper injuries. I felt my heart thud with dread.

I guided us along the wall toward the narrow passage, or where I thought it might be, if memory served.

"If you think your head hurts," I said dryly, "you should see the wall."

Val let out a faint laugh that turned into a groan. "Don't... don't make me laugh."

We stepped into the altar room, then the butchery. I tried not to look at anything, tried to hold my breath. I looked up at him, found his face pale and drawn. He needed Mariana.

In the dining hall, something pricked at the edge of hearing, so I stopped.

Weeping. Soft. Muffled.

I tilted my head, listening until I was sure it wasn't just memory echoing in my skull. I thought it came from the area they'd used as a kitchen.

"Do you hear that?" I asked him.

"All I hear is the ringing in my ears."

Inside the kitchen, I guided him toward a crate near the wall and lowered him down to sit on it. He winced as his weight settled.

"Try not to fall asleep while I find where it's coming from," I said, softer than before.

"This is the last place I want to take a nap," Val said, leaning back against the wall. He pressed the thumb and middle finger of one hand to his temples.

I took a torch from its holder and followed the sound toward the far end of the chamber. The light flickered across blood-stained stone and broken tools. In the corner, it caught on a door—heavy, reinforced with bands of iron. A rusted padlock hung from the latch.

The weeping, faint and muted, came from behind it.

"They're here," I called back to Val. "The women. I wondered where they were."

"Do you need me to—"

"No." I glanced back at him. "You stay there. I'll take care of it."

I crossed to the butcher's table. Among the scattered tools, I found a rusted meat hook and a heavy mallet. Either would do. Together, they'd do better.

I wedged the torch into a bracket beside the door, then pressed the hook's tip into the narrow gap between padlock and hasp. Lifting the mallet with both hands, I brought it down. The impact rang through the room. The lock held.

I struck it again. Metal groaned but didn't yield.

On the third swing, the rusted shell split open. The padlock cracked and fell to the floor with a dull clang. I pushed the door inward, hinges shrieking in protest.

The stench hit me first, rolling out in a thick, suffocating wave of fear and filth layered together and clinging to everything it touched.

Torchlight fell across the room beyond. Gods, the neglect. Animals were treated better than this. The women were hollow-eyed, dirt-streaked, far too thin. A cluster of them cowered in the dark, shackled to the wall, others huddling against the stone floor, arms wrapped around themselves, as if trying to vanish into the cold.

They stared up at me in silence, wide-eyed, wary, and disbelieving.

"It's over," I said in Aeltyrian, stepping carefully inside. "She's dead. They're all dead. You're safe now."

A glance around revealed the keys to their irons hanging on the wall near the door, just out of reach. I took them, moved slowly to the nearest woman and knelt beside her.

"You're free," I said softly. "You're all free now."

One by one, I freed the rest. Some flinched from my touch, their shoulders curling in fear. Others wept. A few stared until their limbs remembered how to move. They rose and followed the others toward the exit.

"When you leave the cave," I said as they passed, "head west. You'll reach Gormlaith by midday."

They didn't speak, just moved silent as ghosts with breath still clinging to them. When the last woman vanished into the dark beyond, I went back to Val. He was exactly where I'd left him, upright and watching me.

"Thanks be to Lithau," I sighed. "You stayed awake."

"I told you I would."

I helped him up, looping his arm around my shoulders again.

"You saved them," he said. "All of them."

I heard what he didn't say, that it was a good thing I'd survived to find them.

"I couldn't leave them," I said.

"I know," he murmured. "Didn't think you would."

I wasn't sure what to say, so I said nothing.

"You're a good person, Aleaia."

I'd let him keep the illusion, this time. "Don't tell anyone," I said.

His lips twitched, a flicker of a smile, half-formed and gone again.

Together, we made our way out of the cave mouth. Dawn bled into the sky, gray and weak. Val blinked against the light. On we went, into the forest and toward Gormlaith.

I worried more with every step that he might go down, and I wouldn't be able to get him up. I'd have to hope someone would realize he was missing and come looking for him.

Lucius would be waking soon, if he wasn't already. And he would be furious.

I glanced up at Val and caught him looking at me, patiently expectant.

"What?" I asked, as if I didn't know he was waiting for the conversation we hadn't finished.

"We have to talk about it sometime," he said.

"I should've left you in there." I meant it in jest. He didn't laugh, so I went on. "Following me into that den was perhaps the most foolish thing you've ever done."

"I don't know if it's the most foolish," he said. "But it ranks high. I just couldn't bear the thought of you facing that alone. Fortunately for you."

He wasn't wrong. Without him, I would never have survived. I'd be—

Gods, I couldn't even think about it.

"You're right," I said. "I don't think I would've made it back without you, either."

"I'm glad you agree. Tell Lucius when we get back, would you?" Val said, his gaze drifting toward the path ahead as he sobered. "I meant it when I said I feared losing you in that place."

"I know," I said simply.

"Did you mean it?" he asked abruptly. "When you said you meant to die in there?"

I breathed in, slow and shaky. The air scraped in like it had to claw its way past everything I couldn't say.

"I don't know," I lied. "I can't answer that."

The silence stretched between us as we walked. Guilt crept in. I owed him more than that silence, more than a lie. After everything, I owed him at least some of the truth.

"My father," I said, forcing the words out. "My grandparents. Everyone who matters to me ends up dead. I almost lost you, last night." My voice came harsher than I meant it to, too bitter. Too bare. "The only thing you all have in common is me. And the things I did. The things I let happen when I was…"

I shook my head. I couldn't finish it. Couldn't name it out loud and see the way he'd look at me afterward.

"Maybe I did mean to die in there," I said, voice quieter now. "Maybe I thought that would make things easier for everyone."

He still said nothing, and the silence felt like judgment.

"I already know what you're going to say," I said, bitter enough to taste it. "You'll tell me it isn't my fault. That I didn't choose any of this. That none of it matters."

When he did speak, finally, it was soft. "I wasn't going to say that."

I stopped walking. Slipped out from under his arm and turned to face him, frowning. "What? Why not?"

He met my gaze without flinching. "I was going to say…" He hesitated, brow furrowed. His hand rose, fingers brushing lightly against my cheek. "What's this? Tears?"

"No," I said quickly. "Just blood, I think." I turned my face away. As if he wouldn't know the difference. Of course he'd be able to tell the difference. He wasn't blind.

"There's blood. But there are tears here too." His thumb followed the trail they'd left on my skin. "Why?" he asked softly.

"I thought…" My voice caught. I lifted a hand to my mouth, trying to hold back the sob that still broke through. "I thought you were... I thought it was just like... that I lost you, too."

"Oh. Aleaia," he said, pulling me close, arms firmly around me, one hand cradling my head to his chest. "I'm not going anywhere."

I didn't answer. Just leaned in, eyes closed, anchoring to the rhythm of his heart, the warmth of him, solid and alive. I let one shuddering breath go, let the tears fall as my arms slid around his waist, then quieter.

And he held me through it.

When I finally pulled back, wiping my face on my sleeve, my voice came smaller than I meant it to. I looked down at my hands. "What were you going to say?"

"I was going to say I don't care."

My eyes snapped up to his. "You—what?"

"I don't care," he said again, softer now. "Not about your so-called curse. Not about how dangerous it might be to stay."

Frustration sparked quick and hot beneath my ribs. "That's reckless."

"No, it isn't." He shook his head. "You're not a curse, Aleaia. You're a storm. And I'd rather be struck by lightning than spend my life watching from a distance."

The words hit somewhere I didn't have words for. Buried deep, beneath the armor I'd made of all the guilt and shame and fear.

"That's not a good reason," I said softly, raggedly.

"It might not be," he said. "But it's mine."

He swayed. I caught him without thinking, hands firm on his arms to steady him. He was too close, his gaze too sharp, too direct. I tried to hold it. Tried not to look away.

My eyes flicked to his lips. Just for a second.

A mistake.

My heart kicked hard in my chest.

I wanted him to—

No. I couldn't even think about it.

His expression shifted suddenly to panic, before he stepped back. "I'm… excuse me."

He turned sharply to brace himself against a nearby tree, then retched, long and hard, as people often did when they took a hit to the head.

Relief and sympathy tangled in my chest, knotted tight. The moment had broken, but maybe it needed to. Maybe neither of us was ready for what it could've become.

I followed without hesitation, hand settling lightly between his shoulder blades. I rubbed his back slowly. "I'm that revolting, eh?"

He wiped his mouth with a trembling hand. "I'm sorry. It came on so suddenly."

"Don't be," I said, softer. Warmer. "You'll feel better."

When he stood upright, I stepped in close again, shifted his arm over my shoulder once more.

"Come on," I said. "Let's get you back to town."

We walked in silence, his words echoing louder than the forest around us. He said he didn't care what standing beside me might cost him.

I did. That much was unchanged.

But I knew I would never again walk into the dark and leave him to find me only in words on a page.

# CHAPTER TWENTY-SEVEN
## *Burdens*

*"The wind does not weep for what it carries—*
*only the ones who must walk against it."*
—Song of the Stars, Cycle V: The Cycle of Storms

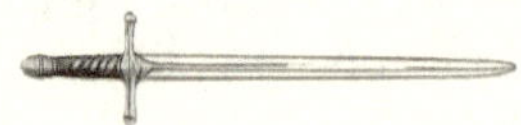

Dēwamos 62, 1230
*Aleaia*

We spent the next two days recovering from what Asena left behind.

It felt wrong, somehow, that people called me Wolfsbane for it. That they lifted their cups in the tavern and sang songs that made it sound like I'd faced the entire den alone.

Val got nothing but a scathing lecture from Lucius for charging in after me alone.

And yet, I understood it, because I felt the same.

On the final evening in Gormlaith, I stepped into the longhouse. Val was inside, under orders to rest, though I doubted he was following them. At the threshold to the bedchamber, I paused, letting my eyes adjust to the dimmer light.

He sat on the edge of the bed, shirtless save for the bandage wrapped tight around his head. He was adjusting it with one hand, fingers working carefully across the cloth.

He looked up.

He wouldn't know the way he looked when the fading light cut across his jaw, or how the tension in his shoulders made every muscle stand out in sharp relief. Bruised and bandaged as he was, the strength beneath it still showed.

"Dieter, about time you got here. It's nearly sundown," Lucius said, rising from a chair beside the bed. I hadn't even seen him there.

I felt heat rise in my face before I could stop it. Had he seen?

"I thought you'd show up earlier," he said. "Give me a little time to prepare."

"Everything's done," I said. "Mariana said he could sit up?"

"She did. I heard it myself. Though he'll probably need to lie back down soon."

"I'm right here," Val muttered, glaring at both of us.

"See? Already cranky." Lucius grinned and clapped me on the shoulder as he passed. "Don't be too hard on him. If you need anything, shout. I'll be just outside."

"I will."

The door shut behind him.

I stepped closer, peering down at Val. "I should let you languish in the wagon for ten days, and then, finally, when you start complaining and threatening, I'll ride up and say…"

I let a teasing edge slip into my voice as I adopted an exaggerated version of Val's clipped Calesian. "You look like you're in need of a rescue."

He groaned, probably at both the impression and the truth of it. "I don't sound like that, do I?"

"You do." I unbuckled my sword belt and dropped it beside the empty chair at the bedside, sinking onto the seat with a quiet exhale. "How are you feeling?"

"My head only feels like it's being hammered on an anvil when I sit up like this." He rubbed the back of his neck. "By the Creator, it's hot in here. How was your day?"

I started on the buckles of my bracers. "Long, but manageable. Not worth the breath to complain about. Nox is sulking. He and Argenti both need a proper run."

"I'm not going to be able to ride for a while."

"It doesn't have to be you, does it?" I moved on to the breastplate. "I'll make sure he gets what he needs."

He still sat too stiffly, his balance off, breathing shallow in that way pain forces on the body, like he couldn't tell which part of his body hurt the worst.

I paused to look at him. "The wagoner finished today. It'll be more comfortable than it was when I was in it."

I eased the breastplate off, sore in all the usual places. The floorboards creaked beneath as I crouched to unstrap the greaves from my shins. When I looked up again, he was shifting, trying to recline.

"Wait," I said, halfway rising. "Not too fast."

He stopped, one arm braced behind him on the mattress.

I stepped in, steadying his shoulders. "Easy. Slowly."

A faint smile pulled at his mouth. "You're starting to sound like Mariana."

"Oh? A high compliment indeed."

"If only you'd been so diligent when you were the injured one."

I laughed. "I follow instructions just fine for other people."

He didn't argue. Just moved with caution, every shift slow and measured.

It was easier to bear everything else, somehow, with someone to look after. Someone who needed me. When I could focus on him, I didn't have to think about everything I couldn't fix. Everything I'd already lost.

I returned to the chair and finished removing the last of my armor. My hands moved with the rhythm of habit, each piece set aside in order beside his. When I was done, I sat back, let the stillness settle, then reached into my satchel.

The book was worn, the brown leather cover thinned and softened by time and use and hands. The gold lettering on the spine had faded almost completely.

Despite the risk of discovery and the consequences that would follow, I had carried my father's copy of *Te Canil atē Aelilí—The Song of the Stars*—with me all my life, ever since my father died. Val's gaze flicked to my hands, curiosity clear in his expression.

"I thought you might be bored," I said, not quite meeting his eyes as I propped my feet on the edge of the bed. "Figured I'd read for us for a bit."

"If I fall asleep," he murmured, "it won't be a comment on your delivery."

"Of course it will be," I said, flipping the book open. "But I'll take it as a compliment, if you sleep well."

I turned to the first page, cleared my throat, and began.

"Ere dawn first broke and time begun,
The world lay still, beneath no sun.
Then Lithau wept, and from her grief,
The waters flowed, both wild and deep."

Val said nothing. Just watched me, eyes steady, silent.

"Her breath became the roaming gale,
Her mind, the spark in fire's veil.
She tore her flesh to birth the land,
The hills and stone, the soil and sand.

Her blood she gave—red, bright, and rare,
To thread the ether through the air.
And when her gift was spent and done,
The world she left, and stars were spun."

It felt strange, hearing it in Calesian, even if I was only translating for Val's sake. The lines felt thinner, like something essential had been scraped off in the translation.

"It sounds different in Calesian," I said. "The rhythm is off."

His gaze flicked to me. "Then read it how it's meant to sound."

I hesitated. "In Aeltyrian?"

"I want to hear it the way you learned it."

My eyes darted to the windows. They were open. Anyone passing could hear.

"The Lithaun version is already illegal," he added, a spark of mischief glinting behind the sincerity. "If we get caught, it should be worth the consequences."

I sighed but couldn't quite suppress the smile tugging at the edge of my mouth.

Sliding my feet off the bed, I pulled my chair closer, propped my arm on the bed, and started again.

*"Bres aura brisin et elenin cauril, Te veriden lanin mar, piteu nae auril..."*

The words flowed without effort. I didn't think about grammar or inflection. They came from somewhere older than memory, a place deeper than blood. When the verse ended, I looked up.

His eyes were closed, but he spoke.

*"Dearel tó, domaviraos."*

I went still.

*Thank you, my lady*. Genuine gratitude, said like I meant something to him.

I watched him for a breath too long. Something inside me twisted in recognition. Of how much he'd listened. Of how much he saw.

My thumb traced the worn edge of the cover. The book felt heavier than usual.

"What's wrong?" he asked gently, as he had done often since we came back from Asena's cave.

I glanced up at Val, then back down at the book. His presence steadied me. The rhythm of his breath. The steadiness of his voice. It was enough to let me breathe again.

In that moment, I thought of the illusions. The memories that had never stopped gnawing, even before Asena forced me to face them again.

And I wondered how much I could tell him.

"I've been thinking about our conversation after the cave."

His brow furrowed slightly. "Which part?"

I picked at my fingernail. "The part where I told you I thought I was a curse."

His expression softened. "What about it?"

It felt like being stripped down in public. Laid bare. Exposed. "If you're too tired, I can wait—"

"I'm fine," he said, voice gentle. "Let me help you carry it."

I exhaled. Set the book on the mattress. Rested my hands on top of it.

Val didn't move. Didn't rush me. Just waited.

"She started with my father. Made me watch him die. Not twisted. Not changed. Just... as it happened. Like I was back there again."

My fingers curled against the spine of the book.

He didn't speak, but I felt his attention, steady and patient as I searched for the words.

"There were other ones," I said. My voice came thinner now. Strained. "Not just him."

I tried to keep going, made a mess of it.

"The terrible... things I did. Taran Caerwyn. From Lhannor. He—he trusted me. I told him they'd be safe." My throat closed around the words. "And the others. Catan Row. Caerlan. I remember their names but not their faces anymore. Just screams. Smoke. Blood on stone." I swallowed. "A boy asked me if I could teach him the sword. And I said yes. And then they—"

The rest broke apart inside me. I couldn't say it. I couldn't shape the memory into anything that would make sense out loud. I covered my face with one hand, not to hide, just to keep something in.

"I'm sorry," I said. "I wanted to say more. I tried. I just... I can't." I lowered my hand slowly and looked down at the book again. "I can say one thing, though. I don't know what would've happened if you hadn't found me. Either night."

My voice caught, but I made myself finish.

"So while I'm furious that you risked yourself and ended up hurt... I'm also grateful."

The silence that followed didn't press. It held.

When he didn't answer right away, uncertainty twisted in my gut. Was he judging me? Did he think less of me?

I dared a glance, swallowed past the lump in my throat.

"Please," I whispered. "Say something."

Val drew a slow, steady breath. "I'm sorry. What she did to you was monstrous. I can't imagine how deeply that must've wounded you."

I don't know what I hoped he'd say, but that wasn't it. My throat closed again. My vision blurred at the edges.

"Look at me, Aleaia."

I did.

"There will never be a moment when you're in danger that I won't come for you," he said, voice low and clear. "No matter the cost. I couldn't live in a world where you didn't exist."

"I'm your guard—" I started.

"Not just that."

He reached out, hand open, palm up.

I placed my hand in his, fingers trembling as his wrapped around them. His grip was warm, strong, roughened like mine, calloused by use, and shaped by everything we'd both survived. Warmth stirred in my chest, slow and unexpected, like the tide coming in.

His thumb moved across the backs of my fingers, steady and light.

"I have to tell you something," he said. "The things you've endured, the things you had to do... they're not your fault. Neither was what happened to your father."

I started to speak, to argue, but he squeezed my hand. "Please. Let me finish."

He had listened to every word I'd forced myself to say. I owed him the same.

"I'm listening."

"We were already nearby," he said. "Traveling south, along the same road we'll take tomorrow. Our camp was two miles from the clearing. Those men, your father's killers, they snuck in, stole weapons and coin. One of our guards failed to raise the alarm."

He went very still.

"We tracked them," he said. "I was young. Impetuous. Newly given command. We had numbers, but we weren't quiet. Too much steel. Too much arrogance. They slipped away from us until you and your father drew them out."

Silence stretched.

"I've wished a thousand times we'd reached you sooner. Especially when I see what it's done to you. How deeply it marked you." He sighed. "I'm sorry, Aleaia."

I shook my head. "You couldn't have done anything differently."

"And neither could you," he said gently.

I hadn't realized I was staring at him until the words reached all the way down.

"You're nothing like I expected a prince to be."

He laughed softly. "What does that mean?"

My hand tingled in his. I could feel the flush rise in my cheeks before I looked down. "You're... open. Warm. Real."

"I wasn't raised at court," he said. "I grew up in the countryside, at my mother's estate. Then Elisedd. Mostly farmers and soldiers. Thank the Creator for that."

The quiet returned. It wasn't heavy this time, but full.

I could feel it again, that weight in my chest. The thing I hadn't asked yet. The thing I needed to. I looked back at him.

"I have a favor to ask," I said.

His eyes met mine. "Anything within my power."

The words echoed my own, spoken to him when I accepted his offer, in Avitum. Now they returned to me, tender, unflinching.

I hesitated, choosing the right place to begin.

"A few days from now, we'll be near the place where my father..."

No. That wasn't right. Too formal. Like I was briefing a superior officer.

I swallowed and tried again.

"Will you go with me to see him? When we pass near his burial site?"

He didn't even pause. "Yes. I would go anywhere with you."

The relief settled into my shoulders like a weight I hadn't realized I'd been holding.

His gaze didn't leave mine. "Did you want to see the village too?"

I shook my head. "No. I think just seeing him is enough."

The hush that followed was the kind that brings all the heavier thoughts back to the surface.

It still wasn't safe for him.

And he... he was beginning to matter more than I could admit, no matter how hard I resisted.

But maybe it had never been my choice to make.

I curled my fingers tighter around his. He didn't pull away.

And neither did I.

# CHAPTER TWENTY-EIGHT
## *What Comes Next*

*"The past is not the path ahead,*
*Though oft we walk where sorrow bled.*
*Lay down thy grief, but not thy name,*
*The stars forget not whence we came."*
—The Song of the Stars, Cycle VIII: The Cycle of Mortals

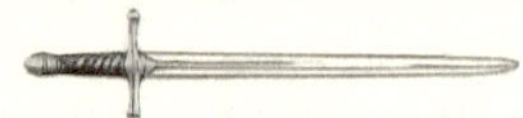

Dēwamos 68, 1230
*Aleaia*

I huffed, swatting at the cloud of biting insects hovering around my face. "Why are they only biting me?"

"You must be delicious," Val said from behind, laughter threading through his words.

"Maybe I just smell better than you do."

He chuckled. "Probably do."

It wasn't lost on me, how often he laughed now. How easily the teasing came. Since Gormlaith, something had shifted between us. His flirtation wasn't subtle anymore, no longer hidden behind formality.

And I liked teasing him, too. Making him laugh.

The memory of his hand in mine lingered like warmth against my skin.

What would it feel like to close the distance between us? To lean in and kiss him?

My breath caught a little. I bit the inside of my cheek and looked ahead, as if the thought might be scrawled across my face.

I didn't live in a world where things like that happened. Physical closeness was one thing—sharing quarters, sparring, bleeding beside someone on the battlefield.

But this?

This was different.

There was no room for affection in the auxiliaries. And after I bought my freedom, there had never been time to want, and even if there had been, it would have been forbidden.

I'd broken the rules and kissed a boy, once. Just once.

He died in Tuath, the next day.

And that was it. I'd never tried again. Never wanted to.

Val hadn't grown up that way. He'd been betrothed. Nobles pretended to value chastity because the Anvallan Temple demanded it, but everyone knew the truth. And he would know all the things I didn't.

Heat crept across my cheeks, and I was grateful for the sunlight that masked what my face might reveal.

"We should be there soon," he said.

I pushed thoughts of him, in that way, from my mind. Did a poor job of it.

Before long, the trees began to thin.

The clearing opened.

I stopped. My breath snagged at the sight.

Where once there had been only bare earth, wildflowers bloomed in a riot of color.

The grave I remembered had been nothing but a shallow wound in the earth, dug through frozen soil and grief. I had scraped his name into a splintering piece of wood with bloodied hands.

A black granite marker stood in its place, tall and carved and polished smooth. A rectangular slab, the length of the man beneath it, marked the grave.

I stepped forward, then again, until I stood at the foot of the grave. My fingers clenched in the fabric of my tunic, the only thing holding me upright while I read the inscription.

*Jurian Dieter*
*Beloved father*
*Brave defender of Aeltyria*

My eyes caught on the last line.

Val stood just behind me, silent.

"Val..." My voice broke on his name. I turned toward him. "How...?"

"The first two lines are yours," he said. "The last, I asked the mason to add after what you told me about him."

I looked at him fully now, the knot in my throat too tight to dislodge. "Why would you do this?"

His brow furrowed slightly. "Because it mattered to you."

As if it were the most obvious thing.

He stepped closer. Wiped a tear from my cheek, cupped my face in his hands. "Because I saw you," he said. "That was enough."

I knew it was because we were on the edge of something I wasn't meant to have.

I had no language for what this was. Only the certainty that it couldn't last. Men like Val did not linger. They passed through lives like mine and moved on.

I stepped back before I could let the moment tip into something else.

He let his hands fall. Rubbed the back of his neck, color rising along it. "I'm sorry."

"There's nothing to apologize for," I said softly. "I'm... I'm just…"

He searched my face, waiting patiently for me to finish.

I sighed. "It's dangerous for you."

His jaw tensed. "I told you—"

"Not that," I said. "What's... what's happening here. This—whatever it is—is not allowed."

He turned away, focused on something in the distance, and nodded slowly. "You'd pay the higher price for it."

That wasn't it. But I'd let him believe it, if it kept him a safe distance from me.

I looked down at the grave. "You've given me more than I know how to repay."

I felt his eyes on me again and lifted mine to meet them.

"Aleaia." His voice was firm. "I don't offer you these things because I expect repayment. I wouldn't accept it if you tried."

"But if your father hears—"

"He's my problem to deal with. And I'll deal with that when it comes. If it comes," he said. "I won't let them use you against me."

That broke something open.

I stepped into him and wrapped my arms around him, my head on his chest.

He pulled me in, steady and warm, chin resting against my hair, and sighed.

We stood in silence, in relief, surrounded by stone and wildflowers and the wind in the trees.

"Thank you, Val," I whispered.

And meant it, down to the marrow.

# CHAPTER TWENTY-NINE
## *Aeldunon*

*"Orphaned children of Aeltyrian blood are to be placed under Imperial care until deemed fit for labor, conscription, or reassignment. Names may be altered for ease of record. Instruction in the Aeltyrian tongue is prohibited."*
—Imperial Decree CXLII, Concerning Native Wards, Year 1208

Dēwamos 76, 1230
*Aleaia*

As we neared Aeldunon, the city rose on the horizon, a mass of towering black granite walls and steep-gabled roofs clustered like the darkened bones of a giant. Sunlight struck the upper quarter, casting long shadows through the narrow lanes. At its heart, Aeldunon Castle loomed, its obsidian spires carved like spears.

Outside the walls, fields stretched across the valley, golden with harvest and scored with narrow irrigation ditches. Roads wound through them like veins, all drawing us toward the open maw of the southern gate.

I rode beside Val and Lucius. For them, this was familiar ground. For me, it was the first glimpse of a city I'd only heard of in the stories my father told.

Aeldunon. The seat of Aeltyria.

Once ours. Now theirs.

The place my father had meant to bring me, seven years past.

"It's so much larger than I imagined," I said, not meaning to speak aloud, but the wonder gave me away.

Lucius turned, the corner of his mouth lifting before he looked away.

I caught the expression too late and narrowed my eyes. Heat crept up my cheeks.

"Oh, spare me," I said.

"No idea what you mean," he said, far too innocent for the gleam in his eye.

Val cleared his throat and urged his horse ahead. "I'm starving," he said. "Let's keep going. I'm ready for a proper meal."

We rode on.

The next two hours passed in practiced rhythm. Three cohorts moved in unison, footfalls drumming against the old road, kicking up dust that settled behind us like ash. Farmers stopped their work to stare. Some straightened slowly. Most only lifted their heads, staring in silence.

A courier had gone ahead to herald our approach, and the South Gate stood open when we arrived. Val rode at the front, every inch the prince of Calesia. His silver armor caught the light like a drawn blade, and the deep blue of his cloak rippled behind him, proud and deliberate.

I followed just behind, black drake-scale armor glinting with a subtler sheen, like a rainbow if you could see one at night. I'd never owned anything like it. The quality was unmatched. Of course it had been a gift from Val, after Gormlaith. He'd intended to give it to me upon arrival to Aeldunon but couldn't wait.

"Since you're determined to run headlong into danger," he'd said wryly when I'd opened the box.

I thought about that moment again, while we rode into Aeldunon. How I'd tried to refuse, because it was too elaborate. What would people think, if he gave me a set of armor fit for royalty?

"I wouldn't invite scrutiny like that," he'd reassured me. "Lucius got one too."

So he had paid a royal sum for *two* sets of armor: one to protect my body, and the other to protect my reputation. The thought warmed me to the core.

The streets of Aeldunon greeted us with the same watchfulness we'd found in the fields. Faces appeared behind glass. Shopkeepers in the market stalls froze mid-motion. Children pointed even as they clung to their mothers' legs, wide-eyed and silent.

Calesian banners fluttered from stone balconies, but here and there, the old city showed through—carvings too deep to erase, faded knotwork along doorways, a broken mosaic in a crumbling wall.

The city was scarred. Maybe with Val overseeing, it would heal.

Halfway down the main thoroughfare to the castle, we passed an old stone building with a crooked lintel and sagging cornice. A group of children stood on the steps with a woman in a plain blue dress. She was likely the matron.

They waved as we passed, small hands rising in eager arcs.

I expected Val to nod or toss them a pouch of sweets, like he had in other towns. Instead, he raised a hand and called a halt. The command rippled down the line. The column slowed until it drew to a stop.

My eyes went wide. This wasn't part of the route. We'd gone over it twice this morning. There was no stop planned at the orphanage.

"What are you doing?" I hissed as he dismounted.

Val was already moving, confident and unhurried, as though this detour had always been his plan.

I slid from Argenti and hurried to catch up. "My lord. Please wait."

Lucius joined me, speaking quietly enough that only I could hear. "Now you see the real Val. The one who doesn't listen."

The matron—delicate, fair-haired, Calesian—turned, gathering the children. "Remember your manners, boys and girls."

She dipped into a curtsy. The children followed, some more graceful than others.

Val removed his helm and tucked it under one arm. His voice was warm. "Good afternoon, madam. Hello, little ones. What brings you out today?"

A few ducked behind the matron's skirts. Others peeked around her, curiosity winning out. I counted seven in all.

One boy, five or six, stepped forward on unsteady legs. "We came to see the soldiers!"

Lucius leaned in, voice dry. "Children adore him, and he encourages it. I'll never understand either."

Val knelt, posture easy. The children edged closer, drawn in without hesitation. He made it look effortless. I pressed my lips together, fighting a smile.

"Did you?" he asked, voice softened at the edges. "Now that you've seen them, what do you think? Do they pass muster?"

"They're so big and strong!" the boy said, bouncing on his toes.

Val chuckled. "They are. But it takes years of training. Strength, yes, but courage, too. And heart."

Another boy squinted up at him. "Are you a knight?"

"I am. My name is Val, and I've been given the important job of helping care for this city and its people." He turned toward me. "This is Aleaia, one of my most skilled warriors. She's one of the bravest, kindest people I know."

My face went hot, though I tried to keep it still.

"*Ara es Aeltyrii, laun em!*" a girl exclaimed, eyes shining with recognition.

The matron turned sharply. "In Calesian, child. Another slip, and it's the rod for you."

The girl's smile faltered. She ducked her head. "Sorry, mistress."

I swallowed the vitriol that came by reflex. I knew that feeling better than I wanted to think about, but I couldn't let my anger get the best of me in front of children.

Before I could speak, Val stepped in. "Yes," he said gently in Calesian. "You're right. She is Aeltyrian. Just like you."

I narrowed my eyes at him. I had been trying to teach him and thought he was a poor student who understood little.

The girl peeked up at him, eyes wide, uncertain, then smiled again.

He turned to the rest. "And this," he said, gesturing to Lucius, "is one of our household guard. His name is Lucius. One of our finest soldiers, even if his face doesn't look like it."

Lucius inclined his head, arms folded, long-suffering to the bone.

A boy peered up at him. "Is he always that grumpy?"

I turned slightly, biting back a grin. Val's mouth twitched, caught between amusement and pride.

Lucius didn't blink. "Smiling's a slippery slope," he said. "First you smile, then they expect you to talk to people."

The children erupted in giggles.

I leaned toward him. "Careful. You're endearing yourself."

"Stars forbid," he muttered.

Another child pointed at his sword, eyes wide. "Is that the Fellglow Blade?"

Val sighed. "I'm afraid not. Just a plain old sword."

The boy stepped forward again, bright-eyed. "When I grow up, I want to be a knight. Not just a soldier."

I felt my heart drop. This poor boy was about to get his heart broken. There had been no Aeltyrian knights since Cadoc Aneirin, the First Sword of Queen Eavan. The order was gone.

His voice stayed calm. "I have no doubt you will be. But remember, being a knight isn't about armor or titles. A true knight is brave, kind, and protects those who can't protect themselves. If you hold to that, you're already halfway there."

One of the boys tugged at Val's arm. When he leaned in, the boy whispered something in his ear.

Val listened, nodded, and flushed faintly above his gorget. "Perhaps one day," he said, glancing at me, "but not yet."

I raised a brow. What was that about?

He only stood and turned to the matron. "Are you in charge of these children?"

"I am, my lord," she said, dipping into a curtsy. "Serena Dumos."

"Miss Dumos," Val said gently, "are there other orphanages in the city?"

"No, my lord. We're the only one. Seventy children, six caretakers."

Val reached into the pouch on his belt and withdrew a small bag of coins. "Use this for their needs—food, clothing, repairs. If more is required, send word to me at the castle."

She accepted the bag, eyes wide. "Thank you, my lord. This is generous… and very much appreciated. And thank you for stopping, my lord. This meant so much to them. I'm sure they'll talk about it for days."

"You're welcome." Val turned to go, then stopped.

"One last thing. Children should never be punished for speaking the words their mothers taught them. If I hear of it, the consequence will fall on the one who raised the rod."

The matron paled and nodded. "I only meant to follow the law, my lord—"

"I am the law here now."

I swallowed. Hard.

She held his gaze for a long moment before dipping into a deep curtsy. "Yes, my lord."

We left them there in the afternoon light and turned toward the horses. Lucius moved to Val's right. I to his left.

"I had no idea you were so fond of children," I said softly.

"They're the most vulnerable of us all," he replied. "And they're our future. If we don't nurture them, we deserve what comes next."

Lucius shook his head as he swung into the saddle. "If we stop for every wide-eyed child, we won't reach the castle until moonrise."

Val mounted with ease. "Afraid of the dark, Lucius?"

The formation shifted. The road opened again before us.

"What did he whisper to you?" I asked.

Val adjusted his reins. "I'll tell you later. Wave to them."

I did, lifting a hand, casting one last smile toward the children.

I glanced back. The children were still waving, Serena gathering them into a neat line. Their joy hadn't faded. The street, once silent, now murmured with cautious interest. I saw faces in upper windows. Shopkeepers leaning out.

The prince had stopped for orphans, and left coin behind.

I turned toward Val as we resumed pace. "Why would you promise the boy he could become a knight? That title's forbidden."

"You're as full of questions as they were," he said, a spark in his eye. "Let's just say I never make a promise I can't keep."

What in the gods' names was that supposed to mean?

"The building they were living in was once a school," I said. "For younger children."

He looked at me, curious. "A school for nobles? All the way down here?"

"No. It was for all children. Until twelve or thirteen, when they apprenticed. That was before my time. But once, every one of our—*their* children was taught in such places."

I caught the subtle shift in his expression when I corrected myself.

"Only tyrants fear educated people," he said.

I gave a small nod. We rode a few paces in silence before he spoke again.

"You needn't correct yourself with me."

My chest tightened. I turned to look at him.

He was watching, steady and quiet. No teasing. No pressure.

I looked away, but the warmth behind my ribs didn't fade.

It pressed there, unrelenting.

Something deep. Steady.

And that's when I realized what it was—the warmth I felt when he was near, the way his presence steadied me, the way my thoughts kept returning to his lips.

It was the most dangerous feeling of all.

Like falling from a high place and being powerless to stop it.

I *was* falling—falling in love with him.

# CHAPTER THIRTY
## *Idle Hours*

*"Idleness gets soldiers killed. If your sword's not in use, sharpen it. If your mind's not in use, gods help the man beside you."*
—Lucius Tutela, during Aleaia's first season in the legion

Dēwamos 86, 1230
*Aleaia*

"Here, carry this," Mariana said, thrusting a chest of medicines into my arms without a hint of sympathy.

I accepted it with a grunt, the weight shifting against my shoulder. "I miss when you cared about my health."

She set a second chest on top.

"What about my back?" I peered around the stack. "Surely I'm too fragile for labor. I could reopen something."

"You've been cleared for duty for several decadia," she said, waving me off. "Time to rebuild your strength. What better way than hauling things for me?"

I narrowed my eyes. "Is that your professional recommendation, as a healer?"

"Aye."

The laugh escaped me before I could stop it.

She hefted another chest for herself and led the way to the infirmary. I followed, careful not to shift the weight too far to one side. The room was clean and spacious with eight patient beds and a private chamber off to the side. Mariana crossed to a long table and dropped her chest with a thud, then began to unpack it. I set mine down next to it.

"I asked his lordship if I might borrow you for the day," she said, already organizing supplies.

My brows rose. "You asked him?"

"He consented."

"No one thought I should be asked?" I said dryly.

"You'd have said yes." She just kept sorting bottles without sparing me a glance. "I need to go foraging. We've barely spoken since Elisedd. I thought we could catch up."

"Today?"

"When else?"

I sighed. "I was planning to wander aimlessly until something interesting happened. Where are we going?"

"The forest north of the city. I'll show you around on the way."

"When should we leave?"

Mariana shrugged. "Now, if it suits you."

I straightened, brushing dust from my palms. "Let me inform his lordship. I'll return shortly."

"I'll be here," she said as I left the infirmary, headed toward the great hall.

Truthfully, I didn't mind the idea of escaping the city for a few hours. The open air would do me good. Since arriving in Aeldunon a decadium before, I'd had more idle time than at any point since joining the legion. I'd thought unfilled hours would feel like freedom.

They didn't. Not entirely.

And Val's distance hadn't helped.

He'd grown more cautious since we visited my father's grave. More still since we'd arrived. Like I'd tugged too hard on a thread I wasn't meant to touch. Maybe I'd broken something.

I shook the thought away as I entered the hall.

Inside, Val was presiding over court. Lucius stood behind and to his left. Marcus perched nearby on a stool.

My heart clenched at the sight of Val. He wore nothing elaborate, just a linen shirt and black breeches, but even that cut through me. Clean lines. Command worn like a second skin. I hadn't meant to feel so much.

I'd stopped pretending, you see, at least to myself. I'd admitted to my soul that my heart belonged to him, but that was as far as it went. Surrendering to that truth would endanger us both.

Maybe he'd realized that too. Maybe that's why he kept his distance.

It was smart, even if it felt wrong.

Val looked up. Our eyes met. He gestured for me to approach.

I moved forward, kneeling at the bottom of the dais steps.

"Dieter, rise," he said softly.

I stood and climbed the stairs. I pulled the mask of indifference into place. My pulse betrayed me anyway. It always did near him.

At his side, I leaned in, catching the scent of leather, clean linen, and bay soap—his, familiar and warm. I tried not to breathe him in and failed. Something in my chest kicked once, hard enough to be inconvenient.

"What did I tell you about kneeling to me?" he murmured, mock-stern.

I didn't smile, but I wanted to.

"I came to say I'll be in the northern woods with Mariana," I said, a little more breathless than I'd have liked. "Likely until sunset."

He gave a small nod. "Be careful. If you're not back by nightfall, I'll come looking for you myself."

"I will," I said.

I left the castle on Argenti with Mariana not long after. The streets of Aeldunon unfurled ahead, cobbled, and winding, carved from black granite like the rest of the city. I let Argenti pick his pace, guiding him through the slow churn of midday bustle.

Calesians often called Aeltyria a land of savages, thinking it provincial and primitive, but the city's design said otherwise. It was practical. Enduring. Beautiful. Thick-walled stone buildings drank in the sun's warmth and held it through the cold months.

We passed market stalls clustered around the square, where vendors called out and Calesian and Aeltyrian children darted between carts. The North Gate's broad arches rose ahead, its squat towers worn smooth by wind and time.

Beyond it, the city gave way to open country. Fields stretched in neat squares, hemmed by hedgerows and stone fences. The Drustan River wound through the farmland, silver-bright as it passed beneath a stout bridge. On the other side, the woods waited.

"What are we looking for?" I asked.

"Hypericum and tanacetum," she said without a moment's hesitation.

There were few times my mind went completely blank. This was one of them. My grandmother would've called them something else.

I looked over my shoulder. "Of course."

Mariana laughed, soft and untroubled. "If you see yellow or white flowers, point them out. I'll tell you if they're useful or just pretty."

The sun pressed down steadily as we rode. Even this far north, the heat lingered. The drake-scale brigandine clung close, flexible but thick, trapping warmth close to the skin. Sweat clung to my spine, sliding beneath the leather. I shifted in the saddle, easing the pressure where the straps bit in.

Still, it felt good to move. To be beyond the walls. To chase flowers instead of blood.

I hadn't dreamt of death or blood or fire in nearly a decadium. Hadn't been reminded of the things I'd done. I'd forgotten what it was like to sleep a full night.

"So," Mariana said behind me, "what have you been doing since we arrived?"

"Settling in. Learning the castle and the city," I said.

She snorted. "Has his lordship not kept you close?"

"Lucius has him half the time. Almost exactly half, actually. He has him today. I'll be with him tomorrow. And you?" I asked. "How's the infirmary?"

Mariana sighed. "Chaos. I'm responsible for the entire household. His lordship, guards, kitchen staff, horses."

"Horses? They have a—"

"You know what I mean. It's busier than Avitum."

I glanced back. "That sounds miserable."

"Depends on the day. Most days, it's tolerable."

"Maybe you need a second healer."

"I'll have one, if I can find a good one. His lordship's left it to me. Maybe I'll request one from the university."

"I think I'd rather pull a plow than lance boils or whatever you do all day."

She laughed. "It's not so bad. I didn't have many choices—but more than most. My father saw to that."

"You've never mentioned him."

"He's Calesian. After I was born, they forced him to marry. He lives somewhere in Lascebar now, with his family. I've never met him. But he petitioned the university for me."

I was quiet a moment. "I'm sorry."

She shook her head. "Don't be. I was born of love. I feel sorry for them."

I studied her. "You've a kinder heart than mine."

We rode in silence awhile. Wind rustled the trees, carried the birdsong to us. What would I do if Val married? Stand by and watch, I supposed. Watch as whatever had started between us burned out before it caught. Watched while some fairer, wealthier, better woman was loved by him.

I'd die, probably.

"Do you think we'll have to go north? To Inveraria?" Mariana asked.

"Maybe," I said. "I haven't heard anything."

"I hope not." Her voice dropped further. "If I'm honest… I agree with them. The Inverarians."

Trouble in Inveraria had a way of pulling soldiers north whether they wanted to go or not. They'd never bent to Calesian rule. Not once.

I looked back. "You're safe with me but be careful who you say that to."

She didn't answer.

We crossed the bridge and followed the forest road, the path narrowing beneath pine and alder. We'd ridden the length of a fieldmark when a flicker of yellow caught my eye, bright petals clustered in a clearing where sun pierced the canopy.

"Are those what you need?" I nodded toward them.

Mariana perked up. "I think so! Let me down?"

I brought Argenti to a halt and reached back. She slid down with ease, striding toward the flowers. Kneeling, she brushed her fingers over the petals.

"These are tanacetum," she said, smiling. "You've a shrewd eye. Maybe there's an herbalist in you yet."

I gave a small smile and shifted in the saddle to keep watch while she worked.

Then she began to sing, light and soft in Aeltyrian, her voice wrapped the clearing in something old and sorrowful.

*"The rivers run red with Aeltyrian blood,*
*Her treasured children lay dead in the mud,*
*O'er the red moors did Calesia ride*

*Queen Eavan the Bles't knew Cadoc died*
*Sacrificed herself in old Aeldunon's hall*
*Her sacred blood spilt to safeguard them all*
*Her spirit roams there, forever restless*
*Seeking—"*

Beyond the trees, I heard men's voices. Distant. Wrong. Too many.

"Mari," I said, sharp and low, reaching down for her.

She looked up, then stood. "What is it?"

"Quiet." I grabbed her hand, firm. "Up. Now."

I hauled her up behind me and kicked Argenti into motion. Not a gallop—I'd lose Mari—but as near as I dared.

The voices vanished.

Then, a crack. The groan of bark tearing from wood.

A tree came down in front of us.

Argenti locked his legs, skidding to a halt just before the trunk slammed to earth with a shuddering crash. I rocked forward, catching Mariana as the dust rolled over us.

Her arms clung tight, breathing fast.

The road ahead was cut off.

And someone had made damn sure of it.

I drew my sword in one smooth motion. Reins in one hand, steel in the other, I pressed my leg into Argenti's left flank.

"*Casson*, Argenti."

He followed my command to pivot, trained to follow my weight without hesitation.

"Today's our lucky day, boys!" The speaker stepped into view—reed-thin, one good eye, the other buried beneath a scarred brand shaped like a 'T' burned deep across his face. "A noble's a noble, even if she's a half-breed."

Sweat prickled down my spine as I counted.

Six with swords. One with a bow. One with an axe. Eight total.

And all I had was a sword and a mean horse.

Fuck me.

"What is the meaning of this?" I called, my voice sharp, even.

They spread into a loose ring around us. Mariana gasped behind me.

"Oh, like to play knight, do ya?" the one-eyed man sneered, stepping closer. "I got a sword to put in your sheath."

I kept my tone flat. "I wouldn't come any closer."

"And why's that?"

He reached for Argenti's bridle.

"Argenti, *adreon*," I commanded softly. *Release.*

Argenti's ears pinned flat. His teeth flashed.

He lunged and bit down on the man's hand.

The scream came instantly. Blood sprayed as the bastard stumbled back, thumb half-torn, dangling like a strip of meat.

Then, chaos.

Hands reached for Mariana. I lashed out from the saddle, blade cutting wide, forcing them back. Argenti reared, striking one in the chest with both hooves. Mariana cried out as she lost her grip and tumbled from the saddle.

I hauled the reins, wheeling Argenti around.

My blade came down in a heavy arc without flourish, meant to split bone or armor. Steel crunched into the one-eyed man's shoulder.

Another blade slammed into me from the side. Pain knifed through my ribs as I was wrenched out of the saddle.

The world tilted sideways. I hit the dirt hard. Breath punched from my lungs.

Still, I held my sword, raised it just in time to catch the blow meant for my chest. Steel screamed against steel as his weight crashed into me.

Above the noise, someone shouted, "Don't hurt the lady or the horse! They'll both fetch a fat purse!"

"What about the armored cunt?"

He bore down, trying to drive the blade through my guard. I locked my elbows, planted my heels in the dirt, trying to buck him. He straddled my legs, pinning me.

I'd been trained to think in movement, in lines and angles. Flat roads. Open fields. Give me room and I could find a retreat, a flank, a way to break through.

But not here. Not pinned like this.

Argenti screamed.

I saw him turn—eyes wild, blood streaking his shoulder—then charge.

His teeth sank into the man's neck where shoulder met throat. Deep. Bone crunched. Flesh tore. The scream that followed cut through the clash of steel and voice, then collapsed into a gurgle as his body slumped onto me.

I shoved him off, breath coming hard, soaked in his blood.

"Good boy, Argenti," I rasped as I stood.

I swept the field.

The axeman was gone. One swordsman lay dying. Two were binding Mariana. Two more were trying to corner Argenti.

One swordsman unaccounted for.

I turned—

Just in time to see him rush me.

His blade met mine in a brutal clash. We locked together, steel on steel, muscles straining.

I braced. Watched the edges. Counted the rhythm of the fight.

"Aleaia, behind you!" Mariana cried.

I dropped low. The first man stumbled past. I turned, caught the second's strike, and kicked him twice, hard, until he staggered back.

The first charged again.

This time he caught me around the middle and drove forward.

We went down together, crashing through the brush and over the edge of the ravine.

The impact jarred through every bone as I slammed into the slope, brambles tearing at my arms and legs. I couldn't stop. I slid hard, picking up speed. The ravine dropped steeply beneath me, and I barely had time to brace before I hit the bottom.

Pain cracked through me. The breath vanished from my lungs. I lay there gasping on the riverbank.

Somehow, my sword was still in my hand.

I forced myself upright, every joint screaming, and looked around for the bastard who did this.

There, crumpled in the grass not twenty paces off. His leg was twisted beneath him, bone punched through the skin. Blood soaked the dirt in slow, pulsing rhythm. He wouldn't get far. He might not even last the hour.

Didn't matter.

I was too angry to let it go.

I crossed the distance without hesitation. My blade rose and plunged clean into the hollow of his throat.

He shuddered once. The blood arced, then poured out in thick waves. His eyes went wide, then vacant.

I stood over him, breath raw in my chest, ribs burning.

I couldn't spare a moment to feel the pain in my... well, everything. Mariana was still up there. Surrounded. Outnumbered. Because of me.

*Maybe this time,* I thought, *I'd be quicker than Vespera. If I could get back.*

The slope behind me was too steep to climb. I wouldn't get back up that way. The Drustan River ran nearby, its surface gold-lit and quiet, winding like a ribbon back toward Aeldunon. I turned and followed it, boots churning the wet earth. My legs screamed with every step.

I gripped my sword's hilt tighter. The curse. I'd felt it for years, dragging its claws through everyone who got too close. Everyone I let in. That ended now.

I ran, pain chasing close behind.

If the curse wanted blood, fine. I'd give it more than it could drink.

But not from her.

Not from me.

From *them.*

# CHAPTER THIRTY-ONE
## *The Armored One*

*"You'll know them by the blood on their boots—not the shine of their steel."*
—Cadoc Aneirin, the last First Sword of Aeltyria

Dēwamos 86, 1230
*Aleaia*

I climbed hard and fast, the trail slick underfoot, sweat burning my eyes. The ravine had cost me precious hours, and the sun was already half swallowed by the horizon by the time I reached the bend in the road.

I stopped cold.

Two bodies. Neither were her. Argenti was gone.

A knot twisted in my gut.

I knelt, fingers brushing the packed earth. Hoofprints. Heavy tread. Mariana's footprints weren't among them. They'd probably carried her.

One of the bodies was the bowman, his bow useless beside him. I picked it up. Decent weight. Five arrows in the quiver.

Not enough, but something.

I pressed on, still aching from the fall. The light was dying fast, and the sky to the west was turning the color of bruised iron. If the rain came before I reached them, the tracks would vanish.

And I would lose her.

So I ran.

That was the only time I can remember being glad for the days I'd spent running up and down hills as a young legionary. I made good time, even when I kept low along the footpath.

I slowed when I saw movement. A man ahead, alone, patrol pattern loose and lazy. He had no idea I was there.

Good.

I took an arrow from the quiver, nocked it, lined the shot, pulled—then slipped.

The arrow released too early. *Careless*, I chastised myself.

It hissed past him, grazed his ear.

"Ow!" he yelped, hand going to the side of his head as he fumbled for his blade. "Who's there?"

Fuck.

No time.

I loosed the next shot on instinct. This one flew true, buried deep in his neck with a wet thump. He dropped without ceremony, blade still half-drawn.

Three arrows left. Four men.

If they'd touched her—

I didn't let myself finish the thought. Had to focus.

I moved on. Fast. Silent.

I kept to the trees, down low, boots soft on wet roots, the bow in my hand and murder in my blood. The foliage was thick enough to cover my approach.

Ahead, torchlight flickered through the trees, weak and sputtering. A ramshackle cabin squatted in the trees, timbers sagging with age. Two men stood on the porch, weapons sheathed, eyes outward. Smoke curled from a crooked chimney.

I crouched behind a thicket of pine and listened.

Every voice. Every step. Every rustle of cloth. Watched every flick of movement, every shadow stretching from the porch.

No good angle on the inside. No knowing how many more waited in there.

I waited. Still as stone. Bow ready.

Inside, someone shouted. "Keep your hands off 'er! She's worth somethin'. Prob'ly more if we give 'er back in good condition."

The words hit like rot on the tongue.

Another voice answered. "Fine. I'm goin' to look for Byr. Should have been back by now."

I watched the bastard step out—tall, unarmored, lazy with his blade. He headed down the path, muttering to himself.

I let him pass, then followed, bowstring drawn.

He spotted the body too late.

Dropped to his knees beside it, soft idiot. I loosed the arrow into the base of his skull. He sagged forward over the other one like a sack of meat.

I turned back to the cabin, blood pounding in my ears. Two left on the porch.

One had a limp. I remembered Argenti kicking him. He'd be slower. Easier to close on with steel if I had to.

That left the other.

I lined up the shot and let the arrow fly. It hit him clean in the eye, and he fell where he stood.

The limping one screamed and clawed for cover behind the porch post. "Lugh, someone's shooting arrows!" he cried, panicked. "They got Doran!"

"Well, find them, idiot!" came the reply.

I was already moving. Nocking another arrow. My last.

"They'll kill me, Lugh!"

"If you don't find them, I'll fucking kill you!"

I shifted position, keeping low and quiet. I watched the limping one emerge, tracing the last shot's trajectory.

He made it halfway before I buried the arrow in his temple. He dropped face-first into the mud.

I dropped the bow.

My sword came clean from its sheath and mounted the porch steps with purpose.

Then I heard it behind the cabin. A snort. A low, impatient whinny. Hooves shifting in the wet dirt. Argenti, complaining as ever, but alive.

He'd have to wait. I had one left. The one with the axe.

And this one would know why I came.

The door creaked.

I startled.

Still, I lunged out of the shadows, seized the bastard by the collar, and dragged him out of the doorway before he had a chance to shout. One quick draw of the blade, a hard pull across the throat. Warm blood spurted over my knuckles. He spasmed once. I caught his weight and lowered him fast to keep him from thudding.

Then I stepped inside.

The door clicked shut behind me.

The stink hit first—sweat, mildew, wet leather. The hearth was cold, the room dim, torchlight from outside flickering through the gaps in the wood. A bed was shoved against the far wall.

The axeman I'd seen on the road stood in front of the hearth. Big bastard. Broad through the back, shoulders like a smith. A mess of greasy black hair clung to the sweat on his neck.

Mariana was tied to the bedpost, wrists bound, knees drawn tight to her chest.

Her eyes found mine. Tear-streaked. Wide. Relieved.

I raised a finger to my lips. *Stay quiet.*

I started forward, slow. The floor groaned.

"What now?" he asked, annoyed.

I didn't answer.

He glanced back and saw me.

His face twisted in recognition, then rage.

He lunged.

I sidestepped and slashed. Quick hit. Caught his arm, drew blood.

He couldn't use the axe in there—too close—so he grabbed a short sword from beside the hearth. We closed in fast, too fast to think. The shack was too small. My blade was longer, his arms thicker. The walls pressed in on both of us.

He came in swinging.

I raised my sword to meet his, steel clanging loud and close. The impact drove me back a step. My boots slid. I bent my knees and dug in.

The wall met my back.

Nowhere to go.

*Stupid. I let him box me in.*

"Who the fuck are you?" he snarled, pressing forward.

"The armored cunt," I growled. "Remember?"

He shoved hard. My arms trembled. Muscles screamed. I braced my heels and held.

Then I ducked, drove upward, and slammed my shoulder into his gut.

He grunted, lost balance, stumbled back. I followed, shoving him into a table. It crashed over, sent pots and plates scattering. I slipped past and put my back to the door.

Clear ground. No corners.

He bared his teeth and dropped the short sword, grabbing the axe instead.

Shit.

Mariana screamed.

He raised the haft and barreled into me before I could move.

The door exploded behind me.

We went through it, and I was half-lifted, half-thrown as the door tore off its hinges.

Then we hit the mud.

I landed on my backside, hard. My sword flew from my grip and landed somewhere in the mud. He stood over me, axe in hand, breath heaving.

I forced myself to my feet, spat, and found my blade.

He grinned.

My gloves were slick with rain and mud. I wiped them on my tunic and gripped the sword tighter. Rain hammered down, into the seams of my armor, soaking the padding beneath. Cold water squelched in my boots.

The torches had gone out.

I kept my eyes on the brute, illuminated by a thread of light from the shattered doorway behind him.

He moved like he didn't feel the cold—axe across his shoulder, broad as a wall. That weapon was made for mass slaughter, not a fight like this. Too heavy. Too long. He'd have the reach, but not the speed.

He planted his feet and bared his teeth.

I heard my own heart beating. Thunderous. Too loud.

And then—

*My father's head on the ground.*

*Blood in the grass.*

*His mouth still shaping his last words to me.*

The memory clung to me. My hand trembled. My breath shook. I squeezed the sword in my grip until my knuckles ached.

Stay calm. Breathe.

I inhaled through my nose, slow and steady for one breath. Cleared my mind.

Not the same. I can save her.

The axeman roared and charged.

I moved fast. Sidestepped.

Boots slipped.

The axe came down like a siege ram, crashing into the earth just behind me. Mud exploded upward, soaking my legs, spattering my face. He grunted, yanked at the haft, stuck in the muck.

I darted forward, slashed at his side. The blade skidded across his armor, bit in shallow. Not enough.

He swore and tore the axe free.

Swung wide—waist-high.

I dropped to one knee. The blade passed inches over my head, wind and steel. Cold rain struck my face. I staggered upright, boots fighting the sodden ground.

Everything was heavier now—my arms, my legs. The rain soaked everything. The mud clung like it meant to drown me.

He laughed. Deep. Ugly.

I let him, just watching him through the rain. His side bled. He was breathing harder now. Slower.

He raised the axe again. High. Another killing blow.

Then his foot slipped. Barely enough to notice.

But I did.

I didn't wait.

I closed the distance fast. My shoulder slammed into his chest and knocked him back. He fumbled. The axe came down behind me, useless. Lodged deep in the earth.

I shoved my blade up beneath his arm, right through the gap.

It sank deep.

Hot blood burst over my glove. He screamed, guttural and raw. His arm went limp. He fell.

His back slammed to the ground. Mud sucked at him.

I stepped over him, planted a boot to his throat to stop the squirming. He twisted, tried to rise, but his strength was gone. He flailed with the dead arm, the other scrabbling at the mud.

"You…" he gasped.

I stepped off.

Raised the sword.

Drove it down straight through the center of his chest.

His body bucked once, then stilled. Blood pooled beneath him. His eyes fixed on the sky.

And then, as if the gods had waited for him to die—

The rain stopped.

I wiped my blade on his tunic, then slid it back into its sheath with a soft click. The tension that had filled me like a forge bellows began to fade, pulled out with the blood. The man had reminded me so much of my father's killer that, somewhere in the fight, I thought ending him might give me something like redemption.

There was nothing.

No triumph. No sense of justice.

Just breath in my lungs and the knowledge that the task was done.

I turned from the body, boots squelching in the churned mud, and made my way around the cabin. Argenti's distress came loud—snorting, stomping, nerves bared.

He didn't recognize me at first. Not beneath the layers of filth and blood.

I scrubbed my face with one sleeve. "Held your ground back there, didn't you, soldier?"

His ears flicked forward as recognition dawned. He neighed and stepped forward, nose nudging the air between us.

I stepped in and wrapped my arms around his neck, pressing my forehead to his shoulder. He let out a soft nicker and leaned into me like he understood.

"Let's get out of here," I said, untying his reins from the post. "I still can't believe you bit off a man's thumb and killed another. Val got lucky, when you bit him."

We walked around to the front of the cabin. I looped the reins over the porch railing and gave his flank a parting pat. "Glad you're on my side."

I mounted the steps. The wood creaked under my weight.

"I'm bloody," I called as I entered, "but none of it's mine."

Mariana's voice cracked with disbelief. "You came for me alone! Why would you do that?" Her face was streaked with tears, wrists still bound to the bedpost.

I drew Val's dagger and made quick work of the rope.

"It would've taken too long to get back to Aeldunon for help," I said. "Couldn't risk what they might do in the meantime."

The bindings fell away.

Mariana scrambled upright and threw her arms around my neck. "You are so foolish."

"And disgusting," I said. My armor clung with gore, and the padding beneath was soaked. I reeked of blood and fear and work.

"I don't care," she said, and held on tighter.

I put my arms around her, slow and light at first, then tighter, and gave her back an awkward pat.

After a moment, I pulled away, my hands on her shoulders while I looked her over. "Did they hurt you?"

She shook her head and wiped her face. "They thought I was a noble. The big one wanted to ransom me. I—I punched one in the nose. For trying to…"

She didn't need to finish. I knew what she meant.

"Did you make him bleed?"

She hesitated, wringing her hands. "Yes. From his nose."

The thought of Mariana landing a punch was so absurd I almost smiled. "Well done."

She waved it off and grabbed a blanket from the bed, dabbing at the blood on my face. "I felt bad about it anyway. Are you hurt? I saw you fall toward the river."

"I'm covered in bruises and everything will hurt tomorrow. But nothing is open or broken. You can see for yourself once we're back. Let's go home."

We were halfway back to the city walls, the road winding through mist-draped fields, when I spotted the flicker of torchlight ahead.

I took a deep breath in through my nose. "I'm in so much trouble."

Mariana gave a tired laugh. "And I didn't even get to keep the herbs. We'll have to go out again. Maybe tomorrow?"

I shot her a look back over my shoulder. "If I'm allowed outside before Succamos, it'll be a miracle."

The lights drew closer. Shapes took form. Riders. Armor.

A search party.

One rider broke free from the column, tearing up the road like it owed him blood. Even before I saw his face, I knew. I slid off Argenti, passed his reins to Mariana.

Nox, Val's destrier, stopped fast, black and rain-slick. Val was already out of the saddle, boots hitting the ground hard as he came for me.

I dropped to one knee.

"No," he said, the word striking like steel.

He reached for me and pulled me upright and into his arms like he couldn't stand the space between us.

I froze for a heartbeat, then melted into him, pressed my face to his shoulder, and gripped his cloak.

"I'm filthy," I said. "You'll get mud and blood all over you."

"I don't care. You're here." He held on like he meant to keep me there. When he finally eased back, his hands stayed on my arms. His thumb brushed a bruise on my cheek where a blow had landed. "Are you hurt?"

"Bruised. Sore. Nothing broken."

"You're never leaving my side again. Not like this." He lowered his head, forehead touching mine, careful as if I might break. "I can't bear it."

My throat tightened. I closed my eyes. The search party waited in silence. I was painfully aware of their eyes on us. Still, my hands stayed twisted in his cloak. I didn't trust them to let go.

When he finally drew back, it was only far enough to see my face.

"Let's get you home," he said.

I nodded. My voice wouldn't come.

We stood there in the half-light, soaked and aching. His hand slid down to lace his fingers tight with mine like he was anchoring us both.

And I held on like the gods might take him if I let go.

# CHAPTER THIRTY-TWO
## *The First Knight*

*"A sword is for war. A horse is for the road. But a ring… a ring is for belonging. You don't give one unless you mean to say, 'You are mine.'"*
—Valerius di Calesia

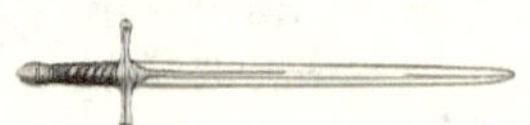

Dēwamos 89, 1230
*Aleaia*

I stood just outside the temple doors, willing my breath to slow and my mind to quiet. The sun was sinking fast. By the time it vanished, I'd be a knight, sworn to protect the Empire and its citizens.

Val had encouraged me to write my oath and told me not to worry. He'd manage the rest. I still hadn't slept the night before, too focused to be afraid, too taut to be calm.

I adjusted the plait down my back and gave it one last smoothing touch. A quick glance at my boots, hose, and black tunic showed nothing out of place. I shook out the cloak over my shoulders—black silk, wholly impractical for anything but ceremony, stitched with the indigo bloom known as Wolfsbane.

It was Mariana's idea. My first moniker, now my sigil.

"Is it all too... dark?" I had asked her.

"No. But darkness is beautiful too. It suits you," she had said.

The heavy oak door creaked as I pulled it open. I drew a breath, steadied myself, and stepped inside.

The temple was dim, lit only by braziers and candles, but I looked into the main chamber and saw the banners: Val's lion, gold on blue, hanging behind the dais. Other than the two guards by the door and a Lithaun shaman, only three others were present: Lucius, Mariana, and Val.

Mariana wore her ceremonial white robes with the hood drawn over her dark hair. Lucius had chosen the crimson of his house, his cloak pinned with a silver eagle. And Val—

He stood before the dais in a white tunic, the deep blue of his cloak sharpening against it. No circlet. No Calesian banner. Just him.

I watched him for a moment, the way he carried on his conversation with Lucius. He laughed at something Lucius said and I felt my stomach flip.

Lucius caught my eye, then tapped Val on the arm to point at me. I ducked out of sight.

I could still leave. Could still stop him from doing this irrevocable thing that would endanger him once his father learned of it. He was reckless—not in the same way I was from time to time, but with his reputation and the law. He'd publicly chastised an orphanage matron for enforcing Imperial law, been seen embracing me in public after I returned with Mariana, and now he meant to make me a knight. When word got out, and it would, he'd pay the price alongside me.

I'd go, I decided. I turned to walk out of the temple, my hand on the door.

"Nervous?" Lucius asked from behind me.

I stopped, letting out a slow breath as my hand fell away. "Just a bit. That obvious?"

"You look like you're headed for the block." His voice was dry at first, then gentle. "Where were you going?"

"Lucius, I can't—I can't let him do this." I turned to face him. "This is dangerous for all of us, but him most of all."

"You think he doesn't know that already?" Lucius folded his arms, looked down at me with a hint of a smile. "He's been walking this line his whole life. He does what he thinks is right no matter the cost."

I didn't know what to say to that, so I just said, "Well, that's foolish."

"I don't think so. Val's many things. A fool isn't one of them. His father would never have let him take command of the Second if he couldn't strategize." He reached out, put his hands on my shoulders. "I think you're just afraid. And you're right to be. Any price would be yours to pay, but we won't let it come to that. So take a deep breath. You look decent. Don't smell terrible. And it's not such a big crowd."

I took his advice, drawing a long breath in through my nose, then out through my mouth. "All right."

He said nothing else, just put his hand on my back and guided me inside. Together we approached the dais and stopped.

"My lord," Lucius said. "It is my privilege to present Aleaia Dieter to receive the honor of knighthood."

When I caught Val's eye, something in his expression settled the last of the restless current inside me. Not a smile, not even a nod. Just quiet pride in his eyes, the kind that steadied me better than any words.

He cleared his throat and began. "Friends, we are here today to honor Aleaia for her exceptional bravery and selflessness.

"In Gormlaith, she defeated the sorceress Asena, ensuring the safety of its people and freeing the captives. And not three days ago, she put down brigands who plagued this land and rescued our healer from their hands. These extraordinary acts prove her valor."

Val turned to me. "Your courage, dedication, and unwavering spirit reflect the highest ideals of knighthood. Kneel before your gods, Aleaia Dieter, and speak your oath."

My legs trembled as I stepped forward, but I lowered myself onto the cool stone. I placed my palms on my thighs and looked up at him.

The oath I'd written was plain. Simple. But it was mine, and I recited it proudly.

"I, Aleaia Dieter, do solemnly swear to stand for the innocent and the defenseless, to uphold justice and honor, and to remain steadfast in the face of adversity. So sworn on the blood of Aelan."

The words felt… heavier than they should have.

"From this day forward," Val said, "you shall be known as Dame Aleaia Dieter, Shield of Aeldunon. This title reflects your vow to protect and serve its people."

He drew his sword.

I felt Lucius's fingertips apply light pressure to the back of my head. I bowed. The correction sat heavy in my chest.

The shaman spoke as the blade was laid on my right shoulder, her voice soft and reverent. "By the will of Lady Lithau, and by the spirits of your ancestors, may you be granted the strength and wisdom to bear it."

Tears stung my eyes as I thought of the trouble he'd gone to, to let me swear this oath in front of a shaman of my faith.

The blade touched my left shoulder. "May She grant you the fortitude to uphold justice and defend our people."

"Rise now, Dame Aleaia," he said. "And stand as a knight of Aeldunon, a true embodiment of courage and honor."

I stood.

Lucius handed Val a small wooden box.

When he opened it, I caught a glimpse of the silver signet ring inside: my sigil engraved in miniature. A shield bearing the Wolfsbane bloom.

"As a symbol of your new rank and the responsibility it carries," he said, "I give you this ring. Let it remind you of your vow."

He handed the box to Lucius and took my hand in his. When his eyes lifted to mine, the rest of the temple faded. He slid the ring onto my finger, and I watched him instead of the silver.

I thought my knees might give way and prayed they wouldn't.

"The first knight in Aeltyria in twenty-four years," he murmured. "Well done."

And then it made sense—the private ceremony, the title tied to Aeldunon and not the Empire, the absence of imperial banners.

The Emperor didn't know. Or hadn't approved.

"Thank you," I said softly, eyes dropping to my hand still resting in his.

"Dame Wolfsbane," he mused, thumb stroking the backs of my fingers. "Shield of Aeldunon. Sounds intimidating."

"I am intimidating."

"You'll always be Aleaia to me." The corner of his mouth tugged up. "Come, there's a feast waiting."

# CHAPTER THIRTY-THREE
## *Dame Wolfsbane*

*"Let the wine loosen what pride has bound—*
*but gods help the fool who listens too closely."*
—Calesian banquet hall inscription, origin disputed

Dēwamos 89, 1230
*Aleaia*

The feast was modest by noble standards, but the hall still brimmed with firelight and sound as we entered. Long tables were piled high with roasted meats, spiced wine, braided loaves, and soft cheese—enough food for twice the number present.

Most of the faces belonged to the Second Army. There were no titles, no court finery. Just soldiers, friends, and more wine than was wise.

I hadn't expected to go unnoticed. I was the reason they were gathered. Still, I hadn't expected quite so much attention.

"So then she comes crashing into the cabin," Mariana declared, lifting her goblet with theatrical flair, "soaked in blood, dripping mud everywhere, and she just says, calm as you like, 'I'm covered in blood, but it's not mine.'"

The table roared with laughter. Tankards slammed the wood.

Val raised his cup. "To Dame Wolfsbane!"

That made five toasts in less than an hour. My cheeks were warm, and the floor had begun to drift ever so slightly under my boots.

"You make it sound like I'm constantly bleeding," I said, not quite keeping the slur from my voice.

Val chuckled. "You usually are, in these stories."

Lucius stood then, raising a hand for quiet. Down the hall, a few soldiers pounded the tables and shouted, "Speech! Speech!"

Once he had command of the room, he began, "With all this talk about Dame Wolfsbane, we seem to have forgotten our equine brother, Argenti. Now, he couldn't be here tonight. He's on duty tormenting the stable hands."

The hall erupted in laughter.

"Someone has to keep them sharp," he added. "But that doesn't mean we can't honor him. Master Bard, if you would?"

The bard, a wiry man with wind-worn hands and a grin full of poor decisions, climbed atop the nearest table. His cloak swung at his heels as he unstrapped a lute, struck a few bold chords, and tapped one boot in time with exaggerated flair.

He let the soldiers settle. Then launched into the song:

*Eight foul men in the forest lay,*
*Blades all drawn for a noble's pay.*
*The trap was set, the kill was neat,*
*'Til death arrived on silver feet.*

I turned sharply toward Val, narrowing my eyes. He sipped his wine like he hadn't a care in the world.

"What is this?" I hissed.

"I want you to know," he said smoothly, "that I had absolutely nothing to do with it. And by the time I found out, it was far too late."

Of course it was.

I downed the rest of my wine in one long, determined gulp.

The bard stomped once, lute ringing, and launched into the chorus, his boot thudding in time atop the table.

*Bite! Bite! Who's he gonna bite now?*
*Duck and run and take your vow!*
*Don't breathe loud, don't make a sound,*
*The man-eating warhorse is back in town!*

*The first was kicked through bark and bone,*
*He died in chunks. He died alone.*

"Argenti didn't… he didn't do that," I muttered, eyeing my wine like it might come to my defense.

Lucius didn't even look at me. "Then write your own version. Make it historically accurate. Sing it for us."

"He took a thumb off one. Bit another to death." My voice came out flat. "Ripped out his throat. It was justified."

Lucius lifted his goblet. "Same story. Just needs a chorus."

I turned to Mariana. "You're supposed to be my friend. Why did you let him do this to me?"

She was breathless with laughter, leaning into the table, one hand clutching her ribs.

Down the hall, the legionaries pounded their tankards in time to the chorus.

*Bite! Bite! Who's he gonna bite now?*

"This is terrible," I groaned. "I need something stronger than wine." I looked around for a server. They'd vanished, likely hiding from the noise. "How do they all know the words already?"

*Broke one's ribs and bent a plow!*
*Guts went up and heads went down,*
*The man-eating warhorse is back in town!*

I tried to rise. The floor shifted under me like a raft on river current. I dropped back into my seat.

*The fourth man dropped his sword in fear*
*So Argenti kicked him through a deer.*
*The fifth one charged with sword held high,*
*Then screamed as both his shins passed by.*

The song was so ridiculously bad. I couldn't stand it. I cupped my hands and shouted toward the bard. "No one screamed about their shins!"

"You were mid-duel," Val said, utterly composed. "Could've happened. Maybe you missed it."

"You're taking Lucius's side?" I stared at him, incredulous.

*She smoothed her cloak and checked her sleeves,*
*While trees were painted red with thieves.*

"I was covered in blood!" I flung an arm toward the bard, wine sloshing near the rim of my cup. "After I rolled down a rav—ravine, climbed back up, and—and fought the biggest man I've ever met!"

*Bit through shields, swallowed them down,*
*The man-eating warhorse is back in town!*

I looked down the table and caught Lucius tapping his fingers in rhythm, not a trace of shame on his face. "Stop that," I growled.

"Catchy, isn't it?" he said.

The world tilted as I narrowed my eyes and pointed at him. "It was you! You... you commish... commishhh... you paid for this!"

Lucius regarded me with the solemnity of a priest. "Yes, we did pay the bard for his performance. That's the way it works."

The bard didn't miss a beat.

*And what of our lady, sword in sheath?*
*She gazed at our lord, her heart to bequeath.*
*She sighed, perhaps, and said his name,*
*While Argenti played his hunting game.*

I stabbed a finger in the bard's direction. "Your... your shong—song doesn't even make sense, sir." I turned halfway in my seat, then, and lifted the cup like a weapon. "I couldn't have been 'gazing at Val' from the northern forest. That's—not how distance works!"

Val reached over and gently lowered my arm before I could slosh wine across the table. "Easy, soldier."

"I challenge you to a duel!" I shouted at the bard.

"He would win, Aleaia," Lucius said, calm as ever. "You couldn't fight your way out of a flour sack right now."

*The last man knelt. He wept and prayed.*
*Argenti waited. Then flayed and flayed.*

I turned to glare at Lucius again, then stuck out my tongue like a child denied supper.

Lucius didn't so much as blink. "Dame Wolfsbane. Your station."

Behind his goblet, Val made a strangled sound—half-cough, half-laugh. His shoulders shook as he tried to contain it.

*And what of our dame, all calm and sweet?*
*She dreamed of steel, both long and neat.*
*Her lord's great sword, she thought to keep,*
*In her sheath, buried good and deep.*

Tankards hit wood like hammers. Mariana nearly fell off her bench, gasping with laughter.

I dropped my head into my hands. "I'm gonna die," I groaned. "I'm gonna die. Humilia… humilia'ded to death by a drunk with a lute!"

"She *dreamed* of steel, Val," Lucius said, dry as bone.

Val tried to maintain some sense of decorum. Gods, he tried.

"It's a powerful metaphor," he managed before burying his face in his hand to hide his smile.

*Bite! Bite! Who's he gonna bite now?*
*Sniffed out blood and bit a brow!*
*Warhorse born of wrath and frown,*
*The man-eating legend of Aeldunon!*

The bard ended with a grand flourish, arms wide as he bowed low.

"I must confess," he announced, "to having taken certain artistic liberties with the details of your adventures, my lady. I beg your pardon for any misrepresentation of your character."

I pushed to my feet, steadying myself with one hand on Val's shoulder. I lifted my goblet with grave purpose—not to fling, but to toast, this time—as I blinked at the bard.

"Fuck. You," I said, clear as a bell. I drained it, then added with all the dignity I could muster, "From the bottom of my heart."

The hall howled. Legionaries whooped, mugs slammed on tables.

"If—*hic*—if there's another verse," I slurred, dragging a hand down my face, "I'm gonna climb the tallest spire in this keep and throw m'self off it."

"It's the north spire," Lucius offered helpfully. "But you couldn't find your way out of your right boot right now."

I leveled a finger at him. "I will ne'er forgive you, Lucius Tutela."

"Yes, you will. And one day, you'll be the one in my position. Welcome to the ranks, little sister." He rose, lifting his mug high. "What a tribute to our courageous Aleaia Dieter. Raise your cups one last time to Dame Wolfsbane!"

More cheers. More pounding mugs. A few chanted my new title like a war cry.

"Wolfsbane! Wolfsbane! Wolfsbane!"

I gave what might have passed for a bow and drained the rest of my wine.

I wondered who had refilled it. How many had that been? And why was it so strong?

*No matter,* I thought as I turned toward the door, doing my best to move with dignity. The floor pitched and almost took me down. I reached out instinctively and found a solid shoulder beneath my palm.

Lucius didn't even flinch. "You're welcome," he said.

"I've… ne'er hated anyone's much as I hate you right now." I clung to him like a drowning sailor.

"Strong words, Dame Wolfsbane."

I didn't answer. I was too focused on the dais steps.

I took a staggering step toward them.

Then another.

My foot missed the top one.

And for a breathless moment, I was flying.

*Valerius*

I moved before I thought. One moment she was upright, and the next, falling. I caught her midair, one arm beneath her knees, the other braced behind her back.

Cheers erupted around us.

"Quick hands, my lord!"

"Smooth as a sword draw, that!"

I barely heard them.

Her head lolled against my shoulder as she blinked up at me, brow furrowing, trying to remember how she'd gotten there. She was warm. Too drunk to be afraid. Laughing—loose with it, in a way she rarely allowed.

"Val," she said, giggling. "Put me down."

"I will," I murmured, low and steady, "once I've delivered you safely to your room."

"I'm not that even—" She frowned. "Even not that drunk. I meant."

My brow arched. "Want to try that again?"

She sighed and slumped against my chest. Her cheek pressed against the collar of my tunic, just above my heart. The scent of her reached me, dulled by wine but not lost in it. Lavender. Leather.

I adjusted my hold and crossed the hall, shielding her the best I could from the volleys I knew were coming.

They came anyway.

"Give her the steel, my lord!"

"Time to sheath that sword!"

She groaned into my tunic, her voice muffled. "Ohhh gods… take me to the north spire."

I exhaled a breath of something like laughter, even as my chest tightened. Every knight faced jests like these during the Rite. But this felt different.

Because the insinuation wasn't the problem.

The problem was how true I wished it was.

I wanted her. Not as a passing thing. Not as some nobleman's dalliance. I wanted the shape of her life folded into mine. I wanted the look she gave me when she forgot to hide it.

I didn't answer. Just held her close and kept walking. Every step made me more aware of every curve of her in my arms. She was mine to protect.

They'd sing their songs and have their night. And I'd have this moment.

"I hate all of you," she mumbled.

"I know," I said softly, smiling down at her. "I've got you anyway."

"Not you, Val. Could never hate you. I lo—"

She hiccupped, and the rest was lost to the haze.

Two syllables. Half a word. Devastating as a hammer wrapped in silk. It knocked the breath from my lungs and left my heart scrambling to catch up.

She wouldn't remember it. I'd be the only one haunted by it, left to turn those unfinished words over in my head. And gods, would I.

Lucius's voice cut through the laughter like a coda.

"Show some respect. That's the Shield of Aeldunon you're harassing." He let the silence hang for a heartbeat. "Only *top-notch* sword jokes for her. I'm noting the best ones."

The doors closed behind us, muting the noise.

She stirred. "Thought Lucius was my friend."

"He is," I said. "That's how he shows affection."

"I hate him."

"So you said."

"He can stick his… 'ffection…"

Her words muddled as I climbed the stairs, her weight shifting easily in my arms. She hiccupped again, cursed under her breath.

The guards stepped aside at my word, opening the door to her chamber without question. I crossed the threshold, kicked the door shut behind me, and laid her down on her bed. She grumbled as I took her boots off, but didn't open her eyes.

"I could have made it up the stairs," she muttered.

"Of course you could have," I said, setting her boots aside.

She huffed, then sighed. "Won't you join me?" she asked.

I straightened.

Her eyes were heavy with drink, her hair a dark spill across the pillow. There was no guile in the question. Just soft, clumsy sincerity.

She stretched, slow and languid, and every part of me answered before my mind could intervene.

Every nerve lit.

Every muscle taut.

My breeches had become… inconveniently snug.

I stood there like a man on the edge of a cliff, weighing whether the fall would be worth the impact.

It would be sweet.

Brief.

The landing would kill me.

I looked away, pinched the bridge of my nose. "By the gods, Aleaia," I choked out. "Would that I were a less honorable man."

She beamed. "I just wanna hug you… in the bed."

My heart thumped in my chest.

Then came her singsong, "You can take your clothes off if you get too hot."

I bit the inside of my cheek so hard it bled, and made a sound somewhere between a groan and a laugh.

"Much as it wounds me," I said, "I can't."

Gods help me, I needed to get out of that room.

"There's water on the table," I added, backing toward the door. "Drink it, or you'll regret surviving the night."

I turned, reaching for the handle—

And there she was, like something pulled her after me, a thread taut between us. Maybe it pulled at me too. Her hands found my chest. Her eyes half-lidded, searching.

"Won't you at least kiss me good night?"

I swallowed hard. Set my hands at her waist to steady her.

My throat was parched. The Pravian Pass had nothing on it.

"Not like this," I said tenderly. "Ask me again when the wine's worn off."

She didn't let go. Instead, she leaned into me. Her cheek against my chest. Fingers curling in my tunic. Her breath warmed the hollow of my throat.

"Oh, Val," she sighed. "You always do the right thing… even when I wish you'd do the wrong one."

Her words landed like a blade between my ribs. I closed my eyes.

*Gods help me.*

I wrapped my arms around her, just tightly enough to feel her warmth through the silk and linen between us. Enough to know what it would cost to let go.

I could indulge her. Gods, I could indulge us both.

I pulled back slightly and tipped her chin with my fingers until her gaze met mine.

Just one kiss.

But it would never stop there. Not for us. We'd wanted this for too long. One night, she'd asked for. Twice.

But she wouldn't remember. The memory would be carved into me. And she would forget.

That wasn't a line I could cross.

I exhaled through my nose, brushed a lock of hair back from her cheek. My hand lingered there. "You'll thank me in the morning," I said softly. "And again when the time is right."

She didn't answer. Just leaned into me again, loose and trusting, like she might unravel if I let go.

"Come on. Back to bed."

"No," she said, childlike and obstinate. "Like it here. It's safe."

Anvallus's balls, she isn't making it easy.

"Your bed is safe too," I said gently, and turned her toward the bed again.

She sighed but let me guide her unsteady steps.

At the edge of the bed, I turned the blankets back and helped her in. She mumbled something about swords and Lucius. Possibly ribbons.

Her eyes drifted shut as I tucked the covers up around her chin.

Then she reached for me, her fingers brushing my cheek—clumsy, feather-light.

"I like when you smile," she breathed.

And just like that, it gutted me. I couldn't answer. If I spoke, I'd say too much, or not enough. I just stood there, leaning over her like a fool until her hand fell away.

I tucked the blanket tighter. Stood.

Made it to the door.

Paused.

Ran a hand through my hair.

And muttered a curse that would've made Lucius proud.

I needed water.

A cold river. A frozen lake. A godsdamned mountain stream. Hel, I'd take a puddle, if I had to.

I just needed to soak in it until morning.

# CHAPTER THIRTY-FOUR
## *Feathers in the Wind*

*"Wine sharpens the tongue, weakens the limbs, and lays siege to dignity. Use only in moderation—or not at all, if your dignity is already fragile."*
—Cura Vitalis

Dēwamos 90, 1230
*Aleaia*

I thought a hammer struck my skull three times in rapid succession, sharp and rhythmic.

"Wake up, you layabout!"

Lucius. At the door.

Of course it was Lucius. I'd almost have preferred an actual hammer.

"There's work to be done, and it's already dawn!"

"I'm going to kill him." I rolled off the bed only to drop straight to my knees. The stone was cool. That helped.

"Let's go!"

*You'll regret surviving the night,* he'd said. And he was right. I smacked my lips, trying to coax up some spit. "I'm up, *tuchlus*. Leave me be. I'll be down shortly."

Tomorrow. Tomorrow was shortly.

Maybe I could just stay here. Val wouldn't mind. Lucius was awake. The Empire would endure without me for one day.

I pressed my forehead to the floor. What great fool did I make of myself?

Memories of the night returned in fragments. I'd already been five—no, six—cups deep when that odious bard had leapt atop the table and sang that ridiculous ballad about me and Argenti. Before that…

*A legionary in a wine-stained tunic kissed my hand, lips lingering as he slurred his devotion.*

*"The Maiden of Mayhem, in the flesh!"*

*Val placed a hand on his shoulder, knuckles white, and said something low. The man blinked like he'd forgotten how to be a person and stumbled off.*

I groaned. How did I even get back here?

*I headed for the dais steps, meaning to dismount.*

*My foot disagreed. Then—*

*Then I was in Val's arms.*

*My cheek against his chest. Warm. Steady. Too close. He smelled like leather, cedar, and a hint of woodsmoke. Someone in the crowd shouted, "Give her the steel, my lord!"*

*"Time to sheath that sword!"*

*And I, elegant creature that I was, muttered, "I hate all of you."*

*Val smiled and said, "I know."*

*"Well, not you, Val. I could never hate you. I lo—"*

My eyes flew open.

Gods, no.

I covered my head with both hands as if the ceiling were about to collapse.

What had I done?

And then the worst of it returned.

*Join me, won't you?*

*Kiss me goodnight.*

*And Val—gods, Val—too gentle, too kind, his breath warm against my skin as he whispered, "Ask me again when the wine wears off."*

I flopped onto my side. "I can't come down, Lucius," I called hoarsely. "I'm… I'm ill."

"If I have to come get you, you'll really be ill," came the reply. "I'll carry you down, and not nearly as gently as his lordship."

I winced. He meant it. Lucius didn't bluff, not when he had a point to make. Best to salvage what remained of my dignity.

"Might I have a little time to make myself presentable?" I asked, pushing myself upright slowly. My palm pressed to my temple, as though I could hold my brain together. "I need to change. Get cleaned up."

"Very well. But if his lordship arrives first, I'll come back. And you'll regret the delay."

"He's not with you?"

"Don't worry about him, he's fine. Hurry up."

I peeled off the wrinkled, wine-scented clothes from the night before and tossed them into a corner. Picking knots from my hair with clumsy fingers, I crossed to the wardrobe and flung it open. Most of what hung inside was black or gray, mercifully interchangeable. I wasn't in any state to match colors.

This wasn't the first time I'd overindulged, though it had been a while. I knew what I needed now—food, water, and a bit of some drink with a bite.

I pulled on a clean shift, black fitted trousers, and a plain gray tunic that fell to my knees. My sword belt cinched it at the waist, snug and familiar. I slid Val's dagger into the sheath in my boot and moved toward the washbasin, bracing one hand on the edge.

The looking glass above it offered no comfort. I looked like death warmed over.

I splashed cold water on my face. It stung, but it helped. Barely.

I dragged a bone comb through my hair, wincing as I tore through a tangle. No patience for braids. I tied it back loosely and let it be. Not my best, but it would do.

I chewed a pinch of mint from my kit, swished a mouthful of water to clear the worst of the night from my tongue, and called it good enough.

I made my way downstairs more from duty than will. The hearth in the great hall had gone cold, the ashes swept. The mess of the night before had vanished.

Lucius and Mariana were already seated at the high table, both looking far too alive.

"Morning," Lucius said cheerfully, as if he hadn't bullied me out of bed.

"Aye. It is that." I collapsed into the chair across from him. Pain spiked behind my eyes the instant I sat.

"Here." His voice lanced through my skull. He slid a mug across the table toward me. "Hair of the dog."

I stared at the watered ale like it might bite. My stomach gave a harsh warning lurch.

"I can make you ginger tea, if you prefer," Mariana offered, her voice far too gentle for the amount of pain it caused.

"Why are you all so loud?" I groaned, pressing a hand to my temple.

Lucius took a slow sip of ale, plucked a grape from his platter, and leaned back like a man who'd slept soundly and regretted nothing. He crossed one ankle over his knee with all the self-satisfaction of a cat in sunlight.

Plotting. He was plotting. I knew it.

He reached into the pouch at his belt, withdrew a folded parchment, and cleared his throat. "I bet you're wondering what happened after you left."

"I'm not. Not at all."

A servant placed a bowl of barley pottage in front of me. The scent of leek and pork rose with the steam and nearly made me bolt.

"I'm going to tell you anyway," Lucius said. "You should be well-informed. For duty's sake." He unfolded the parchment with the care of a clerk reading royal orders.

My stomach turned again.

Mariana shook her head. "Starting in on her first thing in the morning. Shame on you. Please, continue."

I stared at her for a long moment.

"'Things said of Dame Aleaia Dieter, the Wolfsbane, Shield of Aeldunon, by her brothers and sisters in arms of the Second Army.'"

"Please. No," I whimpered, resting my forehead in my palm as I forced down a spoonful of pottage.

"'She's getting that sword nice and wet. For polishing, obviously.' Got some laughter, but I ranked it low. Too easy."

I turned to Mariana. "What's the quickest way to the north spire?"

Lucius didn't pause. "'Have you ever seen those women at the market who swallow swords for coin?'" He tapped the parchment. "'They could learn a thing or two from the Wolfsbane. She got a knighthood.' Bit wordy, but creative."

"You're not even eating," I grumbled, forcing down another bite. "You're just sustaining yourself on my anguish and misery."

Footsteps approached behind me. A chair scraped to my left. I already knew who it was, so I kept my eyes on my bowl. If I looked at him now, I might give away too much.

*"Ask me again when the wine wears off."*

"Now that his lordship's here," Lucius said cheerfully, "I'll skip to the best."

Mariana elbowed him hard. His cup wobbled. He didn't flinch.

"This one got quite a lot of applause. A collaboration between two very imaginative legionaries." Lucius grinned like a man at confession. "'Anything's a scabbard if you're brave enough.'"

"Why are you like this?" I rubbed my temples with my thumbs.

"'I hope, for his lordship's sake, she doesn't bite like her man-eating horse.'" Lucius looked to Val. "They care about his well-being. How nice."

I didn't lift my head. "I want their names."

"Oh? To thank them?" Lucius asked.

"To put their heads on pikes. Right next to that goblin of a bard."

"I thought you liked the bard," Val said dryly as he reached for fruit and bread. He didn't look at me.

"She liked yelling at him," Lucius replied. "In defense of what little honor she had left."

Mariana stood with a sigh and gathered her mug. "Well. I'm off to the infirmary. Don't darken my door if you beat each other bloody."

Once she left, I risked a glance at Val.

His hair was damp. His shirt clung to him in places, not fully dry. His skin held a faint flush—maybe from the cold.

Or maybe not.

The thought struck.

Had he gone to the baths? Or… somewhere else?

A burn caught behind my ribs and spread upward. I clenched my jaw and stabbed my spoon into the pottage harder than necessary.

"Where have you been," I asked, too lightly, "without either of us?"

Val didn't answer right away. He tore a piece of bread, fingers tight on the crust.

"Went for a walk, to clear my head," he said at last.

I nodded like that settled it and kept my eyes on my bowl.

"Must've been a long walk," I added, too coolly.

Val tore off another piece of bread with slow, deliberate care. He took a bite, chewed it like a man stalling for time.

"Long enough." Still not looking at me.

No explanation. No invitation.

I took another bite of porridge I couldn't taste.

Then the door opened.

Lucius leaned back in his chair, plucked another grape, and said, "If we're all quite finished brooding," he said, "I believe the day insists on beginning."

"Good morning, my lord. Lucius," Marcus said as he entered, crossing to the far side of the table.

He didn't even glance my way.

Val looked up, brow arched mid-chew, and locked eyes with him. He hadn't missed the snub.

A long moment passed.

Since Elisedd, I'd seen Marcus often enough. Always in public, always for business. Our exchanges were cold and clipped, tolerable only by necessity.

Still, I couldn't help the smirk tugging at my mouth. I remembered the sound his head made when my fist connected with it. My knuckles had ached for days, but it had been worth it.

Marcus finally looked at me. Then at Val. Then back again.

"Good morning, Dieter," he said, clipped.

"Frugi," I replied.

Val's tone was velvet. "Good of you to join us at this early hour, Marcus."

"I must say," Marcus went on as he settled into his seat, "I'm impressed to find everyone so bright-eyed this morning, after such spirited evening… escapades."

Val stared at him.

"Shall we go over the agenda? First audience begins with the bell," Marcus said. When no one objected, he went on. "The morning looks light. There are shortages of salted fish and firewood. One clerk claims the storerooms are low. The chamberlain says he's miscounting…"

I swirled the ale in my mug, watching it lap against the rim.

Was I sure Val had said those words last night? Or had I imagined it—some desperate dream my heart clung to?

*"Ask me again when the wine wears off."*

I didn't know. Not anymore.

If I hadn't been so inebriated, might he have kissed me? Might he have stayed?

Worse yet, had my drunkenness ruined the night so thoroughly that he'd needed comfort elsewhere?

Regardless, he should've brought a guard with him. Lucius was the obvious choice, and the kinder one, for my sake.

He had gone to the baths before. Probably more than once. And everyone knew what happened there.

But why had my mind jumped there first? Bitterness, maybe. It was easier to chase shadows than sit in silence. The answers drifted just out of reach, like feathers in the wind.

"Your thoughts, Aleaia?" Val asked.

All their eyes were on me, but I looked only at him.

"I'm…" I cleared my throat. "Sorry. I was far away."

"Why ask her?" Marcus asked sharply. "You know what her opinion will be."

Val's head turned. The shift was instant. Cold. Precise.

"Another slight," he said, "and I'll assume your usefulness has run its course. Consider that your only warning."

"Slight? I—"

"You know what he means, Marcus," Lucius cut in. "Stop pretending to be stupid."

Marcus clamped his mouth shut.

Val turned back to me, voice softer, warmer.

"There's a case involving an Aeltyrian craftsman, Cormeth Avenal, and a Calesian noble, Titus Calvus," Val said, hands folded on the table. "Avenal's a builder. Reputable. Experienced. Speaks Calesian but can't read it. Calvus contracted Avenal to build a house."

I tilted my head. "All right."

"Avenal agreed to take the commission," Val went on. "But asked for a contract he could read and reference. So, two versions were drawn up. Same terms, same witnesses, signed at the same time. They were read aloud by a local woman who said she could read both languages. Meant to prevent misunderstanding. And he got to work. Calvus was… disappointed with the result."

"What happened?" I asked.

Marcus said, "A house. Built too small."

I raised a brow. "Do you have the contracts?"

Val gestured. Marcus retrieved them, reluctantly, and passed them over. I laid them side by side, comparing them line by line. It didn't take long to spot the problem.

"Gods." I shook my head. "I see what happened."

Lucius leaned in, sharpening. "Go on."

"The contracts are identical except for the units of measurement. This one uses Calesian footmarks—twelve inches per foot. This one…" I tapped the Aeltyrian copy. "Uses *pedras*. That word translates directly to footmark, but in our system, a *pedra* is ten inches per foot."

Marcus frowned. "That's a two-inch difference per footmark."

"Exactly. Across sixty footmarks? That's ten full Calesian footmarks lost on the footprint. And volume-wise, we're talking about a structure barely half the intended size. A grown man wouldn't even be able to stand upright."

Lucius let out a whistle. "So instead of a house…"

"He'd have a very expensive chicken coop," I said dryly. "Or perhaps a playhouse for children."

Val raised an eyebrow. "Built perfectly. Just to the wrong scale."

"If Avenal built to what he read, based on his version of the contract, then he didn't breach anything. He fulfilled the terms as he understood them." I handed the documents back across the table. "Do you have the plans he was given?"

Val nodded at Marcus, who looked like he'd rather chew gravel than cooperate, but passed over the rolled parchment anyway.

I unrolled it and studied the script. "Exactly what I expected. These use Calesian footmarks—twelve-inch increments—but nowhere is that stated. Not in the margins. Not in the scale legend.

And if the interpreter missed it, how was Avenal supposed to know? You hand a man a string of numbers without context and expect him to divine the system behind them? That's not a mistake. It's a trap."

Marcus shifted in his seat. "If he's a man who regularly works with Calesians, builds things for Calesians and uses Calesian coin, shouldn't he know the difference?"

Lucius made a sound like he was trying not to laugh into his mug. "When we reinforce a camp or fortify a supply post, the builders use drawings just like this, but the scale is always marked. The units always labeled. Without that, you end up with bastions too narrow for siege ladders, or gates too short for a supply cart."

I let that settle before going on. "Cormeth Avenal built a miniature house because that's what he believed he was commissioned to do. If anyone's at fault, it's the noble who saw the price and thought he was getting a palace for the cost of a village well. And where was he during construction? A prudent buyer inspects progress."

Marcus made a vague gesture. "A prudent *builder* would've asked questions. About the units. Or why a nobleman wanted a house so small."

I gave a tight nod. "Fair point. Maybe he did. Those will be excellent questions for the hearing. I will say it's not easy for us Aeltyrians to question Calesian nobles."

Lucius grinned. "Remind me to have you argue my next contract. Marcus, she's going to put you out of a job."

"It's a simple enough issue if you can read both languages," I said, eyes still on Marcus as he pushed to his feet. "I'm happy to assist with any other contracts that need untangling."

"We should, ah, move to the audience chamber," Marcus muttered, straightening his tunic. "I'll go make sure everything is in order. If I might be excused?"

"Certainly," Val said, with a single nod.

The door clicked shut behind Marcus, and for a moment, the silence lingered, fragile. Like a page half-turned.

Lucius stood, brushing his hands together as though the conversation had left something dirty on his palms. "I'll go see if the clerks are squabbling over the rolls or if they're finally ready for you."

He didn't wait for an answer. Just slung his cloak over one shoulder and strode out with a casual wave.

The silence that followed was different. Heavier. Closer.

I reached for my cup again, forgetting it was empty, and set it back down with more care than needed. "What's at stake for the builder?"

"Calvus wants him bonded into service for five years. As penalty for breaching the contract, and compensation for the materials."

I blinked. "That seems excessive."

Then he looked at me—really looked. It landed like sunlight, warm against my skin.

"You were—" His voice dropped. "You *are* extraordinary."

A part of me wanted to bask in it. To close my eyes and let the praise settle. But another part, the one that had kept me alive all these years, tensed against it.

I forced a shrug. "I've spoken both languages my whole life. It's nothing remarkable."

"It is when you wield words like a blade."

It was too much. Too close to the thing I didn't want to name. I opened my mouth to speak, but he beat me to it.

"About last night—"

"I didn't—" I said at the same time.

The words collided and fell apart.

Then came boots in the corridor. A scribe calling names. Duty returning.

Val took a deep breath, then stood. "Shall we?"

I rose, adjusted my sword belt. "I didn't mean to embarrass him. Not really."

"You didn't," Val said, falling into step beside me. "He did that all on his own."

We walked side by side into the day—leaving the moment, like so many others, unspoken behind us.

# CHAPTER THIRTY-FIVE
## *Edict and Echo*

*"A ruling, once made, binds the realm—not merely the subject."*
—On the Authority of Governors

Dēwamos 90, 1230
*Aleaia*

From my post behind Val's right shoulder, I watched the crowd with a soldier's eyes. They shifted and murmured like cattle penned too long, each ready to bray grievances the moment they reached the front.

A year past, the death of Domitian di Alvareti—Val's uncle and former governor—had left Aeltyria in slow rot, passed from one official to the next haphazardly, none of them strong enough to govern properly. Now that the office had passed to Val, everyone wanted their share of justice.

"Dieter." Irinia Norbanus's voice slithered in from the left, clipped and cold, like steel drawn just enough to threaten.

I didn't turn. Her disdain hung in the air between us, pungent and bitter as woodsmoke.

"Norbanus," I said evenly.

Why Lucius had picked her for this, only the gods knew. He stood beside me, close enough to feel his amusement, though he had the sense not to show it. I gave him a look that might've blistered paint.

He dropped his gaze and rubbed the back of his neck. At least he had the decency to look guilty.

Hours dragged. Complaint after complaint rolled forward—food stores raided, boundary markers moved, a half-brother claiming an inheritance that wasn't his.

I kept my eyes on the crowd. That was my duty. Letting my thoughts wander would take me somewhere I'd rather not be just then.

Then came the case I'd been waiting for.

Titus Calvus stepped forward, smug and self-important—until Val read the ruling. Avenal would not be bound, and Calvus would pay him for the work already done, as agreed in their contract.

Calvus didn't take it well.

The man made the mistake of raising his voice, then his hand. Lucius was on him in an instant, dragging him from the chamber as he shrieked threats and curses.

It was all I could do not to smile.

When the chamber quieted again, the steward called, "Is Prefect Darius Rullus present?"

"Here, sir," came the measured reply.

A nobleman stepped forward from the back—tall, fair-haired, broad-shouldered, and polished in the effortless way that came with rank. At his side was a dark-haired Aeltyrian woman in a plain gray tunic. Her every step was measured, head bowed and hands folded before her.

Before the dais, they stopped. He bowed. She curtsied.

"Rise," Val said, lifting a hand.

They did. The man straightened with the confidence of someone long accustomed to authority. The woman kept her gaze lowered, body still. I'd seen that kind of stillness before—restrained, careful, born of too many years spent under the weight of someone else's heel.

"It is an honor to stand before you, my lord," Rullus said, voice ringing clear. "I am but a humble servant of the realm and loyal subject of the Empire, entrusted with governance of her eastern Aeltyrian province of Ostala. I come today seeking justice, and to support the claim of an Aeltyrian woman long denied it." He turned slightly and gestured to her. "This is Eira, formerly enslaved in Lascebar. May she speak for herself?"

Val nodded. "She may."

"My lord," the woman said, voice trembling, "Lord Quintus Varro promised me freedom upon his passing, but his son, Lord Caius Varro, refuses to release my papers and sent men after me when I escaped. I beg you to honor what was given to me and let me live as a free woman."

Rullus stepped forward again. "I vouch for her, my lord. I've spoken with her witnesses and brought them, should you wish to question them. I also carry Lord Quintus's will. He was a man known for keeping his word, and I believe it's our duty to see that his last wishes are upheld."

Val didn't so much as blink. Whatever he was thinking, it didn't reach his face. "Is Lord Caius Varro present to defend himself?"

"Here, my lord," a man's voice called from the back, smooth and practiced.

"Prefect Caius Varro of Lascebar," the steward intoned.

I shifted as the man emerged, already bracing for the stench of entitlement. He had the kind of face that never smiled unless it meant trouble. His hair was clipped short, not a strand out of place. Eyes blue and cold as mountain ice.

He moved like a soldier—the sort who never dirtied his boots. Disgusting.

He bowed at the bottom of the dais.

"And how do you answer Lord Rullus's claim?" Val asked, leaning forward on the throne.

"It is an outright falsehood, my lord," Varro said. "Furthermore, the slave Eira has run away—"

"Seeking protection from you," Rullus cut in, smooth as stone in a riverbed.

"—after being a disobedient, troublesome thorn in my side," Varro finished, unbothered. "She hasn't earned manumission."

"My lord," Rullus said, turning to Val, "Lord Varro's opinion is irrelevant. She was never his property. She should've been freed long ago."

Eira stood motionless beside him. But I saw the tremor she suppressed.

I didn't know Rullus. But I liked him.

"I appreciate your willingness to provide evidence," Val said. "Let me see the will."

Rullus withdrew a folded parchment from his tunic and handed it to the steward, who brought it to the dais.

"That is a forgery!" Varro snapped, voice cracking.

Val didn't flinch. He opened the document and read it in silence.

"If this is a forgery," he said at last, "it's a convincing one. It bears my father's seal."

He passed the will back. As the steward passed, I shifted slightly to glimpse the date: thirty-sixth of Quiestra, 1230. Succamos, as we Aeltyrians call it. Just half a year ago. Too recent to dismiss. Quintus Varro died not long after.

"Lord Varro, what evidence do you have to refute this?" Val asked mildly.

Varro's face darkened, a vein emerging at his temple. "I knew my father," he barked. "He would never have freed her. He meant for all of his property to pass to me."

"I'm sure you believe that," Val said evenly. "But I asked for evidence. A document. A witness. Something tangible. Do you have it?"

"My father—"

"It's a simple question. Do you have proof?"

Varro's mouth opened, then shut. He gulped, and when he spoke again, it was so quiet, I almost couldn't hear him. "No, I don't."

"I didn't quite catch that."

"No, my lord," he said louder, brittle.

"Then it is my judgment that Eira is a free woman. Any further attempt to claim, coerce, or harm her will be punishable by imprisonment on the first offense."

Varro took a step forward, face twisted in fury.

I moved before he could get close, boots cutting the silence on the stone as I descended the dais. My hand settled on the hilt of my sword.

"Don't," I said.

He sneered at me, gesturing like he might brush me off, then looked at Val. "No wonder you're on her side. You've got a weakness for these fucking savages."

"One more word," Val said, sharp from the throne, "and you'll find yourself in the dungeon today. Dieter. Norbanus. Escort him out. Eira, see my clerk."

I'd be lying if I said I didn't enjoy it when I took Varro's arm and turned him toward the doors. Norbanus stepped up on his other side, silent and stiff as always.

Varro yanked free. "I will leave of my own accord!"

"Sorry, my lord," Norbanus said.

I shoved him into the corridor with more force than necessary.

To the guards at the door, I said, "Don't allow him back in without Lord Valerius's permission."

"Who gave you the authority to speak on his behalf?" Norbanus snapped.

My shoulders went taut. She'd challenged me, loud enough for the guards to hear, and with Varro still in earshot.

I turned to her, voice even. "Do you think, if his lordship had him escorted out, he'd let him walk right back in? Use your head. If you doubt he'd back the order, ask him. Or ask Praefectus Tutela."

"Oh, I certainly will," she said, sneering.

This needed putting down before it festered.

"Follow me. We'll sort this out," I said, already walking.

A guard called out, "We'll keep him out, Praefecta!"

I glanced back. "Thank you."

I led Norbanus a few steps aside, far enough the guards wouldn't hear. The chamber began to empty behind us.

I kept my arms loose and my voice low. No heat, just steel. "What exactly is your problem with me?"

"I heard what they say about how you got your knighthood," she said. "It's probably why every ruling today has gone in favor of your kind. Calling you a knight is a farce and an insult to true knights."

I let the silence hang a beat, then laughed, sharp and cold. "So, you think I'm that good in bed? Gods, if my cunt could earn a title, I should've aimed higher."

Her face flushed scarlet.

I didn't flinch. Just folded my arms and stared down at her.

I felt Val arrive and stand just behind my shoulder. He didn't hesitate.

"She earned her knighthood when she killed the creature in the woods near Gormlaith and freed every prisoner that witch held captive," he said. "Earned it when she stood alone against eight armed men to protect a healer. No one gave her a title out of kindness. Certainly not as part of some kind of trade. She bled for it. And she's more of a knight than most who've ever worn the name."

Norbanus stiffened. "It violates imperial statute, my lord. She's—"

Val lifted a hand to silence her. "I know the laws. I also know the difference between a soldier and the kind of person who hides behind them. You won't serve in my household guard."

Her face drained.

"You may return your tabard to Praefectus Tutela before you leave."

She didn't look at me. I didn't look away.

"Dieter," Val said. "Walk with me."

I cut one last scathing look at her before I turned to walk away.

We crossed the hall in silence. At the first landing, he finally spoke.

"I'm sorry about her. I'll speak to Lucius about being more discerning with his selections."

"You don't need to apologize. They were her words, not yours." I paused. "You walked up just in time. How'd you manage that?"

"I didn't catch the beginning," he admitted. "But from the look on your face, and hers, I could guess the rest."

My voice softened before I meant it to. "I appreciate your defense of me."

"I told you I'd stand by you. Not just in words, though I meant every one of them." His eyes found mine. "You didn't need me to speak for you. But I wanted to."

I glanced sideways at him. "You were rather convincing."

The corner of his mouth twitched. "I try."

We climbed the last few steps in silence, the kind that sat easy between us.

Just before the upper hall, he spoke again, his tone casual, almost teasing.

"By the way… I found something peculiar in my chamber last night."

*After the feast? I thought he had—*

"Care to lend me your expertise?"

I didn't answer, just followed him. At his door, he gave the guards a nod, then turned and opened it.

"After you, my lady."

# CHAPTER THIRTY-SIX
## *Inheritance*

*"We do not choose the blood in our veins. Only what we do with it."*
—Caitriona Lennan, High Mage of Aeltyria

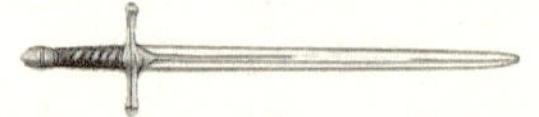

Dēwamos 90, 1230
*Aleaia*

I stepped into the room. Everything bore his mark: simple furnishings, furs piled on the bed for warmth, two leather chairs drawn close to the hearth like they were meant for confessions.

And books. Gods, the books. Some stacked with care, others teetering in half-tamed piles, like he'd stopped halfway through reading and never picked it up again.

The corner of my mouth lifted. In another life, he might've been a scholar.

He crossed to the far corner where the wardrobe had stood. It had been dragged away from the wall and left haphazardly, like he'd forgotten it.

I followed. "So," I said, eyeing the wall, "what's this mysterious discovery of yours?"

"Look here," he said, gesturing to a small cavity carved into the stone. "Some of the mortar here, between these stones, looks different from the rest of the wall. Might be a passageway, but I can't get it to open."

The keep at Aeldunon was ancient. Built in Aelan's time, it was over a thousand years old. I'd grown up hearing tales of it, but seeing it up close, living inside it, felt like walking inside a story.

A chunk of stone rested on the desk nearby. I picked it up, thumb brushing the shallow carving and the Aeltyrian script etched into its surface.

"'To where memory is kept.'" My brow tightened. "At least, I think that's what it says. Sounds ominous. How'd you even find it?"

He shrugged. "Curiosity."

"You were moving furniture out of curiosity? In the middle of the night? It didn't look like this yesterday."

It didn't look like this before I threw myself at you.

"It looked off to me," he said. "Too close to the window."

I raised a brow as I held his gaze.

He shrugged. "There are better places to put it."

"You could've waited. What if something had been behind there?"

"What, exactly, would've posed a threat? It's a wall."

"Something that needed a wall to keep it in."

He laughed. "You have me there."

I leaned in, studying the dark opening where the missing brick had been. The air from within was cool, tinged with stone and something older. "I wonder what lies within?"

I stuck my finger inside to check for a key or anything that might offer a clue.

"A sharp—"

"Ouch!" I hissed, jerking my hand back. Blood welled on the tip of my finger.

Val caught my wrist with that maddening gentleness of his, thumb pressing against the cut. "I was about to warn you."

His touch was warm. Steady. Distracting. My thoughts scattered like embers kicked from a hearth. I looked down at our hands.

"I'm sorry," I said. "Should've been more careful."

He looked at me and something in his eyes softened.

"There's no need to apologize. Your fearlessness is one of the things I—"

A deep, grating rumble cut him off—stone grinding against stone behind us.

Val didn't let go of my hand. We both turned as the wall slid open, revealing a hidden corridor—no, a stairwell swallowed by darkness. Cold, damp air spilled out to meet us.

"We'll need a torch," I said, stepping back slightly.

His fingers tightened, just enough to stop me. "I meant what I said last night. If you remember it."

My pulse kicked. "Which part?"

I could feel the warmth between us.

*Kiss me*, I'd told him. Drunk and bold and aching.

"What do you recall?" he asked quietly.

Damn him.

"Why don't you remind me?" I asked, lower now. "If you meant it."

He didn't look away. "Ask me again, if it's truly what you want. And if you're not ready…" His voice lowered. "I'm not going anywhere."

There was no doubt in me. Only fire.

He lifted my hand to his lips and kissed the backs of my fingers—slow, reverent, his gaze never leaving mine.

My breath caught. That kind of tenderness was dangerous. I didn't move at first.

This was what I had wanted and been afraid of, all at once.

But the dark waited. And so did the godsdamned torch.

I pulled away, crossed the chamber, stepped into the hall, and returned with one, already lit.

Val took it from me without a word and turned toward the passage.

The stairwell beyond was narrow, far older than the rest of the keep. There wasn't room to walk side by side. As we descended, the walls seemed to press inward, worn smooth by time and silence. Torchlight danced along the stone, swaying in rhythm with our steps.

We didn't speak.

My pace slowed as memory crowded me.

He hadn't stayed.

After everything, after the way he'd touched me, held me, *looked* at me, he'd laid me in that bed and vanished into the night. I told myself he needed air. That he wanted space to think.

But part of me, mean and sore, kept whispering he went to the baths.

Because I'd asked and he'd said no. He'd had to.

Because I'd been too drunk.

And maybe he'd needed something I hadn't been able to give.

"Where did you go after the feast?" I asked suddenly, low enough that the stone might swallow it whole.

I hadn't meant to ask. But the question had been clawing at the back of my mind since we sat around the table that morning.

"I brought you upstairs. Put you to bed."

I stopped. So did he. The stairs gave me just enough height for us to stand eye to eye.

"And after that?" I asked. "Once I was tucked in safe and sound?"

"Back here," he said. "I tried reading."

"And?"

"I read the same line six times."

I raised a brow.

His mouth twitched. "Then I decided I didn't like the position of the wardrobe."

I stared at him.

He hesitated. "And early this morning, I went to the river."

I frowned. "You went into the river?"

"To cool off." He rubbed the back of his neck. "I stood in the shallows. Fully clothed. It was… cold."

I exhaled, uncertain if it was disbelief or amusement. "That's ridiculous. Why would you do that to yourself?"

His voice dropped, quieter now. "I needed the cold."

He didn't open up often. Most of him lived behind that careful restraint. For a moment, he allowed it to slip.

"Why didn't you stay?" I asked.

"In the river?"

"No. With me." My cheeks burned. Not long ago, I'd been embarrassed to let him dress a wound for me, and now I was asking why he hadn't fucked me when he had the chance.

"Because when it happens—when it's real, and you're ready—I want it to be something you remember. Not dulled by wine. Not shadowed by doubt. Something that's ours."

It would've taken nothing—half a breath, a step closer, the neck of his tunic clenched in my hands—and I could have kissed him until I forgot what hesitation felt like.

But I didn't.

"Now," he said, his voice steadier again, "if you're done tormenting me, might we see what's down here?"

I gave a faint nod, and we moved on.

The steps tightened as we descended, spiraling deeper into the earth. The air grew colder with each turn, the walls pressing close, damp stone breathing against our skin. Somewhere below, the scent changed, thickened. Old earth. A place long forgotten.

The stair ended in a circular chamber, just large enough to turn in without brushing the walls. Shelves ringed the room, thick with dust. I stepped closer, eyes tracing the titles stamped into warped leather. Treatises on spellwork. Ritual theory. Some bore runes at the spine. Others were bound in hide.

Outlawed texts.

The kind Claudius had banned.

The kind the Anvallan Temple condemned.

My gaze caught on a second door across from the stairs. And held.

The locking mechanism was clearer this time, set into the stone like it had been waiting for me. I stepped forward, braced myself, and pressed my finger to the shallow needle point. It bit. I let it, then touched my thumb to the wound without complaint. A faint click echoed in the dark.

I didn't understand how it worked. I knew the stories—how magic was once sacred to my people, how Calesia had burned it out root and stem. But beyond that, my knowledge was a patchwork of myth and instinct.

Something beyond that door pulled at me. Not violently, just steady, like a hand at my spine.

"They really didn't want anyone getting through," Val said from behind me.

I stepped forward. The chamber beyond was quiet. Still. Nearly empty.

A stone slab filled the center, its surface carved with shallow channels, darkened with old blood. A skeleton lay on it, half-dressed in what might once have been clothes, now little more than threads. A sword had been driven through the ribs, the blade's tip vanishing into a narrow seam in the stone.

The slab's grooves stretched outward like rivers drawn in miniature, all feeding toward a larger cut in the floor. Beyond it stood a full suit of armor—dark, ornate, untouched by time.

I took a slow breath. "Even I can tell this was someone important. And that this is blood magic."

The words tasted strange in my mouth. Like naming it gave it weight. Like speaking it made it real.

Val stepped forward, frowning at the slab. "Everything I know about magic comes from Calesian books," he said. "Which means it's probably skewed. Censored. Or both."

I moved toward the slab and knelt, brushing dust from the inscription carved into the stone. Val stayed a few paces back, quiet.

He lowered his voice as his gaze drifted over the skeleton. "I wonder who this was. And why they died like this."

"Me too," I said. "Maybe someone they didn't want walking back out."

I blew gently across the surface, leaned in, squinted at the worn lines.

"'To seal that which they abhor, I spill my blood,'" I read aloud. My finger followed the line to a chipped section. "There's damage here… but the next line says, 'To take the sword and set it free.' Gods, I think it was voluntary. A self-sacrifice."

Our eyes met as I stood.

*Free me.*

Not my thought, but there all the same.

I gestured toward the blade. "Go ahead. Take the sword."

He raised a brow. "I don't like how readily you volunteered me for that."

"You're bigger than I am. Leverage."

"Aren't you supposed to protect me?" he asked. "Any blade pinning remains to a blood-soaked altar isn't exactly begging to be touched, Aleaia. Let's go upstairs, see if anyone knows who this might be."

I couldn't hear him. There was a sound rising in my ears, soft at first, like wind through a long corridor. Then sharper. A ringing, high and clear, like a bell only I could hear. It pressed behind my eyes, crowded out thought.

His voice faded beneath it.

"I want to—" I said. "I… have to."

I think he answered. Maybe it was just the sound.

My body moved without permission. Each step landed with a weight that wasn't mine, guided by something I didn't understand.

The ringing grew louder, building with every breath until it pushed me forward.

My hand rose.

Fingers closed around the hilt.

It felt… familiar.

My stomach turned.

I hadn't chosen this.

I obeyed it.

# CHAPTER THIRTY-SEVEN
## *Blood & Magic*

*"There is no greater magic than a vow made in love—*
*and no curse more lasting."*
—Caitriona Lennan, High Mage of Aeltyria

*Aleaia*

I stood by the window in Val's chamber.

No. Not his. Mine. The same space in another life.

It was a memory and a dream at once.

The shape was familiar—the scent of it, the slant of light through the high panes. But something was wrong. Outside, the walls of Aeldunon shattered under Calesian siege fire. The shots were the kind only their engineers could design—anti-magic rounds that split stone like parchment, tearing through the city's last defenses with brutal precision.

The door burst open.

"My Queen, grave news from the city walls. King Cadoc—"

"I know." The voice that answered wasn't mine, though it came from my mouth. It trembled, but did not break. "I felt his spirit cross the Veil."

As I turned, something in me recoiled. I wasn't moving on my own.

This wasn't my body.

"Jurian, you know what must be done."

The man in the doorway looked stricken. "My Queen, is there no other way?"

"You know as well as I that there is none. Take my daughter somewhere safe. I will do what I must." My voice held, even as the edges frayed. "Do not mourn for my body. The chamber will be its tomb."

"You know the dangers of blood magic, Your Grace! You'll be trapped here!"

"I know." I looked away, toward the bed Cadoc and I had shared for such a short time. Bittersweet. Where I'd conceived and birthed my daughter. Where I'd hoped to die, an old woman, many years from now.

"I know the dangers well and I accept them willingly. It will only be until my daughter returns. You must ensure it, Jurian. Keep her safe. Love her well. And tell her—" My breath caught, just for a heartbeat. "—tell her the truth. Tell her I did this for her."

"I will," Jurian said. "I swear it."

I turned toward the passage and stepped inside. Before it closed again, I looked back at him one last time. "She must know this came from love. I regret only that I could not save us all."

"You've done all that could be done." Jurian dropped to one knee, head bowed. "For that, we are forever in your debt."

I smiled, small and tired. "It is my duty. You owe me nothing, except to keep my daughter safe. Now go."

I pressed my finger to the blood-lock just inside the door. I didn't wait for it to close before I turned away, toward the spiral stair. Jurian would take care of concealing the lock outside. With a flick of my hand, the torches flared to life.

I descended quickly, crossed the antechamber, and entered the room at the bottom. My fingers trembled as I removed my armor piece by piece, placing each part on the stand. When only my linen shift remained, I took up the sword.

My gaze swept the room once, brief and final. I lay back on the slab.

My breath came shallow. Sweat clung to my skin, a cold sheen across my chest and arms. My hands trembled as I turned the blade toward myself, pressing the tip beneath my ribs.

Mana surged through the metal, lighting it from within—a ghostly glow that felt wrong in every way. It recoiled. We were bound together and now I asked it to harm me. To take my life.

"My lady Lithau, Goddess of All Creation, heed my plea," I whispered. "For my daughter, and for Aeltyria, I offer my life. Let this act cease the flow of magic across the land. Let it shield my people from those who would abuse your gifts."

The sword shook in my grip. My chest rose and fell in short, uneven gasps.

I was afraid.

I was so afraid.

Not of the pain. I could bear that.

I feared what would happen if this didn't work.

I feared what would become of my daughter, if I failed.

I would never see her first steps. Never hear her first words. Never watch her become anything more than a child left behind. She would grow to womanhood never knowing the mother who gave everything for her.

Grief settled in my soul. In my bones. Tears stung my eyes.

I had seen both threads unfurl. One where it didn't work. One where it did.

It would work. It had to.

"May this seal be undone only by the Daughter of Aelan, rightful heir to the throne and my legacy. I give you the blood of your daughter's daughter… and my own soul to seal this vow."

I breathed in.

Held it.

Then drove the blade into my abdomen.

The scream tore loose. Blood spilled hot across the stone, hissing as it met the glowing runes. The sword seared in my grip, sliding deeper, drinking from me. Anchoring the spell.

I almost stopped. Almost.

But I pressed again, hands shaking.

The blade resisted, as if the chamber itself fought back. Fire raced through my veins. Magic howled through my body, not with me, but against me, ripping away strength, breath, self.

My vision blurred at the edges.

I had to do it.

Had to keep going.

With the last of my strength, I drove it home. My blood spilled into the carved channels, racing toward the center. The slab drank it in. The walls shuddered.

And I thought, in those last moments, about the day she was born.

The snowstorm came early—bitter and blinding.

I labored through the last night of Mētanos, gripping Cadoc's hand while the wind screamed through the shuttered windows.

It was agony. Endless.

And then—

She arrived.

Tiny. Wailing. Warm against my chest.

And when I looked into her eyes—those wide, pewter eyes—I forgot the pain entirely.

She blinked up at me as if she'd been waiting all this time.

I remember Cadoc's hands shaking when he first held her. How his eyes were wet as he looked at her as though she were the whole world made small enough to fit in his arms.

As though he had never believed in the gods until that moment.

"Aleaia," I had whispered, voice breaking with joy and fear and awe. "She is Aleaia… the light that endures when all else is gone."

And somewhere behind me, the vault door began to close.

Dēwamos 90, 1230

*Aleaia*

The chamber rushed back around me.

"Aleaia, are you all right?"

I was still on my feet. Somehow. But my breath came in gasps. My clothes clung to me with sweat. My hand clutched the hilt of the sword, white-knuckled.

It was no longer in the stone.

I stared at it, the blade still glowing faintly. A soft pulse shimmered along the edge, beating with my own heart.

It felt alive.

I dropped it like it had burned me. It struck the floor with a sharp clang.

My breath hitched, shallow. Too fast. The world tilted.

She was the queen.

And my mother.

And she had died.

For me.

"I can't… breathe," I managed.

A wave of cold swept over me, sudden and bone-deep. My limbs went numb, heavy and useless. Darkness edged my vision.

I didn't even know I was falling until Val caught me from behind, arms wrapping around me as I collapsed.

"Aleaia, no. Stay with me. I've got you."

He sank with me to the floor, guiding me down.

"You're all right," he said softly, steady as stone.

I latched onto his voice.

"Just breathe. In… and out," he said. "That's it."

One breath.

Then another.

Slowly, the room steadied. I realized I was on the floor between his legs, his arm around my back, holding me upright.

"I'm sorry," I said, sitting forward. I rested my elbows on my knees and pressed my hands to my face.

Val's voice came quieter then, rough at the edges. "It felt like something passed through you."

"I saw it," I rasped. "I saw everything. Through Queen Eavan's eyes."

He didn't move, except to stroke my back. "You dropped like you'd been hit. I—" He exhaled. "You don't do that."

I pressed a hand to my stomach, still half-expecting to find blood.

"It wasn't real," I gasped. "It couldn't have been."

His voice stayed low. "What wasn't?"

The words caught. Then they tumbled out. Raw.

"I was in your room, but it wasn't yours—it was hers. The Queen's. I was her. I saw the walls fall. I saw my Papa—young. She told him to take me and run. I felt it all—the magic, the pain, everything. She died to stop it, Val. To stop the war. To save me. For love… for the love of me."

His arms tightened. He didn't say it wasn't my fault, didn't offer pretty lies.

And I let myself fall against him.

Because there was nothing else I could do.

The sword lay where I'd dropped it. Waiting.

I stared at it. "What… what is that thing?

Val didn't look at it. He looked at me. He reached up, fingers brushing gently along my cheek, turning my face toward his.

"The Fellglow Blade," he said quietly. "I think. My father's been searching for it since the war ended."

"Why?"

"He meant to give it to Cassius, to prove he was the rightful heir. Or at least keep the true one from rising."

"What?" I heard him fine, but couldn't make sense of what he said.

He didn't glance away. "The Fellglow Blade only responds to the Aeltyrian heir. And I think that's you, Aleaia."

# CHAPTER THIRTY-EIGHT
## Playing with Fire

*"The heart does not fear fire when it knows who it burns for."*
—Aeltyrian Proverb

Mētanos 8, 1230
*Valerius*

Aleaia stood just behind me, off my right shoulder. She rarely spoke in this chamber, but her presence steadied me, like a fixed star above shifting seas.

And I sat in the seat her bloodline once claimed. That truth pressed in around me.

"Lord, we must dispatch reinforcements to quell this uprising," Marcus said from the seat beside mine. "It has gone unchecked for far too long."

I didn't answer right away.

The chamber was close with heat and tension, heavy with unsaid things. For the last decadium, we'd received reports—village fires sparked without flint, crops ruined by sudden flood, a child who opened a sinkhole.

It wasn't rebellion, but fright and instinct. Magic, awakening in those too young to know how to hide it.

To most Calesians, magic was not misunderstood. It was dangerous. Corrupt. The first sign of sedition. To the men at the table, those people weren't afraid. They were rebellious. The children were insurgents in the making.

Marcus would have me cull the lot. Make an example of them. I meant to buy time until I found a real solution.

"I *will not* act without a direct order from Avitum," I said at last. "To do so would exceed the authority of my post."

It wasn't true. I think we both knew it.

"With respect, my lord," Marcus replied, "you would be well within your rights. The law is clear regarding the use of magic. You have both precedent and divine mandate."

"Divine mandate," I echoed flatly.

He pressed on. "The Temple's teachings leave no room for ambiguity. Magic, untamed, is corruption made manifest. We cannot allow it to fester. Not if we mean to hold this land."

Aleaia hadn't moved, but I felt her. The weight of her silence. The edge of her stare. She was watching Marcus like a falcon watches a rabbit—sharp and still and entirely without pity.

Before I could speak again, Lucius did.

"There has been no confirmed uprising. Only fear. Scattered incidents," he said evenly. "The people are not armed. They are not coordinated."

"As far as we are aware," Marcus countered. "Forgive me, Praefectus, but you're speaking as though this is a matter of comfort, not security."

The formality didn't go unnoticed. The three of us had grown up together. And now Marcus was drawing lines. Perhaps I'd drawn the first one, in Elisedd. Things hadn't been the same since.

"Security," I said sharply, "does not begin with fire and sword. Not in a land we already rule."

Marcus leaned forward, palms pressing into the table. "Then how many more incidents will you tolerate, my lord? Another fire? A legionary dead from an Aeltyrian woman's curse?"

I gritted my teeth.

Lucius laughed softly. "Marcus, it sounds like you're afraid of the women or the curses yourself. Probably both."

Behind me came the faint creak of leather and metal.

I glanced back.

Aleaia hadn't moved, but she wasn't still. Her fingers flexed around the hilt of her sword once, held in check by discipline and the weight of the room.

"I believe in law," Marcus said. "And in order. Without such principles, we are nothing."

"And I believe that fear is not reason enough to call down steel on civilians," I replied, softer than before.

There was silence, then.

Tight. Brittle. Waiting to crack.

"Well, my lord, if we do nothing, as you propose," Marcus said, his tone edged with irritation, "and unrest becomes open revolt, the consequences will be on your head. Not mine."

"My position stands." I rose. "And this discussion is over."

I moved to the door. Didn't look back. Just gestured to Aleaia and walked. She fell in beside me without a word, boots striking the stone in rhythm with mine. Marcus's voice followed us, urgent and bitter, but we were already at the doors.

"He's vile," Aleaia said once we were clear of the council chamber.

"He wasn't always," I replied.

She sighed. "No one ever is. That's the danger."

"You think I'm defending him."

"I think you're trying to remember who he was before all this." Her voice dropped. "And I think he's brave to call for blood in front of me like I wasn't even there."

I didn't answer at first. It wasn't bravery, but ignorance. He didn't know what we'd learned about her in that hidden chamber.

After a few more steps, I spoke again. "He was the clever one. Better at rhetoric than anyone I've ever met."

"And now he wants to burn villages."

I couldn't expect her to envision a time when he hadn't always been the voice of the Empire. When he'd been a brilliant boy who cared more about being right than about being feared. "He wants to be indispensable to my brother."

She looked ahead. "That'll do it. Where are we going?"

"Would you spar with me?" I asked. "I've been too sedentary. I need the feel of a sword in my hand."

Her brow furrowed. "What if I hurt you?"

I couldn't imagine that. The thought was so at odds with her it drew a laugh out of me. "We're evenly matched, Aleaia."

She shook her head. "I mean the other way. I can't control it yet. Not when I'm angry. Or… distracted."

I knew what she meant, and there was no laughing at that.

After we'd found her mother's repository, magic had surfaced without warning, and the laws left her no safe way to learn. What knowledge she gained had come from scraps—old texts her mother hid, fragments pieced together behind locked doors. No teacher. No guidance. Only instinct. And risk.

Her mother had been able to call upon all the elements, she said. So far, Aleaia had only called fire. Not well. Not cleanly.

It didn't look like any flame I'd ever seen, either—silver, flickering white, almost too bright to look at.

Three nights ago, she'd tried to light a candle and a tapestry had gone up in flames. I remembered it more vividly than I'd have liked.

She'd come to my room near midnight, her hair loose, a streak of soot across her cheek. She hadn't knocked. Just stormed in, wild-eyed, clutching a half-melted candlestick in one hand like it might explain everything.

She hadn't realized, at first, what she was wearing: nothing but a thin linen shift, damp and clinging from the water she'd thrown at the blaze.

I had noticed right away.

And then tried not to.

"We hid the other incident, but I don't know how many more times we'll be able to. Especially if something happens out in the open."

I met her gaze. "Just focus on the swords. The training ground is empty."

I watched her—the tension in her shoulders, the flicker of uncertainty in her eyes. She wanted to give me what I asked, though. She always did.

But this time, fear held her back. That wasn't like her. She was brave by nature. Defiant by instinct. This hesitation was something new.

"It'll draw more attention if we don't," I said, softer now. "We haven't trained together since we found it."

She exhaled, slow and reluctant. "All right. Let's go."

Across the courtyard, the training ring lay tucked between the barracks and outer wall—just packed dirt, worn rails, and a sky full of pale morning light. The chill of Messoris—no, *Mētanos*—lingered in the air, edged with woodsmoke and early frost.

She shrugged off her cloak and slung it over the fence. "Steel or wood?"

"Steel," I said, lifting one. "Try not to poke too many holes in me."

She gave me a look as she drew hers, long-suffering if I ever saw it. "These are so blunt I couldn't poke a hole in you if I tried."

I fought back a smile. "Do you want to?"

"Not yet." She stepped into the ring, blade glinting. "But if you keep talking, I might."

She dropped into a ready stance, loose-limbed and predatory. Her balance shifted like water, never fixed. Each step turned her body slightly, blade tracking as if drawing circles around me. Aeltyrian-trained.

A dancer—one who knew exactly when to cut.

My stance was squared, direct. High guard. Shoulders locked, weight anchored. Legion technique, honed for the battlefield, designed to crush.

"Come on, then," she said.

I stepped in with an overhead cut. She caught it with a flick of her wrist, spun out of reach, and slashed toward my ribs.

"You're slow," she said.

"I'm careful."

"An abundance of caution is a burden."

I advanced again, deliberate and controlled. She slipped past the edge of my swing, pivoted with the easy certainty of someone who knew she was faster, then darted back in with a lunge that nearly kissed my throat.

I blocked—just.

Her eyes glinted. "You're dead."

"That's your opener?"

"I could end you with a flourish, if that's what you're into."

My gaze flicked to her mouth, then met her eyes again. "Only if it's mutual."

She rolled her eyes, spun her blade once, and went for a high strike. I stepped in, turned my blade, and hooked hers clean with the crossguard and wrenched it free. Her sword hit the dirt with a dull thud.

She sighed in exasperation. "Sloppy on my part. Just hit me already. I deserve it."

"Where's the fun in that?" I stooped, picked up her sword, and held it out. "Fight me like you mean it."

She took it, adjusting her grip. "You said no holes."

"You can do both. You have enough control."

Her gaze held mine. "Is that a command?"

I stepped closer. "Would it make a difference if it was?"

Her answer came fast—a strike from the right, sharp and close. I caught it just in time. She pressed forward, relentless, until our blades locked and we broke apart.

"Enjoying yourself yet?" she asked, all breath and bite.

"I am."

She laughed. "Of course you are. Typical. Man enjoying himself while the woman's doing all the work."

My grin came slow. "Then she's with the wrong man."

"Oh?"

I closed the distance again. The space between us felt tighter. Sharper.

"The right one puts her satisfaction first. Every time."

She disarmed me with a clean twist of her wrist. My sword hit the ground, and she stepped back, victorious. Breath quick and even. Eyes bright. "Who are you trying to convince?"

"You," I said, brushing my hands off. "But I could convince better with action than words."

"Could you?" Her brow lifted. "Then one more."

She began to circle, blade twirling with dancer's ease. Loose strands of dark hair fell around her face like strands of silk. She looked wild and untouchable.

"Don't hold back," she said. "I'm armored. You're not."

"I'm bigger." I shrugged. "Seems fair."

"Bigger isn't always better."

"A bold claim."

She gave me a measured look. "Small size can be mitigated with cleverness."

I tilted my head. "Oh, I'm clever, too. Want to test me?"

"Disarm me first."

She came in again—low, then high. Angled strikes, sharp and fast. I met her strike for strike until I caught her momentum, swept behind her knee. She hit the ground with a soft grunt.

I winced. Leaning in, I offered my hand.

She hesitated only for a second, then took it.

I pulled her up, and she didn't let go.

For one breath, maybe two, we stood too close. Lips parted. Eyes on mine as though she were still mid-fight, debating whether to finish me off or fall into me.

And then she made her choice.

She grabbed the neck of my tunic and pulled me in.

The kiss came, breathless and certain. As if she'd finally decided.

Her hands moved to my neck, bracing me, and I dropped the sword, my hands at her wrists. I kissed her back, the hunger I'd kept buried for years breaking loose at last.

Her mouth opened beneath mine, and the world narrowed to the warmth of her lips and the certainty that this—*this*—was real.

Gods, she was more than I ever imagined. Softer. Fiercer.

And then the magic came.

It stirred quietly at first, like heat gathering beneath skin, in my periphery. Then it bloomed silver and shimmering, a warm pulse that swelled outward.

A shield rose around us, silver and luminous. The air within it felt hushed, sacred for a brief moment. And then, as quickly as it had appeared, it dissolved.

She pulled back first, her lips brushing against mine as she exhaled, eyes wide.

"I didn't..." Her voice faltered. "I didn't mean to do that."

I wanted to tell her it was all right.

That I didn't regret it at all.

That I wanted to kiss her again, had wanted to for so long.

But before I could say anything, she stepped back and turned away. Anger, maybe. Or fear.

She picked up her sword as she headed for the edge of the ring, then hurled it. It struck the barrel with a jarring clang. Her gloves followed, flung hard in the opposite direction.

Then she gripped the fence with both hands. Head bowed. Shoulders taut. Her breath came sharp and fast in the cold.

The realization settled in my chest, slow and unwelcome:

I shouldn't have let it happen.

I stood still, watching her for a long moment. Then moved to gather her gloves and both swords. I slid the blades back into the barrel, tucked her gloves into my belt.

Since she'd been with me, she'd always been controlled. Quiet in her anger. Measured. But I could see it now, flaring beneath her skin—not at me. At herself.

I stepped close, slow, and laid a hand on her back.

"You pushed us into this," she said, still facing the fence. "Even after I told you I wasn't ready. That I was afraid of losing control."

I let the words sit. Let her say them.

"The sparring? Or the kiss?" I asked.

She turned halfway, just enough to glance at me. Her eyes were storm-dark.

"The sparring. That was you." She sighed. "The kiss... was mine."

I said nothing, but let my hand fall away. Waited.

"And I don't regret it," she added softly. "I would do it again. And again. And I will, if you let me. But I'm afraid of what it means for you."

That caught me.

"Before, it was just an issue of class. The consequences, when they came, were mine to bear. But now, with magic—if someone saw the shield, and saw us together like that, they'll call you a traitor," she said, her voice breaking on the word. "Not just to the Empire, but the Temple too. You'll be an apostate."

Worse than a deserter. Hunted to the ends of Veridion by the Third Army.

That's what she saw for me now, because she'd kissed me. Because her magic had answered.

No wonder she had thrown her sword.

"You're not—"

"I am, Val. To them. I'm Aeltyrian. A mage. The heir to a kingdom they tried to erase. And now they've seen you with me. That's all it will take." She wiped a hand over her face, let it fall to her side. "I don't care what happens to me," she said. "But I won't let you burn for standing too close."

I breathed out slowly. "I wouldn't have played with fire if I feared being burned."

The truth of it settled between us like ash.

"If someone did see us…" I shook my head. "Then I'll protect you. As I protect all of our people."

She crossed her arms. Held herself still.

"To them, there is no 'our people,'" she said. "There's yours. And there's mine. And the Empire will rip us apart to prove it. Rip you apart to—"

She couldn't finish, covering her mouth with one hand. Her eyes shone.

I reached out, slowly. Arms open.

She leaned in, her head resting against my chest, holding me tight around my middle. I rested my cheek on her hair.

"I hate that the world is this way," I murmured. "I think what's inside you is a gift. If I ever have the power to change how this world treats your people… I will. And I'll stand beside you. Always."

The quiet held. The stillness with it.

And in that stillness, I knew what had to be done.

I only needed to find the way.

# CHAPTER THIRTY-NINE
*The Absence*

Mētanos 9, 1230
*Valerius*

Marcus's seat at the council table was empty the next morning.

No formal notice was given.

No message delivered.

Only a folded scrap of parchment left behind in his quarters, hastily scrawled.

*Val,*
*I have been summoned to Avitum with utmost haste.*
*—Marcus Frugi*

I read it twice. Didn't believe it either time.

He was running.

Because Marcus was, and had always been, a coward.

I folded the note, slipped it beneath my belt, and stood there a while.

I should have told her.

Should have done more when I had the chance.

But I didn't, and I'd never forgive myself.

And now Marcus was gone—two steps ahead of the reckoning he'd earned.

# CHAPTER FORTY
## *To Burn, and Not Regret It*

*"The First Sword must love not only the Queen, but her land. Her fury. Her people's scars. Anything less is treason to the vow."*
—Rites of Coronation

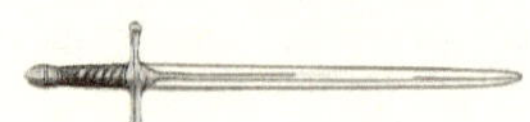

Mētanos 17, 1230
*Valerius*

Something was shifting.

I felt it, subtle and steady, like pressure building beneath the surface, or a storm gathering just beyond hearing.

I shifted on the throne. The carved wood bit into my spine—stiff and unforgiving. It fit the part, I supposed. Power wasn't meant to be comfortable.

The petitioners' voices buzzed at the edge of my hearing. I registered the words, but I wasn't listening.

I was tired of listening.

"Magic use is becoming increasingly and alarmingly widespread throughout the territory, my lord," said Evaristus Pulcher, prefect of the Second Army's Fifth Cohort. His voice struck like cold iron—measured and full of quiet menace. "Some have begun wielding it against our authority when we attempt to enforce His Majesty's law. We need access to Aeldunon's incolumium stores."

Until five days ago, Pulcher had been a name on parchment—Gavius's replacement, stationed in Elisedd. Now I knew him for what he was.

I'd spent my life surrounded by men like him. I knew the type. Arrogant. Rigid. The kind of man who mistook fear for order, and obedience for respect. Polished on the outside. Rot underneath.

He thought authority meant dominion. That rank justified itself.

And he'd come to demand that I use mine like a cudgel.

He stood at the base of the dais as if he owned the hall—shoulders square, tunic immaculate, eyes steady and smug. Everything about him reeked of control.

Rebellion here. Rebellion there. Spoiled nobles cry rebellion any time they're asked to actually lead.

I'd read the reports. I knew the truth. There was no armed resistance in Elisedd. No organized revolt.

Since Pulcher's appointment, the town had bled. Land seized. Livestock taken. Homes stripped from families and handed to soldiers. Heavy taxes laid on the backs of people who had almost nothing. And when they couldn't pay, they were dragged into the mines to dig the same ore meant to bind their magic in chains.

Incolumium, though, was a hard metal to pull from the earth and harder still to smith into usable form.

And now Pulcher wanted more.

He wanted a blank writ.

He wanted blood.

My patience thinned by the minute.

But that wasn't the worst of it.

Then came the rest. The reason the town had turned on the cohort.

My gut twisted, sharp and familiar. A disgust that lodged beneath the ribs and refused to move. What Pulcher had allowed wasn't simply a failure of command.

Pulcher served in the Second. That made it my problem.

It was corruption. The kind that eats through bone and rank alike. The kind the Empire turned a blind eye to, so long as the grain arrived on time and the taxes stayed high.

Several of his legionaries had pursued a young woman. Repeatedly. She refused them every time.

And after the third rejection, they kidnapped her.

Took her to the mines. Brutalized her. Killed her.

Her mother had found out.

And when she did, she set them alight.

A fitting public execution. Loud. Unapologetic. Her grief became fury, and her fury became a rallying cry.

The people of Elisedd drove the cohort out like plague rats. The soldiers hadn't had time to shackle them all, and even if they'd had time, they wouldn't have had enough incolumium to do it.

They had no defense against magic, so they ran.

And ever since, Pulcher had returned to Aeldunon's great hall day after day, demanding reinforcements and permission to take the town by force.

I had denied him. Every time.

Because I knew what Pulcher would do if given the freedom he craved.

He would raze Elisedd to its bones. Hang bodies from the elder tree and call it peace.

He was exactly the kind of man my brother would reward.

I wouldn't let it happen on my watch.

I leaned back. My hands itched with the raw, steady ache of restraint. What I wanted was to throw Pulcher out of the castle. Better still, to throw him out of his position, but his family was too well connected.

Most of all, though, I wanted to be elsewhere. Somewhere far from Pulcher and men like him. With someone else, her mouth beneath mine, the feel of her in my arms reminding me that there's more to this life than denying the rotten souls of men the suffering they desired.

I'd kissed her once.

*Once.*

And now I was here, listening to Pulcher poison the air with words like *authority* and *order*, as if the Empire's hunger hadn't already hollowed out this land.

I exhaled slowly. "As I've explained to exhaustion, Lord Pulcher, I cannot sanction such extensive action against civilians without explicit approval from the crown."

"My soldiers are relegated to the fields outside Elisedd, my lord! They've been expelled from the town. Any attempt to re-enter is met with fire!"

Behind me, Aleaia shifted, her armor creaking. Her posture sharpened like a blade unsheathed. Still as stone.

I knew what kind of storm her silence could carry. I felt it coiling in her, tight as a drawn bowstring, ready to snap.

These were my soldiers. My command. This had happened under my banner.

My voice sharpened. "Why, exactly, were they expelled?"

The silence was answer enough.

I leaned forward.

"Was it because your men murdered a girl of sixteen? They were lechers, rapists, and killers. They received a better death at the hands of her mother than I would have given them."

Pulcher's lips thinned. "If you refuse to enforce order in your own domain, perhaps it is time I appeal to your father, my lord."

I stood.

My voice carried through the hall. "You dare speak to me of order? Your men brutalized an innocent girl—and you have the gall to stand here and demand I give them a second chance?"

"She was Aeltyrian—"

"—and your cohort has preyed on her people since the day they arrived. You're lucky I haven't decimated the lot of them. Yet."

The hall went still. Even the back benches fell silent.

I exhaled through the heat in my chest. When I spoke again, my voice was calm as Vespera's breath.

"Send your message if you must. But the first snowfall is close, and no aid from Avitum will reach you before spring." I stared, daring him to defy me. "It's no secret the Fifth won't survive winter in the fields. So I'll ride to Elisedd myself. Speak to the town. Speak to the girl's family. But there will be no military action against civilians."

I stepped down once from the dais.

"The price has been paid." I said. "Their lives for the life they took."

Another step.

"Either you bring your men to heel, or I'll see you replaced before the year turns. Have I made myself clear, *Prefect* Pulcher?"

Pulcher's jaw clenched. "Abundantly."

I descended the last step and stood a hand's breadth from him, looking down at him. It wasn't often that I used my height to intimidate, but I did then.

My voice dropped to correct him. "Abundantly, *lord*."

He swallowed. "Abundantly, lord."

I held his stare a moment longer.

Then turned and walked out.

Aleaia was, as always, beside me.

The moment we were free of the chamber, the air changed. The weight of the hall peeled off my shoulders like a sodden cloak, leaving only the bite of wind and the pounding in my skull. Each day brought me closer to a decision I could no longer afford to delay.

Aleaia didn't ask where I needed to go. She just took me there. The walls had been too tight today.

"You know, if you decimate a cohort, you'll have half the capital calling for your head," she said as we crossed into the garden.

"I didn't say I would."

She dropped her voice, mimicking mine. "'Yet.'"

I exhaled. "It was a warning."

"Good. Just make sure it stays one."

I glanced at her. "You disapprove?"

"No," she said evenly. "I'm just not ready to watch you get dragged to Avitum in chains. The last decimation was during the war. Your reasoning would have to be rock solid. Beyond reproach."

I let out a short breath of a laugh. Dry. "My reasoning is beyond reproach."

She tilted her head, not quite meeting my eye. "Hmm. I think it's rather reproachable with me in the mix."

We walked in silence, boots brushing frost-stiff grass. The garden felt thinner than usual, like it might fracture if we pressed too hard on the quiet.

"Are you all right?" she asked. "You don't look well."

"Petitions have been heavy," I said, pressing a thumb to one temple, a finger to the other. "My head is killing me."

"You haven't been sleeping either."

I let my hand drop and shook my head. "How could I? I'm half-convinced a coup will arrive before the snow does. Honestly, I almost hope for a blizzard, just to shut Pulcher up."

She let out a breath of laughter, then sobered. "You've made the right calls in Elisedd. From where I stand."

I glanced sideways at her. "Good to know I have the true heir's approval."

"Stop," she breathed as she gave a faint smile. "What will your father do if Pulcher writes to him?"

"Hard to say. He hasn't truly ruled in years."

"When we last saw him, he looked healthy enough," she said.

"He was a figurehead then. Still is." I exhaled slowly. "Any letter signed with his name is written by Cassius. My brother's been circling the throne like a carrion bird for a decade."

She nodded. "His response would be a brutal one."

"I know." I ran a hand over the back of my neck. "That's why I have to resolve this before he gets the chance."

"Do you think the reparations will work?" she asked.

I stopped. Turned to face her. "Well, not if you're asking. Do you have a better idea?"

Her hand brushed mine. Brief. Intentional. The warmth of it stayed longer than the touch itself.

She looked up at me. "I might, as a matter of fact. But it'll have to wait, because we're finally alone."

"By the gods, are we?" I looked around the garden—bare trees, shuttered windows, frost underfoot. No guards. No watchers. Just wind and ivy and her.

I didn't wait.

I turned.

And I kissed her.

I kissed her like I couldn't stand another breath of distance. She met me with equal hunger. Her fingers gripped the front of my tunic, pulling me down, anchoring me to her like she knew I wouldn't hold together without it.

Her lips were cold at first from the wind, but they warmed fast against mine, parting hungrily. I backed her gently against a stone wall, hands settling at her waist, armor firm beneath my palms.

The world narrowed. Pulcher, Marcus, my brother—gone.

There was only her now. Her mouth on mine. Her breath in my lungs.

When we broke apart, I was breathing like I'd come straight from battle.

She stared up at me, dazed, lips kiss-bitten, eyes bright. Then she reached up and swept a hand through my hair. "I thought your head hurt."

"It did," I said, brushing my thumb along her cheek, then lower, to her throat, where her pulse hammered beneath my fingers. "But apparently the cure rests on your lips."

She huffed a breath, blushing prettily. "I didn't know you had such a poetic soul."

"I don't," I said. "It only shows up for you."

Her eyes lifted. Wide. Unafraid.

I kissed her again, harder this time. Messier. Her hands tightened in my collar, drawing me down, mouth parting beneath mine with a gasp I felt in every nerve.

When I pulled back—barely—I murmured against her, "Does your plan involve us running away?"

"You'd never," she breathed.

"Neither would you."

I kissed the corner of her mouth. Then the edge of her jaw. Then lower.

She tilted her head back, breath shuddering. When my lips grazed the skin beneath her ear, she shivered, her whole body coiled tight beneath the steel. A sound escaped her throat. It nearly broke me open.

I pressed closer, lips at her neck. "Gods, Aleaia…"

Her hands slid inside my cloak, beneath my tunic, warm and sure.

I kissed her again—slow and deep. "Tell me to stop."

She didn't, but her hand stilled against my chest.

"Maybe not stop," she whispered. "Just… not right now. Not here."

I held there, heartbeat pounding.

"Then I'll wait," I said.

And I meant it.

Let them say I burned for her.

Let them say I started the fire.

# CHAPTER FORTY-ONE
## *Prelude*

*"To withhold truth from the one who steadies you is not restraint. It is fear masquerading as wisdom."*
—The Song of the Stars, Cycle VIII: The Cycle of Mortals

Mētanos 17, 1230
*Aleaia*

The evening after Val dealt with Pulcher, we sat at a small table near the hearth in his chamber, a simple meal between us.

I wasn't really hungry. My plate sat mostly untouched.

Val lifted his mug, glanced at me. "So. That idea you mentioned."

After the garden, neither of us had quite managed to return to the matter of Elisedd. I had been hoping he'd forgotten. My plan had been to use my birthright to quell the unrest in Elisedd. It seemed like a good idea at the time, but I'd had too long to think about it, and I wasn't so sure anymore.

I held his gaze. "It's nothing. Forget it."

He didn't blink. "Aleaia."

My throat tightened. I traced the wood grain on the table with my finger. "What if the heir stepped in? What if—"

"No."

"—she told them to stand down?"

"Absolutely not." He shook his head. "Do you know what the Empire would do to you? Your existence threatens Calesia's rule more than anything happening in Elisedd. They can't find out what we know."

Heat rushed to my cheeks, sharp and immediate.

"It's all I had to offer," I said, softer. "All I could think of."

He reached across the table, his hand covering mine. Warm. Solid. Gods, I hated how much I needed it.

"There will be a time to reveal yourself," he said. "But not like this. Not yet. Not in Elisedd. Let me handle it."

I exhaled. Long. Tired. I stared down at the table, at the edge of my plate. "If you say so. I just… feel useless, Val."

His thumb moved across my knuckles. "You're not. You steady me."

The door creaked open. We both turned, leaving our conversation to hang there, unfinished, in the space between us.

Lucius stepped in, brushing snow from his cloak. "Hope I didn't miss dinner. Smells better than whatever they're feeding the rest of us."

He had a habit of appearing wherever food was, as if hunger itself were a summons. Sometimes he stayed, if it was his turn. Tonight wasn't. This was purely social.

Val straightened. "I was just finishing up. I have reports waiting, but you should stay." He gave my hand one last squeeze before letting go. His fingers lingered for half a second longer than necessary. "Don't stay up too late. Either of you. We leave early tomorrow."

Then he was gone, leaving me with Lucius, and the echo of his warmth.

Lucius dropped into Val's chair and reached for the bread. He chewed, watching me for a long moment. "All right," he said. "What's weighing on you now?"

"What makes you think something is wrong?"

"I can tell," he said simply.

And I wondered then, if I could share the burden with him too. His opinion wouldn't be colored by the same protective instinct that made Val tell me no.

I hesitated. I'd have to tell him everything for it to make sense. My hand wrapped around my cup, tight enough that my fingers ached. "I found something out. About myself."

He raised an eyebrow. "You're not dying, are you? Because I am not handling this mess alone."

"I'm the heir."

There was a moment's silence.

"To…?" he asked.

"Aeltyria."

A few heartbeats passed.

Then, he said, "Huh. That explains a few things."

I'd just told the Sword of Calesia that I was the heir to the throne of Aeltyria, and that was his reaction? "That's it?"

"You were expecting me to throw the cup? Shout about royal blood?"

"I don't know. Something."

He tore off a chunk of bread. "Honestly, I should've guessed. You do spend an awful lot of time brooding, refusing help, and yelling at people in two languages."

I rolled my eyes, but the pressure in my chest eased a little.

"How long have you known?" he asked.

"Since the day after the knighting."

He nodded like it was no more surprising than bad weather. "Val know?"

"Of course he does," I scoffed. "He was there when I found out."

"And now you want to tell everyone?"

"No," I blurted. "I don't *want* to. Just… Elisedd is ready to burn. And I thought… maybe if they knew Aeltyria's heir stood with them—"

He was already shaking his head. "No. Terrible idea."

So much for that. My cheeks felt hot.

"That's the same thing Val said," I muttered.

Lucius leaned back, studying me like I was a risky wager in a tavern brawl.

"He's right, you know. If you try something like that, they'll arrest you the moment you leave Elisedd. And even if you did get away, there'd be nowhere left on this continent where you'd be safe."

I stared into my cup. "I know."

"Doesn't seem like you do."

I let out a breath. "I—I thought it was the only way I could help him."

"To end your life? Quicker to jump from a tower."

I arched a brow. "Was that supposed to be comforting?"

"No," he said. "Just true."

That earned him a sharp look.

"I'm not being cruel," he added, quieter now. "I'm being clear. You have power—real power. But the second you show yourself, you lose every advantage you've got." He poured the last of the wine into my cup.

"I'm not good at waiting," I said. "I need to do something."

"You're not alone in that." He stood, gathering the plates like it was the most natural thing in the world. "Try to get some sleep. We leave at dawn."

He'd seen right through me. I couldn't let that stand without a little needling back.

"Tell Mariana goodnight for me," I called after him.

"I will—" He stopped, turned. "Wait. How did you—?"

"You smell like her soap," I said, trying not to smirk. "It's a little… floral for you."

"I hate you," he said, though something in the way he said it told me that was a lie.

I raised the cup in mock toast. "I know. I hate you too."

After the door clicked shut behind Lucius, I stayed where I was, alone with my thoughts and the firelight and silence that didn't help a damn bit.

Val was buried under parchment in his chamber.

Eventually, I rose. Barred the door. Checked my weapons. Stirred the fire until it flared a little brighter. Then I unfastened my armor and set it, piece by piece, on the stand beside his.

It looked right there. Natural, even. I stared at it too long.

Stop. It was a few kisses, not a marriage proposal.

I paced the room. Touched the spine of a book on a shelf. Rearranged a pair of candlesticks. Stared into the fire. Then did it all again.

None of it held my interest.

Only he did.

So I let my feet follow where my heart led.

Val sat at his desk near the window, brow furrowed as he scrawled something over parchment. He squinted in the dim light, hunched like a scholar with too many opinions and not enough lamp oil. It was almost exactly how I found him that night in the Aperta Plains.

"Do you need me?" he asked without looking up.

"No. I mean—yes. Always. But I don't need anything from you right this moment."

That made him glance up. He squinted harder at me than he had at the parchment. "Are you all right, Aleaia?"

If I leapt from the window, it would spare me the humiliation of whatever I might say next.

"I tried sleeping on the chaise," I lied, casually enough, "but I'm too wound up about tomorrow. I thought I might borrow a book." I glanced toward the shelves.

He blinked. I don't think he believed me.

"The ones you'd actually like are on the top left," he said, nodding to the shelf behind him.

I crossed the room, let my fingers skim the spines. The titles were impressive—and forbidden.

*On the Ruin of Empires*
*The Breath of the World*
*The Burning Eye*
*The Fire That Remains*
*The Scholar's Guide to Sedition: Annotated Edition*
*A Record of the North: The Lineage of the Daughters of Aelan*

"You just... keep these out in the open?"

Still writing, he didn't glance up. "They're on the highest shelf. Not many people can see up there."

"I can see them just fine."

"Last decadium, I paid the quartermaster extra for your thirty-four-inch inseam. You're not most people."

I stared at him, bristling. "I'm aware I have a long stride."

He chuckled and set his quill down, then leaned back in his chair with his hands folded over his middle. Watching me.

I reached up and tugged *A Record of the North* from the shelf.

"Brave choice," he said.

My voice came dry. "Figured if I'm already under review by the quartermaster, might as well add the Inquisition."

"That's my girl."

My stomach did that little flip he seemed to provoke so often. I didn't answer. Didn't even look at him. Just opened the book with a little too much force and pretended like my heart wasn't halfway up a battlement preparing to jump.

*Eavan Caedmon, daughter of Rhiannon Caedmon and Amund Valdemar, born 18th Rudamos—*

A strangled sound escaped me as I slammed the book shut and shoved it back into place.

*No. Not this. Not right now.*

Val let the silence stretch, eyes sparkling with mischief like he knew exactly what page I'd landed on.

"Not what you were looking for?" he said, voice maddeningly even.

I turned, glare sharp enough to flay. "No."

He smiled and leaned back, crossing an ankle over his knee.

*Gods, he's enjoying this.*

I turned again, trying to shake it off, but my pulse hadn't settled, and his *that's my girl* was still echoing somewhere behind my ribs like a war drum.

I crossed to the bed. I only meant only to sit. To collect myself. To do something—anything—that felt normal.

That's when I saw it.

The small, slim volume on the nightstand. It was nothing like the weighty tomes on his shelves. The cover was worn, the edges soft from use. I picked it up and felt my breath catch.

*A Children's Primer in the Aeltyrian Tongue, Volume Three.*

There was a strip of leather tucked between two pages near the middle. I stood there, fingers curled around that little primer like it might vanish if I breathed too hard. I ran my thumb along the edge of the primer's cover. Once. Twice. A tiny smile ghosted across my lips as I opened to the marked page. Simple words. My mother tongue.

I turned it over in my hands. Blinked back the sting in my eyes.

Val stood, pushed in his chair, and walked around the bed to the far side, near the hearth. Behind me, now.

I didn't turn, just listened.

The scrape of a belt unbuckling.

The soft clink of metal set aside.

The thud of boots placed side by side.

When I turned, his back was to me, firelight casting long shadows over the shape of his shoulders, the clean line of his spine beneath the thin linen shirt.

He folded each piece of clothing with care. Not like a man settling in for comfort. Like a soldier finishing the day.

I watched him in silence.

The crackling fire. The hush of the wind. The quietness of him.

"Is everything all right?" he asked, finally stepping closer.

"Everything is…" I faltered. "It's fine. I'm fine." I set the primer back on the nightstand. "Why?"

"You're welcome here," he said. "I don't mind. It's just… not like you. You usually post up in the anteroom."

I looked at him. "I just don't want to be alone tonight."

He opened his arms, and I walked around the bed to him, tucked myself under his chin.

His heart beat against mine, just as fast. He rubbed my back slowly. Then kissed the top of my head before stepping back. "We should both get some sleep. Early day tomorrow."

"I know," I murmured.

He sat on the side of the bed, swung his legs in, and pulled the blanket up to his waist with all the precision of a man trying very hard not to think about what had just happened. Then, as if to test my limits, he reached behind his neck and peeled his shirt off in one smooth motion. I hadn't expected that to unravel me, but it did.

The sight of him—bare-chested, firelight catching old scars—struck me harder than every confession he'd ever made. All the quiet strength, all the pain he'd carried, laid bare in the curve of his back.

He lay down facing away, one arm tucked beneath the pillow, the blanket drawn up under his ribs. For a few beats, the only sound was the fire.

Then, soft and even, he said, "There's plenty of room on this bed if you get tired of standing there."

# CHAPTER FORTY-TWO
## *Gold & Shadow*

*"Only once was Caedmon brought to his knees, and it was not by sword, nor spell—but by the voice of the woman he loved."*
—Annals of the First Sword

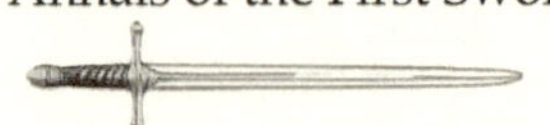

Mētanos 17, 1230
*Aleaia*

I didn't know how to answer. So I didn't. Just turned to the ties of my tunic. My hands trembled, but I moved with purpose. Took a soft, shuddering breath.

You do this all the time. You're only getting undressed.

I stripped down piece by piece, folding each item with the same care he had, placing them beside his on the chair. I untied the cord at the end of my braid, shook out my hair.

Barefoot, I padded around the room, snuffing out candles until only the fire remained. Then I slipped beneath the blanket.

The warmth of him hit me first.

Then the shape of his body, outlined by flickering light.

I reached out, fingertips grazing a line that ran from his shoulder down across the muscle. He stilled.

So did I.

*Was that not allowed?*

"You don't have to stop," he said quietly.

I traced the line of his spine, slow and curious. Bit my lip when I felt him shiver beneath my hand. Then, bolder, I let my fingers drift to the small of his back.

Val exhaled hard through his nose. One hand gripped the edge of the blanket like it might steady him.

He laughed softly. "Are you trying to kill me?"

I smiled. "I thought you were unbreakable."

"Not from this. Not from you."

He rolled onto his back and opened his arm to me. I slid closer, tucked myself against him, head on his shoulder, hand resting on his chest. His skin was warm beneath my palm, the hair soft under my fingertips.

His heart was racing. Mine was too.

"I'm sorry," I said, warmth rising in my cheeks. "I don't… know what to do. I know what I want, though."

He reached up, tucked a lock of hair behind my ear. "And what's that?"

"You," I said, resting my hand against his cheek. "Us."

"That's good," he murmured, brushing his thumb along my jaw. "Because I've wanted 'us' for a long time."

He tipped my face up to his, pressing his lips to mine, gentle at first. I sighed against his mouth, parting for him without thinking. His hand found the back of my neck, warm and steady, fingers weaving into my hair.

I traced the thick line of his shoulder, the plane of his chest. Muscle shifted beneath my touch, dense and responsive. Alive.

When I touched his middle, he jerked just slightly and let out a breathless laugh, breaking the kiss.

I pulled back. "Sorry."

He shook his head, still smiling as he took my hand, returning it to his stomach. "You tickled me, that's all. I didn't know I could laugh like that… with you here. With us like this."

I smiled too. The tension eased out of my shoulders, replaced by the warmth of his hand over mine.

*You're only learning him,* I told myself, as I let my hand wander again. *You're allowed to want this.*

His breath deepened, and his eyes closed as his fingers flexed where he gripped the covers.

"Do you…" My voice barely cleared my throat. "Do you like it when I touch you? Like this?"

"Aleaia, I like it when you *look* at me," he said, rough with honesty. He lifted his hand, brushed his thumb along my cheek. "Gods, yes, I like it when you touch me."

Then lower, his thumb ghosted over my lips, trailing down the line of my jaw, across the hollow of my throat. I drew in a sharp breath, startled by the rush of heat his touch left in its wake.

"When I touch you…" His voice softened to something close to wonder. "It feels like learning you, one breath at a time."

Heat climbed my throat. I didn't know where to look.

When it came again, his voice was so soft, I barely caught it—whispered like a prayer, a confession. "You don't even know what you're doing to me."

"Show me," I breathed.

His hand slid to my wrist, gentle but sure, guiding my hand lower.

My palm met warm, solid muscle. The faint dip beneath his ribs. The smooth heat of skin drawn tight over strength. He went still when I touched him there. Not rigid, just alert. Like he felt every inch of it.

I forgot how to breathe. Had to remind myself that this wasn't a dream but him, letting me touch him like this.

"Keep going," he said roughly.

"Don't you want to touch me… more?" I asked, breath quickening as my hand moved lower still.

"I do. More than anything." His hand tilted my chin up until I had no choice but to meet his eyes. "But I want you to feel it first. How much I want you."

Then he kissed me, claiming my mouth. Tongue sweeping in, deep and slow, coaxing mine to meet him. I opened to him with a soft gasp, clinging to him, baring myself to him, wholly and without fear.

My hand followed the lines of him downward, until I reached the loose knot of his braies at his hips.

I'd be too embarrassed, later, to admit what I expected.

That it might be veiny and pulsing and awful, like the healers' sketches that looked more like tumors than anything anyone would want inside them.

But then I slipped beneath the fabric. Touched him.

He was hard—so much harder than I'd imagined. Hotter than I anticipated. Thick. Flushed. The skin velvet-soft over steel.

Val sucked in a breath through his teeth, jerking under my hand.

I stopped. "Am I doing it wrong?"

He looked at me for a moment like he was trying to decide whether to laugh, cry, or kiss me senseless. "Aleaia," he breathed. "No, you're doing everything right."

His hand curled around my wrist again and held, thrusting into my hand with a low, broken sound.

I froze.

*Was that because of me?*

The heat of him pulsed in my hand, alive and insistent, and something hot and dizzying flared in my belly.

With a rough exhale, he shoved the covers down past his hips.

Then he lifted them just enough to push his braies down.

I let go of him to help, fingers trembling as I eased the fabric lower over the hard lines of his thighs.

And then he was bare.

The firelight painted him in gold and shadow.

I swallowed hard.

Once, in Avitum, I'd seen a statue in the old gardens—some ancient warrior-king, bare to the waist, all muscle and power captured in stone. Val looked like that. Like something carved, a weapon made flesh.

Heat flushed up my neck. I couldn't look away.

I had never seen a man like this before. Naked yes, but usually dying or wishing they were or so drunk it was surprising that they weren't dead already.

And I had certainly never *touched* one like this.

I reached again for the heat and weight I'd held before, my hand closing around him once more. A sound escaped him—caught between a groan and a gasp.

I felt powerful. Unsteady, with him twitching in my palm, thick and hard and slick at the tip.

And for one sharp, silent moment, all thoughts of romance or longing fled my skull like startled birds.

I realized—

That's not going to fit.

My hand stilled.

This was… more than I had any reasonable capacity for.

No mortal woman could possibly be built to survive that.

I stroked him once, slow. There were worse ways to go.

"Gods. How will it—?" I hated how small my voice sounded.

Val blinked, then exhaled hard, like the question had physically knocked something loose in him.

He rose onto one elbow beside me, pressing me back into the pillows. "You'll see. Trust me."

His hand slid up the back of my thigh, deliberate and certain. He pushed the hem of my shift higher, baring me to the air. I shivered and let my knees fall open.

"First I'll put my mouth on you." It was a vow against my skin. "Until you're dripping. Until you're grinding against my tongue and shaking in my hands."

My heart pounded in my chest.

My hand found his shoulder, holding there as he leaned in, his lips grazing the line of my jaw. His breath was warm, his hand warmer where it slipped between my legs, tracing a line up and down my thigh.

My fingers tightened without meaning to.

"Then I'm going to open you with my fingers," he said, voice rough at the edges now. "Stretch you slow. Make you feel it."

I felt his teeth at my shoulder and gasped at the shiver it sent through me.

"I want you soaked," he murmured. "So desperate you can't stand the thought of not being full."

My thighs pressed closer around his hand.

His eyes met mine, dark and sure of what he was doing to me.

"I want you ready. So all you'll know is pleasure. Until you tell me to stop."

Something unclenched in my chest.

He eased the hem of my shift higher, his hands skimming my waist as he leaned over me. I arched to help him, arms lifting without thought. He drew the fabric over my head with care and let it fall somewhere behind him.

He hovered for a moment, breath shallow and uneven as his eyes moved from the slope of my shoulder to linger on my breasts, then to my stomach, my thighs.

And between them.

All of me, bared beneath him.

My breath caught. Heat rushed to my face.

For one terrible heartbeat, I wanted to fold in on myself. To hide.

"You're…" he said, whatever word he'd been about to say falling away, his gaze lingering like he couldn't look away.

I shifted, suddenly too aware of the pale line just below my breast, proof of the old wound that had once nearly ended me. My hand hovered there before I could stop it.

"Scarred?" I said, trying for humor. "Sorry to disappoint."

His gaze flicked to the mark, then back to my face.

"No," he said, voice low. "That scar is why I have you."

He set my hand aside and touched it, barely, his fingertips warm and reverent.

"You fell into my arms, bleeding. This is the scar that brought you back to the world of the living. To me."

Then he looked at me—really looked at me. And I thought that whatever he saw in that moment unraveled something in him.

"Aleaia, you're written in starlight. You're—"

He stopped himself. His throat worked. When he spoke again, his voice was unsteady. "You're the most beautiful thing that's ever happened to me."

My eyes burned.

Not from the words, but from the way he said them. Like he meant every one.

He touched his mouth to the scar, his lips soft and comforting against it.

Then higher, over the swell of one breast, his tongue tracing the peak before drawing it into his mouth. His hand cradled the other, thumb sweeping lightly across the sensitive tip as his mouth worked.

I wasn't prepared for the jolt of sensation it sent through me—how quickly pleasure flared, heat pooling fast.

He moved lower—over my stomach, my hip, the inside of my thigh—until I was trembling beneath him. His hand slipped between my legs, fingers stroking gently, finding where I was soft and wet.

My whole body tightened. I couldn't breathe. Couldn't think. There was only him, his fingers, the heat of his mouth on my skin. I would have begged for more, if he'd asked.

"Val," I sighed.

Then, without warning, his mouth replaced his hand.

I gasped when I felt his tongue, slow and deliberate—hips jolting, thighs clenching tight around his shoulders. He circled where everything seemed to gather, once, then again, with firmer pressure.

Heat bloomed low, spilling from the center of me outward. I felt it in my spine, in the soles of my feet, in places that had never ached before now.

I didn't recognize the sounds coming from my mouth.

*Gods. Am I dying? Is this what it feels like to die?*

My hands found his hair, threaded tight through it, clinging to him.

"Val," I gasped, trembling. "I—I don't know what's happening. Help me."

His hands only tightened on my thighs, steady and grounding, his tongue pressing right where I needed it, over and over, until the panic twisted into something else. Something hotter. Deeper.

The world narrowed to him—his mouth, his hands, the rising, unbearable ache he'd built in me.

Then—gods—he looked up at me.

Eyes dark and hungry, lit with the pride of a man who knew he had undone me.

Pleasure surged hard and hot, tearing through me like lightning through open sky.

My cry was raw as I clutched him, fingers tangled in his hair, hips lifting toward his mouth.

He held me there, coaxing every last shudder from my body.

And then I couldn't take it. I needed him. I needed him inside me, though I couldn't have said how my body knew it.

I reached for him, found his shoulders. "Come here," I breathed. "Please—come here."

He did, slowly, kissing his way up my body until his mouth found mine.

And when he settled against me, I cradled his face and kissed him.

Tasted what he'd done to me.

Salt. Heat. Me.

His mouth moved over mine, deep and slick, tongue sliding against mine as his fingers slipped between my thighs again.

I gasped into his mouth. My legs parted instinctively. I was too sensitive but still craved more.

"You're shaking," he murmured against my lips. "Still with me?"

"Yes, please—"

I didn't know what I asked for but knew he could give it to me.

Another kiss, slower and deeper.

His fingers moved—testing, easing in with careful pressure. Two. Deep.

I gasped into his mouth as he curled them just right, hitting something inside me that pulled a helpless sound from me.

Every nerve still hummed with what he'd just done. Each stroke built on the last, pressure mounting, until I was writhing beneath him.

I was slick, aching, stretched open, and it still didn't feel like enough.

His smile brushed my lips, dangerous and beautifully sure.

"That's it," he whispered. "Let me feel you."

I clutched at his back, his arms, anything to hold on, my hips rocking into him as I moaned into his kiss. My hands found his shoulders, then his face. I kissed him hard, breathless, my thighs still trembling from the last wave.

"Val," I whispered against his mouth. "I want you. Inside me. Now. Please."

He inhaled sharply, withdrew his hand slowly, then moved over me, fitting his body against mine.

He rubbed the head of himself against me, against the slickness. "Tell me if I hurt you."

Then he pushed in, slow, steady.

The stretch startled me, sharp and sudden. Not pain, not exactly. Just… fullness. My body tensed.

I held my breath, eyes squeezing shut against it.

"Look at me," he whispered.

I did, focusing my eyes on his.

"I've got you. Just breathe."

He sank into me with aching care, until our hips touched and I could feel all of him, deep and warm and right.

It was too much.

And still, I wanted all of it.

He didn't move. Just held there, breath shallow, forehead resting gently against mine.

His voice was careful. "Am I hurting you?"

At first I said nothing. Couldn't.

He kissed me—tender, searching, like he needed to feel my answer. "I'll stop if you—"

"I don't want you to stop," I whispered. "Don't."

"I won't, then," he breathed, lips grazing my cheek.

He began to move—slow—and a low sound tore from him.

My breath hitched. A sound escaped me—half moan, half prayer.

My legs wrapped around him, shifting the angle enough that he brushed a sensitive place inside me. Heat flared. I cried out.

A breath left him as he pulled back, then slid in again, slow. "There?"

"Yes. There. But please—" I reached up and touched him, my palm flat to his chest. "Please let me see you."

He shifted, pushing up onto his knees, pulling my hips into his lap, hands beneath my thighs, holding me wide open as he thrust into me again.

Harder. Faster.

Each movement sent heat rushing through my spine. I felt every inch of him inside me, every grind of his hips against mine.

And he was so godsdamned beautiful, moving like that above me, I could cry.

I rose to meet him, my body aching toward something I didn't want to rush. Didn't want to end.

"I want to feel you come around me," he gritted. "Gods, you're so beautiful when you fall apart."

The pressure built, steady and hot.

My hands clutched his arms.

Not from pain. From everything.

The weight of him, the warmth, the devastating joy of him being mine.

My body trembled. My heart raced.

And I felt something deep—not lightning, but a wave.

Consuming me. I thought I might drown.

"Val—I can't—I—"

He breathed something like a laugh—not at me, but in delight. "It's all right, Aleaia. Let go—just let go. I've got you."

And then I went under—crying out his name, breaking apart around him.

Felt molten heat spreading from the place where we joined outward, to every part of me.

Somewhere, distantly, I thought I heard him swear.

And when it was over, he was still with me—every inch, every heartbeat.

His rhythm faltered, once. He groaned and pulled out fast.

"Aleaia—"

I reached for him, still trembling, my hand wrapping around him, stroking as he spilled across my stomach.

I understood, then, why he chased my pleasure so intently.

Saw it in the way his pupils blew wide. In how he held his breath at first, then released it all at once. Felt it in the way his hand braced on my thigh, the other fisting the sheets as I stroked him through it.

I had done that. Given him that.

It wasn't a taking. It was a vow, spoken in skin and breath.

I had given him everything, and he had worshipped me for it.

Afterward, he stared down at me, breath still ragged, loosening the hand on my thigh.

His gaze moved over me—my flushed skin, my parted lips, the tremble still in my thighs. And lower, where his release streaked my belly.

Then he leaned in, cupped my cheek, and kissed me.

Slow. Tender. The kind of kiss that says *you're mine.*

"I'll be right back," he said softly against my lips.

He rose and crossed to the washstand, dipped the cloth in the basin, wrung it out, and came back to me, quieter now.

The cloth was warm when it touched my skin, sweeping carefully across my stomach. When he finished, his hand lingered just above my hip, and something in me softened at the care in it. He leaned down and kissed the scar on my ribs, under my breast. A soft press of his lips.

When he looked at me again, there was nothing but tenderness in his eyes.

"Too much?" he asked softly.

I shook my head. "No. Just… a lot. And new."

"I didn't go too fast?" he asked, brushing a bit of damp hair from my temple. "You're all right?"

I nodded, my hand lifting to touch his cheek. My chest ached with warmth. "It was—"

How could I even explain what it made me feel?

"It was good," I said, and immediately regretted how small I'd made it sound.

Val pressed his lips together, trying not to laugh. "Good?"

I pushed his shoulder. "It was the best thing I've ever felt. Now don't make me say anything else about it. Please. Gods."

He chuckled. "I told you once, a real man sees to her pleasure first."

He stretched out beside me and rested his head on my chest. I put my arm around him, then brought one hand up, threading my fingers into his hair.

He sighed, sinking into me like he'd never been held this way before, and had only just discovered how much he needed it.

For a time, neither of us spoke. I thought about what had happened. I was a novice. He had to have noticed. I bit my lip and exhaled through my nose harder than I meant to. My hand stilled in his hair.

He lifted his head, met my eyes. "What is it?"

"I just... hope I didn't disappoint. I've never—" I swallowed. "I don't know if I was any good."

He leaned up on one elbow, brushing his thumb over my cheek.

"You've ruined me," he said, smiling. "I'll never recover."

A sound escaped me—half mortified groan, half laugh—as I hid my face behind my hand. "You shouldn't say things like that."

"Why not?" he asked, completely unbothered. "It's the truth."

"You're impossible."

He kissed my temple. "Suppose I'll have to prove it to you."

I turned my face toward him, dazed and breathless. "Again?"

"If you're ready." He took my hand in his, laced our fingers together. "If you want to."

I searched his face for some sign that he was teasing. "I just thought... once you..."

His smile came slow. A little wicked. But behind it, I saw something raw. Honest. His.

No. *Ours*.

"That wasn't the end, Aleaia," he said softly. "It's just the beginning."

He kissed me again. Light. Sweet.

A thing of gossamer wings and quiet promise.

I didn't yet know what this would cost us—only that there was no way back to who we had been before.

# CHAPTER FORTY-THREE
## *Nine Days*

*"What is young love, if not the first rebellion? A heart choosing for itself—not by law, but by fire."*
—The Breath of the World

Mētanos 18-27, 1230
*Aleaia*

Val woke me with a kiss to my brow and a whisper against my skin. "It's time to go."

I blinked up at the canopy overhead, rubbing the sleep from my eyes.

It was real, even if I had a hard time believing it.

I sat up, swung my legs over the side of the bed—and winced. Proof. "Fuck me."

Near the hearth, Val smirked. "Again? Three times wasn't enough?"

I groaned as I stood, bracing a hand against the bedpost. "I meant my legs ache. My everything, really."

He was already half-dressed, tugging on his boots. His hair was still damp from a quick wash.

"Gods, you let me sleep too long," I scolded.

"The fiercest warrior I know," he mused, "felled by my sword."

"That's a terrible joke." I took a step. My thighs were on fire. "Gods, I feel like I was trampled. And now you're both going to be waiting for me."

He crossed to me and brushed a loose strand of hair from my face. "I waited seven years to make you mine," he murmured. "I can wait a few more minutes for you to dress."

*Waited seven years?*

We didn't have time to discuss that but I tucked it away for later.

My mouth twitched as I bent to pick up my shift. "You were less patient last night."

His voice dropped, quiet as the embers behind him. "Oh, I thought I was very patient. Especially with my mouth."

I shot him a look, but my pulse leapt as I remembered his hands. The press of his mouth. The way he held me through every shudder.

I turned away, turning my shift the right way and pulling it on, heat prickling across my face. "*Aelan, gavel melior en tuchos,*" I said under my breath.

*Aelan, have mercy on my arse.*

I started when I felt him behind me—closer now, his breath skimming my ear. "If you thought that's where my mouth was, maybe you need a demonstration to clarify."

Everything in me went still.

Except my pulse, which bolted straight into my throat.

I didn't turn. Just cleared my throat. "Valerius," I said slowly, "put your boots on."

He stepped back but I caught the flicker of satisfaction in his eyes, the bastard.

I reached for my tunic, and the pressure hit me.

The very real, very inconvenient need to relieve myself.

Urgent. Immediate.

I glanced toward the screen in the corner. No. Not with Val still in the room, calmly stuffing the last of his gear into his satchel like he hadn't spent the night making me forget how to breathe.

I yanked my tunic over my head, shoved my legs into trousers that stuck to sore thighs, and buckled my belt. "I need to fetch my things," I said, a bit too fast.

Val looked up. "Didn't you already pack last night? Your pack is right—"

"I left something in my chamber."

Arching a brow, he looked at me for one long moment before tightening the flap on his satchel.

I cracked open the door—

And found Lucius just outside, hand raised mid-knock.

Aelan's mercy. No.

Our eyes met. Then he looked me up and down. Hair a mess. Tunic wrinkled. Bare feet.

His brow lifted, wicked with delight. "Well. You look… rested."

I pushed past him. "I need my things so we can leave. Move."

Lucius barked a laugh. "Gods. Finally."

I paid closer attention to my steps, trying to figure out if I had a limp or not. I didn't think so.

He kept on anyway. "Should I saddle your horse or send for a litter?"

"Oh, would you saddle Argenti? Please?"

Lucius narrowed his eyes. "You answered that too quickly. Won't bite me, will he?"

I felt a twinge of mischief stir at the back of my mind. "Just tell him *nimon.*"

"*Nimon*? What's that supposed to mean?"

"To be still," I said as I disappeared into my room.

By the time I'd used the chamber pot, packed, and gotten into a clean tunic, my legs were starting to loosen. Still, every stair was a lesson in pain. I cursed—quietly, but with conviction—at each one.

Val followed just behind, mercifully silent.

We reached the bottom of the stairs just in time to hear, "Godsdamn it!"

Something crashed in the stables, followed by a yelp and a string of colorful swearing.

Lucius stormed out, rubbing his hand. "He bit me anyway, the dumb bastard! Tell him *nimon*, she says. Forgot to mention he doesn't listen."

Val looked at me. "Isn't that the command to bite?"

I kept walking.

Argenti stood perfectly still in the stables—calm, obedient. For me, at least. I bridled him, hauled his saddle into place with a grunt, and fastened the girth straps.

"Next time," I muttered, cinching the last strap, "aim higher."

Mounting was its own kind of torment. Val stepped in to steady the bridle and offer a boost.

I swatted him away. "I've got it."

I didn't. Not really. But I managed, barely, to swing into the saddle.

Val stepped close, his hand settling on my thigh.

It didn't stay there.

He slid it higher, fingers tracing the seam where my legs came together. Possessive. Warm. Nowhere it should've been in public.

I stared at him.

"I know he teases you," Val said softly. "But he cares about you, and he offered to help you."

"He didn't get hurt that badly—"

"I don't mind the needling," he interrupted. "But that was low. I can't have you hurting each other. At all."

The words struck cool and heavy in my gut.

I looked down at the reins in my hand. It had been childish. I wasn't sure what had gotten into me but it was gone now. "Yes, *my lord*."

"Stop that." His mouth twitched. Almost a smile.

Right on target.

I leaned down, letting my voice slip into his accent—too careful, too polished to be accidental. "My lord," I said sweetly, "won't you kiss me, before anyone sees?"

His hand came around the back of my neck. "That's not what you called me last night, princess."

"You are despicable," I said, laughing against his lips.

"Another thing you did *not* say last night."

And then he kissed me, full and passionate, with everything we didn't have time to say.

When he pulled away, he whispered, "I could never stay angry with you, you wild, reckless thing."

When he let go, I sat up straighter, any chance I had of thinking clearly ruined for the next ten miles.

And I didn't regret a single moment.

Where the road was only wide enough for two riders, Val sometimes rode ahead with Lucius, discussing terrain and pace, but his gaze flicked back toward me often.

On the second day, he dropped back beside me and handed over a strip of dried meat.

"How are you feeling?" he asked.

"Not too sore," I said.

"Good." After a quick glance at Lucius—well ahead of us—he leaned in conspiratorially. "Let's sneak away when we make camp."

We didn't. A full day of riding and three without a bath took the edge off our enthusiasm.

The third day was much the same. Stolen kisses, a shared bedroll, fully clothed. We stayed awake talking. I told him about the farm where I grew up—how the mornings smelled like damp earth and bread, how I used to run barefoot through the fields until Jurian yelled at me for tracking mud inside.

On the fourth night, Lucius took last watch. Once he slept, Val lay beside me, palm warm against my spine beneath the shared cloak. His hand rubbed the soreness from my back, then lower, easing the ache from my legs.

And then it stopped.

"Why did you stop?" I murmured against his throat.

He exhaled, whispering into my hair. "You know why."

We didn't do more than hold each other, but gods, we wanted to.

By the fifth day, I couldn't stop watching him. The set of his shoulders. The shape of his back in the saddle.

I thought, not for the first time, that I'd very much like to ride him.

On the sixth, I ached for him. He held my hand while we walked for a bit. He told me about his home—Letia. The sound of the sea in the mornings, the moon shining across the water in long silver bands. He wanted to take me there.

"Maybe next Dēwamos," he said, like it was already decided.

On the seventh day, we passed a yarrow field touched by frost. Val plucked a bloom and tucked it into the buckle of my cloak.

"For luck," he said, and kissed me.

I didn't answer. My throat had gone tight.

It wasn't the flower. It was the gesture. The softness behind it.

I already loved him, that wasn't new, but when he did things like that, it settled deep, becoming an ache I couldn't name.

I tucked the bloom away in my copy of *The Song of the Stars*—not because it meant something, but because *he* did.

On the eighth day, fog clung to the hills and rolled low across the road. We rode in tired, companionable silence, our shoulders brushing now and then. Once, Val reached for me, took my hand and pressed a kiss to the back of my fingers. No words. Just warmth. Just him.

And on the ninth day, Elisedd came into view like a memory sharpened by cold: stone walls washed in gray, smoke curling from unseen hearths. The road narrowed, drawing us back into the world.

# CHAPTER FORTY-FOUR
## *The Principle*

*"Fear commands obedience. Only respect earns loyalty."*
—Aelan, First Queen of Aeltyria

Mētanos 27, 1230
*Aleaia*

We entered through the northern gate just after midday, cold wind snapping at our cloaks. At the stables, I handed off Argenti's reins with a parting scratch between his ears. He snorted, flicking them toward me.

Val entered the command tent, shoulders set. He would speak to Pulcher alone first.

Lucius lingered nearby, flexing his wrist under the edge of his bracer. I knew exactly why it ached.

I shifted my weight, cleared my throat. "About Argenti."

He didn't look at me. "Ah yes. The part where you gave me a false command, got me to tell your horse to bite me."

I folded my arms. "It was meant to be a joke."

"Oh, it was," he said.

I exhaled. "Val thinks I should apologize."

Lucius smirked like he'd just won a wager. "Does he now."

"And I think you should learn Aeltyrian for yourself if you don't want to be tricked again."

He spread his hands, shoulders drawn up against the offense. "I'm trying! It's a difficult language!"

It was so hard to keep a straight face. But I did, because I had amends to make.

"I didn't think Argenti would listen to you," I said. "Didn't think he'd acknowledge you at all."

"Not the point," he said, drawing himself up with mock solemnity. "It's the principle. I trusted you."

He said it like a jest, as he did most things, but I was serious.

I sighed. "I'm sorry. I shouldn't have done it."

He snorted. "See? That wasn't so hard."

"It was, actually."

"Good," he said. "I already told the bard, though. There's a new verse."

I groaned, regretting every life choice that had led me to think Lucius Tutela was my friend.

Before I could respond, the flap of the command tent stirred. Val stepped out, grim as ever. He didn't speak, just motioned for us to follow.

We moved through the camp, snow falling in soft flakes that melted as they kissed the wool of my cloak.

"Pulcher left Aeldunon before us," Val said at last. "He should be here, but he's not."

"Here's hoping the midden took itself out on the road," Lucius said as if we were only discussing the weather.

I bit the inside of my cheek. I shouldn't have found it funny, but I did.

The outer gate loomed ahead, towering iron-clad doors coated in frost, closed tight. A message.

Val slowed, turned to me. "You know the language better than I do. And I'd rather not risk offense. Will you translate for me?"

I stopped walking.

My breath puffed once in the cold, then stilled. My feet felt suddenly too heavy. It should've been an easy thing—just words. A voice. A task I'd performed hundreds of times. I knew what he was asking.

I also knew what it had cost me before. The memories came swift as cold water.

Villagers ushered into halls with promises of peace, only for the Calesians to come down on them days later.

Val was watching me, carefully. "If it's too much, say so. I'll find another way. I won't add to what you already carry."

"I'll do it," I said, hoping I wasn't giving myself away. "Of course I will. I was just thinking that before we go in, we need a fallback plan. If things turn in that hall, we can't be caught guessing."

He nodded and motioned Lucius in. Snow settled in our hair, our cloaks.

"Any ideas?" Val asked.

I glanced toward the wall. "I remember hearing something once, in passing, last time we were here. I don't know if it's true. But the new castle was built over the old stronghold. The dungeons might still connect to the original tunnels. There could be a way out."

Val nodded. "It's not much, but it's something."

"I suppose," I said. "Lucius and I will look for exits once we're inside."

"We're close enough to the Fifth Legion to send a bird if we need to," Val said. "But I don't want this to begin with a show of force."

"Then we'd better find Riogal quickly," I replied.

Val looked toward the gate. "He sounded reasonable in his letters, but if the town wants blood, reason won't hold them long."

Lucius exhaled, his breath clouding the air. "Has Pulcher broken any actual laws? I mean, he *is* a bastard, but the Empire's tolerated worse."

"He's destabilized the most cooperative province in Aeltyria," Val said. "That may not be treason on parchment, but it's a failure of command. And for now, that's enough."

"I hope so," Lucius said.

"Elisedd isn't unmanageable. Triarius governed it well," Val went on. "From the time we were boys. His son married Riogal's daughter, for gods' sakes. The people accepted Calesian rule."

I watched him, taking in his sincerity. He had more conviction about this than many of my own countrymen.

I folded my arms. "So Pulcher broke the unspoken pact of clemency in exchange for loyalty."

Val's gaze met mine. "Exactly. And if I can answer that breach with lawful justice, I will."

Lucius eyed the gates again, skeptical. "Assuming they let you in at all."

"Time to find out," Val said.

He stepped forward and raised his voice, clear and firm. "I come under the banner of peace, with two guards, to speak with your ealdorman and seek resolution for our people."

When there was no reply, I stepped beside him and called up in Aeltyrian, crisp and sure. *"Calam natha te draevelleth a selaeth, sen dua gardí, taran sen tóa celmavir et thalel gaerfineth ana só virií."*

The words echoed back from the stone—heavy, formal, chosen with care. The language of diplomacy, not command.

We waited. Snow drifted through the silence.

Let them look down and see we came without blades drawn.

Let them remember what peace could look like.

Let them decide.

Aelan, please, let them, I prayed silently.

One of the guards laughed. "We can understand you just fine, Calesian. No need to get your lapdog to translate."

*These arseholes.*

I raised my voice. *"Essa alaren nimes. Witatí valethan nain cá dummat?"*

*This lapdog bites. Want to find out how hard?*

"Aleaia," Val warned.

Lucius muttered, "That didn't sound diplomatic."

I didn't listen to them. I listened to the blood rushing in my ears.

Then another voice, a different guard, leaning over the parapet with a grin that promised nothing good. *"Au, gavam sumtaenge ana tó sidan in tóa clia, noív banoch."*

*Oh, I have something for you to put in your mouth, little bitch.*

The others laughed, far too sure of themselves.

"Come down, then," Val said.

He didn't shout. Didn't have to. His voice cut clean through the air, controlled and lethal.

The laughter died like a snuffed flame.

"Come down here," he repeated, colder now. "Let's see how funny it is face to face."

My breath left me slow. Measured.

Gods help me, he hadn't even drawn a blade and still they stepped back. He didn't have to shout or posture. He'd spoken a few words, sharp as drawn steel, and that was enough to silence them.

And I had never wanted him more.

*Get it together,* I told myself. *This is not the time.*

Another figure stepped into view behind the guards, snow dusting the shoulders of his cloak and landing in the darkness of his beard. The sentries were still smirking when the newcomer spoke—flat, unimpressed. *"Vaet es te arvoreth a essa?"*

"He asks, 'What is the meaning of this?'" I translated for Val and Lucius.

Lucius crossed his arms. "An excellent question."

One of the guards straightened, already flinching. *"Te Calesii esesí harē taran, ser. Esamí gavinge ó noív a halar sen enen."*

"They say we're here to talk. Called him sir. Say they're having a bit of fun with us," I said softly.

The newcomer's expression darkened.

He stepped forward and struck the speaker hard, open palmed, across the head. The guard reeled, clutching his ear.

"What do you think this is?" the commander snapped in Calesian, his glare slicing through the others like a lash. "You're on duty, not gutter-born thugs. These are guests at our gates. You think that kind of filth is fit for soldiers under my command?"

No one answered.

"Report to the barracks. Send your relief. I'll decide later if any of you are worth posting again," the commander said coldly.

Then he turned toward us.

"Sir, I'm here to speak with the ealdorman," Val called.

"Are you an emissary of the governor?"

I raised my voice again. "He *is* the governor, Lord Valerius di Calesia."

The man's posture shifted. "My lord, I'll let you in, but I can't guarantee your safety. If that's a risk you'll accept, we'll open the gates."

"Very well," Val said, calm as ever.

"Easy for you to say," Lucius muttered.

At a barked command, the doors creaked open just wide enough to admit the three of us.

Inside, the chill settled deeper. The portcullis loomed ahead, iron teeth casting long shadows over the stone. I looked at the murder holes above, silent and empty, but no less ominous.

"This is a bit different than the last time we visited," I said under my breath.

The doors thudded shut behind us.

Chains groaned overhead, then the portcullis began to rise. Rust drifted down like ash.

Val leaned in. "What does *banoch* mean?"

I shook my head once. "Later."

He gave me a look.

I kept my eyes forward. "Because if I told you now, you'd kill a man in the street. And we've only just been let in."

The man who'd silenced the guards was waiting for us on the other side of the arch.

"Branoc Riogal," he saïd, extending a hand to Val. "I'm the ealdorman here. My apologies for the conduct of my men. They're young."

Val clasped his forearm without hesitation. "Your security is excellent. Well done."

"That credit belongs to Lord Triarius," Riogal replied. "He reinforced the gate before retiring to country life."

Val inclined his head. "Allow me to introduce my guards—Dame Aleaia Dieter and Sir Lucius Tutela."

Riogal raised his brows, looking at me.

I shrugged. "So he says."

"The Wolfsbane and the Sword of Calesia," Riogal said, nodding toward them. "An honor. I know why you've come, and what needs discussing. Might we speak by the fire? Over ale?"

"Certainly. Lead the way," Val said.

We fell into step behind them. The streets were quiet between the stone buildings. Snow clung to rooflines, caught in the curves of gutters and worn stone.

Faces watched from windows, doorways, alleys. Some turned away when I met their gaze, but most didn't. Their eyes followed me with a weight that settled under my skin.

And then, I saw it.

It layered over everything, thick and sudden, like a shroud tugged loose in my mind. The snow fell, but felt like ash. I saw the scorched lintels, collapsed beams, bodies half-covered by broken thatch. A child's shoe in the street. An older man holding a girl's hand as they were pulled apart.

I blinked hard. Forced my shoulders back.

Not here.

Not this town.

Not this time.

This wasn't some cold general with a translator at his side.

It was Val.

It was *him*.

He wasn't here to punish them. He was here to stop the bleeding. And I wasn't walking ahead to demand surrender—I was walking beside him.

*Beside*. I had to remember that.

I took a long breath, deep enough to burn. Kept walking.

I didn't pull up my hood. Tempting as it was, it would only narrow my vision. Better to endure the stares. I'd borne worse, and their eyes didn't burn half as much as the memory still clinging to my ribs.

So I forced my focus back where it belonged—on the streets. The line of the alleys, the choke points, the paths we could take if the crowd turned.

Two cross-streets behind us. One alley blocked with crates and broken wood. Useless. A side gate stood ajar near a courtyard well. I marked it. Another, tucked behind a shuttered bakery.

Every alley, every window, every shutter left askew—I noted them. Not out of fear. Habit. One doorway led into a tannery, the stench of brine clinging to the stones. Another lane curved behind a row of outbuildings. Too narrow for a horse, maybe good enough for a fast escape on foot.

Lucius came up alongside me. "Something bothering you?"

"Just watching our exits."

He grunted. "Good. I'd hate to die in a town this ugly."

I flicked a look his way. "I thought you said you liked Elisedd."

"I'm fond of its women."

"Probably best not to say things like that given the reason we're here," I said.

"Its ale, too." His tone was easy, but his eyes had already gone to the rooftops, watching the shadows in the eaves.

We reached Riogal's home. Humble, not poor—timber and stone, with thick beams and a thatched roof that hadn't sagged under the first frost. Shutters were tight. Smoke rose clean from the chimney, and firelight leaked through the cracks between the slats, soft and golden.

The scent of burning wood and dried herbs hit me as we stepped inside, wrapped around me like a familiar old cloak. The main room was plain, but warm, with crossbeams overhead and woolen tapestries hung to trap the heat. A broad hearth blazed at the center, casting flickering light across a wooden table and several sturdy chairs.

A woven rug stretched before the fire, worn but clean. Benches lined the walls. Stacked chests sat in the far corner beside shelves of preserved herbs and sealed jars. A carved stool. A folded blanket over a chair. Little things. The sort of things that told me this wasn't just a place where people talked politics. Someone lived here.

"Please, sit," Riogal said, gesturing to the table.

Val took a seat without hesitation.

Riogal moved to a keg by the hearth and filled several thick-handled mugs. As he handed one to Val, he caught the raised brow I didn't bother hiding and offered a faint smile.

"Old habits," he said. "I was the town's innkeeper once, before the duties of ealdorman claimed me. There's a kind of peace in pouring a proper ale."

Lucius took Val's mug, took a drink, then gave it back to him. "Probably wish you could go back to that," he said to Riogal.

Riogal chuckled as he passed the ale around to me, then Lucius, and settled across from Val. The firelight caught on the lines of his face, deep and weathered.

I stood behind Val's chair, just off his right shoulder.

Lucius took up position near the door, leaning his weight against the frame, sipping like it was just another night at camp. He raised his mug in my direction, nodding. "Not bad."

Riogal took a long pull from his mug before setting it down. "I'll speak plainly, my lord. You're not the one I wanted to see, but I'm not sorry it's you."

Val nodded once. "I imagine you've every reason not to trust us."

"More than I'd like," Riogal said. "Three of your soldiers dragged a girl from this town into a cellar. She refused them. They didn't care. They left her body in the snow for her mother to find."

My fingers tightened around the mug in my hands.

Val didn't move, but I saw the stillness settle over him like a cloak, sharp and cold.

Riogal went on. "That woman took her vengeance. And I won't condemn her for it."

"You won't have to," Val said, voice low. "The men responsible are dead. I read the report. And I agreed with her choice more than I should admit."

That startled something behind Riogal's eyes. Still, he didn't soften. "It was a long time coming. Pulcher's made a habit of punishing hunger with forced labor. Flogging men for trapping rabbits. Throwing women into his bedchamber like grain into a bin. These aren't soldiers, lord. They're thugs under an Imperial banner."

"I don't dispute that," Val said with a shake of his head.

"You're here to bring them back into Elisedd," Riogal said. "Tell me, how do you plan to protect my people from them if you do?"

Silence stretched just long enough for doubt to prick hot in my gut.

Val didn't answer right away. He didn't have to. I knew that look. The stillness in it. The tightness at the edges.

He was thinking of the Empire. Of his father. Of how little room he had to maneuver.

When he spoke, his voice was measured. "I came to mediate. I hoped I could convince your people to allow the cohort back in, under stricter oversight, at least until the snow makes the roads passable."

"And when they start again?" Riogal asked. "When the next girl doesn't come home? Will you mediate that too?"

That landed like a slap.

I held my breath, watching Val. Waiting.

He looked down at the ale in his hands for a long moment. Then he set the mug aside.

"No," he said. "You're right to ask more. Mediation won't fix this. Pulcher's conduct, what he allowed to happen under his command, can't be overlooked."

He looked across the table, his voice steady. "I want to deliver justice. But if I move too quickly or too harshly, I risk bringing Imperial scrutiny. My father would send inquisitors. Replace me. Strip this province bare."

That was the truth of it. I felt it in my chest like a stone.

"So you'll do nothing?" Riogal leaned back slightly, studying him.

My heart kicked.

"No," Val said. "I'll hold him accountable. But I'll do it in a way the Empire cannot reject."

He glanced my way—just briefly, but there was something in it. Like he wanted me to see the line he'd found in the dark.

"I'll call a tribunal," he said. "It will be public. Witnessed. Pulcher will answer for his actions in front of his own men and your people. I'll summon the other prefects. I will preside. And the judgment will be mine."

I exhaled, slow and careful. It wasn't everything. But it was more than I'd dared hope.

Riogal nodded once. "That will satisfy my people, if it's real. But I need your word, my lord, that this won't be a farce, and it won't end with incolumium shackles."

"You have it," Val said. "I won't use incolumium here."

Something eased around Riogal's mouth. Not quite a smile. Just less tension.

"And the cohort?" he asked.

Val didn't look away. "I still need them brought in before the freeze. But I'll station them outside the inner quarter until the tribunal concludes. No unmonitored contact with the townsfolk. Any violation of order, and I'll remove them myself."

Riogal considered. Then he nodded again, slower this time. "It's a hard line you walk."

"I know."

"You'll make enemies," Riogal said. "In Calesia and here."

"I already have," Val said. "I'd rather make the right ones."

Riogal raised his mug again. "Then we'll hold the line together."

Val took his own, raised it, and they drank.

I let myself breathe.

Because for a moment, I hadn't been sure they'd find a path at all. For a moment, I'd been afraid Val would back down. That there were too many weights pressing him from above.

But he hadn't.

He'd chosen a middle road, yes, but not a coward's one. Not a placating one.

I was proud of him.

# CHAPTER FORTY-FIVE
## *Down the Steps*

*"All stairwells within Imperial detention facilities must be regularly inspected for loose stones, uneven grading, and any hazard likely to result in prisoner injury or fatal incident."*
—Imperial Infrastructure Code, Section IX, Subclause 17.4, Amended Quiestra 25, 1231

Mētanos 30, 1230
*Aleaia*

In the days that followed, while we waited for the prefects from Ostala and Lascebar to arrive, an uneasy quiet settled over Elisedd. Val spent long hours conferring with Riogal on local grievances, meeting with the cohort's centurions to gather testimony, and drafting charges.

I kept to the streets, watching the townsfolk, gauging their mood. Most still eyed me like I had a blade tucked behind my teeth. Suspicion trailed me with every step.

*Mathdraenir,* they sneered, when they thought I couldn't hear. Kin-killer. All auxiliaries-turned-Calesian citizens bore it, but it cut me deeply.

Riogal had proven himself honorable. After the cohort's expulsion, he'd ordered the castle sealed and left undisturbed. He could have picked it clean.

Most would have, but it stayed secured until Val requested its reopening.

I hadn't asked why, but he offered the answer anyway.

"Two reasons," Val told us one evening, just Lucius and me, gathered in the keep's hall. "First, I don't mean to impose on Riogal's hospitality. More importantly, there are workers assigned to the keep. They don't get paid if they don't work. Leaving them idle too long would be a cruelty."

That night, after a plain supper the castle cook had managed, I talked him into a game of Talon. Lucius paced the hall as we played, offering smug observations every time one of us hesitated.

I placed my last piece with a small, deliberate flourish.

Val stared down at the board. "Again?"

I lifted my mug. "You're the one who taught me."

He leaned back with a sigh. "And I've regretted it ever since."

Lucius chuckled from his spot near the hearth. "You might consider yielding next time. Spare yourself the humiliation."

Before Val could answer, the door swung open hard enough to rattle its hinges. A scout burst in, cloak and boots crusted with snow.

Val stood at once. I rose with him, hand already on the hilt at my hip.

Lucius intercepted the boy before he reached us, one arm snapping out to bar his chest. "Easy. No charging nobles like a stray goat. Start with a name."

"Mine? Arthen Vyga," the youth gasped. "Been watching the camp two days now, by order of Ealdorman Riogal." His eyes flicked to Val. "My lord, Pulcher's returned. Ealdorman said to tell you the moment I saw him."

Val nodded to Lucius, who gave the boy a coin from the pouch on his belt. "Well done, Arthen. You may go."

The boy left, and Val turned to me. "I hate to ask you to do it, but I need you to bring him in tonight."

"Better me than you. You're too recognizable," I said.

He nodded. "Take Lucius. Keep it quiet, and have him in the cell before dawn."

I fastened my cloak, fingers quick on the clasp, then paused. "You shouldn't be left alone."

"No one will know you're both gone. And I trust Riogal." His voice was even, measured.

It was still a risk. I thought, briefly, that I might request a couple of guards to post outside his door, but the request itself would draw attention. And we could trust neither Aeltyrians nor Calesian legionaries.

"I'll be fine," he said, gentler now. "You're the ones I need out there. You're the only ones I trust to do this right."

I nodded and turned to go.

His hand caught my wrist, and he leaned in and kissed me. Quick. Certain.

His voice was low, meant for my ears alone. "Be careful."

"He's only one man," I said, letting him adjust my cloak. "We'll be back before you know it."

We slipped through the halls and outside, past shuttered windows and cold stone, past the carved lintels no one had bothered to clean since Triarius left, and toward the storehouses. Among faded banners and crates of spare kit, we found what we needed—standard-issue tunics from the Second Army, Fifth Cohort—Pulcher's cohort. Forgettable. The sort of uniform no one looked twice at.

I pulled the surcoat over my head, down over my armor, and rolled my shoulders, settling into the shape of someone I no longer was.

"Let's hope no one looks too closely. Auxiliaries aren't exactly in favor these days."

Lucius gave me a once-over. "You're right. Let me do the talking. You've got the wrong cheekbones for this army."

"That almost sounded like a compliment."

"Don't read too much into it. And wear a helmet."

I did.

We slipped out the sally port. Snow had been falling steadily for most of the day and evening, light and steady, softening the ground and the sound of our steps. The town slept behind us. Ahead, the camp rose quiet and orderly, tents lined in rows, their edges blurred in white.

We didn't hurry. Straight backs, even strides—just two legionaries making their rounds.

No one stopped us.

Pulcher's tent sat where it always had, dead center, larger than the rest. One lantern burned inside, just enough to cast his shadow across the canvas, hunched over a desk.

Lucius shook his head. "This piece of shit."

"*Petten a sca*," I whispered.

"What?"

"*Petten a sca*. Piece of shit." I glanced at him. "I'm determined to teach you Aeltyrian."

He snorted.

After a few more moments of watching Pulcher, we stepped inside. He looked up as we entered, eyes narrowing, hands pushing back from the desk as he recognized Lucius.

Lucius crossed the space in two strides, clamped a hand over his mouth, and held him tight. I moved behind him and twisted his arms back. Bound his wrists quick and tight before he could even grunt.

When Lucius let go, Pulcher tried to shout. Lucius leaned in and gave him a cuff to the back of the head, just hard enough to take the fight out of him. I shoved a rag in his mouth, bound another around his head to keep him quiet.

"No fuss," Lucius said. "Unless you want us to get creative."

Pulcher glared, red-faced and sputtering behind the gag. I finished the knots, cinched them hard, and reached for his belt.

"Help me strip him," I said.

In moments, we had taken his fine winter cloak and cut away the tunic marked with Imperial insignia. All that remained was a plain linen shirt and trousers—exactly the kind of thing worn by prisoners dragged out for lashes.

"Now he just looks like a man about to be disciplined," I said. "Appropriate."

Lucius grunted as he hefted Pulcher over one shoulder. "Bit heavy for a punishment detail."

"Try not to throw your back out, old man."

"I'm only five years older than you," he said, adjusting his grip.

We stepped out into the cold with Pulcher slung like a sack of grain. One of the night guards glanced over as we passed, his brows drawing together. Lucius met his gaze squarely.

"Directive from the prefect," he said, flat and sure. "Prisoner's to be processed." He made a neat little throat-slitting gesture. "Outside the walls."

The guard hesitated. Nodded. Said nothing.

We kept walking, crossing the perimeter and slipping back through the sally port. The iron door scraped shut behind us, loud enough to echo through the keep.

Neither of us spoke as we descended into the dungeon.

Lucius dropped Pulcher into the empty cell without a word. He landed like a side of beef.

We replaced the ropes with manacles, bolted to the stone behind him. No sooner had I torn the gag from his mouth than he decided to use it.

"He gave you a sword," Pulcher sneered, "so he wouldn't feel like he was fucking an ashborn slave."

White heat ripped through me. It wasn't anger but something older, sharper. The kind that didn't leave room for thought.

*Burn him,* my instincts said.

"Say it again," I snarled, stepping toward him.

Pulcher flinched, chains rattling as he skittered back. I'd be lying if I said I didn't like it, that *he* was afraid of *me*.

Lucius stepped in, catching my wrist.

"Not him," he said. "You're better than that."

I stood motionless, jaw tight, breathing hard through my nose.

He was right. I released the heat back into the room.

Lucius let go. "Go. I'll finish this."

I narrowed my eyes at him.

"I won't kill him," he added. "But I'll make sure he remembers what he said."

I didn't answer. I turned and walked out, jaw clenched against my temper.

The door thudded shut behind me.

Then came the crack of bone.

I took my helmet off, tucked it under my arm, and pinched my nose against the headache that was forming behind my eyes.

A second strike.

A third.

A grunt. A curse. Another blow.

Sniffling. A plea. Another strike.

I stopped counting.

When Lucius emerged a few minutes later, he was wiping his hands on a bloodied kerchief, nose wrinkled like he'd handled something rotten.

"He won't insult anyone," he said, "for a long time."

I looked down at his knuckles. Split. Bruised. Then back at his face.

"What did you do?" I asked.

"Me? Nothing." He shrugged, tucking the cloth into his belt. "He's clumsy."

I gave a slow nod. "Pity he fell down the dungeon steps."

"Fought us the whole way down. We're lucky he didn't take us with him."

We locked eyes for half a second. Nothing more.

No smile. No wink.

Just the same lie, carried between us.

# CHAPTER FORTY-SIX
## *This Quiet Violence*

*"Law without memory is tyranny. Memory without law is vengeance."*
—On the Ruin of Empires

Mētanos 31, 1230
*Aleaia*

Elisedd Castle's great hall held the kind of hush that stretched, waiting to snap.

The townsfolk lined the walls, eyes flicking toward the heavy doors. Tension settled over the space like a held breath. Just the thick silence of expectation.

Val sat at the center of the long table on the dais, calm on the surface, but I knew better. I'd heard him tossing and turning last night, the huffs of annoyance at his inability to sleep.

Riogal sat to his right, while Caius Varro lounged to his left, drumming his fingers against the carved armrest with the kind of impatience that made me want to break one of them.

I stood behind Val's right shoulder, the way I was meant to. Spine straight. Hands clasped. Still and watchful. Lucius stood to my left, his stance just as rigid, though I knew better than to think he wasn't already picking apart every person in the room.

Riogal leaned slightly toward Val. "Lord Rullus should be here by now, shouldn't he?"

"I've had no word," Val answered, shaking his head. "I don't know what's kept him."

"Perhaps he's busy encouraging ashborn slaves to defy their masters." Varro flicked a speck of dust from under his nail with all the lazy venom of a spoiled child.

The slight landed square. Casual on the surface, meant to needle. Still nursing his bruises from Aeldunon, if I had to guess.

"Watch yourself," Val said quietly.

"Yes, *lord*," Varro replied, as if the words hadn't slithered like a serpent out of his throat.

Time dragged. Morning turned to midday. Val sent a scout for Rullus. No one spoke of the delay, but we were all thinking the same thing—that Rullus was never late. And the last missive from him said he'd be there.

When the doors finally opened, the tension in the room shifted.

Rullus stepped through, snow in his fair hair, his expression taut and face pale. A boy walked close beside him—no more than twelve, soot on his cheeks, eyes wide and red-rimmed. His tunic hung in tatters beneath a legionary's cloak—too large, poorly fastened, clutched tight around his thin frame. He froze just past the threshold, gaze darting across the hall like a cornered animal.

Val stood. "Rullus. What happened?"

Rullus gave a short bow, though his eyes never lifted. "My apologies, my lord. We were delayed." His voice was flat. Frayed.

Something crawled down my spine, slow and cold, like the frost that had crept across the dungeon floor the night before. The kind of chill that settles in your gut when you know something's gone very wrong.

"On the road, we came upon what remains of Ardhmor," Rullus said. His gaze flicked to the boy beside him, then back to Val. "There's nothing left. The village was razed. This child is the only one we found alive."

I knew Ardhmor.

A cozy little village. Just a handful of cottages, a well-loved Elder Tree, and people who never caused trouble.

Razed now.

Smoke and ash and ruin.

I tasted bile.

A shocked murmur swept through the hall.

Riogal didn't speak. Didn't move. His shoulders sagged, hands clenched in his lap, gaze fixed on the boy like he couldn't quite process what he'd heard.

My fingers tightened around the hilt of my sword. So tight the leather of my glove creaked under the pressure. I couldn't let go. Couldn't trust myself to.

Rullus kept going. "We searched the remains. Every home, burned. The longhouse was filled with people. Locked. Set ablaze. The tree..."

He faltered. Looked only at Val.

"The bodies were left in the open," he said. "We found House Pulcher's banners there."

From the corner of my eye, I saw Varro shift. He looked away, fingers drumming too fast. Too loud.

"A prefect of the Empire would never—he wouldn't do such a thing without provocation," he said.

Rullus turned on him. "What provocation warrants murdering children?"

"Anyone could've taken his banners." Varro shrugged. "Planted them there."

The air in the hall turned thin. Brittle.

Val's voice cut through it. "Go ahead, boy. Speak for your people."

His voice was raw, trembling. "They… they screamed, my lord. I heard them. But I couldn't… I couldn't help. I was too… too small."

The words hung there, suspended like smoke in winter air. I breathed them in.

And they suffocated me.

*You're one of us—how could you?*

Bile rose again. I brought a trembling hand to my mouth.

I'd been powerless for so much of my life.

And when I hadn't been powerless, I'd been complicit.

Translated. Negotiated. Spoken the words the Empire needed, and my people had listened because I wore their face, spoke their tongue, and carried their sorrow in my voice.

*But you're one of us!*

They'd trusted me. I'd let them die. Been complicit in their murder.

I'd told myself it was for survival.

Told myself the Empire's law was stronger. Cleaner. That it brought order. That they deserved to win because they were better at making war.

Val turned slightly, just enough to catch me in the corner of his eye.

I couldn't meet his gaze.

Something twisted behind my ribs. Cold. Jagged. Like broken glass against bone.

The memories rose like a tide.

*Fires.*

*Screams.*

*Bodies piled where elders once sat.*

*Aeltyrian voices begging for mercy.*

*And always, always, that same voice in my head, the thing that led to all of it—*

*"She's skilled with a blade."*

Papa had said it. Steady hands on mine as I learned to parry. Sharp words correcting my footwork. His face when I landed a clean strike—never surprise. Just pride.

They'd taken that.

Taken everything he taught me.

*Skilled with a blade.*

And used it to turn me into something useful. Obedient. Theirs.

A weapon turned inward.

I hadn't held the torch, no. But I'd spoken the words that made the torch bearers welcome. I'd made it easy.

*Skilled with a blade.*

My tongue was the blade.

I'd told myself I wasn't like them. I didn't have a choice. Law and victory made it right.

Something cracked inside me. Deep.

Not enough to break.

But close.

And through that fracture came the faces of those who'd died trusting the words my father taught me—words I'd used to lull them into peace.

Peace that never came.

Then I was back in the hall. Mostly.

Everyone there could probably tell I held myself still by force. Every joint locked. Every muscle tight. If anything loosened, if I let go for even a breath, I didn't trust what would come next.

The boy looked up again. Lips trembling. "They had torches," he said. "They burned the longhouse with my ma and sisters inside it. Their banner was black… with a red serpent, I think."

Armor clinked.

Mine. From the tremor I couldn't stop.

Lucius noticed. Of course he did.

He stepped in close, spoke quiet near my ear. "If you need to leave, I've got him."

I shook my head before he could finish. Sweat slicked the back of my neck, rolled down my spine beneath the weight of the drake-scale. My temples were damp.

My hands wouldn't stop. Fucking. Shaking.

Gods I tried to make them stop and they wouldn't.

I exhaled, long and ragged, like it might hold something in place.

Ceri stepped forward then, laying a gentle hand on the boy's shoulder. "My lord, if you require nothing further of the boy, may I get him something to eat?"

"Yes, of course. I'll speak with him later," Val said. He turned to one of Riogal's men. "Fetch Pulcher."

I watched them go.

The boy's cloak dragged behind him as he was led from the room, quiet and small.

My jaw ached from clenching. When I looked back to Val, he was watching me—brow furrowed, eyes searching. Whatever he saw in my face, he didn't like it.

The smaller doors opened then. Not the grand ones that led to the courtyard, but the plain set used by guards and messengers. Two soldiers stepped through, Pulcher between them.

His wrists were shackled in front.

He didn't stumble, but he didn't look well, either. One side of his face was mottled with bruises, lip split, one eye nearly swollen shut. Dried blood crusted near his temple, and the fine wool of his tunic hung crooked and torn, the neckline stretched.

Shocked whispers rippled through the hall.

"By the Creator. What happened to him?" Rullus asked. When had he taken his seat?

Sloppy on my part. The man had mounted the dais and I hadn't noticed, blinded by memories. Occupied with ghosts.

Pulcher kept his gaze straight ahead. Mouth set. Shoulders squared. Daring anyone to look him in the eye.

A current of unease wound through the chamber, like the hiss before a strike.

Val's gaze shifted—not to Pulcher, but behind him.

First to Lucius. Still as a statue, not a flicker of expression on his face.

Then to me.

I met his eyes.

Just looked at me, question buried in the weight of it.

The guards brought Pulcher to stand near the tribunal table. He kept his chin lifted. Arrogant even now. But the whispers followed him, crawling through the hall like smoke under a door.

My ears throbbed with my own heartbeat, so loud I didn't hear the first questions Val asked Pulcher.

I forced my fingers to move, and only then realized they'd gone numb.

"Prefect Pulcher," Val said, tone level, "where were you before you returned to camp?"

"Riding my horse," Pulcher said, voice sharp with scorn.

"Where?"

"Through the countryside."

Val didn't rise to the bait. "You had no guard with you?"

"I gave them leave to remain in camp," Pulcher replied. "I required no escort."

"You left Elisedd with a full century," Val said. "You returned with fewer. Where are the rest?"

Pulcher sniffed, shrugged. "Scattered. Assigned duties as needed."

"You kept no ledger?" Val asked. "No report of where your men went?"

"I don't have it with me. I was removed from my tent by force and without warning, you'll recall."

Val's voice stayed calm. Steadfast. "You took them with you to Aeldunon. And somewhere between there and here, you lost some of them—and an entire village in your territory was reduced to ash."

Pulcher's sneer twisted back into place. "Coincidence is not evidence, Legate."

"No," Val said quietly. "But it demands explanation."

Pulcher spread his hands, the chain between the manacles tugging taut. "Then go chasing after it in the snow. I'll wait here."

Val's jaw tensed. He had hoped for something—remorse, a slip, anything he could use to avoid what came next. All he got was that accursed smirk.

He stepped back. "This tribunal is postponed until I've investigated the razing of Ardhmor. In the meantime, Pulcher remains in custody. No visitors. No privileges. No exceptions."

The tension was near to boiling over.

"Justice!" someone shouted. "We want justice!"

More voices joined.

Too many. Too close.

The sound scraped down my spine.

They pressed in, rising loud and sharp around the edges—rattling my ribs, clawing at the last shred of control I hadn't yet lost.

I could hear my father's voice in that moment.

*Breathe.*

Val lifted a hand. The hall went still.

*In.*

"We will not act on accusation alone," he said. "Not without proof. What's been described here demands more than outrage—it demands truth. And I intend to see it with my own eyes."

*Out.*

He turned toward Rullus. "Prepare a small party. We ride to Ardhmor at dawn."

Rullus nodded once. "Yes, my lord."

# CHAPTER FORTY-SEVEN
## *Storm Surge*

*"Press a blade long enough, and it will cut without being wielded."*
—The Fire That Remains

Mētanos 31, 1230
*Aleaia*

Val moved toward the back stair. "Dieter. Tutela. With me."

I felt Lucius's eyes, but I couldn't meet them. Couldn't bear it. If I did, I might shatter.

We followed Val out. Up the steps. Through the corridor. Toward the chambers we'd been using since the castle reopened.

My feet were numb. I wiped sweat from my chin.

My thoughts wouldn't settle. They spun faster, tighter.

Everything I'd forced down—kept pressed beneath the surface—was rising. Hot. Loud. Unstoppable.

Inside, Val moved to the table and poured a cup of wine with steady hands. "Close the door," he said.

Lucius followed me in and shut it with a soft click.

Val leaned back against the table, swirling the wine before sipping. Watching.

"So," he said, "what happened to Pulcher?"

"I suspect he wasn't disciplined enough as a child," Lucius offered.

"What happened *to his face*?"

"Ah. See, when an ugly young man and an ugly young woman love each other very much—"

Gods, the fucking jokes. They were his way of dealing with the world, but it wasn't the time.

"Lucius," I said, too tight.

The taste of ash still lingered at the back of my throat.

I smelled it. Fire. Burnt flesh. Everything Ardhmor was now.

Val set the cup down.

The sound was quiet.

Final.

"This isn't about scolding you," he said. "I'm asking because I need the truth. I need to know what I'm walking into. How much explaining I'll have to do. And to whom."

My mouth was dry. My breath, shallow. I couldn't tell if I was standing still or holding myself upright by habit.

"If you mean the bruising all over his face," Lucius said flatly, "he did it to himself."

Val didn't move. Waiting.

"Your integrity," he said, "matters more to me than your obedience. Lying to me would disappoint me more than anything you might've done."

I didn't want to speak.

But the words came anyway.

"We got him without a fight," I said. My voice didn't sound like mine. "He was in the dungeon. It was over. Chained him. Took the gag off. He opened his mouth."

I swallowed, but it didn't clear the taste.

"Said you only gave me a sword so you wouldn't feel like you were—like you were fucking an ashborn slave."

Val went very still.

"I nearly burned him alive," I forced out. "Lucius stopped me. Then he made sure Pulcher didn't say it again. And I stand by him. I would, even if he'd killed him."

My voice caught but the words kept coming. Rage had cracked something open inside me, and now it refused to shut. Refused to let me breathe around it.

"My whole life—my *whole fucking life,* Val—every time I've bled for something, fought for it, clawed my way toward it, someone's whispered that I must've fucked the right man."

I heard my voice shake, and I hated it.

"They don't care what I've done. Don't care how hard I've worked, how many scars I've earned. The things I've had to do just to stay standing. They see a woman with a sword and assume someone put it in her hand. Especially because I'm Aeltyrian."

I hadn't noticed my fists had clenched, my nails biting into leather.

"They all said it. In whispers. In jokes. 'She's skilled with a blade.' Even you said it, once." I scoffed. "It's not praise, or pride. Just proof that I was useful. A weapon. Nothing more."

I dragged in a breath that didn't fill my lungs.

"Lucius knows. He was there when I earned the things they said I didn't deserve."

Val turned away, bracing one hand on the table like he needed something solid to stay upright. For a heartbeat, I thought he'd leave.

"He said that to you?" he ground out.

Too calm. Too quiet.

"Yes." I swallowed hard. "And I've heard worse. Every command, every promotion—every step I took toward something they thought I wasn't meant to have—someone said it. Or implied it.

Or hinted at it when they thought I wouldn't hear. I've never even fucked anyone but—"

I stopped myself.

Laughed.

The breath at the end hitched. I brought my hand to my mouth to stifle it.

"I'm skilled with a blade, all right. Steel, when they need killing. My tongue, when they need lies. And a man's cock, they say, when they can't stand that I did it better than they could."

Lucius stepped forward and placed a hand on my shoulder.

I flinched. Heat crawled up the back of my neck, made my skin raw. It surged under my skin, hot and sick, like it was trying to burn its way out.

When I looked up at him, he nodded. I knew what that meant.: *You're relieved. I've got it from here.*

"Aleaia's right," he said, turning to Val. "It wasn't that long ago I had to treat her very unfairly for something similar."

He didn't wait for permission. Didn't soften the edges.

"She was supposed to enter the tournament to earn her place in the Imperial Guard. Some bastard from the First Army made a foul comment. Put his hands on her. She defended herself. She was punished."

His gaze didn't waver.

"Dungeon. Then a work party. If the guard had died, her life would've been forfeit. But he lived. So she served her time. A decadium. And on the last day…"

He paused. Let the silence do its work.

"You remember that day, I think. The day she took an arrow for you."

The silence stretched again, taut as a bowstring.

"If she'd been a Calesian man, the worst she would've faced was a stern lecture. If it had been you or me? We'd have been praised."

Lucius took a deep breath.

"She's telling the truth," he said. "The way our legions treat the women who dare to fight for the Empire is disgraceful. Worse if they're from up north. And I'm sorry if I've made this harder for you, Val. But this time, I had to do the right thing."

Val didn't speak. He folded his arms. Stared at the floor like he was hoping the answers might rise up through the stone. Then he exhaled. Ran a hand through his hair.

Then searched my face for answers, maybe, or forgiveness.

"I'm sorry he said that to you," he said. "I'm sorry any man ever has."

He lifted his cup and drained it.

"I want to believe the tribunal will be enough. That a fair trial and judgment will somehow balance the scales." He shook his head. "But knowing what he said to you, what you've endured, I don't know how I'm supposed to sit there and pretend this is objective."

Tears stung at the corners of my eyes.

"You did the right thing," he said. His gaze shifted to Lucius. "Both of you. And if I'd been there… I don't know that I could have stopped."

"I didn't want to, either, but I knew who would carry the blame if I didn't." Lucius glanced at me, then back to Val.

"Could you give us a moment, please?" Val asked him.

"Gods, yes. Decency is exhausting and I need a drink," Lucius said, already heading for the door. "Something stronger than fucking wine."

He stopped in the doorway.

Glanced back at me—brief, steady.

Then slipped out and closed the door behind him.

Val half-sat on the edge of the table and took a deep breath. "What am I to do? Either way, I condemn myself."

"I'm no scholar of the law," I said, "but it seems clear enough that Pulcher should lose his head."

He shook his. "If only it were that simple. First there has to be an investigation. These charges are heinous, and the consequences must be harsh if he's guilty. But this isn't just about justice for the girl. Or Ardhmor. It's about what comes after—for your people, for the Empire." He hesitated. "For us."

My brow furrowed. "What?"

He lifted a hand. "Hear me out."

I didn't interrupt. But the words cut through me like a blade.

*No. Val. Don't.*

"If I execute a Calesian official—no matter how guilty, no matter how monstrous the crime—my father may see it as an act of defiance. The court will say I've yielded to Aeltyrian pressure. Some will call it treason. And if they do…" He exhaled. Looked away. "We'd be lucky if they only came for me. They might clamp down on all of Aeltyria."

I stared at him.

I couldn't speak. Couldn't even think. Just stared.

*No justice for them. For any of them.*

*I was part of things like this so many times. Why does this one hurt, when I wasn't even there?*

The answer came quickly.

Because it's my responsibility.

Because they are my people.

Because I'm one of them.

"So that's the choice," I said. "Spare a monster to spare the Empire's pride."

His expression hardened, but he didn't look away. "If I push too hard, they'll say I've lost control. That I've turned rebel."

My voice dropped, cold and cutting. "Then say what you really mean. That a village full of dead Aeltyrians is a price you're willing to pay! He burned a village to the ground!"

I didn't look away.

I have to convince him. I have to.

"He let his men *rape* and *kill* a girl and did nothing. Nothing! You want to talk about destabilization? He didn't just undermine order—he shattered it. With his own hands. And left corpses behind to prove it."

Val said nothing.

"And you're worried what your father will think?" I sneered, looking him over once, as if to measure him against what I'd thought he was.

"It's not about approval," he said, quiet now. "It's about what the Emperor will do. My father just happens to *be* the Emperor. And then there's the court. Every loyalist in the Empire waiting for an excuse to crush this territory—"

"And you think not punishing him will stop them?" I snapped. "That if we play nice, if we bow and scrape and hold our tongues, they'll show mercy next time? They never do!"

"This..." He stopped. Started again, slower. "It's bigger than Pulcher. Bigger than this tribunal. I thought I was prepared, but the stakes grew. But I don't, Aleaia. And I'm running out of room to move."

"Then make. Fucking. Room," I said through my teeth.

His voice came faster now. Hard. Heavy.

"We don't have anything to defend with," he said. "No soldiers. No supplies. No plan. Nothing. They'd kill me, because that's the only way they'd get to you. They'd bind you in incolumium, and then they'd do to you what they did to your father—hang your body in the capital square. As a warning."

He stepped closer. His voice softened, but the heat remained. "You'd be used, Aleaia. Just like before. Only this time, you wouldn't walk away."

I stared at him.

Then let out a breath that caught on something sharp and bitter. Half a laugh, half a sob.

It tasted like ash.

"So what do you call this?" I asked. "Because it feels like being used."

My voice faltered on the last word, but I didn't stop.

"I bled for this Empire! I watched it burn my people, strip us of our names, our gods, our language—and I still fought for it! For you!" My hands clenched at my sides. "And now the man who saw me, who made me feel like I was more than a weapon, wants me to sit there and smile—"

"I would never—"

"—while the bastard who razed a village walks free? Because it's *easier*?"

"No," he said quickly, "because I don't want to waste the one chance—"

"You were supposed to be the one who didn't ask that of me!" My head shook of its own accord, my breath hitching hard. "You were—you were supposed to be different."

He was just like them after all. A son of the Empire.

He stepped toward me, close. Too close.

I felt the heat of him. His presence, his steadiness. Like standing too near the sun.

Bright and beautiful. It'll burn you alive if you get too close.

His hand found my arm—light. Warm. Steady.

I couldn't breathe.

"Aleaia." His voice was soft. Measured. "Come back to me."

Val's voice was too kind on the heels of betrayal, and I couldn't bear it. I flinched like he'd struck me.

*Come back? From what?*

I didn't even know where I was anymore. Only that I needed out.

Out of that room.

The castle.

My skin.

The walls pressed in. The fire roared in my ears.

I backed away.

"I can't," I whispered.

He reached for me.

I pulled back—harder.

"How can you look at me and not see the part that's just as monstrous—as terrible—as the Pulchers of the world?" I rasped.

"You aren't—"

"I am." The words cut out of me like blades. "I see it now. I was the vanguard for the evil they did."

Val's brow furrowed.

"I told villages to surrender," I said, the words spiraling faster. "Told them to trust the Empire. I translated lies while soldiers waited outside with torches and steel. I did it to survive."

I drew a breath, ragged and sharp.

"No. No. That's not true. I did it because I believed. Believed in the legion. The law." My chest ached. My ribs felt too tight. "And now I'm standing here, again, watching another monster get away with it, because politics are delicate and justice is dangerous."

He stepped forward. "That's not what I'm—"

"Don't." I held up my hands, as if to physically hold him back. "Not while the bodies are still burning."

His face fell. "I'm trying to protect you."

"No," I said. "You're trying to protect what's left of your place in this Empire. And I'm not sure there's room for both of us in you."

I couldn't catch my breath. The air was wrong. The light was wrong. Everything was wrong.

I turned.

*Get out.*

*Get out get out get out.*

He reached for me again. "Don't go."

I didn't answer.

My feet were already moving.

Out the door. Into the corridor.

"Aleaia!" Val's voice behind me.

"Leave me alone," I snapped, my boots hard against stone.

His followed. Echoing. Fast.

"Where are you going?"

"I said leave me alone."

I didn't think it—I just knew.

The stables.

"No," he said.

The word hit me like a lash. Not loud. Not shouted. Just low and fierce. A refusal. A plea. A fear.

I moved faster.

"Aleaia, stop."

I didn't.

"That's an order."

I kept walking.

"Aleaia," he said again, sharper now. "I said stop. Come back inside. Now."

I didn't turn around.

"Dame Wolfsbane!"

"Going for a ride."

"A ride where?" His voice was fraying now—too tight to hold.

"Maybe I'll translate another lie of peace," I barked. "Show off my skill with a blade."

I shoved open the outer doors. The stable yard was slick with slush and half-melted snow. I crossed it fast, threw open the door to Argenti's stall.

He stepped forward the moment he saw me.

I grabbed his mane and swung up bareback.

*"Brison!"*

He launched forward at the command to break, hooves striking mud and gravel, flinging snow in every direction.

The sentries at the gate saw me coming. They hesitated.

*"Immon!"* I barked. *Move.*

They didn't.

But the fire did.

It surged from me like it knew my fury, like it shared it. The gate caught with silver flame—not rage, not aim, just release—and went up like kindling. The guards, terrified, ducked to either side of it.

Behind me, I heard Val's voice rise above the wind, right before it vanished under Argenti's pounding hooves. "Shit. Get my horse. Now!"

I didn't look back.

I just rode.

# CHAPTER FORTY-EIGHT
## *Shattered*

*"When the world was young and the gods still walked among us,*
*Lithau named the elder tree her witness.*
*Beneath its boughs, all oaths are heard. All love is bound. All prayers rise.*
*To burn it is not only desecration. It is rebellion against the heavens."*
—The Song of the Stars, Cycle VIII: The Cycle of Mortals

Mētanos 31, 1230
*Aleaia*

The world blurred.

Wind lashed my eyes, my cheeks, my lungs. Snow stung every inch of exposed skin. I didn't stop. Couldn't. My fingers clenched tight in Argenti's mane, my thighs locked hard against his sides as he thundered over frozen ground.

*You're a weapon.*

*A weapon.*

*A weapon.*

The thought pounded in time with each hoofbeat.

*Not a person.*

*Nor daughter.*

*Not even…*

*… a woman.*

*Just a blade.*

*Drawn and swung.*

*And sheathed on command.*

I had spoken Aeltyrian to soothe frightened villagers.

Softened my voice. Crouched to meet the eyes of children.

Told the elders there would be no harm.

That the Crown only sought peace.

I did it while prefects behind me counted how many could be taken for labor, how many left to die.

They had trusted me.

*Trusted* me.

I looked like them.

I was one of them.

*One of them.*

And still I had stood by while the doors were barred from the outside. While the crimson dragon demanded names, family ties, loyalties. While the screaming began, and never quite stopped.

I had watched.

Better it came from me.

More merciful than the others.

I was Aeltyrian.

*Skilled with a blade.*

My breath came hard and fast. My vision blurred—not from wind, not from snow. From memory.

It rose like bile, thick in my throat. I could still hear them—half-remembered voices, sharp with fear.

*"But you're one of us!"*

My stomach turned.

I didn't know where I was going.

Only that if I stopped, I might never move again.

My jaw ached from clenching so hard. My thoughts were fire and smoke, snarling in my head—no room for reason.

The road narrowed. Trees closed in, then broke again.

And then, I smelled it.

I reeled in the saddle.

I knew that smell.

Smoke.

Flesh.

Blood.

Argenti slowed without a word.

He knew it too.

I'd buried the rot—wrapped it in steel and forced it down where it couldn't reach me.

I thought.

Told myself there was no time, no choice. That I'd done what I had to do.

But it had always been there.

In every order obeyed.

In every lie told.

In every time they sent me first. Because I could look like peace and speak like home.

I was useful.

I had made myself useful.

Because I was one of them.

I didn't break when they called me traitor.

Flogged me.

Took my horse, my breath of freedom.

Not when they handed me a staff.

But this—

—broke me.

Because now I understood.

What I'd been made for.

My legacy had been stolen before I ever knew I had one. Twenty-four years ago, they started carving it out, and never stopped.

I was supposed to be their protector.

Heir.

*Queen.*

Instead, I'd been their executioner.

Their broker.

The hand that offered peace and marked them for slaughter.

I guided Argenti down the slope into what was left of the village. Where homes had once stood, only blackened skeletons remained—timbers scorched, roofs caved in. In places, the fire had been so hot it still smoldered. Ash drifted to the ground, where patches of blood melted the snow.

No building was spared. Some were razed entirely. Others bore marks of the cruelty—doors barred from the outside. Windows nailed shut.

It hit me again.

I wasn't their protector.

I was the hand—

—with the blade.

The voice before the fire.

The lie they believed.

Bodies littered the road.

And those that didn't lie were impaled on pikes, limbs limp, heads bowed like broken saints. Ravens picked at the dead, slick black feathers and beaks stained red. Their wings beat softly overhead, croaks low and wet with blood.

They tore the flesh softly.

As soft as my voice had ever been.

In Lhannor, Catan Row, Caerlan.

But I heard it.

Lithau help me, I heard it.

I slid from Argenti's back.

My knees buckled when my boots hit the ground. He whickered, stepped closer, nosing gently at my shoulder.

I didn't look at him.

I couldn't.

I took a step forward.

Another.

My boots crunched through ash and frost. My cloak snagged on splintered wood, tore slightly at the hem when I didn't stop to free it.

The elder tree—or what was left of it—stood at the center of the village.

They'd hanged them.

From the elder tree.

The sacred one.

The tree where villagers tied ribbons for blessings.

Where children played.

Where rites were sung.

Where sweethearts wed.

Creaking now, under the weight of corpses.

Become the gallows tree.

I felt it deep in my gut.

What little I'd eaten surged up—hot, bitter, sour. I doubled over, retched into the ash and snow, the vomit hissing as it hit. Wiped my mouth on my sleeve, hand trembling.

Moaned. Gods it hurt.

Somewhere I couldn't name.

Took one step back.

Spun.

Movement beneath the tree.

Not ghosts.

Men. Living.

Five. Dressed in tattered remnants of Fifth Cohort tunics. Half-armored. Laughing, like the dead around them weren't real. One knelt by a corpse, picking through a pouch strapped to the belt, shaking coins loose, tossing scraps aside. Another leaned against the roots, sawing a blackened, swollen finger to take the wedding ring. One of them pissed against the trunk.

*Why are they still here?*

*Waiting, maybe… for what?*

*No matter.*

They didn't see me. Not at first.

I slid my sword from its sheath.

One looked up. "Well, look at that. One came back."

I didn't speak.

I walked toward him.

I'd show them I was skilled with a blade.

"Oi, ashborn," another called, pushing to his feet. "Here to have some fun, girl?"

I killed him first.

Not like my father taught me.

Not with honor.

Not with style.

Hard, short thrusts.

Like the legion made me.

Straight in. Blade low, up beneath his ribs. He gasped. I yanked the sword free and kept walking as he dropped.

The others scrambled. One drew steel. I took his arm off at the elbow.

He screamed. I kicked him in the chest and left him.

The third swung wide—panic, not skill. I caught his wrist, wrenched his blade aside, and drove mine deep into his gut. Twisted.

He groaned. Folded. Fell.

Two left.

One ran.

I let him. I'd find him later.

The last backed toward the tree, shaking his head, babbling something—an apology, maybe. A plea.

I didn't care.

I swung.

Steel bit bone. He went down.

My blade rose.

And fell.

*Skilled with a sword.*

Again.

Not praise. Not anymore.

Just a reason. An excuse.

A way to justify what they made me do.

Again.

I'd been useful.

Precise.

Efficient.

Good at ending lives.

That's what they'd seen.

That's what they made.

Once.

Skilled.

Again.

Good for killing.

Again.

Just a weapon.

Again.

*Esam Aeltyrii.*

*I am Aeltyrian.*

And again—

Then came the sound.

Low at first. Broken.

A moan, warped and wrong, clawing up from somewhere too deep for language. It rattled in my chest. Climbed my throat. Twisted as it rose—

And became a scream.

Not grief.

Not rage.

Ruin.

Then silence.

My sword slipped from my fingers.

My breath came in short, ragged gasps. The tears fell hot and soundless, streaking down my cheeks.

The old tongue tore from me, half-choked by sobs. "Lithau… my lady… have you forsaken us?"

Two staggering steps forward.

"The children…" My voice broke. "My lady, they killed the children—why?"

*Valerius*

I kicked Nox into a gallop, reins slick with sweat and snow in my grip. The village blurred past, a smear of soot and ruin as we thundered toward the center.

Corpses littered the streets, some blackened from flame, others left to rot in the frost.

A woman with a charred arm curled around two children.

A man whose neck had been opened nearly to the spine.

My soldiers—

Then I heard it.

A scream.

Hers.

Ragged. Wordless. Sharp enough to shatter glass.

My heart climbed my throat.

The elder tree loomed ahead, blackened, split by fire. Ropes hung from its thickest branches—eight, maybe ten. Bodies swayed in the breeze. Old men, women, children. Some scorched. Others split open. Most naked and blue. None a threat when they lived.

And at the base of the tree—

Aleaia.

She stood over a butchered corpse in Calesian armor, Fifth Cohort insignia still visible through the blood. One of Pulcher's men.

Three more lay scattered around her.

One missing an arm. One split to the spine. Another still clutching a broken blade.

So much blood.

My eyes swept the tree line—instinct.

And there he was.

A man—bloodied, limping, sword drawn—burst from the trees with a snarl.

Toward her. Fifteen paces. Maybe less.

I didn't think. I ran. Closed the gap and slammed into him just before he reached her.

We hit the ground hard, rolled through frozen muck. He grunted, swung wild. Steel bit into my left shoulder—cut through cloak, tunic, skin. Pain bloomed, hot and instant.

I sucked a breath through my teeth.

Caught his wrist. Slammed it against the ground—once, twice. His sword clattered free, skidding into the slush.

We both dove.

I got a hand on the hilt. He drove an elbow into my neck, kneed me in the gut, punching the breath out of me. Then he scrambled on top of me, fist raised.

I smashed my knuckles into his throat. He reeled back, choking.

I clawed for the sword—missed. We rolled, tangled in limbs and wet cloth, breath steaming.

He lunged for the blade.

I caught his arm, wrenched it back until I heard the pop.

He shrieked.

I didn't wait. I grabbed the sword, planted a knee on his chest, and drove it down. The blade sank deep. He bucked beneath me, wailing, so I pushed harder. Twisted.

He went still.

I let the sword go and staggered upright. Breathing hard. Drenched to the skin. My cloak hung heavy, soaked in blood and ice. My shoulder screamed. Copper filled my mouth.

I spat, wiped my mouth on my sleeve, and turned.

Back toward the tree.

Aleaia was still kneeling. She hadn't moved. Her hands were in her hair. Her cloak was soaked through, spread around her like a dark pool. Her back bowed under the grief. She rocked slightly. Swayed under the weight.

I could only make out half of what she said.

"My lady…" Her voice was hoarse. Raw. Nearly gone. "Lithau… have you *anatretiet* us?"

I stepped forward, slow.

"The children…" Her voice cracked. "My lady, they *mathin* the children—why?"

I was close enough to hear her breathing. Shallow. Shuddering. Like something inside her had cracked.

"You let them *mathel* the children—why?"

"Aleaia," I said quietly.

I don't think she heard me.

"I'm one of them," she whispered. "I told them to surrender. I told them it would be safe…" Her shoulders shook. "I translated the lie."

My chest tightened.

She hadn't been here. But it didn't matter—not to her.

I'd only seen a glimpse of it, once, but I knew enough. I knew that guilt doesn't care about truth when grief gets there first.

I dropped to my knees beside her. Wrapped my arms around her.

"I know what they made you do," I said. "But this wasn't you, Aleaia."

She was stone, at first. Then the tremors started—slight. Uneven. She collapsed into me. Her fingers clutched at my tunic. Her face pressed into my chest. Her whole body shook—not from cold, but from something deeper. Older.

Grief that had lost its name and festered.

I just held her.

And for the first time since I met her—

Aleaia shattered.

The sobs tore loose. Raw. Unstoppable.

"Val," she choked. "I can't—I can't fix this. I can't make this right."

"No." I swallowed. "You can't."

She dragged in a shaking breath. "Then what am I supposed to do?"

I cradled her head to me, my voice careful at her ear. "You make sure it never happens again."

That made her look up. Her eyes were red. Her lips cracked. Ash streaked her cheek like war paint. She looked like the warrior she was and the queen she would become.

"I will help you do it," I said.

Her mouth opened. No words came—just breath. Just pain. "Val—"

"You don't have to carry this alone." I brushed my thumb along her cheek. Soot lifted away like shadow.

Her eyes closed.

"I know," she whispered. "That's what scares me."

My brow drew in. "What do you mean?"

"I'm afraid my fucking birthright is going to demand your life as the blood price. And I—" her voice cracked. "I can't bear it. Not you, too."

I took her face in both hands. Made her look at me. "Aleaia—"

"How could I choose?" she asked. "Between you and my people?"

I wiped a tear from her cheek. Gentle, where everything else was wreckage.

"I know what this is. What it could cost."

I pulled back, my forehead against hers. Let her see it all. Every crack. Every fear. Every choice I'd already made.

"The price of your people's freedom will be steep. But I won't make you choose. If the gods demand a blood price," I said, "I'll pay it."

I leaned in and kissed her. Tasted ash and sorrow.

A warlord's oath made flesh and sealed with blood.

"Don't let go," she murmured.

Not a command. A surrender. Soft as snow, quiet as breath.

And when I wrapped my arms around her again, it wasn't just a promise. It was my answer.

I would hold her through this. Through all of it.

Until the end.

# CHAPTER FORTY-NINE
## *Confessions*

*"I did not mean to tell you everything.*
*But you were warm, and my heart forgot how to lie."*
—The Breath of the World

Mētanos 31, 1230
*Valerius*

I found her sword first. It was half-buried in bloody snow near the elder tree, where she'd dropped it. The metal was cold in my grip. I wiped the blade clean on my sleeve.

She was still sitting on the ground, arms wrapped around her knees, face buried in them.

"Come on," I said gently, helping her up with a touch at her elbow.

She didn't resist. Didn't speak as I slid the sword into the sheath at her hip.

I lifted her into the saddle, then mounted behind her, one hand on the reins, the other steady around her waist. She leaned into me, face pressed to my chest just under my chin.

Blood still trickled down my arm. I tried to ignore it as we rode back toward Elisedd. Argenti followed, tethered by a slack rein.

The gates of the town opened without question. The ones to the castle were wide open, being repaired by a few men.

No one met my eyes.

Lucius stepped forward, then stopped.

I dismounted, then reached up to help her down.

She didn't resist, but the moment her boots touched the ground, she sank, as if her bones couldn't bear the weight. And that's where she stayed—in the dirt outside the stables, cloak pooled around her, head bowed, hands limp in her lap.

I crouched beside her.

"Aleaia," I said softly. "Let me take you in."

She didn't look at me. Just sat there, still as stone.

So I gathered her into my arms and lifted her carefully, as if she might break all over again. I carried her up the steps, across the threshold, into the keep, and up to our chamber, calling for hot water the moment we entered. The servants scrambled, hauling buckets from the kitchens.

I sat her near the fire and stripped off her cloak—soaked, cold. She didn't move, staring down at her hands.

I pulled the bandage roll from my satchel. The linen stuck briefly to the torn fabric of my tunic, already damp with blood. I eased it off. The cut wasn't deep, but it was wide. Sloppy. Gritting my teeth, I doused it with wine, pressed a folded rag to the worst of it, and bound it tight.

I'd do better later, when we were cleaner and I'd seen to her properly.

I fetched a clean shift from her pack. By the time I returned, a servant waited in the doorway with bath sheets, soap, and rags clutched to her chest, accompanied by two boys who carried the tub, and a third with two buckets of hot water.

"My lord," she said softly, eyes averted. "Shall I help Dame Dieter with her bath?"

"No." My voice was steady. Final. "You may go."

Servants came and went with more hot water, until the tub was full. And then we were alone.

Word would spread. It always did. They'd say Pulcher broke Dame Wolfsbane. I wouldn't let that be the end of it. I would bring her back.

I crouched in front of her and unlaced her boots, setting them aside.

"Aleaia," I murmured. "I'm going to help you undress."

She didn't look at me, but she didn't pull away either.

I stood her up and eased her trousers down first, slow and careful. Then reached for the fastenings of her tunic. The laces were stiff. The fabric peeled away in brittle folds, and underneath, her shift clung to her, damp from sweat and blood. I slipped it over her head and added it to the pile.

I stripped quickly, laying my own clothes aside. Took up the bucket that had been left, dipped it in the tub until it was halfway full, then used a rag to clean the thickest smears of blood off her first, then me.

I gathered her again—one arm beneath her knees, the other around her back—and stepped into the tub. Steam rose around us as I sank with her into the water.

She rested against me, back to my chest, head tucked against my shoulder.

The heat of her hit like a fist.

My body betrayed me.

*Godsdamnit.*

Not now. Not with her like this.

I shifted, jaw clenched, and reached for a bath sheet, folding it between us.

"I'm sorry," I said quietly. "I didn't mean for that to happen."

She said nothing. I'd keep trying.

I reached for the pitcher.

"Close your eyes."

She did.

Relief bloomed in my chest. I'd seen soldiers broken by less, men and women who never came back to themselves after a break like the one she'd had. Some of them couldn't even follow simple commands.

But she was still in there, somewhere.

I poured water over her hair in slow passes, smoothing it with my hand. Then worked in the soap, steady and gentle.

A sound escaped her—a small sigh, so I worked the soap into her hair a little longer than I needed to, then rinsed the lather and moved on.

Her neck. Her shoulders. Her arms. Her hands.

The places that still held tension.

The places that refused to let go.

"May I wash your back?"

She shifted, leaning forward onto her knees.

I reached for the cloth again.

And saw them.

The scars.

They were raised and uneven. Some wide, some crossed. As if whoever held the lash hadn't cared where they landed, only that they did.

I'd seen a glimpse before. A flicker in the woods, when I bandaged her shoulder. But never all of them. This was the first time I'd seen her back in full in the daylight.

I followed the curve of each scar as I ran the cloth over her back—not to trace, but to witness. Water slid down her spine in rivulets.

I said nothing.

Gradually, I felt the shift. Her body, once rigid, began to soften.

The water was cooling, so I washed myself, then stood and reached for a bath sheet.

She took my hand when I offered it, let me help her from the tub. I dried her gently, then wrapped the sheet around her. I wrung the water from her hair, rubbed it between two folds of a bath sheet.

That was when she looked at me—just a glance.

I didn't reach for the shift. I knew what she needed.

My shoulder burned when I lifted her—one arm behind her back, the other beneath her knees again—and carried her to the hearth. Sat in the old armchair and settled her in my lap, still wrapped in the sheet.

She curled into me, a hand on my chest, head beneath my chin. Her hair, now clean, lay damp against my skin. I let it fall over the side of the chair to dry by the fire.

I held her. One arm around her shoulders. The other across her lap.

The fire snapped softly in the hearth.

After a long while, she spoke. Her voice was quiet and even.

"There were three. Others too, but these were the worst."

I didn't ask. I just waited to bear witness.

Her voice had that clipped cadence I knew too well. The tone used in debriefings. When detachment was the only way to survive the telling. "Lhannor. Catan Row. Caerlan. Lhannor was pine country. A hill village north of Gormlaith. Small. Isolated. They'd sheltered rebels—three men. Starving, half-dead. Gone before we ever arrived."

She took a shallow breath.

"Prefect didn't care. Shelter was treason."

I stroked her arm as she spoke.

"I handled the negotiation. Said if they surrendered their arms, no harm would come to them. That's what I'd been told. So that's what I told them. And they listened. There was an ealdorman—Taran Caerwyn. He had a son who couldn't have been more than twelve. They both laid down their blades."

Her throat worked.

"There was a girl. Lira. Maybe seven or eight. She gave me a bundle of dried flowers. Said I looked tired." Her voice snagged on that. "Her hair was tied with a yellow ribbon."

I felt her body tense. Memory dragging her under.

"Night fell. Then the fires started. No orders. Just torches. They went door to door—dragged people out. Set the roofs alight. I saw Taran fall—tried to protect his son with a rake. He didn't last long. They strung him up like a warning."

She blinked, slow and heavy, as if trying not to see it again.

"Lira died with her family. I found the ribbon the next morning. In the square. Black with soot."

A yellow ribbon. I'd seen one tied around the pages of her old copy of *The Song of the Stars* she always carried. Marking the start of the eighth cycle, *The Cycle of Mortals.* I hadn't known what it meant.

Not until then.

"I was twenty," she said. "I told them they'd be safe."

She let that hang. Then continued.

"Catan Row was different. That one, I made worse."

Her voice stayed flat.

"The prefect wanted names. Rebels, sympathizers, smugglers. We weren't even sure there were any. But we were ordered to find them anyway. There was a boy, Emrys Danwyn. Seventeen. He'd been keeping a journal of passing riders and supplies. Thought it might help prove they *hadn't* given aid."

She exhaled.

"I convinced him to hand it over. Told him if he cooperated, he'd be spared. He asked if I'd teach him to fight once it was over."

That's when the tears came. She didn't wipe them away.

"They found him the next morning. Pinned to the chapel door. Nailed his tongue—"

She took a trembling breath.

"And then they lit the granary. People were inside. I remember the smoke more than the sound. I found Emrys later. In the barn. He'd hanged himself. Still kicking." Her hands fisted in the sheet. "I made it to the threshold. That's it. I stood there and let him die. Less cruel than what they'd do to him."

I held her tighter. She didn't resist.

"Caerlan came last." Her voice was thinner now. "They gave tribute. Rings, trinkets, melted scrap. I remember a man who gave us his wife's wedding ring and the last coin he'd been saving to buy seed the next year. The shaman asked if it would be enough."

She was shaking.

"I told her it would be. That it had to be."

I felt what was coming before she said it.

"Varenius spat on their tribute. Then gave the order. I couldn't—I couldn't follow it. The others did. They went for the children first. One girl—"

She went still in my arms, sobbed hard, once.

"A man tried to run toward her. Her father, probably. They caught him and struck him in the head with a mace, then left him—just left him there."

After a deep, shuddering breath, she went on.

"Varenius flogged me for insubordination. Took my horse, sent me to the First Legion. Said, 'Congratulations on your promotion.'"

Then silence. The kind that wasn't peace—just aftermath.

When she finally spoke again. "There were more, Val. Those were just the worst."

She didn't speak again after that. Just breathed—quiet, uneven, through the tears.

I held her while she wept, her confession settling between us. My thumb traced slow, steady lines along her shoulder. Not to fix anything—gods, I couldn't. Just to anchor her. To remind her she wasn't alone in the ruin.

Her tears dried, but the tension remained, and so did I. So, when the silence had stretched long enough to dull the sharpest edge of her grief, I shifted just enough to press my lips to her temple.

"I need to tell you something," I said.

She didn't move. A breath. Permission.

"I knew the kind of men who commanded you," I said. "Even if I didn't know everything they sent you to do. I knew the kind of work they'd ask of you. And I knew what it does to people. And I told myself that if it was quiet—if it never reached me—then it wasn't mine to interfere with."

I let the fire crackle. Let the truth sit between us.

"That was a lie," I went on. "One I lived with because I didn't yet know how to defy them."

My fingers trailed a slow, grounding line along her arm.

"I asked about you," I said. "More than once. Maybe too often. But I asked the wrong questions. Where you were posted. If you were assigned to negotiations or patrols. How dangerous the postings were."

The words tasted like failure. I swallowed it down.

"I never asked what we were doing to you. Told myself I was being careful. That I was protecting you by not drawing attention to…"

I stopped, searching for the word. I'd never given it a name before.

"… to my weakness for you. And in doing so, I let it blind me, and you paid the cost.

I realized I was holding my breath. I let it out, slow.

"When you saved my life," I said, "I never meant for you to guard me. I only wanted to keep you close, where I could protect you. And even then, I kept my hands to myself. I gave you space. I gave you choice."

My eyes burned. I took a deep breath. Blinked.

"Seven years of wanting to reach for you, and choosing not to, because I didn't want *my* choices to cost you everything. But I did anyway."

I rested my cheek against the top of her head.

"You don't owe me anything," I finished. "Not for the past. Not for surviving it. But if you're here now, with me, it's because you chose to be. And I will not fail you twice."

Then she said, quiet as breath, "I love you, too, Val."

A tear slid down her cheek. I caught it with my thumb. She stayed curled against me. And I just held her.

She had no idea what it meant—that she loved me. No idea what it did to me to hear it. I'd spent my whole fucking life holding the world at arm's length. Keeping only what I knew I could protect. Never what I couldn't bear to lose.

And now, here she was. Wading out of her grief to give me the one thing no one ever had.

I kissed her temple. Said nothing.

She'd given me those words without hesitation. As if I was something worth loving. Gods, I wanted to say them back, but some part of me still believed that if I spoke them aloud, they'd vanish.

That she would vanish.

But I couldn't let her carry this alone.

My voice was quiet when I spoke, rough with truth.

"Aleaia, I can't undo what was done. Not to them. Not to you." My hand found hers. Laced our fingers together. "But I swear to you, I will not be another silence. Not another weight."

Her fingers tightened around mine.

"This country gave me you. And whatever I am now, whatever I will become, I swear it will be someone who stands for them. For you."

My heart thudded, and I was sure she heard it.

She pulled her hand from mine to touch my cheek, tentative, as if unsure I'd still be there. I reached up, covered her fingers with mine, and turned my face just enough to press a kiss into her palm.

A vow sealed in silence.

One I hoped, just for tonight, might be enough.

# CHAPTER FIFTY
## *Enough*

*"We carry each other, or we break."*
—The Fire That Remains

Mētanos 33, 1230
*Valerius*

Two days had passed since she saw the ruins of Ardhmor.

Since I went into that place after her.

The morning light was pale, bleeding into cold stone without ever warming it. Frost rimed the corners of the high windows.

Lucius sat by the fire in the small solar overlooking the courtyard, eyeing a plate of untouched bread and cheese. "You should eat something."

I stayed near the window, arms folded. "Not hungry."

"You haven't slept either."

He wasn't wrong. "I just want it done."

"You're no good to her half-dead, Val." Lucius exhaled slowly through his nose. "Grind yourself down like this, you'll be useless before the tribunal even starts."

I kept my thoughts to myself. They staggered, drunk on sleeplessness, colliding without order. I thought about the nine days' travel to Elisedd. Those early days of courtship, as much as I could give her.

And now, she was… not herself. All I could do was wait for her to come back, if she did. Even then, nothing would be quite the same.

"How is she?"

"Hurting." I kept my eyes on the courtyard beyond the window. "I can see it. In how she moves. The way she avoids looking at me."

Lucius leaned back. I didn't need to see him to know the look he wore—watchful. Measuring.

"She hides it well," I said, softer now. "But it's there. Not just grief. Guilt."

"She's a soldier," Lucius said. "She'll come through this."

I shook my head. "I hope so."

Lucius's voice dropped a register. "So why's it hitting *you* this hard?"

I didn't answer right away. Just touched one finger to the glass. Traced a line through the condensation. Cold burned the pad of my fingertip.

"I failed her long before Ardhmor."

That got his attention. I turned. Met his eyes. Then looked away again. I didn't want his sympathy.

"I never gave her direct orders," I said. "She was too far down the line. But the orders I gave still reached her."

Lucius stayed silent.

"I issued directives. You know the kind. 'Secure the region. Bring the villages into compliance. Contain unrest.' I never followed the chain. Never asked whose hands were doing the work."

"You're not the only one," he said.

I glanced at him.

"I was only her tribune that last year. She never said much about what came before, but I heard things. The kinds of assignments she'd had. The ones that don't get written down. I should've asked questions. But I didn't. Not soon enough." He leaned forward, elbows on his knees. "Because it worked."

I nodded. "That's the worst of it. It did."

Lucius gave a short, grim nod. "So what now?"

I dragged a hand down my face. "I don't know."

"Well," he said, sitting back, "whatever you decide, I'm with you."

A bell rang through the keep. One clear note. The summons.

Footsteps sounded on the narrow stair behind me.

I knew the rhythm before I saw her.

She entered in full drake-scale, polished to catch every sliver of light. Her cloak was fastened with her wolfsbane brooch. Her hair had been braided tight to her scalp, narrow plaits pulling the black strands back from her face. I'd never seen her wear it that way before.

Lucius raised a brow. "Nice of you to join us, Dame Wolfsbane. Thought you might sleep through the tribunal."

That was the thing about Lucius: he treated you the same no matter what you were carrying. I was grateful for that. Grateful he gave her something close to normal when everything else was fractured glass.

She adjusted her belt without glancing up. "Lucius."

He gestured between them. "At least you had the sense to match me. Very intimidating. Very grim. Like a couple of terrifying bookends."

She met his eyes, unimpressed. "It looks better on me."

Lucius snorted. "If you say so."

"Ready?" she asked both of us, testing the draw of her sword—just an inch—before sliding it back into place.

I nodded. "As we'll ever be."

I watched her a moment longer.

I'd been with her nearly every moment since Ardhmor. I'd helped her dress, tended the bruises she wouldn't speak of, sat beside her and held her through hours of silence.

This, though, was the first time she looked like herself again. Armored. Steady. Sharpened into purpose. I didn't know what it had cost her to wear it all again.

But she had done it, and gods, I was proud of her.

Not because she was ready.

Because she refused not to be.

And for the first time in two days, I let myself believe she might survive this whole.

# CHAPTER FIFTY-ONE
## *Reckoning*

*"I saw him choose justice over safety. Over comfort. Over his own crown. And gods help me, I wanted him for it."*
—The Writings of Aelan

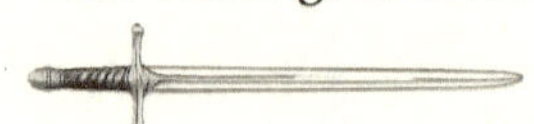

Mētanos 33, 1230
*Aleaia*

The tribunal had been called for Pulcher's abuses in Elisedd—tax theft, unlawful reprisals, and his failure to discipline the legionaries who murdered a girl.

But Ardhmor had changed everything.

The first witnesses were called. Soldiers from Pulcher's own cohort stepped forward, heads bowed like condemned men. Each gave their account with the hollow rhythm of a tolling bell, recounting the moment Pulcher gave the order to raze Ardhmor.

The first boy couldn't have been more than seventeen. He reminded me of Emrys. His hands clasped together until his knuckles were white, and his voice shook like he hadn't slept since.

"We… we didn't understand at first, my lord. We thought it was just a threat, something to scare them. Thought we might burn a few houses, drive off the livestock. Make an example of the place, not… not destroy it or kill people."

He dared a glance at Pulcher, then looked away. "But he ordered us… 'no mercy,' he said. 'No survivors.' I… I have no excuse, my lord," he said. "I did what I was told. I didn't question it."

The words cracked the still air like a snapped branch. He met Val's gaze. Silence followed. Tight as a noose. The townsfolk didn't move. I don't think they even breathed.

Val gave a single nod. "Your testimony is heard. Your name is recorded."

The boy nodded once and went with the guards. I watched his back until the door closed behind him.

Another stepped forward. Older. Broader.

"When he gave the order," he said, "I didn't think. That was the problem. We just... followed. We were more afraid to disobey than we were to do what we did."

"Your testimony is heard," Val said. "Your name is recorded."

One by one, six legionaries—one of them a centurion—stepped forward. Their stories blurred. Orders barked. Torches raised. Screams. Children crying for parents who would never rise. Farmers throwing themselves in front of their kin. Magic too faint to do more than lift stones or ripen grain was no match for imperial steel.

With each account, the hall grew colder. I felt it behind my ribs, in my teeth, like the cold had come up from the floor to hollow me out.

I didn't move. Not a whisper of breath or shift of stance. Just stood there beside Val, hand on the hilt of my sword.

I stopped watching the witnesses. Just kept my eyes on him.

*Pulcher.*

I tracked every breath, every twitch of that smug, rotting mouth. I wanted to see the exact moment he stopped pretending not to care.

Wanted to put a blade in his gullet for the things he'd done.

He sat through it all as if none of it concerned him. As if they were describing a harvest, or the weather. His eyes stayed fixed on nothing, and his expression didn't change. Only his mouth moved once, just once, and not with guilt or shame.

It twitched. A whisper of a smirk, like the whole thing amused him.

My vision narrowed.

Not in rage, though I could feel the fire gathering there, silent and waiting—but in something colder. Something that came after grief, when even fury stopped having edges.

One of the soldiers, his voice hoarse and eyes sunk deep in his skull, spoke of the gallows tree. It sent me back to that village. Back to the quiet after, when the flames had gone out and only smoke remained. Back in the stillness that came too late, the wind whispering through the trees, ash rising in slow spirals from the ruin.

I remembered the bodies, just left where they'd fallen. Some clutched each other. Some hadn't made it that far.

When the final soldier stepped back, silence reigned—one that dared anyone to breathe.

Val waited, watching them all, then turned his eyes on Pulcher. The hall seemed to tilt with it.

"These are the accounts of your own men, Prefect Pulcher," Val said. "They have confessed to following your orders—orders issued in violation of Imperial law, in betrayal of their oaths, and in defiance of the most basic human decency. Do you deny these charges?"

Pulcher lifted his chin. "I did what was necessary," he said, contempt dripping from every word. "Those people were rebels—every one of them."

Val didn't rise to it. He only turned his head to his right. "Ealdorman Riogal."

Then to the left. "Lord Varro. Lord Rullus. Do any of you have anything to add before I pass judgment?"

Varro cleared his throat.

I didn't look at him. I didn't have to. I knew that sound too well. It was the false hesitation of a man about to say something foolish with far too much confidence. The heat had already started crawling up my spine.

I kept my eyes on Val. Steady, righteous Val. Being near him was all that held me together.

"Perhaps we're being too harsh, my lord," Varro said, smooth as oil. "Prefect Pulcher did what was necessary to maintain order. These Aeltyrians have always been difficult. They don't understand strength, or authority, or order as we do. Pulcher exercised the power needed to bring them in line. Sometimes, examples must be made. Such was the case in Ardhmor."

The hall erupted before he even finished.

"Fuck you, Calesian dog!" someone shouted from the back. "We should make an example of you!"

I stepped forward without thinking, placing myself between Val and the fury building in the room. Lucius moved up beside me, calm as ever, though I caught the flick of his hand toward his belt.

"Anvallus's balls," he muttered.

The noise swelled—shouts, benches scraping. The crowd was cresting, frothing like a wave about to break.

A strange cooling drifted across the dais. Slow. Focused.

Magic.

The elements were always present. Magic didn't come from nowhere. It had to be gathered. Concentrated. Commanded.

So if the room was cooling, someone was pulling heat out of it.

"Lucius," I said, voice tight, "I think someone's drawing fire."

His eyes skimmed the hall, narrowed. "That's... not good."

I stepped forward and raised my voice.

"Enough!" I commanded. "We are here under the banner of peace!"

For a breath, it worked. Heads turned. Noise faltered.

"You are one of us, but you sit up there with your Calesian masters! Fuck you, traitorous bitch!"

*One of us.*

It landed clean. Because it wasn't wrong. Not entirely.

I stood frozen, heart hammering. I breathed in. Out. Tried to steady the noise inside. But my fingers itched with the need to act.

And the room kept cooling.

Too fast now.

Then it struck.

A spark flared midair, like a whip cracked from the crowd—thin, searing, streaking toward the dais.

I didn't think. Didn't choose.

I moved.

The magic came like breath after drowning.

It exploded from my palm in a wide flare, catching the flame midair. The shield snapped into place, hardening into a curved silver veil that rippled once and held, thin as glass and strong as stone.

The fire hit it and scattered, embers hissing against the warded air.

Gasps rippled through the hall. Someone cried out. Chairs scraped back.

"Stand down!"

Riogal's voice cracked through the chamber like thunder. "There will be no magic summoned here. We will have order!"

It worked.

The pressure in the air relented. The heat withdrew. Slowly, warmth crept back into the room.

The shield dissipated and I stepped back. My limbs felt hollow, but I stayed upright.

Riogal went down the steps, crossed the hall in a few long strides, and seized a boy near the back by his collar. Didn't shout. Didn't speak. Just dragged him out.

The door hadn't even closed behind them when Pulcher laughed—a foul, brittle sound. Like something rotting through.

"A traitor to the Empire, right here beside you, Valerius di Calesia," he said, voice slick with venom. "It proves I was right. These people can't resist their baser instincts. And you—you presume to pass judgment on me?"

"He does because you're a waste of flesh and fresh air, Pulcher," Rullus said, bone-dry. "She shielded you, too."

A few people actually laughed at that. Short. Bitter.

"My lord," Rullus continued, addressing Val, "might I have your permission to arrest Lord Varro if he opens his mouth again?"

Val didn't blink. But something in his face tightened.

"If Lord Varro speaks again with the clear intent to disrupt these proceedings," he said coolly, "you have my permission to arrest him."

Then, to the room, Val said, "This tribunal is in recess. We will resume in one hour, once tempers have cooled."

With a nod to Rullus and a pointed glance at Varro, he stepped down from the dais.

"Tutela, stay with Rullus," he added, not breaking stride.

"Yes, lord," Lucius replied.

Val walked toward one of the side corridors, and I followed.

He led me back to the small chamber off the hall—the solar, small and dimly lit, with a hearth and high windows. No guards. No ears.

He crossed to the table and poured two cups of wine from a decanter left behind. Wordless, he sniffed the wine, then handed me one.

"I'm sorry," I said, softer now. "For what I said before. About you being just like them."

He swirled the wine in the cup in his hand, looking down into it.

"I know you're not," I added. "I shouldn't have pushed you like that."

"Don't be sorry. You were right to." He met my gaze. "I'm the one who should apologize. For making you think I sided with him."

I'd forgiven him already, even if I hadn't said it aloud. Even if I hadn't forgiven myself for the things I said before I left.

"I just needed time," he said. "That's all I was trying to buy. If I execute him, I strike the flint and show them we're not afraid to burn what needs to burn."

I didn't look away.

"Then strike it," I said.

No fear. No hesitation. Just fire.

He didn't answer at once, but I saw the shift in him. A man done running from truths he already knew.

Then, slowly, he stepped closer and took my hand.

Warm. Solid. Familiar.

He brought my fingers to his lips and pressed them to my knuckles.

Then he let go.

"Now to go argue with Varro," he said, draining his cup and setting it aside.

When we returned to the great hall, it was empty, save the tribunal—Riogal, Varro, Rullus—along with Lucius and a few guards posted along the edges.

Val walked around the front of the table. He wouldn't sit for this argument. He'd need to move.

"We've heard the testimonies," he said, composed and steady as he looked at each man in turn. "The evidence is undeniable. Pulcher's actions disgrace the Empire. For his crimes, justice demands his life."

Varro exhaled sharply, already shaking his head.

"Pulcher may be guilty of overstepping, of failure, but he is Calesian. An officer. Execution would deepen the divide between our people and these..." He faltered. "These conquered lands. Banishment would punish him without risking rebellion."

"Banishment is not enough," Rullus said. "This wasn't one mistake. Pulcher became an enemy to those he was sworn to protect. His orders violated the oath we all swore. If we let him walk away, we tell every other prefect they can do the same and expect mercy."

Varro's jaw clenched. He kept his voice calm, but color rose in his neck. "And where is mercy, Rullus? Or has justice become so simple? Pulcher wasn't as well behaved as he should have been, but he is one of ours. He comes from a loyal house, one that supports the Empire. If we begin turning our swords on our own, what message do we send? The Empire does not and should not bend to barbaric cries for blood."

"'Barbaric cries'?" Riogal leaned forward, planting his elbows on the table, his voice low and cold. "It was Pulcher's order that soaked Ardhmor's soil in blood. His men butchered families. And before that, let us not forget, a girl died because he refused to restrain his soldiers. Banishment?" He scoffed. "We Aeltyrians are not fools. If you want us to believe justice still exists, he must suffer the consequences."

Varro made a disgusted sound. "And now we take justice lessons from ashborn? Creator preserve us."

Val stopped in front of him.

"Watch your fucking tongue," he said, voice quietly lethal. "Unless you want it removed."

The room stilled.

Except me. I hadn't known what it would do to me, to see him like this, but I was soaked straight through, listening to him snarl at Varro that way.

Val didn't stop. He advanced a step, shadows deepening the lines of his face as he leaned on the table. "You think station protects you? That your title gives you license to speak like that in *my* hall?"

His voice was deadly now. "Riogal is here because the blood spilled within the walls of Elisedd and at Ardhmor was Aeltyrian. And because *we* failed to stop it. If you think justice belongs only to men like you, then you don't deserve your post."

I pressed my thighs together, but it didn't help. I was going to have to burn my trousers.

Varro sat back, a flicker of unease tightening his mouth.

"My lord," he said carefully, "would you throw Calesian blood to the wolves for some ideal? Today it's Pulcher. Tomorrow it could be any of us, condemned by local sentiment and Aeltyrian spite."

*Spite!*

The word struck like a jolt. I didn't move, but my shoulders went rigid. My hand drifted an inch toward my belt before I caught myself. Every time he spoke, my pulse kicked harder.

What was wrong with me? I wanted to stab Varro and fuck Val all at once.

Val's voice was calm. Too calm. "This isn't about appeasement. It's about accountability. Pulcher's crimes stain Calesia itself. If we want any hope of respect, we must prove that imperial authority doesn't shield the guilty. He didn't fail his duties. He destabilized our rule. He harmed innocents. He dishonored us."

He met Varro's eyes. "If you fear the same fate, I suggest you don't follow his example."

Rullus nodded. "To hesitate now would show weakness. If we protect our own at the cost of justice, we become what they call us—tyrants. I won't be counted among them."

Riogal's voice was firm and final. "Aeltyria has suffered enough under men like Pulcher. Let his death be a warning—and a peace offering, if peace is still what you want."

Varro didn't flinch, but when he spoke again, his voice was cool and precise, like a blade drawn slow. "You speak of justice as if it's a clean line. But when the Emperor or Prince Cassius demand answers, will you tell them you chose blood over a more measured path? Pulcher's death won't end unrest—it'll fuel it. And you'll answer for it."

*Measured path.*

The only thing measured about Ardhmor was the spacing of the corpses.

Val cleared his throat and looked to each man seated before him. When he spoke, it was with no trace of doubt.

"I understand the risk, Lord Varro. But we cannot betray our oaths by turning a blind eye. Pulcher's life is forfeit—for the lives he destroyed, for the trust he broke. Justice demands no less." He let the silence linger long enough to settle in the bones. "Pulcher will pay with his life. That is my judgment."

I should have wept. For the girl. For the town. For all of it.

But all I could do was stare at him, breath caught somewhere between grief and ruinous hunger.

Varro leaned back, arms crossed, expression unreadable. But there was something in his eyes. Weight, perhaps. Or warning.

"Seems your mind was made up the moment you walked in," he said, flicking a glance toward me. "I only hope you know what this will cost you, di Calesia. And I hope she's worth it."

Varro believed Val's closeness to me had swayed him.

And gods help us, he wasn't entirely wrong.

Val's voice came low and razor-edged. "Be very, very careful, Varro."

He stepped forward just enough to cast a shadow over the table again—just enough to make Varro shift in his seat.

"If you think this was done for her, then you've not only misunderstood me—you've exposed yourself. What you're really saying is that the blood spilled at Ardhmor was acceptable. That justice should serve your comfort, not the truth.

The next words fell like steel.

"She's not the weakness in this room. You are. And if I hear you speak of her again like she's a stain on your tongue, I will personally see you removed from this tribunal and this province."

Silence. Heavy as stone.

Then he looked up at me. Met my eyes.

*Aelan's mercy.*

Every inch of me was heat and heartbeat, slick with want and something fiercer. He was fury given form—sharp, merciless, and so godsdamned beautiful it made my knees weak. I could've drowned in that voice, that wrath—like the crack of thunder that splits the sky and doesn't apologize for the storm that follows. He was mine, and the whole room had just been made to remember it.

I bit my lip.

Riogal's mouth twitched, barely, and he offered Val the kind of nod men give other men after a particularly well-landed blow. "Shall I open the doors, my lord?"

He didn't look at me, but I saw the breath he took to calm himself, the flicker of restraint as he forced his fury back beneath the surface. Then he nodded. "Let's get this over with."

Riogal signaled the guards. The great doors groaned open. Townspeople began to file in—slow at first, then in a wave of bodies and boots on stone.

Pulcher was brought in last, shackled and flanked by legionaries. Head high. That same smug twist to his mouth. No shame. No fear. Just venom.

My hands clenched at my sides, nails biting skin.

If it were up to me, he'd already be dead.

Val took his place behind the tribunal table, facing the crowd, but he didn't sit.

"Evaristus Pulcher," he said, voice steady, clear enough to carry, "I was summoned to address the abuses committed in Elisedd—abuses that led to the death of an innocent girl. Your failure to act incited unrest, and as consequence, your men were expelled from the town. You destabilized His Majesty's rule."

I kept my eyes on him.

"That alone demanded justice. But your crimes didn't end there. Witness after witness named you in the razing of Ardhmor. Your orders were depraved, the evidence abundant. There is no doubt of your guilt." He turned to the tribunal. "Do we stand in agreement?"

Rullus gave a single nod. Riogal followed. Varro said nothing, stone-faced and silent.

Val faced Pulcher once more. "You are guilty of dereliction of duty, abuse of power, incitement of unrest, destabilization of imperial holdings, mass execution of civilians, and crimes against the people of the Empire."

Each charge landed like iron on stone.

And then—

"The punishment for these crimes is death. Sentence will be carried out at first light. By my blade."

A murmur swept the hall, and this time it wasn't outrage.

Satisfaction.

Pulcher laughed. "Incitement of unrest? This is a joke. What do you think this will do?"

I didn't look at him.

I was still watching Val.

He didn't blink. "Secure him in the dungeons."

It was done.

And I felt it—tight in my throat, sharp behind my ribs.

Justice. Spoken aloud. Clear. Unapologetic. Final.

I had learned two things during that trial.

First, that Val was as good a man as I had ever known.

And second, that there was nothing in this world or the next as ruinous as Valerius di Calesia standing in judgment.

# CHAPTER FIFTY-TWO
## *Wildfire*

*"He did not break me. He watched me fall apart and called it beautiful."*
—The Breath of the World

Mētanos 33, 1230
*Aleaia*

The doors closed behind us, shutting out the crowd, the whispers, the rot of Pulcher's name. I didn't speak as we climbed the stairs toward our chamber.

I couldn't stop seeing him there, standing on the dais like he was forged for command. The sound of his voice, low and lethal, still echoed in me.

My heart pounded like a war drum.

I wanted him. I ached for him the way wild earth longs for fire—to be stripped bare, burned clean, born again from ash.

I wanted the weight of him—his hands gripping, pinning me in place, his mouth at my throat.

Gods, I wanted him.

I shoved the chamber door shut behind us.

He barely had time to turn before I seized him, shoved him back against the wood. His eyes went wide for half a breath. I dragged him down by the front of his tunic, knuckles whitening in the fabric, desperate for the taste of him. My teeth grazed his bottom lip, and he groaned into my mouth.

Then the wildfire caught, ready to burn us alive.

He turned us and drove me back against the door hard enough to steal the breath from my lungs, kissing me like he meant to devour me.

I arched into him, hips rolling without permission against the thigh he wedged between my legs. The friction dragged a sound from me that I hadn't meant to make. His hands moved to the buckles of my armor until each piece was discarded.

He dropped to one knee—one boot aside, then the other—his fingers at my waist, untying my trousers and dragging them down. They clung, damp with want. Heat wound tight in my belly.

His hands stilled as he looked up at me through his lashes, voice catching on something dark and hungry. "Gods, Aleaia..."

Heat crawled up my throat, across my chest, spreading under his stare. I braced one hand on the door behind me as he eased my trousers off the rest of the way, then tossed them aside.

He pressed his mouth to the inside of my thigh, then bit down hard enough to make my knees tremble. The strength drained from them so fast I had to brace harder against the door.

I *liked* the way pain and pleasure blurred together.

My hand flew to his hair, fisting there, holding him to me.

He groaned against my skin, licking where he'd left a mark. His teeth grazed me again, slower this time.

"That's it," I whispered, the words slipping out before I could stop them.

I let go as he rose, watching him, heat pulsing low and steady in my belly.

My shift was damp, clinging to every curve. I reached for the laces, but he caught my wrists.

"No," he said, voice rough. "Let me."

Something in my stomach tightened at the command.

Then he grabbed the neckline and tore it, splitting it down the seam with a sound that hit low in my spine. Cool air skimmed over my breasts. I felt suddenly exposed—and hungrier for it.

"Fuck," I whispered as the ruined pieces fell like shed skin around my feet. I fisted the front of his tunic and pulled him back into a kiss. "Get rid of these godsdamned layers."

He yanked it over his head and let it fall, then kissed me again, hotter and wilder. More collision than kiss, breaking only to kiss along my jawline.

"Bed?" he asked against my ear.

I bit his shoulder, hard enough to make him grunt. "Here. Now."

He dropped his trousers, kicked them off with his boots, and lifted me, my legs locking around his waist. My back hit the door with a thud—his mouth at my neck, hands gripping my thighs. The wood pressed hard between my shoulder blades as he settled his weight into me.

"Gods." My breath came fast, fingers digging into his shoulders. "You don't even know what you looked like up there."

He pulled back to meet my eyes—his green gone molten. "Tell me."

"Like vengeance incarnate. All I could think about was how it would feel to be beneath you. To have you inside me," I said, something intoxicating unfurling inside me. I took his jaw in my hand and kissed him—fierce and sure—then held him there. "Don't be gentle, Valerius."

The admission left my pulse racing in my throat.

With a groan, he drove me higher against the door, pressing my spine against the wood. One arm braced beneath my thigh to hold me there, the other sliding between my legs without hesitation. His fingers pushed in slow, slow at first, then deeper. The curl of them sent a sharp pull in my belly, and my knees squeezed instinctively around him. I gasped, head tipping back against the wood.

A pleased hum rumbled in his throat. "You're so fucking wet for me."

I laughed, the sound vibrating low in my chest, heat pooling heavier between my thighs. I caught his lower lip between my teeth. "Have been since you told him to watch his tongue."

He pulled his fingers free—slick, glistening in the firelight.

I met his gaze, bold and unrepentant.

I wanted him to see. To know exactly what he'd done to me.

So I leaned forward.

Held his gaze.

And took his fingers into my mouth, down to the base.

His breath left him in a shudder. "Fuck."

His reaction sent satisfaction flaring hot through my core.

I let his fingers slide from my mouth with a soft, wet sound and smirked. "You want to ruin me, don't you?" I whispered. "So do it."

The words spilled out before I could pull them back, heat tightening deep in my gut.

He rolled his hips once, the thick heat of him stealing my breath as it pressed against me where I was already aching. My back arched, chasing the pressure.

"Feel what you do to me?" he asked, voice low and ragged as he reached between us and rubbed himself against me. "I'm so hard for you it hurts."

The admission made something inside me burn hotter.

My control snapped like a pulled thread.

"Please," I rasped. "Now."

He drove into me in one hard, unrelenting thrust, filling me. The stretch flared hot and deep, almost too much and not enough all at once. A hoarse cry tore from my throat. My back arched clean away from the door, my body clenching around him.

"Hold on to me," he grated out.

My arms locked around his shoulders before I could think, fingers digging into muscle.

Then he pushed into me again—deeper. Rougher.

I could only feel him inside me, his hands gripping my thighs, his mouth at my throat. Each thrust knocked the air from my lungs, leaving me gasping.

"You feel like fire," he growled at my ear. "Like you were made to be fucked like this."

"I was," I gasped, head tipping back as the haze closed in. "Just for you."

Saying it sent a thrill straight through me.

His mouth curved, slow and knowing. "Is that so?"

I slipped one hand around behind him and smacked his arse. "You know it is. Harder."

His mouth found my ear and nipped it. "You wicked little thing," he growled. "Don't start what you can't finish."

I laughed, panting. Then I did it again, sharper.

He laughed, too, low and dangerous. "If you want me to do it to you," he said, "just ask."

He caught my leg and brought his hand up harder than I had, the smack sharp enough to tear a raw, involuntary cry from me. The shock of it made my hips buck against him.

"You like that?" he ground out.

"Yes," I whispered. My thighs trembled where they held him.

He drove into me—harder, deeper—grinding until the ache and the hunger bled together.

And gods, his face. Tight with restraint, eyes wild with the effort not to fall apart. Just heat and hunger and need.

"Fuck—Aleaia—you're so—tight—"

The pressure built at the center of me, a blaze licking up dry timber. Every muscle in me tensed, straining toward something inevitable.

"Right there," I cried. "Don't stop—gods—don't stop—"

There was only him—his relentless rhythm, the world narrowing to sound and weight and burn. I moaned, the sound ripped from somewhere deep.

I came hard, a cry torn from me as my body clamped down around him, spasming, straining. I went tight as a drawn bowstring before snapping loose. I arched, ankles locked behind his back, nails digging into his shoulders.

"Fuck—finally," he groaned, ragged with need. "Made me work for it, didn't you? Godsdamn, I love how hard you come for me."

Then he tore me from the door and carried me to the table, clearing it with one arm, scrolls scattering, a goblet clattering to the floor and rolling into the hearth. The sudden movement made my head spin, my limbs weak and shaking.

Then he laid me out hard, like a feast he'd starved for.

The cold of it shocked my overheated skin, making me shiver despite the burn still moving through me. I lay there stretched across the table, legs slack, heart galloping. Skin flushed. Limbs loose. Every inch of me humming.

He leaned over me and kissed me, lips just brushing mine, fingers grazing the hollow of my hip. I shivered, every inch of my skin raw from him.

"What are you waiting for?" I asked.

"Just slowing down," he murmured. "Savoring this. You."

"Fuck me," I said, bucking my hips toward him. My body still thrummed, restless and unsatisfied.

His hands were reverent as he smoothed a lock of damp hair from my face, laughing through his breath. "So impatient. Just let me please you."

He bent to press a kiss to the center of my chest.

Over my heart.

Soft. Feather-light.

My throat tightened, breath catching high in my chest.

"I know what I'm about, Aleaia." One hand held fast to my hip, the other slid up my ribs, dragging across sweat-slick skin until it found the curve of my breast. "And I know what you need. Enjoy it."

I looked up at him through the haze, half-wild and fully his.

"You do. Because I am yours," I said, hoarse from the cries he'd torn out of me. "Because I gave myself to you."

The admission left me breathless as my fingers drifted between my thighs, still slick, the ache there throbbing in time with my heartbeat.

His breath hitched as his eyes followed my hand, watching what it touched.

"Give myself to you still."

He exhaled sharply, a sound of awed hunger.

The sound of it sent a thrill through me, and I realized he liked it when I spoke to him like that.

I crooked a finger, beckoning him down to me with a smile.

He leaned in.

I brushed my lips against the shell of his ear, fingers catching the line of his jaw. "I'm not fragile," I whispered, my hand firm. "I trust you not to break me."

"Careful," he said, too softly. "That's not something I take lightly."

I met his eyes. "Nor I."

He sucked in a breath through his teeth. Rolled my nipple between his fingers until I cried out. Heat shot straight down my belly, making my hips lift off the table as he claimed the other with his mouth.

His lips and hands made their way down my ribs. My stomach. My hip.

My thighs parted wider without being told.

Then he knelt between them, leaving cool air to brush my skin where he'd just been.

He kissed the inside of my thigh, just above the bend of my knee. Then higher.

My back bowed, anticipation tightening every muscle in my body.

His mouth moved higher still.

I inhaled, shivering as his breath ghosted over the heat of me.

My hand drifted down again, fingers slipping between until he batted them aside.

"No," he growled. "That's mine."

The denial left me restless and aching.

"Please," I sighed, trembling with the effort of staying still for him.

He lowered his head.

Touched his mouth to me.

The first stroke of his tongue split me open. My back bowed off the table before I could stop it. I cried out, hips jolting. Every nerve felt exposed, oversensitive and throbbing.

He spread me open and devoured me. Slowly. Thoroughly. As if nothing else in the world existed but me. My hips lifted helplessly to his mouth.

"So greedy," I whispered, my voice unraveling. "You want to taste how good you fucked me?"

His grip tightened and he groaned into me.

*Oh. He liked that, too.*

I throbbed under his mouth.

He slid two fingers inside while his mouth stayed locked on me, relentless. The stretch was sweet and overwhelming.

My hips rocked. My body bowed into him, hungry, unmade, hard enough to lift my shoulders off the table.

"Val—fuck—right there—don't stop—please—"

My hands fisted in his hair as it tore through me—bright, unbearable, and all the more intense for the things we said to each other, not just the things we did.

My vision blurred at the edges as every muscle in me clenched. I cried out his name.

He didn't stop until I lay there shaking beneath him. Then he rose, eyes locked on mine as he wiped his bottom lip with the pad of his thumb.

My chest rose and fell too fast.

Before I could speak, he sat me up, fisted my hair, tilted my head back, and kissed me. The pull at my scalp sent heat straight through me. His tongue slid into my mouth once before he pulled back.

"You belong to me," he said against my lips.

"I do," I panted.

He slid me off the table, turned me, and pressed a hand between my shoulder blades to bend me over it. My palms gripped the worn edge in anticipation as he pressed his chest to my back, breath searing my neck. My legs felt unsteady, still weak from him.

"You gave yourself to me," he said hungrily. "I'll teach you what that means."

His palm dragged up to my shoulder blades, fingers tangling in my hair near the scalp. The sharp pull—harder than before—forced my head back and sent heat flooding through my stomach.

I gasped. Why did that feel so fucking good?

His other hand slid around, palming my breast as he nudged my thighs wider with his knee. My thighs quivered where they braced against the table.

"You're shaking." I felt his teeth at my ear, his thumb flicking across my nipple. "Need it that badly?"

"Val—"

"Say it," he growled. "Tell me how you want it."

I tried to push back, my breath coming thin and uneven as I fought for words.

"I want you," I breathed. "To take me."

He exhaled, rough and close. "Not good enough."

He let go of my hair. Let me fall forward, helpless, then cracked his palm across my arse in one punishing smack. The impact sent a jolt straight between my legs.

I gasped, high and startled, as heat bloomed fast and hot across my skin.

"Now, tell me what you really want," he said.

The words scraped out of me, heart pounding in my throat.

"Hard," I cried. "I want it hard—I want you to use me—"

Another smack, across the other cheek. Harsher. My whole body jolted.

And I wanted it. Every strike. Every word. I wanted him like this. Wanted him to handle me.

He leaned in, mouth grazing fire just below my ear.

"Never using," he said darkly. "Claiming."

My chest tightened at the sound of it.

I tried again, but no words came. My thighs shook. My hands held tight to the table's edge.

He laughed, delighted and triumphant. "What happened to that sharp little mouth? Say it. Tell me how you want me to fuck you."

A moan broke loose from me.

"If you don't answer, I have to guess," he said as he gripped my hips.

And claimed me in one brutal thrust.

My fingers slipped on the wood before tightening again.

He yanked me upright by my hair—pulling me flush to him, back arched—his other hand sliding down my belly. Heat streaked down my spine.

I loved it. Every savage bit. I *wanted* to be taken like this.

His breath tore ragged across my ear.

"You're not coming," he growled. "Not until I let you. I'll keep you here all godsdamned night—stuffed full and shaking—if that's what it takes to hear you beg."

My hips rocked back toward him instinctively, chasing what he denied me.

"Val—please—"

"No," he snarled. "Like you fucking mean it."

The words burst out of me, breathless and shaking. "I want it. Want you—to fuck me—until I can't stand, can't breathe, can't think—"

I felt something break in him.

"That's it. Good girl."

He pressed me down against the tabletop, pulled out, and slammed back into me with a vicious, bone-deep thrust.

He stayed deep, one hand wrapped in my hair, the other braced at my back, pinning me there, holding me open.

"You're mine," he said, pulling back, his voice ragged with want.

Then drove into me again. Hard. Devastating.

"Every part of you."

Again—deeper, rougher. I gasped, greedy for it.

"Mine to take."

I moaned, thighs parting wider, open for him. Only him.

"Mine to ruin."

A shiver ran through me. My nails dug into the wood. I craved this. Needed this.

"Mine to keep."

My chest ached at that one.

He pounded the truth into me again and again, until it wasn't just words. Until it was worship. Until there was no space left between my skin and his voice.

"Harder," I begged. "Please—don't stop—"

The table groaned beneath us, legs scraping stone with the rhythm of him.

"You feel that?" he panted at my ear. "Feel what you fucking do to me?"

"Val—I—" My voice broke. "I love you."

The words tore through my chest, leaving me bare. I'd said it before. I'd say it again. A thousand times.

He stilled for a heartbeat. Panic flickered through me.

Then he leaned over me, bracing himself close, one hand on the table, the other sliding up my belly, up my ribs, until his fingers curled beneath my jaw and tilted my face to his. He kissed me deep, his tongue claiming the words from my mouth.

The tension drained from my shoulders, replaced by something molten and steady.

When it broke, he didn't speak.

He just looked down at me through his lashes, hungry and undone.

Then he held me to him and moved in me again—measured now—his hand still at my chin, watching my face as if memorizing what he did to me.

And when I came, it wasn't a cry.

I clenched hard, then broke in waves that left me open and shaking.

Heat pulsed outward from where we were joined, spreading through me until there was nothing else.

He was close too. I knew it from the ragged snap in his breath, the deep, helpless sounds he made. One hand gripped my hip, the other braced beside mine on the table.

Then he pulled free, drew back just far enough to spill across my back, gasping like it hurt to be torn from me.

Warmth streaked over my skin, intimate and unmistakable.

Satisfaction settled low in me.

I lay flat on the table, cheek against the cool wood, trying to catch my breath. He dipped his head to rest between my shoulders.

We stayed like that for a long moment, breathing, shaking.

He reached for a crumpled cloth on the table. Didn't speak. Just cleaned me, tenderly and thoroughly. When he finished, he pressed a kiss to my shoulder.

I pushed myself up, my legs wobbling beneath me.

Val noticed.

He lifted me and carried me to the bed. Laid me down, then slid in beside me. I turned to him instinctively, curling into the warmth of his chest, the thud of his heartbeat under my ear.

His hand found my hair, this time only to soothe. Long, slow strokes through it. The fire in me dimmed to embers, my muscles going heavy and loose beneath his hand. For a moment, I didn't have to burn.

"Was that too much?" he asked gently. "Not just your body. All of it."

My fingers splayed across his chest, thumb brushing lightly through the hair there. "No."

I felt his breath catch beneath my hand, the faint tautness in his shoulders.

"I mean it," I said. I touched his chin, turned his face to mine. "It wasn't too much." I leaned in to kiss him, slow and soft now.

His hand slid from my hair to my cheek when he pulled back. "You'd stop me if I did?"

I nodded. "I would."

I meant it. Because he didn't want to tame me, didn't want my obedience. He loved my fight.

I thought about when he'd said *good girl,* how I should've spat fire. Should've torn away, snarled something sharp. But I hadn't.

Because I liked it.

What did that mean about me? I wondered.

"You didn't hurt me," I said, softer. "You gave me what I needed."

He didn't answer, and I said nothing more, just let him make peace with whatever was inside him.

"Come here," he said as he pulled me closer, tighter, until I was half-sprawled across him, my face tucked into the hollow of his neck. His arm curved around me, fingers tracing circles on my back.

We stayed that way a long while. I could've drifted off. I wanted to. But there, in the quiet, I thought I figured out what bothered him—and once I knew that, I had to comfort him.

"I meant it," I said. "When I said I love you. I do."

His hand stilled.

I lifted my head, and our eyes met.

"I know," he said softly.

But he didn't say it back.

That struck like a blade to the heart. Heat flooded my face. My eyes stung. I ducked my head, hiding from the humiliation.

I'd thought he loved me but didn't know how to say it. Thought to give him space to say it. To lead him.

Maybe I'd been wrong.

*Good,* I thought. *Better this way. Safer for him.*

He tucked a strand of hair behind my ear, then touched a finger under my chin.

"Aleaia, look at me," he said softly.

I did, willing the tears not to fall.

He brushed his thumb across my lip.

"I need you to understand something," he said. "About the way I feel about you."

I held my breath.

"Every second I'm with you, I feel peace. Warmth. I don't feel like I'm surviving. I feel whole. And every second I'm not, all I think about is getting back to you."

His hand slid to my cheek. "But every time I've named something I couldn't bear to lose, it's been taken from me. And if I say it—if I give it voice—I have to believe—"

His voice cracked. Not from weakness, but from weight.

"I wouldn't know how to survive it if it—"

I kissed him. Soft. Certain. Silencing him.

It didn't make sense to me, but it did to him. And I knew what he needed to hear then.

"You don't have to," I murmured. "I'm not going anywhere. Say it when you're ready. I feel it in everything you do. It doesn't change a thing for me."

He breathed in deep and held me tighter.

And when my eyes closed at last, I didn't fall asleep. I surrendered.

To firelight.

To silence.

To a love too dangerous to name—and too fierce to deny.

Wrapped in the arms of the only man who could tear me open, and still hold the pieces like they were blessed.

# CHAPTER FIFTY THREE
## *The Line*

*"Draw the line once. Make them bleed for crossing."*
—Cadoc Aneirin to Queen Eavan on Calesia's declaration of war

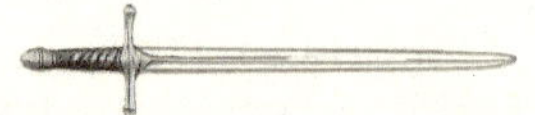

Mētanos 34, 1230
*Aleaia*

Morning broke gray and cold—the kind of chill that bit through furs and made your fingers ache if you didn't keep them moving. Snow drifted down soft as ash, blanketing Elisedd in a silence too clean for what we were about to do.

The crowd had already gathered in the square. Silent. Still. Like mourners, though this wasn't grief. It was anticipation. A reckoning long overdue.

I stood beside Val on the scaffold. Lucius stood just behind us, close enough to reach either of us in a heartbeat, his cloak dusted with snow, his eyes sharp and unreadable.

I'd gotten up early to braid my hair the old way: tight, severe plaits, pulled back from my face and bound close to the scalp.

War braids.

They left nothing loose. Nothing that could be seized or used against me.

I needed clarity. Control. The kind that doesn't shake.

I felt still. Calm, even in the deepest parts of me. I just watched the ones who'd gathered for this. The farmers and elders, children clinging to their mothers, soldiers stiff-backed in the snow.

Some had bled for what Pulcher did.

Some had buried what was left.

They were here to see it end.

It was justice. Simple as that.

The castle's outer gate groaned open. Riogal came out first. Pulcher followed, between two guards wrists bound,. What passed for his pride was just his fear wearing a better coat.

He missed a step halfway up the platform and caught himself. When they forced him to his knees, he stared at the crowd, then locked eyes with Val.

Val ignored him. This was the part when the judgment was read from a parchment, but Val had committed it to memory. "Pulcher, for your crimes against the people of Aeltyria, you are condemned. For the burning of Ardhmor. For the slaughter of innocents. For the abuse of your office and the laws you swore to uphold."

His voice rang through the cold.

"Have you any last words?"

Pulcher bared his teeth. "You're a traitor, Valerius di Calesia. A disgrace to the Empire."

His spit hit the boards at Val's feet.

Val drew the longsword from his hip.

Then he turned and offered it to me, hilt-first.

I took it, unsurprised. He'd asked me if I wanted to wield the blade of judgment. And I'd accepted.

It was heavier than mine. Calesian-forged, meant for a man's arm and a two-handed swing. But it was balanced. And deadly sharp. That was all that mattered.

I hefted it, resting it on my shoulder, and looked to a woman in the front row—eyes red-rimmed, dressed in the shapeless black robes of mourning.

*"Maethir,"* I said in Aeltyrian, *"vaet esin tóa genaé nem?"*

*Mother, what was your daughter's name?*

Not once during the tribunal had she been named. The proceedings had started with her death, and been eclipsed by the tragedy of Ardhmor.

She deserved better, and I'd give it to her.

"Thalenna," the woman said. Her voice was clear, even through her tears.

I nodded.

I looked first to Lucius, who stepped forward and pushed Pulcher's head down roughly onto the executioner's block.

Then to Val, who nodded.

I stepped up beside Pulcher. He was shaking, and a sour stink hit the air. He was pissing himself. Of course he was. A man can shout and bluster all he wants, but the body always knows the truth.

I moved Val's blade off my shoulder, raised it.

*"Ana Thalenna Eliseddii!"* I called.

*For Thalenna of Elisedd!*

The blade came down in one clean arc.

It bit deep, straight through the bone, and parted his head from his neck with a spray of blood so fine it hung in the air like mist. The head hit the boards with a hollow thud. The body sagged forward, limbs twitching, blood steaming in the cold.

I looked down at what was left. Not out of remorse. I wanted to see the truth of it. The stillness. The end. One better than he'd ever deserved.

My pulse pounded.

They were watching. All of them.

My voice had once been a weapon wielded against them.

Blood still steamed from the severed neck. The sword dripped red. It was heavy to hold in one hand, but I did, bending to grab the head by the hair.

I lifted it high so every soul in the square could see. Blood on my gloves. Blood on the snow. Dripping down my arm as I held it high.

I gave them my voice now, raised in vengeance.

*"Ceareth!"* I shouted. *"Essa es ceareth, bi te delen a Valerion di Calesia!"*

*Justice. This is justice, by the hand of Valerius di Calesia.*

It was bloodlust, yes. But it was also a message.

He had delivered justice. Not through tribute. Not through orders from Avitum. By the blade.

*"Valerion!"*

The chant rang through the square—loud and raw, born of grief, of rage, of something that almost sounded like hope.

Lucius stayed to my right, one hand on the hilt of his sword, holding the line as the chant rose like thunder.

I looked at Val, standing there, shoulders braced like he was waiting for a blow.

But I knew better. That wasn't guilt.

It was calculation.

The crowd had cheered for justice.

But what they wanted wasn't justice. It was vengeance. It always was.

And whether he liked it or not, he'd just given it to them.

In public. On record. With my hand and his sword.

There would be more hiding behind diplomacy. No more pretending Aeltyria was compliant.

I let the head fall with a thud against the boards.

Let the last echo of Pulcher's life bleed out into the snow with the last vestiges of our illusion.

Then I cleaned the sword on Pulcher's back. Slow. Precise. No shaking hands. No second thoughts. When the steel shone again, I offered it back, hilt-first.

Val took it. Silent.

Our eyes met.

He turned to the crowd and lifted a hand in acknowledgment.

And I stood beside him.

Not behind.

Not beneath.

Beside.

# CHAPTER FIFTY-FOUR
## *Atonement*

*"I know I don't deserve your forgiveness.*
*But I'll die for the love of you, and hope that's close enough."*
—Cadoc Aneirin to Queen Eavan before the fall of Aeldunon, 1207

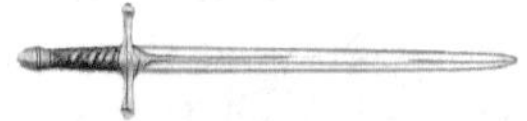

Mētanos 35, 1230
*Valerius*

We left Elisedd the morning after the execution, under a sky the color of iron.

The wind had stilled. The clopping of hooves was a steady rhythm on the road. No one spoke. And I didn't think about Pulcher, or the mess I'd created in Elisedd. There was nothing I could do about that, for now.

I was consumed with thoughts of one person. Just one.

And she rode just ahead of me, her braid swaying down her back, catching what little sun pierced the cloud like a raven's wing. Every line of her body was sure and balanced.

I couldn't look at her without remembering.

The way she'd bent under my hands. The way she'd taken me—all of me—and begged for more.

It had been two days, and I still couldn't stop feeling it. Her. Every gasp. Every word. Every yes that undid me.

I'd had lovers before. Measured. Distant. But I had never lost myself. Not like that.

I'd said things. Done things. Things I hadn't thought myself capable of.

*Mine to take. Mine to ruin. Mine to keep.*

How the fuck could I have spoken to her like that?

The memory hit like a punch to the gut. Heat surged through me, sharp and unwelcome. Revulsion followed on its heels. I shifted in the saddle, shame curling in my gut. My body remembered too well.

And still, she'd told me she loved me, during and after. That should've steadied me. Instead, it terrified me. What if she'd only said she wasn't hurt? What if she'd been strong enough to endure it, but hadn't felt safe enough to tell me I'd gone too far?

She always bore pain in silence, chin held high.

If she had told me to stop, I would have. But she hadn't. She had taken my restraint. My control.

No. That wasn't true. I had given it freely.

She wasn't just under my skin. She was inside my every breath.

I was hers. Utterly and completely.

Ahead, she turned in the saddle. A glance over her shoulder, the glint of a smile tugging at her mouth. Slid her eyes over me from head to toe, like she knew what I was thinking. What I was reliving. What I was feeling.

Lucius fell back a pace, even with me, eyeing me sidelong. "You're thinking too hard."

I couldn't answer.

He smirked. "Usually means trouble."

"Just thinking about where to stop for tonight," I said.

"We're almost to the turnoff for Dicowica," Aleaia said, falling back to ride beside me. "Up here on the left."

The road narrowed as we entered the village, flanked by sagging rooftops and shuttered windows. Dicowica was small and poor. The snow had settled thick on the thatch, softening the edges of stone and wood, but it couldn't hide the wear.

Most of the buildings were dark, hearths long since gone to embers. Only one, near the village center, glowed faintly with firelight and movement.

"That's the inn, most likely," she said, pointing to the squat building with smoke curling from its chimney. "Hopefully there's room for us."

We dismounted in silence. As I stepped onto the worn stone stoop, Aleaia brushed past me.

"I'll do the talking," she said.

The tavern was too warm. Heat pressed in from a hearth along the far wall, smoke curling from it in lazy ribbons. The scent of roasting roots and old ale hung like smoke. Light flickered more from fire than candle, but the place was far from empty.

A dozen people filled the room. Near the hearth, a young, lean man half-heartedly plucked a lute. Some looked up when we entered, but no one stared long.

This was a place where strangers passed through often enough to earn only a glance. The murmur of the room was steady. Familiar. Spoons in bowls. Boots scraping floorboards. Voices hushed and close.

We found a table near the back wall. Tried to stay inconspicuous. As soon as we sat, the air shifted. The kind of shift that meant something had been noticed, and not kindly.

Heads turned. We caught sidelong glances and furtive looks over mugs, through the haze of firelight, from corners where men hunched around their ale. One nudged the man beside him. Said something low. Both of them chuckled.

Didn't matter that I wasn't wearing Calesian colors, or that my sword stayed sheathed. I didn't look Aeltyrian. Neither did Lucius. For some people, that was enough reason to hate us.

"We shouldn't stay," I said. "They don't want us here."

"That's ridiculous." Lucius pushed back the hood of his cloak. "Let them stare. You want a drink or not?"

Before I could answer, a barmaid approached, young and buxom with callused hands and eyes that sought Aleaia first. Her smile was thin. Measured.

*"Vaet roa keram tí?"* she asked in Aeltyrian. I caught the rhythm of it, if not the meaning. Too fast, and the dialect was different than I'd been learning.

Aleaia answered before I could glance her way. *"Sumtaenge tesau, vethel. Sidra, hetha, vaetacin gavató."*

I could understand Aleaia. Her Aeltyrian was crisp and clear, not slurred together like the barmaid's. *Something warm, please. Cider, soup, whatever you have.*

The girl lingered, eyes narrowed—not with suspicion, exactly. Something sharper. Then she leaned in and spoke again, quieter this time, the words shaped with care. *"Domaviraos, esató harē adrai, sen essía virí?"*

I caught maybe half of it. *Sen essía virí* stood out—*with these men.* And *domaviraos* was *my lady*. The rest slipped past me too fast, but the tone didn't need translating. She was asking Aleaia if she needed help.

Aleaia didn't flinch. Just held the woman's gaze.

Then came the real warning. *"Avídiros es ó talen immatha. Eun murron enen ap an te manen. Cear taron te taril."*

I understood even less. Mostly the common words—cousin, earth, something about moving.

Wait. Was she saying her cousin could *bury us*?

Aleaia replied without hesitation. *"Esam bau. Te delsum aur es vedrānos, et te anthau aur es draeth-brathiros."*

*I'm fine. The something one is… something, and the loud one is…*

I was lost.

The barmaid narrowed her eyes at me, then leaned toward Aleaia. *"Esató vedrin an Calesii?"*

Aleaia didn't miss a beat. "Aye."

The woman made a sound of disgust in her throat. *"Lo ar naeroa ervel vethril."*

Aleaia, still looking at the table, replied flatly, *"Nae."*

The barmaid tilted her head, a grin spreading. *"Grau carnas?"*

*A big what now?*

Aleaia didn't flinch. *"Drai. Et ta es vethrilun. Lo naetaenge es grautha elau frelioros."*

*Very. And it is magical. But nothing is bigger than my appetite.*

The girl laughed, loud and sharp.

I didn't know all the words, but I knew enough. And I knew the sound of Aleaia's voice when she was being a menace.

She glanced at me then, eyes sparkling with something bright and dangerous.

Mischief.

Lucius leaned in. "What'd she say?"

"Bunch of words I don't know," I lied. "And I'm not sure I want to."

Still laughing, the girl turned to fetch our order.

Lucius cocked a brow.

"She asked if I was with you willingly," Aleaia said.

"And?" I asked, though I already knew.

"She offered to kill you. Politely. Said her cousin could bury you."

"I knew it," I said. It didn't feel like a victory.

Lucius chuckled. "Nice place."

The girl returned with three mugs of ale and three bowls of what might have started as soup a season ago. It was thin, gray, vaguely cabbage-scented. A single leaf floated on top. I didn't touch it, but I ventured a sip of the ale. It wasn't much better—tasted like half-fermented bread.

Aleaia ate like someone who hadn't had a meal in two days and didn't care what it was now. Efficient. Completely unbothered.

"Sounded like more than just two sentences," I said.

"Just women's talk."

Lucius poked at his soup like it had betrayed him. Looked like he had two leaves—twice as revolting. "Can't wait to get back to Aeldunon. Say what you want about the city. At least the food doesn't look like it died twice."

"Better than nothing," Aleaia said.

He took a bite anyway. Grimaced. "*Tastes* like nothing."

He set his spoon down, muttered something about needing to take a piss, and stood. The chair scraped back from the table, loud and graceless, before he made his way outside.

I waited until his footsteps faded, started to ask, but before I could ask, she spoke.

"She was surprised I had a Calesian man, since you can't use magic. Asked if you had a big…" Her eyes dropped to my lap, bright with mischief. "To make up for it."

I froze, spoon halfway to my mouth.

She said nothing else. Just sipped her ale.

"That's it? You're not going to tell me what you said?"

"I thought I used familiar enough words for you to figure it out," she said with a smile. "But I told her yes. And that it was magical." She wiggled her fingers in a parody of casting.

I huffed a laugh, and she nudged me under the table with her knee.

Gods. She was impossible. And I adored her for it.

Lucius returned looking vaguely suspicious and wholly unimpressed.

"Miss anything?" he asked, dropping back into his seat.

Aleaia lifted her spoon, utterly composed. "Just more soup complaints."

I forced myself to eat. It wasn't good, but it was hot, and the heat helped. Gave my hands something to do.

"It's dark already." Lucius drained half his mug, then looked toward Aleaia. "Almost the solstice. What do your people call it again? The Light Festival?"

She glanced up, spoon halfway to her mouth. "Aelan's Day."

Lucius snapped his fingers. "That's it. That means your birthday's coming up, right? Isn't it close to the day?"

"First of Succamos," she said softly. "Same as Aelan's Day."

"That's not what your record said. Did you lie on your documents?"

"I did," she said casually. "I did my whole life, in Rhaelaith. Didn't want anyone getting any ideas about me." She took a sip of her ale. "All kinds of prophecies about a child born on Aelan's Day."

"Like what?" Lucius asked.

"Oh, I don't know. My father never told me what they were."

He leaned in. "So did you lie about your age, too?"

"No. I'll be twenty-four."

I didn't move. Lucius had remembered. And I hadn't even known it to start with.

"Wait, you're older than me?" I asked.

"I suppose I am. By two seasons."

So she knew mine but I didn't know hers. The realization landed like a stone in my gut.

"How do you celebrate?" Lucius asked. "Should I call your favorite bard?"

"He's not my favorite and you'd better not." She stirred her broth slowly. "I don't celebrate anymore. Last time was when I was sixteen."

Lucius leaned back, sighed, waving away his annoyance. "Anvallus's balls, I made her broody."

"That year," she said, "the village invited us back. Just for Aelan's Day. No one said why. Maybe they pitied my father. Figured he'd been punished enough." She paused. "It was the only time they ever welcomed us."

She didn't look at either of us. Just stared into the soup, like it might ripple with something lost. "There was music. Firelight. Cider. My father had too much ale and tried to teach me the harvest steps." She took a deep breath, laughed softly. "He was awful at them."

She took a drink from her ale, looked down into it and said, "He died the next Mētanos."

As if it were a comment on the weather.

I stilled.

I'd been there in the aftermath of his death, but hearing it like this—wrapped in warmth, then cut short—hit differently. She hadn't just told a story. She'd shared the last time.

Near the hearth, the bard let the last notes of his melody fade. Then, without fanfare, he began another. The new melody was soft. Mournful. Aching.

Then the bard began to sing.

*In Mētanos' thaelil, piteu grau alvilí,*
*Te celmabreath threnin breu et draveu.*

I caught fragments of the verse. *Gray skies. Tree.*

Not enough to grasp the whole. Enough to feel it crawling beneath my skin.

*Nae colvia ta morvin, nae wula, nae sula,*
*Lo narnin sen atrenethí a draelirí.*

*No fruit. No leaf. Hung. Kin.*

Aleaia blinked, spoon halfway to her mouth. Held it there for a breath, then set it down carefully.

*Nae vetharil esin tariet, nae palda esin dorin,*
*Nae maethir ulvin, nae canilí esiní canilin.*

*No prayers. No bells. No mother wept.*

She stared at the bard for a long moment, then shook her head once and reached for her mug. Downed its contents.

*Te succa esin ruau, te alvil esin ulthau,*
*Et naur vo silin mirin a revau.*

*Red snow. Black sky. No one came back.*

She went still, her face pale, her eyes fixed somewhere far from the table. Far from us.

She'd vanished inward, drawn to some place only she could see.

Lucius caught it too. His gaze cut to me. Then the bard. "The fuck is this?"

I didn't answer.

*Esí calin in bleu, esí calin in aeleu,*
*Sen aena in delen, et anarethí ancalin fuau.*

*Blue and gold. Fire in hand.*

I understood enough.

I stood. Slow. Careful. My chair scraped back against the floor.

*Esí venin nae nem, esí melin nae draeliri,*
*Esí narnin enen lir te celmabreath, ralau.*

*No name. No kin spared. Hung from the elder tree.*

Lucius shifted beside me. "Val."

Too late. I was already moving.

When I got to the hearth, I stepped in close to the little bardling and spoke low enough that only he could hear.

"Stop."

His fingers stilled, hovering just above the strings, a familiar kind of defiance in his eyes. The kind that had never learned what it cost to be brave.

"It's just a song," he squeaked. "Truth ought to be heard."

My gaze didn't waver.

"I don't care what you think it is," I growled. "If you play one more note of that song, I'll break your fucking fingers. One for each verse."

He stared at me, searching for any hint of jest, looked away when he found none. Sitting a little straighter on the stool, he let his hands fall from the strings, then reached for his mug instead of the lute.

"And they weren't wearing blue and gold," I added, voice flat. "It was black and red. 'The truth.'" I scoffed as I turned away.

Every step back to the table was measured and silent.

Aleaia hadn't moved. She sat just as I'd left her, ale untouched, looking down at the table.

"Aleaia," I started, gentler now than I had been with the bard.

Lucius gave me a look. Sharp. Knowing.

"Come help me with the horses. Let her sort the room."

I looked back at her, met her eyes. After a moment, she gave a small wave, just two fingers off the mug. Barely a motion.

A signal that said *I'm fine.*

I didn't believe it, but I nodded anyway and followed Lucius out.

The cold met us like a slap. The wind had picked up again, dragging snow in lazy spirals around the hitching post. Our horses stood patiently, steam rising from their flanks.

Lucius moved to the nearest one, taking his horse's lead from a post. "We putting them in the stable?"

I nodded, doing the same for Nox and Argenti. "Yes."

We were halfway to the stable before he spoke again. "You going to tell me what's chewing you up, or am I supposed to guess?"

I didn't look at him. "Elisedd took a lot out of me."

Lucius snorted. "That much I figured. Everyone heard the two of you."

"Gods, Lucius."

"But this?" He interrupted as he gestured toward the inn. "This is something else."

I gave a half-smile. Humorless. All edge, no warmth. "You talk too much."

"Maybe you don't talk enough."

We left it at that.

*Aleaia*

The tavern was quieter now, without the lute.

My head wasn't.

I sipped my ale, trying to ignore the bitterness on my tongue, the colder sourness beneath it. I needed to move, to do something.

I'd get us a room.

I stood and made my way toward the bar to speak with the innkeeper. Not two strides from the counter, a man stepped in front of me. Drunk. Middle-aged. Broad shoulders. Narrow mind.

"You want to get out of here with a real man?" he slurred, swaying as he leaned in too close.

His breath stank of rot and cheap ale. His hair was stringy and slick. The kind of man who'd never seen a battlefield but liked to tell stories like he had.

I stared at him. Blank. Unimpressed. "You see one around here?"

He laughed loudly, like he thought I was flirting.

Then, without warning, he grabbed my face. Fingers dug into my cheeks, sudden and hard. Shoved me back until my spine hit a wooden beam with a dull, hollow thud.

He leaned in. Close enough that I could smell every sour note of him. "You a traitor on purpose," he growled, "or just too dumb to know better?"

I didn't move. Didn't flinch. I'd heard worse.

And part of me—the part that still remembered every village I'd marched through in Calesian armor, every order I'd carried out without question—believed he had a right to say it.

Ardhmor hadn't been the beginning. It had just made me remember everything that came before.

I'd worn the Empire's armor and expected loyalty from people who had none left to give.

And there I stood, jaw in a stranger's hand, and thought—

*Maybe this is the cost.*

*Maybe this is how it balances.*

I felt the fight slip right out of me, like a soul fleeing a corpse.

Behind him, the maid's voice cracked the heavy air. "Leave her alone!"

He didn't move.

The innkeeper did—toward her, hand raised. "Get back to work," he snapped at the girl.

She hesitated, then disappeared through the back door.

I stayed where I was.

Numb.

Still.

Not because I was afraid.

Because I deserved it.

Didn't I?

*Valerius*

After the horses were stabled, we went back to the inn, saddlebags slung over my shoulder.

I stepped back inside, the warmth hitting like a wall after the cold. And that's when I saw it.

Aleaia, pressed against a support beam.

Eyes wide. Lips pressed tight.

A man's hand on her face.

Gripping her like something he owned.

She just stood there.

No blade. No spell. No shout.

*Why isn't she fighting? She fights everyone.*

Every instinct in my body flared hot and violent.

I said nothing. Just thought—

Actually, I didn't think much at all.

Just let the saddlebags fall with a thud.

Behind me, Lucius hissed, "Shit. Here we go."

Three strides.

Caught the bastard by the shoulder, ripped him around and drove my fist into his mouth.

There was a wet crunch. He staggered back, blood blooming from his lip, crashing into a table hard enough to scatter tankards and send a stool clattering across the floor.

The tavern froze for a heartbeat.

One more.

Someone cursed. A chair scraped.

And the room erupted.

One of them lunged at me. I ducked, drove him into the nearest wall with a full-body shove. Another fist came out of nowhere—cracked across my cheek. Hard. My head snapped sideways. Light burst behind my eyes. Blood pooled on my tongue.

I turned, slammed my fist into the man's gut.

He folded. I grabbed his collar, yanked him forward, and brought my knee up into his face. Dropped him.

Lucius knocked one man across a table with a shoulder-check. Another came in swinging. He ducked, caught the stool he'd just knocked over, and drove it into the bastard's shins.

"I just wanted a drink," Lucius grunted, shoving the stool aside and ramming a tankard into a man's skull.

Someone grabbed my cloak from behind. I twisted, drove an elbow into their throat, slammed their face against the edge of a table.

Another came at me, tankard raised. I caught his wrist mid-swing and hit him. He crumpled, crashing into a bench.

Wood cracked. A chair toppled. Someone slipped in the spilled ale and took two others down with him.

Chaos.

I looked around for Aleaia. Found her standing back, out of the fray.

*Fine.*

Lucius took a hit to the ribs and let out a grunt. He grabbed the nearest broken chair and shoved a man backward toward the hearth.

"Don't kill anyone!" I shouted to him over the din. Aleaia would never let us live it down.

Lucius slammed into another man shoulder-first. "Why not?"

"Fucking don't, Tutela!"

Shouting. Boots. Fists. Splinters. Broken mugs.

And then—

A wall of a man entered. Broad as a doorframe. Scar-split scalp. Shoulders stacked like quarry stone. He moved like he'd never needed to move fast in his life.

Lucius saw him a second too late. The brute's fist came in low and mean, and caught him full in the jaw. Lucius dropped like a felled tree over a bench. He didn't get up.

I lunged.

We met like stags, weight against weight. He was bigger but I was angrier.

I struck first, sharp to the ribs. He grunted. Didn't slow. His counterpunch hit my side like a hammer.

Something cracked, took the wind out of me. "Fucking Hel."

Another blow to the face. White-hot flash. Vision swam. Blood filled my mouth.

I staggered.

I saw Aleaia starting forward.

"No," I snapped, hoarse. My hand came up, bloodied and shaking, warding her off. "No. I've got him."

She hesitated for a moment. Then stopped.

Because she knew.

It wasn't about the fight anymore.

I needed this.

Needed to break something—or to be broken.

To find out if the violence in me was something I craved, if it could be beaten out of me.

The brute caught me by the collar and slammed me backward into a table. It cracked in half beneath me.

I held tight to his collar, and we hit the floor hard in a mess of limbs, spit, blood, and curses.

Rolled. Swung. Landed a few.

My head hit the floor—once, twice—before I managed to jam my forearm under his throat and shove him off.

We scrambled up just enough to keep swinging.

Breathing like warhorses on the field.

I struck first. A clean shot—center mass, just below the ribs.

Felt it land. Felt the air leave him. He staggered back. Just half a step. But I didn't wait.

Drove my knuckles into his face.

Felt it jar my wrist and ring through my shoulder.

Then a hook to the side of his head. Another, hard to the gut. He grunted. Spat blood. Came back swinging.

Caught my side. I twisted away, off-balance, vision flashing red at the edges.

Didn't matter. I pressed in. Shoved him back into a table. It groaned under the weight.

He threw a wild punch. Missed.

I buried my fist in his stomach again.

He folded forward, and I cracked my elbow across the back of his neck.

We tumbled down again, both of us hitting the floor.

Grim and bloodied and spent.

The next punch I threw landed soft. Weak.

His came back slower still.

We kept going—grunting, bleeding.

Trading pitiful blows that didn't leave marks.

Like dogs too proud to lie down.

My fist scraped his jaw.

He swatted back, grazing my cheek.

Again.

Sad little punches.

Two men with nothing left to swing but spite.

Then I heard her voice, low and clipped as she crossed the floor.

*"Fachinge Hel... drenná glavil... Vai gavel te devethí fachin am?"*

Was that a prayer or a curse?

Boots crunched over crockery.

She stopped beside us and looked down with that flat, exhausted stare I'd seen aimed at idiot recruits and stubborn horses.

*"Etta es eithich,"* she hissed.

I knew that one. *That's enough.*

The brute groaned, sagged against a cracked table leg, and didn't get up.

Neither did I.

I let myself fall back onto the floorboards—bloodied, breath ragged, too filthy and spent to keep pretending.

Didn't even close my eyes.

Stared up at the rafters, seeing nothing.

"Get up," she said, in Calesian this time. "I have to go wake Lucius."

She turned on her heel, flung one hand skyward in sheer exasperation, and launched into a furious stream of Aeltyrian.

I caught maybe two words. Neither of them sounded complimentary.

*"Fachinge tuchlusí et eó drenná sca... keron tóa sca ancravatha, Lucius! Bi Lithaué tuat, nare draetható en calwenós!"*

She stormed to the basin, sloshed water into a bowl with what could only be described as divine aggression, then stomped across the room to Lucius, still draped over a bench, facedown.

The litany didn't stop.

*"Te devethí fach sú. Am esin mirin ana bellior, naet essa sca! Am sude gav laethel enen laenon inan te lus!"*

Then she dumped the water over his head.

Lucius bolted upright with a gasp and a snort. "Wh—what the fuck—?"

"You died," she snapped. "And I dragged your sorry soul back with the last cup of clean water in this godsdamned place."

He blinked, stunned and dripping. "Did we win?"

*"Fachinge virí mirel ó bura, et esam venin glanan ta ap!"*

She dumped the rest of the bowl on him.

"Am I cursed?!" Lucius shrieked. Never heard him make that sound before.

She stalked back across the room.

I watched her go, still breathing like I'd climbed a mountain.

And in the quiet that followed, I didn't feel proud. Didn't feel righteous. I'd purged nothing from myself.

I just felt tired.

There was no great epiphany waiting in the wreckage. No revelation. No absolution.

But bruised, half-broken, sitting in the carnage I'd waged in her name, I could finally admit to myself what I'd known for a long, long time.

I loved her.

Not the heir.

Not the warrior.

Just her.

The woman muttering furious curses in the language of her people while reviving the man who'd just been knocked out cold in a tavern full of strangers.

The woman who stitched torn edges back together with bloodied hands.

I loved her like it was written into my bones.

I just hadn't said it yet—because I couldn't.

Something hit me in the chest.

A rag.

Wet. Warm.

I looked up.

Aleaia stood over me, one hand on her hip, the other holding a second cloth.

"You're bleeding," she said.

I blinked. "I know."

"Then stop sitting around and do something." She tossed the second rag at my head. "Clean yourself up. We're leaving before someone wakes up and decides to assemble an angry mob to chase us out of town."

She turned, already muttering something sharp and sacred under her breath.

I wiped my face.

Stood, slowly.

And followed her.

Of course I did.

We crossed the broken floor toward the door. But before we could reach it, the barmaid—the same one who'd once offered to bury us—moved to block our path.

She looked younger now in the firelight. Braid half undone. Eyes darting between the blood on my knuckles and the stillness in Aleaia's face. She spoke Calesian.

"My father won't throw you out," she said. "Not if you pay well."

The words barely made it through the ringing in my head.

"We have a room," she went on. "Bandages. I'll make you something warm to drink. Something to eat better than that soup. Stay. Please."

Her gaze stayed on Aleaia.

She gave the faintest nod.

And we stayed.

# CHAPTER FIFTY-FIVE
## *Vedrānos*

*"Love does not ask for penance.*
*It waits in the quiet after, and reaches."*
—The Breath of the World

Mētanos 35, 1230
*Aleaia*

The tavern's kitchen was warm and shadowed, the water in the pot rolling gently as it came to a boil. I waited nearby, sleeves pushed back, watching steam thread through the air.

I'd offered to help clean the wreckage Val and Lucius had left behind, but the innkeeper's daughter had waved me off.

"The ones who started it will be the ones putting it back together," she said simply.

She nodded toward the table. "Help yourself to the clean cloths. There's honey up on the shelf, and a jar of salve my mother made. Good for stopping bleeding."

Then, without another word, she took Lucius by the hand and led him away.

I shook my head. He was a reckless fool, but I didn't have time to say anything to him just then. I had another reckless, foolish man to care for.

When the water was ready, I tipped the pot on its hanger to pour water into a pitcher, tucked a bundle of cloths under one arm, and cradled the jar of salve in the crook of my elbow. It was awkward but manageable as I climbed the stairs, bumped the door open with my shoulder, and closed it again with a careful kick.

Inside the room, everything was still.

I crossed to the table and set the supplies down, one by one: pitcher, basin, cloths. Steam rose from the basin as I poured into it. I dipped a cloth, let it cool just enough that it wouldn't burn me, and wrung it out until it barely dripped.

"Has it stopped bleeding?" I asked quietly as I turned to him.

Val sat in a chair by the small table, a crumpled rag pressed to his cheek. He didn't look up. "Think so."

I stepped closer, took his hand, and peeled the cloth away. It clung, tacky with half-dried blood, before giving way with a soft pull. He hissed through his teeth as the air hit broken skin. His fingers clenched just slightly, there and gone before it could harden into a fist. "Anvallus's balls."

The split along his cheek was deep, already bruising dark, but it needed to be cleaned.

"Never been hit in the face before?" I asked, teasing.

"Many times. Just not…" He trailed off.

I pressed the warm cloth gently to the wound. He flinched but didn't pull away.

"Sorry," I said, easing the pressure. I steadied him with my other hand on his shoulder.

He glanced up at me, then down again.

"What's happening, Val?" I asked. "This isn't like you."

"Just tired."

I raised a brow. "I've seen you tired before. You don't usually punch people in taverns."

He drew a breath. The kind men take before charging a wall. "When I saw him grab you, and you just stood there…"

His voice cracked. He closed his eyes, hands gripping his thighs tight.

He'd never get it out on his own. I'd have to help him. "Out with it, before it eats you alive."

"First of all," he said, crisp and clipped, the way he always was when he had something to defend. "I can't stand to see anyone put their hands on you like that. It just…"

Another breath. Shallower.

"You didn't do anything. So I thought—" he whispered, then swallowed hard. "What if you didn't stop me that night—in Elisedd—because—because you didn't feel safe enough to?" Val looked down at his hands, at the blood still crusted across his knuckles. "You said you wanted me—told me you did. But what if I missed something?"

I dipped the cloth again, wrung it out, pressed it carefully to the cut on his temple. I'd let him get it all out before I said anything else.

"You always bear pain in silence," he said. "I can't stop wondering if I hurt you. If I—if I did. If I *liked* it. If there's something wrong with me."

In silence? That wasn't true, but this wasn't the time to correct him.

I set the cloth back in the basin, put a hand on each of his shoulders, and looked at him fully.

"When I think about that night," I said, steady as stone, "I think about how you made me feel. Desired. Loved, even if you can't say the words. I meant what I said. Every word. Every time I touched you, every time you touched me, I wanted you."

I brushed a strand of hair back from his brow. "That man grabbed me because he wanted to punish me for refusing him. And I didn't react because I can't…"

The words caught in my throat, sharp as glass. But he needed to hear them. Not just his truth, but mine.

"I can't hurt my people," I said softly, willing my voice to be steadier than it wanted to be. "I can't raise a hand to them. Not after the things I've done. And in a way, I thought I deserved it."

It hurt to say aloud.

I cupped his face in my hands, thumbs brushing the edges of the bruises on his cheeks. I leaned down and kissed his forehead. "You touched me because you wanted me. To please me. And you did, so many times."

He was trying not to cry. I felt it in the way he breathed.

"There is nothing wrong with you," I said. "Except that you're despairing over a night I felt beautiful and loved, and *you* suffered in silence while you waited days to tell me."

Val leaned forward, wrapped his arms around my waist, and laid his cheek against my chest. I held him to me, cradling his head and stroking his hair as he held on.

And then I knew exactly what he was afraid of. I saw it, suddenly. Not just shame but terror. That he carried the same rot that lived in the other men of his line.

"You are not your father," I said softly. "Or your brother, or your uncle, or the Empire."

He took a deep, shuddering breath, and I felt his tears on my tunic. My fingers threaded lightly through his hair.

It was strange, how natural this reversal felt. To be the one offering comfort. The one anchoring instead of clinging. To hold him like this. To let him need me. To be needed not as a weapon or a warrior, but simply as a woman who loved him.

A word rose in my chest before I spoke it. Old. Heavy. Sacred. I'd seen it in my mother's journal once.

Vedrānos, she'd written. It means more than husband, or lover, though Cadoc is both of those to me. It is deeper. My bonded one. The soul I chose, and would choose again and again, in happiness or ruin and everything between.

Something deeper.

I knew what it meant. I'd said it to the barmaid when I described him.

"You are mine. And I am yours, *vedrānos*." I kissed the top of his head, resting my cheek against the loose curls. "And if you still have doubts, I'll show you how rough I can be with you too. Let you see it the way I do. But not tonight," I said, smoothing his hair back. "You've been beaten enough."

He laughed—broken, but real—his shoulders shaking against me.

And he held me tighter.

# CHAPTER FIFTY-SIX
## *Defiance*

*"A single flame can change the dark—but it cannot choose what follows."*
—The Breath of the World

Mētanos 45, 1230
*Aleaia*

Word traveled faster than we did.

By the time we reached the outskirts of Aeldunon, the story of the tribunal had already taken on a life of its own. They spoke of the younger prince of Calesia who had stood before an Aeltyrian crowd and ordered the death of one of his own.

Some called it treason—Calesians, usually.

Others called it justice—Aeltyrians, mostly.

I knew it was dangerous.

For those who remembered what it meant to resist—old rebels, hedge-witches, battered healers—it lit something they'd thought long dead. The stories weren't clear, not yet. But whispers stirred. Of change. Of defiance. Of someone on the Empire's side willing to break the rules.

And when they reached my name, they were murkier still.

I hadn't drawn the Fellglow Blade. I hadn't called the storm. But someone had seen what I *had* done when I cast the shield and that was enough to start rumors, to spark a flicker of suspicion in a cold season.

If the heir of Aeltyria lived, they said, she would not hide behind a Calesian shadow.

But if she never claimed her throne, perhaps the defiant son of the Empire would do.

Where hope began to glimmer, fear pressed close behind. In noble halls and garrisoned towns, incolumium restraints were dug from dust-choked crates. In some households, slaves were shackled again. Not because they'd done anything, but because someone thought they might. Varro's orders came swiftest. Others followed.

Every fresh report settled hard in my chest.

It had been Val's voice that condemned Pulcher, and his blade that struck the final blow, but it was my hand on the hilt that made it irrevocable. And the weight of it—what we'd stirred, what might follow—dug in deeper with every mile we rode.

By the time Aeldunon's gates came into view, that weight pressed heavier than the cold.

Mariana was already waiting in the courtyard. Arms crossed. Hem soaked. Her face set like thunder on the edge of breaking. The moment she saw Val's bruised cheek and Lucius's black eye, she stormed toward us.

"What happened to you?" she snapped.

Lucius slid from his saddle with a grunt, landing hard enough to hiss through his teeth. "Taverns," he said, then spat into the snow.

Val dismounted more carefully. Every motion betrayed the bruises he wasn't talking about. "We're fine."

I swung down from Argenti's back, rubbing his flank as I caught Mariana's glare.

"I'll tell you later," I said, just loud enough for Lucius to hear.

His look over Argenti's back was part warning, part plea not to tell her. Whether he meant the girl or the fight or both, I wasn't sure.

I didn't look away. Whatever he owed Mariana, it wasn't mine to collect for him, but it was mine to remember. Some truths demanded to be spoken by the one who broke them, or they curdled into something worse.

We limped toward the keep—cold, stiff, sore in places we hadn't known could bruise.

Toward home.

# CHAPTER FIFTY-SEVEN
## *Foundations*

*"The work of surviving begins long before the first blow is struck."*
—On the Ruin of Empires

Mētanos 83, 1230
*Aleaia*

The last of the firelight clawed at the stone walls of Val's chamber, stretching long across the floor.

Across the table, he pushed a sealed letter aside and pulled another map toward him. His fingers absently grazed the shadow of stubble along his jaw. Since our return, this had become his rhythm—daylight spent ruling in the name of the Empire, nightfall spent laying plans to undo it.

He didn't say much during these late hours, but I watched him all the same.

Gods, but I loved looking at him like this. My eyes traced the lines of his face—high cheekbones, the Calesian-straight line of his nose casting a shadow over his mouth. I followed it without meaning to, down to lips that would open under mine, if I leaned in. Beautiful, yes, but more than that. Everything in him sharpened when he focused, and sometimes I wondered if that was the real him—the man made of strategy and silence.

I set my goblet down and leaned forward, elbows braced on the edge of the table. "What are you doing?"

It was the kind of question I asked when I wanted to understand and he never minded when I asked. He meant to teach me things in these quiet hours—leadership, command—but duty always dragged him away before he could finish the lesson.

Val looked up at me. "Building a resistance," he said, as if it were the simplest thing in the world. "Carefully. One stone at a time."

"We're rebels now?" My heart raced.

He sealed another parchment with the ring on his hand, slid it aside while he stifled a smile. "We're not calling it that. I'm just laying the groundwork. Finding allies who won't crumble under pressure. Securing places we can hold when it comes to war."

*When*, not *if*.

My tongue felt thick as wool.

I'd seen skirmishes. Been in Tuath Forest, which was more massacre than battle. I'd never known true war.

"Your people have a saying," he said. "You don't call the storm until you're certain you can survive it."

I leaned in, the words settling like frost beneath my skin.

"All right," I said.

Val shifted one of the newer maps aside, revealing another beneath it. It was older, its edges softened and worn. Aeltyria before the conquest. He tapped a point on the map—Aeldunon, ink-ringed in coarse strokes.

"Not long after the Empire took the capital," he said, "the clans of Caermora and Dun Erian rose."

He dragged a finger across the map, along the coast, over narrow fields and thin passes I recognized.

"They had numbers. Six or seven thousand between them. Fierce, loyal fighters. Before the war, they would've had strong mages—some of them your kin. But the magic was gone, and nothing replaced it. No fortresses. No siege lines. No supply routes."

He tapped a point near the sea, so faint it was nearly lost in the parchment's age.

"The legions came through the Varenne Pass. Trapped them between the cliffs and the tide. No retreat. No cover. Nowhere to rally."

I traced the shape of it in my mind. The failure wasn't in their courage. It was everything else. Everything they hadn't planned for.

"Three hundred died that day. Villages burned after. The Empire hunted the survivors. Salted the fields when they were done." He let the map fall flat again, folded his hands in front of him. "Their mistake wasn't heart. It was thinking heart was enough."

Val looked at me then, steady as ever. Unsparing.

"I don't want numbers," he said. "I want readiness."

I sighed. "You say we aren't rebelling but—"

"We aren't. Yet. That's the point of the story." He reached across the table, covering my hand with his. His palm was warm, solid. Unshaking. "You have to be ready, first," he said. "To lead. If I fall."

The words hit like a sudden blow. I flinched, pulling my hand back. My throat closed hard.

"Don't say that," I whispered. It came out broken. Too soft. I couldn't stop the ache tightening beneath my ribs. "I don't want to do this without you. I can't."

He reached for me again, palm up, open, waiting.

I hesitated. Then I set my hand in his. "It sounds like you're planning on dying."

His voice softened, but the edge was still there. "There's no promise any of us walk away from this."

He waited. Gave me silence to absorb it.

I didn't like it. He wasn't telling me something. I could see it in his eyes, hear it in the softness of his voice.

"If it comes to it," he said, thumb brushing the back of my hand, "it has to be you who survives."

I tried to speak. The protest stuck, thick and useless. He squeezed my hand gently, quieting me.

"You're not just a woman with a sword. Not just the Shield of Aeldunon. Or the Wolfsbane. You are the last Caedmon. The *Daughter of Aelan*. You're what they've waited for, all this time."

He sounded like he'd already made peace with it, somewhere deep inside himself.

"I'm just a man," he said. "A sword. A shield. I can be replaced."

"No you can't," I said quickly.

His hand tightened over mine. "I can."

The silence that followed could've drowned us both.

I pressed my lips together hard. My eyes burned. He'd tried talking to me about this before and I'd refused to listen and left the room. Once, I'd sat in his lap and reminded him exactly how much easier it was to fuck me than to talk about dying.

This time, though, I stayed, and let him speak aloud the shadow that lived in his heart.

He smiled. Faint. Real.

"But until that day comes," he said, still holding my hand like it was the only thing anchoring either of us, "I'll stand between you and the dark. As long as there's breath in my body."

# CHAPTER FIFTY-EIGHT
## *Scarlet & Silver*

*"I gave birth on the coldest day of the year. She wailed like a storm—and I knew the world would never be quiet again."*
—the Writings of Queen Eavan

Succamos 1, 1231
*Aleaia*

Aelan's Day came colder than expected, the sky gray and brooding like it wanted to press the breath from my lungs. The wind knifed through wool and leather, slicing deep enough to sting. I'd been out in it most of the day.

First in the poorest quarter of Aeldunon, where I learned what city-poor looks like.

Then, beyond the walls, where I went hunting. I dressed the stag where it fell—a fine animal, broad in the chest—quartered it, loaded Argenti, and led him back myself.

Because no child should go to bed hungry on Aelan's Day.

I'd returned to the keep, intent on having a bath but found Val waiting for me. So off we'd gone to light the fires for Aelan's Day. Afterward, he'd kissed me on the stairs and told me he'd see me at dinner.

*Thank the gods, I can finally bathe,* I thought. *I smell like blood and dead things.*

I opened the door to my chambers and found Mariana fussing over something on the bed. She started, standing stiffly upright to face me.

"Oh, Aleaia!"

And then I saw what she'd been fretting over.

A dress lay spread across the bed. Deep scarlet, it was threaded with fine silver work that caught the firelight and scattered it like breath.

"Where have you been?" she asked with a laugh. "I've waited at least two hours for you."

I shut the door behind me, keeping the draft at bay, and crossed to the basin near the hearth. The water had long gone cool, but I splashed it over my face and hands anyway, scrubbing until the worst of the cold and grime were gone.

"Val dragged me up to the battlements," I said, drying off with a linen cloth. "He performed the Rite of Warding. Lit the fires himself."

Mariana's brows lifted, wide-eyed and uncertain.

"Val?" she asked, thin as a blade's edge.

I nodded, letting the fire warm my hands.

"He didn't say a word. Just offered me his arm and said we had somewhere to be. And then..."

The memory rose fast—hot and disarming.

He had stood above the city, shoulders squared against the cold, saying the sacred words.

And when he turned toward me...

*Gods.*

I wasn't dressed for ceremony, or anything else. My cloak was damp, my cheeks raw from wind. My hair probably looked like it had tried to strangle me on the way up.

But he looked anyway.

Let his gaze move over me, slow and deliberate, like he was taking stock of something rare and already his.

A smile—small, maddening—ghosted across his mouth. Just enough to say, *Yes, I did this for you. You're welcome.*

And damn him, it worked. I had to look away.

A flush crept in while I tried to find the words to tell Mariana.

"He honored it," I said. "Properly."

She watched me a long moment.

"That's dangerous," she said finally. "Val honoring the old rites in front of witnesses? The Empire won't look the other way."

I shrugged, barely. "You know he's always been the wayward one."

"After Elisedd, he should be more careful."

"Try telling him that."

For a moment, I thought she might argue. Instead, she took a deep breath as she turned toward the bed and the waiting dress, smoothing her hands over the fabric.

"My mother altered this for you," she said, lighter now. "It was Queen Eavan's. We found it tucked away. Hidden under cedar wood and linen. Whoever packed it meant for it to last."

I didn't dare move.

The dress shimmered—scarlet with silver vines and stars and runes curling along the hems. The bodice looked low. Scandalously low. Val would love it on me but he'd love it more on the floor.

"How did you know?" I asked. "That..."

"Lucius told me," Mariana said, waving a hand like she could bat the awkwardness away. "And we thought you might want something of hers. Tonight."

I stepped forward, slow.

When I reached out, my calloused fingers brushed the fabric and found it softer than it looked. Heavier too. The weight of it—fabric and meaning—pressed against my ribs.

"I can't—" I started. "I've never… I don't know—"

Mariana's voice gentled. "It's just a dress," she said. "It doesn't make you anything you're not." She smoothed a fold near the hem. "But it's yours. If you want it."

I drew a slow breath, feeling the fire blur around the edges of my vision. My mother's dress, lovingly altered for me to wear. When I looked up, I nodded.

Mariana didn't say another word. She only lifted the dress from the bed with both hands, as careful as if she were holding a relic.

"Well," she said. "Hurry up. Time's wasting."

"What?" I asked.

"Put it on," she said simply.

"I have to wear it now? Why?"

Mariana grinned. "Strict orders not to tell. But you'll want to look your best."

"I can't put that on without a proper bath first," I said. "I already called for one."

As if summoned by the words, a knock sounded at the door. "Dame Dieter? We have your bath ready," came the voice of one of the young kitchen hands.

Once they brought the tub in and filled it, I stripped off my tunic and boots, stiff from travel and long wear, and washed quickly, careful not to wet my hair since it was still reasonably clean. When I was done and dry, I tugged a fresh linen shift over my head. The fabric clung for a moment before settling, and the cold air found every inch of bare skin.

Mariana moved briskly, shaking out the gown and gathering it in both hands. Together, we lifted it, and I ducked into the silk, letting it fall across my shoulders with a whisper. Mariana tightened the laces at my back with sure fingers.

"There," she said, stepping back.

It rippled to my ankles. I ran my palms down the fabric, feeling the unfamiliar weight settle over me. By the hearth, a pair of black slippers waited—simple, soft leather, but finely made.

I stepped into them carefully, flexing my toes, then sank onto the stool she dragged close to the fire. The heat pressed against my spine, a welcome thing, while she gathered a comb, a few ribbons, and a handful of silver pins.

I raised an eyebrow at the implements.

"You're not getting some matron's crown of braids," she warned. "Not tonight."

She wove small braids through the fall of my hair, loose enough to keep the weight off my scalp, tight enough to hold their shape. Most of it she left down, to cascade across my shoulders and back. For a time, the only sounds were the fire snapping in its cradle and her hands whispering through my hair.

"I'm glad you're back," she said. "It's different when you're not here."

I watched the firelight shift against the stone. "I'm not that important."

"You are," she said, certain and easy. She tied off another braid, smoothing it back with care. Then added, softer, "Lucius has been… odd, lately."

That landed heavier than it should have. I pressed my hands into my lap. "What do you mean?"

Mariana shrugged, fiddling with a coil of ribbon she hadn't used. "He's different. Since you were gone. And even after you came back. Distant, like he's still carrying something he won't put down."

I thought of the tavern. Of blood on stone, on his boots. Of Lucius slipping into the night with the barmaid.

I folded my hands tighter. I couldn't tell her now, not when she'd gone through all this trouble to have her mother alter a dress for me and make me look decent. I'd clout him later for making me complicit.

"He's carrying a lot," I said after a moment. "We all are. I'm sure he doesn't mean to be that way."

Mariana tied off the last braid and let her hands rest lightly on my shoulders, warm and steady.

"It was a hard journey," I said. "I'll tell you about it someday. But it's too long a story for right now."

The words caught under my ribs like broken glass.

*I'm going to kill Lucius*, I thought grimly.

Mariana gave my shoulder a squeeze. "You're so serious lately."

"I know," I said. "Lucius calls me broody."

"He's right."

I sighed. "I'm starting to understand why hedge witches live in hedges."

She laughed. "All right, stand up and let's have a look at you."

I rose and brushed the skirts down with both hands. The silk shimmered as I moved, scarlet and silver shifting with each breath.

Mariana stepped back, shaking her head. "You look…"

"Ridiculous?"

"No, you—"

"Like I'm trying too hard?"

She laughed softly. "No! Like he's going to forget how to breathe."

Heat rose up my neck, and I bent to fuss with the hem to hide it.

"I'm going to trip over this and land in someone's lap."

"With any luck," she said, "that lap will be his lordship's, lest he start another brawl defending your honor."

Evidently Lucius had told her some of what happened in Dicowica but not what came after. I was *definitely* going to kill him.

A firm knock sounded at the door.

We both turned.

Mariana winked. "Speak of the lion."

# CHAPTER FIFTY-NINE
## *Sanctum*

*"No fortress falls faster than the one that thought itself safe."*
—On the Ruin of Empires

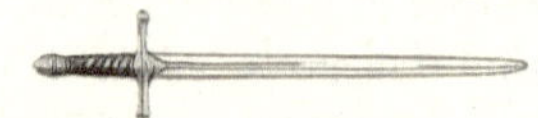

Succamos 1, 1231
*Aleaia*

I crossed the room and opened the door.

Val stood there, freshly shaven, boots polished, dressed in deep blue and black. For a moment, he didn't say a word. Just stared, as if whatever he'd meant to say had been swept clean out of his skull.

Then he smiled. Slow and warm and so full of quiet awe it landed in my chest like a blow and a balm at once.

"My lady," he said, and took my hand, lifting it to his lips, soft as silk against the back of my fingers.

I looked over my shoulder at Mariana. She smiled and waved me forward, smug as a cat in cream.

I turned back to Val, eyeing him warily. "Where are we going?"

He shook his head, a smile tugging at the corner of his mouth, nearly scattering my thoughts like leaves in wind. "Trust me."

"That's what you said earlier, and I ended up on the battlements in the freezing cold thinking about—"

I stopped myself but it was too late. He already had the hook.

"Thinking about what?" he asked.

I slid my hand into the crook of his arm. "Wouldn't you like to know?"

Val chuckled. "I think I already do."

"Then you tell me," I said.

"Me, of course."

Sixty days ago he would have had to think about the words. Now the Aeltyrian came easily.

I turned my nose up, mimicked his accent. "'Me, of-a course.' Sorry to disappoint, but I was thinking about dinner. I'm starving."

He laughed—really laughed—and it felt like stepping into sunlight.

Val led me through the corridors of Aeldunon Castle. Only when we reached the massive double doors of the great hall did I realize what he'd done.

The scent of roast meat and spiced wine thickened the air. Music spilled through the doorway—lyre, drum, and voice, tangled in something joyful and wild. Blue banners hung from the rafters, stitched with silver stars and holy flame. Garlands of holly and winter ivy wound around the pillars. Every brazier blazed, chasing shadows from every corner.

The place was packed, mostly with auxiliary soldiers, but townsfolk too. Near the long hearth, Lucius spotted us and raised his mug, grinning like a man who knew exactly what Val had pulled off.

Aelan's Day in all its glory.

And my birthday, as it had never been.

I turned to Val, wide-eyed. "What did you...?"

He only smiled, guiding me up toward the high table, pulling out a chair to seat me at his right hand.

We barely had time to sit and be served before the steward rapped his staff against the stones. The room stilled. Conversations died like sparks in snow.

Val stood. He lifted his goblet, speaking in clear Aeltyrian. "Tonight we honor the return of light, the promise of hope for the Aeltyrian people on Aelan's Day."

The hall quieted.

"But there is another light here tonight." He turned toward me. "You know her as Dame Wolfsbane, the Shield of Aeldunon. I know her as the one who reminds me what is worth protecting."

He lifted his goblet higher.

"To the light of my heart—Aleaia Dieter."

For a moment, as I watched him, everything else fell away. No noise. No people. Just my heart pounding for him, and the maddening, wonderful fact that he'd done it all without telling me. He'd given my people back their day, and made sure I had mine too.

Gods, I adored him for so many things, but just then, it was for the way he saw me. For the way he carried the weight of my people's hope.

The hall roared back to life. Chairs scraped on stone. Goblets clanged together with a hundred toasted echoes.

When I looked up at Val, I caught the smile teasing his lips.

Heat bloomed low and fierce in me, a wicked thrum I couldn't ignore.

He sat down beside me and I just... stared.

"What is it?" he asked.

"You know damn well what *it* is," I said as my fingers grazed his knee—slow, measured, drifting higher, trailing along the inside of his thigh.

Just enough to test the line.

Just enough to feel it stretch.

I felt him grow hard in his breeches, and gave his thigh a squeeze.

He didn't flinch. Only sipped his wine like nothing at all had happened.

Then I felt his hand clamp around my wrist to guide my hand higher.

Right over the hard length of him.

My breath caught.

Then he met my eyes, releasing my wrist. Cool. Measured. And so godsdamn sure of himself I wanted to crawl into his lap and throw my wine at him at once.

I did neither.

Instead, I buttered my bread with the same hand that had just palmed his cock under the table.

We made it through a few courses. He refilled my wine. I licked honey from my fingers just to watch his eyes go dark and hungry.

Then the musicians struck up a slower rhythm. Val pushed his chair back, rose, and extended his hand to me.

"May I have this dance?" he asked—low, formal.

I smiled, sweet as honey, and placed my hand in his. "Of course, my lord."

He led me out to the floor. His hand rested at my waist. Mine was light against his shoulder.

We danced properly at first, each step precise and measured. We still remembered how to pretend, but with every slow turn, every pass of fabric against fabric, the space between us thinned, stretched until it threatened to snap.

Val's breath was hot against my ear. "Keep teasing me, and I'll have you bent over a table before the next song ends."

A shiver of anticipation raced down my spine. I tipped my head, let my lips brush close to his jaw. I let my fingers drift along the back of his neck, curling into a lock of his hair. "Promises, promises."

The corner of his mouth twitched.

When the music faded, he led me from the floor, weaving through the crowd to the far end of the hall. We reached a velvet curtain, thick and dark. He drew it back enough to guide me through, into the shadowed alcove beyond.

The curtain fell. The feast faded like a dream left behind.

I laughed, knowing what he meant to do.

Before I could speak, my back struck stone as he pinned me and his mouth took mine—hot, insistent, tasting of wine and desire. His hands pulled my skirts higher with frantic urgency, fingers finding bare skin, sliding up until they gripped me hard behind the thighs.

"You," he growled against my lips, breath ragged, "have been tormenting me all night."

I fisted both hands in the front of his tunic to pull him close as I laughed again. "I know."

He lifted me easily, my skirts caught between us, bunched around his arms. I locked my legs around his waist, gasping as the press of him found me.

The kiss turned messy—breath catching desperately, hands grasping without care for grace.

He tore away to blaze a trail down my throat, finding the hollow between neck and collarbone. One hand tugged at the low neckline of my gown, baring me to the cold air.

Then his mouth was on my breast, hot and insistent.

I moaned aloud at the feel of his tongue on my nipple, clutched at his hair.

"Please," I whispered.

He growled, set me down only long enough to fight with the fastening of his breeches, hands shaking against the ties. He shoved his breeches down just far enough and caught me up again like I weighed nothing at all.

He pressed against me, lined himself up—

"Lord Valerius!" The steward's voice cleaved through the air, sharp and urgent.

We both stilled.

"Maybe he'll go—" I started.

The music faltered. Then stopped entirely.

Val's breath hissed between his teeth as he lowered me to the floor.

"Gods. Why?" He dragged a hand down his face.

He tried to fix his clothes, fingers fumbling the ties of his breeches. I reached out and tied them for him, tugged his tunic's hem back into place.

"Thank you," he murmured.

He leaned in one last time, a finger under my chin, mouth brushing against the curve of my ear. "Later. I swear it."

"Go," I whispered, pushing him toward the curtain.

He kissed me, quick and fierce, then stepped back. After one last look at me and a muttered, "Anvallus's balls," he left the alcove.

I fixed the bodice of my gown while I listened.

I heard his footsteps, calm and measured. Somewhere well beyond the curtain, he asked, "What is it?"

"A missive, lord. For your hands only."

There was a pause, then muffled voices I couldn't catch.

Val's voice rang out again, crisp and clear. "I'll be in my chambers. Carry on."

I waited a few breaths—just long enough to be sure the steward was gone and let the music start again—then slipped out from behind the curtain, wove through the crowd, and climbed the stairs toward his room.

When I opened the door, he was already there, seated at the desk, quill scratching across parchment, brows drawn in thought. Same urgency, different task.

I closed the door behind me and leaned against it for a moment, watching him work.

Val didn't look up. "I'm sorry," he said, still writing. "This required… urgent attention."

"Oh?"

Whatever that letter said could wait. I'd nearly had him against a wall, and I wasn't done yet.

My skirts whispered as I crossed the room to settle into the chair across from him—far enough to appear innocent, close enough to be dangerous.

I caught his gaze and held it as I sank back with a sigh, legs relaxed, knees falling open just enough to make the air between us feel sharp. I slid my palms down the front of my skirts, smoothing the silk languidly, then gathered the fabric bit by bit higher up my thighs.

The snap of the quill between his fingers was immensely satisfying.

I bit the inside of my cheek to keep from laughing.

"Come here," I said, letting the command land in my voice.

For a moment, he only stared at me. Then, slowly, he rose, moving toward me like he owned every step between us.

I tried to look smug, even as my heart pounded. When he stood between my open knees, I let my fingers trail up the length of his arm.

"On your knees," I said, hushed and steady.

He arched a brow, eyeing me for the briefest moment. And then he obeyed, damn him, sinking with maddening grace in front of me. The heat of his hands resting lightly on my thighs bled straight through the thin fabric.

I swallowed, fighting to keep my face composed.

"Now you're going to—" I began, but the words tangled, and a laugh escaped instead, sudden and helpless. I slapped a hand over my mouth, mortified.

Val looked up at me like he already knew how this would end and saw no need to hurry.

And that only made me laugh more. Maybe I'd had too much wine.

After he cleared his throat, his voice was unbearably patient. "You were saying?"

"I'm trying to be commanding," I gasped, helpless with laughter. "But I sound ridiculous."

"You do," he said. Before I could move, he stood, scooped me up, and flung me over his shoulder like a sack of grain.

"Val!" I kicked lightly, fists thumping against his back. "Put me down, you bastard!"

After flipping my skirts up, his arm locked around my thighs, his hand drifting over the now-exposed curve of my rear.

"Oh, what's this?" he said, utterly unrepentant as he gave my arse a firm squeeze.

I laughed helplessly, breathlessly. "You degenerate!"

"I'm carrying you to bed and you're scolding me?" he said, all innocence as his hand caressed me. "You started this."

"If you don't stop fondling me like a prize roast, I swear—"

"You are one, and I mean to feast," he said, and gave one sharp slap to my backside before tossing me onto the bed.

I landed on my back with a squeal and a soft thump. He bent forward, eyes locked on mine as he pushed my skirts up, baring me. His mouth followed, lowering to the place already aching for him.

I gasped.

One hand flew to his hair, the other to the blanket beneath me, clenching hard. Heat burst through me at the first stroke of his tongue—slow and sure, just enough pressure to make my hips lift, to make me moan.

His hands held my thighs apart, mouth working in steady rhythm—tongue circling, flicking, drawing sounds from me I didn't know I could make.

It didn't take long.

Pleasure coiled sharp and quick, pushing me to the edge. I broke apart with a cry—hips jerking, thighs tightening, body melting under his mouth.

He didn't stop until I sagged back, panting and dazed.

"That was fast," he said, clearly pleased with himself.

"Did you think I was teasing you for no reason?" I reached for him, sitting up. "I've wanted you since we stood on the battlements."

He leaned over, flushed and beautiful, and kissed me, his lips warm and wet with the taste of me. Fingers at the laces of my bodice, he untied them as I tugged at his tunic.

"I want to see you," I murmured against his mouth.

We fumbled slightly—too eager to slow down—but managed quickly enough.

I pulled the tunic over his head, and suddenly, I forgot how to breathe.

The firelight gilded him from behind, outlining the hard cut of his body, the tension in his stance. And for a moment I just looked—stared, really—at the man I loved.

Gods, he was stunning. Devastating.

I sat up and slid forward so he stood between my legs.

While I worked the ties of his breeches, I trailed my mouth over his chest. He watched as I pushed the fabric down his hips, then moved off the bed to kick them away.

I kissed a trail down his abdomen. Warm skin. The taste of him. Just him. He shivered, groaned softly, like he had tried and failed to hold it back.

I loved that. That I could do that to him.

Then he reached for me. Took my gown and shift in both hands and pulled them up over my head. The silk whispered across my skin, then vanished from his fingers.

I wrapped my arms around his waist. Pulled him close.

His skin was warm against mine, the length of him caught between my breasts, and all I could think—all I could feel—was him. The weight of his body, the way he held me like nothing else existed. It wasn't possessive. It wasn't even prideful.

It was need. Fierce. Focused.

I leaned up and caught his nipple in my mouth.

He inhaled, sharp and sudden, as his muscles tensed beneath my hands, hips jerking just enough for me to feel the full press of him against my skin. But he didn't stop me. Didn't pull away.

Just stood there, breath ragged, hands trembling faintly as he cupped my breasts. I covered his hands with mine, pressed them together, and let him thrust between them. Once. A second time.

I looked up, met his eyes. "Gods, I love you," I whispered.

I said it all the time now. In moments like this, in the quiet place just before sleep, when we first woke up in the morning. I'd say it again and again until he felt safe enough to tell me he loved me, too.

He looked down at me through his lashes. Took my jaw in his hand and kissed me.

My whole body answered, every nerve lit and reaching. There was no room for breath, no room for thought.

Only this.

Only him.

"Turn over," he said softly against my lips.

I obeyed without hesitation, limbs trembling as I rose. Turned. Braced myself against the mattress. Thighs flush to the edge. Feet on the floor.

Behind me, I heard it—a soft grunt of approval, low in his throat as he ran his hand down my spine.

"Beautiful," he murmured.

Then I felt him—his hands firm at my hips, his body lining up behind mine.

He slid into me in one long, deep thrust that stole what little air I had left.

The stretch of him was sudden. My body clenched around him, taut and aching, desperate to keep him there. I sucked in a breath through my teeth.

He moved with steady, devastating rhythm. One hand found my breast, the other pressed between my shoulder blades.

He bent, mouth at my ear. "I want to feel you break," he breathed, voice rough and steady in my ear.

"Harder, then," I said, breathless.

And he gave me what I wanted, what I needed, driving into me again and again.

The pleasure built fast—heat, yes, but something deeper, too. Like sunlight through storm clouds. Like the world righting itself.

It didn't feel like losing control.

It felt like coming home.

I cried out as it hit—my body tightening, clenching around him as the pleasure tore through me in waves.

He caught me, his arm locked tight around my waist, holding me to him as I shook, as I shattered.

When the tremors finally eased, he dragged in a ragged breath.

"Up on the bed," he panted. "On your back."

I climbed up, legs unsteady, chest still rising hard with every breath. Laid back. Let him in. Let him pull me to the edge of the mattress and fill me in one smooth, perfect thrust.

I tried to wrap my legs around him. Tried to move with him, but the angle was wrong. I could feel it. Too low, or too loose, like we were just missing the mark, and gods, it made me want to scream.

I shifted again, stubborn. One leg slipped. The other hooked too high. I cursed under my breath, cheeks burning.

I'd once hit a moving target from horseback at fifty-eight paces with a bow. And now? I couldn't even position myself to hit this one target that actually fucking mattered.

Elegant. As always.

Without a word, he caught both my ankles in his hands. Lifted. Hooked them over his shoulders. Slid a pillow beneath my hips.

The change was immediate.

I gasped, back arching as he drove deeper.

He groaned as my body clenched tight around him.

Then he looked down at me.

And godsdamn him, he smiled. Just a little. Just enough to be smug about it. Like he'd performed some complicated maneuver and *of course* it had worked.

"Better?" he murmured.

He always knew what I needed when I didn't.

He moved with aching care—long, steady strokes that filled me completely, over and over, each plunge drawing pleasure out like honey and fire. I arched into him, breath catching, mouth parted beneath every slow, deliberate press of his hips.

Leaning down, he braced on his forearms, and his mouth found mine, kissing me like he couldn't bear to stop.

"Aleaia," he whispered hoarsely against my lips. "I can't remember a night I didn't want this. Didn't want you."

My fingertips brushed his cheek, and he turned into the touch.

"I dreamed of you," he said. "Long before I had the right to."

He kissed me again, slow and searching as his hips rolled into mine.

I clutched at his back, nails digging into his shoulders.

His arms slid beneath me—around me—holding me close as he moved.

Like he was giving himself to me.

"I belong to you," he said against my mouth. "Even if the world tears us apart. Even if it tries to burn it out of me. I'll still be yours."

My throat closed. I couldn't speak. Couldn't breathe for how much I felt.

And then, so quiet I almost missed it, he whispered, "Sometimes I think I was made for this. To know you. To touch you. Even if only for a while. *Luce mea.*"

He moved within me, slow and devastating, each thrust striking that hidden place that unmade me.

Then I felt it again—the unfurling deep in my belly, like something ancient waking in the dark.

I clutched him to me, every muscle locking tight around him as the release tore through me. It wasn't soft. It wasn't gentle.

It was fire and blood and pressure beneath the skin. I felt it echo through my thighs, down my spine, in the pulsing center of me, then rippled. Each wave dragging me deeper, pulling me apart.

I cried out, every nerve lit and thrumming, until I wasn't sure where I ended and he began.

And then I felt him lose control.

He pulled out with a groan—breath ragged, rhythm breaking.

And I reached for him.

Wrapped a hand around him. Stroked him through it.

With a deep, guttural moan, he came hard across my stomach, hands braced on either side of me as he shuddered through it.

Gods, the sound of it.

Raw and unguarded. Like he forgot how to hold anything back.

He leaned in and kissed me, fierce and breathless as his mouth moving over mine.

"I—" he started.

Whatever he meant to say, he buried it.

I touched his cheek. Light. Steady.

"I know," I whispered.

He went still. Just held himself there, silent.

A flicker of something crossed his face. Shame, maybe.

His eyes shone in the low light. He blinked, once, hard.

Then he reached for a cloth. Wiped me clean with careful hands.

When he finished, he set it aside and leaned in to kiss me, softly this time.

My lips. My cheek. The corner of my eye.

I reached for him, but he was already gathering me close, tucking the blanket over us both as he lay beside me. I curled into his chest, head tucked under his chin.

"Thank you," I said softly. "For today."

His hand slid up my spine, fingertips trailing over my flesh.

"I wanted to give you something that would last. A night you could carry with you."

His voice was warm, but something about the way he said it made my chest tighten.

Still, his arms were around me.

I was safe. Home. So I let it go.

Let myself have that fleeting thing called happiness.

Closed my eyes.

And slept.

# CHAPTER SIXTY
## *No Chain*

*"Love makes fools of warriors. Leave them alone long enough and they will burn the world looking for you."*
—The Fire That Remains

Succamos 2, 1231
*Aleaia*

*I have to save him.*

The thought echoed like it always did—old as bone, sharp as the first breath of winter. I clenched the hilt of my sword tighter, knuckles white, fingers slick with blood. The blade dragged behind me, gouging a crooked line into the marble floor—too bright, too polished, too wrong.

Pain was everywhere. Hot. Blinding.

It burned behind my eyes, blotting out the edges of my vision in pinpricks of light. Blood filled my mouth, thick and metallic. I could taste it. Smell it. Feel it sliding in a slow line over one swollen eye.

Most of it was mine. I was sure of that.

Didn't matter.

I kept moving. Step by step. One foot. Then the other.

Somewhere ahead, just out of reach, he lay crumpled on the floor.

Blood spread beneath him in a wide, glistening pool. Dark as pitch. His limbs were bent wrong, like a puppet half-cut from its strings. One hand lifted weakly, trembling in the half-light.

A warning. A plea.

"No," I gasped. The word tore itself from my chest.

"No, no—"

The mist closed in—thick, choking, alive.

It dragged at my limbs. Pulled at the air in my lungs. My sword scraped along the stone, carving through blood and marble both as I stumbled forward.

Too slow.

Too far.

I couldn't reach him. Couldn't stop it.

A blade flashed ahead—gleaming, merciless.

Then it fell.

He arched once under the strike. His body seized, then stilled.

I was too late.

Always too late.

Pain split through my chest like cracked stone, the soundless echo of a scream I couldn't force out.

The mist devoured everything—his blood, his body, the world itself—and I fell into darkness, still reaching for him.

I woke with a violent jerk, gasping like I'd been drowning.

The chamber was gray with dawn's first light. The hearth held nothing but ash. Damp bedding tangled around my legs, clinging to my skin like it meant to hold me down.

I turned blindly, reaching across for warmth, for him, for anything solid.

My hand found only a cold, empty bed.

I knew it was wrong and that knowing pressed in like a weight.

"Val?"

My heart pounded. I sat up, stiff and aching. I paid it no mind as I shoved the bedding aside and stood.

My feet touched stone. Cold enough to numb.

My heart ran colder.

The chamber was empty.

No whisper of leather shifting near the door.

No quiet creak of bootsteps.

No him.

Just stillness.

I pressed my palm flat against the mattress where he should have been, like I could will him back into the space he'd left.

*Gone.*

And something was terribly wrong.

I knew it, the way my mother knew when my father fell. Deep in my soul, like ice in my core.

I moved through the room without thought. First to the cold hearth. Then the window seat. The narrow chest nearby.

Nothing.

No boots.

No cloak.

No sword propped against the wall.

Panic scraped at the edge of my mind, sharp as broken glass. I shoved it down. Forced myself to breathe. To think.

I hadn't seen the raven recently.

That was a good thing, wasn't it?

If he left, he would've said something. There had to be a message. I turned to the desk.

And there, just off-center, one thing out of place.

A folded scrap of parchment. The broken quill stub beside it. My hands were shaking as I snatched it up. My name was written on the front. Nothing else. Just *Aleaia,* in his hand. No seal. No flourish.

I fumbled it open, throat tight, and the air left my lungs in a rush. The letter shook in my hands. The world narrowed to the cramped lines inside.

*Aleaia,*
*Forgive me. I would not ruin your night with talk of duty, nor burden you when you should have been celebrated. It is no fault of yours. Had I stayed, it would have meant unbearable consequences. I go to delay what cannot be stopped, and to buy us what time I can. I will not abandon the people who placed their trust in us.*
*I will return to you.*
*Wait for me, if you can bear it.*
*Yours always,*
*—V*

I stared down at the page, reading it again. Then again.

Was this what he'd been writing last night? The one he said was too urgent to wait?

Had he been trying to slip away, before I'd come upstairs?

The words blurred. Wavered.

*Wait for me, if you can bear it.*

My breath tore at my throat like broken glass.

I didn't cry. I didn't scream. Not yet.

I only thought one thing, clear and cold—

*I have to save him.*

The thought struck me hard and fast. Was this *the* dream? Would I go to him, find him bloodied and broken with Vespera's fingers around his throat?

Without thinking, I grabbed the linen shift I'd worn beneath my dress and dragged it over my head. My feet carried me across the stone. I flung the door open and bolted across the hall, heart hammering so hard I thought it would claw its way out.

"Praefecta!" The startled word came from the guard outside Val's door. I ignored him.

I burst into my own chamber so hard the door hit the wall.

The drake-scale armor waited for me, dark and gleaming where it caught the dim morning light.

I moved fast.

The shift shoved up over my thighs. Padding hauled into place—breeches, linen, the thick gambeson. Boots yanked on tight.

Then the armor. Pauldron straps buckled roughly. Vambraces cinched with trembling fingers. The breastplate came last, hauled into place with a grunt. The weight settled across my chest like fury made solid.

I had done this a thousand times, just never like this.

Never with my teeth clenched and my heart in pieces. Never chasing after a man who had held me with soft hands, then vanished into the dark.

Only when I reached for my sword did I hesitate.

My old blade waited by the bed. Plain. Battered. Reliable.

If I was going alone, I needed something more.

I left it behind and turned, nearly stumbling over my own feet.

Gods help me figure out how to use the damn thing.

I stormed back across the hall, to Val's chambers, and made straight for the archive.

The blood lock flared as I shoved my finger into it. I felt nothing when it pricked me. Heard nothing as the hidden door ground open.

The torches along the stone walls of the stairwell ignited with my descent, blazing to life in a sudden flare of silver flame that made me flinch. My magic had answered my panic before I'd even called it. Just like in my mother's memory, the one that had told me who I was.

The Fellglow Blade waited at the bottom.

I seized the hilt without ceremony. It fit into my hand like it had never belonged anywhere else. It hummed faintly hungry.

For blood.

For mana.

For me.

It was starving and would take whatever it could get. The blade shivered eagerly once in my grip and then stilled.

Sword belted at my hip, heart raw and bleeding inside my chest, I turned and fled back up the stairs.

Lucius's door wasn't locked. I slammed it open hard enough to rattle the hinges.

The room was dim, lit only by the spill of hallway torchlight. Lucius jerked upright in bed, half-tangled in his blankets, hair wild, his sword halfway drawn before his eyes adjusted.

"Where is he?" I shouted.

"What the—Aleaia?" He scrubbed a hand down his face and swung his legs over the side of the bed. "Gods, what—?"

"Where is Val?" I roared again, already moving across the room to stand at the foot of his bed.

My hand clenched around the hilt at my hip. The Fellglow pulsed beneath my palm, starving and ready.

Lucius grabbed a tunic from the back of a chair and yanked it over his head with clumsy fingers. I hadn't even noticed he was naked until then. "I can't—"

"You can," I snapped. "And you will."

We stared at each other for one long moment.

My voice dropped, cold and cutting. "There's no reason for me to stay here without him. So either you tell me where he went, or I track him blind. Alone. In the middle of a godsdamned Aeltyrian winter."

He hesitated. "I swore to him," he said finally.

My hand twitched on the hilt.

"Swore what?" I hissed. "To lie to me? To stand there and scheme while I slept?"

The thought burned through me, hot and bitter.

*He fucked me into sleep, and left me behind.*

"I swear on Galdorin's blade I will run you through if you don't tell me, Lucius Tutela!"

Lucius grimaced. Swore softly.

"Avitum," he said. "He left—" He glanced toward the window, where the light had begun to pale the sky. "Six hours ago. Maybe more. Took eight men."

"Why didn't he take you? Or me? Or tell me?"

He looked at me again. His voice lowered, reluctant.

"He thought he wouldn't come back. And if he did—"

I turned toward the door.

Lucius lunged, grabbing my wrist before I could bolt.

"You're not going after him," he said sharply, tightening his grip. "He told me to keep you here. Protect you."

I yanked against him, struggling hard.

"You think I need protecting? By you?" I snarled, jerking my arm.

He didn't let go. His grip shifted—both hands now, bracing, trying to hold me like he could anchor me in place. "You don't understand what's waiting in Avitum—"

I didn't let him finish.

I slammed the heel of my free hand straight into his nose.

It wasn't graceful. Wasn't even the blow I wanted. I'd meant to punch him—really punch him—but it landed. *Good enough.*

Lucius staggered back, blood already spilling between his fingers as he clutched his face, more stunned than hurt.

I tore free and bolted for the door.

"You should've known," I shouted, not caring who heard. "No chain you forge could ever hold me."

I paused in the doorway just long enough to glance over my shoulder.

The sight of him standing there—bleeding, stunned, trying to do what Val had asked—only sharpened the fury.

"So much for brotherhood," I grated out.

Then I turned.

And I didn't look back.

# CHAPTER SIXTY-ONE
## *The Bloody Moor*

*"She brought the old war with her. And the moor welcomed her home."*
—The Ashes of Aeltyria

Succamos 2, 1231
*Valerius*

The cold had long since numbed the gash along my ribs.

The rope binding my wrists to the wagon wheel bit deeper every time I shifted, sawing into flesh gone raw hours ago. I sat slumped in the mud and snow, breath escaping in shallow, steaming gusts.

I couldn't draw in more than that. Something inside—bruised, cracked, broken—pressed tight against my lungs. Every breath felt borrowed.

My cloak was gone. My sword was gone.

My dignity felt not far behind.

Blood slid warm down my side, soaking into the linen of my tunic. I couldn't tell how deep it ran. I just knew it hurt.

Around me, the wreckage of everything I'd planned stretched in every direction.

Men I once commanded—men who had once carried my banner—circled nearby, speaking in low, harsh voices. They wore no insignia now. Only scraps of mismatched armor, tattered cloaks, and the kind of bitter, directionless hunger that clings to a man who's lost everything but the memory of rank.

The ones I'd brought with me lay sprawled in the snow.

Bloodied. Still.

I leaned my head back against the wagon. Forced myself to breathe slow and as deep as I could manage.

It had been a simple plan.

Answer the summons. Delay what couldn't be stopped. Buy time—for Aeltyria, for her—while the seeds I'd planted in the dark, nurtured in toasts and laughter, began to bear fruit.

Instead, I'd led good men to their deaths. Been captured by the deserters of my own damn army.

I bit down hard on the sourness. Shame burned hotter than the wound in my side.

*She'll stay,* I told myself. *Lucius will stop her. She knows how dangerous this is.*

I'd thought, if I didn't say the words—if I didn't tell her—she'd follow the order. I'd tried to protect her.

But the voice in me—the one that had always known her better than I knew myself—whispered the truth.

No order could hold her back.

Not from this. From me.

I closed my eyes. Poor Lucius. He'd tried to warn me. A bitter laugh caught in my throat.

Footsteps crunched in the snow nearby. I let my head hang forward, feigning unconsciousness. Listening.

"He's not worth the risk," one said—close enough I could've cut the bastard's ankle if I weren't bound like a dog. "The Empire'll gut us the second they find out."

"Not if we sell him first," another said. "Somebody'll pay. Family. Army. Someone."

A snort. "More likely to kill us for capturing him than to give us an award."

"He's a traitor anyway."

A new voice—older, rougher. "Better alive. Fetches more. Send word south, see who wants to buy him."

"And if no one bites?"

"Then we bury him deep and forget it happened. Sell the armor. That's worth something."

"Too bad about the horse. I always wanted a stallion like that."

"You couldn't've ridden him, you stupid arse. He's loyal to his master. Or was."

Their laughter scraped against the air like a blade on bone.

I kept my eyes closed. Flexed my fingers again.

*Stay away,* I thought bitterly. *Stay where it's safe.*

But I knew the truth. Knew it in my bones. Knew she would tear the world open to reach me. I gritted my teeth as something sharp and aching hollowed out my chest.

Then I saw it, through my eyelids.

Light.

Bright. Alive.

I opened my eyes. Squinted against it.

The men around me faltered, voices tapering off as they turned toward the hill.

Then it flared as it burst from the tree line.

Silver.

Searing.

Blinding light that cut through the gray like a blade drawn by the gods.

Over the frozen moor, a black-cloaked figure barreled toward us on a silver stallion, unflinching. Her sword burned in her hand. It spit and cracked in the air, twisting heat into the cold like a living thing starving for blood.

*Aleaia. Godsdamnit, woman, why don't you listen?*

The mercenaries stumbled, swore, scrambling for weapons, shouting orders too late.

She didn't slow.

*"Bracon!"*

Her command—*strike*—tore across the field like a war cry, raw and thick with bloodlust.

Argenti obeyed.

He crashed into the first man like divine judgment, hooves shattering bone with a crunch. The man folded backward, limbs limp, his weapon flying from useless fingers.

Then she was among them.

Aleaia carved through the next two as though she were built for nothing else—wide, vicious arcs, the blade moving faster than they could react. Steel sang. Flesh split. Blood sprayed warm against the snow.

The sword burned brighter with every kill, light flaring white-gold and silver from its edge. Holy fire. It hissed against blood and snow alike, unquenched.

One man lunged for her cloak.

Argenti lunged back, jaws snapping shut on the man's forearm, leaving splintered bone behind. Then Aleaia turned him to cleave his head from his neck in one brutal slice.

She was outnumbered. Gods, she was so badly outnumbered.

I fought against the cords at my wrists. Useless.

They swarmed her—dragged her out of the saddle with snarling hands and a hail of shouts. She slammed into the ground hard, her breath knocked from her in a ragged gasp.

Argenti shrieked a war cry. Savage. Unforgiving.

One man raised his shield too slow. A hoof sent him flying into the mud, limp before he hit.

Aleaia rolled to her knees and stood, cloak saturated with blood and muck, armor scored and slick. Her sword flashed—parrying, cutting, searing, again and again. Just survival and fury.

Each swing left a trail in the air—embers and sparks and ash caught in its wake, like the gods themselves marked every stroke.

A mercenary charged with a short axe. She let the blow glance off her vambrace, then rammed her blade beneath his ribs. He folded, choking on blood.

Another came from behind.

She turned fast, cracked him in the face with her hilt. Bone snapped and he crumpled at her feet.

They kept coming.

Argenti barreled into one, biting deep at the thigh. The man shrieked, tried to crawl—too slow. Aleaia drove her sword deep under his arm without a word.

Another grabbed her. Aleaia turned, twisting her arm free to shoulder check him, then plunged her blade into his gut.

She kept cutting them down.

I couldn't move. Couldn't breathe. My body ached to do something—anything—but all I could do was watch. Watch and pray she wouldn't fall.

The moor was a butcher's yard. Steam rose off blood-slick mud. The stench—iron, bile, burnt leather—hung thick. Men screamed, wept, bled into the churned snow. With every kill, her sword burned brighter still.

Every swing was slower now. Every breath cost her.

Then the last man broke, bolted, stumbling through the snow.

Aleaia staggered after him—limping, panting—but she couldn't match his speed. She slipped once, caught herself, kept moving.

I thought he might make it. Then his boot skidded in the blood-slick mud and he fell, scrambling on hands and knees.

She was on him in a heartbeat, raising the burning sword overhead to bring it down with all the wrath left in her, plunging deep into him. The blade flared with holy fire as it struck, searing through flesh and snow alike. She crashed down with it—elbow, hip, knees into the slush—landing hard beside the corpse.

Slowly, she shoved herself upright. Her arms trembled under her own weight.

"*Te devethí raviresí tó*," she said, then spat on the man.

*The gods reject you.* A curse.

It was quiet then. Only the faint crackle of the embers that remained, Argenti's breathing, and my own heartbeat remained.

Aleaia stood in the ruin. Cloak torn. Armor spattered. Braid half-unraveled. Her body was a testament to violence—mud to her knees, gore dripping from her gloves.

She looked around once to ensure her work was done, bent to clean her sword before sheathing it. Then she turned toward me, untying and yanking off her helmet.

And came for me, dragging herself forward in stiff, limping steps, her sword trailing behind, burning a faint line into the slush.

Every part of her was trembling.

When she reached me, she dropped to one knee, setting her helmet and gloves aside.

She didn't speak. Didn't look at me. Just breathed, raw and shallow, like her rage was the only thing holding her upright.

Her fingers fumbled with the bindings, clumsy and slick. She pulled a dagger from her boot and sawed at the ropes until they split.

She let the dagger fall from her hand.

Then she stood over me, shaking.

"Get. Up." Her voice, deadly quiet, tore through the silence. "Face me like a man."

# CHAPTER SIXTY-TWO
## *Like a Man*

*"A man may command nations, but if he confesses love, he confesses weakness."*
—Emperor Claudius di Calesia, privately, to Valerius

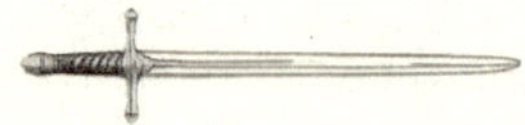

Succamos 2, 1231
*Aleaia*

Val braced himself against the wheel and hauled himself upright, left arm clutched to his side.

He barely found his balance before I shoved him. Both hands to the chest. Hard.

"You fucking left me!" I shouted. "You left without a word, without a plan, without a godsdamned chance!"

He didn't argue. Didn't flinch. Just stood there, head bowed and shoulders set, like a soldier awaiting judgment.

"Just look!" I said, gesturing to the carnage around us. "You should have brought me with you! You know how many dangers lie between here and Avitum! You know how many would kill you just for your name!"

My voice cracked. I forced it steady.

"I'm not a fool, Valerius. I know the risks. I've lived them every day of my life. But to wake up and find you gone—" I stopped. The memory sliced deep. "To find nothing but a letter in your place—"

I pressed thumb and fingers to my eyes, as if I could hold the ache there. Contain it.

"You know what you mean to me. You know what it is to get a letter like that. What it felt like to find me gone, once," I said, quieter now. Shaking. "You *know*. And you… you left anyway."

He stepped toward me.

I shoved him again, harder. He staggered.

"No! You stupid, stubborn, beautiful bastard!" The tears that blinded me finally broke, hot as they streaked down my blood-smeared cheeks. "You could've died. You could've left me alone in this godsdamned world. And for what?"

The last of my strength failed me. My armor dragged me down like stone until my knees gave way. I sobbed as everything I'd held back—fear, rage, grief, love—broke loose and swallowed me whole.

"For… for what?"

He was beside me in an instant. Kneeling. Gathering me into his arms, careful despite the shiver running through him.

I fought him, pushed him, hit his chest twice. Fought him with what little I had left, until I collapsed against him, my fists knotting into his tunic.

For a long time, we didn't speak. Only my ragged breathing filled the quiet.

He tipped my chin up with a finger.

Then, gently, he took the edge of my cloak and wiped the blood and dirt from my face. His hands shook.

My eyes met his, blurry and burning.

"I love you, Aleaia," he said.

Simple.

Unflinching.

I stared at him, stunned. For a moment, I thought maybe I'd taken a blow to the head. That I hadn't heard right. That the world had tilted and left me behind.

"That's why I left without you," he said, voice thick, eyes shining. "And why I couldn't tell you before."

"Say it again," I whispered.

"I love you because you never bow to the world," he said, softer, breathless, like the words had waited too long. "Because you fight for everyone but yourself. Because you're fierce, and reckless, and full of heart."

His thumb brushed along my jaw.

He paused, struggling for breath, but forced the rest out, raw and shaking. "Because you're everything I was too proud to reach for."

I surged forward and kissed him.

Eager. Fierce. My hands held his tunic, anchoring him to me, to the moment before it could slip away. I kissed him like it might fix something. Like it might change everything.

He kissed me back.

Slowly. Like the strength was bleeding out of him even as he gave it to me.

Then he broke away, panting.

"Should've… told you," he rasped.

His lips parted again.

And then—

The weight of him collapsed into me, sudden and heavy. I caught him with both arms, staggering under the shift, my shoulder pressed hard to his chest. No resistance. No tension. Just limp bone and blood.

I caught him as he buckled. "Val!"

He didn't answer.

Didn't move.

And in the frozen silence that followed, I thought my heart might break clean in two.

# CHAPTER SIXTY-THREE
## *Vicious Oaths*

*"A vicious oath is still an oath. Watch what you promise in your rage."*
—Maren Dieter

Succamos 2, 1231
*Aleaia*

I caught him before he could fall forward, gritting my teeth as I shoved him back against the wagon wheel.

Too pale. Breathing too shallow. Sweating too much for the cold.

For a moment, I knelt there, heart hammering in my throat, terrified he might crumple sideways and never rise again. That the last thing I'd ever hear from him would be those words—*I love you.*

"Stay with me." It came out like an order, not a plea.

He grimaced, nodded. "Trying."

I jumped at the sound. "Fuck, you scared me. Let me see." I took the hem of his tunic in hand.

His hand twitched to push me away. I slapped it aside and peeled back the torn edge of his tunic, my fingers gentler than they had any right to be with everything that still boiled in me.

The wound was a mess. Thick blood welled from the gash—dark, steady. Not immediately fatal. I leaned in. No froth. No bubbling. Maybe the lung was spared.

"You're lucky," I said. "Missed the lung. I think."

He gave a soft grunt that might've been a laugh. "I am… lucky… but not… because of… that."

I tore two strips from my cloak, folded one, and melted snow into it.

"Deep breath and hold it," I told him, blotting his blood with the folded strip.

Val obeyed, though I could see how much it pained him to do it.

I pressed the cloth to the wound, sealing it with my hand, then bound it hard around his ribs with the other strip.

"Keep breathing," I said. "That's all you have to do."

"We have to get… to Avitum," he rasped.

My head snapped toward him. "No. We need to get you home."

"If we don't… Cassius will burn Letia… strip my command… and give it…" Another breath. Another wince. "Give it to… someone like him. Running out… of time."

"You're running out of *air*, too. Stop talking and let me think." I stood, scrubbed a shaking hand over my face. "Fuck."

*What do I do with you?*

*No cart. No healer. No road back.*

And of course he wouldn't turn around. Not Val. Not when the path ahead bought time for the people he cared about.

I remembered riding patrols here. Memorizing maps until I knew them better than the lines of my own hand. There was a village nearby. Cortueca. Reminded me of Rhaelaith. They weren't one of the places I'd betrayed. Maybe they'd have someone willing to help who knew what they were doing. Or someone who could use spirit magic in a way I couldn't.

And if nothing else, they'd have somewhere for us to sleep. Food. Supplies. It was better than nothing.

"All right," I said, forcing steel back into my voice. "We go to Avitum. But we stop in the nearest village for a healer on the way."

Every part of me ached as I moved—shoulders tight, ribs sore, a sharp throb where someone's blade had caught me earlier but hadn't pierced my armor.

The wagon was useless. Its yoke was snapped clean through, wheels shattered. Even if it hadn't been, Argenti wasn't bred for pulling. He was built for riding. We'd have to ride double until we reached Cortueca. He stood a few paces off, bloodied and blowing hard, foam streaking his flanks, his hide slick with gore. Not his, thank the gods.

I went to him, stroked his neck and wished I could care for him better just then.

My left saddlebag—the one that had contained medicine and bandages, of course—was slashed open, contents strewn gods knew where. The right one—the one with maps, spare underclothing, and my copy of *The Song of the Stars*—was whole, though.

Argenti and I picked our way through the field of Val's captors. They lay scattered like slaughtered cattle, limbs bent at unnatural angles, guts steaming against the frozen earth. Some were charred, blackened meat clinging to bone.

I'd done that. I didn't know what to think of it, so I offered the killing as a sacrifice. "Galdorin, let this be enough," I murmured.

When I reached Val again, he was still upright—barely. Head bowed. Left arm braced against his ribs.

"Still alive," he grated.

"You're welcome," I said, sharper than I meant.

I looped Argenti's reins over what remained of the wagon and turned back to the dead.

The Calesian soldiers who'd ridden with him—good men, most of them—lay scattered where they'd fallen. They'd followed their commander into the jaws of death.

I checked each one. Felt for breath first, then supplies. Found only quiet.

With the last, I knelt for a moment in the red-streaked snow. The smell of blood clung to the back of my throat. Cold gnawed anywhere it found my flesh.

*They deserved better than this. I could give them better. And it'd only take a moment,* I thought, *if the flame burned hot enough.*

My mana felt thin. Probably had enough for one shot.

I gritted my teeth and rose to walk back to Val. He watched me through half-lidded eyes.

I brushed a sodden lock of hair from his brow. "What would your people say?" I asked. "For funeral rites, in a time like this?"

"Not much," he said. "Consign them… to the flames… honor them… carry their names." His voice faltered at the last.

So no different than a funeral in quieter times. I could do that. I nodded.

"You remember their names," I said. "I'll do the rest."

I went back to our fallen, dragging them close, laying them side by side with limbs straight, hands folded over the middle.

I drew my sword and the moment I gripped the hilt, power surged—raw and furious—but I didn't resist. I welcomed it. I raised the blade toward the line of corpses.

"Rest well," I said. "You are not forgotten."

Flame answered. A clean, hungry blaze leapt across the field in streaks of silver and white. Despite the cold and wet, they went up like dry tinder. Smoke roiled skyward, thick and black at first, then gray as the heat burned purer. The scent was hideous, but I didn't balk.

I fed it everything I had left. Until the fire burned white-hot. Until my head swam and my gut twisted. Until there was nothing but ash and the hiss of cooling bone.

Only then did I sheathe the Fellglow Blade and stumble back to Val.

He was watching me. His brow creased. "Your nose."

I touched my fingers to it. They came away streaked red.

*Mana depletion,* I thought. Everything I knew of magic came from books, but I was sure that's what this was. Too much, too fast.

"I'm fine," I lied. "What'd they do with your armor?"

"Wagon. In a crate."

There were several crates. Stolen goods, probably. Nothing I could use. It cost precious time to find it but leaving his armor behind was never an option. It might save his life—again.

Once I found it, it took everything I had to get him into it. Cold metal, stiff straps, every buckle a battle. He winced with every touch but didn't complain.

When I was done, I bent to brace his right arm across my shoulders, squatting deep and bracing myself. "On your feet, *vedrānos.*"

Up we went, difficult as it was. As we walked, he sagged into me with a grunt, nearly taking us both down. I staggered under the weight but held firm.

"What's that... mean, anyway?" he asked.

I tightened my arm around his waist. "Means I won't leave you out here to die, even while I'm furious with you."

He made a sound—half groan, half laugh. "A single word... for all that, eh?"

"Efficient language," I said. "Stay alive and maybe I'll tell you when you're better."

Getting him onto Argenti was worse than standing him. So much worse.

He was too tall, too heavy, too damn stubborn. The first try nearly broke my back. The second, he almost toppled us both, and I thought that's how I might die—under him, and not the way I liked. By the third, I was swearing vicious oaths my grandmother would've cuffed me for as I threw everything I had into one final heave.

He landed in the saddle with a grunt. Finally.

I breathed hard, my hand on the saddle horn. "You're a big bastard, you know that?"

"You think so?" he asked with a huff of a laugh.

I hauled myself up in front of him, and gripped the reins in one hand.

"Gods, I'm fucking tired. Put your arms around me."

When he did, I pinned them under mine, hoping it would be enough to keep him on. We weren't going far—just far enough to hand him off to someone who could do better than I had.

# CHAPTER SIXTY-FOUR
## *Bradarcam*

*"Born of her blood. Bound to her line."*
—Inscribed on the Fellglow Blade

Succamos 2, 1231
*Aleaia*

We reached Cortueca just past dusk, cold and soaked to the bone. Argenti whickered as we rode into the square, hooves sloshing through the half-frozen muck. I held Val upright as long as I could, waking him when he threatened to drift off.

He started to slide sideways again, just inside the gate.

"Val?"

No answer.

I slapped his thigh hard. "Wake up!"

Nothing.

"Shit." I tried to hold his arms around my waist, but he was too heavy, too slippery in armor, too limp.

We slid out of the saddle, crashing hard to the frozen ground. I landed beside him, trying to catch the breath that had been knocked out of me.

He lay still.

I scrambled to my knees. Yanked my gloves off. Leaned over him to feel for breath.

A faint tickle at my ear, thank the gods.

"Val, stay with me. Stay with me, please," I said, fervent as a prayer.

I ignored my tears as my clumsy fingers worked at the buckles of his cuirass, trying to free him.

"Someone help me!" I called.

A few doors creaked open. Lanterns flickered. A handful of villagers gathered at the edge of the square—Aeltyrian faces, all of them.

We were the same people. But we saw very different things.

I saw the man I loved, the man who was willing to risk everything for all of us. They saw his deep blue cloak. His silver armor. His ash-brown hair and Calesian steel.

"He needs a healer," I said, loud enough to carry. "Please!"

No one moved.

"He's dying." I looked around, frantic now. "You have someone here. You must."

A woman shook her head. "Not for him."

A man beside her spat into the snow. "Let him die. His kind gave us no mercy."

"You don't know what he's done," I said. "He's not like them."

"No, you're not like us," a younger man said. "Just another dog of the Empire."

"Please," I said again. "I'm begging you. Help me!"

He laughed, low and cruel. "Let the Calesian bleed. Good riddance."

"Gods damn you!" I shouted.

They were turning away now. Closing doors. Pulling back.

That was it. If they wouldn't help because I asked, because I *begged*, they would do so on my order.

I stood, drew my sword. The soft sound was unmistakable. Pale light flared, casting flickers over the snow.

They turned back. One by one.

"You know what this is," I called out, voice steady now. "I am Aleaia Caedmon—Daughter of Aelan, Shield of Aeldunon, Bearer of the Fellglow Blade."

No one spoke. I leveled the blade at them.

"I asked you twice." "Now I command you. Save him."

For a heartbeat, I thought they'd laugh at me. Or worse, swarm us, pick us clean, and leave us in the mud.

But they obeyed.

Someone shouted for a runner.

I barely heard it as I sheathed the blade and knelt beside Val again. He reached for my hand weakly. I caught it. Clutched his cold, clammy fingers tight.

His eyes fluttered open, unfocused, searching the blur of sky overhead—the way soldiers did when they lay dying on the field—until he found me.

"I'm here," I whispered, pressing my other hand against his cheek. "You're not alone."

The rest of the world narrowed. Just blood and breath and this man clinging to the edge.

If they failed him, he would die.

I wouldn't let that happen. Not here. Not for things he did to protect these people. My people.

Boots splashed through the slush. Voices rang out, urgent and clipped.

A woman in healer's robes dropped to her knees beside me. Her apprentice followed close behind, satchel already open.

"He's still in armor," she said sharply. "Get it off. Now."

Two of the villagers moved to help me wrestle with the straps and buckles. The cuirass was soaked through and stiff with half-frozen blood. Every time we shifted him, he groaned faintly but he didn't wake.

I tossed the breastplate aside, then the pauldrons, then held his hand tightly as the healer worked.

"What happened?" she asked, already tearing away the ruined linen I'd bound the wound with earlier.

"Ambush," I said. My throat felt scraped raw. "He's been bleeding for hours. I think," I swallowed. "I think maybe his lung—"

She pressed her hand to his ribs and closed her eyes. Her brow pinched.

"Broken ribs. Pretty sure none of them punctured the lung. It's collapsed though," she said grimly. "Bleeding inside, too."

"Can't you heal him?" The words snapped out, sharper than I meant, edged in fear.

She didn't look at me. Her hands were already moving, fast and steady. "I can't fully heal him," she said. "Not with what I have. Magic's too weak, and it's the wrong kind."

*The wrong kind?* I frowned, not understanding.

She glanced at me, likely saw the confusion written on my face. "Water mage. I can ease the worst of it, but his body has to do the rest."

She didn't wait for permission. Her hands moved fast—vials, cloths, tinctures. "Hold him steady. I need to purge the blood."

I nodded and moved to Val's head, bracing his shoulders. He was so cold.

I bent to his ear, teeth clenched against the ache in my chest. "You have to be still now, *vedrānos*. No matter how much it hurts."

Mana stirred, cool and methodical. Not wild like mine. Her hands glowed as she pressed them to his side, coaxing the blood outward.

There was so much pooling under him.

He gasped.

Stilled.

Then breathed deeper.

"What do… what do I do?" I asked, hating the way my voice wavered.

"You're doing all you can," the healer said, casting me a quick, sympathetic glance. "Stay with him. Talk to him."

Around me, she ordered people to help her carry him inside. I followed as they brought him to the longhouse, stood back like a wraith, and hoped—no, *prayed*—that what she did would be enough.

I never left him.

Not when they peeled his clothes from him, slick with blood.

Not when the healer spoke grimly about torn muscle and the slow trickle of blood inside that might yet drown him.

Not that night, when she crouched beside me and offered to take a watch so I could rest.

I refused. Wanted to punch her for asking.

Wanted to punch every person in that town.

Wanted to punch Val.

But I struck no one.

I just sat beside him in the dim light while snow gathered outside the narrow windows. Pressed a damp cloth to his brow when fever took him. Changed his bandages. Forced a trickle of water between his lips when he couldn't rouse enough to drink.

I did that for hours.

The hours stretched into days.

I barely drank. Didn't eat unless someone forced food into my hands and said, "Please, Your Grace, for us."

I was afraid if I moved, if I looked away too long, if I left, he'd stop breathing.

When I wasn't hovering over him, I cleaned our armor and swords. Laid each piece in order with the quiet discipline the legion had drilled into me. I told myself we'd need it when he woke.

Because he *would* wake.

Because I wouldn't be able to stand it if he didn't.

The hearth burned down to coals and was rebuilt twice on the second day before I finally closed my eyes without meaning to, head resting on my folded arms beside his bed.

For the short while that I slept, I dreamt nothing.

I woke to movement.

The creak of the bedframe.

My head snapped up, hand already flying to the sword still sheathed at my hip. I was on my feet before I was fully awake.

Val was struggling to sit upright, his face a drawn mask of confusion.

I was confused too—why was he up?

He swung his legs off the bed, made it halfway to standing before I caught him. Gods, he was fast for someone who had been near death not two days before.

"Val!" I circled quickly around the other side.

He blinked at me, glassy-eyed. "I have to—she's out there—I have to stop her—"

"Stop who?" I put my hands on his shoulders, to stop him from trying to stand again.

"Aleaia. She's going to get herself killed!" he pushed back weakly, but enough to twist something in my chest.

"No, Val," I said softly. "I'm right here. I'm safe. You're safe. It's over."

He stared at me, as if the words took time to land. Then the confusion gave way to awe.

"Aleaia?" he whispered, his voice breaking. "What're you doing here?"

I gave a shaky laugh and brushed the damp hair from his brow. "Where else would I be?"

He didn't answer right away. Just let me grab his legs to help him back in bed, and watched me tuck his blankets around him like he couldn't quite believe I was real.

I sat again, close enough that he could touch me if he wanted, my hand on his chest.

His hand found mine, clumsy and warm.

"*Luce mea.* You love me," he said, thick with disbelief. "At last."

I flushed but didn't look away. "Of course I love you, you stubborn, reckless bastard. Much to my detriment."

His smile was soft. Tired. Gods, it hurt me.

I couldn't stop myself from leaning in and kissing him. Just once. His lips were warm now, thank the gods.

For a moment, neither of us spoke.

"Get in," he murmured. "There's plenty of room."

I laughed. Choked and quiet, but real. "Nice try. Go to sleep."

"I will," he said. "Just... promise you won't leave me."

"Where else would I go, *bradarcam*?"

Outside, a storm clawed at the walls. But in the longhouse, there was only the steady beat of his heart beneath my hand.

Eventually, his breathing deepened. A faint snore escaped him, ragged and uneven.

Only then did I move.

I stripped off my boots and belt, set them aside. Laid my sword on the table by the bed, within reach, and slid beneath the covers. I curled beside him, resting one hand over his heart, my head on the pillow.

His hand came up, fumbling, and patted mine twice as if he meant to comfort me, then laid over mine before falling still again.

I still couldn't sleep, so I thought about the things I knew to be true.

I was sore but alive. And his.

He was alive, too. And mine.

And no power in this gods-forsaken world would tear me from him now.

# CHAPTER SIXTY-FIVE
## *Respite*

*"The body's not sacred.*
*It's a leaking, screaming thing that'll stay alive just to spite you."*
—Mariana Gallo, on the sacredness of the body

Succamos 5, 1231
*Aleaia*

That was the only time Val woke for nearly three full days after our arrival in Cortueca.

On the fourth morning, when he finally, *truly* woke, he blinked up at me with the hollow-eyed look of a man not entirely convinced he was still alive.

"Anvallus's balls," he rasped. "I have to piss."

Not exactly the declaration I'd been waiting for, but I'd take it.

"You're not getting up," I said, already reaching for the chamber pot. "Try it, and I'll knock you out myself."

He didn't argue. Just shifted to the side of the bed and set to it, utterly unfazed.

The sound was… not subtle.

I tried not to pay attention. Like I hadn't spent three sleepless nights willing him to live only to be rewarded with what sounded like a waterfall hitting the inside of a copper basin.

How much *could* the human body hold?

"What the fuck? Why does it look like that?" His voice was hoarse and raw with sleep, but the horror in it was very much awake.

"Healer said it's red because you nearly bled out," I said. "Be glad anything is coming out of you at all."

He grimaced. "Fair point."

I hoped he wouldn't ask how I had learned why it was red in the first place. I could never tell him I'd changed his linens. I had refused to let anyone else see him like that.

I handed him a cup of water. "Drink. Slowly."

He did. When he finished, he sank back onto the bed. I tucked the blanket tight around his chest. He was clammy and pale. But he was also awake and making sense, and that was all that mattered to me.

"How long?" he asked.

"Three days, after you fell off Argenti."

"I fell off a horse?" he asked, as if that was the most unbelievable part.

"Yes." I stared at him, bracing for the next ridiculous question.

He exhaled, slow. Like the weight of it had just caught up to him. "Gods. I'm starving."

"The healer says broth. Anything heavier and you'll throw it right back up."

He shut his eyes for a moment, then opened them again. "We can't stay long."

Maybe he wasn't making sense after all.

"You're not going anywhere until you can sit a horse without falling off," I said.

"I'll crawl to Avitum if I have to."

"The fuck you will," I scoffed. "Not after what you just put me through."

He huffed a breath of laughter, then winced and clutched his ribs.

I hoped it did hurt. Nothing about this was at all humorous.

I sat beside him, my voice low. "Don't you ever do that shit to me again."

His gaze met mine. "I know. I shouldn't have gone alone. I knew it even as I left. I just..." He hesitated. "I was trying to protect you."

I looked away. Swallowed. Took a breath.

"In the future," I said, when I could speak again, "remember that I go where you go. Every time. No matter what."

His hand found mine and lifted it to his lips, a reverent press against my knuckles. He held my gaze the entire time. My anger slipped, just a fraction.

*Damn him.*

"They didn't want to help you when we first got here," I said quietly. "Not until I made them."

His brow furrowed.

"I asked twice. Third time, I drew the Fellglow Blade and gave orders."

He looked at me for a long time. Then, gently, "I'm sorry."

"I'm not telling you to earn an apology," I said. "I'm telling you because when we leave this healer's hut, you need to know what to expect."

"All right."

"Rest," I told him. "We'll leave when you can ride. Not a moment before."

This time, he didn't argue.

I sat back and watched as sleep claimed him again.

When I was sure he was truly asleep, I stepped outside and sent a message to Aeldunon.

*Lucius,*
*Found him. Alive.*
*We'll rest a few more days, then onward.*

*Hope your broken nose didn't make you uglier.*
*Still hate you.*
*—Aleaia*

When I returned to the longhouse, the fire had burned low, casting the walls in soft orange light. Val hadn't moved.

I stood just inside the door, unsure what to do with myself. There was nothing left to fight. Nothing left to fix. Only the waiting.

I crossed the room, sat in the chair by the bed, and folded my arms on the edge of the mattress. Rested my head there.

Outside, the winter sun dipped behind the mountains.

We had miles yet to cross.

A pass still to brave.

But for a moment, we could afford this one quiet peace.

I finally slept.

The next morning dawned gray and bitter.

I was up before first light, loading the last of our gear onto the horses. Argenti shifted beside me, ears flicking at the wind but steady. Val's new horse—a lean Aeltyrian courser, barely broken—stood nearby, eyes sharp.

It wasn't much. But it was the best Cortueca had. Hardy. Fast. Bred for frost and steep country.

Val emerged from the longhouse slowly, steps measured. His cloak was drawn tight, armor strapped over fresh bandages. I'd helped him into it. He hadn't asked.

"You ride Argenti," I said. "Can't let you get thrown off your first time in the saddle."

He only smiled that small, maddening smile he always wore when being stupid, and swung stiffly into the saddle of the new horse.

"Better me than you. One of us has to be whole," he said.

I dragged a hand down my face.

This man and his inability to listen would be the death of me.

I mounted Argenti and guided him close. Val's hands were steady on the reins, but his posture was too straight. Controlled. His legs trembled, just slightly.

"You're going to kill yourself trying to impress me," I said under my breath.

He leaned in, the corner of his mouth lifting just enough to make something twist deep in my chest. Then he grabbed the neck of my cuirass and kissed me, firm and full.

"Too late," he said. "I've been trying to impress you for years."

I smacked his arm and turned Argenti toward the road.

We rode out through the gates and onto the long road south. I didn't look back. There was nothing left behind us. Only what lay ahead.

He would go, broken or not. So it fell to me to keep him upright, to get him to Avitum with breath in his lungs and blood in his veins.

Even if it cost me everything.

No matter what waited when we got there.

# CHAPTER SIXTY-SIX
## *Gone*

*"What is lost leaves shape behind.
We walk in the outline of old selves, wearing them like armor."*
—Aeltyrian funerary inscription

Succamos 10-21, 1231
*Aleaia*

From Cortueca, we crossed frost-choked hills and half-frozen streams, winding through lands so quiet it was as though the world had forgotten how to speak. Neither of us said much, both subdued by pain—his in his side, mine in my heart.

It took five days to reach Gormlaith.

Nearly ninety gray miles, cold and constant. We moved as quickly as we could with Val still healing.

When we arrived, I found the stablemaster myself. He was an older Aeltyrian man with shrewd eyes and a clean yard. I told him exactly what I expected: Argenti was to be exercised daily, fed properly, and kept away from anyone who didn't know how to handle a warhorse. No whips. No crops. No loans. No riders he doesn't trust. No mistakes.

He gave a single nod. I gave him nearly all the coin I had, then walked Argenti to the far end of the paddock, where it was quiet enough for what I had to say.

I pressed my brow to his, fingers twined in his mane, and stood there for a long moment.

"I'm not taking you through that pass," I said. "I'll see you when I get back, all right?"

He just stood, ears twitching, breath fogging in the cold.

"Be good. Or at least don't be awful," I said. "I'll come back for you either way."

Then I turned and walked away. Told myself not to look back. Blinked hard. Told myself I wasn't a hypocrite for using the same excuse Val had given me. Argenti was a horse, not a person who could make decisions about the danger they'd accept.

When I reached the stable gate again, Val was still there. I caught a glimpse of a heavy purse in his hand as he passed it to the master.

"For the horse," he said. "See that he gets everything she asked for."

"This is enough to buy him again," the stablemaster said.

"Not quite, but close." Val turned as the man looked past him at me. "Ready?" he asked.

And he must've known I was about to tell him it wasn't necessary to thank him, because he cut me off.

"Don't," he said. "He saved your life when you came after me. And it's just gold."

*Just gold.* I'd never even held a gold coin before, and he'd just handed the man a bag full to take care of my horse.

I swiped at my eyes, but he only put his arm around my shoulders and gave a small, firm squeeze.

We rode hard after Gormlaith, through Elisedd and beyond, pushing the horses and ourselves past reason. Taking too long would look like defiance.

I hadn't said anything more about his leaving. Not since Cortueca. Not about riding into that village with his blood soaking through my cloak. Not about how many times I'd replayed the moment he left me behind. Not about how close I'd come to losing him without ever getting to hear him say he loved me.

I kept it quiet. Locked it down tight. It was the only way I knew how to keep moving.

We stopped only when we had to. Ate in near silence. Slept little. The closer we drew to the mountains, the colder it got.

Just off the road on the last stretch to the Pass, tucked behind a stand of bare trees that broke the worst of the wind, we found a small clearing. It wasn't much, but it would do.

I swung down stiffly, legs sore from the ride. Val dismounted slower, one hand braced against the saddle to steady himself. He tried to hide the strain, but I saw it.

"You sit," I said. "I'll take care of the rest."

He didn't argue.

I led our mounts to the edge of the trees, unsaddled them, brushed them down with brisk, practiced strokes. They were steady, obedient, and that was enough for now.

When I came back, I crouched beside the kindling Val had gathered—I let him do that much—and exhaled slow. Held out my hand. Summoned flame.

It caught easily, silver and white hot. I'd been practicing control. It wasn't like a normal flame, the kind you had to stoke and feed until it licked blue and white at the base. It just arrived that way, ready to incinerate whatever it touched.

I'd destroyed a few piles of kindling before I summoned it small enough to be practical.

Val sat nearby on the blanket, cloak pulled tight, hands tucked beneath it for warmth. Watching.

That done, I set about staking the tent, working fast before the light failed. He didn't offer to help, and I didn't want him to. Not after the last time. I'd yelled at him for lifting the cookpot, and we'd both decided, without saying it, that he was done trying to prove anything.

When I finished, I dropped to the blanket beside him, sore clear through.

He opened his cloak and shifted closer, drawing me in. I let myself lean, head settling against his chest, his arm curling around me.

I felt his hand tracing circles along my back. Closed my eyes. Let myself fall into the rhythm of him—the rise and fall of his breathing, the steady beat of his heart beneath my cheek, the quiet that lived between us now.

He exhaled, soft against the top of my head.

"What's wrong?" I asked.

He didn't answer right away.

"Just thinking," he said at last. "When I was fifteen, my uncle Calpurnius, who was my mother's brother, was the governor of Aeltyria. When Cassius took command of the First Army, his presence was expected in Avitum. So was mine. So, twenty of us went into the Pravian Pass, including my mentor, Gavius Triarius, Lucius, and me. Only the three of us came out alive. Damned harpies and wyverns."

"I'm sorry, Val," I murmured.

"Don't be," he said. "He deserved worse. He's the one who arranged my mother's marriage to Claudius. And it was still a better end than what Cassius's mother got."

"How so?"

"Your mother and Cassius's mother were sisters. Eavan and Orlaith."

"Oh that. Wait a moment." I wrinkled my nose, pulling back to look up at him. "We're not related, are we?"

I knew we weren't, but I loved teasing him. He couldn't always tell when I was serious.

"What? No!" Val laughed, a short bark of sound that fogged in the cold.

"Just making sure we're not about to turn the family tree into a wreath," I said flatly.

A real laugh broke from him, low and rough, like it had been trapped too long. He dragged a hand over his face, shoulders shaking.

"Fucking Hel. You get me every time," he said once he could breathe again.

"I know." I smirked. "I think certain… proclivities run in your family."

"You might be right. We do have a tendency toward mouthy Aeltyrian women who think they're clever," he said, one brow lifted.

I scoffed. "Good thing the women in my family apparently like cocky Calesian royals."

His smile widened, slow and unrepentant. "Cocky, is it?" he said, his voice dropping just enough to make the word linger. "Funny. You've never complained about the cock part."

I shot him a look, but the heat flaring in my cheeks gave me away. "Not what I meant, you arse."

"Admit it," he said, eyes glinting. "You *like it* when I'm cocky."

I narrowed mine, though the corner of my mouth twitched. "Depends."

He tilted his head, curious. "On what?"

"The setting."

He brushed his fingers lightly down my arm, the barest graze along my sleeve. Just enough to make the air between us feel warmer than it should. "Hmm… tell me more."

Traitor that it was, my mind dragged me back to Elisedd—the tribunal, the rush afterward, the way I'd thrown myself at him without hesitation. The way it still thrilled me.

*The door.*

*The table.*

*The way he pulled my—*

I cleared my throat hard. "You're a good orator."

Val laughed again and leaned in, his breath warm against my ear. "Is that what we're calling it now?"

Before I could stop myself, I said, "Whatever *you* call it, I want more."

His hand stilled. Then resumed, slower, more deliberate.

"Noted," he said with that quiet satisfaction that always gave his pride away.

"Anyway," I said, louder than I meant to, "what were you saying about Orlaith?"

His smile lingered a beat before fading.

"Orlaith and Eavan were close. Too close, maybe. Orlaith was gifted in spirit magic, but not the healing kind. Prophecy, some said. After Cassius was born, her health began to fail. My father believed your mother cursed her."

"My mother wouldn't do that," I said. "'Curses are the work of hedge-witches and cowards,' she wrote in her journals."

"I don't believe it either," he said, voice softening. "But my father did. Orlaith allegedly killed herself. My father called it a sign that magic was evil. The Inquisition followed."

The fire snapped. I stared at it, unmoving.

"Maybe…" I said quietly. "Maybe Orlaith thought *herself* cursed. Maybe she blamed Eavan, even if it wasn't true."

"Being married to him would feel like a curse," he agreed.

The past was a tangle of blood and whispers. And it had led us here, to this fire, this night.

After a while, Val said, "Living in Aeltyria… feels like I escaped something. I thought about ignoring the summons altogether."

The note he'd left behind had said he had to buy time, to stall while the rebellion aligned. At the time, I couldn't see the logic. All I saw was that he was gone.

I still couldn't believe he thought I wouldn't follow him. That I'd stay behind and find some other path, once I realized he'd left me behind.

Like I'd just wake up that day and go, "Oh so that's where he went." Shrug my shoulders and move on.

Sometimes, I thought he knew me better than I knew myself. Other times, like that one, it felt like he didn't know me at all.

And it still stung.

"Leaving you was the hardest thing I ever thought I had to do," he said. "But you're the future of your people. This is dangerous. Not just the Pass. What comes after. After Avitum, after we go home."

I shook my head. "You have a lot of faith in me."

"Yes," he said simply.

I looked away. That kind of certainty should have steadied me. It didn't. It pressed down, heavy and suffocating.

"I'll make a disastrous queen," I murmured.

Val caught my hand and squeezed. "Why would you say that?"

I shrugged. "Because it's true. I wasn't raised for it."

"Were you taught to read and write?"

"Aye."

"Taught to fight?"

"Aye."

"Then you're already better suited than half the people sitting on thrones now."

A breath of laughter escaped me as I shook my head.

"You're courageous. Smart. Fair. You've got more honor than the entire Calesian court put together," he said. "You'll be a good queen, Aleaia. And if you aren't, I'll still stand beside you, and hopefully advise you well."

I looked at him. Then away. "Well, I almost lost you, didn't I?"

The words came quiet. Flat.

His brow furrowed. "Aleaia… what does that have to do with it?"

"If I had more… I don't know, guile, maybe I could've seen through…"

The words faltered.

Understanding hit him a heartbeat later.

"Oh. Aleaia, I'm sorry. I didn't mean—" He pulled me tighter. "I meant what I wrote in that note. I just wanted one good night for you before everything unraveled."

If I hadn't gone after him, he'd have died in the snow. Just another noble fool who thought his death would cost less than his defiance.

My gaze dropped, pulse tapping hard beneath my skin.

And not for the first time, I thought—

*What happened to that simple country girl?*

*The one who hunted with her father.*

*Who carried water. Fed the goats.*

*Helped stir her grandmother's tinctures.*

*The one who had a simpler life. An easier one, in many ways.*

*Gone.*

A shiver climbed my spine.

"It's cold," I said softly. "I'm going in now."

# CHAPTER SIXTY-SEVEN
*The Balm*

*"Truth, when calmly offered, is no sword but a balm—
it does not cut fear away, but renders it visible, and thus, bearable."*
—Of Truth and Reason

Succamos 21, 1231
*Valerius*

I followed her into the tent and let the flap fall shut behind us. Neither of us spoke as we undressed and slid beneath the furs. The wind pressed against the canvas walls, and the fire outside hissed low into embers.

I lay still for a long while, listening to her breathe. Listening for the tears she thought I hadn't heard every night since Cortueca. Then I shifted, slowly and carefully, brushing my fingers down the length of her spine.

She turned to lay on her back and looked up at me.

Gods, the *way* she looked at me, her eyes red-rimmed and burning, like she saw the edge I was standing on. Like she knew I was one breath away from falling.

She raised herself on her elbow, pushing me onto my back. Her hair fell across her shoulders, onto my chest.

I reached up, brushing a stray strand behind her ear. My hand lingered, my thumb stroking along her cheekbone.

She leaned into it. Just barely. Just enough.

Then she moved.

She rose to her knees and straddled my hips, the furs sliding off us both. Her shift clung to her like water, outlining every curve. My mouth went dry.

"You should be resting," she murmured.

I managed a slow, aching smile. "I'll rest," I said hoarsely, "after."

Her hands moved between us, untying my breeches just enough to free me. My breath hitched as her fingers brushed me, feather-light and maddening. I gripped the furs at my sides, every muscle straining not to flip her beneath me and bury myself in her.

She made a low sound—part disbelief, part hunger—and peeled her shift over her head, casting it aside.

I forgot how to breathe.

Even with the shadows under her eyes, she was the most beautiful thing I'd ever seen.

Not in the way court women tried to be. No polish or pretense.

She was strength and scars and starlight.

The woman I loved.

The life I never thought I'd get to keep.

I couldn't look away. The ache coiled tighter, sharper. I needed to touch her. To taste her. To take her to prove I was still allowed.

Then she leaned down, skin to skin. Her breasts grazed my chest, soft and unbearable. Her heat poured into me, and my hands found her waist.

She kissed me hard. Fierce. Angry. Her teeth caught my lip, and I groaned into her mouth, helpless beneath the weight of her and everything she hadn't said. My arms closed around her.

She hadn't forgiven me.

Not fully.

I shifted, intending to roll her beneath me, but she pulled back from me and pressed me down with both hands, bracing against my chest. Keeping me pinned.

"Let me take care of you, *vedrānos,*" she said, voice catching. "Please."

Gods, I couldn't have denied her if I tried.

My hands slid up her back, rough and urgent, then forward to cup her breasts. I caught each in my palms, thumbs teasing until she gasped and rocked against me. Still kissing me, she shoved my breeches lower, just far enough to free me completely.

Then she reached between us and stroked me once. Slow. Firm. Devastating.

"Fuck—Aleaia—"

She shifted her hips and guided me into her, sinking down in one long, relentless stroke.

I groaned, half-broken. Gods. She was so tight, so hot, it nearly undid me.

At first, she moved slow. Savoring. Her hands slid over my chest as if memorizing every inch, anchoring herself here, to me.

I cupped her breasts again, teasing until she whimpered, her rhythm faltering as need overtook restraint.

She moved faster, riding me hard. Like her body was chasing something she hadn't named.

I was already close, too close. Gods, it hadn't even been that long, but it felt like years since I'd been inside her. Every breath scraped the inside of my ribs. Every muscle pulled taut, ready to break.

I had to see her fall apart first.

"That's it, *amor mea.*" I gripped her hips harder. "Take what's yours. Take all of me."

She opened her eyes.

Gods.

That look. Raw. Aching. It knocked the air from my lungs.

But then I saw it. A shimmer at the corner of her eye—a tear, sliding down her cheek. Then another. My stomach dropped.

My hands flew to her hips, catching her, stilling her.

"Aleaia, wait. Just—wait, a minute. Stop."

My voice came out frayed with heat.

She blinked down at me, dazed. Confused.

I reached up, cupped her face gently, brushing the wetness from her cheeks. "What's wrong?"

Her throat worked. I felt something cracking just beneath the surface, a pressure she couldn't hold much longer.

Then she grabbed my jaw hard, her hands shaking.

"Don't you dare leave me again." The words spilled out in a rush, breathless and broken.

The guilt sliced deep, hollowing me, carving through bone and breath. There wasn't a word in any tongue that could make it right. What had I done to her?

So when she moved again, brutal and desperate, grinding down on me like she could fuse us together. I didn't stop her. I let her take what she needed.

She rode me hard. Dragged broken sounds from both of us. Her hands held me fast, pulled me into a kiss, fierce and claiming. Then she grabbed my wrists and crushed them into the furs above my head, holding me down.

Binding me.

Keeping me.

Owning me.

The furs twisted beneath us, but I hardly noticed. The world had narrowed to breath, to heat, to her. I gave her everything, every jagged piece of what was left. Every apology I didn't deserve to speak.

She ground down harder, her breath catching. A choked cry tore free as she came, tightening around me, trembling as she shattered above me.

I thought she'd collapse into me. Rest.

She didn't.

Still shaking, she slid down between my thighs, her hair brushing my stomach like silk. Then her mouth was on me—hot and slick.

Her hand stroked in rhythm as she took me deeper, and my hands flew to her head before I could stop them. I held her there, hips jerking helplessly.

No one had ever done this for me.

Not once.

Not ever.

She hummed low, like she knew exactly what it meant.

When she took more of me, I lost the last thread of control. My fingers tightened in her hair, pushing her farther than I meant to.

She gagged, just once, and I flinched, loosening my grip instantly.

"Aleaia—" It tore out of me, half-plea, half-apology.

She didn't stop. She swallowed me down again, and again, dragging me to the edge with need and vengeance all at once.

I came with a broken groan, my body locking tight before collapsing into the furs, undone by pleasure, guilt, and the kind of love I didn't know how to carry.

She wiped her mouth with the back of her hand. Crawled back up to me like she hadn't just broken me completely.

I pulled her close, wrapping my arm around her waist, holding her tight.

We lay tangled in silence, the furs clinging to our sweat-slicked bodies. I didn't move. Just kept her there, tight against my side, like I could hold the pieces together if I didn't let go.

I slid a hand through her hair, smoothing it back from her damp brow. Then pressed my mouth to her temple—no smile, no teasing. Just a quiet, reverent kiss.

"I'm sorry," I murmured against her skin. "I was too…"

I didn't know what to say, so I let it hang.

"You didn't hurt me," she said, fierce and sure. Her voice was hard against my chest. "I wanted you. I still do."

I shut my eyes, breathing her in.

Still, guilt gnawed at me. Dull. Merciless.

I didn't deserve this.

Didn't deserve her.

And the ache in me was like something cracked wide open and left me hollow.

"Not just that. I'm sorry I hurt you, when I left you. I don't know how I'll make it up to you. But you are everything to me, Aleaia, and I'll spend my life trying, if that's what it takes."

I thought she'd pull back, but she pressed herself tighter against me, daring me to move. Daring me to try and run again.

"I need to tell you something," she said softly. "About why I was so frightened. And angry. Something I've never told another living soul."

I said nothing, just stroked her hair.

"I've had this dream," she said. "Since I was a child."

My brows drew together, but I didn't interrupt.

"I'm in this place…" Her voice faltered. "I don't know where it is. I've never seen it outside the dream. The floor is stone. Cold. I can't see the walls or the ceiling, but I know it's big. And there's blood. Gods, there's so much blood."

She shuddered. One trembling hand rose to scrub at her face.

"My sword's covered in it. Sticky. I'm wounded, dragging it behind me, and all I can think is, I have to save him." She let out a broken breath. "But I never knew who he was."

She sobbed, ragged and breathless.

"And then I watch a man kill someone on the ground… and I think it's you, Val. I think he kills you, and I'm so afraid."

I pulled her tighter, wrapping my arm fully around her back. The silence stretched, long and sharp.

Aleaia didn't fear anything. I'd seen her defiant, angry, annoyed—but never afraid.

But this? This had lived inside her for years. A child, waking with blood on her hands and no name for the grief. And now, gods, now she thought it was about me.

I didn't believe in that sort of thing. Dreams. Fate. Prophecy. I believed in steel. In tactics. In the choices we made. But she believed it, and she'd been carrying it like a blade buried deep in her ribs.

I couldn't let her keep bleeding from it. So when I finally spoke, I kept my voice steady. Gave her something solid to hold.

"I don't believe in premonitions," I said. "Or fate. Or destiny."

She didn't pull away, but I felt her still in my arms.

"I believe in choices," I went on. "In control. In fighting for what matters. In fighting for you."

She didn't answer right away.

Then, almost too quiet to catch, she said, "Then how… how could I have had the same dream since I was a child?"

I trailed my hand down her back in steady rhythm. "You started having it before magic came back."

She tensed. Just a breath, but it was there.

"If it was a vision," I said, keeping my tone even, "if you had some kind of gift—prophecy, foresight, whatever they call it—it wouldn't have worked back then. Magic was sealed."

I let the silence settle for a moment. Let her absorb it.

"You couldn't have seen the future, Aleaia," I said gently. "There was no magic to show it to you."

A long, shaky breath escaped her.

"You grew up in the early years of the occupation," I said. "Raids. Executions. Things like that happened all the time. You were young. Your father didn't talk about those years much, did he?"

She was still for a long moment. "Maybe I saw someone else with a sword that way. And I just… thought it was me. And you."

I felt the tension begin to bleed out of her.

So I just held her. Kept my breathing slow. Steady. Let her match it. Let her feel it. Let her feel me right there with her.

"Then maybe that's all it is," I murmured. "Just a memory. Not something waiting to happen."

She didn't argue. She only curled closer and tucked her face against my neck.

The tightness I'd carried in my ribs since the day I left her eased, just a little.

I'd given her something real.

A little of her own light, reflected back at her.

Enough to cut through whatever shadow had haunted her all these years.

And maybe, gods willing, that would be enough.

# CHAPTER SIXTY-EIGHT
## *The Tether*

*"A tether is not a weapon. It is a reaching. Skin to life, will to breath.*
*All living things hold mana—*
*it is the heir's right to draw it, but not without care.*
*Let it come like a thread drawn through silk. Gentle. Intentional.*
*Never in anger."*
—from the journals of Queen Eavan, written for Aleaia

Succamos 22, 1231
*Aleaia*

I woke to the steady weight of Val pressed against me, his breath warm against my collarbone. His head rested on my shoulder, his arm slung low around my waist, like even in sleep, he wouldn't let go.

Dim light seeped through the tent walls, soft and gray. I stayed still, listening. The wind stirred outside, brushing bare branches against the canvas in slow, rasping strokes.

It was cold. Thank the gods he'd listened when I told him to put his clothes back on before we slept.

It was quiet.

No dream.

No blood.

No helpless, gut-wrenching terror.

I should've felt relief.

Instead, I felt dread, crawling through my gut, cold and shapeless.

Val thought the dream was a memory. Something I'd witnessed as a child and twisted into something darker with time. Maybe he was right. Maybe I had seen something like it. Someone dying. Someone I couldn't save. And I'd carried it with me so long my mind had made it mine.

But there was still that moment. Always the same. Always so clear. The man on the ground. The other one standing over him, sword raised.

And the knowing.

It's *him*.

He said he didn't believe in fate or visions.

But I did.

I hadn't told him that. I didn't want to take from him the thought that he could anchor me with nothing but words.

And he tried. Gods, he tried. I saw it. Felt it. He wanted so badly for me to believe, as he did, that nothing lay ahead but what we chose. That he could shape the future the same way he shaped himself—with strategy and discipline.

I wanted to believe it too.

But I couldn't.

He made me feel safe. When he held me, the world quieted. The dreams stilled. Grief didn't press so hard. That feeling had nothing to do with magic, memory, or choice. That was just him.

I shifted carefully, tracing a slow line down the curve of his back.

Even after a full night's sleep—the best I'd had since we left Aeldunon—my strength hadn't returned.

There was nothing to replenish my mana.

The ether was there, just dimmed. It was like trying to see by a sliver of moonlight.

That, more than anything, made my skin prickle. Other places, it hummed, low and constant, like a breath beneath the earth. Here, there was nothing.

The land felt hollow. Leached.

*Why was that?* I wondered.

If I could pull knowledge the way I pulled ether, maybe I'd know what in Lithau's name to do.

I wish I could call a storm. Command the wind like the harpies did. Or manipulate the earth. All the things my mother could do.

But I wasn't her, and that wasn't the kind of magic I had. I could do exactly two things: fire and a shield. Maybe I could buy us enough time to ride hard and hope the monsters were slower.

My mother's book had mentioned some kind of thread, something I could tease from other living things to recover mana. Maybe *that* would help sustain a shield.

It wasn't much of a plan, but it was what I had.

"You've sighed four out of eight breaths," Val said against my skin, voice thick with sleep.

I glanced down. His cheek was warm where it rested on my shoulder, his eyes half-lidded. Without thinking, I brushed my thumb across the curve of his cheekbone.

"Trying to figure out how to get us through the Pass without getting eaten alive," I murmured. "It's not going well."

"What have you got?" He groaned as he shifted, stretching with the graceless misery of a man twice his age.

I rolled my own shoulders, sore from the cold ground. Sleeping beneath the stars had its freedoms, but not comfort.

"I have an idea," I said. "Not sure I'd call it a *good* one."

He grumbled again, dragging himself toward the tent flap like a soldier forced to rise too soon.

I waited until he ducked out, then crawled after him into the biting morning air.

He straightened with a grunt, working one shoulder gingerly before turning back and offering his hand.

I batted it away and gave him a look. He should've known better, with his wounds still healing. I pushed to my feet, brushed the dirt from my knees—

—only for his arm to snake around my waist and pull me flush against him.

A breath caught in my throat, but not enough to stop him.

"I just wanted a kiss," he said.

Then he stole it, quick and maddeningly smug.

"Now tell me about your plan," he said, still close enough for his breath to brush my cheek. "While we get dressed."

I shook my head as he let me go. A smile tugged at the corner of my mouth despite myself. I turned to fetch our armor from the end of the tent, where it had been stashed with our other things.

"I was reading one of my mother's journals before we left," I said, teeth chattering. "It mentioned something she called a tether. A way to draw mana from living things. I thought I might try taking ether from the creatures we'll have to fight anyway."

"You're going to draw mana from a harpy?" His voice caught somewhere between disbelief and admiration.

"If I can." I brushed a hand over my cuirass, crusted with frost and grime. "If I can't, we stick to the edges, take cover, and hope the gods favor fools."

"I trust you," he said, and reached for my armor first.

We moved through the routine easily, without needing to speak. It was something we knew now—how to buckle and strap each piece into place, how to brace, how to adjust. His hands were steady, practiced. He didn't fumble, didn't second-guess the weight of a strap or the angle of a plate.

He just worked beside me like he didn't remember a time when we hadn't done this together.

When I reached for his arms to fasten his vambraces, he leaned in toward me.

"Before we go," he murmured.

Before I could pretend to object, he stole another kiss. Fast. Playful.

I flushed but laughed softly and caught him by the neck of his breastplate before he could escape. This time, I pulled him down harder.

The kiss I gave him wasn't hurried. It was slow. Intentional. He let out a low, satisfied grunt against my mouth, and the cool edge of his armor pressing into my palm as I held him there, reluctant to let go.

"I love you, *vedrānos*," I whispered, just as I pulled away.

He smiled. "And I love you. But what does that mean? '*Vedranos*?' You still haven't told me."

"It's *vedrānos*—veh-DRAH-nos. Not VED-ran-os."

"Ved-raaah-nos?"

He said it wrong on purpose, slow and exaggerated, his Calesian accent curling around the word. The glimmer in his eye told me he wanted to grin and wouldn't allow me the pleasure. My irritation slipped sideways into something warmer.

"Broad ā," I said. "You'd know that if you kept up with your lessons."

Val laughed. "I've been a bit busy. And that was a *broad* ā."

"You dragged it out too much," I said with a wave of my hand.

"'Make it broader,' you say, and then tell me that's too much." He shrugged lightly. "Perhaps I'm not such a hopeless student after all."

"Not hopeless. Just stubborn," I said lightly, reaching for my sword. "If you don't figure it out yourself, I'll tell you when we reach the other side."

"That's what you always say," he grumbled, fastening the last buckle on his cuirass. "Then you never tell me."

Now I laughed. "When have I ever done that?"

"Any time you use Aeltyrian I don't understand and I ask about it."

"I'll tell you whatever you want if we survive this."

"Oh, *whatever* I want? High stakes for you. Maybe you don't want me to make it."

Someone was in a mood today. "Means you'll have to live if you want to know."

He shook his head, but a smile tugged faintly at the corner of his mouth.

"Cruel woman," he muttered.

I flashed a quick smile. "You knew what you were getting into."

We packed quickly. I saddled our mounts without thinking, falling into the rhythm of preparation. Val tightened the girth on his horse beside me, but I caught the slight grimace when he shifted his weight. He was still sore, though he hadn't said a word.

He swung into the saddle easily enough. Then paused.

I stood beside my horse, staring at the snow like it might offer an answer.

"What is it?" he asked.

I didn't look up. "What I told you earlier, about tethering. I read about it, but… I've never actually done it. I don't know if I can. There are so many things she could do that I can't, and if I can't—" I broke off, inhaling deep. "We might die because of it."

"Well," he said lightly, "if that happens, we earn a quick, valiant death and find ourselves in Aetheria. Peace, wine, endless sun."

I shot him a look scathing enough to kill weeds. "That is not helpful."

"How about this?" He patted the breastplate I'd just finished securing. "Try it on me."

I grimaced. "I was afraid you'd say that."

He shrugged. "I'm the only other living thing here besides the horses. You don't have a better option."

He wasn't wrong. I just didn't like it.

I did have another option—to go in without testing this idea first. And that was worse than attempting it on Val. I sighed and fastened my gloves to my belt, leaving my hands bare. The book had said tethers worked best that way.

Reluctantly, I closed my eyes and reached out with one bare hand.

I pictured it the way she'd described: threads of life-force, invisible and delicate, stretching between all things. Tethers.

Nothing.

Just cold air.

Empty.

My hand dropped to my side, and a knot twisted tight in my chest, sharp and bitter. Failure.

"Aleaia."

I opened my eyes.

He was watching me. No fear. No hesitation.

Just that same maddening calm. That same trust.

"I told you I trust you," he said, voice softening. "And I meant it."

I drew a deep breath. Steadied myself.

And tried again.

This time, I saw them. Thin silver strands shimmering faintly from my palm into the space between us, threads seemingly spun from starlight, delicate and alive.

I reached.

Val tensed. His spine arched, a low curse dragging from between clenched teeth. He sucked in a breath and shifted in the saddle like the contact had jolted straight through him.

The moment it connected us, I gasped. Heat pooled in my belly and I moaned softly before I could stop myself.

*Gods.*

My face burned. Mortified, I nearly dropped the tether on instinct, but the mana flowed too fast, too warm, too good.

He squirmed again, fists clenching around the reins.

"Aleaia," he bit out, voice ragged. "Whatever you're doing—fuck—"

I closed the connection, heart hammering.

He sagged in the saddle, then looked down at me. His pupils were blown wide, dark and dazed. He was breathing hard, flushed beneath the stubble and the cold.

I stared up at him, breathless, my thighs tight with longing. When had I gotten this close?

"It works," I said, voice hoarse.

"You think so? *Deia mea…*"

I nodded. My cheeks still burned. I couldn't bring myself to speak.

His eyes dropped to my mouth, then lower. Slowly. Hungrily.

And I couldn't help it. I stepped closer. Pressed one hand to his thigh.

He stripped off a gauntlet, leaned down, and caught my chin in his hand.

"Not now, *luce mea,*" he murmured. "But when we make camp…"

*Luce mea. My light.*

"Gods, I love it when you call me that, *vedrānos*."

I put a foot in his stirrup, lifted myself, and caught him around the neck to kiss him. Hard.

He sighed, his arm locking around my waist, holding me tight as he kissed me back.

When we finally pulled apart, I rested my forehead against his.

"Aelan's mercy," I breathed, "I hope it doesn't feel like that every time I draw from something."

He chuckled as I slid back down and moved to my horse. "I hope it doesn't either. You'd have no use for me anymore."

"I'm just glad it works."

"Of course it does," he said softly. "You're brilliant."

The words caught me off guard. I wasn't used to being praised like that, especially not for something I barely understood.

The magic still hummed faintly in my blood, warm now, not overwhelming. Manageable.

I could work with this.

He caught my eye again and gave me a wry half-smile. "Let's go. Before I ask you to do it to me again."

Heat rushed back to my face. "You are unbelievable."

I mounted, my fingers tightening around the reins.

Whatever waited in the Pass, I was ready for it now.

# CHAPTER SIXTY-NINE
## *Consequence*

*"It is not the initial surge that ruins the mage. It is the moment after—the heartbeat where they believe they can take more."*
—Last words of Magister Corvin, Battle of Daran Hold

Succamos 22, 1231
*Aleaia*

By midmorning, the pass narrowed. Craggy walls closed in around us like the jaws of a giant. Every sound echoed: hooves striking frozen earth, the clink of armor, and, somewhere ahead, screeching.

I threw my cloak back over my shoulders, one hand near the hilt of my blade. The hair at my nape rose. They were close.

Shrieking split the air. It didn't just cut the ears. It sank straight to the marrow.

Val reined in nearby, sword already drawn. His horse sidestepped, snorting, ears pinned flat.

"They're coming," he said.

I reached for my mana. The ether here was worse than before, like the Pass was starved for it. My hand trembled, fingers digging into my palm.

"Stay close," I hissed, unsheathing my sword. The Fellglow Blade shimmered, dim in the gray light, but alive. Waiting.

A shadow swept over us.

The first harpy dove.

Wings tucked. Claws out. The stink of rot and rust hit like a blow.

My horse was no warhorse. She reared with a sharp snort, teeth bared. Val's mount danced sideways, ears flat, wild-eyed.

I threw up my hand, the tether flaring hot through my palm, and pulled. Its mana tore loose like meat from bone, raw and burning. If Val's mana was a delicacy, this was hardtack and gruel. Coarse. Ugly.

The creature shrieked, ragged and choking, then dropped like a stone. Hit the rocks, wings torn and smoking. It twitched, sprang up, took to the air and fled.

I staggered but stayed upright, breath shuddering with the aftershock. My blade stayed raised, glowing faint in my grip.

Another scream ripped the sky open.

The second came faster.

Val spurred forward, shield high. He caught it midair, its claws striking the metal with a bone-jarring crack. His arm buckled for a breath, then he swung.

The rim of his shield smashed into its skull. Bone crunched. The thing collapsed into the snow, stunned.

If there were more—

"We have to move!" he shouted, wheeling back toward me.

"They'll just chase us!"

I twisted in the saddle, thrust out my hand toward the writhing thing in the snow and pulled.

Its mana surged into me like a flood. No resistance. No thought. Just raw energy, slamming through my limbs, searing hot. I breathed through it. Held it.

Barely.

A third shriek tore the air. Another shape loomed overhead, circling in for the kill.

I didn't wait. The moment it crossed into range, I pulled.

Again, mana surged hot and furious. The creature shrieked once, then went still. Smoke curled from its chest, harsh and acrid.

When I was younger, after lean times passed and there was finally food again, I'd eat like it might vanish tomorrow, until my stomach hurt and Papa joked that he'd have to roll me out to the barn for the night. You never knew when the next tribute would starve you.

That was what I did then.

I gorged myself on mana.

It was the only way I knew to survive the hunger that might come next.

I looked up. Five—no, six—circling, shrieking to each other in sharp, angry bursts.

"They're learning," I said. "They know to stay out of range."

Val gave a dry, humorless laugh. "Smart little fuckers."

One broke off and dove.

I didn't think. I reached.

The siphon surged, hotter this time. My palm burned like I'd pressed it to a forge.

I looked down. Red. Angry. Not blistered but close.

My horse tossed its head, snorting. Val's mount pawed the frozen ground, skittish and wild.

"Aleaia?" he asked, eyes narrowed at me.

"Let's ride," I said, and kicked ahead. The need to cast something gnawed at me.

We kept to the jagged wall, weaving between snow-choked stone and the rotted bones of those who'd come before. Splintered shields. Rusted blades. Bits of armor half-swallowed by ice.

A graveyard stretched beneath our hooves. We didn't look down.

Twice more, they dove.

Twice, I reached.

And twice, I tore.

Both dropped hard, limp and lifeless.

But each pull dragged more into me than the last.

My hand burned, white-hot and swollen, veins dark beneath the skin. Mana surged through them like a waterskin stretched too tight. My chest clenched, high and suffocating.

I couldn't catch a full breath.

My vision ringed black. A pounding started behind my eyes, and my heart—

Too fast. Too hard.

Val's voice cut through the wind. "Aleaia, what's wrong?"

I didn't answer.

Couldn't.

Nausea surged. My mouth filled with copper.

"Aleaia?" Closer now.

"I—" It choked out of me. My vision faltered.

*Do something.*

*Cast. Cast something.*

I didn't plan the release. Didn't shape it. It just broke free.

The shield burst from me in a crackling wave of pure, radiant force. A dome flared to life around us, blinding-bright, burning with my mana.

Two harpies dove at that moment.

They slammed the barrier like birds against glass and dropped into the snow.

Then, silence.

Cold. Sudden.

My lungs opened. The ache in my chest vanished. The pressure faded.

I breathed, finally. Deep. Clean.

I had mana in my blood, a flaming blade in my hand, and the next breath in my lungs.

And for one terrible second, I felt strong. Untouchable.

I straightened in the saddle, still trembling, but sharp. Ready.

*Let them come. Let them burn.*

"What *was* that?" His voice had gone softer. Not afraid. A warning, maybe.

"I don't know, but it felt good, Val."

He let out a slow breath through his nose.

I shrugged, flexing my fingers once against the reins. "Would you rather I exploded?"

"Not today," he said, dry as kindling.

He kept watching me, though, and under the humor, I felt the weight of it.

*Fear.*

By the time we saw the narrowing mouth of the pass, the harpies had fallen back. They circled wide, shrieking now and then, but none came close.

They knew better.

I let the shield fall. My mana was dipping fast.

A bitter wind rose, carrying the iron-salt stink of blood.

Fresh.

I jerked my horse to a halt.

Val rode up beside me, visor lifted. "What is it?"

I caught his arm, eyes scanning the sky.

No screeching. No wingbeats. It was too quiet.

"Do you hear that?" I asked.

His eyes narrowed. "No, I don't."

A massive, winged lizard plummeted from the clouds and slammed into the pass with a sound like the sky itself cracking open. It landed hard on its hind legs, snow billowing in all directions. Its roar made my ears ring.

I reacted before I could think, throwing up a shield just in time to catch the blast of flame from its maw.

"What is that?" I shouted.

"A fucking wyvern," Val growled. "I hate this place. If we get in close, it won't use fire."

"I'll keep the shield up—"

"I'm the bait. You're the sword. Drop the shield when we're close, then kill it." He slammed down his visor.

"I should be the bait. I'm faster—"

"No, Aleaia," he snapped. "Listen to me, just this once."

I hesitated. Then nodded.

"All right," I said, tightening my grip on the blade. "Ready?"

"Always."

We moved.

The wyvern didn't charge. It watched, unblinking, steam curling from its nostrils.

"Stop here," Val said. "Drop the shield. Now."

I obeyed, veering right, light in the saddle. My horse danced beneath me but didn't bolt. I rode fast across the snow, harrying its flank. Val charged straight in, shouting, hammering his sword against his shield.

The tail whipped fast. It slammed into Val's shield with a crack like splitting timber, then tore it from his arm and flung it aside.

I had to do something. The next hit would land, would hit him unshielded.

He would be angry but he'd be alive so I'd take it.

The tether snapped from my palm, silver and crackling.

I pulled.

The wyvern staggered. Its wings faltered. The roar that followed was hoarse, off-balance. Val was still moving, but I wasn't watching him anymore.

The mana flooded in.

Heavy. Wild. Endless.

Not like Val's. Not like the harpies'.

It was too much, but I wanted more.

One thread wasn't enough.

The tether thickened. I pulled harder.

The air screamed.

I lost track of what was happening around me.

The wyvern reeled. And then it died.

But the mana didn't stop.

And I couldn't stop it.

*What the fuck?*

The last surge tore through me like a storm through canvas.

My hand wouldn't release. The mana kept coming.

My palm blistered.

Heat exploded through my arm, like lightning in my blood, sparking and searing as it climbed.

Up my shoulder.

Through my chest.

I dropped the reins. Slid from the saddle. My knees hit snow.

*It burns it burns it burns—*

I screamed.

The smell hit next. Burnt flesh. Sour. Metallic. Wrong.

"Val! I can't—let go!"

I clawed at my arm. Tried to tear my hand free. Nothing worked.

The tether wasn't a thread anymore. It was a rope.

It may as well have been a noose. Because I knew—*I knew*—this would kill me.

Val reached me at a run. Caught my wrist as I staggered. Steadied me before I fell.

He reached for the tether, his fingers passing through it like mist.

All he could do was watch as every drop of the wyvern's mana poured into me.

It pulsed. Once. Bright as the sun. Sharp as a scream.

Then it snapped.

I swayed.

My breath came fast and shallow.

Too fast.

My lungs couldn't keep up.

My hand—gods, my palm was ruined. Blistered, red and weeping, steaming in the cold. Fingertips white. Cracked. Joints stiff. Too swollen to move.

Then the second wave hit.

Not a flare. A deepening. Pain crawled inward now, burrowing through the veins of my arm.

Everything blurred.

The world was distant. I wasn't fully inside it anymore.

My knees gave out. Val didn't let me fall.

"Hold still," he ordered.

I doubted the *Cura Vitalis* recommended what he did next. But then again, I doubted it covered guzzling mana either.

So he did the only thing he could.

He shoved my hand into the snow.

The shock split through me.

I screamed, hit him once, then slapped my good hand over my mouth to muffle it. My body shook. I turned away and retched into the snow.

"It's all right. You'll be all right," Val said, too fast.

He tore off his gauntlet, packed snow into it with his bare hand.

"I'm sorry for this," he said, and forced my hand deep into the gauntlet.

"*Fuck!*" I gasped, stamping the ground. I tried to pull away, but he held me fast, even when I clawed at his fingers.

"It's done now. It's done," he said, far from my hearing.

The mana was still burning its way through the channels of my body.

My vision whitened at the edges. Ears buzzed. Pressure built behind my eyes like they might burst.

"We have to go. The harpies can smell blood. They're coming."

I was shaking now, badly. Tears slid down my cheeks. I didn't remember crying.

I forced breath through my teeth. One. Then another.

*Stay here.*

*Stay upright.*

*Stay in your body.*

Val guided me to my horse. Said something I couldn't hear. One hand at my back, the other catching the stirrup.

I braced. Lifted my leg.

Slipped.

"Got you," Val said as he caught me, then pushed me up into the saddle.

He mounted fast, clean, eyes already skimming the ridge.

The harpies weren't diving.

Not yet. But they would.

"Go," he said.

It sounded like he was underwater.

The horses bolted, fast and hard.

Neither of us looked back.

# CHAPTER SEVENTY
## *Nothing to Give*

*"The man who weeps in front of others reveals his weakness—and invites defeat."*
—Maxims of Command and Discipline

Succamos 22, 1231
*Valerius*

We cleared the pass at a gallop.

The cliffs fell away behind us, jagged stone giving way to open white and brittle trees. The road widened by degrees beneath the snow. We didn't slow. Not yet.

Aleaia hadn't said a word since we fled the wyvern's corpse. Just made those little barely audible, tight gasps she couldn't quite bite down. I'd heard that sound before, in legionaries trying not to beg for mercy.

I glanced back once.

She was upright. Eyes fixed ahead. Her reins slack in one hand, the other buried in snow inside my gauntlet, packed around that mangled, blistered palm.

It wasn't right.

Aleaia could ride for days. Could fight bleeding, freezing, half-starved. She'd done it before.

But now, she looked like she was about to fall apart in the saddle.

*Damn it, woman, you weren't supposed to tether yourself to the fucking wyvern.*

She'd agreed to the plan. I was supposed to be the bait. She was meant to be the blade. And then she'd done whatever she wanted anyway and nearly immolated herself in front of me.

I gripped the reins tighter.

Later. I could shout at her later, when she wasn't halfway to collapsing.

I wished there was somewhere closer than Praedia, which lay half a day south. I knew the town. It was small, fortified, the kind that had a healer and half a dozen people who owed me favors. Just a little farther—

There was a thud behind me.

I turned.

Her horse was still moving, barely a few paces behind mine.

She wasn't in the saddle.

"Ah fuck! Aleaia!"

My heart slammed once, hard against my ribs.

I reined in and wheeled around, dismounted fast and hit the snow at a run.

She lay face down in the drift, hair tangled, limbs half-curled like her body hadn't known which way to fall.

*Gods.*

*Gods, no.*

I dropped to my knees beside her.

No blood. No visible wounds.

I touched her cheek, her neck—warm. Too warm.

"Aleaia. Wake up."

I turned her onto her side.

Her lips were parted. Breath shallow, too fast. Sweat beaded at her temples despite the cold. Her pulse kicked against my fingers, wild and erratic.

Not bleeding. Not injured.

Something else.

Her arms twitched. Muscles jerking beneath her skin in tiny spasms. Her jaw clenched. Her eyes drifted, lids half-lowered, fluttering.

I took her good hand in mine, pinched down on a nail.

Nothing.

*Fuck, that's bad.*

I didn't know what this was. No training had prepared me for it.

"Come on, luce mea," I whispered, leaning close. "Stay with me."

She didn't answer.

I slid my arms beneath her and lifted her from the snow. She was limp. The weight of her full, unresisting body.

My horse hadn't bolted. He stood steady, waiting.

I slung her in front of the saddle, belly down, torso draped over the horse. It wasn't graceful, but it was fast.

I vaulted up behind her.

Once I was seated, I pulled her upright into my lap, her head tucked tight against my chest, legs dangling over one side. Her burned hand pressed between us, radiating heat through both our cloaks.

"Got you," I murmured.

I gathered the reins with one hand.

And we rode.

Her horse had slowed to a walk ahead, saddlebags still strapped tight.

I should've kept going. Every second counted, but I knew what was in there.

Her father's copy of *The Song of the Stars.* The only thing she'd never let go of. The last thing he ever gave her. She would never ask. Would never even mention it. But if she woke up and it was gone—

I nudged my horse forward, guided him alongside hers. Leaned down over the saddle, found the right pouch. Unbuckled the flap.

There it was. Leather-worn, weather-darkened, strap still looped around it like always. I grabbed it and tucked it into my own saddlebag.

Then I turned the horse south and spurred hard.

The snow blurred beneath us.

The horse breathed hard, flanks heaving beneath us, hooves pounding like war drums against the frost, but I pushed him faster. Harder.

I was running out of time.

I could feel her heat where her cheek rested against the edge of my gorget—unnatural, wrong. Too hot, even through steel and padding, like iron pulled straight from the forge. Her breath was shallow against the hinge of my cuirass.

I shifted her against me, cradling her weight with one arm, reins gripped tight in the other. Her head lolled beneath my chin. She didn't stir.

"Come on," I grated out. "Just hold on."

The horse stumbled once. Recovered.

I didn't slow. I wasn't thinking about the animal. I couldn't. If it died beneath me, I'd walk the rest of the way with her in my arms.

*Is this what it felt like?* I wondered. *For her, back in Cortueca, when I was half-dead and burning with fever? When she found me and dragged me back from the edge? When she slept beside me while I raved?*

She'd carried me. Carried me in a hundred ways I hadn't seen.

Her body jerked once in my arms—small, a twitch.

I leaned forward into the wind, sheltering her with my body, and kicked the horse again.

It was foaming at the mouth. I couldn't stop until we reached the town.

Praedia came into view just as the sun began to sink. Low stone walls. Smoke curling from chimneys. A watchtower barely visible through the snow haze. The gates were open. A few guards stood at the entrance, already turning as they heard us approach.

"Hold!" one of them called.

"Gods, it's Prince Valerius! Make way!" another shouted, already stepping back.

The horse was flagging beneath me, foam slicked down his flanks, breath coming in gasps, hooves striking the stone with less rhythm now, more desperation. Every stride shook.

He got us through the gate. Into the square. And then I felt it—the falter. The give.

I pulled hard on the reins. Hauled him to a stop.

Dismounted.

Pulled Aleaia into my arms as I slid from the saddle.

The moment her weight left his back, the horse collapsed, dropping hard to his knees, then over onto his side. Probably dead, but I didn't have time to check or to care.

The guards shouted. One of them ran toward us—a younger soldier, reaching instinctively.

"Here, let me take her."

I shifted back, tightening my grip.

"She needs a healer!" I snapped. "Now!"

A voice answered behind me—clipped, feminine, Aeltyrian accented. "Here. Bring her in."

I turned. A woman stood in the doorway of a squat building just off the square. Simple tunic. Gray cloak. Hands already outstretched. Incolumium manacles locked around her wrists. Older, weathered skin, lines carved deep.

"I'm Amareth. The healer you're yelling about."

I carried Aleaia up the stairs and straight through the door. Inside, the air was warm. Herbal. Clean.

The woman shut the door behind us, bolted it, and swept a hand toward a table. "Lay her there," she said. "I need to see the wound."

"She's not wounded." I eased Aleaia down carefully. "It's… something else."

The woman brushed back Aleaia's hair, then reached for her hand and removed the gauntlet.

She froze. Not at the burn. At the blade. Her eyes were locked on the sword at Aleaia's hip. Then her face. Then me.

"The Fellglow Blade?" she whispered. "I thought it was a myth."

"*She's* real," I said. "And she's dying. Please, help her."

The healer studied me for a long moment. Then gave a single, resolute nod. She rolled up her sleeves and went to work, fingers already moving to the buckles of Aleaia's cuirass. Her voice was brisk, professional.

"She's burning." The healer rested her hand on Aleaia's forehead. "We need to strip her down."

I obeyed, hands shaking as I unbuckled her belt.

"What happened?"

I unfastened the straps of her cuirass. I'd done this dozens of times traveling with her. Never like this. Never without her awake, smiling, teasing, pulling me close. Things I'd done before in love, I did now out of fear.

"She's not wounded. Not like you're thinking." My voice shook and felt thick.

A sharp look. "How, then?"

The healer loosened the underlayer at Aleaia's throat. Her fingers brushed flushed skin, still radiating heat. She looked up at me. How could I explain without condemning her?

"What happened to her, boy?" she asked in Aeltyrian. "Stop being scared. I can't help her if you don't tell me. And I think I already know the most dangerous part."

I hesitated. Calculated the risk. Then answered in kind, though I wasn't quite as fluent. "She… she can pull magic from things. She calls it a tether."

The woman stilled.

"She drew from a wyvern. She didn't stop when it died. Now she's like this."

The healer exhaled. No more questions. She folded a cloth beneath Aleaia's head, dipped another into cool water, and laid it across her brow.

Aleaia's left hand twitched. Just the fingers at first. A spasm. Barely visible. I froze.

The healer's voice changed. Calm. Quick. "Roll her onto her side. Now."

I moved without thinking. One arm behind her shoulders, the other at her knees. I shifted her carefully onto her left side.

Her arm jerked again. Then the whole limb went stiff, locked straight as a blade.

"What's—what's happening?" I swallowed hard.

The healer braced her head. "She's fitting. Don't panic."

Her back arched. Legs kicked once, then again, harder. Uncontrolled. Her breath came fast—

Then stopped.

She wasn't breathing.

I couldn't either.

"She's—" I said. "She's not breathing!"

"Hold her." Amareth was quiet but firm. "Keep her from falling. I'll do the rest."

I wrapped my arm around her middle, pulled her close enough to feel every tremor. Every spasm. Every jolt that threatened to tear her from me. Her teeth clenched, grinding with effort.

"Stay with me, luce mea," I whispered. My voice caught. "Please… don't leave me in the dark."

The convulsions worsened.

And I couldn't stop it.

Couldn't shield her.

Couldn't fight it.

All I could do was hold her. And pray she didn't die in my arms.

Then—

Stillness.

An awful, breathless stillness.

And—

A gasp.

Another.

Her ribs rose under my arm. Shallow. Uneven. But real.

She was breathing.

The healer touched her throat, feeling the pulse. "I need to stop a second fit."

She turned to the shelf behind her, grabbed a small glass vial, pulled the stopper with her teeth, and leaned over the table.

"She can't swallow," I said hoarsely.

"I'm not giving her anything to swallow, lad."

She dropped two clear drops onto a curled leaf and tucked it beneath Aleaia's tongue.

"Absorbs faster. Mouth's dry. She won't choke."

I nodded. Or tried to.

"She's through the worst," she said. "But she'll be slow and confused if she wakes."

The room tilted.

Slight. Sudden.

Not around her. Around me.

Everything was too quiet now. Shadows crept at the edges of my vision.

The healer glanced up. Her face tightened.

"You need to sit. Now."

"I'm fine."

She didn't wait. Dragged a stool from the corner. Kicked it behind my knees. "You're white as milk. *Sit.*"

I sat. Elbows braced on my thighs. Head bowed over her good hand, held between mine. I could still smell her skin, her sweat. Still feel the twitching beneath my arm. Still hear the sound of her breath stopping.

I'd thought the worst moment we'd have was the arrow. I was wrong. This was worse. This wasn't bleeding I could stop with my hands. Wasn't a wrong I could right with a judgment. Wasn't a dream I could dispel with logic. Couldn't draw my sword and fight it off. Couldn't even name it. All I could do was hold her and feel it tear through her.

And when the panic finally drained—

When the only sound left in the world was her breathing—

I bent forward.

Touched my forehead to the back of her hand.

And cried.

Not loud, but deep.

Violent. The kind that shatters a man from the inside—slow and wrenching, until the sound finally breaks free.

I had never cried like that.

Hadn't known I could.

She was alive. But what would be left?

I had never been so afraid in my life.

# CHAPTER SEVENTY-ONE
## *First Sword*

*"The First Sword does not lead with strength, but with discipline.*
*He does not pull the heir to safety—*
*he stands where the danger is greatest, and clears the path."*
—Annals of the First Sword

Succamos 22, 1231
*Aleaia*

Darkness.

Heavy. Thick as wool. Pressing in around me like fog that wouldn't lift.

Heat licked beneath my skin. Wrong. Sick.

My chest ached.

Bees were in my bones, buzzing.

My mouth tasted like metal and ash.

And then—

Sound.

Not clear. Not sharp.

Just pain, made voice.

Not quiet tears. Not the kind men hid behind their hands.

Real weeping. Raw and guttural. The sound of someone breaking.

He was close. Kneeling maybe. Or sitting on the floor.

I wanted to reach for him. My body wouldn't move. Nothing did. But the sound tore through me all the same.

A woman's voice spoke evenly. Calm. A gentle weight in the air. "You did everything you could."

*Am I dead?*

A pause. His breath hitched. "What if—what if she—"

"She's still here because of you."

*I am still here.*

Wherever *here* is.

I fought the fog. Pushed against it with everything I had left. My throat burned. My chest was a cracked cask, leaking heat and light and something worse.

And I spoke. Dry and broken and thick on my tongue but it was the only word I could think of to say.

*"Vedrānos."*

A gasp. His.

I forced my eyes open. The world swam, blurred with firelight and shadow. He was there. At my side in an instant. Hands cupping my face like I was something fragile.

"Aleaia?" His voice broke around my name.

I blinked slowly. Heavy-lidded. Couldn't keep them open long. But I saw him.

And I said it again. Stronger this time. Slurred, but sure. *"Vedrānos…* who hurt you?" My voice dragged. "I'll kill 'em. Give me m'sword."

His breath caught. One sharp, helpless sound, and then he clutched my hand tight, pressing it to his heart like it was the only thing tethering him in place. He bent over me, shoulders shaking, and I felt him kiss my hand, soft and reverent as a prayer.

*"Putaevim amirim ti aetarnem, amor mea."*

Another kiss, warm against my knuckles.

*"Adorat esa itara, vesae."* His voice cracked. *"Arim tam teraris. Areo tam teraris."*

And again—his lips brushed the backs of my fingers like he could anchor himself through touch alone.

I wanted to hold on. I did. But something was wrong. The pressure—

Gods, the pressure.

It coiled beneath my ribs like molten rope, hot and climbing, and I couldn't hold it much longer.

"She's going to have another fit if she doesn't purge some of the mana," a woman said nearby. I tried to find the source but couldn't see well enough.

He sniffed, wiped his face roughly with his hand, then leaned in close to my ear.

"Aleaia, luce mea," he said, voice still shaking. "You have to let some mana go, or it's going to kill you."

I understood some of the words. But they didn't make sense. They floated, detached and strange.

"I don't know." My words ran together. "I don't know."

"Then listen to me. You have to bleed it slowly. Not all at once. Just enough to stop the surge," he said, steady now. Calmer than I felt. He cupped my cheek. "You've been doing so well, controlling your spirit fire. Use that."

I blinked up at him.

Fire. Yes.

I could do that.

I thought I could.

I nodded, barely.

Behind him, the woman's voice cut through the haze again. "Not in here," she said firmly. "She'll burn the roof off."

Val didn't hesitate. "Let me take her outside. Is there somewhere safe?"

"The back courtyard. Through there."

He lifted me. My head drooped against his shoulder. My pulse still thundered. The pressure behind my ribs climbed again with every heartbeat, sharp and wrong.

"It hurts, Val," I said softly.

"I know. We're going to fix it."

He carried me through a narrow corridor, kicked a door open, and walked down a short flight of steps into the open dark. Snow crunched beneath his boots. The wind bit hard against my skin. And still, the mana surged. Boiling, it crowded me from the inside out.

He didn't hesitate. Didn't set me down. He dropped into the snow himself, settling me in his lap like he'd done it a hundred times before. One arm wrapped around my waist. His chest braced my back. I could feel the rise and fall of him, the steadiness of his breath against the chaos in mine.

Then the rasp of leather and the whisper of steel drawn free—the Fellglow Blade.

He laid it across my lap, its glow faint but unmistakable. Then he wrapped my hand around the hilt, his hand covering mine where the wrapping met the crossguard.

The blade flared the instant I touched it, bright enough to throw silver across the stones. Val's arm tightened around me for half a breath.

"This'll help," Val said softly. "Don't think about how. Just… point where you want it to go."

It was strange, casting this way. I usually needed my other hand to direct the flow properly. But that hand throbbed uselessly, too raw to use. I swallowed, hard. "I can't—"

"You can." His voice was steady. "Just listen to me. I'll aim. You bleed it."

"Where?" I asked.

He guided my hand, pointing the blade outward toward a patch of half-frozen grass along the garden's edge.

"There," he said. "Focus on that corner. Don't force it," he said softly at my ear.

I focused. The pulse rose again. Not panic now—power. Twisting behind my ribs. Crawling up my spine.

He spoke quietly at my ear. "Just breathe."

I looked at the place Val had chosen.

Then he whispered, "And let it burn."

I tightened my grip on the blade. A thin line of spirit-flame ignited from the blade to the grass. Steam hissed up from the wet ground. I shivered from the release. The surge bled out in a wave—not all of it, but enough.

The pressure in my chest ebbed. My head cleared, just a little. I leaned back against him, gasping.

Val let the blade drop into the snow beside us, his arms tightening around me.

"You did it," he murmured into my hair.

"No," I whispered. "You did."

# CHAPTER SEVENTY-TWO
## *Open Wounds*

*"I've seen men torn open by blade and spell—*
*but nothing prepared me for what I saw, knowing I couldn't make it stop."*
—the private journal of Valerius di Calesia

Succamos 25, 1231
*Aleaia*

The door creaked open. The evening light hit me like a blade. Too bright. Too loud. Even the air felt raw. I stopped on the threshold, blinking against daylight's last rays, my bandaged hand drawn to my chest. The healer had warned I might feel weak for a few days, but this wasn't weakness.

It was hollowness. Like I'd poured out too much, and now I was smaller.

Val hovered beside me, not quite touching, but never more than half a step away. He hadn't said much since the courtyard. Just stayed close. Guarding the perimeter of me like I was something still at risk of breaking.

The town of Praedia stretched out quiet and cold. Low-roofed homes. Thin trails of smoke curling into a slate-blue sky. It looked ordinary. Safe. Nothing about it felt that way.

Behind us, the healer said something about rest, herbs, and more salve for the burns. I nodded without really hearing.

Val took the bundle from her hands, thanked her softly in Aeltyrian, and reached for me. His fingers brushed my palm before he laced them with mine.

We crossed the square in silence. My legs didn't feel like mine.

"I can walk," I said after a few paces, because I could feel the tension in him. The urge to catch me with every misstep.

"I know," he said.

The Second Prince of the Calesian Empire. Legate of the Second Army. Holding my hand as we crossed to an inn, like it was nothing. Like he wasn't risking whispers, questions, sedition charges.

Reckless. But I couldn't think about that right now.

I couldn't stop thinking about the blistered skin of my hand, red and swollen and slick with weeping fluid. I kept running through all the things I needed my hands for. Gripping reins. Drawing a blade. Pulling a bowstring.

Touching Val.

I hadn't slept after the first day, not truly. Just drifted in and out beside him while he stroked my hair.

Val was angry. He hadn't said so, but I knew. He didn't show it in the way most men did. Not with shouting or sharp words or brooding silence.

Just more restraint. The kind born of fear, or grief he hadn't figured out how to bury.

I remembered none of it, but he'd seen me have the fit. The way the healer described it gave me chills. And I remembered what it was to be the one sobbing at his bedside.

I hated knowing I'd put him there, crying for me.

"Maybe we'll stay out of an infirmary for a solid season now," I said, trying to lighten it.

He didn't so much as crack a smile. That's how I knew I really fucked up this time.

We crossed the muddy street to the inn. Val spoke briefly with someone at the door, then led me up the outer stairs to the second floor. He unlocked the room and held the door like always.

It was simple. Modest.

Darkness pressed at the windows. I lifted my right hand—the good one—and summoned a small silvery flame. It came quickly. Naturally. Light and warmth flared into the room.

I could feel my mana like a deep well now, not the shallow trickle it had been before the wyvern. The hollowness made sense then. There was more room than I needed.

As the firelight spread, I took in the modest space. A bed just large enough for two was tucked in the corner. A small table and two chairs stood before the hearth. Our armor and saddlebags were stacked neatly along the wall. No luxuries, but everything we needed.

Everything his saddlebags had carried.

Mine were gone, lost when I fell. Which meant everything here—from the new bags to the fresh linen shifts inside them, to the tunic folded over the chair—had been bought by him. Chosen by him. For me.

And they weren't just practical. They were soft and warm and expensive.

*He spoils me,* I thought, blinking hard.

Maybe he didn't know how to buy plain things. Or maybe he just loved me.

Val set the healer's parcel down on the table.

A knock followed a moment later. He opened the door to receive two steaming buckets of water and a stack of clean rags from the innkeeper.

"That was fast. Thank you," Val said.

The innkeeper nodded and pulled the door shut.

Val set the buckets down and pulled a bar of soap from one of the saddlebags. He shaved off thin curls with his belt knife, dropped them into each bucket, and stirred until the water frothed.

Then he nodded to one. "This one's yours."

He didn't wait for a reply. Just stripped off his shirt and stepped to the other bucket to wash, quiet and methodical.

I lingered near the hearth, eyeing the steam. My skin prickled with cold and sweat. I peeled off my tunic and shift, wincing at the stiffness in my muscles. They joined the soiled pile near the fire.

Unlacing my braies was easy. Pulling them down with one hand was not. After a few silent, frustrating attempts, I gave up.

"Val."

He paused mid-wash, water dripping from his face, a rag in hand. His eyes met mine—steady. Waiting.

I gestured toward the garment clinging to my hips. "Please."

Gods. I hoped I wouldn't need him every time I had to piss.

Or shit. I would die if he had to pull them down so I could shit.

Val set the cloth aside and dried his hands. He crossed to me without a word or hesitation. He eased the trousers down with care, focused on the task. Then he helped me step free.

"I'm sorry," I said softly.

"No need to apologize," he said. His smile was faint, soft, almost sad. "Anytime you want me to take your clothes off, just ask."

He kissed my brow and turned back to his own washing.

I cleaned myself with slow, careful movements, then knelt beside our bags, digging through the weight of new fabric. My fingers brushed something rigid—too solid to be cloth. I pulled it free.

*The Song of the Stars.*

My throat tightened. He'd thought about this—remembered it in the panic—and saved it. I pressed it to my chest for a breath, then slid it back into the saddlebag.

Then reached for the shift and managed to pull it free. It was hard to sort out one-handed but my pride wouldn't let me ask him again.

Val crossed the room without a word, took the shift gently from my hands, and helped me into it, guiding my bandaged arm first, then tying the delicate laces at the neck.

"Thank you," I murmured.

He smiled again, smaller this time, and kissed my cheek.

I sank into one of the chairs by the fire, comb in hand, and reached for the leather strip binding what was left of my braid. My fingers fumbled. The knot gave way with effort, leaving the thick rope of hair tangled and limp over my shoulder. What had once been a source of pride—long, dark, and glossy—now hung dull and snarled, heavy with dried sweat, blood, and days of neglect.

Val had just finished dressing when he looked over. He took in the comb, the state of my hair, the tension stiffening my shoulders. Without a word, he crossed to me.

"I can—" I started.

"Not one-handed," he said. "It needs a wash."

Then he knelt beside me, reached into the cleaner bucket, and dipped a tin cup into the water. He poured it gently over the back of my head, angling the flow so it ran into the empty washbasin he'd placed beneath me. His fingers followed, working through the tangles first, then lathering in soap. He massaged it gently across my scalp, rinsed, poured again. Over and over. No rush. No words. Just warmth, water, and the steady hands of a man trying to do something, anything, to make it better.

I thought about his words in my waking moments.

*"Putaevim amirim ti aetarnem, amor mea. Adorat esa itara, vesae. Arim tam teraris. Areo tam teraris."*

I hadn't understood the words at the time. But now, with a clearer head, I knew what they meant.

*I thought I lost you forever, my love. Don't do that again, please. I was so afraid. I am so afraid.*

Gods. I had wounded him so badly.

A wave of guilt rose in my throat. "I'm sorry to be such a burden."

Val didn't answer. He just picked up the comb and kept working at my hair.

I let out a breath. "Are you still angry with me?"

His hands slowed. Not long. Just a moment. "Yes," he said.

The honesty of it made my stomach twist, even if it was unsurprising and well-deserved.

"You didn't follow the plan," he said. "You weren't supposed to tether to it."

"I didn't know what it would—"

"That's right. You didn't. You weren't supposed to take that kind of incalculable risk. And I had to watch it nearly kill you."

He resumed combing, slower now. "I've seen soldiers bleed out on the field. I've seen men die by fire and frostbite and every kind of blade. None of that prepared me for—for *that*."

It hurt him so much, even now, that he couldn't say the words.

"You are not just the heir," he said, quieter now. "You are not just some—some weapon with legs. You're *Aleaia*. You're *luce mea*. You're—you're *it* for me. Losing you would be—"

He took a deep, shuddering breath.

"And you nearly died in my arms because you didn't trust me to do my part."

I bit the inside of my cheek. "I did trust you. I do."

"Then why didn't you listen to me?" That hurt more than I expected. I would've rather he shouted than deliver it so softly. "I've encountered wyverns before. I knew what to do. What works."

I turned toward him slowly.

"I didn't know if you'd live long enough to strike," I said, voice unsteady. "I saw the tail go through your shield. I saw it knock you back. I thought—" I swallowed hard. "I thought if I didn't do something, you'd die."

His mouth tightened. His eyes didn't leave mine. "I told you I could handle it."

"I know," I said. "But I couldn't take the chance. Because you're it for me, too, *vedrānos*."

His brows drew together. "You would've sacrificed yourself."

"I wasn't trying to," I said.

"Are you sure?"

I realized that he thought it was like Asena's den. Thought I'd made the same choice again. Walked in alone, ready to die. And maybe once, he would've been right, but not this time.

"I was trying to end it." I shook my head. My thoughts were still cloudy, and it had come out wrong. "Fuck. End the wyvern, I mean—not my life. Fast. Clean. Before it could kill you. Before it could kill both of us. And if not that, I thought I might keep it paralyzed."

He sat back slightly, comb still in one hand, the other resting on his knee. The firelight flickered across his face.

"You don't get to do that," he said firmly. "Not alone. Not when you already agreed to the plan we made together."

"You made that plan," I said.

"And you agreed to it."

Gods, he was so fucking sharp, and so damned calm about it.

"I didn't mean to cut you out."

"But you did," he said. "You made the choice alone. And I had to carry your half-dead body through the snow, wondering if you'd ever open your eyes again."

I felt my temper swell, up from my gut and out of my mouth before I could check it. "Well now you know how it feels, don't you?"

Val went still.

I regretted the words the moment they left my mouth. My stomach dropped. Gods. What had I done? "Val—"

"How it feels," he said, voice flat. "You think I don't remember—" He stopped. Shook his head. "Don't do that. Don't use that against me. I've apologized so many times."

I closed my eyes. Shame hit fast and hard. "I didn't mean it like that."

"Yes, you did." He wasn't cruel. Just honest. "You were trying to hurt me because you felt guilty. And you did."

I opened my mouth. Closed it again. There was nothing I could say that wouldn't make it worse. So I said the only thing I had left. "I'm sorry."

A few heartbeats' silence passed between us.

Then, he said, "I know."

He didn't move right away. Didn't touch me. Just let the hush settle between us, raw and open. Eventually, the tension softened. I felt it in his next breath.

"I think," he said slowly, "we're both terrified of losing each other. And we're both terrible at handling it."

My lips pressed into a line. He was right.

"I love you," I said softly. "That's all I was trying to do."

"I know." His hand squeezed mine just once, firmly. Then, steadier, he said, "And I love you."

He set the comb aside and stood, then offered me his hand. I took it, let him guide me to the bed, let him help me under the cover. He climbed in after me and pulled me against his chest. My head fit beneath his chin. He wrapped one arm around my waist, the other behind my shoulders, holding me like something precious and breakable.

His breath warmed my hair. I could hear the rhythm of his heart, steady and solid beneath my cheek. His fingers slipped through my hair again in slow, absent strokes. "Go to sleep, amor mea."

My eyes closed. The warmth of him beneath me, the sound of his heart, the rise and fall of his chest, lulled me toward sleep.

I wanted so desperately to go home.

Home.

Aeldunon.

I thought about when we first arrived there, how different things had been.

"You never told me what that boy said to you," I said, voice thick with exhaustion.

"A boy?"

"At the orphanage. In Aeldunon. You said you'd tell me later."

He chuckled softly, breath stirring my hair. "I did, didn't I? I suppose it wouldn't hurt to tell you now."

I waited.

"But I won't."

My eyes cracked open. "Why not?"

"Because you haven't told me what *vedrānos* means."

I groaned. "You're going to make me tell you, aren't you?"

He didn't argue. He just waited, calm and vexingly patient, the way he always did when I tried to deflect.

I sighed.

"*Vedrānos* is..." My throat tightened. "It's a... noun form. From *vedran*—'to bind.' And the suffix *-os* means 'my,' but in this case it's not... not ownership. Not like... um... a goat. Or boots. A person, but—gods—not like a slave—fuck, I'm making a mess of this. It's sacred. Because you say it with a long 'ā,' you know. It means... bound-one. Sacred-bound. My sacred-bound one." I took a breath. "You."

There. It was done. Said aloud. No taking it back now. My heart pounded. My mouth was dry.

"I read it in my mother's journal," I added quietly. "The way she talked about my father. One word to say so much."

I couldn't meet his eyes. I wanted to sink through the mattress. My face burned. My hand pulsed. And my heart, laid out like a fool's, was raw and vulnerable.

Then I felt his hand, the careful slide of his fingers beneath my chin. He tilted my face up until I met his eyes. There was no anger in them now. No teasing, either. Just something stunned and quiet and achingly full.

"You've been calling me that," he said softly. "Since Dicowica."

And then he kissed me. When he pulled back, he didn't go far. His forehead rested against mine.

"I hoped it meant something like that. Part of me worried you were just calling me an idiot, but that didn't make sense."

He drew me closer. His arms wrapped around me, tucking me beneath his chin. He held me like I'd just handed him something priceless.

After a moment, he mercifully shifted the subject.

"The boy said, 'She's very pretty. Are you courting her?'"

I latched onto it like I was drowning. "And you said, 'Not yet,' as if you were so confident you'd win me over?"

"Was I wrong?" I could hear the smile in his voice.

"No," I said. "No, you weren't. Though I loved you already. Even then."

His sigh, low and warm, settled into my skin like a promise.

"Wait," he said suddenly. "What does *bradarcam* mean?"

My eyes narrowed. "Where did you hear that?"

"So it's a real word, then?" He didn't answer the question. Not that I needed it. I knew where he'd heard it.

At least this was easier to explain. "Long time ago, it was *bradarcaram*—*brader* for 'fool,' and *caram* for 'I love.' Somewhere along the line, it shortened to *bradarcam*. It means 'beloved fool.'"

He laughed. "You called me that in Cortueca."

"I did," I said. "You were trying to get up and come find me."

"I don't remember that part. Just your voice. Calling me that."

"You couldn't even stand," I said.

He was quiet for a long moment. "Oh, I believe you. I would've tried anyway."

"I know."

He stroked my hair once, still damp from the washing, then let his hand rest there, on the side of my head. His palm muffled everything else, and all I could hear was the slow, steady beating of his heart.

I didn't know what waited for us in Avitum.

But that night, there, in that room, in his arms—

I wasn't afraid.

# CHAPTER SEVENTY-THREE
## *Homecoming*

*"The hearth remembers even those who come back changed—*
*though its fire may not burn for them as it once did."*
—The Breath of the World

Succamos 38, 1231
*Aleaia*

"Ah. Home. Cassius has been busy, I see." Val eyed the staked corpses lining the road like milestones of horror.

The road to the capital should have been alive with traffic—carts burdened under sacks of grain, herders swearing at bleating flocks, merchants' wagons rumbling over the road. Instead, it was still. Near silent. The only sounds were the clack of our horses' hooves on cobblestone and the harsh caws of the ravens feasting on the dead.

It was no surprise that people were staying away. If I'd had the choice, I wouldn't have come near the place either.

"At least it's cold," I muttered, shuddering as we passed another bloated corpse.

The face had half-sloughed away, jaw hanging in a black-lipped scream, eyes already pecked out until only cavernous pits remained. The gut had ruptured, spilling viscera in ropes down the stake. It reeked of spoiled meat, shit, and iron.

I pulled my cloak up over my nose, muffling my voice. "This is more..." I couldn't find the word in either of the languages I knew. "It's *more* than usual."

"Vinculatores' work," Val said.

As we neared the gate, something moved on the battlements—a flicker of white against the gray.

The fucking white raven. Eyes like obsidian, watching. Staring at me.

*It's just a bird,* I told myself. *Strange, yes, but nothing to fear.*

Val drew a long, slow breath, then nudged his horse forward.

Ahead, the guards lowered their halberds into ready position.

"Halt, stranger!" one shouted.

Val pushed back his hood. That was all it took.

Recognition flickered. The guard lowered his weapon and pressed a fist to his chest. "Your Highness. Forgive me. I didn't know."

The gates groaned open, and the stink of death followed us in.

The capital felt just as lifeless as the road that led to it. We took the main thoroughfare toward the center and the castle beyond.

I glanced around, uneasy. Life, or something like it, carried on, but the rhythm of the city was gone. Black cloth shrouded the eaves. The few people we passed hurried with heads down, wrapped in mourning grays and blacks. There were no barkers shouting prices. No music drifting from taverns. No children chasing dogs through alleyways.

Even the air felt wrong. Heavy. Waiting.

A town crier's voice rang out across the square, clipped and precise. "His Majesty lies in state. Only essential business is to be conducted until the forty-fourth day of Quiestra. Any violators of this decree will be punished according to their station."

That was how Val learned his father had died. From the town crier. I wondered if I should offer condolences or congratulations.

I turned to him, searching his face for some sign of what he felt. I knew he hated this place, but his face was unreadable, eyes fixed ahead.

"Well," he said at last, voice clipped, "we'll go to the castle. The infirmary first. Then we deal with my family."

We passed through the city without hindrance.

At the stables, we dismounted and I took both horses' reins and led them to the stablemaster, keeping my face shadowed under my hood. I hoped, between that and the road dust, that my face was unrecognizable. Just for good measure, though, I left my sword with Val, stooped my back and limped slightly.

"Whose animals are these?" the old man asked.

"Caius Varro's," I rasped. He was abominable, so I didn't feel even a little bad for using his name.

"Didn't know he was in the city. Huh. Never had much of an eye for horseflesh, I suppose."

I bit back a smile. "I'll collect them in a few days."

Val had lingered near the edge of the yard, tucked in shadow where the risk of recognition was lower. I joined him, and together we crossed the courtyard toward the infirmary.

"Convincing," Val murmured. "Though the limp may have been a touch theatrical."

"Next time I'll let them recognize you," I said sweetly.

I glanced up and caught the twitch at the corner of his mouth.

When we reached the infirmary, I peered through the frosted glass and caught sight of Hesta at her desk, hunched over parchment. My heart gave a nervous flutter. The sight of her, familiar and kind, hit harder than I expected.

I left the window and eased the door open a crack.

"Hesta," I said softly.

No response.

Just a bit louder, I called again. "Hesta."

"What can I—" She looked up. Bewilderment flickered across her face for half a second before her eyes widened. Her voice caught. "Aleaia Dieter?"

"Shhh! Keep your voice down," I hissed, glancing over my shoulder. "Is anyone else here?"

Hesta shook her head as she stood and moved toward the door. "No, but what in the Creator's name are you doing here?"

I waved to Val. He slipped inside, shutting the door behind him without a sound.

"I need you to look at my hand," I said, already unwinding the bandage with careful fingers. "I burned it… about fifteen days—"

"Sixteen," Val corrected from his place near the door.

That made her look up sharply. She hadn't really seen his face until then. Her expression shifted, and she dipped a quick curtsy. "Your Highness."

He returned the nod with quiet formality.

"*Sixteen* days ago," I confirmed.

I didn't mention the wyvern, or my inheritance. Not because I didn't trust her—I did—but saying it aloud would make her complicit. If the Vinculatores came asking questions, I wasn't about to give them a reason to drag Hesta into it.

She took my hand. As she peeled back the layers of cloth, her eyes narrowed at the sight of the healing flesh of my palm.

"Couldn't get to water in time," I said, guilt lining the edges of my voice. "We packed it with snow. A healer treated it with honey in Praedia. We've been changing the dressings twice a day since."

My heart skipped a beat, remembering the care in his touch, the steadiness of Val's hands, how he never once flinched from the sight of it.

"You're lucky," she said, angling my palm toward the light. "Snow can make it worse. But it looks good. You took good care of it."

"Should I keep using honey?"

"Just on the open spots." She gestured for me to sit at the table. "I'll dress it and send you with more. How long are you staying?"

"A few days," Val said. "We're here for the funeral."

Hesta turned back to her task—cloth rustling, water trickling, the practiced rhythm of her work. When she finished, she bundled up salves and fresh bandages, then looked at me again—not as a healer this time, but as someone who had once known me before the blood, before the frost and fire.

She reached for me suddenly and pulled me into an embrace.

It knocked the breath from my lungs. I stiffened, then returned it, steadier. Firmer.

"I wish I had come to see you under better circumstances."

"I expect this with you," she said, a rueful laugh warming the words. "Take care, my dear. I want to see you before you leave."

"I will, I promise."

Val and I stepped back into the gray morning, and the cold slapped my cheeks the moment the door shut behind us. Together, we crossed the bailey toward the great hall. I could feel the tension gathering in him like a tide.

At the base of the steps, just around the corner and out of sight of the guards, Val stopped.

I looked up at him.

I never forgot how beautiful he was, but sometimes, it caught me off guard—how hard-cut and elegant, even when the weight of duty pressed into every line of his posture. The sharpness of his cheekbones, the clean line of his jaw, the deep green of his eyes—like they'd always known me and were still the only place I had ever felt at home.

Sometimes I wondered if he ever looked at me that way—if something in him ever stilled, breath held tight, just from seeing me there.

I could feel how tightly he held himself in the quiet.

He needed something from me.

I wasn't good at this kind of thing. Not like Lucius. But I tried anyway.

"Just think," I said gently. "When we're done here, we can go home. Back through the pass, in the last leg of winter. And then, shortly after we get home, it'll be Rudamos. Everything will be blooming and green and beautiful."

The corners of his lips twitched. "Can't wait."

I reached for his hand. Didn't take it—just brushed my fingers over his knuckles. "You don't have to prove anything, vedrānos. Not to him. Not to me. Not to anyone. You're already the man I chose. The one I'd choose again. Every time." I drew a slow breath. "So whatever happens in there… I'm with you."

He turned his hand and laced our fingers together.

"I know," he said, voice low and steady. "I remember every time I breathe. Every time I look at you." He hesitated, just a second. "Luce mea, you are the only thing that's mine."

Then he lifted my hand and kissed it, barely a brush of his lips, but he lingered there. Eyes closed, his lashes dark crescents against his skin, his face suddenly soft with something unguarded. Something sacred.

"All right," he murmured, releasing my hand. "Let's get it over with."

Together, we climbed the steps.

At the top, Val pushed back his hood once more. The guards recognized him at once and opened the doors without a word.

"His Highness Valerius di Calesia and his guard, Legionary Aleaia Dieter, Your Majesty," the steward announced.

I almost laughed aloud. I didn't expect them to call me Dame Dieter—but Legionary? Not even Praefectus?

I leaned toward Val and whispered, "Demoted the second I stepped through the door. Impressive efficiency. Think they'll make me polish Cassius's boots?"

The faintest smile ghosted across his lips. Just for a second.

Inside, it was colder and darker than the street—fitting, given that Emperor Claudius lay in state at the center of the dais, wreathed in herbs and flowers that did little to hide the sickly-sweet rot of death. None of it had helped much.

Cassius sat nearby in mourning black, the picture of somber nobility. He didn't rise.

"Ah, brother," he said. "I wasn't sure you'd bother."

I'd never seen him up close, never heard his voice before. It was disconcerting, how alike they sounded. Cassius was older, colder, and crueler, and it came through in every word.

We knelt at the foot of the steps. It galled me that Val had to kneel to this man.

"Rise," Cassius said.

We did.

"Didn't have a choice, did I, Cash?" Val said.

Cassius scoffed. "No, I suppose not. And this must be the one the ashborn call *Dame Wolfsbane*?" He didn't bother to hide the sneer. "Explain to me what's been happening in my province. Knighting the locals now? Beheading respected prefects from good, wealthy families?"

*His province. Disgusting.*

"Ah. Well, to the first, it might be difficult for you to understand, but I recognized her exceptional service," Val said evenly.

"The northerners are servants, Valerius. Raising them up only confuses them. And you."

I kept my eyes forward. My fingers itched for the Fellglow Blade. Just to see the look on Cassius's face when it answered my call.

While I drained the life from him.

But I didn't draw it or set it alight or burn him, as I wanted.

"Pulcher ordered the slaughter of an entire village. He needed putting down." A muscle ticked in Val's cheek. "I stand by my decisions."

"You'll address me properly," Cassius said coolly. "You're in my house."

Val bowed, deeper this time, with a flourish. "I stand by my decisions, *Your Majesty*. My sincerest apologies. I wasn't aware I'd already missed the coronation."

Cassius laughed. Hollow. Joyless. "Come. Say goodbye to our father." He gestured toward the corpse.

Val climbed the dais with slow, measured steps. I think he would rather have shoveled a camp shit-trench after a season-long siege.

I remained below, eyes on him as he approached the bier.

He spent a long moment, standing there, staring. I couldn't see his face. Couldn't guess what was going through his mind.

Then he turned away and faced his brother.

Cassius wrinkled his nose as he looked him over, gaze lingering on Val's hair. "You look like a savage. I'll send someone to clean you up."

My brow furrowed. He looked fine to me. The longer length suited him.

"No need," Val said. "I'll be in my chamber, if it pleases Your Majesty."

"Nothing would please me more."

Val bowed once more, then turned and descended the steps. His eyes found mine.

I bowed to Cassius for a long moment before I fell in beside him. We passed into the corridor. "A heartwarming reunion indeed."

He didn't answer, but the curve of his mouth said enough.

We reached his chambers, and the moment the door shut behind us, he dropped the bar into place. The thud echoed like a seal between us and the rest of the palace.

It felt like stepping into another world, one that still remembered warmth and comfort. The fire was already lit. A tray of food and wine waited near two chairs, and the bed looked like it could fit five grown men with room to spare. Shelves lined the walls, each one heavy with books.

I crossed to the corner with the armor stands and began stripping off my armor, piece by piece. My hand still twinged when I flexed it, but at least I could use my fingers again. Val did the same beside me.

Once free, I snagged a piece of cured meat from the tray and bit into it. Val came up behind me, arms sliding around my waist, breath warm against my neck. He kissed just beneath my ear, and I tilted my head without thinking.

"With the household in mourning," he said, "we're to stay in here. Five days until the procession. Until then…"

"Well, before we do anything else, I absolutely must have a bath," I cut in, wrinkling my nose. "You too. We're filthy."

"You're right," he said, laughter threaded into his voice. "But by tradition, we're not supposed to bathe during the mourning period."

I stared at him. Though we'd arrived only for the last half, a full mourning period lasted a decadium. "No bathing for ten days?"

He nodded.

"That's…" I didn't even know how to finish the sentence. A decadium of sweat and grief in heavy wool was practically a war crime. Anvallans did love self-flagellation, though.

"One of many traditions I have no intention of following," he said. "But I can't exactly summon a tub up here without drawing attention."

"Then we're just not going to—"

"I have a plan. I know a place."

I glanced at the Fellglow Blade. "Is there somewhere I can stash my sword? I don't think it's wise to keep it in the room. Not with… everything."

"Bring it," he said.

We gathered clean clothes, soap, bath sheets, my sword, and a lantern. Then he took my hand and led me from the room.

Sneaking through the castle proved easier than expected. Grief hung thick in the corridors, and those few we passed were too deep in their duty to notice us.

Val led me down the servants' stairwell. At the bottom, the air turned still and damp. We passed into a forgotten cellar, where dust coated every beam and barrel and cobwebs hung like lace from the rafters.

To the left, a heavy wooden door waited.

Val unbarred it and stepped through first, holding it open for me.

I hesitated at the threshold. "What happens if someone bars the door after us?"

"That's only happened to me once," he said, then frowned. "Actually… twice. But neither time was recent."

I gave him a long look.

"No one comes down here. We'll be fine."

I followed him. I would have anyway.

The passage narrowed as we descended further, the stone walls slick with condensation. Somewhere in the dark, water dripped in slow, rhythmic beats. Each drop echoed sharp and hollow.

Then we stepped into a cavern that stole my breath.

A vast pool stretched out before us, its surface steaming gently in the lantern light. The water was clear enough to see the stone beneath, and a fine mist curled upward into the vaulted dark like spirits rising from the deep.

Stalactites hung from the ceiling like the teeth of some sleeping giant. Droplets fell from them, catching and fracturing the light. Pale fungi bloomed along the far wall, glowing with a soft blue-green shimmer.

"It's beautiful." I stepped forward slowly.

"It's my secret," he said, voice quiet. "I used to come here when I was younger. No one ever thought to look for me in the undercroft."

"No one else knows about this?" I asked.

He shrugged. "I'm sure someone does, but I've never met them or heard anything about it."

Whatever misgivings I'd had about mold and locked doors vanished. I let go of his hand and ran down the natural stone steps in my bare feet, drawn like a moth to flame.

"Careful," Val called after me. "It's slippery."

I barely heard him.

I set my sword aside and stepped straight into the pool, still fully clothed. The water climbed fast up my legs, my hips, my ribs. It was deep enough to swim. I longed to float and let it carry me, but my hand couldn't get wet.

Still, I wasn't about to waste this. I sank beneath the surface, careful to keep my injured hand lifted, and came up with a gasp. The heat wrapped around me like a second skin. Scalding. Soothing. The ache in my back and shoulders began to melt, drawn out of me as though the spring itself knew what I needed.

"Gods, this feels so good," I said.

Val followed more cautiously, setting the rest of the supplies on the flat rock near my sword. He stripped and stepped into the water with a hiss.

"You're supposed to take your clothes off first," he said, mock-chiding. "And are you even allowed to get your hand wet? Hesta's going to kill you."

"First of all, my clothes are filthy, too."

"We could have them laundered. Like civilized people."

"And my hand is dry." I lifted it for inspection. "See?"

I splashed water at him with my good hand. That earned a quiet laugh.

I found a smooth shelf of stone near the pool's edge and settled onto it, the water lapping just beneath my chin. My injured hand rested on the ledge, safely dry, while the heat soaked into the rest of me, easing knots I hadn't known I'd been carrying.

My gaze drifted toward Val, and stayed.

He wasn't trying to tempt me. He was just bathing. Focused. Methodical. Scrubbing the road from his skin, his neck, the long lines of his arms. There was nothing performative in it.

Still, I couldn't look away.

"Enjoying yourself?" he asked, not even glancing back.

Heat climbed into my cheeks. "Yes, actually."

"Glad to be of service."

When he finished, he crossed the pool toward me, water rippling at his waist. He offered me his hand. "All right. Your turn."

I took it, let him pull me gently to my feet. He peeled the soaked fabric from my body and tossed the garments aside. Then he lathered soap on a cloth and handed it to me. I scrubbed until my skin was pink and the grime was gone.

"If you turn around, I'll wash your hair," he said.

Of course I did. I'd never give up an opportunity to let him knead my scalp.

He worked up a lather and began massaging the soap into my hair, slow and careful. His fingers were patient, coaxing the tension from my skull as if they'd always known how. I closed my eyes and let them.

"You're so good to me," I murmured, drowsy from the warmth, from the quiet.

He shifted behind me, smoothing his hands down the length of my hair, working the lather through until it clung in pale, dripping ropes.

"You should rinse," he said softly.

I ducked beneath the surface and came up blinking water from my eyes.

He was wading into the shallows now, his back to me, lantern light catching on the wet line of his shoulders, the long sweep of muscle down his spine. Every movement was effortless, like he had no idea how ruinous he looked.

And maybe he didn't.

But I did.

I wanted to climb into his lap.

To ride him until we were both shaking.

I wasn't thinking about softness. I was thinking about how long it had been since he'd been inside me. About how I didn't care if the stone scraped my back or bruised my knees. I just needed his hands on my hips and his mouth on my throat and the weight of him, real and heavy and mine.

He turned then, slow and unhurried, and caught me staring.

His eyes darkened. No smile. No teasing.

Just a quiet, "Come here."

And I did.

# CHAPTER SEVENTY-FOUR
## *Divine Order*

*"Let the union of flesh reflect divine order—measured, sober, and silent. That which arouses frenzy belongs to beasts, not to men."*
—On the Duty of the Faithful, Temple Doctrine of Anvallus

Succamos 38, 1231
*Aleaia*

Val sat on a shelf of stone near the edge of the spring, head tipped back, hair clinging wet to the curve of his neck. Mist curled around him, lantern light sliding over wet skin and deepening every shadow.

The water carried me to him, slow and silent.

He watched through lowered lashes. Held out a hand as I neared.

I took it.

He pulled me onto his lap, letting me straddle him. His hands found my waist. Mine, his jaw.

My mouth opened against his, tongue brushing his in bold, wordless demand. He moaned low, arms locking around me.

I felt him harden beneath me. Felt the slip in his control when I bit his lower lip.

I pulled back, met his eyes. "If you're going to take me—then *take me*."

His expression darkened. He knew what I meant: I didn't want gentle. I wanted *him*.

The water rippled as he shifted, rising from the stone in one fluid motion, lifting me clean off his lap. My breath caught. He turned, laid me down on the edge of the pool. Warm stone met my bare skin.

Then he was on me, kissing like he'd waited too long. Like he'd forgotten how to stop.

I reached for him. He caught my wrists and pinned them overhead.

"You sure about that?" he growled. "Because if you want slow and sweet, now's your chance to say so."

I arched up against him, breath sharp. "I said what I meant, vedrānos."

He kissed down my neck, my throat, every word pressed into skin. "You're playing with fire."

I laughed. "It's the only element I know."

His teeth scraped my neck, then sank into the curve where shoulder met collarbone. I gasped and he licked the sting away, slow and careful, like he wanted me to feel every heated pass of his tongue.

Then lower, to my breast. His mouth latched on without warning, tongue circling, sucking, gliding across skin until I writhed beneath him.

My hips lifted, seeking friction, but he held me still.

"Already squirming," he said.

Then he released my wrists, only to take my hands and guide them to the edge of the shelf beneath my hips. His touch lingered on the bandage on my left hand.

"Doesn't hurt?" he asked.

"It's fine," I whispered. "I'll tell you if it hurts."

"Hold on, then," he said. "Don't move unless I say."

I gripped the stone, pulse hammering. "What if I do?"

He looked up through wet strands of hair. "Then you'll have to wait."

I met his gaze. Said nothing.

He knelt in the water, hands gliding down my thighs to push my knees apart.

"Keep them open." He dragged his thumbs up the insides of my thighs, feather-light, until my hips twitched. "Let me see you."

He didn't touch where I needed him. Just looked, as if memorizing the flush of my skin, the way heat pooled between my legs. His breath came sharp, drawn between his teeth.

"I should take my time with you," he murmured. "Make you beg for it."

"I won't."

"Oh, you will."

And then—finally—his mouth found me.

My gasp echoed off the cavern walls, head tipping back as his tongue caressed the center of me in long, deliberate strokes that left me trembling. He started slow, circling that sensitive knot of nerves like he meant to worship and punish at once.

When I moaned, he pulled back.

"Val," I sighed.

"You asked for this," he said, dark and steady. "That means I get to tease. You'll take what I give you, when I decide you've earned it."

I nearly cursed him.

He knew exactly what he was doing—drawing me up and pulling back again and again like it meant nothing.

And the worst part?

He enjoyed it.

It wasn't cruelty. It was control—precise, intentional. The more he held back, the more I wanted to fall apart for him.

He kissed the inside of my thigh, then bit down just hard enough to make me gasp.

Then his mouth was back on me, hands gripping my thighs to keep me still as his tongue moved in measured rhythm, until my toes curled and I started to shake.

And then he stopped.

"Tell me what you want," he said against me.

"You know what I want," I gasped.

"I want to hear you say it."

I clenched my jaw. Shook my head.

He didn't move, didn't speak. Just watched me.

"Fuck—Val, please," I choked out. "Let me come."

*So much for holding the line.*

He looked up, mouth wet, eyes smoldering, laughing softly at my broken defiance. "There she is."

Then he was back—tongue sure, fingers relentless, mouth drawing every sound I didn't mean to make out of me.

I came with a cry, legs tightening around his shoulders, body arching so hard I nearly lost my grip on the stone. He didn't stop until I was gasping, spent, thighs twitching.

He rose from the water—muscles tight, skin flushed, cock hard, eyes locked on me. He looked like restraint made flesh, every line of him strung taut with ravenous tension.

"Turn over," he said, voice raw.

I obeyed, limbs shaking as I shifted into position, knees on the shelf.

Then he hauled me to the edge, bent me forward over the stone, my palms catching on the slick surface. His hand skimmed down my spine—possessive, claiming.

I arched into it, panting.

He wanted my defiance. Needed it. He didn't know it. Not fully. But I did, and I'd give it to him.

My legs still trembled from release, but I braced on my elbows, glanced back over my shoulder, and smirked. "That all you've got?"

His eyes flashed. "You want to test me?"

Fire bloomed across my arse before I saw him move, a sharp crack echoing through the cavern.

I yelped—more shock than pain—but gods, the heat it left behind, the dizzy rush of sensation surging straight between my thighs.

"Gods, yes!" I laughed, breathless. "That's it? I thought you were trying to break me."

The second landed harder. Perfectly placed.

My hips jerked as I moaned. "Fuck!"

Then I felt him behind me—his grip on my hip tightening, the other hand twisting into my hair and tugging my head back just enough to bare my throat.

And then he thrust into me.

One hard stroke, buried to the hilt—without warning, without mercy.

The stretch was sudden, aching. I cried out, my fingers scrabbling for purchase on the stone.

He filled me completely, dragging fire through every nerve.

"You like it like this?" he growled against my ear. "Bent over. Dripping for me. Too full to think?"

"Gods, yes—harder—"

He drove into me again—deep, ruthless.

"Say it louder."

"Yes—fuck me, Val—don't stop—"

He grabbed my shoulder, holding tight to my hair like he meant to break me apart, driving into me. Each thrust landed fierce and devastating. The sound of us filled the chamber, wet and obscene, every slap of skin an echo of what he was doing to me.

"You think you're in control?" he said, voice low, dangerous.

"I am," I laughed, breathless.

"That how you think you got me here? With that fucking mouth?"

My voice came sharp enough to cut. "You're here, aren't you?"

The next slap landed harder. Controlled. Flawless.

I laughed again, half-gasping. Gods, it felt so good when he did that, especially while he was still inside me.

"You're just begging me to break you open," he said, voice tight with need. "Say the word."

He gripped a handful of my hair and tilted my head back. Not cruel. Just enough to hold me exactly where he wanted me.

"What did you think I wanted, vedrānos?" I gasped.

His hand found the center of my back, pressing me down, arching me into position. My hips hit the stone. I bent forward with a gasp, belly pressed to the warm, wet surface.

"Val—"

I barely got his name out before he drove into me.

Hard. Deep.

"Gods—" I cried, voice breaking.

He didn't give me time to adjust. He just took relentlessly, like he meant to leave his name inside me. Carve it into my spine with every stroke.

"This what you wanted?" he ground out. "You want it rough?"

"Yes—Val—"

"You'll be lucky to walk out of here," he rasped.

His grip twisted in my hair, dragging me upright just enough to bare my throat again.

"All you had to do," he said, grunting between thrusts, "was ask nicely."

I laughed, mocking. "Never."

"No?" he echoed, incredulous.

I smiled over my shoulder. "No, *my lord*."

"Say it," he growled. "Beg for it."

"No," I said, breathless. "You want it too badly."

He let out a low laugh of disbelief and thrust into me so hard my breath caught. It spilled into a moan as he rutted into me with everything he'd been holding back.

He grabbed my wrists, twisted them behind my back with one hand, and used the leverage—pulling me back onto him, forcing every inch deeper.

I cried out and he pressed his other hand over my mouth, palm flush to my lips, smothering the sound.

"You think you can keep smarting off like that?" he growled into my ear, breath hot against my skin.

My eyes rolled. I whimpered against his hand.

I could have broken free if I wanted to.

But I didn't want to.

He released my wrists only to grab my hips, pinning me in place as he drove into me over and over—deeper each time, chasing the part of me I hadn't given yet.

Then he bit—shoulder, neck, the curve of my spine. Not breaking skin, but hard enough to make me cry out.

I moaned into his palm—then bit *him.*

He laughed. Dark. Delighted.

I think that's what he wanted all along.

He let go just enough to pull my arms back, hooking his forearm through the crook of my elbows to keep me upright as he drove into me from behind. His other hand clamped across my throat—not choking but feeling.

"You feel that?" he panted. "This is what happens when you don't say please."

"Then I'll never beg again," I panted.

He drove into me, hips snapping against my arse in a bruising rhythm. Each thrust was more ruthless than the last. Every stroke hit deep, angled to tear another sound out of me.

"You love this," he snarled. "Being taken like this."

His hand slipped from my throat to between my thighs, fingers finding that swollen, desperate place—working it in tight, punishing circles.

"Tell me what you want," he demanded.

I gritted my teeth. Shook my head.

He pulled out and released me all at once.

I dropped my forehead to the stone. Hit the ledge once with the flat of my hand. I trembled. "Not yet."

"So defiant today," he growled.

A breath later, the thick weight of him smacked against my arse—once. Twice. Three times. Slow. Filthy.

I shuddered.

"Say it," he whispered, brushing my hair aside. "And I'll give it to you."

I looked back at him, saw his smirk. "Fuck you," I panted.

"No, *I'll* fuck *you* till the only word you remember is my name."

"Then do it."

He didn't touch me at first. Just leaned in—slow and close—his body crowding mine, cock hot and hard between my thighs.

Then he kissed me, soft and sure, right between the shoulder blades.

I shivered.

His mouth brushed the same spot again, and his voice dropped. "I won't let you come again until you beg me for it."

Then he grabbed my hips and thrust into me again—harder than before, savage and deep. My hands scrabbled against the stone, barely catching hold, my body jolting with every thrust.

One hand slid forward, cupping one breast, squeezing until I gasped.

A broken sound caught in my throat, traitorous and thin.

He let go of my hip to press my upper body down, chest to stone, spine arched into the curve of him. One hand clamped around my hip again, the other sliding to the back of my neck.

Heat flashed low in my belly, made my fingers curl against the stone.

"You love this," he rasped. "The way I claim you. The way you give yourself to me—every time."

He pinched one nipple between his fingers with enough pressure to make my back arch. I clenched tight around him.

I whimpered—writhing, panting, so close again—but still defiant.

"Say it."

I shook my head, cheek scraping the wet stone. "Make me."

His hand left my neck long enough to slap my arse—sharp and flawless. I cried out. He did it again. Then once more.

I moaned—gods, I moaned—and he bent over me, mouth brushing my ear.

"You're already trembling," he said, rough with heat. "Already soaked. And you still won't give me this one thing?"

"Never."

"You're going to remember this," he murmured. "Every time you mouth off. Every time you make me work to hear it."

Then he thrust into me.

I didn't know how long it lasted—his voice in my ear, his hand in my hair, driving into me like he meant to erase every trace of defiance.

And maybe he was.

Because I felt it slipping—my will, my breath, everything but him—until there was nothing left but the rhythm of his body in mine.

"Is this what you wanted?" he snarled at my ear.

"Yes," I moaned. "Yes—Val—gods—"

I felt his hand in my hair, holding tight, close to the scalp.

"You're mine," he growled. "Say it."

"I'm yours," I gasped.

Harder.

Faster.

"Louder."

"I'm yours, I'm yours, vedrānos! Please," I gasped. "Please, Val—please—I need it, I need it—gods, let me come—please—"

He inhaled sharply and I felt it, the words striking something deep in him. A jolt. A shiver in his breath. "Good girl."

Another wave rolled over me, ripping through me like lightning through a tree, splitting me from the inside. His name tore from my throat, jagged and raw, as my hands scrabbled uselessly at the stone, trying to hold on to something, anything. My body clenched hard around him, pulsing with each crashing wave.

And when it had passed, he pulled out, leaving me whimpering at the loss—empty, aching.

His mouth brushed my ear. "On your knees."

Then he guided me down to kneel in the water before him. One hand slipped into my hair, threading wet strands between his fingers as he tilted my face up.

I knew what he wanted. And gods, I wanted to give it to him—every breath, every sound, every part of myself. I hadn't done it often—only once—but I didn't care.

I wanted him undone. Wanted him to come for me. *Because of* me.

I looked up, heart racing. "Tell me what you want."

His fingers tightened. "Your mouth," he said, voice rough. "And don't look away."

I parted my lips and leaned in, tongue flicking slow across the tip. He hissed through his teeth. I kept my gaze on him as I circled him, savoring the weight, the heat, the way his breath trembled when I drew him in.

"That's it," he managed, already unraveling. "You ask, and I—fuck—just like you're… doing… now—"

I must have been doing a good job of it, if he couldn't even speak.

My hands braced against his thighs, anchoring me as I took him deeper, watching his composure slip.

"That's it," he groaned. "Just like that. Gods, you look—"

He didn't finish. I hollowed my cheeks and pulled back, teasing the head with a flick of my tongue.

"Let me see," he choked out. His hand tightened. "Let me see how much you can take."

I sank without hesitation—took him *almost* to the base. He twitched. His thighs tensed beneath my palms.

Then, he moved. Just a little.

An instinctive thrust.

Too far.

I gagged.

He let go immediately. "Aleaia—shit—I didn't mean to—are you all right?"

I coughed once, eyes watering, throat tight, but I nodded. "I'm fine."

He looked stricken. "I shouldn't have—"

"No." I laughed softly. Swallowed. "It's all right. Actually… I think I liked it."

He blinked. "What?"

Heat flared in my cheeks, but I held his gaze. "If you want to do it again… I don't mind."

He stared at me, something raw and worshipful in his eyes. Then his hand came to my cheek.

He understood.

This wasn't about control. It was about trust.

"If it's too much," he said, "push me away. I'll stop."

My heart ached. "I will."

His hand slid back into my hair and guided me forward again.

This time, he moved slowly. Testing. Listening.

A ragged groan tore out of him.

I matched his rhythm, let him guide me. Moaned around him. Felt him twitch again.

"Fuck," he gasped. "Your—mouth—"

I pulled back to tease him, tongue slick, savoring the way he looked at me. Then I took him again—to the back of my throat.

He jerked, hips twitching. His hand fisted in my hair, breath catching on a hiss.

"Aleaia," he groaned. "Just like that."

I let him use my mouth the way he needed. His rhythm grew hungrier, each thrust deliberate and possessive. Spit slicked my lips, my chin. I could feel it drip down my neck.

And gods, I wanted it. Loved it.

He was quiet for a moment—lost in it—but he kept his eyes on mine. Wild. Awestruck. "I've never—fuck—never had anyone like this. Only you. It's always been you."

Then—suddenly—he pushed deeper.

My throat stretched full. I looked up, breath held, eyes locked to his as his whole body went still, like I'd knocked the air from his lungs. He held me there. Just a heartbeat.

Then he started to pull back.

I didn't let him.

I braced my hands behind his thighs and pulled him deeper, tighter. My throat fluttered around him.

"Fuck, Aleaia—look at you—taking me like you need it."

He shuddered hard, hips jerking, fingers tight in my hair.

Then something broke.

He lost the rhythm. Gave in.

"Let me," he rasped. "Let me—finish like this."

A plea.

Eyes locked to his, I gave the smallest nod I could.

That was all he needed.

His grip turned desperate. Hips snapped forward—sharp, instinctive. I gagged once, then again, and he groaned, a guttural sound ripped from his chest.

"That's it," he choked. "Gods—I love you—I love you—"

His body coiled tight, every muscle trembling. He gave a low, broken cry—my name torn from him like a vow—as he buried himself to the hilt.

"Aleaia—*amor mea*—luce mea—" he groaned, voice cracked and reverent. He pulsed against my tongue.

And gods, the way he came apart for me—trembling, giving himself over—

Made me feel like a goddess.

When he finally stilled, I eased back—slow, careful. I swallowed every drop, eyes never leaving his.

He didn't speak at first. Just knelt there in the steaming water, one hand steady at the back of my head, thumb of the other moving slow along my chin, wiping away what he'd left behind. Reverent. Careful. Like he still couldn't quite believe I'd let him come apart that way.

"I'm a mess." My breath hitched on a smile.

"No," he said, eyes softening. "You're radiant."

He cupped water in his hand, rinsing my chin and neck in slow passes, as if tending something sacred. Then he kissed me, warm and full, like he meant to give back every piece of what I'd given him.

When he pulled back, his brow rested against mine. His hands trembled.

"Are you all right?" I asked.

He nodded, then hesitated. "That night in the tent… when you…" He swallowed. "That was the first time anyone ever did that. Ever."

My eyes widened.

"And it…" His gaze swept over me. "It wasn't even something I knew to want."

"You're serious?"

He gave a single, tight nod. "It's against the Temple's teachings. 'Copulation is for duty. For heirs. Procreation, not pleasure.' That's what they teach. Especially for women. Purity, restraint, and discipline."

"I know those are the teachings. Didn't seem like anyone followed them."

"Most don't. They just make an offering to compensate." He shook his head, gestured between us. "But this? No one does this."

*No wonder my aunt died here,* I thought.

I leaned back a little. "That's tragic. But you had other women before me. What was the point, if it wasn't like this?"

"There weren't as many as you think," he said at last. "I was with Liora, five, maybe six times. We were betrothed, but even then… After her, I never saw the same woman twice."

I blinked. "Why?"

"They always wanted something. A betrothal. A title. A child they could name 'di Calesia.'"

"Which you did not give them?" I prompted.

He didn't answer right away.

"Right?" I asked. Gods help him if I found out he had secret bastard children all over Calesia.

"I did not." His breath left him slow. "It was just easier not to stay."

My brow furrowed. "So, what are brothels for?"

He looked away. "Release. Same as pissing or eating. You pay, you finish, you leave."

I frowned. "That's not what I heard about the camp followers."

"They're different," he said. "They stay for coin or protection. The men talk. Boast. But it's never real. They don't love those women. They don't even see them. Just something warm and willing between the legs."

"Where did you learn…?" I arched a brow, let my gaze drift to his lips.

He huffed a laugh—soft, a little embarrassed. "I can't believe I'm saying this to you."

I waited, patient. The same way he always waited when he knew I was hedging.

He rubbed the back of his neck. "Some women let me. Some were horrified. Sent me straight from their rooms like I'd offered them plague."

I laughed. "No!"

His eyes lit up then. He must have realized I wasn't as scandalized as he thought I would be. "Yes. And there was this book, *On the Proper Bearing of a Gentleman*. Forbidden, of course. Incredibly useful."

"You really are a scholar at heart."

He gave a crooked smile. "The point is that what I have with you is unheard of." His hand came to my jaw again, still tender despite the heat that lingered between us. "I never thought it could be like this."

Something flared in me. Hot. Triumphant.

"No wonder so many of your men want to stay in Aeltyria," I said. "If that's what they leave behind. We don't have those kinds of inhibitions. We're taught to love with everything we have. Life is short, sometimes it's miserable, but with the right person, it can be beautiful too."

He smiled faintly. "That explains a great deal about you."

I arched a brow. "Meaning?"

"You're free."

I brushed his hair back. I didn't know what to say. I'd thought he was so polished, inscrutable. But he was just a man. Undone by kindness and hunger and a little bit of heresy.

I wasn't even angry about the others. I thought I would be, but it just felt sad. What did any of it mean without love? He had the experience, but not the freedom. My heart had always been free, even when my body wasn't.

Maybe that's what made us work.

He took my hand from his hair and held it to his chest. "I love you."

"Oh stop, you're only saying it now because I—"

"No." His thumb grazed my knuckles. "I'm saying it because it's true. Because I love you in a way I didn't know was possible. Because you let me love you as myself. Because you're chaotic and wild, and you make me feel freer for it. I love you, Aleaia."

Something shifted in me. Not a falling. Not a surrender. A recognition. Like hearing a song I'd always known, and just forgotten the words.

I leaned in, arms circling his neck, and pressed my lips to his.

"I love you," I whispered. "Utterly. Without end."

# CHAPTER SEVENTY-FIVE
## *Quiestra's Twilight*

*"Beneath the weight of Quiestra, all things are made still—*
*by grief, or by fire."*
—Book of Hours, Funeral Canticle

Succamos 43, 1231
*Aleaia*

I'd stood through Calesian funerals before, but never one like this.

The procession wound through the capital in hollow pageantry. Hundreds of professional mourners led the way, tearing their hair, flinging themselves to the ground, wailing like Claudius's death had torn the sun from the sky. I supposed they'd earned their coin.

Succamos's twilight—Quiestra, the Calesians called it—cloaked the city in gray as we marched through it. I kept pace behind the bier, eyes on the back of Val's cloak, and let the spectacle move around me.

Ahead of me, he bore the weight of the father who had cast him out and cursed his name. The man who had blamed him for his mother's death and made him pay for it his entire life.

I hoped Claudius was screaming in Hel.

At the edge of a snow-dusted field, the bier was raised onto a vast wooden pyre. The vesperatorius—guardian of the dead—circled it once, inspecting the angles of the timber, the wrappings on the corpse, the tilt of the dead emperor's chin. Satisfied, he gave a shallow nod to one of Cassius's aides.

Val fell back beside me, face unreadable. He'd donned the mask the Empire made him wear.

Our fingers found each other beneath the folds of our cloaks.

Cassius stood closest to the pyre, his princely crown gleaming cold and menacing in the evening frost. He looked regal—still as stone, and just as lifeless.

It wasn't just loyalty to Val that set me on edge. There was something wrong with Cassius. Beneath the polish, beneath the solemn mask of heir and sovereign, I felt a deeper malice. Something dark and coiled. Something patient.

The monster was gone.

And something worse had taken his place.

Then I saw him.

Marcus, flanked by four slaves—two men, two women—approached the pyre. They wore nothing. Their wrists and ankles were shackled in incolumium.

Even the sight of that cursed, magic-stifling metal made my skin crawl.

I tapped Val's hand. He glanced at me, then dipped his head slightly.

"Marcus is here," I whispered.

He followed my gaze. "One would assume he's here to mourn, but…"

He didn't finish. He didn't need to.

We both knew what came next.

A human offering. Rare. Reserved for the deaths of emperors. I'd read about it in texts so old the parchment crumbled. But I'd never seen a funeral like this. Claudius had always loomed so large over my life—over Aeltyria—that he'd felt immortal.

The words scraped out of me. "How can we just… stand here?"

Val leaned close—probably closer than was wise in front of so many—breath warm at my ear. "Careful, luce mea. We're unarmed. We cannot stop this."

The fury hit so fast and hot it staggered me. The blade. I'd left it hidden in the cavern beneath the castle. *Godsdamnit.*

I'd cut Marcus's throat with the dagger in my boot if I had to.

I moved to step forward.

Val caught my wrist. Firm. Silent.

"Aleaia," he said softly. "If you move now, we die with them. Please."

It was the *please* that stopped me. That broke me.

He was afraid for me. I couldn't do that to him again.

So I'd swallow it down—the rage and the pain and the bloodlust. Save it for another day.

The slaves were led to the pyre. Bound to it.

The younger man lost control of his bladder. The vesperatorius struck him hard enough to knock him sideways.

I let every detail carve itself into my memory. The curve of the girl's cheek. The way the youngest man trembled. The older man whispering comfort through chattering teeth. The tilt of the older woman's chin, high and proud.

I would not forget them.

The vesperatorius touched a torch to the base of the pyre.

It caught fast.

Wails turned to high, terrible screams as flame kissed flesh. Hair shriveled. Skin split. The air soured with the smell of burning fat. And something in me cracked.

The smoke hit the back of my throat—and suddenly, it wasn't Claudius's pyre I smelled.

It was Ardhmor. And Catan Row and Caerlan and Lhannor.

The sick-sweet stench of charred wood and roasted flesh. The wind tugging at a scorched blanket still wrapped around a child's shoulders. The bodies hanging from the Elder Tree like some grotesque harvest—limbs rigid, eyes open.

And me, splattered in blood, hacking down Pulcher's men as they screamed, begged, fled. I hadn't stopped. Not when they fell. Not when they wept. Not even when they cried for mercy.

Val didn't look at me. He couldn't. But he clasped my hand in his, steady and sure.

My hand went slick with sweat. I knew he felt it.

I stood, rigid and shaking, as the pyre devoured them.

As it burned this, too, into my memory.

Every pop of rendered fat.

Every crackling bone.

Every scream—

Never again.

# CHAPTER SEVENTY-SIX
## *The White Raven*

*"She walks the threshold clothed in silence, feathered in white. The mother who does not weep—only watches."*
—The Song of the Stars, Cycle IX: The Cycle of the End

Succamos 44, 1231
*Aleaia*

I walked beside Val, silent and sore, exhaustion rooting itself deep in my limbs. My thoughts barely held together, haunted by images of the night—bodies thrashing against ropes, blistered skin blackening and splitting, mouths gaping around screams. I could still see the way their hair had caught, gone in an instant. Could still smell it. Burned flesh and scorched silk and the sweet rot of incense meant to hide the truth.

It clung to me. I'd carry it until the end.

When I first came to this city, I thought it was beautiful. Clean. Full of order and wonder. But I was a child then and that was a child's belief, the kind that dies quiet and early.

Avitum wasn't a marvel. It was a corpse—the decay inside hidden by nice clothes and a good wash.

Val's voice cut through the haze. "You look exhausted. Go on ahead and gather our things. I'll finish here. Then we can leave."

I stopped. Turned toward him, incredulous. "What is wrong with you? Are you ill?"

He blinked once. "What?"

My voice sharpened. "I'm not leaving you here. Aren't we staying for the coronation?"

He sighed and raked a hand through his hair. "I don't want to. I have a bad feeling about it—about all of it. Cassius was cruel enough as regent. Now that the crown is truly his…"

He didn't need to finish. I knew.

Cassius, encouraged by Renatus, had been gnawing at the leash to bring back the Inquisition. To purge the Empire of whatever he deemed impure. Of whatever frightened him most, especially if it lived in his own veins.

I thought of Mariana. Half-Calesian. Kind. Before we left, her magic had begun to stir.

If Cassius could use magic too, what then? Would he choose to crush anything that mirrored what he hated in himself?

"Aleaia?" Val's voice pulled me back.

"Forgive me. I was just wondering if he's… like me."

His expression went dark. "Gods help us if so." He glanced toward the mausoleum. "I wonder what my uncle would do to him. Or with him."

I shook my head. I didn't want to think about it.

Val exhaled through his nose. He didn't want to either.

We walked in silence, the weight of the last two days pressing down like armor made of stone. I could feel it in my joints, in my ribs. Each step slower than the last.

As we crossed the inner bailey, I stopped short. My gaze snapped upward.

The bird. Exactly the kind of omen he claimed not to believe in.

"Val," I said, voice pulled tight. "Do you see it? Up there?"

I pointed to the rampart. The white raven perched against the pale stone, feathers like polished bone in the morning light. It cawed once—sharp, hollow.

Val followed my gesture. "A white raven," he said, brows furrowing. "They're rare, aren't they?"

"We have to leave." My hand found his sleeve, gripped it. "Something isn't right."

He straightened, already adjusting course. "All right. I'll speak to Cassius."

"No." My voice caught, brittle in my throat. "No, we can't go in there. Something terrible is waiting, Val. I know it. We should just leave."

He didn't argue. Just let out a breath. "What about your sword?"

Val was right. I couldn't leave it in the castle, no matter how well I'd hidden it. Claudius had tried, for the last twenty-four years of his reign, to find it.

I pinched the bridge of my nose, muttering, "*Drenná glavil et sca, etta es aon cethí rodasí fie te tirven.*"

He raised a brow. "What's that about wheels and a cart?"

"'Endless rot and shit, that's all four wheels off the cart.'" I looked up at him, saw the way his brows knit. "Means we're thoroughly fucked."

"Eloquent. What do you want to do about your sword?"

"Could we leave, then try to retrieve it later? I'm out of ideas, Val, and we're running out of time."

He wiped a hand down his face, fingers lingering at his mouth. "I can't leave. They'll know I'm running and come after us both. There's probably a passage out of the keep and into the city for egress but…" He shook his head. "I wouldn't know where the endpoint is. It could come out anywhere. Somewhere worse."

I closed my eyes for a moment. Breathed deep. Panic wouldn't help either of us.

"All right," I said. "We go to the coronation. That gets us inside, at least. And if there's a feast afterward… that might be our time to slip out."

He didn't answer right away. Just stared at the ground, weighing it.

"It's the best we can do. Can't leave now. Might be able to leave then. What else could we do, Legate?"

He scoffed. "Adapt."

A curl of cold wind slipped through the bailey, threading past us like a whisper.

"Wait," I said. "Is there a servants' stair?"

Val didn't hesitate. "Yes. South wing, near the old laundry passage. Comes out in the scullery, just past the larder."

I stared at him.

"What?" he asked.

"You answered that suspiciously fast."

He kept walking. "I used to sneak out."

"Really?"

He glanced over. "Didn't want to be in the castle. You met my father."

I huffed. "Good point. In the arena, I thought I would rather fling myself off the balcony than be near him another moment. Did you get up to mischief?"

I just wanted to talk about something else, to stop the walls from closing in.

"Sometimes." He shrugged. "Not really. It was just the only time no one watched me."

We crossed the bailey without drawing notice. Mourning left everything heavy and slow. Most of the household was already inside preparing for the coronation or stationed in the upper halls. No one questioned us.

The servants' stair was exactly where he said—tucked behind a low door set into the stone. Val tried the latch. It creaked open on hinges that likely hadn't been oiled in a decade, and the scent of lye and old smoke wafted out.

The stairwell beyond was narrow and steep, lit only by a thin shaft of gray light from a slit window near the top. We slipped inside.

And stopped.

Voices. Footsteps. Then—

"Hold there."

Two guards waited at the bottom. One older, clearly a career soldier; the other barely grown into his armor.

Val moved ahead, slow and composed. "Checking security here. You really should have two men posted outside this door."

The older one looked uncomfortable. "Ah. See, I suggested that, Highness. No one listens to me. I'm just another name on the payroll."

Val didn't miss a beat. "Fix it."

He started down the steps.

The guard held up a hand, shook his head. "No one in or out this way today. Not even you, Highness. You'll need to return to quarters through the front hall."

He wasn't being disrespectful. Just careful. Almost apologetic.

The younger guard cleared his throat. "Begging your pardon, Your Highness. But it's strict today. Ceremony protocol."

Val kept his features carefully neutral, but I saw the flicker of resistance in him, the urge to press. He nodded once. "Well done. I was testing you."

"Thank you, Your Highness," the younger one said as they both bowed.

Val turned, ushering me out of the narrow stair ahead of him.

Outside again, I let out a slow breath. "Well. That went nowhere."

"They're locking things down," he muttered. "Cassius is nervous."

"Or smart."

He didn't disagree.

Then he offered me his arm, all calm civility. "Back through the front, then."

"Not like that, vedrānos," I said, patting his arm lightly. "We should maintain some pretense that I'm just your guard."

"Everyone has to know I'm fucking you," he said flatly.

*"Valerius di Calesia."*

"What? Anyone with eyes can see it every time I look at you."

I sighed. "Just walk. Next to me."

He didn't argue. I let him lead me inside.

Servants were already stripping away the mourning cloth from the great hall and replacing it with garlands. Banners. Gold. The keep gleamed with celebration It turned my stomach as we climbed the stairs.

Val opened the door to his chambers and barred it behind us.

It struck me then—the fierce need to feel his arms around me, to tuck myself into him and feel safe.

"I'm terrified, Val," I whispered. "Please… just hold me for a moment."

He didn't hesitate. He stepped forward and wrapped his arms around me, warm and solid and still.

"I know you don't think the dreams meant anything," I said, pulling back just enough to see his face. "But there's something else."

He nodded.

"The raven. The white one. When I was a girl, out hunting with my father, it came to me for the first time. I fainted the moment I saw it. Couldn't be woken until the next morning. No dreams. No visions. Nothing. And not long after… my grandparents died. Then Papa."

Val's brow furrowed, but he didn't speak.

"I've seen it since. A few times. In Tuath Forest. The day your own men tried to kill you. Twice since we approached Avitum. I know you don't believe in omens, or visions, or any of this, but I do."

He drew in a breath and let it out slow. "It could be coincidence. Maybe it was just… there."

I held his gaze. "You don't believe that."

"I do," he said. "The first time you saw it, when you didn't wake for a day—that was around the time of the plague, wasn't it?"

"Yes."

"I know you have a connection to things like that." He made a small gesture, fingers fluttering in mimicry of the way I cast. "Maybe that's why you survived. When they didn't."

"Papa didn't get the plague," I said flatly.

Val's mouth pressed into a line.

Even if he wanted to argue, he didn't. "Even if it is as you say, what can we do? We're stuck here."

"I think it warns of death," I said. "Or change."

He brushed his knuckles across my cheek, slow and tender. "Or it's just a raven. Beautiful. Unusual. But not a herald of doom."

"I've never told anyone this." My voice dropped, softer than it had been all day. "Only Papa. And only because he was there. And I was afraid. And until recently, I didn't have anyone I trusted enough. But I know what I saw. I know what followed."

His voice gentled. "Then I believe you. I just hope it's not what you think."

"So do I," I said. "But I'm not wrong."

He pulled me close again, arms tight around me, steady as always. "Then the best thing we can do is rest. I'll take the first watch."

After we parted, I lay down on top of the bed, cloak still wrapped around me, boots and belt untouched. The soldier's sleep. Ready to rise, to run, if we had to.

Val moved to the hearth, silent as ever, and coaxed the fire to life with flint and steel.

He didn't sit. He stood in the half-light, arms folded across his chest, eyes on the flame. The fire cast shadows across his face, drawing hard lines over his cheekbones, softening at the mouth.

Always watching. Always calculating. Always carrying more than he said.

Vedrānos.

I didn't tell him I loved him again. I didn't need to. It was in the way I let my eyes linger. The way my breathing quieted. The way sleep came not as escape, but as surrender—because he was there.

The last thing I saw was Val, still standing at the hearth.

Awake. Watching.

# CHAPTER SEVENTY-SEVEN
## *The Last Peace*

*"A heart chooses. A heart endures. And then it breaks."*
—The Breath of the World

Succamos 44, 1231
*Aleaia*

When I opened my eyes, the light had faded. Evening.

Val never woke me for my watch.

He let me sleep.

I should have known better.

He'd already dressed. Shaved, too. The basin still steamed on the stand beside the fire.

My clothes were folded nearby—a deep blue tunic, tailored to match his own. His colors. I moved to them, stared longer than I should have.

"How did you get this on such short notice?" I asked, brushing my fingers over the fabric.

He shrugged. "Coin is a strong motivator."

I washed, then dressed. The tunic lay soft against my skin, but the cloak felt heavier than it should. When I fastened it at the shoulders, my hands trembled. I flexed the left one, still tight from the healing.

The scar stretched across my palm like a pale starburst.

"Ready?" he asked from where he stood by the door.

I crossed to him and straightened his tunic, smoothed a wrinkle from his collar. He had to look perfect.

"There," I murmured. "Now we're ready."

I reached for the door.

His hand caught my arm.

"Wait."

Before I could speak, he stepped in close and brought his hands to my face.

Then he kissed me. Thoroughly. Like he meant for it to last.

My back met the door as his mouth moved with mine, his hands steady at my cheeks. I closed my eyes and wrapped my fingers around his wrists. Held on. As if the world might fall out from under us and this was the only thing keeping it in place.

When he pulled back, he didn't step away. He pressed his forehead to mine, his breath warm between us.

"I love you, Aleaia," he said. "I've loved you since the day we met. And I always will. No matter what."

My heart twisted. It sounded too much like goodbye.

"I love you too, Val," I whispered. I rose onto my toes and kissed him again—harder this time. Certain. Then I wrapped my arms around him, clutching him close.

He held me just as fiercely.

"You and I know what comes next. I'm going to do my best to convince him of our innocence," he said against my hair. "But if things go awry, I want you to focus on getting out. Get back to Aeldunon. Tell Lucius what's happened."

"Val, no—"

"We talked about this, luce mea. You can rally your people in a way I never could. They're yours. You don't need me to lead them." He swallowed. "I can't—not without you. If it comes to that, you run. And you don't look back."

I bit the inside of my cheek. I wouldn't cry. Not yet.

"I'm sorry I pulled you into this," he said. "I tried to protect you."

I pulled back just enough to meet his eyes. "You never forced me into anything. Not your service. Not your trust. Not this. Everything I did—for you, for us—was my choice. And I don't regret a single breath of it. Because I love you, too. Don't carry guilt for it."

"I won't," he said softly. "But I'll do whatever I must to keep you and Aeltyria safe."

He kissed me again—quieter now. Slower.

Like he meant to memorize me. Like the shape of my mouth might be the last thing he ever touched.

And I knew that no matter what he said, I would do whatever I must to protect him.

# CHAPTER SEVENTY-EIGHT
## *The Dragon's Maw*

*"The Creator alone commands the unseen.*
*All others who reach for it steal from the divine.*
*Let their names be forgotten, their souls sealed."*
—The Edict of Purity, 1205

Succamos 44, 1231
*Aleaia*

We parted reluctantly and made our way to the great hall.

The heavy oak doors stood open. A guard flanked either side, ceremonial stillness wrapped in polished steel.

The last time I'd walked through those doors, Claudius's corpse had dominated the room, the air as chilled as a tomb. I hadn't noticed how vast the space was then. The towering columns were draped in banners bearing the crest of Calesia—the crimson dragon, claws outstretched, snarling against a field of black.

At the far end, the dais waited like a gallows dressed for ceremony. Black velvet lined the steps. The dark ebony throne loomed like a challenge. Beside it, a pedestal bore the crown and ceremonial sword, jeweled and gleaming, scattering flecks of light across the chamber.

Nobles lined the carpet in perfect rows, perfumed and polished, their eyes sharp behind veils and jewels. Behind them, the Legates of the First and Third Armies stood at attention, crimson and black cloaks crisp beneath the dragon's glare.

Then the herald's voice resonated through the hall.

"Valerius di Calesia, Second Prince of the Empire and Legate of the Second Army, accompanied by his Aeltyrian mistress, Aleaia Caedmon, the last of House Caedmon."

The words landed like a blade.

Not Wolfsbane. Not Shield of Aeldunon. Not Dame. Just a man's whore in his colors.

The whispers slithered behind fans and gloves, rippling like rot beneath fine silk. I felt every eye like a knife under the ribs.

Discipline carried me forward where pride might have broken. I kept my face still, my spine straight.

A steward stepped forward, bowed to Val.

"This way, my lord," he said, gesturing toward the dais.

We followed, taking our place in the front row.

Each step felt heavier than the last. Val's posture was calm, if tense. He knew exactly what this was. Knew what would happen before we even entered.

This wasn't just a coronation.

It was a calling. A calling for their enemies to kneel.

"It wasn't me." His voice was low, urgent. "I don't know how they know."

"I do," I said.

Marcus. It had to have been him.

My heart pounded like a war drum. I could feel my magic stirring, hot beneath the skin. It wanted out. I forced a slow inhale. Buried it.

A trumpet blast split the air.

The great doors opened again.

"His Imperial Highness, Cassius di Calesia, Heir to the Throne, First Prince of the Realm, and Legate of the First Army, who shall today take his place as Emperor!"

A slow, rhythmic drumbeat began. Each strike echoed through the hall like a heartbeat muffled by silk and stone.

Cassius entered.

His retinue followed in the measured pace he set, armor gleaming beneath ceremonial silk. The procession looked less like a coronation than a military inspection.

As Cassius climbed the steps, trumpets blared again—sharper this time, a crescendo that struck like steel on steel—then cut off, clean.

Renatus was already there, beside the throne, cloaked in crimson and gold, robes sweeping the steps like blood pooling at his feet. Acolytes flanked him, robed in the same colors as the banners above.

Renatus raised his hands and voice, every word shaped for echo.

"By the will of our Creator Anvallus and the law of the Empire, we are gathered here on this hallowed day to witness the ascension of Cassius di Calesia, firstborn of Emperor Claudius, to the Imperial Throne…"

I barely heard the rest.

Cassius had dragged me into the light. Laid it out for the Empire to see.

*Here is the last heir of Aeltyria. Look where she stands.*

The damage was done. The rest was pageantry sharpened to wound.

Renatus turned to the throne. "This throne, carved over five hundred years ago, stands as a testament to the unity, strength, and eternal dominion of our Empire…"

Claudius had ruled from it with fire.

Cassius would wield it like a sword.

Renatus faced him. "Cassius di Calesia, you stand before the throne not as a man, but as a vessel of divine will."

There was nothing divine here.

Cassius stepped forward, regal in his polish, voice smooth as tempered steel.

"I stand before the Creator and the Empire to claim this throne as my birthright. I pledge not only to guide this realm, but to command it..."

The air had shifted.

Cold that didn't come from winter.

My mouth went dry.

My heart pounded like a war drum.

I wanted to scream.

To burn the castle down, starting with him.

Instead, I stood still.

"I accept the burden of this crown so that the strength of Calesia will endure, unshaken, unbroken." He paused. "Let the gods and the people bear witness. Today, our empire rises anew."

*Burden.* He meant authority. Control.

Renatus lifted his hands. "Kneel now and receive the blessings of our Creator."

Cassius lifted the ceremonial sword, turned, and lowered himself to one knee, the blade's point touching the polished floor, hands folded around the hilt.

A man swearing fealty to himself.

Renatus placed a hand on Cassius's head and began the invocation.

"Lord Anvallus, our Creator, we humbly beseech You to bless Your servant, Cassius di Calesia."

My eyes locked on the crown as Renatus lifted it from its pillow and held it high.

That thing would make him untouchable. Would cost us everything.

My gaze swept the hall.

I should've planned for this the moment we stepped inside.

Main doors barred.

Side exits flanked by Imperial Guard.

Windows narrow slits.

Archers in the upper balcony.

Too many eyes. Too many weapons. No armor. No sword.

We'd die before we reached the door.

I shifted. Loosened the clasp of my cloak.

I could shield Val. Maybe I could get him out. If not, buy him time.

Renatus lowered the crown onto Cassius's head. A shroud settling over the room. A moment sealed.

Renatus stepped back, voice ringing. "Rise, Cassius di Calesia, Emperor of the Eternal Empire, the Creator's chosen, and wielder of the sword of divine will!"

Cassius rose and stepped forward three measured strides, then turned to face the court. The throne loomed behind him. Every motion calculated. Polished to gleam.

His gaze swept the room. Found Val.

Held.

"Behold, Emperor Cassius di Calesia!" the herald proclaimed, voice like a blade unsheathed.

I dropped to one knee, cloak fanned around me, head bowed. Hiding.

I glanced sideways, just once, and saw Val, kneeling beside me. Head lowered. Faultless.

Cassius sat with the slow grace of a man who believed the world had been built to give him its throne. The ceremonial sword lay across his lap, gleaming. His fingers curled around the arms of the throne like he meant to mold it to his will by touch alone. Like it belonged to him by divine right. I suppose he thought it did.

Renatus stepped forward. "The Creator's will has been fulfilled. His chosen ruler sits upon the throne. Let none question his authority."

Cassius's eyes were still on Val.

"Rise," he said.

The assembly obeyed.

Renatus's voice rang out again. "Lords of the Empire, step forward and kneel before your Emperor to swear your oaths of loyalty."

The room held its breath.

Val stepped forward first.

Of course he did. He thought it might save us. Save me.

His cloak trailed like dark water, every step measured, back straight, gaze fixed. I felt the tension beneath the silence, beneath the stone. It clung to my skin like frost.

Every noble watched him. Every soldier measured his stride.

He reached the dais, dropped to one knee.

And then, I watched as he offered a vow he didn't mean.

"I, Valerius di Calesia, Second Prince of the Empire and Legate of the Second Army, do solemnly swear by the Creator Anvallus and upon my honor to remain true and faithful to His Imperial Majesty, Cassius di Calesia. I pledge my sword, my life, and my loyalty to the service of the Calesian Empire. May the Creator guide my hand and strike me down should I falter."

Cassius regarded his brother like a sculptor eyeing flawed marble. Cold. Measuring. The pause dragged just long enough to cut.

Then came the answer. "Rise, Valerius. Your loyalty is... acknowledged."

*Acknowledged.*

Val rose and walked the long path back to me in silence. I couldn't look at him.

Because I knew—

They were watching *me*.

Waiting for the last Caedmon to kneel.

If they wanted spectacle, I'd give it to them. I stepped forward.

As I passed Val, I whispered, "Forgive me, vedrānos."

He didn't move, but the air tightened between us.

"Aleaia," he warned.

He would hate this. He'd understand it, but still hate it.

They wanted a Caedmon. They'd get one. Just not the way they expected.

I walked to the base of the dais and stopped.

I lifted my chin and met Cassius's eyes across the gulf between us.

I did not kneel.

I let my voice carry.

"I am Aleaia Dieter Caedmon. Wolfsbane. Shield of Aeldunon. Daughter of Aelan. Bearer of the Fellglow Blade. I am no one's whore, and I kneel to no man. Not even one who styles himself Emperor. Congratulations on your ascendance, cousin. May it bring you all the blessings you deserve."

No oath. No false pledge. No fealty.

I'd named myself.

I let the words ring.

As I turned and walked back, I felt sweat break out on my back, on my palms.

When I reached Val's side, I felt it before he spoke. He didn't look at me.

"What in the name of every fucking god have you done, Aleaia?" he whispered.

Not angry. Just resigned. The kind of voice a man uses when remembering his fate was always sealed.

He exhaled. Slow. Measured. Pinched the bridge of his nose as he muttered, "Of course. I fell in love with a woman who picks fights with an entire Empire."

One by one, the nobles stepped forward. Some gave their vows with pride. Others spoke them like a confession. Cassius received each oath with the same lifeless cadence. "Rise. Serve the Empire with honor."

When the last vow fell quiet, Renatus stepped forward again, voice swelling to proclaim, "Long live Emperor Cassius di Calesia!"

The crowd echoed the cry.

I flicked a glance at Val. His head was bowed, but tension radiated off him.

Cassius's gaze swept over us. Lingered just a heartbeat too long before moving on.

"Let all who kneel here today remember their oaths," Renatus said, his voice smooth as oil on a blade. "You serve the Empire, and the Creator's will. Let loyalty guide you, for treachery will not be forgiven. Nor will it go unpunished. The strength of Calesia lies in its unity. Betrayal fractures it. We will not permit it."

Cassius sat back in the throne like a man sliding into armor. His council formed behind him. Marcus was among them, silent as a shadow.

Then Cassius spoke. "Before the feast begins, there is one final matter that weighs upon the soul of this Empire."

"Valerius di Calesia," Cassius said. "And Aleaia Caedmon. Step forward."

I followed Val's lead. My legs were too light, breath too shallow, fingers twitching near the phantom weight of a sword I didn't have.

"For the preservation of the Empire's unity and the protection of its people," Cassius said, rising, "It is my duty to inform you that you are both under arrest on charges of heresy and treason."

Val let out a bitter, humorless sound. Not quite a laugh.

"Heresy and treason," he repeated flatly. "Do you know what we endured just to stand here today? To witness your coronation and kneel before you?"

The room rippled—motion like dry grass before flame. More guards stepped forward.

I looked at Val.

Then I looked at Cassius.

"These charges have been carefully investigated," he said. "The evidence is undeniable. Your actions threaten the Empire's stability."

Val's voice cracked like a whip. "You told me that if I came here of my own accord, you would spare Alvaretia and Aeltyria. I obeyed the summons, brother."

Cassius gave a nod. "So you did. And they will be spared of a worse fate than they would have received if you had been disobedient."

"You start your reign this way, by falsely charging and imprisoning your own brother?" Val asked, incredulous. "When I have done everything—*everything*—that you've asked of me?"

The great doors closed behind us with a heavy thud. I turned, found that the court had been ushered out while I'd been focused on the confrontation between Val and Cassius.

As a girl, I'd set traps for hares with my father. I'd later come upon the creatures, find them writhing and terrified at my presence, and I'd often set them free. When I was caught and chastised for it, I told Papa that to let them die in fear of me, shrieking and wide eyed, seemed cruel. After that, he taught me to shoot a bow, so they would die as they lived—free and unafraid.

I learned, in that moment in Avitum's great hall, that I was right. That to be trapped by something much larger, something you're near powerless to fight, something that will certainly be your end is cruel. No one would be coming to free us from this trap. It would be left to us to do it for ourselves.

Cassius only nodded to the steward, who stepped forward, hands trembling as he unrolled a scroll. Then he began to read.

"Aleaia Caedmon—also known as Aleaia Dieter—under Calesian law, you stand accused of the following: magistry, unlawfully accepting knighthood as an Aeltyrian, consorting with a Calesian royal, sedition, impersonating a noble, swearing false oaths, blasphemy, and heretical worship of the northern gods."

The steward's voice rang with ceremonial clarity, each word dropping like a stone.

"Valerius di Calesia, you are charged with failure to report magistry, unlawful bestowal of knighthood upon an Aeltyrian, sedition, concealing a false identity, failure to report noble impersonation, consorting with an Aeltyrian subject, blasphemy, false oaths, heretical worship of the northern gods, and dereliction of duty."

Val didn't flinch. "Quite the list. And the evidence?"

Cassius descended a step from the dais. "I understand this is painful, brother. I wish it were otherwise."

"Then show us the evidence," Val snapped. "Or at least give us the—"

Cassius raised a hand. "The law will be followed. You'll stand trial. The evidence will be presented."

The trap was closing. I felt it in my bones.

"Please. Cooperate," Cassius said. "Let the law take its course. The truth will emerge. The Creator will judge."

Then he turned to the guard at his right hand.

"Guards. Seize them."

Val moved the moment the order was given.

Steel whispered free of its scabbard. One guard went down before the club even finished its arc, Val's blade opening his throat in a single, efficient cut.

He turned into the next strike like he'd been waiting for it all along.

Another guard on my side moved without hesitation—club swinging for Val's head.

I stepped into the blow.

Pain ignited up my left arm, white-hot and blinding, but I caught the club, wrenched it free and drove forward, smashing the wood down on her wrist. Bone cracked. She screamed.

I didn't stop.

My elbow caught her jaw. She dropped, limp, and another guard rushed me from the right. I shattered his fingers and drove the club into his throat. He fell choking, clawing at his neck.

I discarded the weapon.

Fire answered my call instantly—hot, liquid, hovering above my palm like molten ore. I flung it.

It struck the guards nearest Cassius and clung where it landed, spreading, burning through armor and flesh alike. They screamed and fell, rolling, the flames refusing to die.

It wasn't enough.

Val was fighting to my right—two down at his feet, a third closing fast behind him.

I reached for their mana and pulled. All three collapsed in the same heartbeat, gasping, arms clutching their middles like they'd been gutted.

Val was already moving again.

He stepped over the fallen without looking down, blade rising and falling in tight, ruthless arcs.

One guard lunged.

Val took his arm at the elbow and drove the sword up under his arm before the man could scream.

Another came in from the flank. Val pivoted, shielded my side with his body, and cut him down with a single thrust to the face.

"Left," he said calmly.

I turned just as the next guard broke through.

Another guard rushed me.

I caught his sword, stepped inside his guard, and drove my blade up under his ribs.

He sagged.

I wrenched the steel free and let him fall.

Val took a blow meant for me, steel scraping across his ribs, biting deep. He grunted once and smashed the guard back with a savage upward strike. Steel rang. The man went down.

Blood ran down Val's side, dark and fast, but his stance never faltered. He wiped his face with the back of his hand and kept killing.

I turned and ran for the dais.

Pain seared into my left side.

I staggered, breath tearing from my chest, and looked down. A bolt jutted from beneath my ribs—dark metal, unmistakable.

*Incolumium.*

With a cry, I tore it free and flung it aside as another guard charged. I met her with the hilt, drove my boot into her chest, and sent her tumbling down the steps.

Above, Cassius's household guard locked into formation—shields raised, a wall of steel braced to sweep the hall.

We wouldn't make it.

Not unless I ended this.

I was already fraying. I'd siphoned, but I burned through mana faster than I could replenish it. My control was instinct then, not discipline.

I looked up. The rafters loomed high above—heavy beams, dry with age, thick with banners and paint. They would burn.

I turned and ran back down the steps toward Val.

He was fighting at the foot of the dais, sword flashing. Three guards pressed him hard, two more closing from the flanks. He cut one down. Then another. He stumbled, caught himself, and raised his blade again.

I slammed into the guard behind him at full speed, shoulder first, knocking him off balance.

"Stay close to me!" I shouted, gathering fire above my left hand, sword raised to guard Val's back.

"Aleaia, what are you doing?" Val yelled as he reached me.

"Saving us!" I snapped.

"You need to get out!"

"I go where you go, bradarcam! Now stay with me!"

I hurled the liquid flame upward. It struck the rafters and spread.

Not like normal fire—this was alive. It crawled along the ceiling in burning veins, hungry and relentless, and I felt it still tethered to me, still drawing from my mana as it consumed beam after beam.

I cast a shield around us—silver light snapping into place, tight and shimmering.

The castle groaned.

Paintings tore free from the walls. Stone cracked. A chandelier shrieked as it fell behind us, raining iron and flame. Guards scattered, some running, some frozen in terror as the ceiling began to fail.

I plunged my blade into the throat of the guard in front of me, then reached out a hand and drained him dry. He collapsed, boneless.

I fed the stolen mana into the shield.

Into the fire above.

Blood streamed from my nose. My mouth filled with iron. My stomach lurched, but I held.

The shield shimmered, but guards still forced their way through it, shields raised, weapons driving in.

Panic clawed up my throat. *Why isn't it working?*

Val grabbed my shoulder. "Aleaia, stop! You're going to—"

His hand was ripped away.

Pain snapped tight around my throat.

I gasped, clawing at the cord biting into my neck as the world tilted. Gauntleted hands slammed me to the floor. Shackles clamped around my wrists. Then my ankles. Chains yanked tight.

My mana was gone, like embers scattered on the wind.

The pressure eased.

Air came back in broken gulps. I coughed, spat blood, vision swimming.

Marcus Frugi stood over me, whip in hand, black coils faintly shimmering.

"Just as the artificers promised," he said, eyes bright with glee. "No more casting for you, little witch."

Cassius descended the dais. He clapped slow. The sound echoed through the wreckage.

"The whip works perfectly, Lord Frugi. Well done. I think we all see that no trial is needed after all. She is a mage. And my brother," he gestured to Val, "has clearly fallen under her spell. Do you agree, councilors?"

Most of his council was dead. Those that still lived stared, stunned and bleeding.

Except Marcus, who said, "Yes, Your Majesty."

I was hauled to my knees. Val knelt nearby, chained, blood trailing from his temple.

I looked from him to Cassius.

"That's right! It was me!" I shouted, straining against the shackles. "He knew nothing! I charmed him!"

"Aleaia, don't—" Val started.

The club came down on the back of his neck.

He crumpled for a moment. Shook his head.

"Don't worry, mage," Cassius said, voice bright with cruelty. "We will purify him. The spell will break and his soul will be clean again."

*The fuck does that mean?*

I thrashed. "I'll kill you for this, Cassius di Calesia!" I screamed. "And you, Marcus Frugi, you treacherous pile of shit!"

Something slammed into my skull.

The world buckled—

—but not before I turned my head. Just a little.

Val's eyes were on me.

I couldn't reach him.

And then they began to drag me away. I dropped my weight. Dug my heels in. Bucked.

"I swear to you, vedrānos," I shouted. "I will come for you! I will burn everything to get to you!"

Two more guards came to lift each of my legs. Carried me out the door.

The last thing I saw before the doors shut was Val's face—and I knew that loving me had finally destroyed him.

# CHAPTER SEVENTY-NINE
## *In the Belly of the Beast*

*"Pain purifies. Magic sears the soul—
let it be scoured with flame, silence, and steel."*
—Doctrine of Purification, Vinculatores Codex

Succamos? 1231
*Aleaia*

I never could get used to the smell.

Thick and rotting. Blood. Mildew. Something older. Putrefied. It clung to the air like rot to bone.

The damp coated my skin like mold.

I shivered. Every inch of me felt raw.

They'd hung me from the ceiling like a carcass left to drain.

My side throbbed, wet and leaking. I didn't need to look to know the blood—and whatever else seeped out—hadn't stopped.

Somewhere, water dripped.

No windows. No fire. No light.

Time blurred. I slipped in and out.

Each time my weight sagged forward, the chains snapped me back—wrists yanked, steel biting deeper into torn skin.

My feet were bare on cold stone—numb, then burning, then numb again. My fingers were too stiff to move.

The quiet hum of my magic had gone silent.

I was hollow. Not just from the loss of my mana.

Val.

My throat clenched.

*Where are you?*

*What have they done to you?*

*Was it worse than they were doing to me?*

Tears came, unbidden.

Somewhere deep inside, I clung to the same thread my mother must have once clung to—that I would know if he crossed the Veil.

Then—footsteps on stone. Measured.

I tensed. Every time it had opened, someone had brought pain.

I was tired, and hungry, and sore, and sad. Every time they came to hurt me, I had less and less strength to help myself.

The door groaned open. Metal scraped. A figure entered, haloed by torchlight.

Marcus.

I didn't move.

Didn't speak.

He'd already taken my magic. He wouldn't have my fear.

He stopped a few feet away, light casting his face in long, cruel shadow.

"What a piteous thing you've become," he said, voice smooth as water over a blade. "The lost heir to Aeltyria, if we're to believe the word of a bewitched man. But what does it matter? There's no one left to ransom you back to."

He began to circle me.

As if appraising livestock.

I said nothing. Believed nothing.

"I did consider proposing a match," he went on. "Marrying you to the Emperor would've solidified his claim. But he couldn't overcome his revulsion."

He stopped in front of me, his gaze sliding over me.

"Shame. You are quite beautiful, when you're not screaming. Or fighting. Or fucking your superiors."

Still, I said nothing.

He stepped closer.

His hand rose to clamp around my jaw. Fingers dug into my cheeks, forced my chin up.

"The pain you'll suffer in the arena will be exquisite," he said. "But nothing compared to what your precious prince will endure."

I stared him dead in the eye.

And spit in his face.

It landed thick, just beneath his eye.

His hand whipped across my face so fast I barely saw it coming. The crack echoed. My head snapped sideways. Pain flared hot along my cheek, and the copper sting hit my tongue.

I didn't cry out.

He grabbed my jaw again, leaned in—and crushed his lips to mine.

And I, in return, bit him.

Hard.

His scream tore through the cell, high and undignified. Blood filled my mouth, hot and thick. He staggered back, lip torn, clutching his face.

I laughed.

Delirious.

Wild.

Terrifying, I hoped.

"You bitch," he snarled, voice muffled by his own hand. Blood ran between his fingers.

I stopped laughing abruptly, leaning forward as much as the chains would let me.

"He was your friend once," I rasped.

"Yes," Marcus snapped. "And then you came along and ruined him!"

"I set him free. Fuck you and your empire of stone."

His face twisted into a mask of rage and pain mingling with something older.

He reached for his belt, drew a key, and stepped forward.

The lock above me clicked.

My arms dropped like dead weight.

I collapsed. Hard. Limbs too numb to catch me. Agony screamed through my shoulders as blood returned—prickling, stabbing all the way to my fingertips.

I lay there, teeth gritted against the pain.

Didn't move when he shackled my wrists close to the floor bolt. Didn't flinch when he chained my ankles.

The chain clinked once. Final. Unyielding.

He straightened. Brushed invisible dust from his tunic. Touched his lip—now bloodied, swollen, torn.

Then turned and walked out.

The door groaned. Clicked shut.

Darkness swallowed the room again.

I lay there, trembling. Limbs useless. Face pressed to my knees.

Quiet. Shaking.

And when I was sure I was alone—when the echo of his boots was gone—I let the tears come.

# CHAPTER EIGHTY

## *The Hollow Season*

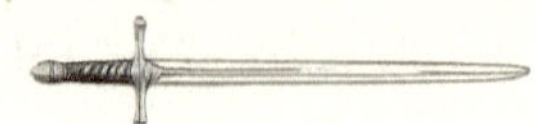

Succamos? 1231

*Aleaia*

There was nothing to mark the sun's passage. The days bled together into one long, unbroken night.

There was only darkness.

And cold.

And pain.

They gave me only rancid water and bread mottled with rot. Most days, I couldn't keep it down. When I vomited, the guards laughed. Sometimes they jeered. Sometimes they just watched.

On the worst days, they forced me to swallow it again.

There was no bucket. No chamber pot. No dignity.

When my body gave out, I collapsed into filth.

*Not even animals are kept like this*, I thought.

My lips split with thirst. My joints screamed from the positions they forced me into. Punishment, they called it, but I knew the truth.

Sometimes, it was for fun.

I cried once.

Just once.

I tried to remember what it felt like to be warm.

To be safe.

To be held.

The memory felt farther away every day.

Until—

It hit sharp and sudden. Not pain. Not grief. Something deeper. Like breath drawn too fast under a broken rib.

*Val.*

*Barefoot on cold stone at dawn, half-dressed and still waking, pulling a blanket from his shoulders to wrap around me. I'd been soaked and shaking from patrol, too proud to admit how cold I was.*

*He didn't speak. Just pulled me close.*

*I remembered the press of his chest against my back. The slow rise and fall of his breathing. His chin resting lightly on my shoulder.*

*The way he held me like he couldn't believe I'd let him.*

*I remembered how my fingers clutched the edge of his sleeve. How his hand covered mine without a word.*

*How I let my weight sink into him.*

*Not because I had to.*

*Because I wanted to.*

*Because in that one quiet moment, I wasn't a soldier, or a symbol, or the daughter of anyone.*

*I was just Aleaia.*

*And I was loved.*

*Even before he could say it.*

*Before he knew what to call it.*

The memory flickered.

The dark closed in again.

My fingers found only chain.

My teeth clenched.

They could beat me. Starve me. Strip me down to nothing.

But they would not break me.

Not here.

Not like this.

# CHAPTER EIGHTY-ONE
## *Anarethos*

*"They fear love because it is the only power they cannot chain."*
—Reflections on Rebellion, 1218

Succamos or Rudamos, 1231
*Aleaia*

I jerked awake as icy water sloshed over my face. A choked gasp tore from my throat, the cold stealing the air straight from my lungs. Another bucket followed. I tried to flinch away, but the chains snapped taut, iron biting into bruised wrists.

Marcus stepped into view, nose wrinkling. "By Anvallus, you're revolting. You can't present yourself to the Emperor like this."

Two guards hauled me upright. My legs dangled for a breath before they remembered how to stand. A third dumped another bucket over my head. I didn't react this time. They were looking for pain. They wouldn't find it, if I could help it.

Someone unlocked the chain just long enough to shove a coarse shift over my head—sackcloth, wet and stinking. The lock snapped closed again.

I was half-dragged, shivering, down a corridor that stank of blood and smoke. My bare feet scraped across stone, every step agony in places I could no longer feel.

The next room was worse. Wider. Wetter. Torchlight flickered off red-streaked walls and rusted iron. The stink of copper clung to the back of my throat.

A rack loomed on one wall. Cages lined the others. And in the center—

Val.

Chained to a support beam. Stripped to ragged smallclothes. His ribs jutted like broken blades under bruised skin. Some of the wounds still bled.

There was a table beside him. Lined with whips. Hooks. Brands. Implements of pain arranged with ceremonial care.

My knees nearly gave out.

"Val," I rasped.

He lifted his head. Just barely. But enough for his eyes to find mine.

I saw pain. And fear. And anger.

"Ah. All the guests are here," a voice said smoothly.

Cassius. Reclined like a noble at the theater. Legs crossed, goblet in hand. Perfectly at ease.

"Cousin," he said, mocking, "I thought you might like to see what your treasonous, indecent conduct has wrought."

I said nothing. I wanted to. Gods, I wanted to. My throat ached with it. But I'd learned what speech cost here.

Val hadn't.

"Fuck you," he spat.

A guard stepped forward and pressed a finger into the open wound on his side. Val jerked. His whole body tightened—one long, shaking line. But he didn't make a sound.

Cassius sipped from his goblet. "What an odd arrangement, the three of us. Brother. Cousin. And the two of you entangled in such a… licentious affair." He clicked his tongue. "You spent too long among the savages, brother. You should have known better."

One of the guards stepped forward and selected a whip from the table. My stomach turned.

"No matter. I'll have you purified." He set his cup aside and stood. "I had considered scourging you myself, but Marcus reminded me—noble blood and all. So a whip will have to do."

I couldn't breathe.

Cassius's voice sharpened. "Forty lashes, Decimus. Shoulders to hips."

Forty would kill him.

The whip cracked.

Val grunted—sharp, guttural—but stayed upright. The second landed harder. By the third, his arms were trembling. I stood frozen, my breath locked in my throat. I couldn't do anything. I could only watch.

I remembered the feeling of leather on skin. The burning. The despair.

My eyes stung.

By the twentieth lash, I began to pull at my restraints. Pointless. Weak. I couldn't stop.

"Twenty-one," Cassius's steward counted. "Twenty-two… twenty-three…"

Val slumped forward. Body slack.

I didn't know if he was unconscious. Or worse.

The words erupted from me before I could stop them. "I will take the rest of his lashings! Please, Your Majesty!"

Cassius raised his hand. The whip stilled.

Val stirred. Even half-dead, he fought to lift his head. "No."

Cassius strolled to me, steps echoing across stone. "How badly would you like to?" he asked, stopping in front of me.

I was trembling—cold, afraid, fury burning beneath it. "Very m-much, my lord."

"Aleaia, stop!" Val's voice cracked.

Cassius looked to Val, then to me with a smirk as he leaned in. Close enough I could smell the wine on his breath. "Then beg."

I stilled, my heart in my throat.

I had knelt for Val. Hands on his skin. My name on his lips.

I had begged before, too. For pleasure. For mercy. In the sacred, quiet way you beg someone to keep touching you.

This wasn't that. This was shame. A man trying to drag love into the mud and make it kneel.

But I did it anyway.

For him.

I dropped to my knees. Placed my hands on my thighs. Lowered my eyes.

"Please… let me t-take the lash for him."

"Aleaia, I said no! Godsdamnit, woman!" Val snarled.

"Lower," Cassius said.

I touched my forehead to the floor.

"Say it."

I let out a long, shuddering breath in the silence. "Please, Your Majesty," I sobbed. "Let m-me take the lash f-for him."

Val wrenched against the post with a hoarse snarl. "You'd better pray I die here, Cassius, because if I don't, I will see you dead for this."

Cassius looked at Val and laughed. "Oh, there you are," he said softly. "Willing to suffer for this meaningless construct you call love. No. Continue, Decimus."

The whip cracked again. I flinched, still kneeling, wrists chained, body shaking with fury.

"Twenty-four," the steward counted.

Val didn't cry out. His silence was worse than any scream.

Cassius's gaze returned to me.

"This sniveling creature is the last issue of my Aunt Eavan and Uncle Cadoc? Are we certain?" He spread his hands to the room in mockery. "What a shame."

He turned and walked back to his seat.

I bit my tongue. It didn't stop the tears.

"Twenty-five."

Cassius's gaze slid to Val, then back to me. "He could have been something great, you know. A prince of the Empire. If only he hadn't betrayed his own for some ashborn with a corpse's claim."

Maybe I could draw his attention to me. Keep it on me.

"I'm your cousin," I spat. "Do you even hear yourself? The same 'ashborn' blood courses through your veins."

He laughed. "Oh, I hear myself. But let me remind you what I saw, little cousin, of the last First Sword of Aeltyria, just in case you have designs to lay such a burden on my brother. I watched your father's corpse as it was paraded through the street, eyes burned out of his skull, put on a pike outside the arena gates until the sun bleached his bones. That was a First Sword. That was Aeltyria."

Something in me shifted—something violent and horribly familiar.

"And now you—filthy, chained, soaked in your own piss—pretend love makes you strong?" He gave a dismissive flick of his hand. "It just makes you pathetic."

And then it tore. Not soft. Not slow. Like the crack of splitting stone—the moment before eruption, the breath before a battlefield charge.

"You think love makes me weak?" My voice was cold. Steady. "You think your godsdamned Empire knows anything of strength?"

I surged to my feet, chains screaming, blood running, teeth bared.

*"Cassius di Calesia duscam bi Galdoriné valer—ancane aenon cintaenge tóa paethir tegin!" Cassius di Calesia I swear by Galdorin's blade—I will burn everything your father built!*

I kicked backward at the post, yanked the chain again, threw my entire weight into it. The anchors groaned.

*"Sola tóa nem es brisaniet! Sola atrató násen genirí! Násen ó nem a tóa etó genim! Nameniet!" May your name be broken! May you die without heir! Without a name of your own creation! Forgotten!*

"Remove her," Cassius said flatly.

The guards approached.

I spun. Threw myself into the first one. Headbutted him hard enough to knock him sideways.

A second reached for my arm. I tore free and drove my elbow into his gut. A third caught my wrist. I bit him. Deep. He screamed.

"She's out of her godsdamned mind—"

"Val!" I screamed over them. "I love you!"

Everything stopped for a breath. Val's head lifted—barely. His eyes found mine, dazed, blood-matted.

I shouted again, throat raw. *"Caram tó, anarethos, vedrānos! Ane sirevató em, Valerion? Caram tó!" I love you, my heart, my bonded one! Do you hear me, Valerion? I love you!*

Cassius stood, wine glass in hand, watching like a man observing a storm battering itself to pieces against his walls.

"You think that shames me, *tuchlus*?" I spat. "You think love is weakness? He made me stronger. He made me whole!"

A gauntlet slammed into the side of my head. I hit the ground hard. Fists found my ribs. My shoulder. I curled, snarling, spitting blood.

"You can't unmake it," I gasped. "You can't unmake us."

"Get her out of my sight," Cassius said coldly. "And make her quiet."

*"Te corvethí ancane elgarest en tóa atreneth! Ancane noram en tóa draeth!" The ravens will feast on your corpse! I'll bathe in your blood!*

They dragged me toward the door, kicking, fighting. I caught one last glimpse of Val.

Still breathing.

Still chained.

Alive.

# CHAPTER EIGHTY-TWO
## *Shield of Calesia*

*"Caramin tó in tautharil. Caramin tó in aena.*
*Et ancane caram tó esmirau te Velil."*
—Aleaia Dieter Caedmon

Rudamos?, 1231
*Aleaia*

*Resist.*

The word pulsed in my skull, weak as the rhythm of my heart in the dark.

*Resist.*

A boot slammed into my side. "Get up!"

Another.

"You deaf bitch? No wonder the ashborn lost the war. I said get up!"

Bone cracked against bone.

I curled up, arms clutched around my ribs where the wound had reopened—hot, weeping, stinking of pus. Every breath burned, thin and white-hot. But I forced myself upright, trembling under the weight of fever.

A pair of sackcloth trousers hit the floor near my feet.

"Put those on."

I reached for them, fingers clumsy with cold and the stiffness of too many days hanging by my wrists. The fabric was crusted stiff. The boots were too large. I had to brace against the wall just to pull them on.

Without a word, the guard threw a cracked cuirass over my tunic, then jammed a rust-stained helmet onto my head. The weight of it dragged at my neck. Antlers—real ones, jagged and tarnished—had been bolted into the crown like some grotesque parody of a war helm.

The collar cinched tight around my neck as he yanked the chain to drag me down the corridor.

I stumbled once. Then again.

The second time, he struck the back of my skull hard enough to ring my ears.

I was used to it by then. If I reacted, it just encouraged them. So I didn't.

At the end of the passage, he undid the bolt on a heavy door and shoved me forward into a narrow antechamber. Iron groaned shut behind us. Another opened ahead.

Light.

Blinding. Brilliant. I flinched. Squinted as I welcomed the sun's heat on my face for the first time since I'd stood in that courtyard with Val.

I drew a breath—rust and dried blood and morning air thick on my tongue.

Then I saw where I stood.

The arena.

If they meant to execute me, I supposed it was better to die with a sword in my hand.

The visor narrowed my view. I turned as far as the collar would let me.

And looked up.

Cassius lounged on the balcony, draped in decadence, smugness gleaming in his eyes.

And beside him—

*Val.*

*Gods. Alive.*

Thin. Shackled. Pale as death. But standing.

His eyes found mine.

Relief. Raw and real.

I swallowed hard and raised my chin.

A herald's voice boomed through the stands.

"And now, to close these illustrious games in honor of our late Emperor Claudius, we present a reenactment of his greatest triumph—the conquest of the Aeltyrian savages!"

The crowd erupted.

*Done mourning him, then. Must be Rudamos already.*

A gate beneath the balcony groaned open.

From its shadowed mouth came Aristides Canina—a mountain of a man, famed across the Empire for the way he killed. Brutal. Unbeaten. A living relic of every war Calesia had ever waged.

The man who killed my sire.

He was enormous—at least two heads taller than me, with rope-tight muscle and skin that was more scar than flesh. Sunlight struck the polished plates of his armor. His shield bore the black serpent of House Canina. His sword dangled from one calloused fist.

He took one step forward.

I stepped to the center of the sand—small and fevered and gaunt by comparison. The rusted metal sagged from my bones.

A match, they called it.

I scoffed and shook my head.

A guard stepped forward and flung two swords into the dirt.

Two. No one fought with two swords. Not if they wanted to live.

I crouched slowly. My hands felt far away, numb from cold and sickness, but I closed them around the hilts. The worn leather bit into my raw palms.

The crowd quieted. The announcer's voice rose, echoing over stone.

"Thirty years ago, the Aeltyrians defied Lord Anvallus, our Creator, time and time again."

Jeers swelled like thunder.

"King Claudius sought peace. He offered union. A marriage to one of their own. But the savages refused. Instead, they laid a curse on Queen Orlaith. A curse that killed her!"

Louder now. Screaming. Spitting.

"Only three years old, the young Prince Cassius watched the betrayal unfold. Queen Orlaith's murder demanded justice. King Claudius—righteous in his fury—gave it. Aeltyria was set ablaze, its resistance purged by fire and steel!"

The voice reached a fever pitch, triumphant.

"In the final siege, Claudius's champion met the famed First Sword of Aeltyria, and bested him with ease!"

My father.

"We now bring you that historic battle, for your enjoyment. But this time, Cadoc Aneirin will be played by someone with even more to lose—his daughter, the princess of the ashborn herself, Aleaia Caedmon!"

The arena roared.

One by one, the collar and shackles were removed. The guard stepped back through the gate.

I smiled. Shook my head.

Huffed a soft laugh.

I could feel the thrum start beneath my skin.

Not rage. Not panic.

Clarity.

Settling over me like a mantle.

Let them watch. Let them cheer. Let them mock.

My breath deepened. I flexed my fingers around the hilts. The sting grounded me. Kept me here. And the crowd fell away.

"Emperor Claudius will be represented by no other than the captain of his guard, the Shield of Calesia—Aristides Canina!"

The crowd howled for blood.

And above it all, from the balcony—

Val's voice cut through like a blade.

"Dame Wolfsbane!"

My head snapped up.

There it was—

Pride. Fierce and unyielding. Burning in his eyes.

"Show them what you're made of!"

I raised a sword in salute.

A guard struck him across the back of the head. He staggered, caught himself on the rail.

And then I bound myself in an oath to Galdorin.

*I will win.*

*And when his blood is spilled for you, I ask for you to give me the means to free us.*

*And when I am free, I will kill them all, for you.*

"And, begin!"

The trumpet sang.

He came at me with his shield up. Sword low. Every step measured, balanced.

Not a brawler. A soldier.

The one who killed Cadoc Aneirin. My father.

I didn't rush him. Let the crowd think I was afraid. Let him think I was broken already.

I held my stance—low, blades loose in my hands—and watched.

He moved like he knew the ending. Like he'd already buried me in his mind.

*Good.*

He tested left. I let him. Slid just out of reach. Circled again. Kept my guard high. Waited.

We clashed once, steel ringing—a clean, brutal rhythm.

He tried to force the opening with his shield.

I twisted away, slashed low, and caught the inside of his wrist. A shallow cut. But it bled.

His eyes flicked to the wound. Then to me.

He didn't follow—not yet. He wanted the next blow to end it.

I held my ground. Circled again.

"They gave you your father's helmet," he said, pacing now. "Did you know? The antlers. Stag of House Aneirin. He wore it the day Aeldunon fell."

I said nothing.

"I thought I killed you back then," he went on. "The baby in the nursery. Nursemaid tried to run. Didn't get far."

Another child, dead in my place.

He said it like he was naming the weather. As though it hadn't haunted my people for twenty-four years.

"You're a ghost. Fitting. Your father died screaming, and you came back wearing his bones."

He lunged. I met him, blade to blade.

Our weapons locked. Strained. He twisted, trying to drive me off balance. I let him.

Shifted my weight and slipped out, slicing upward as I passed. The blade cut into his bicep.

Blood followed.

He slammed into me with his shield.

I flew back. Hit the ground hard. The helmet cracked against my brow. Stars burst in my vision.

He didn't wait. Boot to my ribs. I rolled, gasping.

Then he straddled me. Held his sword high, meant to plunge it into my throat.

*Fight from the ground if you must.* Papa's voice in memory. *Use the bastard's weight. Let him think you're finished. Then take his eyes.*

I grabbed a fistful of sand. Flung it into his eyes. Rolled away.

That bought me space.

I scrambled upright.

He charged—half-blind—swinging wide.

I ducked, slashed upward, and opened his thigh from knee to hip.

He bellowed, stumbling.

I drove one blade into the gap beneath his arm. Wrenched it free.

Blood sprayed, hot across my hand.

He struck back—fist to my gut.

The world folded around me. I hit the sand again. Hard.

My breath stuck. Limbs refused to move.

Pain surged in waves. The sky tilted above.

"Aleaia!"

Val's voice.

It broke through everything.

Then again. Louder.

"Aleaia!"

Then his command—

"GET UP!"

The sound ripped through me.

I blinked. Light reeled. Blood filled my mouth.

I rolled again—just in time for him to miss killing me with his shield.

My fingers brushed the hilt of the second blade. I took it.

Slashed Aristides's calf open.

He dropped to one knee.

He swung—wide, desperate. I ducked. Drove my shoulder into him and sent him sprawling into the dust.

I stood over him, breath ragged.

Blood poured from his wounds. His sword lay near his hand, untouched.

He looked up at me. Drew his hand away.

"I yield," he rasped.

I reached up. Tore the helmet from my head.

Held it at arm's length and just looked.

The antlers that jutted from the battered crown were cracked and blackened from years of staged defeat.

Not just any helm. His. Cadoc's.

Turned into a prop.

A costume.

A lie.

I dropped it in the dust at my feet.

"Is that all you have, Cassius?" I shouted. "That's your champion?"

No one answered me. In my periphery, the guards began to close in.

I turned back to Canina. "Get up," I snarled.

He looked at me, unsure if he should comply.

"Get up or I'll kill you where you are."

He rolled onto his side, then got to his knees. He couldn't stand. Just as well.

I grabbed the plume of his helm, yanking his head back.

"For you, Galdorin," I murmured in Aeltyrian.

I swept the sword in a clean arc across his throat. A fine spray of blood misted the air.

He collapsed forward a moment later. Blood pooled thick in the sand.

Cassius stood and stormed from the balcony, his personal guard at his heels.

No cheers followed. Only silence.

I let the blade fall. Found Val's eyes. He was at the railing—held back, straining. His nose trickled blood.

They'd beat him for calling out to me during the fight.

His voice rang across the arena.

"That's my girl!"

They struck him for it. Pulled him away.

"My heart is yours," I called up to him, so loud that even the godsdamned stones would know. "It always was. It always will be."

Let them drag me. Let them break me. Let this be the last thing he hears.

"I loved you in silence," I called to him in Aeltyrian now. "I loved you in fire. And I will love you beyond the Veil."

Hands seized my arms. Chains clicked back onto the incolumium manacles at my wrists. The collar yanked. I didn't fight them. Just took one last look at Val.

The love of my life. The best thing that had ever happened to me.

What I'd done in that arena—standing over their prized dog, defying the Emperor's plans—there'd be no walking that back.

And Val… after shouting for me like that, after letting them see—

If I lived, he probably wouldn't.

They dragged me back into the bowels of the prison. Deep into the stone. To a new cell. They stripped me again. Shackled my arms to the wall. Then left.

I slid down the stone as far as the chains allowed, resting my head on my knees. I didn't cry. Not then. I just sat there, spent and hollow in the quiet, and tried to breathe.

And waited for the gods to decide what came next.

# CHAPTER EIGHTY-THREE
## *The Cell*

*"She called me vedrānos.*
*Don't forget her voice. Don't forget her voice. Don't forget—"*
—scratched into the stone of the Avitum dungeons

Rudamos 27, 1231
*Valerius*

This cell was marginally better than the last. A sliver of moonlight cut through a slit in the stone. A bucket for waste. A pallet of straw gone soft with mildew, sagging on a creaky old wooden frame.

Rotten, like everything else here.

I'd rot here, too.

After surviving Cassius's so-called *purification,* I'd been informed my life would be spared. Freedom would not. My mind, my body, would waste away behind stone and silence.

The pain in my back had dulled to something distant. Numb. What lingered was worse.

What they'd made me watch them do to her when I couldn't stop them.

*"See what love does, Valerius?" Cassius said softly in my ear.*

My stomach turned. I pressed a hand to the wall, bracing against the rush of nausea.

And then I remembered the arena.

Cassius had meant it as an execution. Her death, dressed up for spectacle. A gift to the crowd. But she lived. Fought. Triumphed. I could still see her, bathed in sunlight, helmet in the dirt, eyes burning with defiance. That image was the only reason I was still breathing.

I was going to kill him.

For what he did to her. For what he did to us both.

I glanced down at the tally scratched into the bedframe. Twenty notches on splintered wood. Two full decadia since the arena. Twenty days without a sign of her. Maybe she was already dead. Maybe they'd parade her body through the streets of Aeldunon, a warning writ in blood.

Alive or dead, her absence was a wound no cell could match. I wasn't just prisoner to these walls. I was prisoner to every imagined ending I couldn't stop picturing.

And that was the point, wasn't it?

To leave me alive long enough to imagine every way she could've died.

To make me regret loving her.

My vision blurred. I leaned my forehead against the cool stone beneath the window, pressing into it like pressure might silence the thoughts.

Then, faint as breath—

"Val."

I didn't move. My mind had played this trick more than once. It was usually her voice. Wouldn't surprise me if it started conjuring other ghosts too. This one sounded like Lucius.

A key scraped in the lock. The bolt slid back. The door creaked open. A figure stepped into the cell. I blinked.

Looked like Lucius, too.

"No." I shook my head. "I've finally lost it."

"Very likely," the figure said, and pulled me into a tight, familiar embrace.

I stood frozen, arms limp at my sides. "Lucius is in Aeldunon," I said flatly. "This isn't real. There's no rescue coming."

"Quiet, you fool. It's me." He stepped back just far enough to meet my eyes. "And we're getting you out. Get dressed."

He shoved a bundle into my arms—boots, tunic, cloak. I stared down at it. Solid. Real.

"You just slow now? Too many hits in the head?" Lucius snapped. "Move!"

I yanked the sackcloth off over my head and dressed fast, every muscle stiff from cold and disuse. "I can't believe you're actually here."

"Believe it later. Gods, you're a skinny bastard now, aren't you?" He shook his head. "You've got a beard, Val."

I touched my jaw. The hair there was thick, coarse—proof of time I'd lost.

"No worries. I'll fix you up when we get out of here," he said. "We've got a queen to rescue."

"A queen?" Gods, how long had I been a prisoner?

"A princess. You know who I mean. Move."

"This is reckless. Why would you come here?"

"Because if I don't have you, all I have are three sisters by birth and that pain in the arse down the hall.

"Lucius, that's enough," Mariana said, brushing past him to me.

"Mariana," I said. "You shouldn't have—"

"I know. Had to make sure you're well enough to travel, though." She smiled, soft and warm, as she pressed a hand to my chest.

Mana spilled through me like rain on parched soil, soothing some of the aches in my limbs.

"There you are, my lord," she said softly.

My legs steadied. The haze in my head cleared. "Aleaia's down the hall?"

"That's what our man says. Someone's hunting for her sword. We'll get it back to her."

I thought I knew where it was, once.

Maybe it would come back to me.

"We were told—right at the next corner, then left at the end," Mariana added in a whisper.

I followed down the long, dark corridor.

Voices echoed ahead.

"I never get a turn," one of the guards was whining as he stepped out of a cell.

I felt sweat break out. My mouth went dry. I knew what they meant. I didn't want to know it, but I did.

I'd kill them too.

"That's because you never shut up about it," the other replied. "His lordship doesn't like whiners."

Footsteps faded down the hall.

We pressed into the shadows. Lucius raised a hand, listening.

My heart thundered with equal parts fear and hope.

She was close. I could feel it, like a thread pulled taut through my ribs. And gods help the men between us.

# CHAPTER EIGHTY-FOUR
## *Already Gone*

*"They should have killed me first."*
—the private journals of Valerius di Calesia

Rudamos 27, 1231
*Valerius*

The sound stopped us.

A grunt.

A choked breath.

The sick rhythm of—

*No.*

I knew, because they'd made me watch, before, but now—

"Go on then," Marcus said, laughing, breathless. "Cry. I like it when they cry."

I hit the door like a battering ram.

And there she was.

Chained to a table. Blood streaked her mouth. Her wrists were torn raw. Her legs were bound. One twitched, weakly. The last echo of resistance. The collar still clung to her throat. Her head turned aside, staring at the wall, like she'd tried to leave herself behind.

Her chest rose.

Alive.

Then I saw Marcus.

Eyes wide at having been caught.

His hands.

His stance.

His body—between her legs.

And I knew.

So did he.

Everything inside me snapped.

I moved without thinking. Without sound.

The roar ripped out of me—guttural, louder than I knew I could be. It tore through my throat and straight into him as I hit. I drove him away from the table and straight to the floor.

He shrieked—too late. "Val—what are you—"

*No.*

*No words. Not now.*

I slammed his head against the floor.

Again.

The stone split his skin.

I straddled him.

This man had touched her.

Had smiled while she screamed.

My fist drove into his face.

Once.

Twice.

A third time—until his eye split open.

Skin burst. Bone crunched beneath my knuckles.

He spat blood. Tried to crawl away while I wiped it from my eye.

I dragged him back.

Leaned in close.

Pressed both thumbs to his eyes.

And drove them in.

The scream tore from him—raw, animal, choking.

He thrashed, heels drumming against the stone.

He clawed at my arms, nails ripping skin, but I didn't stop.

I wanted him blind when he died.

I wanted him to *remember me* in the dark.

"Go on then," I snarled. "Cry. *You* like it when *they* cry, don't you?"

Then I wrapped both bloodied hands around his throat and squeezed.

I couldn't stop.

Lucius seized my shoulder. "Val. He's gone."

I kept squeezing until my arms trembled.

Until I couldn't feel my fingers.

Until Lucius hauled me off him, dragged me across the room, and forced me to sit on the floor. Planted himself between me and what was left of Marcus—

Between me and *her*.

I didn't fight him.

I couldn't.

Mariana was already at the table, her hands glowing faintly with mana as she worked on Aleaia.

Lucius kneeled in front of me. "She's alive. We've got her. She's safe now."

He paused, my breathing ragged between us.

"Val, look at me. I need you. *She's* going to need you."

I couldn't speak. My whole body shook. My jaw clenched so tight it ached, holding back the sound clawing its way up my throat.

But I nodded.

Behind Lucius, she moved.

I dragged in a breath. Ragged. Wet. The kind of breath a man takes after drowning.

And still, I couldn't look away.

The worst of it was already over.

And still, I knew that what I'd seen then, what they'd showed me before, was only the surface. A glimpse.

"Lucius. He… they…"

The words caught. Thick. Wrong. Too monstrous to force out.

Lucius's voice cut through the fog. Steady. Unyielding. "Get it together. She's still breathing."

He handed me a cloth before he moved away from me and unfastened his cloak, laying it over Aleaia before he returned to Marcus's body, checking his pockets.

I wiped my face, my hands. Felt nothing.

"I've given her all I can," Mariana said, her voice thin and frayed. She looked pale from the effort.

Lucius rose, returned to her side.

"These manacles… even now, they're fighting my magic." She shook her head. "She needs warmth. She needs medicine. She needs to be free."

I stepped closer. My hands trembled as I reached for Aleaia—

Then stopped.

I didn't know if I had the right. Not yet.

*This is what happens when you love.* Cassius's voice.

It wasn't. This was what happened when people *didn't* love. Only that could create such monsters.

"Stay with her," Mariana said. "We'll keep searching. There might be something for the cuffs."

They left.

Beside her, I sank to my knees and gripped the edge of the table to keep from falling apart.

Hollow.

That was what I felt.

Scraped empty to make room for all of it. Rage. Sorrow. Guilt.

Love.

"Aleaia," I whispered. "Luce mea, I'm here."

Her lashes twitched. Her head turned just slightly toward the sound. Her lips parted.

"Val?" Dry. Shaky. Barely there.

"I'm here," I said again, steadier now. "Right here."

Her brow furrowed. She tried to lift her arms, and the manacles dragged them back down. She gasped, but even through the pain, she fought. Pulled against the chains with a hoarse, broken sound that still carried something of her old fury.

Her gaze drifted toward the wall.

"Am I dying, finally? Are you dead?" she asked, voice slurring, unfocused. "They weren't supposed to…"

I reached for her. My hand brushed her shoulder.

She flinched.

I stopped, pulled back like she'd burned me.

"You're real," she breathed. "Sorry. Just… not so sudden. Please."

"Never," I said softly. I moved my hand to hers instead, letting it rest there. She squeezed it. "Only when you want me to."

Footsteps returned. The jangle of keys.

"Fucking Hel. Nothing for the manacles." He moved to the iron ring fastening the manacles to the chains and slid a key into the lock. It clicked. The chain slipped free. "We'll have to cut them off later."

Aleaia pushed upright.

I stepped forward, but she lifted a hand. The smallest gesture.

"Don't," she said. "I can do it."

"Help me dress her," Mariana said quietly. "We need to move."

"I said I can do it," she snarled. "I'm not a fucking child."

Mariana didn't flinch. Just inclined her head, and set a parcel of clothing next to her on the table. "No. You're not. Let us know if you need help."

Her body betrayed her with every movement. Her arms trembled. Her knees gave. Twice. Still, she fought to stay upright, gripping the table like it might anchor her to herself.

Only when Mariana knelt to tug her boots on did Aleaia give a small, reluctant nod.

She was so thin.

*So, so* thin.

Lucius offered her a warmer cloak. "Here. You'll freeze otherwise."

She took it without a word. Pulled it around herself. "Where's my sword?"

"Someone's fetching it," Lucius said.

"Can you walk?" I asked, trying to keep my voice steady.

She nodded. Her body didn't agree. She swayed, knees buckling. I caught her elbow—and let go the moment I felt her tense.

Mariana stepped forward. "Let Lucius carry you, Aleaia. Just for now."

There was pride in her eyes—fierce, flickering.

Another step.

When her legs gave again, she collapsed against me, her weight catching hard against my chest.

"Not Lucius," she said. "Val. But not like I'm made of glass."

My brow furrowed. "What does that mean? Do you want me to sling you over my shoulder like a sack of potatoes?"

Her fingers twisted in the front of my shirt. She didn't answer right away. When her voice came, it was soft, cracked, barely above breath. "Just don't look at me like I'm already gone."

Her gaze tracked toward Marcus's corpse.

"That him?" she asked, voice pulled tight.

Lucius gave a short nod.

I helped her forward, steadying her just long enough to stand over the body.

She stared down at him. Her lip curled. She spat on him.

*"Gen aó galvra. Glavató in Hel."*

*Son of a whore. Rot in Hel.* A curse.

Then she looked up at me. Her voice was raw. "You did this?"

I nodded. "I did."

"You didn't stop."

"No," I said softly. "I didn't."

She nodded once, then looked back at me. "Vedrānos, I'm ready."

I said nothing. Only bent and lifted her into my arms.

I'd carried her before.

The knighting feast, when she'd been too drunk to walk, laughing against my shoulder and threatening to fight the bard on her way out.

Her birthday, when I'd thrown her over my shoulder and smacked her arse just to hear her laugh.

So many times, I'd lifted her to the bed, to the bath, to the wall—when she'd gripped me tight and kissed like she'd never let go.

Back then, she was fire and steel in my arms. Now, she… wasn't.

She didn't speak again. Just laid her head against my chest and let me carry her out through the winding corridors of the prison.

We emerged into a cramped hovel at the end of some forgotten tunnel. A hidden way out. A smuggler's path, maybe.

Lucius opened the door and peered into the street. "Wagon's still there. Good thing it wasn't confiscated. You two will lie in the back until we're clear of the city."

I followed him out.

It was warmer than the last time I'd been outside. The air smelled of smoke. Something sharper beneath it—metallic. Blood.

The streets were too quiet. No merchants. No drunks. No barking dogs.

"What's happening?" I asked.

Lucius didn't look back. "Martial law. First bell rang hours ago."

I stiffened. "First Army?"

"Third. Vinculatores. Inquisition. We'll talk later. Right now, we move."

At the wagon, he climbed into the driver's seat. Mariana climbed into the back and reached for Aleaia.

I adjusted my hold, meaning to place her into the wagon, but she stirred.

Lifted her head. Just barely. "I can climb in," she said.

I hesitated. Then gently lowered her to her feet. "You shouldn't—"

She turned toward me, though she didn't meet my eyes. "I said I can do it."

Mariana helped her up. I steadied the other side as she swung one leg up and hauled herself into the back.

It wasn't graceful. She hissed in pain but didn't cry out. She never did. Not the whole time—

I swallowed. Didn't let myself think about it as I climbed in after her.

I lay flat beside her, staring up at the sagging canvas above us.

Mariana dropped the canvas shut.

The wagon lurched forward.

I turned on my side to face her. I wanted to touch her—needed to—but I wouldn't without her leave. So I just watched her.

Her body was drawn tight, arms folded in, guarding something that hadn't quite broken yet.

"I missed you," I murmured.

She said nothing. Maybe it was too soon.

"We're safe," I whispered instead.

"No," she said. "Not yet."

The wagon creaked onward, wheels bumping over uneven stone as we crossed market square. I shifted just enough to peer through a crack in the slats.

I saw them, charred bodies, twisted grotesque atop tall stakes. Limbs blackened and outstretched. Mouths frozen in final screams.

I turned back to Aleaia and reached toward her just enough to cover the space between us with my hand.

Not touching. Just there, in case she needed it.

From the front, Mariana's voice cut through the silence.

"The gates will be closed to us. Especially at this hour. If they figure out what I am… who she is…"

"Then they'll die by my sword," Lucius said.

Mariana started to ask, "Do you think our papers will hold?"

"They'll hold," Lucius said. "Don't fidget. It'll give you away."

The wagon rattled forward, pulled deeper into the belly of a city that no longer slept.

"By order of His Majesty Emperor Cassius di Calesia," the town crier's voice echoed over stone and silence, "all citizens are to remain inside their residence until otherwise directed. The only exceptions are to seek a healer, or to bury the dead."

*He's keeping them in,* I thought.

Locking them down so he can hunt them in their beds.

Kick in doors.

Drag out the accused.

We jolted over a rough patch of cobblestone. Pain lanced through my back, my ribs, but I hardly noticed. I could only hope we made it out alive. To real freedom. Whatever that looked like.

The deeper we moved into the city, the worse it got. The smoke thickened. The air soured. The stench of burning flesh clung to everything. Bitter. Sweet. Inescapable.

I glanced over at her. She was still. Hands folded over her belly. Her breath came shallow.

Her eyes were open, fixed on something far away.

"You're cold," I said softly. "Would you like to…"

I lifted the edge of the blanket. It was big enough for two but we'd be warmer if we were closer together.

She blinked.

And slowly, she nodded.

But she didn't move.

So I did. I shifted toward her, slow and careful, closing the space.

My arm brushed hers.

She flinched. Tensed.

A dull ache opened behind my ribs. "Is this all right?"

She didn't answer right away. Then, at last, she nodded.

We stayed like that, quiet and only inches apart, for a few breaths.

Then she asked, "Did you see the square?"

"I did."

"I smelled it first. Like Ardhmor."

Her voice didn't waver. She might've been remarking on the price of lentils.

I nodded once. "As did I."

She was quiet a moment. Then, quick as always, she said, "You're covered in blood. It's on the fresh clothes Lucius brought."

Even now, she noticed everything.

"It's not mine," I said.

"Good," she said.

The silence stretched. I let my eyes trace the lines of her face—not just the bruises, but the straight nose, the fullness of her lips, the sharpness of her jaw. Gods, she was still beautiful to me.

"You must have seen," she said, eyes everywhere but on me. "What had been done… to me."

"I did." I wouldn't tell her how much, unless she asked.

I reached out, slow and careful, and touched her hand, just barely.

"My heart is yours," I said softly, "As it always has been. Nothing could ever change that."

Her next words weren't angry or broken. They were worse.

"You should have just let me die."

The sentence dropped like a stone between us.

My throat closed. I swallowed against it.

"I could never do that," I shook my head. "You mean too much to me."

She took a deep breath. Bit her lip to stop its quivering. "Wouldn't you put down a lame horse?"

The way she said it—quiet, thoughtful—stole my breath.

"Aleaia—"

"I don't feel like talking." Her tone didn't change. "Leave me alone."

She turned her back to me. Pulled the blanket up to her shoulder. Curled in on herself.

It wasn't rejection. I knew that. It was survival. The only way she could hold the pieces together.

So I said nothing more. Just lay beside her in silence. I watched the way she curled tighter, the blanket trembling slightly with each breath. My heart ached.

Gods, I wanted to beg her to hold me. To let me hold her. To say *anything*. To share the weight of it. But I knew what she needed now wasn't words.

It was space. Stillness. But not solitude.

"I'll be here if you change your mind," I murmured. "Always."

"Quiet down back there," Lucius called. "We're approaching the gate."

I wiped my face. I hadn't even noticed the tears.

We shifted onto our backs, breaths held, limbs arranged like the dead. The wagon jerked to a stop.

A guard—I assumed—grumbled, "I don't know what I did to get this detail…"

The blanket lifted.

Neither of us moved.

My eyes stayed fixed on the fabric overhead.

The blanket dropped.

"Let them through!" the guard barked.

The wagon creaked into motion again.

We were still for a long while—until Lucius finally called back, "It's safe now. We'll make camp once we're past the farmlands."

# CHAPTER EIGHTY-FIVE
## *First Watch*

*"I will wait. That is the vow."*
—The Breath of the World

Rudamos 27, 1231
*Valerius*

Behind a curtain of old blankets strung near the fire, Mariana tended to Aleaia's wounds. Even if I couldn't make out the words, her voice was soothing. Familiar.

I sat just on the other side, cradling a tin cup of warm water in both hands. The heat barely reached my fingers, let alone the cold deep in my bones. After decadia of hard bread and dirty water, anything else would be too rich and sour in my gut.

"All right. Once more," Lucius said, pressing a hot, damp cloth to my face for the third time.

Lucius hadn't asked if I wanted a shave. He knew.

I'd be lying if I said it didn't feel good after so long without even the barest care. I held the cloth there while he checked the edge of his razor, the soft rasp of steel being sharpened against stone steady and practiced.

When I lowered the cloth, he rubbed the bar of soap between his hands, worked it into a thin lather, and smeared it across my jaw. It smelled clean. Fresh. Gods, I hadn't smelled that in so long.

"Don't move," he said, stepping close behind me. Two fingers settled beneath my chin, his thumb firm at the angle of my jaw.

Then the blade touched skin. Slow strokes along my cheeks first. Then my jawline. Then my throat.

I heard Aleaia sniffle behind the curtain and started at the sound.

"Ah, ah. I said be still," Lucius admonished, holding firm. "She's all right. Just being tended to by the gentlest woman we know."

I drew a breath in through my nose and out through my mouth. Nodded once. Let him finish. Each swipe of the razor left me lighter than the one before.

When he was done, it was the most human I'd felt in a long time.

"Thank you," I said, wiping my face with the cloth.

Lucius clapped me on the shoulder. "Anything to make you more bearable to look at."

Then I sat, waiting for Aleaia.

She emerged after a while, steps slow and careful, and came to sit beside me.

Mariana gave me a pointed look and nodded toward the curtain. She wanted to look me over, I knew, but I just wanted to be with Aleaia. To sit quietly beside her. To comfort her, if she'd let me.

I shook my head. "I'm fine." The smile I gave her didn't reach my eyes.

Too tired to argue, she crossed the fire and sank onto the bedroll Lucius had laid out.

I looked to him, raising an eyebrow in silent question.

He offered a half-shrug, then moved to slide under the blanket with her.

I could feel Aleaia's nearness, even when we didn't touch, and it eased something tight in my chest.

I didn't want to speak. Not with the others still awake.

I cleared my throat.

"I'll take first watch," I said.

"Figured you would. Wake me when you get too tired," Lucius mumbled, already shifting to get comfortable.

Silence settled around us. The fire crackled softly. Its glow danced over Aleaia's face, deepening the shadows beneath her eyes.

"An unlikely pair if I ever saw one." I nodded toward Lucius and Mariana across the fire.

"They've been together a while," she said softly. "Longer than you and I."

Still us. I hadn't realized how tightly I'd been holding my breath.

"Really? I had no idea."

Lucius hadn't told me, but he rarely talked about the women he courted. Still, I would have thought he'd mention her.

Aleaia didn't answer. Just reached out, brushed the edge of my blanket with her fingertips.

I shifted to make space, lifting my arm and the blanket.

She leaned against me, and I wrapped the blanket around us both, resting my chin lightly atop her head.

I took a deep breath. I needed this as much as she did.

The silence between us wasn't heavy. It was refuge.

"They cut all your hair off," she said, voice small.

*Cold stone beneath my knees.*

*Incense.*

*The priest reciting the rites.*

*The rasp of shears at my scalp.*

I shoved it away. No time for that.

"Apparently it was impure," I said. "Cassius mentioned it often enough. His pet butcher sheared me like a sheep, as if you were only with me for the curls."

That earned a soft laugh. Faint, but real.

She sat up and met my gaze. "Would you be upset if I said I was glad your beard is gone?"

"Not at all," I said. "I'm glad it's gone too. It was itchy. Would've gotten in the way."

"In the way?"

"If you wanted to kiss me," I said. "Now it won't be like kissing a sheep."

Her hand covered her mouth, like she was afraid she'd laugh.

I couldn't help myself. "Unless you wanted to kiss a sheep. I could let it grow out again."

"No," she said, laughing—just for a moment—before it turned to a hitched breath.

I knew better than to ask what was wrong.

"I'm sorry," she whispered.

She wrapped her arms around me then, breath hitching again. Once. Twice. I just held her and let her breathe through it.

"You've nothing to be sorry for," I said. "It wasn't your fault. None of it." I held her tighter. Braced both of us against everything we couldn't undo. "They are evil, Aleaia. Nothing you did—nothing you didn't do—brought this on you."

Her shoulders began to shake. Silent sobs soaked into my tunic, the sound of them buried in my chest.

"All I thought about, the whole time we were there… was you," she choked out. "And then when we escaped, I pushed you away. I'm sorry. Please—please forgive me."

"There's nothing to forgive, amor mea." I lifted her chin with gentle fingers, met her eyes, wet and red-rimmed. "When you're ready, let me carry some of it. I'll bear whatever you give me."

She nodded, breath catching again. "Not now… but maybe later."

I brushed my thumb across her cheek, wiped the tears clinging there.

"I don't mind your touch," she said softly. "I just… I can't. Not all of it. Not right now."

The thought that she might worry I'd ask her for that—after everything—turned my stomach.

"Only what you give freely," I murmured. "That's all I want. But—"

The words rose—*you're safe with me*—heavy and urgent, pressing at the back of my throat.

I swallowed them down.

When I could trust my voice again, I held her gaze. "Promise me something. Just one thing."

"What?"

"That if I ever do something that hurts you—something you don't want—you'll tell me. Right away. I'll stop. No questions. No hesitation. Like before. Like always."

"I promise," she said.

Then she leaned in and wrapped her arms around my waist, tight and fierce.

Like she was afraid to let go.
I would wait.
For whatever she chose to give.

# CHAPTER EIGHTY-SIX

## *Seventy-Three Days*

*"Even after I was free, the days stayed with me."*
—Healer's journals of Gormlaith

Rudamos 28, 1231
*Aleaia*

I sat in the back of the wagon, eyes fixed on the road behind us. It blurred—ruts dissolving into one another, as meaningless as the rest of it. My body rocked with the motion, but it didn't feel like mine.

I was a ghost, riding the shell of the person I used to be.

Val lay beside me, finally asleep.

I wanted to wrap myself around him. Press my forehead to his back and hold him tight until the world made sense again. Until I was me again.

But I couldn't.

Not when my own skin felt foreign. Fouled. Untouchable.

To keep the silence from swallowing me whole, I asked Lucius and Mariana, "What day is it?"

The question tasted strange. Distant. Like I'd borrowed it from someone else.

"Sationem—"

Mariana smacked his arm.

"Sorry. *Rudamos* twenty-eighth," Lucius said.

I swallowed. Then asked the one that frightened me most.

"And the year?"

Lucius looked over his shoulder at me. "Still 1231."

I met his eyes and held them for a long moment before nodding and looking away at the road behind us.

*Seventy-three days.*

The breath left my lungs.

"What happened in Avitum?"

Lucius glanced at Mariana, then back to the road. "Well," he said, "we found his lordship first."

"Not that." My voice cracked. *Gods, not that.* "The city. What led up to the rescue?"

He exhaled, slow. Tension bled from his shoulders in degrees. "We received word of your arrest. Inquisition activity surged overnight. The Third Army reactivated the Vinculatores."

My throat closed. Just hearing the name stirred something dark and cold in my gut.

Third Army. Anvallan soldiers under the command of the High Priest. They didn't answer to the crown—they served the Temple. Their elite force, the First Legion, were called the *Vinculatores Magorum*. Mage binders. After the Aeltyrian War, they'd been disbanded, pushed to backwater garrisons and ceremonial duties.

I wasn't old enough to remember the last Inquisition. But the stories lingered like smoke—household raids, midnight arrests, people who vanished without trial.

"Some of the old noble houses fled," Lucius continued. "The city gates were closed. No one in or out without a special permit."

I looked at him, brow furrowed. "Then how did you get inside? How did you even find us?"

He didn't answer right away. Kept his eyes on the road. "I acquired one of those permits."

Mariana nudged his arm. "We had help. A scribe inside the Imperial household. Trusted. Discreet. He could mimic Marcus Frugi's hand, and he had access to the seal. That got us in."

Everything stopped.

*Marcus.*

The name struck like a lash. My throat closed. My breath turned shallow. Bile surged. My vision narrowed. The world muted under the rush of blood in my ears.

I clapped my hands over my ears. Closed my eyes.

Too late. The memories were already there.

*Chains clinking.*

*The stink of wine and sweat.*

*Something sour in the air.*

*Stone scraping beneath my knees.*

*I couldn't breathe.*

*I couldn't move.*

*Trapped.*

"Aleaia."

A voice. Familiar. Steady.

A hand found mine—warm, calm. He didn't pull. Just stayed there.

"You're safe," Val murmured. "I've got you."

I blinked. The blur receded just enough to find him in front of me. Calm. Watching me. Holding still. His voice was careful.

"They're not here. Not now. Just you and me, and Lucius, and Mariana. In a wagon."

My hands fell from my ears. They shook. All of me shook. But the world returned: the creak of the wagon, the scent of pine and dust and horse. No stone. No blood.

"I'm... in a wagon," I said slowly. "With you. And Lucius. Mariana. We're... going somewhere."

"To Letia," he said. "Where I grew up. It's safe, and it's near the sea. You'll rest there. Then we'll go home."

"Home. To Aeldunon." A ragged breath escaped me. "But... won't they look for us in Letia?"

"They won't," Val said softly. "Lucius sent decoys—pairs dressed like us, heading for every obvious place. Ports, cities, even the road to Aeldunon. We've moved slow on purpose. They'll have searched Letia by now. Found it empty."

I reached up with a trembling hand. Touched his cheek.

He caught it. Held it to him. Turned into it and kissed my palm.

"Thank you," I whispered.

I didn't pull away.

Instead, I leaned into him. Tucked myself beneath his chin. Let the blanket shift. Let his warmth take some of the cold from my skin.

I rested my hand on his chest. Fingers fisted lightly in the front of his tunic. I still didn't feel like myself. But the coil inside me loosened, thread by thread, until my breath came easier.

He stayed still. Matched my breathing. Held steady as I unraveled. I didn't stir again.

I listened to his heart, beating steadily. Felt his hand cradle my head to him.

The tension seeped out of me, a little at a time.

For the first time in seventy-three days, I slept.

# CHAPTER EIGHTY-SEVEN
## *Rot & Ash*

*"What survives is not always what lived."*
—The Breath of the World

Rudamos 53, 1231
*Aleaia*

Val spent two and a half decadia tending to me. He bathed my wounds, held me while I slept, and never once asked for more than I could give. He sat beside me when I needed silence, held my hand when the nightmares wouldn't let go. He was patient. Gentle. Steady.

And still, I felt filthy. Wrong in my own skin.

Trees gave way to sun-bleached stone walls and tall, arched windows catching the last gold light of afternoon. The villa stood above the cliffs, the hush of distant waves rising to meet us. The wagon jolted to a halt.

Lucius jumped down from the driver's bench without a word.

Mariana followed, stretching her arms overhead with a soft groan. Lucius caught her around the waist and tugged her in, pressing a quick kiss to her mouth. The kind that didn't need ceremony to mean something.

"I'll check the grounds," he said, heading for the gate. "If I find anything that doesn't belong, I'll gut it."

"I'll head into town. I need some supplies. You two stay here," Mariana said.

I nodded, looking away from all of them, toward the sea.

It wasn't jealousy. Just a sudden, hollow ache. A kind of emptiness that came all at once.

There'd been a time I might've reached for Val like that—easily and instinctively. The thought of touching him felt forbidden. Even if he'd held me since we left Avitum, my body didn't feel like something he should be near.

Whatever was left of me, it wasn't the woman he'd known.

I was corruption. Rot. Ash.

The villa was beautiful the way nature was. Not polished marble and stone like Avitum.

"You said you were a country lad." I glanced toward the whitewashed villa. "Look at this place."

I meant it as a jest. It didn't land. Too thin. Too practiced.

Not really a joke—just the ghost of one.

Like everything else about me.

Val stood beneath a tree, arms loosely crossed, gaze turned to the sea. At the sound of my voice, he looked back.

"This place pales in comparison to Aeldunon," he said. "I hope it doesn't disappoint you too much once we're inside."

I didn't answer. The sun caught his profile, like that day we got lost in the woods. Still unfairly attractive, but no curl at the corner of his mouth. No smugness. Just a sadness that lingered, a slight downturn of his lips.

I had done that. That was the result of loving me. Maybe Cassius had broken something permanent.

It felt like another life, those days on the road to Aeldunon. Another form of me had laughed there, rode wildly with him, dreaming up the future like it was something we could shape with our hands.

That woman had been reckless. Brave. Full of aching hope.

I didn't know where she'd gone.

I wanted to take his hand. Just for a moment. Pretend we were still those people. But my arm stayed rooted at my side.

It was too close inside the wagon. I moved through the flap and down to the ground.

Marcus's voice echoed through my mind, cold and certain.

*"You're repulsive. Defiled and corrupted. Unworthy."*

I squeezed my eyes shut. My stomach turned. I bent forward, bracing my hands on my thighs. My breath came tight and shallow as bile rose. I forced it down.

I would not break.

Not here.

Not again.

Still, his voice clung like grime I couldn't wash away.

I felt Val move beside me, quiet as a shadow. He rubbed my back gently until the nausea passed and I stood upright again.

He took my hand slowly, without pressure. When I didn't pull away, he gave it a light squeeze. "Is this all right?"

"It's fine," I said. The lie was bitter in my mouth, and the truth wanted out. "I just… I don't feel worthy of it. Or of you. I never did. And now… even less."

He didn't speak. Just moved his thumb across mine, steady and soft. Waiting.

I drew a deep, shaking breath.

"There's pain. Everywhere. Inside. Outside. Exhaustion, but when sleep comes, I see it all again. Him. That place. The things he did." I pinched the bridge of my nose, hard. "And when I wake, I still hear him. I can't stop it. He's in my head."

Val said nothing. He didn't try to fix it. Just held my hand.

"It's like rot buried deep inside me. I know it should be cut out. But I can't reach it. It's the only enemy I've ever faced that I can't fight. It's in me now. And it's eating me alive." I swallowed hard. "Then there's fear."

The words stuck. But I forced them out.

"Fear that I might be with child. His. Theirs. I don't know. I can't eat. I can't move."

My breath faltered. My chest tightened.

I lifted both hands to my face, cupping my mouth and nose, trying to force air into my lungs. An ache twisted low in my belly.

I didn't hear him move. But I felt him.

Val's thumb stroked mine.

"You're the strongest person I've ever known," he said. "You've faced worse than most ever will. You'll survive this, too. And I'll be here. Every step."

I blinked hard. Turned away from him.

"I don't know how to love anymore, Val," I shook my head. "All I feel is despair. I'm not a soldier. Not heir to anything. I'm nothing. Just… hollow. He won."

I looked down, but all I saw was dust. Shadow.

"You should have let me die there." My voice cracked. "What's left of me isn't worth saving."

I had clung to life because he'd needed me to. Because there'd been a chance they'd spare him. I bargained myself for his safety.

I wasn't supposed to survive it.

And all that remained was the echo of what I couldn't forget.

I couldn't give him that weight. Not on top of everything else.

"I don't know who—what—I'm meant to be anymore."

Val reached out and gently lifted my chin.

"Then I'll love you until you remember who you are," he said. "I'll show you joy again. Teach you love, the way you taught me. I'll give you memories so strong they drown his voice. I'll help you find your way back, even if it takes all my years, and all of yours."

I searched his face—for what I wasn't sure. Disgust, maybe. Some indication that he was only being kind, that he didn't mean it. But all I found was the truth. And love.

"I won't give up on you, luce mea," he murmured, a faint smile on his lips.

And something stirred. Small. Fragile.

Not hope. Not yet.

But something warmer than the cold that had hollowed me out.

# CHAPTER EIGHTY-EIGHT
## *At The Table*

*"We are not healed when the bleeding stops.
We are healed when we sit down to eat."*
—The Breath of the World

Rudamos 53, 1231
*Aleaia*

The villa, contrary to Val's modest description, was no simple country farmhouse.

When we entered the atrium, I saw that the interior was tended with the same care as the grounds. Though the villa bore the patina of age, it was immaculately kept. The tapestries had softened under sun and time, threads dulled but not frayed. The furniture was old and heavy, carved wood worn smooth at the arms and edges. Preserved. As though someone had chosen comfort over display.

This place hadn't bent to the world. It had endured.

It was a sanctuary.

Even the gardens beyond the atrium showed the same care.

The stone paths were swept clean, flowering vines pruned, hedges trimmed with purpose. Alive with late-spring color, they had been shaped in the old style. Not clipped to angles like in the capital, but allowed to spill and twist where they willed.

The reception Val received was unlike anything I'd seen in a Calesian household. There were no silent lines of slaves, no steward waiting for orders like a statue carved from fear. The Inquisition had been there, just as Val said. But the people who remained bore the dignity of survivors—not as servants, not as prisoners. As themselves, even in incolumium manacles.

Laughter echoed through the courtyard as we entered through the atrium. Two dark-haired children—barefoot and shrieking with joy—raced each other beneath the colonnade. Their shouts bounced off the stone, bold and bright and heedless.

Silver glinted at their wrists when the sun caught it. Incolumium. Light enough not to slow them. Heavy enough to matter.

I watched them run, my breath catching.

They were free.

As free as Aeltyrian children could be in Calesia.

I understood, then, why Val had been willing to give his life for this place.

They didn't notice us at first. But the moment the children spotted Val, their game ended in delighted squeals. The boy barreled straight into Val's legs while the girl jumped—perhaps a bit too early—to throw her arms around his neck. He caught her with a grunt, held her for a moment, smiling into her hair, while he patted the boy's hair.

The girl pulled back, her wide brown eyes fixed on him for a long moment. "Val, you're so skinny!" she declared. "Davena's going to shout at you."

"And your hair's weird," the boy said. He narrowed his eyes at Val, nose wrinkling as he tipped his head.

Val nodded, trying not to laugh. "I've had a hard season."

The girl poked him in the chest with a finger. "You'd better not skip dinner. Davena said she made that stew you like."

"And pudding," the boy added. "She made extra because you always steal it."

Val narrowed his eyes. "Told you that, did she?"

Then he turned to me, and something in his face softened.

"Aleaia," he said, "these two are Bren and Lysa. Bren can be bribed with sweets. Lysa will boss you around if you let her, and she can't be bribed with anything."

"It's because I'm seven years old." Lysa gave me a once-over. "Are you the warrior Davena talks about?"

"Depends." I folded my arms. Did my best to look severe. "What has she said?"

"She says Lucius told her you're very brave," Lysa answered, like it was a formal report. "And that you don't like being fussed over, but you need it anyway. And that Lucius said you like honey cakes too."

Bren stepped closer, head tilted. "You don't look scary. And I'm only six."

I knelt, slowly. "That's because I'm not trying to scare you."

He didn't flinch. Didn't look afraid. Just curious. Honest.

*"Calon, genirí!"* a woman's voice called from the portico. *Come, children!*

At once, they darted off, quick and light as leaves blown down a path. Their laughter trailed behind them as they disappeared into the villa.

The woman who stepped forward was broad-shouldered and strong, her hair wrapped in a kerchief patterned with mountain flowers. Her hands looked like they could lift a cauldron as easily as they could cradle a child.

"Val?" She turned to call over her shoulder. "Rasmus! Val's home!"

She went straight to Val and pulled him into her arms.

He didn't resist.

An older man followed behind her. He said nothing. Just laid both hands on Val's shoulders and pulled him and the woman into a silent embrace.

I looked away.

Not from discomfort. From something quieter.

I'd seen Val bleed. I'd seen him love. I'd seen him furious. But this—this homecoming—struck a different chord. The affection here wasn't tentative. It had deepened in his absence, blooming without waiting for permission.

It didn't belong to me.

I would never know anything like it.

The thought passed through me quietly, like a shadow crossing water.

"Davena. Rasmus." Val stepped back, gesturing to me. "This is Aleaia."

He opened his arm to me, beckoning me closer.

"The woman who holds my heart. Come, amor mea."

Not his guard. Not the Daughter of Aelan. Not heir of Aeltyria.

I forgot how to breathe.

I let him draw me in, bowing my head in respect. "Hello, grandmother. Grandfather."

Davena's eyes narrowed. Measuring.

*"Maisau eithich,"* she said with a tilt of her head. *Pretty enough.* Then, with an edge sharp enough to catch, *"Nare bris ta." Don't break it.*

My gaze dropped to my hands. Calloused. Still dusty from the road. Trembling.

*"Taes araié rean sen dos ara vorest,"* Val said in Aeltyrian, smooth and steady. *It's hers to do with as she wishes.*

The words were for Davena, but his eyes stayed on me.

Something caught in my throat. His defense of me landed deep, in that hollow place inside me. It was the sort of kindness that made everything ache. Like the floor had shifted beneath me and I hadn't noticed until I was already falling.

I swallowed hard, fighting the burn in my eyes.

Davena blinked, caught off guard. Then her expression shifted to something closer to delight. She bowed her head, just slightly, in concession.

"You've learned our tongue at last," she said. "Forgive me."

"I had good reason," Val said, glancing toward me.

Davena's gaze drifted down to my wrists. The manacles.

She and Rasmus wore them too.

Her face sobered with recognition.

Rasmus, silent until now, turned to me. His brows drew together. The look he gave me was clear. Measuring.

His gaze flicked between the two of us. "What brings you here like this?"

Val exhaled. Slow. Soft.

"We're in some trouble. It's a long story. We should eat first. Use the caldarium. Then we'll talk."

"You're in luck. I made that mutton stew you like," Davena said, firm and final. "And enough of it to share. You both look like you've been carved down to the bone."

"I'll get the furnace going," Rasmus said, already turning toward the door.

Mariana stepped beside me and slipped her arm through mine, light and familiar as we walked across the courtyard.

"Well," she said, a sly smile curving her mouth, "you've earned Davena's approval. That's not nothing."

"I hope so." A faint smile tugged at my lips. "She knew you when you arrived."

"We passed through here on the way to Avitum. Lucius insisted we take a ship. Said it was safer than the pass. Took the first vessel from Nuala after Succamos."

I nodded, remembering the Pass. The things that followed. "It is."

I didn't mean to touch it, but my fingertips curled to brush the scar on my palm anyway. Pale and faint now. I had survived the thing that made it. Maybe I'd survive this, too.

Even if I didn't know how.

I couldn't let myself think like that right now. I forced myself to take in the things around me. The stone walkway under my feet. The dummies in the training yard at the far end of the courtyard. The sea breeze. The sun on my face.

And when I felt steady enough—more like myself—I spoke again. "Lucius's family lives here, don't they? Did you meet them?"

Mariana nodded, then flushed slightly. "They do. And I did. They were kind, though…" She shook her head. "His sister was less thrilled to meet me. I thought she might call the guards."

I arched a brow.

"She took one look at me and decided I didn't belong," Mariana said with a shrug. "I think she expected Lucius to show up with a Calesian noblewoman on his arm. Maybe one with shoes worth more than everything I own."

I huffed, almost a laugh. "She doesn't know him very well, then."

Mariana smiled. "Must not."

"I'm glad you have each other," I said softly.

She pulled my arm closer and leaned her head against my shoulder. As close to a sister as I'd ever have.

The warmth of the kitchen met us as we stepped inside.

"I haven't had time to prepare the dining room, my lord," Davena said, already moving between pots and ladles with practiced grace. "But I'll have it ready for dinner. For now, I hope you won't mind something simple, here in the kitchen."

She gestured to the worn wooden table at the room's center—hearth-lit, comfortably scuffed. The kind of table where real things happened. Tunics mended. Knees bandaged. Stories traded over burnt crusts and late wine.

The kind of table meant for the ones who kept a house alive.

The offer, so casual, said more about Val than he ever would. That he belonged here—not by title, but by love. The way Davena spoke to him. The way Rasmus had embraced him. The way the house itself seemed to settle around his presence.

My chest tightened. Not with envy. With pride.

He called me his light, but he was the one who illuminated everything around him for so many.

The scent of stew drifted from the hearth in curling ribbons. Herbs and mutton. Onion, maybe. Thyme. I hadn't felt hunger since Avitum. As if my body had forgotten how to want anything.

But something stirred.

The warmth. The scent. The nearness of people I trusted.

My stomach growled loud enough to earn glances from Mariana, Val, and Lucius.

"Gods, it smells good, Davena," Val said, as he pulled out a chair for me.

Once I sat, he took the seat beside me. Lucius and Mariana settled across from us. Davena moved with the rhythm of someone who had done this a thousand times—ladling stew into bowls, setting one in front of each of us.

I scooped, then lifted the spoon. Blew across the surface. Took a bite.

Rich, earthy flavor. Tender meat that fell apart on my tongue. Salted root vegetables. Herbs still fresh enough to brighten the edges.

It tasted like… *Rhaelaith.*

*Like the weight of my grandmother's cooking pot and my father's boots by the door.*

*Like coming home from the fields in silence, knowing there would be something warm.*

*Like… home.*

I finished the bowl faster than I meant to.

"Could I have a bit more, grandmother?" I asked, careful with the words.

Davena's brows lifted. "Of course," she said, and refilled the bowl. She set it down in front of me with a gentle smile.

That's when I noticed the others watching.

Lucius. Mariana.

Val—thoughtful and still.

I looked around the table at each of them. "What?"

"I've marched with legionaries all my life and never seen anyone eat that f—" Lucius began, only to grunt as Mariana's elbow found his ribs.

"Never mind him," she said quickly, shooting him a look sharp enough to cut.

Val hadn't said a word. Hadn't touched his bowl. He just watched me.

I met his gaze. "What is it?"

He studied me for a moment, then smiled and turned back to his food.

"Nothing," he said in Aeltyrian, and took a slow spoonful of stew.

"Your entire childhood, I tried to teach you the old words," Davena said, standing near him with a cloth in hand. "You sound almost like you were born in Lascebar."

"He does not," I said at once. The hills might claim me, but I had never let them claim my tongue.

Davena's mouth twitched.

Val made a strangled sound that might have been a cough.

"He does," Mariana said. "Probably because you taught him, Aleaia."

I fixed my eyes on her. Stared for a long moment. "He taught himself. With books."

"I did learn pronunciation from you," Val offered.

I turned to him slowly. "You were doing so well."

Lucius and Mariana laughed. Something tugged at the corners of my lips—soft, reluctant.

I ate in silence for a while, listening to the conversation around me. I took in the familiarity between Val and Lucius, the way Mariana smiled without restraint at something Val said. Everyone had connections to each other here, except me.

Lucius leaned back in his chair, eyes on me. "So. Where'd you leave your sword?"

"Me?" I blinked, then wiped my mouth with a cloth near my bowl. "In the springs. Under the castle. I had a feeling that Val's room wouldn't be safe."

"Good thinking," Lucius said with a nod. "When our man searched his room, it was stripped clean. I'll send a bird to let him know he's earned a soak."

I'd be glad to have the Fellglow Blade back, but—

My father's book.

*Gone.*

The thought lodged deep. I drew a thin breath. My eyes stung. I pressed a hand to my mouth before I could stop it.

"He'll get it back," Lucius said, his brow furrowed. "Don't worry."

"It's not… not that. There was a book." I swallowed. "It was important to me."

Lucius leaned forward. "What was it?"

My voice wavered. "My father's copy of *The Song of the Stars*. Old. Brown leather cover. He left notes in the margins. It was in my saddlebag."

A moment passed. No one spoke.

Then Lucius gave a single, solemn nod. "I'll tell him to search harder."

I shook my head. "Don't trouble him—"

"Stop. You're no more a thorn in my side now than you were before you left Aeldunon, Dieter," Lucius said with a shrug, like that settled it.

Mariana cast a pointed look at him. "I've been trying, unsuccessfully, to teach him manners. As you can see. What he means is that you're no trouble at all, Aleaia."

I smiled, though it didn't quite reach my eyes.

The warmth in the room only sharpened the ache in my chest. As if I haunted them now, a ghost of the woman I used to be.

Val knew. He always did.

"Aleaia," he said gently, "if you're finished, I can show you to your room. Then to the caldarium, if you like."

*My room? Alone?*

"I'm done now," I said quickly, grateful for the excuse to stand. My chair scraped back across the stone floor, louder than I meant.

"Come see me after your bath, both of you," Mariana said.

"We will," Val replied.

We stepped into the corridor together, leaving the warmth of the hearth behind.

He offered me his hand.

I hesitated, just a breath.

Then I took it. And I didn't let go.

# CHAPTER EIGHTY-NINE
## *The Drop*

*"Love does not begin with certainty. It begins with presence."*
—The Breath of the World

Rudamos 53, 1231
*Aleaia*

"This was my mother's home," Val said as we moved through the quiet halls. "The ancestral home of House Alvareti. I'm the last of its line."

It struck me then—how much he knew of me. My fears. My failings. The blood I carried. And how little I knew of him by comparison, beyond what the world demanded he be.

The image of Val with Lysa on one hip and Bren's arms around his legs flitted through my mind.

I pushed it down, buried it under a less intrusive question.

I glanced over at him. "What was your mother's name?"

"Astraea," he said. "Everything I know about her, I learned from Davena and Rasmus. They were here when she was born. Cared for her until she left for Avitum."

He led me through a side door into a narrow courtyard overlooking the sea. Tiny shoots of new plants peeked up above the soil. Lavender and rosemary, cut back the previous year, were beginning to wake.

"This is the kitchen garden," he said, nodding toward the herb plots. "It's nothing much now, but in Dēwamos, it smells like basil and thyme and rosemary."

We kept walking, side by side beneath a long portico. To our right, a narrow pool stretched beneath the sky, still as glass. The silence here felt softer than anywhere else we'd been.

I had no right to the question. But I needed the answer.

"The children. Are they yours?"

"Mine?"

Understanding flickered across his face. He stopped, keeping a gentle hold on my hand so I did too.

Heat flooded my face. I couldn't meet his eyes. "Are they?"

"No," he said, steady and certain, his thumb brushing lightly over mine. "They're Rasmus and Davena's grandchildren. Their mother died when Bren was born. Their father…"

Something sharp flickered across his face.

"He was sold years ago. To the mines. Not by me."

The words settled heavily between us.

"They love you," I said quietly.

"They're mine to look after. Family. But they're not *mine*."

I swallowed and looked down at our hands. "I'm sorry."

"Aleaia." His voice was steady.

I looked up, met his gaze.

"If I had children, luce mea, you would know."

I searched his face for hesitation and found none.

He had never lied to me.

I believed him.

I let him guide me forward beneath the portico.

"Your room is at the end," Val said. "I'll take the one across from it, so I'll be close, if you need me. Or we can share a room."

"Don't be foolish," I said, sharper than I meant. Then, softer, "Of course I want to share."

I wasn't sure it was true. I knew I didn't want to be apart from him. It wasn't him I feared. It was the silence. The dark. The things that came when there was nowhere left to run.

He'd seen the worst already. Perhaps he feared the same.

"Me too," he said.

When we reached the door, he opened it.

The room was warm. Books lined the shelves. Linen curtains drifted on the breeze. A worn blanket lay folded over the arm of a chair near the hearth. Lived in.

I lingered by the bed. Too large for one man.

The door stood solid behind me. The walls rose unbroken on either side. No open sky. No easy path out.

*Or in*, I thought.

Val moved to the balcony doors and opened them wide, letting in a rush of cool, briny sea wind.

"I want to show you something," he said.

I stepped outside with him. Rested my hands on the cool stone railing, the wind lifting my hair. Water stretched to the horizon.

"I've never seen the sea before," I said. "It makes me feel… small. Not in a bad way. Just… like I'm not the center of anything."

"Humbling isn't it?" He stood next to me, arms folded, close enough to lean on, if I wanted. "But it frees you, too. The world's vast. And what we carry—our pain—is smaller than it feels. Especially if you swim in it."

I looked up at him. "You swim here?"

"Every summer I'm here. I used to dive off the rocks, when I was younger. The water's freezing at first, but you forget that once you're in."

I imagined it: the climb, lungs burning. The wind in my hair, the sun at my back. One step, and there would be no taking it back.

Only the fall.

The cold.

The moment before you remembered how to breathe.

"I think I'd be afraid of the drop."

"I was. But Gavius told me once that fear is just the body remembering it wants to live."

That landed like a fist to the gut.

Was it the fall I feared—not the water, but the instant before it, when there was no turning back?

A shaky breath escaped me—half laugh, half sob.

He wrapped his arms around me, gently, as if waiting for me to pull away. I leaned into him, my head against his chest.

And I cried. Not all at once. Not loud.

The tears slipped down my cheeks into his tunic, sudden and unstoppable.

And he said nothing. Just held me.

I don't know how long we stood there. But eventually the tears slowed. Dried. Left behind only the ache.

His heartbeat was slow. Steady.

*You don't deserve this. You don't deserve him.*

My shoulders tensed.

Val's voice was soft against my hair. "What is it?"

I shook my head. "Nothing," I lied.

But when I looked up at him, needing something I didn't know how to name, he was already there—eyes searching my face.

I raised myself on my toes and leaned in, touched my lips to his.

A quiet, tender sound escaped him.

And then he kissed me back.

Soft at first. Careful. I slid my hand into his hair.

Still, he hesitated. I could feel it.

I pulled back just enough to whisper, "Kiss me like you used to."

His hands rose to cradle my face, and his mouth found mine again—fierce now, full of everything he couldn't say. My knees weakened, and he wrapped his arms around me to hold me as I swayed.

When we finally broke apart, breathless, he rested his forehead against mine.

"I love you, luce mea," he murmured. "I can't remember what it was like not to."

I closed my eyes.

"I said I wasn't sure if I could feel anything anymore," I breathed. "That wasn't true. Isn't."

He stilled. Listening.

"I don't know if it's love. I don't remember what that feels like. Not yet. It's buried under…" I couldn't finish. "But when I'm with you… I feel whole. Pulled toward you. Like I still exist." I pulled back enough to meet his eyes. "Maybe that's what love is. I don't know. I just... I don't want to say something wrong. I don't want to hurt you."

Loving him was touching something white with blood on my hands. And if I never said the words again—if I didn't bind him to me with them—then maybe, one day, he could still choose a life that didn't end here.

He brushed a strand of hair from my face, his touch unbearably gentle.

"Then don't," he said. "I'll wait. Like you waited for me. Gods, you waited so long. I can, too."

My throat tightened. I swallowed hard.

"I want you to know," I said, "it isn't your fault. The way I feel. It's not because of you. You didn't do this to me. You've only ever made me feel safe."

His breath shuddered as it left him, and something in him eased—just a little.

I tucked myself against his chest, beneath his chin, and he held me tighter.

Below us, the waves whispered against the shore.

The voice in my head hadn't stopped.

But for now, I buried myself in his warmth and tried to believe that maybe, just maybe, it could be silenced.

# CHAPTER NINETY
## *What We Carry*

*"There is no shame in weeping.*
*The gods wept when they shaped the world."*
—Sermons of the Elder Flame, banned scroll

Rudamos 53, 1231
*Aleaia*

"As much as I'd really rather stay here all day," Val said, his cheek resting against my hair, "we should go."

He drew back just enough to meet my eyes.

His were beautifully clear and warm, the kind that saw me without judgment. The way he looked at me, like I was something worth holding on to, softened a part of my chest I hadn't realized was still hardened.

"I had Rasmus prepare the caldarium," he added. "And we're both in need of a bath."

Reluctantly, I let him go. We made our way through the villa, down a mosaic-lined hall that opened into a tiled chamber full of golden light and rising steam. The warmth hit first, then the quiet. Someone had already laid out clothing and bath sheets along a stone bench.

I stepped forward and picked up a tunic, light and silky in my hands. I held it up, studying the drape.

"Whose are these?" I asked. "It's kind of them to lend them to me."

Val laughed under his breath as he reached for his belt. "They're mine. Or they were. From when I was younger. Davena must've kept them from falling apart."

He pulled off his tunic and folded it neatly before reaching for the ties at his waist.

His fingers faltered.

Just for a breath.

His eyes dropped to the water, fingers hovering where they'd stilled.

I glanced over and saw the set of his shoulders, the tension there, the slight bracing curve of his spine.

It wasn't modesty.

He thought I'd flinch.

He didn't say a word. Just took a breath and finished undressing in silence—leaving on his smallclothes—and stepped down into the water, sinking low, as if the steam might hide whatever shame clung to him.

I didn't look away. Instead, I stepped to the edge of the pool near him. I squatted, one hand resting lightly on the warm stone.

He didn't lift his eyes.

"You don't have to hide from me," I said. "I'm not afraid of you."

Val let out a breath. A dry, unconvincing shell of a laugh.

But something flickered across his face. A stillness. His gaze dropped, watching something only he could see.

Then it passed.

I lingered a moment longer, then stood and turned back to the bench. I untied my boots in silence. Then my trousers.

When they were off, I stood there, clutching the hem of my tunic.

*What's underneath is disgusting.* The thought came easily, as naturally as breathing.

"Aleaia?" Val asked gently, glancing over as he scrubbed his shoulder with a sea sponge. After a moment, he added, "Take your time. There's no rush. The caldarium stays hot for a long time."

I hadn't seen my own body naked in a season. Even when they stripped me, even when Mariana looked me over, I'd refused to look. Not once.

I didn't know how to explain that away to Val. So I gave him the truth.

"I haven't… seen myself since. Even when Mariana checked my injuries, I didn't look."

He stilled. "You're afraid of what you'll find."

I nodded, fixing my gaze on a hairline crack in a distant column. I didn't dare meet his eyes. If I did, I might start crying again.

And I didn't want to cry. Not now.

Val waded to the bottom of the steps, water up to his waist.

"What do you want me to do?" he asked, searching my face.

I hesitated. The question settled deep.

"Would you look first?" I asked. "And warn me?"

He lifted his hand to me in quiet invitation.

I took it.

The stone was warm beneath my feet as I stepped into the pool, stopping on the bottom step. The water lapped against my calves, steam curling up between us.

"This feels a little like the hot springs," Val said, offering a tentative smile.

"Without the thrill of possibly getting caught," I said, trying for levity.

It didn't quite land.

"I'll wash your hair for you, if you want," he said.

I nodded. "After."

I just wanted the worst of it to be over.

His hands still held mine. "Do you want to close your eyes?"

I took a breath and closed them.

He reached for the laces at my neck. "I'm going to take this off now."

I covered my chest instinctively as he lifted the tunic and my shift over my head and eased them away.

He said nothing.

"That bad?" I asked, bracing.

He cleared his throat. "Nothing new. Just the scar on your side. That must've hurt."

"It did," I said. "Festered a long time, too. I've never been sick in my life. That was the first time and it was awful."

"Turn around?" he asked.

I did.

"Let's see… there's the scar from the arrow you took for me," he said, voice soft as he brought the sponge to my back. He moved slowly, gently rinsing my skin.

Then he set the sponge aside.

His fingers came next. Light. Careful.

"Just these marks here." His voice thickened as his fingers traced a line from my right shoulder blade to my left hip. "But nothing new anywhere you can't see."

I swallowed hard. Turned toward him. Reached for the sponge. "Thank you."

He didn't hand it to me. Instead, he stared at the water. "I was… there. And I couldn't stop them."

I stiffened.

His breath left him slowly.

"When they—" He cut himself off. Voice cracking.

Then he turned away, bracing his hands against the pool's edge, steam curling around his shoulders.

"I should've kept you out of Avitum. Or kept my distance from you. I knew Cassius would use you. Should've done… something." He bowed his head. "I hate myself for it."

I stared at his back.

Not just the bones beneath his skin, or the scars that matched mine. But the way his shoulders hunched in on themselves. Drawn tight around a pain I recognized.

The kind that didn't bleed.

The kind that stayed.

"I'm sorry. It's nothing compared to what you went through. I have no right—" He stopped.

My own grief hadn't lifted. Not even close. But his broke through the steam like a bell, insistent and impossible to ignore.

I hesitated for a moment. I had to be careful.

Maybe I didn't know how to feel the right way anymore.

But I knew two things to be true.

Firstly, that I couldn't let him hurt like this and not say something.

And secondly, I was very bad at being careful.

"I chose you," I said. "I chose you, knowing what it might cost. And if I had to do it again, I would choose you again. Every time."

A tremor passed through his shoulders.

"There's no shame for you to carry," I went on. "These were my choices. Mine. You always gave them to me."

I stepped closer. The water whispered between us.

"You've been carrying all of it," I said. "Like it's your job to make sense of everything. To protect everyone but yourself."

I remembered the way he'd said the same to me. I remembered how much it had mattered.

I placed a hand on his back, just between his shoulder blades.

"You don't have to do that with me. You don't have to hide your tears. You don't have to hide anything."

His head dipped, as if the words struck somewhere deep.

"I cry," I said. "Gods, I cry all the time. When it's too much. When I'm angry. When I'm scared. I used to think it made me weak."

He let out a tight, ragged breath, as though holding something back.

"But it doesn't. It makes me human. It lets me breathe." My hand stayed firm on his back. Just there. "You don't have to speak. Just—don't hold it in. Not from me."

For a long moment, nothing moved. The only sound was the hush of steam and water.

Then a sound broke in his throat.

A sob, torn from somewhere deep.

His hands gripped the stone edge of the pool as his body shook—once, then again.

He didn't try to speak.

He just wept. Shoulders hunched. Face turned away.

I stepped forward and wrapped my arms around him from behind. Rested my cheek against his back. Listened to the way he broke.

Just warmth and pressure and presence until the shaking began to slow.

His fingers loosened. His head bowed lower.

And still, I held him.

# CHAPTER NINETY-ONE
## *Saessir*

*"The heart is not a kingdom—it cannot divide its land without blood. Nor can it choose who it calls kin, or who it kneels for."*
—The Breath of the World

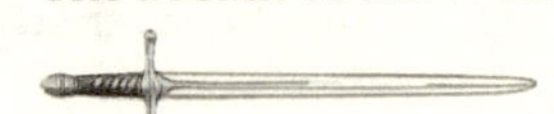

Rudamos 70, 1231
*Aleaia*

We rode in silence for the last stretch on a pair of bay geldings. The ridges above the estate offered a kind of peace, and for once, my thoughts weren't at war. It felt good to ride again. To focus only on the motion beneath me. To remember I still had a body that knew how to move forward.

When we reached the stables, Val dismounted first and stepped to my side. I didn't need help but I let him take my waist as I slid down. His hands lingered a heartbeat longer than they had to.

"Not too sore?" he asked.

"I'll live."

I gave him a faint smile and reached for his arm, my fingers trailing down until they found his hand. Just to anchor myself for a moment.

He looked at me like he wanted to say something more, but didn't. So neither did I.

He hadn't kissed me since the day on the balcony.

But then, I hadn't kissed him either.

Lucius waited at the edge of the stable yard, a bundle of cloth in his hands. He looked like someone smuggling a secret under his cloak and doing a poor job of it.

I met him halfway.

He held it out. "Here. You might need this."

I knew what it was before I even touched it.

My belt, and in the sheath—

The Fellglow Blade.

My mother's sword.

My birthright.

My throat tightened as I unwrapped it and gripped the hilt. It didn't hum in my hand—not with the incolumium still clamped to my wrist—but the weight was comfort enough. Solid. Familiar.

I looked up at him. "Lucius, I…" I didn't know what to say.

He didn't meet my gaze. Just shifted like he meant to walk off. I caught his sleeve.

"I never said thank you," I said. "For Aeldunon. For Avitum. For everything."

He looked down at his boots. Shook his head. "It was my duty."

We both hated conversations like this. I'd thank him in the only way that made sense.

I stepped forward and wrapped my arms tight around his waist, my head resting lightly against his chest. And I held on.

Lucius froze for a breath, then sighed and patted my back once before his arms came around me.

"You're welcome," he said. Then, in careful Aeltyrian, he said, "*Saessiros*."

I drew back just enough to look at him. "You're finally learning Aeltyrian?"

"When this is all over, Aeltyria'll be the only place I have left to live. Seems practical."

"Well… your pronunciation was good, *brathiros*. Better than I expected, anyway."

Lucius squinted. "Are you feverish? That almost sounded like a compliment."

A laugh caught in my throat, tangled with something warmer. I wiped at my cheeks, but the tears had already come. Brief. Uninvited. Entirely mine.

I had no real family left. But I'd made one.

Mariana, my sister of the soul. Kind. Gentle. Smart.

Lucius, my brother in arms. Gruff. Infuriating. Stubborn. And steady in ways that never needed proving. He'd stood beside me in the worst of it. I could always count on him.

And Val.

Vedrānos.

The man I couldn't live without.

The man I loved, even if I was afraid to say it anymore.

And still, somewhere in the back of my mind, that voice coiled close. Whispering that I didn't deserve any of them, least of all him. That what we had was already spoiled by what I'd become. That loving him might drag him down with me, might spread whatever rot still lived in my bones. Just like it could touch Mariana. Or Lucius.

I didn't want to ruin what was still whole.

Maybe, in time, I could make myself clean again. But not yet.

"Try not to leave it lying around again," Lucius said as he pulled away, already turning. Gruff again. But I heard the softness under it.

"I hate you, Lucius," I called after him as I fastened the belt around myself.

"I hate you too." He raised a hand to wave but didn't look back.

I turned and caught Val watching.

I held his gaze longer than I meant to. Something flickered in his eyes. There, then gone.

For a heartbeat, my stomach dropped. The old reflex rose.

*I've overstepped. I've taken too much. I should have known better.*

I searched my own memory—my arms around Lucius, the way I'd held on without thinking. Heat crept up my neck.

Then I saw it.

Not anger. Not distance.

Hurt.

I let it go. For now.

We didn't speak at first on the walk back to the villa, though he kept close. I glanced at him. Studied the set of his mouth. The distant look still clinging to his eyes.

"What is it?" I asked.

He didn't answer right away. A few steps passed in silence.

"I'm fine," he said.

"Was it Lucius?" I asked, voice even.

He blinked. Looked at me, startled—then away.

"Wait. Are you jealous?"

"I'm not."

He stopped. So did I.

And then he went very still. Quiet for a long moment.

When he spoke, his voice was tight. "I never was before. But after what they did… I see things differently. It's harder, sometimes. Watching you laugh—really laugh—for the first time… with someone else. Even him."

I knew what he meant. I had laughed in camp after we escaped, breathless and shaking, half-mad with relief. But that hadn't been joy. Not yet. It had been survival, cracking at the edges.

He swallowed.

"I just…" His voice dropped to almost nothing. "Wish it was me."

I took in the way he stood—the bend of his shoulders, the way he clasped his hands behind his back so he wouldn't reach for me. The ache in his silence. The pain he tried to bury even now.

I could never let him hurt alone. Not if I could fix it.

I reached for his collar, rose onto my toes, and pulled him down, pressing my mouth to his before he could say another word.

A promise I didn't know how to speak aloud.

When I drew back, my breath came unsteady.

"It is you," I whispered. "It's always you."

Then I turned away before I could see his face. Walked faster.

Guilt crept in, slow and stinging.

*I shouldn't have done that,* I thought. *Shouldn't have kissed him like that.*

Not when I was still broken.

Not when I hadn't yet earned the right to touch something good.

# CHAPTER NINETY-TWO
## *The Quiet Return*

*"There is no freedom without fear. No healing without memory."*
—Aeltyrian Proverb

Rudamos 70, 1231
*Aleaia*

The dining room was quiet, save the clatter of dishes, the murmur of voices, and the occasional snap of the hearth. The long table was set with the scent of roast mutton, herbed greens, and fresh-baked bread. Lucius was in his usual place—halfway through his first helping, wine in hand. Next to him, Mariana waved us over.

I slid into the seat beside her. Val took the chair to my right and poured wine into my goblet before filling his own.

Bren and Lysa sat across from us, elbows on the table despite Davena's stern glare. Rasmus stood, slicing the roast mutton and serving portions to each of us. When he was done, he served himself and sat.

"Lucius says you fought off twenty men to escape the dungeons," Bren said to me through a mouthful of greens.

Lysa giggled and pointed her spoon at Val. "And that you punched a priest in the face."

Val looked down the table at Lucius. "You've been busy."

Lucius shrugged, unbothered. "They asked."

Early on, just the mention of fighting off men might have sent me running from the table. But it had been nearly half a season since we were rescued, and I was starting to feel my feet under me again.

"I didn't fight *twenty* men," I said to Bren as if offended. "It was *thirty*."

The boy's eyes widened. Val laughed softly beside me.

"You didn't hear that," Mariana said to the children, smiling as she said it.

For a breath, it felt… normal. Or close to it.

The scent of food. The flicker of firelight. Forks tapping plates, children giggling at things they didn't fully understand.

Val beside me, through all of it.

I picked up my wine cup—

And stopped.

The metal was cold. As cold as the bare skin of my right hand.

My ring—the one Val had given me—was gone.

I stared down at my hand like it belonged to someone else. Turned it over as if I'd find the ring in my palm. Then back again.

Tried to remember when I'd taken it off. If it had slipped free.

Wondered why I was just now realizing it was gone.

A low roar rose in my ears as the memory rushed back all at once.

*Get out. Get out. Get outside. Get out.*

I stood.

No excuse. No words. Just the scrape of my chair as I stepped away from the table and walked out through the open doors to the terrace.

*They can't see. They can't. I can't let them.*

The sea wind hit me, cool and sharp. I braced my hands on the low wall and tried to breathe.

*In.*

*Out.*

*They have to think I'm stronger. I'm better. Less corrupted.*

My breath hitched. Caught. Refused to come.

I stared at my finger. Flexed my hand.

It had been broken.

The memory hadn't been there a moment ago. If I'd tried to recall it before seeing the empty space, it wouldn't have come. But now it flooded in, bright and full.

*The table under my back.*

*The smell of mold. Of shit. Of fear.*

*The taste of blood in my mouth as I bit down—hard, so I wouldn't scream. Not when he opened my fist, bent my finger back and snapped it. Not when he pried the ring from me like spoils from a corpse.*

"Luce mea, come back to me."

When I looked up, Val was kneeling in front of me, where I'd sunk onto the stone terrace.

My voice shook. "How—how did you—"

"You looked at your hand." He pressed a handkerchief into my palm. "Got a look on your face. Bolted."

Shivering, I wiped my nose, then curled the cloth into my fist. "I didn't—I didn't want anyone to—"

"I told them to let me handle it." He tilted his head toward the dining room.

"He took it," I said flatly.

"Who took what?"

"That bastard broke my finger to take my ring," I said, wide eyed as I thrust my hand toward him. "When I wouldn't give it to him. Now look at it."

He took it gently, as if humoring me, and turned it over. "It doesn't look different."

"Look at it next to the other one!" I held both hands up, side by side. "Why can't you see it? It's obvious."

He took both in his hands, studying them. Then lifted them, kissed the back of each, and brushed his thumbs across my knuckles.

"I don't see anything wrong," he said softly. "But I believe you. I believe you, amor mea."

I swallowed hard.

"I'm sorry. It's just—" My voice cracked. "I'm so angry. Even when I try not to be."

"Then stop trying not to be. I'd be surprised if you weren't. I am too. When we found you, I—" His voice faltered. His jaw worked for a moment, before he shook his head. "You have every right."

"I can be sitting next to you, and things almost feel normal again. Then something small—something no one else would notice—pulls me right back there." My hand clenched. "It's like I can never fucking leave."

"It will get better," he said softly. "With time."

I turned on him. "How can you possibly know that?" I demanded.

His gaze didn't waver. "Because I've seen it. Good soldiers. Strong ones. Men and women who came back feeling like you do now. Some healed. Not all. But those who did..." He drew a breath. "They were never the same, but they found ways to live again. Ways that were different, not less."

"I don't feel strong, Val." I looked down. My hands still trembled in his. His were warm. Mine were ice. "I feel... broken."

"Strength isn't being unbreakable. It's putting the pieces back together when they fall apart. Some things are stronger when they mend." He smiled faintly. "Like bones. Ask Mariana."

A laugh, wet with tears, caught in my throat.

How was he so... *good?*

And how had I ever deserved him?

I reached for him. He sat back and pulled me in, arms folding around me, his hand settling at the back of my head.

"I miss the woman I was." I sniffed. "The one who would've flirted with you over dinner. Mocked Lucius without thinking. The one who knew how to want things."

"She's still there," he said. "That woman didn't disappear in Avitum. She's bruised. Quiet. But she's still inside you, Aleaia. I see her now, as I always have."

"I don't." I pulled back and met his eyes. "Even here, with you, I still feel like I'm... tainted," I whispered.

"You're not." His hand came up and brushed a strand of hair behind my ear. "I know what you survived. I saw what it did to you. What *they* did to you. But nothing about it makes you less."

I exhaled. "I don't know how to live with it."

"You don't. Not alone. We figure it out together," he said. "Together. One day at a time."

I looked down. My fingers curled in the fabric of his sleeve.

I don't know what made me decide this was the moment it had to come out. Maybe it was the terrace—the nearness of laughter, the waves crashing below, the warmth of him around me. Val held me like nothing had changed, his cheek resting against my hair, his hand moving slowly over my back. Like it was before we went into that place.

If I didn't tell him, though, it would rot me from the inside. Hollow me out until nothing was left. Whatever we would become would be built on a lie.

But if I did, maybe he wouldn't touch me again. Not after this. Not once he knew.

And maybe that was better.

Before I could think about the words, about what they might do to him, they tumbled out. "I have to tell you something, Val."

His hand stilled on my back but he didn't ask what. So on I went.

"I… I let it happen."

He probably thought he was quiet enough to hide it, but I heard the sharp intake of his breath.

"After the arena," I said, "they brought me to that room—the one you found me in. Kept me shackled to the table when they meant to use me. Chained me in the corner when they didn't."

My throat tightened. I forced the next words out.

"The first four or five times, I fought. Bit Marcus. Tried to tear out his throat. If I was going to die, I wanted to take that son of a bitch with me."

I drew a ragged breath, the memory foul as bile.

"But then he said if I didn't start cooperating, they'd bring you in. Do worse to you than they ever did to me. Cut you apart. Make me watch while they broke you. And I—I couldn't," I choked, voice cracking. "Couldn't stand the thought of them hurting you. Just watching them take the lash to you was—was already too much. And I knew if they did what he said—"

The tears hit without warning. My fists clutched the front of his tunic, clinging to him like the only solid thing left.

"So I gave him what he wanted. Traded myself. Because I could survive that. I could survive being torn apart. But not you. Not watching them…"

I pressed my face to his chest.

"I thought it would end with me dying," I gasped. "And that I'd see you in Aetheria."

My breath came faster—rough and uneven, high in my chest.

"I did this… to myself."

And then it all broke loose. The tears came hard and ugly, raking through me without grace—just sound and pain and everything I'd kept locked away.

"I'm sorry—I thought—I don't know what I thought. Maybe if I buried it deep enough, it wouldn't come back. Maybe I thought I could have this… us… without it touching you."

Val's breath hitched once.

"Gods, I ruined it," I whispered. The words splintered in my throat. "Everything we had. Everything we were."

He exhaled slowly. I felt it more than heard it.

"Do you think I'm—I'm disgusting now?" I looked up at him, terrified of what I'd find. "You must. You haven't said anything."

His hands came up to cradle my face.

"I think," he said softly, "that you survived something unimaginable."

My lip trembled. I put my hands over his wrists. I'd shatter if he stopped touching me.

"I think," he went on evenly, "that what happened to you isn't who you are. It never was."

I shook my head.

He didn't understand. How could he?

"I think you're the strongest person I've ever known," he said. "Not because you didn't break. But because you kept going anyway."

My chin wobbled. I sniffled. I didn't want to cry again—not yet—not when his voice held something so beautiful. I needed to hear.

"Because you still choose to love me," he added, "even after that. Even if you can't say it, I know you do."

The words hit something I hadn't known was still raw.

"You're not ruined," he said. "You're not cursed. And if I could take what happened from you—bear it for you—I would. Every second of it."

I let him pull me in. Closed my eyes. Let the tears fall. I pressed my face to the warm place between his neck and shoulder.

"You didn't ruin anything, amor mea," he said, soft and steady. "You've never ruined anything. All you did… was survive."

But the thing still lived in me. The rot I couldn't name.

"But I *am* cursed," I whispered. "Rotten."

His arms tightened.

"You're not," he said. "This didn't happen because of who you are. It happened because of who he was."

I could hardly breathe.

The things inside me—he thought they were walls he could tear down if he was persistent enough, if he hit them hard enough.

But I knew they were living things. Vines that clutched tighter, the more I struggled. Hungry for motion, they clung tightest when I tried to break free. Wrapped themselves around my throat and strangled when they thought I might.

"I should've stopped it. Fought harder—"

"No." His voice was quiet, but there was steel beneath it. "You did what you had to do to survive."

I sobbed. "I let it happen."

"No. You endured it. That's not the same."

The cry that broke from me wasn't loud. It was low. Long. Tired. My whole body shook with it.

It was grief.

"You're not broken," he said. "You're not dirty. You are not the thing that was done to you."

Something tore free, deep and raw. I clung to him, because it hurt less when I did.

"Aleaia, amor mea, look at me and listen." He lifted my chin. I didn't want to meet his eyes, but he made me. Gently. Steadily. "You didn't have a choice."

I blinked, my breath catching. "I could've—"

"No."

"I should've—"

"No." His voice was iron now. "You were forced. Threatened. Cornered. That's not surrender. That's survival."

"But I let him—"

"No," he said, cutting me off. His hands cupped my face, trembling. "You outlasted him. That's not the same. It's not."

I tried to look away. He wouldn't let me.

"If you had fought harder, they would've killed you," he said. "If you hadn't given in, they would've hurt me just to break you. There was no winning. No mercy. No choice."

The tears ran hot and constant. Still, I shook my head. Like a child refusing the truth.

He spoke every word like a vow. "You. Did. Not. Choose. This."

I choked on the words that tried to come.

"It wasn't your fault," he said again. "I'll say it a thousand ways. A thousand times. Until you believe it."

And—somehow—I did.

The words didn't just land—they struck. They split something open in me. Cut through the rot. Drove into the hollow where I'd buried every reason, every whisper, every lie that said it had been my fault.

Val was right. They weren't vines. They were walls, built of every hurt and every lie they'd mortared into my soul to keep Val from reaching me.

Realizing that was like the moment at the end of a long siege, when the gates open, when you know that even if this place won't ever be the same, you won't be locked in, starving.

A sound tore from my throat, and I collapsed into him, arms tight around his ribs, clinging like the truth might slip through my fingers if I didn't hold fast. Like he might.

I buried my face in his chest, fists twisted in his tunic like it was the only thing keeping me tethered. The weeping came raw and deep, clawing out of me in waves. My whole body trembled, but he didn't let go.

He didn't tell me to stop. Didn't say I was safe or that the pain would pass.

He just held me.

Let me break.

Let me feel. Finally.

"You're not alone," he said, his voice low against my hair. "Not anymore. Never again. I go where you go. Even into the dark. Especially there."

He pressed a kiss to the crown of my head and rocked me, anchoring me with the strength of his presence, until the storm inside me passed.

And for the first time since we left that place—

I felt it.

Not hope.

But the space where hope might grow again.

# CHAPTER NINETY-THREE
## *Cracked Armor*

*"Get your head out of your arse, lord. Or I will do it for you."*
—Lucius Tutela, Letia

Rudamos 70, 1231
*Valerius*

The stars were out, clear and bright above the sea. It was the kind of night that should've felt peaceful.

I hadn't gone to bed.

I stood at the terrace railing with a cup of wine in hand, the carafe half-drained beside me. The villa behind me was still. Everyone else had long since turned in.

I hadn't meant to think about it again.

What she'd told me.

But it came anyway, and it brought memories of the things they'd made me watch them do to her.

Done to protect me.

Spared because of her.

And I hadn't been strong enough to give them what they wanted.

To renounce her and make them believe it.

I took another sip of wine. It tasted like nothing.

I heard Lucius before I saw him—the creak of the door behind me, his boots on the stone.

"It's late," he said. "What are you doing out here?"

"Can't sleep. The usual." I stared into the dark swirl in my cup. "Maybe it's too warm."

*Maybe I can't sleep next to her, knowing what I cost her.*

"She all right?"

I nodded. "She's asleep. Better than most nights."

Lucius came to lean beside me against the wall. "She didn't come back to dinner."

"She needed air."

"And?"

I glanced at him. He might have gotten us out of Avitum, but that didn't give him claim to every part of her.

"She looked at her hand," I said. "Realized her ring was gone. It... brought it all back."

Lucius stilled.

"She talked to me about it," I added, just to needle him. "For the first time."

"That's good." A long moment passed, filled only by the sound of the waves. "Have you told her yet?"

He meant the truth about Marcus.

The man who let his post go unguarded.

Who failed to stop the ones that killed Aleaia's father. Let them steal from the legion and disappear. They'd crossed paths with Jurian and Aleaia in the woods and did what monsters do.

I should've put Marcus to the sword then.

And since I hadn't, I should've told her.

If I had, she would've killed him long before he ever laid a hand on her again. I'd have stood with her then, too. Everything would have been different. Maybe not worse. Maybe better.

Lucius had been pushing me to tell her since last year. Since she agreed to go to Aeldunon with me. I could never find the right time. And I never wanted to think about it.

I didn't look at him. "No."

"Why the fuck not?"

My fingers tightened around the cup. "I *can't*."

Lucius's voice dropped. "You don't think she can manage her own mind?"

"She's finally starting to come back to me." My throat felt dry. "I can't shatter that now. Not when she's this close."

"Close to what? Being cured of what ails her? It doesn't work like that and you know it, Val." He shook his head slowly.

I scoffed. Drank again.

"I mean it." He stepped in front of me, full height now. "Don't do this. Don't keep things from her because you think you know better."

I braced one hand against the railing, felt the stone dig into my palm.

"You think this'll break her? It won't. What'll break her is finding out *after* and realizing she could've stopped him, if only the man she trusted most hadn't kept her in the dark." He sighed and shook his head. "No. Not man. Men. Because I'm as guilty as you are."

I stared past him. The ocean wind stung my face, but it didn't ease the pressure building behind my ribs.

"She already thinks it's her fault," Lucius said. "You've seen it too. The way she still carries it. The way she talks about it—like she should've been stronger, faster, *something*."

She'd just started smiling. Laughing, this afternoon. Letting me hold her without flinching. How could I risk that?

He took a step closer. "You're not protecting her if you keep hiding this. You're just making sure she blames herself for something *we* let happen. Trust her to decide what to do with the truth."

I gripped the edge of the stone rail until my knuckles whitened.

Truth.

The truth was, I'd chosen for her.

Again.

That landed.

Hard.

And I didn't have an answer for it.

"You know what?" Lucius said, voice rising now. "If you don't tell her soon, maybe I will. She has a right to know it's not her fault."

That cut deep.

I turned, eyes sharp. "You wouldn't."

Lucius stepped closer. "Wouldn't I?"

I shoved past him roughly, pacing the terrace. "You don't understand."

Lucius turned. "What don't I understand?"

"She *hugged you*. First time she's ever done that."

He looked at me like I'd lost my mind. "What does that have to do with the other?"

Nothing. It had nothing to do with it. I just wanted to shut him up.

That wasn't right either. I wanted *him* to shut *me* up.

I turned on him, heat rising in my chest. "You touch her like that again, and I don't care what history lies between us—I'll break your fucking jaw."

Lucius just stared at me. "Touch her like what, Val? She hugged me, because I gave her sword back to her. There's room in her for more than just you, Val."

I exhaled sharply, the words catching on the edge of something I hadn't meant to say aloud.

"I've barely seen her smile since we got her back. Then you hand her a sword and say one fucking word in her language and suddenly—"

"—she's happy for half a second?" Lucius snapped.

"—Mariana's not enough for you."

The words tasted rotten the instant they left my mouth.

The second I said it, I hated it.

Because it wasn't true.

Because I'd seen her fall apart in my arms hours ago, raw and real and still bleeding, and now I was standing here spitting filth like she owed me something. Like I hadn't failed her ten times over.

His face changed.

No amusement now. Just cold, stunned revulsion.

"Say that again. And say it plainly." His voice dropped, low and deadly. "Because it sounds like you mean something else. And I don't like it."

"What do you think I mean?"

"I'm not doing that with you. I'm telling you to say what you fucking mean."

He was.

And he was right to.

And that infuriated me.

Lucius and his goodness. His competence.

Against me and my failures.

I hated myself for it.

"You know," he said, voice tight, "for someone who says he loves her, you really don't trust her. That you'd say that about her, after everything—" He broke off, gave me a once over and snarled, "Disgusting."

"It's not her I don't trust."

He stepped in again, less than a hand's breadth from me. "Then who? Me? *You?*"

I shoved him—hard, flat-palmed to the chest. "Fuck you."

He staggered back a step.

Lucius's eyes narrowed. "I know you don't mean me. I'm the one who dragged you out of that godsdamned dungeon when the mission was to get *her*. *You* were saved for her sake, Val. So you better remember that before you start accusing me."

I shoved him again, harder, because the truth was too close now. "Don't pretend like you haven't wanted her. You still do."

Lucius straightened. Shoulders squared. His hand came up, fingers flat and tight, aimed at my chest. Not a strike. A signal.

"You're angry. Fine. Be fucking angry." His voice was cold now. Clear. "But listen to me. I am not your enemy. She is not your possession. And if you can't tell her the truth—that *we* failed her—then you are not the man she thinks you are."

My breath came hard and fast through my nose.

Lucius took one step back.

"Get your head out of your arse, *lord*," he commanded. "Or I will do it for you."

Then he turned and walked away, boots sharp on the stone.

The door closed behind him with a weight I felt in my ribs.

I stood frozen with shame.

What had I become?

A man who heard what she had endured, and hours later turned around and accused her of giving affection too freely.

Like she hadn't already bled herself dry for me.

Like I hadn't failed her first.

My hands shook. I tasted bile.

Lucius was right. She deserved the truth.

And better than me.

# CHAPTER NINETY-FOUR
## *The Edge*

*"You don't have to carry this alone."*
—Valerius di Calesia, Ardhmor

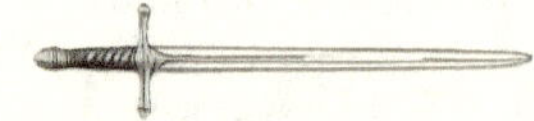

Rudamos 70, 1231
*Aleaia*

I woke fast.

No sound. No dream. Just the unmistakable thrum of wrongness beneath my skin.

I reached across the bed.

Cold sheets.

Untouched.

*No. Not again.*

I sat up sharply, heart hammering. No boots by the door. No belt on the hook. No sound of him moving around the room.

No Val.

His sword was still here. That was somehow worse.

Had someone taken him?

I was already moving.

Barefoot, still in my shift, I slipped out into the night. The stone was warm underfoot, the summer air drifting through the villa.

The courtyard—empty.

The kitchen—dark.

The garden—silent.

My pulse roared in my ears.

The last time he'd vanished like this, he'd left me. Slipped away into the night, chasing some doomed mission he hadn't let me share. I'd woken alone. Reeling. Abandoned.

I padded down the hallway, searching.

And then I heard it.

A sound too soft to be anything but human—ragged and broken. It came with the salt wind, from the terrace off the dining room.

I'd know him anywhere.

I ran.

The doors were open.

And there he was.

Sitting on the railing. Legs dangling into open air, one hand braced beside him, the other holding a goblet. Carafe tipped over on the ground, empty. Head bowed. Shoulders shaking.

My eyes went wide. One strong gust of wind and he'd blow right off the damned thing and into the sea. What the fuck was he thinking?

I had to be careful. If I startled him, he might go over anyway.

A single sob escaped him, and he mumbled something I couldn't make out. His hand went to his face.

Was he thinking about… doing it on purpose?

Seeing that kind of despair was like looking into a mirror. I'd been there once, not long ago.

I didn't call his name. Didn't dare.

Just moved.

Two fast strides.

One solid grip on his shoulder and the back of his tunic.

I yanked him backward with all my weight.

He toppled. Hit the stone hard, flat on his back, wine streaking across the terrace in a dark red arc.

I stood over him, breath ragged. "What the fuck do you think you're doing?"

He blinked up at me, dazed and tear-streaked. His eyes were red. Smelled like a winery. He'd been at it for a long time.

"I—I wasn't—"

"Don't you fucking lie to me."

He sat up slowly, hands bracing behind. "I wouldn't do that to you. I wouldn't leave you. I wouldn't—" he said, hoarse and slurring.

How would he have handled this if he found me this way?

"That's not what I asked you. I asked what you were doing." I gestured to the railing. "Were you just having a drunken think while dangling off a cliff?"

He looked away. "I wasn't—I wasn't going to jump."

I'd tried.

But I wasn't him and he wasn't me. I'd never denied what I'd felt when I thought to take Vespera's hand and let her lead me away. And I couldn't keep calm if he kept denying it.

I dropped to my knees in front of him and shoved him. Not hard—just enough.

"I know exactly what you were doing and you were going to jump," I said, trembling. "How dare you try to leave me here? I need you."

"I wasn't—" His voice broke. "I—I didn't know what else to do. I'm not good for you. For anything anymore."

My veins turned to ice. "What?"

"After what you told me—"

"I would never have told you if I knew this would be the result, Val."

He covered his face with his hands. "It's not just that."

Gods, I was so bad at this. That wasn't the right thing to say either. I had to try again.

"You don't get to go first." I took his wrists in my hands, pulled his hands from his face. "You don't get to give up. You don't get to die when I just got you back."

"You're better off without me." He pulled away like I'd burned him. "You don't—you don't know what I did. What I didn't do."

I did know that this was the time to be quiet. So I bit my tongue. Let him speak.

"You gave yourself to save me," he said hoarsely. "And I couldn't even give them the lie they wanted to save you."

"The fuck are you on about?" I clenched my teeth. Wrong. Again. "I'm sorry. What are you talking about?"

"The priests—they wanted—wanted me to—" He pressed the heels of his hands to his eyes and rocked himself once. "And I couldn't—and they kept—fuck—"

I had never seen him like this. Not even in Praedia.

"Val." My voice was softer now. Careful. "Val, what couldn't you do?"

"They told me to renounce you," he rasped. "Just say you meant nothing. Just say you were a witch who tricked me. And I almost did it. Gods help me, I almost did. And maybe if I did, they wouldn't have hurt you anymore and—*areo tam culpis, amor mea, lo ara peccace mea.*"

*I'm so sorry, my love, it is my fault.*

Aelan's mercy, he really thought they were honest. That there was a shred of honor in them, that they'd have kept their word.

"Val..." I breathed, stunned. "They were never going to stop. You could have renounced me a hundred times and it wouldn't have changed anything."

His face crumpled. One of his hands found my side—fumbled for it, really—and clung there, gripping the fabric of my shift like it was the only thing keeping him upright.

"I'm sorry," he gasped. "I'm sorry. I'm sorry, please—luce mea. Don't shut me out."

I knelt between his legs and gathered him in, pulling his head to my chest. He collapsed into it—like something in him had been waiting to fall apart in someone's arms. My arms.

"Breathe, Val. Breathe with me. In through your nose."

We did.

"And out through your mouth. There you go, vedrānos," I said, rubbing his back. "Cry all you need to, as long as you're breathing."

His sobs came hard and shaking against me. Messy, aching, everything he never let anyone else see.

And I didn't let go. I held him. I rocked him, kissed the top of his head.

Telling him I needed him, that he didn't get to go first—that wasn't enough.

I had to tell him the truth. A different truth than the one that had brought this.

"Val. Listen to me." I took a deep breath. "They would have done what they did to me either way. I just thought I could… maybe use it. To protect you. If it was going to happen anyway."

His arms tightened around me. I almost couldn't breathe.

My voice shook. "It's not your fault. Just like you said it wasn't mine. They are evil. They hurt you. And me. And us."

I rested my cheek on his hair. Breathed him in.

"I need you. But more than that—I love you. I don't want to. Because I am corrupted. Cursed. Doomed to be the end of anyone who loves me. I've been…" My throat was tight. I swallowed. "Broken. Beyond repair. But gods help us both, I love you more than anything else in this godsforsaken world. And I'm sorry it took me so long to say it."

His breath shuddered, like the words cracked something open in him.

"I don't know how you can still love me," he said through his tears. "I've done everything wrong. I let it happen. I didn't stop it. I didn't protect you. I failed—over and over—and you still…"

I pulled back just enough to brush his hair back from his forehead and rest a hand on his cheek.

"You don't get to decide what I feel. You don't get to carry the blame for things that were never yours to begin with. And you don't get to rewrite the love I give you just because you don't think you've earned it."

I tilted his chin up toward me. I looked into his eyes, wiped the tears from his face, and gave him the rawest truth of all.

"You're not perfect, Val. Neither am I. But you are mine. And I am yours. I choose you. Every godsdamned time."

And then I kissed him.

Not to prove anything.

Just because I could.

# CHAPTER NINETY-FIVE
## *Immortelle*

*"Immortelle blooms where nothing else can.*
*It clings to life in the harshest places, bright and unyielding."*
—Field Notes of a Wild Botanist

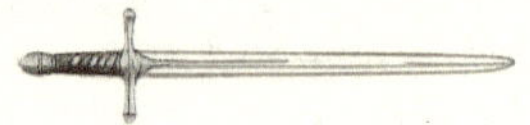

Rudamos 71, 1231
*Aleaia*

Morning came early, pulling me from sleep with the hush of waves on the shore and pale light through the shutters. Birds called softly from the trees, their songs mingling with the scent of fresh bread drifting in from the kitchen. The chamber was warm—salt-sweet, familiar, and still.

I'd nearly lost him last night.

Not to blade or battlefield, but to the darkness gnawing at his thoughts. Guilt. Grief. The kind of sorrow that doesn't shout, only sinks in deep and slow until everything else collapses around it.

In the wake of it, nothing else felt quite as urgent.

I took a slow breath and let the thought drift—for now.

Careful not to wake him, I eased from the bed and dressed quickly.

I couldn't resist pressing a light kiss to his temple.

He stirred briefly, eyes heavy with sleep. That boyish, unguarded smile on his lips—soft as breath, and just as fleeting. It always struck something tender in me.

He called me his light. I would be that for him.

Hard as it was, I pulled my eyes from him and made my way to the kitchen, where the air was thick with warmth and spice.

"Good morning, grandmother," I said.

Davena turned from the hearth with a smile. "Morning, child. Take care of those eggs, would you?"

I nodded and stepped in without needing more. The rhythm came easily—cracking eggs into a bowl, whisking while Davena checked the bread. We moved around each other in a silence that wasn't empty, only comfortable.

She'd kept her distance when I arrived. I'd thought she disliked me. But somewhere along the way, that had changed. She welcomed me now, in her own way.

It started after my first visit to the caldarium. Val had suggested I ask her for help with my hair. I'd nearly refused. The idea of someone else's hands, of the questions it might raise, tied knots in my stomach.

Still, I asked.

And Davena had only said, "Come, sit. I'll get you sorted."

Since then, we'd spoken of many things. She'd grown up in Baeddan, not far from Rhaelaith, and remembered it as more than a Calesian outpost. Her stories were rich with color and defiance—Queen Eavan's last stand, battles nearly won, the day the tide turned.

She'd never once asked about the bruises, or what had happened in Avitum. Her hands had simply worked through my hair with practiced care, easing out the tangles without a word.

For a fleeting moment, I'd wondered if that was what it felt like to have a mother.

I'd come to help in the kitchen early the next morning, and every morning since.

Once breakfast was served, I joined Lucius and Mariana for a walk around the estate. Mariana swore fresh air helped rebuild strength, and she was probably right. This morning, Val joined us too, skipping his usual swim.

He kept the conversation light, steering us toward safe topics like someone afraid the wrong word might break the footing we'd just begun to find.

"Dogs or horses?" he asked as we rounded the far edge of the olive grove.

I shot him a look. "What says I can't have both?"

"Say you had to choose." His mouth twitched.

"A dog," I said after a breath.

His brow furrowed. "Really?"

I nodded. "We had one when I was young. Sage. She was my only playmate most days. Kept the village brats from teasing me too much."

His expression softened. "They didn't know what they were missing."

I snorted. "Perhaps they did. Maybe they were better off avoiding me."

"I doubt it," he said. "I would've picked horses for practicality. But you've convinced me."

"Dogs are loyal. Lovable. And they'll keep you warm on the coldest nights." A smile tugged at my mouth. "Pity they don't live as long as we do."

We walked in silence for a time.

Then, with a tentative edge, he asked. "Will you be sitting under the olive tree again later?"

I glanced at him. "Probably. After training."

He kept his eyes forward. "Would you mind if I joined you?"

"You don't have to ask."

"I know," he murmured. "But I wanted to. It's the closest I can come to courting you properly."

I smiled then, full and warm. Even if it felt foolish, after all we'd been through, the idea of him wanting to court me made something in my belly flutter. "In that case… I would love it if you did."

The sun had climbed higher by the time Val and Lucius split off to spar in the courtyard. Mariana and I stayed behind, collecting herbs from the garden and mixing tinctures in the stillroom. When the bell rang for midday, I returned to the kitchen and rolled up my sleeves beside Davena.

I was wrist-deep in dough when Val walked in. Fresh from training, hair still damp, his tunic clung in a way that made it hard to focus on anything else. He slipped his arms around my waist, pressing a warm kiss to my cheek.

I felt myself flush under his attention.

That only encouraged him. He leaned close, his voice barely above a breath.

"You make it very difficult to remember that I'm supposed to be behaving myself."

I turned to look up at him and saw a faint bruise starting to bloom beneath one eye.

I straightened. "What happened to your face?"

He gave me a smile, waved it off. "Didn't duck fast enough. Caught a hit. Nothing worth fussing over."

I frowned but let it go. For now.

"Your turn, amor mea," he said, low and easy.

Color crept up my neck. I wiped my hands on a cloth. "Right. Let me finish up here."

"That's right, you rogue! Let her finish up!" Davena gave him a swat. He only laughed, like she hadn't even touched him.

A little too cheerful. But I didn't say anything.

When Davena finally released me—with a pointed finger and firm instruction to return in time for the meal—I slipped off my apron and met Val near the door. He fell into step beside me.

"Don't watch," I warned as we neared the courtyard. "It's bad enough Lucius has to see me like this."

My pride still stung from how much strength I'd lost, even if I was clawing it back one day at a time.

Val bent to kiss my cheek again. "I won't. But I look forward to the day you'll allow it."

As I crossed the courtyard, I only glanced back once to see Val retreating into the villa.

Lucius waited for me to stretch. My muscles were loose from the morning's errands but still needing the wake-up. As he turned to fetch a practice blade, I caught sight of the bruise darkening along his jaw. Faint. But there.

I raised a brow. "What happened to *your* face?"

He didn't miss a beat. "Took a hit I didn't see coming. Happens."

"Val said the same thing."

Lucius shrugged. "Well. He's not wrong."

I didn't believe it when he said it either, but I let it go, for now.

The courtyard was quiet, save for the rustle of wind through the olive trees.

Training with Lucius reminded me of my first days in the Calesian military. We started with footwork—simple, brutal drills to hone balance and reaction. He used the same dry, clipped tone he always had, correcting my form with maddening precision.

Then came sword work. Not speed. Not strength. *Control.*

He set up targets and made me strike slowly, each swing judged not by force, but by cleanness. Intent. When we sparred, he kept the pace deliberate, always pressing me to the defensive. Every block sent a fresh ache through my arms. Every sidestep bit deeper into muscles that hadn't yet remembered how to endure.

By the time we finished, sweat plastered my tunic to my back, and I was breathing hard enough that words took effort. But a faint, steady satisfaction curled deep in my chest.

"You're doing well," Lucius said as we made our way back toward the kitchen.

"That bad," I said with a sigh.

He laughed but offered no correction.

"What are your plans for the afternoon?" I asked.

"Mariana wants to hunt down some obscure mushroom that only grows around here. I swear she spends more time outdoors than a legionary."

"A mushroom. Right."

He laughed. "Not that kind of mushroom, you deviant."

I smiled. "Will you be back in time for dinner, or should I make excuses to Davena on your behalf?"

He shook his head. "I'd hoped to take her to see my family again, maybe eat there, but my sister's still narrow-minded. Makes it difficult. We'll be back."

"If you're not back by sundown, I'm coming after you," I said.

His mouth twisted in that familiar, knowing smile—the one that echoed an old promise neither of us would forget. "Not that you could find us. With your sense of direction, we'd be dead by nightfall."

I smacked his arm. "That's just mean."

He snorted.

I slowed without meaning to.

"You know," I said softly, "you and Val gave me the exact same excuse earlier today."

Lucius glanced over. "For what?"

"The bruises." I lifted a brow. "You both said you took a hit you didn't see coming."

He let out a slow breath through his nose. "Well. It wasn't untrue."

I didn't smile.

"Why does it matter?"

"Well," I said. "After everyone went to bed, I woke up and Val wasn't there. I went looking for him."

Lucius stopped walking.

So did I. I turned to face him.

"Found him on the terrace. Sitting on the railing. Crying. Drinking. Said he wasn't going to jump, but..." I shook my head. "I don't know. He didn't look far off."

A muscle in his cheek twitched, but he didn't speak.

"I didn't tell him I was going to tell you. I haven't told anyone. But then I saw the two of you with new bruises and I can't help but wonder if they're somehow related."

Still, nothing.

"I just—" I swallowed. "I know you care about him. That's all, *brathiros*."

Lucius nodded once. "Thank you for telling me. I'll check on him."

"That would be good, I think. He might tell you something he won't tell me."

We walked on in the kind of silence that comes after trust.

After the midday meal, I rested for a little while, more out of habit than need. My body no longer ached the way it used to, but the tiredness lived deeper than flesh.

When I rose, I didn't think about where to go. My feet already knew the way.

The olive tree stood at the garden's edge, sprawling, old as the gods. Its roots twisted deep into the hillside, its branches stretched wide, as if reaching for the wind. I had sat beneath it every day since we arrived. But today, something about it felt... different.

The breeze stirred the silvered leaves overhead, whispering through them like surf on distant shores. Dappled gold and green danced across the grass. I lowered myself to the earth and leaned into the trunk, my fingers brushing its bark, coarse and familiar.

I'd brought a book with me. *The Song of the Stars.*

Not my father's copy. That one had been lost in Avitum.

This one Val had given to me last night, between dinner and bed. No ceremony. Just a quiet, *"I want you to have this,"* and a look that told me he understood exactly what it meant.

I opened it.

*From the library of Astraea di Alvareti.*

His mother's. Why would she have had this?

And then it hit me.

Not the answer to my question, but the realization.

He'd given this precious bit of his mother to me as a parting gift. I'd known enough people who despaired to recognize what this kind of gift meant.

My eyes burned. If I hadn't woken up when I did, if I hadn't gone looking for him—

I didn't read. I just sat.

The book lay open in my lap while the wind turned its pages. I barely noticed.

He had seemed lighter this morning. Almost easy.

I had seen legionaries like that before.

Laughing. Talking more than usual. As if something had finally settled in them.

And then they were gone.

I was beginning to wonder if he would come—if he'd only been pretending to be better this morning, and was off devising the next plan to disappear. I was just about to stand and go find him, when the garden gate creaked open.

He stepped through, carrying a small bouquet of yellow flowers. Their blossoms were like captured sunlight—fragile but bright.

The sharp pang of relief hit me low in my gut. *Thank Aelan.*

He knelt beside me.

I swallowed hard. Willed my voice steady. "What've you got?"

"Immortelle. They symbolize eternal love. Resilience. They bloom bright when everything else fades."

He held them out to me.

Color climbed his neck toward his ears. "They reminded me of you."

"Oh, Val..." I took them carefully, cradling them as if they might vanish. "They're beautiful. Thank you."

He smiled at me with that gaze of his—quiet, reverent.

Before I could overthink it, I reached for him.

Our lips met, soft and certain.

The sea moved behind us, steady and endless. The wind stirred the leaves overhead. I could feel his breath against mine when we parted. I let my forehead rest against his, eyes closed.

Gods, he'd scared me.

Then a voice cut through the stillness.

"Caught you two, have I?"

We turned. Rasmus approached, his smile full of mischief. "Young love. A beautiful thing."

I laughed, warmth blooming in my cheeks. "Hello, Grandfather. Just enjoying the afternoon sunshine."

"Enjoying it very much, I see," he said, giving us a wink.

Val chuckled beside me. "Can you blame me? Look at her."

His voice—rough velvet, thick with restraint—made the words feel like worship.

"Val," I hissed, elbowing him in the ribs. But my smile betrayed me.

"Hard to resist the lips of a beautiful woman. Ask Davena. She's been fending me off for forty years." He glanced at the flowers in my hands. "Those immortelle?"

"They are." I followed his eye to Val, who put down the finger he'd had over his lips. I looked back at Rasmus. "Why?"

"Oh no. Ask *him* where he got them." Rasmus turned to head back to the villa, waving over his shoulder. "Don't be late for dinner."

"We won't," I called, then looked at Val. "So. Where'd you get them?"

He looked up at the branches of the olive tree. "Oh, look, I think I see a ripe one."

"Valerius."

He sighed. "They grow in the limestone on the southern shore."

I thought about the location. A place where I'd seen vegetation sticking out from the seams in the limestone. Vegetation that could only be accessed by a narrow goat track that wasn't meant for humans.

Loose gravel.

No handholds.

The sea pounding below.

"You went down the goat trail to pick flowers for me?" The question came out flat, drawing a laugh from him. "Why would you do that?"

"As I said earlier, I'm trying to court you properly."

"Gods, I hope we get forty years."

He leaned in, kissed my cheek. "I'll take every day you'll give me."

"We won't make it that long if you insist on climbing cliffs for flowers. They're beautiful but I'd rather have you. Alive."

I laid the immortelle gently beside me, then leaned back against the tree. Val lowered his head into my lap with the kind of trust that didn't need asking anymore.

I held up the book. "This was your mother's?"

He shifted slightly in my lap, looking up at it.

"I don't know why she had it," he said quietly. "It's not an Anvallan copy, and it's written in Aeltyrian. But I think she read it often. Kept it hidden. Maybe… it meant something to her that she never told anyone."

I wanted to ask him if he'd given it to me because he hadn't planned on being here anymore but I didn't. My grandmother always said not to ask questions when you already know the answer.

Instead, I just asked, "Will you read it to me?"

He took the book and opened it carefully, his thumb brushing the worn edge of the page. When he began, his voice slipped into the hush like it belonged there—rich as warm velvet. His Aeltyrian carried the shape of his first language beneath it—each word rounded and careful, imperfect in a way I loved, as if he tasted every syllable before letting it go.

And gods, I would've stayed there forever just to hear him read like that.

*"With wrath and sorrow intertwined,*
*He fought the beast with all his power,*
*The creature slain, Isolde confined,*
*To death's cold grasp, a bitter hour.*

*"'Great Aelan,' Alaric cried aloud,*
*'Grant me strength, your mercy lend,*

*Restore my love, beneath this—'"*

He paused, brow furrowing slightly. "*Quid ara osa verce?*"

It took me a moment to pull my thoughts back. I hadn't spoken Calesian since we arrived in Letia. I opened my eyes and glanced to where he pointed. "Shroud," I said. "In Calesian, *sindium*."

He nodded once and returned to the Aeltyrian.

*"Restore my love, beneath this shroud,*
*Let her life not find its end."*

I stroked his hair as he read on, letting the cadence of his voice wash over me.

For a little while, nothing else existed.

Only this.

# CHAPTER NINETY-SIX
## *By Blood, By Steel*

*"By blood, by steel, and by the life I give freely,*
*I swear this oath before crown and gods.*
*I am the shield that does not falter, the blade that does not bend.*
*My life for the heir. My strength for the realm.*
*My soul for Aeltyria—until death, until ruin, until the world ends."*
—Oath of the First Sword of Aeltyria

Rudamos 81, 1231
*Valerius*

Another decadium passed, slow and sun-drenched.

Long enough for the bruises to fade. For the worst of the nightmares to ease their grip just enough to let sleep come. Long enough for something like a rhythm of normalcy to settle between us.

Beneath it, a question lingered. Neither of us dared say it aloud.

I always noticed when she got her courses, even before we were together—the way she turned prickly in the days leading up to it, the way she devoured greasy food like it was her birthright the day before, the way she hunched over the saddle for the first two days after.

But they didn't come.

I wouldn't ask.

I wouldn't even know how.

*What if he got you with child?*

That would go over like a skinned goat at a wedding feast.

But gods, the thought of her carrying another man's child—his child—tightened something in my chest like a fist that wouldn't unclench. I'd told myself it didn't matter. That love wasn't about blood. That she'd been hurt enough without my pain and jealousy compounding it.

I would've stood by her, if it had come to that. I would've loved her still, without question. But I'd have hated every moment of it—of watching her belly swell with the last remnants of the things that had devastated us both.

And then her courses came—finally—and went.

I thought she would have told me either way.

Maybe she didn't talk to me about it because, in my guilt and grief, I'd nearly thrown myself into the sea.

And that shamed me.

That I'd been weak, though she told me I wasn't.

That I'd scared her, which she admitted I did.

Despite it all, that had made everything so much clearer. It had shown me that I wanted her to be mine. Completely. Unequivocally. In name. In bond. In the bloodline that would follow us.

Not because I needed an heir. I didn't.

But because I needed *her*.

I couldn't ask her yet. I had no claim. No title. No land or rank. Just the love she let me carry—unspoken, unbound.

But someday, when I did, I'd ask her to put her name beside mine—not for tradition's sake, but so that when the world spoke of her, they'd speak of my love for her, too.

Rain tapped the window in a slow, steady cadence. I didn't know how long I'd been sitting there. Long enough to lose the thread of the book in my lap, to read the same line a dozen times and retain none of it.

The door clattered open.

I looked up.

She stood in the doorway, arms full—bread, fruit, wine. The scent of rosemary and baked figs drifted in with her.

I felt the corner of my mouth twitch at the sight of her. "What's the occasion for this feast?"

She nudged the door shut with her foot, barely managing the bundle in her arms as she crossed to the table. Still, she didn't answer. Just moved, laying out cheese, olives, goblets, and the amphora. She poured generously, handed me a cup, and raised her own.

"Freedom."

I lifted my cup to meet hers, arching a brow. "Freedom? The blacksmith didn't get your manacles off, so it must be something else."

"He tried. Incolumium's stubborn." She took a deep breath. Smiled at me. "I'm not with child. And no… other remnants either."

Relief hit me so hard I had to swallow it down, like a man who knows better than to trust mercy when it's finally offered. Instead, I exhaled. Slow. No movement. No nod. Just stillness.

"Good," I said quietly. "That's good."

I waited. Surely there was more to it than that.

She sat, finally, like someone easing back into a body that hadn't felt like hers in decadia. "And Mariana says I'm… well enough for other things."

I didn't know what she meant. What that meant.

Was she inviting me? Was this some fearful way of asking me to bed her?

I didn't press. Just watched her eat.

She didn't wear dresses often. But today she had—soft, dusky blue, cut just low enough to remind me she was a woman before she was anything else—and the sight of it lodged behind my ribs, tight and aching. As if the world had been briefly entrusted with something fragile and had not, this time, broken it.

I couldn't *not* look at her. Gods, she was beautiful like that. Not in silk. Not in armor. Just… herself.

I let the moment stretch before setting my goblet aside. Tried to think of something else to talk about, to distract myself from necklines or whether she had invited me to bed her or not.

It struck me. Now that we knew she'd be well enough to travel, we had plans to finish.

"I've been planning our return to Aeldunon," I said. "Should we make port at Clodagh or Nuala?"

She just tore a piece of bread and chewed, weighing the question like a commander reviewing a field report.

"Clodagh's closer to Elisedd," she said. "Could we take the river from there all the way in? That would land us near the legion."

I'd chosen wrong. I wasn't sure I was ready for this. I didn't want to lose the softness between us—the part where she was just Aleaia.

"We could," I said. "Though we've no guarantee of any cohort's loyalty. My command of the Second Army is over. Landing near them might result in…"

"… undesirable consequences," she finished.

Clever as always.

I inclined my head. "It's nearly six hundred fifty miles by river. Then another decadium north on horseback. The terrain should be favorable. Late Dēwamos brings long days and dry roads. It's feasible."

"And the drawback?"

"Delays your coronation. Nuala's closer, about a hundred miles shorter, and near a Drustan tributary. We could sail upriver and reach Aeldunon directly."

Her fork stalled halfway to her mouth. "My what?"

Carefully, I said, "It should be fairly obvious we're on the brink of rebellion. Calesia can't imprison and torture the heir to Aeltyria with impunity."

Only then did I meet her eyes.

"They'll be lucky if we don't invade them."

She swallowed hard, chased it with wine. "You mean to crown… me?"

"Yes." I sat forward and set the book aside. "We need you at the head of your forces. That means crowning you first."

*Even if you can barely look at it yet.*

*Even if it marks you for every enemy eye.*

*Even if I have to bleed to keep you standing.*

She stared at me. "You still want me on the throne? After everything?"

I placed my cup on the table. "It's not about what I want. You're the rightful heir. This is your birthright. No one else can wear that crown."

Her gaze sharpened. "You mean for me to be queen."

"Your mother meant it for you. And the gods."

She didn't blink. Didn't soften. "Did you come up with all this yourself?"

"Lucius and I discussed it," I said carefully. "I needed to know it was viable before bringing it to you."

Her brow ticked downward. "So you planned it together."

"I planned for you. There's a difference." I held her gaze. "I mean you to win. You're the heir. And there's no vengeance without power."

She looked straight through me. "You did it without even asking me."

*Oh. Oh, no.*

"I should've asked you first," I said quietly. "I'm sorry."

Her gaze didn't soften. A slight incline of her head—acknowledgment, nothing more.

"And what of Cassius?" she asked. "If we defeat him, and you take the Calesian throne, you'll be guilty of killing your own kin. Your own countrymen."

I ticked each point off on a finger as I spoke. "First of all, Cassius showed no regard for shared blood when he imprisoned and tortured us. I'll treat him as he treated you. Unless you order me otherwise. Secondly, I don't want any throne, anywhere. And thirdly, we're not talking about invading Calesia. We're talking about freeing Aeltyria."

She didn't answer right away. Just watched me. That look used to unnerve me. Now I knew better. She wasn't withholding. She was calculating.

Then she leaned back, exhaled slow. "I wasn't planning anything… organized," she said. "Just vengeance. Blood for blood. I thought I'd do it myself."

My brow lifted. "Alone? You were going to walk into Avitum and kill my brother by yourself?"

She didn't respond.

"You've seen the castle," I said. "You know what's waiting. The Vinculatores are everywhere. You'd never reach him."

"And you've seen the power I can wield," she said, laying it down like a challenge.

Silence stretched between us, thin and taut as drawn wire. I'd leave it alone for now. Outside, the rain softened its rhythm against the window. But inside, the air stayed sharp, filled with everything we hadn't said.

I wanted to blame her for the recklessness of it—for even thinking of going alone. But I didn't.

Because I hadn't taught her yet. Not enough, anyway.

All this time, I'd meant to show her how to lead an army. How to plan a campaign. How to hold the weight of strategy the way she already held grief and fire and justice.

But I hadn't. There had been so little time.

So I reminded myself to be patient with her.

Still. I couldn't believe she thought I'd let her walk back into that place without me. Not after what they did to her. To us.

She looked down at her wine.

"You speak of war like it's a calculation," she said, finally.

"It is."

Her gaze snapped to mine—cold, unflinching.

"You weren't there for the war, Val. Neither was I. But I've lived every day in its shadow. I grew up with empty fields. Burned homes. Children whose parents didn't come back. It may just be numbers to you—pieces on a board, like some bloody game."

Her voice was quiet but edged with iron.

"But I remember it for what it was: a slaughter."

I didn't look away. My voice stayed steady. "That's why we can't let it happen again."

"Then stop talking like a strategist," she said, "and start speaking like a man who knows what it costs."

She stood and crossed to the window.

"I'm not shying away from my duty. I'll take the crown," she said. "I'll take the sword. I'll take every broken piece of Aeltyria they tried to bury with my mother, and I'll forge it into a spear long enough to run the Empire through the heart."

The fading light caught the glass and etched her silhouette in shadow—sharp at the shoulders, soft at the hips.

"I'll fill their rivers with tyrants' blood," she said. "Carve our anthem into the stones of Avitum. Let them build walls. Let them call their god. It won't matter. The earth will remember what we were before their chains. And by the time I'm through, so will they."

Then she turned toward me.

Calm.

Composed.

Lethal.

She was terrifying.

And I loved her for it. Not despite the fury, but *because* of it. Because it wasn't empty. Because she meant every word.

I knew, with something deep and cold and certain, that nothing after this would be the same. There was no one else I'd follow into fire.

"Gods," I said. "Remind me not to get in your way."

Wine in hand, she crossed the room toward me, each step slow, unhurried. The kind that set my pulse hammering long before she reached me.

She stopped in front of me, set her wine on the table next to me, and gathered the hem of her skirt in both hands.

Her bare legs slid to either side of mine, warm and close.

She settled on my lap.

My breath caught. Words failed.

Every part of me said I was hers.

And unfortunately, that included my cock.

Betrayal, sharp and immediate.

I didn't want her to feel it—not now, not like this. But I already knew she had. Of course she had. And she didn't say a word. Maybe she wanted to feel it.

Then—

She plucked a grape from the table and dropped it into my open mouth.

I chewed.

Stared.

Wondered what in the gods' names she was doing to me.

She sipped her wine like it was any other evening. Unhurried. Composed. Set it down again, and laid her hands on my shoulders.

"If we're going to war, you need a title. I mean to give you one."

My hands were already on her hips. I hadn't even realized I'd moved them there.

"What sort—"

Gods, my voice. Thoroughly undignified. I cleared my throat. Tried again.

"What sort of title?" Hoarse. Stretched thin.

She looked straight at me.

"The one my ancestor, Caedmon, was the first to bear. And my sire, Cadoc Aneirin, was the last. First Sword of Aeltyria. The blade of the crown. The last shield between the throne and its enemies."

Her thumb brushed the side of my neck, right over the place where my pulse jumped.

"I want you to bear it now."

Something inside me buckled.

This wasn't a gesture. It wasn't ceremony. The title wasn't a crown of words. It was weight. Duty. Legacy. A role forged in blood and sharpened by loss.

It was trust. Raw and terrifying.

My throat tightened. "Aleaia… you know the First Sword was bound to the Queen," I said, voice thick. "They were wed."

She didn't flinch. "I know."

The room suddenly felt smaller. Not confining, just full. Like it couldn't hold what pressed between us now.

"Is that what this is?" I asked, careful to keep my voice soft. "A marriage proposal?"

She met my gaze. Her thumb traced the line of my jaw.

"We don't have to do everything the way my ancestors did," she said. "But I'm asking you to stand at my side. As sword. As shield. As the one I trust above all others."

I couldn't breathe.

Not when she touched me like that, not when her gaze held mine like the truth she was about to speak had always lived there.

"I don't need a ceremony to know what we are," she said. Then, softer, "This is enough for me."

It wasn't. Not really.

She'd tried to say it like she meant it, but I heard the shadow beneath. The hurt she hadn't named. The hope she was trying to swallow before it could betray her.

She wanted me.

Not just to bear the title. Not just to fight the war.

*Me.*

And she didn't think I would ask.

I wanted to ask her. Right then.

*Marry me.*

I wanted to say the words and damn the timing, damn the war, damn everything—because no moment would ever feel more like a beginning.

But I didn't, because she deserved more than a warbound promise in a quiet room. And I had nothing to offer her. Just a ruined name and a blade she already held.

*If I win this war for her,* I thought, *maybe that will be offering enough.*

So instead, I gave her what I could.

"I swore it the day I cut down the man who tried to kill you in that forest," I said. "Before I knew your name. Before I knew who you were. I've been your sword since the moment we met. All this does is make it official."

I reached up, threaded my hand into her hair and rested it against the back of her neck. She leaned in close enough to kiss. Close enough to ruin me.

And I gave her the words—the ones I'd read, once—though I made them my own.

"By blood, by steel, and by the life I give freely, I swear this oath to you, Aleaia. I'll be the shield that does not falter, the blade that does not bend. I'll give my life for you. My strength for our people. My soul for Aeltyria—until death, until ruin, until the world ends."

She looked at me as if memorizing the moment—every breath, every line of my face, every piece of me that belonged to her now.

"Good," she whispered. "Because I've always been yours."

She let out a slow breath and leaned into me, resting her head on my shoulder, face tucked into the curve of my neck.

I wrapped my arms around her without a word, holding her like she was the only solid thing left in the world.

And for a long time, we stayed like that.

Still.

Together.

Until she shifted.

She lifted her head, guileless now, all trace of the vengeful queen gone.

And then she asked, "Would you want to be… with me… like we were before?"

# CHAPTER NINETY-SEVEN
## *Reclamation*

*"Love is not proven by desire, but by patience—*
*by waiting when taking would be easier."*
—Song of the Stars, Cycle VIII: Cycle of Mortals

Rudamos 81, 1231
*Aleaia*

I kept my face tucked against his neck for a long while, breathing him in, gathering the courage to ask. To tell him I was ready for this—for us—again.

When I finally lifted my head and met his eyes, the words were already waiting there.

"Would you want to be… with me… like we were before?"

He searched my face.

"Of course," he said gently. "But only if it's what you want too, luce mea. And only as much as you want."

I needed him to understand how much I wanted him—not with more words, but with closeness. I shifted in his lap, just enough to feel his breath hitch, just enough to remind us both what we make of each other.

I leaned in and kissed him.

Slow and deep, threaded with the ache of everything we hadn't said. My fingers slid into his hair, and his mouth answered, opening against mine, hungry in a way that left no room for doubt. My hips moved against him without my telling them to.

His arms came around my waist, drawing me close until there was nothing between us but warmth, pressure, and the careful restraint of two people afraid to move too fast.

When he pulled back, my breath caught at the sudden, unmistakable pull low in my body. His fingers traced my cheek, gentle as breath.

"I don't want to hurt you," he said quietly. "I don't know what you need yet."

The old thought tried to rise—*I didn't deserve him, not after—*

*No.*

I shut the door on it.

I wanted this. For him, for me, for us. I needed to make this choice.

"Touch me, vedrānos," I breathed. "Just… touch me."

His finger traced the line of my neck, then followed the edge of my dress, skimming the curve of my chest without pressing.

"May I?" he asked, fingers touching the laces of my bodice, tentative.

I swallowed. "Not… maybe not yet."

He didn't hesitate or retreat—just leaned in, mouth warm against my throat.

I clutched his hair as my head tipped back, opening myself to him.

One arm stayed firm around my waist as his other hand found my ankle, then traced upward—light and measured—until it reached my thigh.

"Please," I breathed, the word slipping out before I could stop it.

I needed his touch.

Needed it in the place I feared most now.

Needed to know I was still allowed to feel.

"Please touch me… there."

The words burned. I couldn't even name what I wanted—not after Avitum, not after everything that had been taken and twisted. Shame flared bright and sudden.

My eyes stung. If he pulled away, I didn't know how I'd survive it. If he didn't pull away, I didn't know how I'd survive that either.

His hand moved inward.

Would it hurt? Would it feel like it did before?

I leaned forward and wrapped my arms around his neck, my chin on his shoulder, holding tight, eyes closed, bracing myself for whatever came next.

"I've got you," Val murmured. "Always."

Then his fingers touched me—gentle and familiar. Small, careful motions, back and forth, light as breath.

"Does that feel good, amor mea?" he said, warm at my ear.

"Yes," I said, breathless.

And it was true.

The smallest sound—the start of a moan—slipped out of me. I hid my face in the crook of my elbow and felt Val's hand still beneath me, waiting. When he didn't continue, I lifted my head and looked at him. My heart hammered. Had I ruined it with the memories I carried?

"You don't have to disappear," he said softly, brushing his lips over mine. "Stay with me."

"I was afraid to…" I whispered, trailing off. "I was just… afraid."

His thumb traced my cheek before he tucked my hair behind my ear.

"The sounds you make," he said softly, "when they come from being here—with me—they're beautiful. Not because of what they are, but because of what they mean."

The words settled deep, warm and steady. Something in my chest loosened.

"Do you want to keep going?" he asked.

I nodded—because it was true. I still wanted him. Us.

When his hand moved again, I let myself breathe.

Let my forehead rest against his.

Let myself stay.

"Just like this?" Val asked softly.

"Yes," I breathed. "Just—just like—"

There it was.

The familiar warmth I'd been so afraid to name.

It gathered slowly this time. Not a spark—but an ember coaxed brighter with every touch.

A sound left me—soft, open—and this time I let it.

"That's it," he whispered. "You can let go."

My fingers tightened in his shirt as the feeling swelled—too big, too bright—

My breath quickened. My body followed.

I clutched at him as the wave took me—no thought left, no fear—just sensation, just release, tearing through me and leaving me shaking in the wake of it.

And he held me through it. Didn't move, except his fingers, to see me through. Didn't rush.

"There you are, luce mea," he murmured. "Gods… seeing you like that—it's beautiful."

"I missed this," I whispered. "I didn't even know how much."

I leaned into him, tucking my face into the warm curve of his neck. He held me close, one arm firm around my back. His other hand slipped beneath my skirt, just to rest against the bare skin of my lower back.

"Is this all right?" he asked softly, his mouth warm just below my ear.

"It's wonderful," I breathed. "And if you want to touch lower… I don't mind."

His hand moved leisurely, deliberately—down, then back again—tracing my back, my hips, my shoulders, as if committing me to memory all over again.

"You are everything to me," he said against my hair. "I love every part of you."

"I love you so much," I whispered, my voice breaking as tears spilled free.

He turned his head and kissed me then, light and sweet—the kind of kiss that asked nothing and offered everything. When we parted, I rested my head against his shoulder, safe and warm.

"This is nice," I said before I could stop myself. "Just being held like this."

He tightened his arms around me a fraction. "I like holding you," he said. "You're warm. You always have been."

My fingers threaded into his hair.

He hesitated, then added, softer still, "And you smell good."

"Do I?" I asked, a quiet smile in my voice.

He hummed softly. "Like lavender. And sunlight."

The sound of it—that hum—went right through me.

For a while, I simply existed with him. Breathing in the scent of soap and leather and him. My cheek rested against his shoulder. I felt his breathing where our bodies met—slow, unhurried. His fingers moved idly along my back, raising gooseflesh wherever they passed.

I sat up so I could see his face—and so he could see mine—my forehead resting against his.

"Will you… touch me?" I asked softly. "The way you used to."

He stilled, eyes softening. His hand slid beneath my skirts, careful and familiar, his touch returning to the place he had touched me earlier—light, attentive, meant to please. "Like this?"

Just not quite right.

He slowed, reading the tension in me.

"Not quite?" he asked softly.

I shook my head, breath unsteady. "No. I want you inside."

He was so careful. One finger first. Gentle, careful strokes, the way he knew I liked before.

His eyes never left me. I could feel their weight even when I closed mine.

"Another?" he whispered.

"Yes," I said—and gasped when I felt him again.

And then I felt other things—things I'd thought I'd lost.

The way his breath changed—how it quickened with mine.

The way the ache that had lived in me for decadia finally loosened its hold.

But mostly, I felt his love for me.

I wanted more. I wanted him—all of him.

"Val," I whispered.

His hand stilled at once. "I'm here."

I swallowed. My voice trembled, but the truth held. "I want you. With me. Like before."

His gaze traced my face. "Are you sure?"

"I am," I breathed, nodding.

I rose onto my knees and rocked my hips forward, pressing into him. His hands came to my waist to steady me—and to follow, if I asked.

I cupped his face and leaned down to kiss him again.

When we parted, he folded into me, arms circling my back, his cheek resting against my chest. He drew a deep, shuddering breath, and I held him there—just holding—for a long moment.

Because he needed healing too.

When we finally pulled back, he smiled softly, lashes dark with tears.

"You're beautiful, vedrānos," I said, breathless.

He shook his head, color rising to his ears.

I tipped his chin up and made him look at me. "I mean it," I said softly. "Not just how you look—but how you look at me. The way you're careful. The way you touch me. Like I'm still whole."

"Amor mea, you *are* whole," he said.

I felt the hitch of his breath when he pulled me down into another kiss. As our mouths met, my fingers went to the ties of my bodice. I loosened them and let the fabric fall away.

"You'll stop us," he murmured between gentle presses of his lips, "if anything feels wrong?"

"I will," I breathed as his mouth brushed my skin. "If you promise you will, too."

"I do."

His hands cupped my breasts, reverent, his mouth following.

I reached for the hem of his tunic.

He didn't hesitate—only lifted his arms so I could pull it free. I let it fall aside without looking.

I leaned into him again, pressing my body to his, easing him back against the chair. Rolled my hips, feeling the way his breath changed beneath me.

My fingers slid into the waistband of his trousers. He lifted to slide them down.

I raised myself over him, then lowered again, until I felt him there—warm, familiar, waiting.

"Only as much as you want," he murmured, hands at my hips. "As slow or fast as you need. I'm yours."

Then I sank onto him.

Slow, just in case.

And the moment we came together, I gasped—not from pain, not from fear—but from recognition.

*Oh.*

*It was him.*

*It was still us.*

"Gods," I breathed, startled by my own voice. "I forgot how good it feels. To be with you like this."

"You feel so good," he said, ragged and low. "I missed this... so much."

I lifted and sank again, feeling the way we fit—deep and unchanged. Then I began to move, finding a rhythm as natural as breathing. My hands traced his chest. His followed the line of my thighs, my hips, my back.

And then it rose.

The warmth spread through me, the pressure building into something full and bright. I was being drawn under, into something familiar and unmistakably ours.

I moaned, long and soft, as my body remembered how to belong to me.

As we remembered how to belong to each other.

When it crested, the sound that broke from me wasn't a whimper or a cry, but a sob.

Grief leaving me through pleasure.

"Gods... seeing you like this—" His breath dragged, his voice breaking. "I love seeing you like this. Hearing you like this."

I leaned down and kissed him, tasting the salt of our tears as I moved with more urgency, until his breath turned ragged and his hands tightened at my hips.

"Aleaia—" His voice broke, hands loosening as if he meant to pull away. "I—I'm going to—"

I shook my head. "Don't," I whispered. "Please, stay with me."

I leaned forward instinctively, my arms winding around his neck. His grip tightened, like he needed the weight of me there to stay anchored.

"Let me hear you, too," I said softly.

A low sound tore from him as it crested, his hands sliding from my hips to my back, drawing me closer until there was no space left between us.

I slowed while he finished. While the moment passed through him—not as release, but as relief.

I let my tears fall as we held each other, listening to the quiet shudder of his breath. I rested my cheek against his hair, cradling him to me.

"You're all right, luce mea," he murmured. His arms tightened. "Still you. Still with me."

*Still with me.*

The words hit somewhere deep. Not like praise—but like being named. A hard, healing sob rose before I could stop it, and I covered my mouth as it broke free.

"Oh, Aleaia," he said softly, brow furrowing. "What is it? I'm sorry—what did I do?"

"Nothing," I said quickly, pulling back to take his face in my hands again, smiling down at him. I gave a soft, wet laugh. "Nothing is wrong, vedrānos. Everything is right."

# CHAPTER NINETY-EIGHT
## *Letian Ash*

*"They weren't soldiers. They were a lit torch with orders."*
—On the Ruin of Empires

Rudamos 85, 1231
*Aleaia*

"Aleaia, wake up," Val whispered, edged with steel. "We have to go."

I woke slow and thick—too much wine, not enough time for it to wear off. My limbs felt sodden. My thoughts lagged, sluggish and heavy, behind his words. He was already pulling on his boots, voice clipped, urgent.

"What's happening?" My mouth was dry.

"Vinculatores. They're here." He shoved a tunic and trousers into my hands. "Grab what you can. If we're separated, head for the inlet. There's a ship waiting. Lucius and Mariana have gone to wake the captain."

I yanked on the tunic. Shoved my legs into the trousers. My hands fumbled at my belt, but I got it buckled into place, the Fellglow Blade at my left hip and quiver on the right. Pack on my back. Bow in hand. No thought, just motion. Training.

Then we moved.

And stepped straight into chaos.

Everything outside our chamber glowed red. Smoke billowed high from the courtyard. Somewhere across the villa, someone screamed—a high, choking wail that ended too fast.

"The children," Val said.

We headed north, up the portico, toward the servants' wing. An oil lamp burst, fire licking across the ground. One of the maids ran past the far end of the corridor.

A blade took her across the throat, the blood spraying across the stone before she fell into the reflecting pool.

We kept low along the portico, sticking to smoke-shadowed edges. Ash drifted like snow. Embers flared and danced as the roof to the stores collapsed in on itself, the wood hissing.

Then we heard Rasmus in the training yard.

"My lord is not here, sir. I know not where he is, not having seen him for more than a year now. It is not the place of a slave to question the whereabouts of his master—"

"Silence, ashborn."

Steel.

Flesh splitting.

A body hitting stone.

Davena's scream—raw, primal—worse than any war cry.

A second strike. Another fall.

Then silence.

They'd cut her down too.

My blood went white-hot.

Rasmus had raised Val like a son. Davena had fed us. Washed the blood from my tunic. They were kind to me. Spoke to me like I was still worth saving.

I would remember.

Val's expression hardened. "Bastard."

Then came the call.

"Valerius di Calesia, you are charged with high treason and the murder of Marcus Frugi! Resistance will only lead to a harsher punishment! Show yourself—spare the people of your estate!"

I knew that voice.

Had heard it spit filth from behind polished teeth—*You've got a weakness for these fucking savages.*

Now it rang out, gloating and eager.

Caius Varro.

I'd kill him.

Put an arrow right through his gullet. I reached for my quiver.

Val caught my arm, mouthed it: *Not. Now.*

I bit the inside of my cheek. Shook my head. Let him lead me away.

Because he was right, even if I hated it.

We didn't stop.

The servants' quarters came into view, smothered in smoke.

Then, movement.

Two small figures sprinted from between the columns, southward toward us.

Bren. Lysa.

Val didn't hesitate. He scooped the boy up in one arm and kept running.

I caught Lysa mid-step and pulled her tight against me.

"Don't look," I said, tucking her face into my neck. I didn't want her plagued by the things I saw in the dark.

We ran through the kitchen gardens and down the stairs along the cliff face that led to the docks. Arrows hissed past us. One struck the railing just beside my hand. Another buried itself in a fleeing man's back—dropped him mid-stride. He fell over the railing and onto the beach below.

At the bottom, a ship loomed ahead, slick with sea-mist. Behind us, screams rang out—more voices cut down. More blades doing the Emperor's will.

They weren't arresting anyone. They were purging.

The ship rocked in the inlet, sails half-unfurled, gangplank down.

Lucius stood on the deck, waving us urgently. He leaned over, ready to take the children.

I lifted Lysa—hoisted her by the waist and passed her into Lucius's arms, then turned to deal with the Vinculatores close on our heels.

Nocked, drew, loosed.

Again.

And again.

"Aleaia," Val said, prompting me to board before him.

"You first," I said, loosing another arrow. Return fire flew past my head, stuck in the side of the ship.

Lucius reached down and caught Val by the forearm. I heard his boots hit the deck behind me. Then—

"Up you go, luce mea." Val caught me under one arm while Lucius grabbed the other and hauled me over the rail like it was the most natural thing in the world.

Another arrow flew past me, clipping Val in the arm as it stuck in the deck.

"By Galdorin's bloody sword, you'll die for that," I muttered—a curse harsh enough to blister stone—as I stepped to the rail and nocked another arrow.

I raised my voice and shouted, "You missed, you limp-armed shit stain!"

And then I loosed it. Caught the arsehole right in the throat.

The sailors rowed us out of the inlet as fast as they could, until the sail caught. The ship turned.

And the estate behind us burned.

Stone and olive trees. Screaming courtyards. Blood-soaked gravel. Bodies bleeding beneath firelit skies.

Another razing. And I knew, much as I wished otherwise, it wouldn't be the last.

Lucius spat over the side. "That bastard should've been put to the sword when he got your father killed."

# CHAPTER NINETY-NINE
## *Crack in the Rail*

*"When the rot runs deep enough,*
*even the weight of a single word can break the beam."*
—Shipwright's Wisdom, Aeldunon Docks

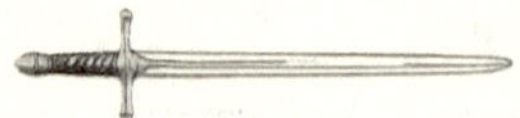

Rudamos 85, 1231
*Aleaia*

I turned away from watching Letia burn, the smoke still trailing like a noose into the night sky, and—for the first time—looked over the wreck someone had the audacity to call a ship.

The vessel groaned with every swell. Its hull was a patchwork of graying timber—warped and bleached, brittle where it wasn't outright rotted. The sail looked like a beggar's rag, stitched from scraps and held together with prayers. The rigging tangled and frayed more each time the wind caught it.

The ship was a deathtrap. Every cracked beam and flapping line screamed it. But it had gotten us away from shore. Away from certain death.

"Who? Varro?" I asked, dropping my pack at my feet. I'd kill him the first chance I got, but if he had anything to do with Papa—

"Sail astern!" a voice shouted from the crow's nest. "Closing fast!"

One of the Calesian ships had broken from the dock and was cutting across the water—sleek, fast, and ruthless. And unlike this pitiful vessel, that one was tightly run. Efficient. Merciless. We weren't outrunning them.

I glanced around the deck, heart hammering. What could I do? Steel wouldn't stop a ship. Words wouldn't either. Then the thought came—sudden, certain.

The enemy of a ship isn't water. It's fire.

When a ship is on fire, there's nowhere to run. Nowhere to hide. Just wind in the sails and timber underfoot. You could jump into the sea, but you risk drowning, or the cold stealing your strength before you ever reach shore.

Let them taste what they gave Letia.

I needed flame.

And a way to carry it.

My hand went to the quiver at my side.

I looked along the deck. A rag lay crumpled near the rail—used, stiff, black with grease. I snatched it up. Found a barrel of pitch lashed near the mast. Pried the lid free. The smell hit like a blow.

I wrapped the rag tight around an arrow shaft and shoved it deep into the pitch until it bled black. Perfect.

"I need a flame!" I barked.

Val held a lantern nearby. "What are you doing?"

"Fixing the only thing I can."

I lit the arrow from the lantern. Watched the fire take.

The enemy's sail loomed pale in the moonlight, wide and waiting.

"Hold her steady," I called to the helm. "Just give me the shot."

The ship groaned, wood straining against the wind. I braced against the rail and raised the bow.

*Distance. Wind from the east. Target low for spread. Fire climbs.*

I drew the string. Felt the pitch drying against my fingers. Breathed once.

"Put that up your arse," I snarled, and let it fly, fire trailing in its wake.

It struck low on the mainsail. Hung there. Then flared. Pitch caught. Flame bloomed. Smoke boiled black as the fire climbed.

Shouts rang out. Shadows scrambled.

Let them burn.

I set my bow with my pack and turned back to the others, pitch on my hands and heat still in my veins.

"You were saying?" I asked Lucius. "Should have killed Varro?"

Lucius shook his head. "Shouldn't be me who tells you. Should have been Val, a long time ago."

"Lucius," Val said. A warning.

"What is it?" I asked, watching their faces.

The fading bruises.

The silence.

They were hiding something. My stomach turned. Whatever this was, it had torn through *even them.*

"Right now?" Val asked Lucius.

"Might never get another chance," Lucius said.

"Mariana," I said, glancing back. "Take the children below. This isn't something they need to hear."

Mariana hesitated, but nodded. "Come on," she said, coaxing Lysa to her feet. Bren clung to her skirt, wary but silent. "Below with me. Just for a while."

She gathered them both with practiced care, then disappeared toward the stair.

Then I turned back to Lucius and Val. "All right. Out with it."

As soon as they were gone, Val swore and pressed the heel of his hand to his brow. "Gods. I never wanted to tell you like this."

Lucius scoffed. "You never wanted to tell her *at all.*"

"Don't," Val said, voice cold as a blade.

"Oh, I think I will," Lucius snapped. "Because I begged you to tell her. Before Letia. Before Avitum. *Before any of this happened.* And you kept saying you would. 'When the time was right.'"

My gaze flicked from Lucius to Val and back again. "Someone had better tell me."

Val looked at me like the words might break him. "Come here," he said quietly.

I should've refused. Should've made him say it loud—made him own whatever it was. But he looked like a man about to gut himself, and I thought maybe he meant to spare me the sting. So I went to stand apart from the others with him.

He exhaled like it hurt. "I'm sorry, Aleaia."

"Stop apologizing and *say it.*" The delay only made me angrier.

"Do you remember what I told you? About the night your father died?"

I nodded. I didn't trust my voice, so I kept it to myself.

"And how my men and I had been tracking his killer? That he got into our camp, killed a sentry, stole weapons, slipped out again?"

"Aye."

"There were two sentries that night," he said. "One of them was Marcus."

I held my breath.

"He didn't fight. Didn't sound the alarm. He hid. That's how they got in and out clean. That's how they found you and your father."

The world narrowed.

So all I could see was the chain of events—

Everything that unfolded because Marcus had continued to exist.

My father's head, lifeless on the forest floor.

Me, marching beneath the banner of the Second Army.

The things they made me do.

Lhannor.

Catan Row.

Caerlan.

Ardhmor.

The way he'd touched me.

The things he whispered.

Avitum.

My grip had tightened on the rail without realizing it.

I couldn't feel my fingers.

Just heat building in my throat—thick, blistering, and rising fast—

I didn't answer. I couldn't.

I'd fought so much, so many things and people in my life. Always straightforward. This was my first taste of betrayal and it had come from the man I loved more than anything.

The ship lurched beneath my feet, dragging me back to the present.

"Could've aimed for the hull," the captain said behind me somewhere, voice rough as old rope. "But the sail was clever."

*Good. Something else to think about.*

They called him Erik. He looked like he'd been a warrior once. Broad shoulders now bowed by time. Hands like old stone. Whatever strength had lived in him had long since dried up with the color in his hair. He moved like a ghost, haunting his own deck.

I was a ghost now, too. Maybe I'd just join him.

"I need a drink," I muttered.

The captain pressed a skin into my hand without a word. I took a long draught.

It wasn't wine. It was sweet at first—*too* sweet—then hot and biting, like fire forced through honey.

I coughed, hard. "What in the gods' names is that?"

"Mead," Erik said, as if that explained anything.

It didn't. But I drank again anyway.

Because my father was dead.

Because Marcus had lived.

Because Val had lied.

That lie had set the chain in motion—every single thing that had ever hurt me.

And because if I didn't keep drinking, I was going to start screaming.

I couldn't think about what had just been said—what it *meant*.

The truth sat like a thorn in my throat, daring me to choke on it.

I couldn't even look at Val.

So I turned instead. Toward the open water. Toward anything else.

To the west, the jagged silhouette of the mainland shrank with every stroke of the oars, its peaks fading into the haze of early dawn. To the east, the horizon blurred into a low smudge of land and light. A dark shape, half-hidden in the mist.

"Captain," I called, raising my voice over the groan of timber and the steady churn of water. "What's that island?"

Erik glanced up from the steering oar, squinting into the distance. "Dunno what it's called. Folk say to stay away. Shrouded in mist and mystery, they say."

Of course they did. Everything cursed was always wrapped in fog and fairytales.

I stared at it a little longer anyway, willing my thoughts to stay out there, adrift. Anything to keep from circling back to the blade Val had just buried in me.

Movement tugged at the edge of my vision.

Val was watching me. I caught the stern look he wore. The one he donned before stepping into a fight he didn't want.

I met his gaze as I took another pull from the skin.

The last mouthful burned on the way down, fierce in my empty stomach. My head felt lighter with every breath, like I could float right out of myself if I let go long enough.

Val stepped closer. "Don't you think you've had enough? There's still another ship, and you'll need a clear head if they board us."

Before I could answer, Erik's shout cracked across the deck. "Row! Put your backs into it!"

I turned.

A second Calesian ship was closing fast, their sail full, their crew a blur of motion. Unified. Focused. Ruthless.

Too far for another shot.

And now I was too drunk anyway.

Another mess of my own making.

"If they catch us," I said, "I'd rather be too far in my cups to care."

"I need you to care," Val said, closer now. "You're one of the best fighters we've got on this floating pile of kindling."

I turned on him.

"Don't," I snapped. "Don't you *dare* pull that commander's tone with me."

He straightened, looked down at me like I might bite if he reached too fast.

"I trusted you," I said, my voice like flint. I stepped in, close enough that he couldn't look away. "Told you everything. You knew the pain I bear. I laid it at your feet like an offering, and you said nothing."

Around us, the deck quieted. No one spoke, but I felt their stares like pricking needles.

Pretending not to listen. Not to look.

"Nothing! Even after—"

I stopped. I couldn't let everyone hear the rest. Not the words. Not the shame.

It wasn't true. He hadn't just stood by. He'd called Marcus out. Fought him. Beaten him bloody more than once. And in the end, he was the one who killed him.

I didn't care then, though. I just wanted to hurt him the way he'd hurt me.

"You didn't think I could handle it. Not just you. Lucius knew. Everyone must have. Except *me*. Because what, I'm too fragile? Too volatile? You think I'd have slit his throat in the night and left you to clean it up?"

Val stepped forward, voice tight. "I didn't tell you because I was trying to protect you."

Wrong answer.

"Of course you were." I laughed—a hard, bitter sound—and mocked him. "Poor Aleaia. The girl in the woods, who lost her papa and everyone she loved. Can't give her the truth, can we? Better let her die thinking it was just fate. Destiny, to see his head in the dirt."

"I didn't want to add to what you were already carrying," he said. "You were barely—"

"No," I cut in. "You don't get to decide that."

"Aleaia—"

"I've followed you through blood, fire, and ruin. I've *killed* for you. Nearly *died* for you. And you still think I need protecting? Like I'm something delicate you keep wrapped in silk until your hands are clean again?"

Tension gathered in his face. He looked like he wanted to speak, but I didn't let him.

"You think you get to decide what I can bear?" I said. "What if I did that to you? What if I made choices about *your* life in secret because I thought *I* knew better?"

He didn't answer.

"You didn't protect me," I said. "You *undermined* me. You made Lucius keep it from me because *you* didn't trust *me*. You talk about loyalty. Respect. But when it mattered, you treated me like a child."

I looked away, fighting the tremor in my breath. My shoulders ached with the effort of holding it in.

Then, my voice dropped lower still, barely audible. "You, of all people, should've known better."

He reached for my hand.

I yanked it back, stepping away. "Don't."

"Aleaia, just—"

"I said don't fucking touch—"

I backed away. My hip slammed into the rail.

A dry crack.

Deep.

Wrong.

For a breathless instant, everything held.

The rotten wood gave.

Then I was gone.

No time to scream.

The sky twisted. The deck vanished.

Then—*cold*.

I hit the water hard—flat, jarring. The breath slammed out of my lungs. Salt water filled my nose, my mouth. The burn was immediate and blinding.

And then the sea swallowed me whole.

# CHAPTER ONE HUNDRED
## *Not Enough*

*"The worst betrayals are quiet.*
*They come dressed in silence and wrapped in love."*
—The Breath of the World

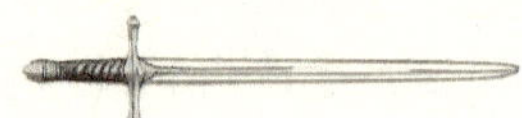

Rudamos 85, 1231
*Valerius*

I lunged, fingers grazing the edge of her sleeve—too slow, too late.

For a breath, I stared at the space she'd left. Just broken wood. Spray. Silence.

Then I moved.

Dropped my belt.

Climbed the rail.

"Lucius!" I shouted. "Don't come back until it's safe!"

I dove.

The sea struck like a hammer. Cold. Punishing. I drove forward through the crush, lungs burning, heart thundering behind my ribs.

When I surfaced, she was far from the ship.

Her arms flailed, legs kicking wide. She was trying to swim, but she'd had too much to drink. No rhythm. No sense of direction. Her strokes fought the water instead of moving through it.

She slipped under.

I swam harder. Three long strokes and I went under after her.

My boots dragged. I kicked harder, driving myself beneath the surface.

My chest burned—not for lack of air, but the knowledge that I would run out.

I opened my eyes. The salt seared. Darkness blurred the edges of everything.

I got close enough to reach her.

Missed.

Tried again—and my fingers caught cloth.

I locked my grip around her middle, hauling her against me, and drove us upward with everything I had left.

We broke the surface again. She coughed seawater, jerked hard against my hold—striking water and me without aim or mercy.

I held tight with one arm around her chest, gasping with the effort of keeping us both afloat. "Stop. Stop fighting."

Her hands clawed at my arms, desperate and blind. Her elbow caught me hard in the ribs and I hissed but didn't let go.

Panic had her now. Pure and wild.

"Aleaia, it's me," I said, louder, closer to her ear. "You're all right. I've got you."

She shook her head, sputtering, still thrashing.

I shifted my grip, pinning her back against me despite the struggle. Not gently.

Slowly—too slowly—her movements lost their fury. The blows softened. Her breath hitched, then dragged in, rough and ragged. She sagged against me, trembling. Her head lolled against my shoulder. Her breath came ragged, shallow.

Exhausted. Cold. Drunk.

I turned us, searching.

*There.*

The island she'd asked about earlier. A low, dark rise on the horizon, wreathed in fog.

The ship was already gone. Its sail pulled full, fading fast into open sea.

*Good. That had been the order.*

I turned back to Aleaia and adjusted my hold. "Look at me."

She did, her eyes searching my face. Gods, I wished I'd taken her swimming in the sea before now.

"Breathe with me. In," I said softly, holding her gaze. She did. "Now, out."

We breathed like that together, until the panic left her.

Once she was calm enough to listen, I loosened my grip, just slightly. "Feel that?"

She nodded.

"It's not like the lakes and rivers you grew up with. The sea wants to hold you up. Let it."

"I'll try," she slurred. "Where are we going?"

Still too drunk to swim on her own. Very unfortunate for me.

"Current's pushing east, toward an island," I said. "We'll try to get there. Kick when I kick. Don't use your arms."

We swam like that for a while. Not well, and not far. I asked her questions now and again—if she was tired, if she was awake.

By the time we crawled ashore, every muscle ached. My lungs felt raw. Salt stung my eyes, my skin.

She collapsed, tunic clinging to her.

I dropped beside her, the taste of salt and failure thick on my tongue.

We breathed heavy in the silence.

"We need to find fresh water," Aleaia said, sitting up. She pulled off her boots stiffly, then stood, tugging at the ties of her soaked trousers. "Need fire and shelter, too. Before sunset."

I stripped, wringing out what I could, fingers slow from the cold. I glanced at her, watching the way she moved.

Tense. Controlled.

She'd been getting stronger. Eating. Sleeping. Laughing, even. Letia had given her space to breathe. Now she looked like she had the day we left Avitum—withdrawn and sharpened at the edges.

It was my fault.

Lucius was right.

I opened my mouth—closed it. Nothing I could say would change the shape of what lay between us.

Pale sand curved up the shoreline. Inland, a mountain loomed—green at the base, white at the peak. Olive trees twisted along the slope, gnarled and weathered. Wild citrus bloomed in patches between flowering vines. Somewhere above, a stream cut down the rock face in narrow silver lines.

It should have been a safe place to regroup.

"You done gawking?" Aleaia snapped.

She stood barefoot in her smallclothes, sodden clothes clutched in one hand, belt and blade in the other.

"Yes." I pushed to my feet.

She didn't look at me.

"There's a game trail," she said, pointing toward a narrow gap in the brush. "If we're lucky, it leads to water."

I already knew that, but saying so would only make things worse. I nodded and fell in behind her. I'd let her lead. Let her keep that. It was the only ground I could give back.

The trail was tight, overgrown in places. We moved through tall brush and twisted roots, beneath trees high enough to mute the light. The canopy cast everything in gold and green. Leaves softened our steps. Loam and moisture thickened the air.

I said nothing. I could be counted on to do that much right.

She'd survived so much. And now she was surviving me.

The trail opened into a clearing, and the sound reached us first—rushing water, steady and loud. A waterfall spilled over a rock face, misting the air. Below it, a clear pool widened out.

Aleaia dropped her bundle without a word and circled the pool. She knelt, cupped her hands, and drank deeply.

"Drink up," she said, not looking back.

I watched her shoulders tense with a shiver. My instincts screamed to cross the space, to offer warmth, apology—anything. Instead, I crouched, drank beside the pool. The cold bit at my teeth and throat. When my thirst was gone, I stood and picked up my bundle.

"Where to?"

She studied the slope west of the pool. "That rise is easier. Less rock."

I nodded and followed.

We climbed into thicker forest. The trees here were older—close and heavy, their canopy thick, their roots rising in knotted shapes. A hush settled over the woods, weighted and close.

Then we saw it. A stone tower at the height of the slope, half-veiled in ivy, hidden in shadow. Ruined. The door hung half-rotted, grayed with age. Moss crept over the threshold, and the path that once led to it was long gone.

It was a place someone had left behind. A refuge.

Aleaia stepped forward, parting the vines. Symbols lined the lintel, half-buried in growth. She shoved the incolumium manacles higher on her arms with a hiss and traced a carving with her fingers.

"Aeltyrian," she murmured. "Or close."

I stepped beside her, drawn to the worn marks. "What do they say?"

She didn't answer at first. Just studied them, brow furrowed, her fingertips moving with that same focused calm she always wore when decoding language.

She'd call it instinct. Or guessing. But it wasn't. She saw patterns. Understood what wasn't written.

"It's an older dialect," she said. "But I think it says, 'Enter and find safe refuge.'"

I looked at her. "Sounds like something people write when they don't want you asking questions."

She almost smiled. Almost.

She tested the door's handle. The wood groaned but didn't resist.

I followed her inside.

The hearth stood against the far wall, already stacked with kindling. Flint and steel rested on the mantle. Beside it lay the remains of a ladder, long since rotted away. I wondered what we might find if we could reach the upper floors.

Dust clung to everything. The scents of dried herbs, old paper, and smoke long settled into stone. The bed was rough-hewn but solid. Homespun linens. No comfort, but maybe no lice either.

Aleaia took the bundle from my hands.

"I'll light the fire and hang these to dry," she said. "You gather more wood."

No warmth. Just instruction, plainly given. I nodded and stepped out.

Deadfall lay scattered around the tower. I gathered what I could carry, one armful at a time, and stacked it beside the hearth. She worked silently nearby.

I didn't speak. Didn't ask if she was all right.

I could see it in her shoulders. The way she kept her back to me. She was angry or breaking—probably both—and didn't want me to see it happen.

She was only holding herself together because she thought she had to.

I turned away, tried to find something else to do so she wouldn't feel me staring at her.

The ache in my gut reminded me we hadn't eaten since the night before. I opened one of the cabinets near what I guessed was meant to be a kitchen. I don't know what I expected to find.

"Hungry?" she asked, still facing the fire. Her voice was even. Not cold. Just… distant. "If you can wait, I saw trout in the pool at the falls. We'll catch some for dinner. Let these dry first, so we have clothes to wear."

I glanced over. She hadn't turned.

"If that's what you want," I said.

I didn't mean anything by it. Was just trying to give her the space she needed.

She was quiet a long time.

Then her voice came, softer than I thought it would be. "Why would you say it like that?"

I didn't answer. Didn't move. I wasn't sure what would come out if I tried.

Like the calm before the storm, I felt it coming—and knew I wouldn't like it.

And then she said it.

"If you didn't trust me," she said, voice tight, "you should've just let me die in that dungeon."

# CHAPTER ONE HUNDRED ONE
## *Seven Years*

*"To withhold truth is to serve fear.*
*To share it is to trust love will survive the fire."*
—The Breath of the World

Rudamos 85, 1231
*Valerius*

I braced a hand on the edge of the cabinet. "Aleaia—"

"You don't get to look at me like that. Not after what you kept from me," she said, turning at last.

Her eyes were dry. but the look in them—flint-edged and cold—scraped straight through me.

I crossed the space between us, slow, careful. Like one wrong step might shatter the ground. "You think I wanted to keep it from you?"

"I don't care what you wanted." Her voice didn't rise. But every word cut clean. "You had seven years."

I flinched. Couldn't help it.

"Seven," she said again, louder, as she stepped toward me. "Seven years of knowing what he did. Of letting me think he was just another spoiled noble. Just part of your retinue."

I opened my mouth. Nothing came. There was no defense. No justification. Only the truth, and the wreckage it left behind.

"You've known every secret I've buried. Held me when I couldn't breathe. You've—" Her hand moved between us, trembling. "You've fucked me until I couldn't stand, Val. I let you—I wanted to for the first time since—since Avitum—four days ago. And through it all, you didn't think I deserved the truth?"

I reached for her.

She stepped back.

"You were there when I learned who I am," she said. "About Aelan. My mother. I let you see what I am. Who I am. What I can't control. Everything."

Her voice wavered. But she didn't.

"And you couldn't even tell me that the man who stood watch that night hid and let those men slip in and out of the encampment. That he didn't even try, because he was a coward."

My heart slammed against my ribs. "You don't understand what you're asking," I said, forcing my breath to steady. "He was a noble. His father was my father's advisor."

She shook her head. A bitter sound broke in her throat. "Lucius was right. You should've put him to the sword."

"I wanted to!" It ripped out of me. Too loud. Too fast. "You think I didn't? I was sixteen, Aleaia. My first command. My first failure. You think I liked walking into that clearing and seeing you nearly dead and your father already gone?"

"Maybe then, that was true, but what about all the years since then?" she snapped. "Why lie by omission? Why watch me serve near him like nothing had happened? He was so fucking cruel to me, Val. And I put up with it. And you *let me*. Fucking Hel, at least if you'd told me, I would have understood why he was so awful!"

My breath caught. I said the only thing I knew might save us. "I did it to protect you."

She gave a brittle, humorless laugh. "You did it to protect *him*."

"No," I said, teeth clenched. "I did it because you would've slit his throat the moment I told you. In camp. In public, probably. In front of the wrong people."

"Maybe I would've. Maybe I'd have died for it. But that should've been *my* decision."

"I *was* trying to protect you," I said again.

"No," she hissed, stepping forward. "You were trying to control me. You didn't trust me to choose."

My hands curled at my sides. "I've trusted you with everything."

"Except this," she said. "The one truth that mattered. The one that would've changed everything."

Silence stretched, tense and fraying.

Then she said the thing that broke me.

"Maybe you shouldn't stand beside me if you don't believe in me."

It landed like a blade between the ribs. Clean. Deep. True.

And suddenly I saw it.

A future where I still served her. Still followed every order.

But wasn't hers. Not anymore.

She'd become what she was meant to be—Queen—and I'd fade into her shadow. Forgotten. Unwanted. Watching her smile at another man. Carry his child. Love someone who hadn't lied to her.

"Don't say that," I managed. "That's—gods, that's cruel."

She didn't flinch. Her voice was ice. "No crueler than what you did."

"I do believe in you," I said, too fast. "Gods, Aleaia, I believe in you more than I believe in anything."

"Then why didn't you act like it?"

"Because I was afraid!" I snapped. "Afraid of what it would do to you. Of what it would cost. Of what I'd see on your face when you looked at me and realized I knew and said nothing. Did nothing."

"That's not fear," she said. "That's cowardice."

"I'm the coward?" The words came out sharp, unthinking. "Remind me which one of us thought it might be better to walk into a wolf's den alone because they couldn't bear the pain of living because they were so gods-damned sure they were a curse?"

Silence. Her eyes welled.

The stinging pang of regret pounded in my chest. "Gods—Aleaia—"

"No worse than you," she said. "Ready to leap from the balcony because you wanted so desperately to be blamed for what happened to me."

I winced.

"You know what? Fine." My voice dropped, sharp as glass. "Call it what it is. I'm a coward. I didn't want to lose you. I didn't want to watch the rage swallow you. I didn't want to give you one more thing to carry. One more reason to give up. So I waited. I waited for a time you might bear it easier."

"And now?" Her eyes glittered. "Is it easier, now that I want to scream every time I look at you?"

I flinched. She saw it.

"Gods," she muttered, shaking her head. "I should've known. It was always too good to last. Even you—" Her voice caught. "Even you were just a lie I let myself believe."

"No," I said, stepping forward. "I'm sorry."

"Don't say that unless you mean it." Her voice cracked. "Don't say it unless you understand what you've done."

My head pounded. I pinched the bridge of my nose between a finger and thumb while the silence stretched.

Then, quietly, her words landed. "You were supposed to be my safe place."

I reached for her hands. She let me take them, but her fingers didn't close around mine. I bent to look her in the eye.

"I'm sorry I didn't know how to tell you," I said, softer now. "And then too much time had passed. And then I couldn't bear to see your face when you knew."

"You still should've told me."

"You're right. I should have."

Her hands trembled. "I don't know if I can trust you again."

"I'll earn it," I said. "Every day. For the rest of my life, if that's what it takes."

She looked up at me. Broken. Brilliant. Furious.

Her hands tightened. Just barely.

"You're a bastard," she said, tears streaking her cheeks.

"I know."

"I hate you."

I sighed. "I deserve that."

She groaned, frustrated. "I still love you."

I breathed again. "I love you, too."

Then her weight came into me all at once, like the fight had gone out of her. She pressed her cheek to my shoulder. Let her arms wrap around me and stay there.

"I can't forgive you," she whispered. "Not yet."

"You don't have to," I said.

We stayed like that. Fire cracking. Her tears falling on my shoulder.

Then, softly—

"You *were* going to jump. In Letia. When I pulled you back. Weren't you?"

I didn't answer. She lifted her head, cupped my face in both hands.

"Was it because of this?" Her voice trembled. "Because just a few hours before, I told you everything—what they did to me. That was it, wasn't it? You and Lucius fought over it, too?"

I couldn't meet her eyes. Not with the tears burning in mine. Not when she'd see everything there, because she could see through me. I looked down. Let out a breath that almost sounded like a laugh.

"I told you," I murmured. "I'm a coward."

"Oh, vedrānos." She kissed me, fierce and shaking. "It was killing you. And you still didn't tell me."

Another kiss, unsteady.

"I don't hate you," she said, mouth against mine.

Her lips on mine again.

"Gods help me, I don't."

Again. Just love, ragged and stubborn, breaking through the rubble.

"I love you. I'll always love you. But if you ever hurt me like this again—"

"I won't," I said, catching her face in my hands. "You're my light, Aleaia. Luce mea. The only thing between me and the dark."

Then I kissed her.

Slow. Full. Like it was the only way I knew how to speak.

She folded into me with a sound that cracked something open in my chest. Her breath faltered when I deepened the kiss—just once.

When I pulled back, she just let her forehead rest against mine. Breathing. Holding on.

"I'm still angry," she said, voice hoarse.

"I know."

Her arms slipped around me again. Tight. Steady. "You don't get to die. Especially not like that."

"I won't."

"Good," she said. And for the first time, she sounded tired. Not broken. Not furious. Just tired.

She stayed there, pressed to me like she needed to feel my heartbeat under her cheek.

And I held her. Quiet. Still.

As long as she let me.

# CHAPTER ONE HUNDRED TWO

## *Measured*

*"A gentleman makes no claim upon a lady's future until he is certain he can carry it."*
—On the Proper Bearing of a Gentleman

Rudamos 86, 1231
*Aleaia*

I woke to birdsong. Wind in the trees. Light pooling beneath the door in a slant of gold. The fire was little more than embers and ash, but the stones still held a trace of warmth.

Val was behind me, one arm draped over my waist, his breath steady against my neck.

The bed was too narrow for two. But it kept us close, and we needed that more than anything.

Then the memory came. The fight. The words we'd hurled like blades.

I stared at the wall. How awful we'd been to each other because of love and a secret.

I turned toward him and found him already awake.

Not already awake. *Still* awake.

"You didn't sleep," I said.

"No. Couldn't." He reached up and touched my cheek. Exhaled through his nose. "This place feels… wrong. Familiar, somehow. I can't explain why."

That wasn't like him. Val didn't say things like that—*feels wrong* or *can't explain why*. He didn't believe places held memory, or that ghosts lingered in stone.

And yet… he didn't try to justify it. Just brushed the back of his fingers along my jaw. Slow. Careful.

"Gave me time to think, though," he said.

I didn't like how that sounded.

"If you ever decide you need to walk away," he said, quiet as breath, "from all of it—from me—I won't stop you."

I stilled.

He meant it.

"I'd still fight for you," he added, fingers sliding into my hair. "Still carry your banner. You don't owe me anything."

I pushed up onto one elbow and looked down at him.

"I owe you everything," I said. "Every part of me that's still here. Every part that knows how to love. You make me furious, you absolute godsdamned idiot, but my heart is yours for as long as I live. And after, too."

He didn't speak, so I went on.

"I've lost everyone I've ever loved. I won't lose you. Not if I can help it. Not over something that happened when we were still children. Papa would be so disappointed if I let his death come between us."

He said nothing. Gaze steady. Still offering the exit. The clean break. No blame, no anger—just that same impossible mercy.

Maybe he wanted to be free of me.

"But if you want to go—" I said.

"No."

I waited, but nothing else came. No reasoning. No plea. Just that single word.

I leaned in and kissed him. Soft. Light.

We probably kissed too often. But sometimes, it was the only way to say what lived too deep for words.

His hand rose to the back of my neck, fingers steady as he pulled me in, deepening the kiss. When we parted, I pressed my palm to his cheek.

"No more hurting each other," I said. "We get hurt enough from other people."

He exhaled, steady and quiet. "Then we do better," he said. "Both of us."

It shouldn't have hurt to hear, but it did, because it was true.

We'd hurt each other. But gods help us—we'd keep choosing each other anyway.

Silence settled. Full, not empty.

Unlike my gut.

My stomach growled. Loud. Traitorous.

Val huffed a laugh, eyes still half-lidded with exhaustion. A smile creased his face, worn and real.

"We need food," I said. "And you need sleep."

"I'm fine," he said, shifting to get up.

"You were up all night. Stay." I pressed him gently back down.

He let me, even as he muttered, "I don't want to sleep in the strange tower without you."

"I'm not a talisman," I said mildly.

I slipped out of the blankets and stood, stretching before tugging on my trousers. The fabric was stiff, but dry. My boots waited near the door; I pulled them on, then crossed back to the bed.

He hadn't moved.

I drew the blanket higher over his chest, tucking it around him with care. He didn't open his eyes, but I caught the faint exhale when I sat down on the edge of the bed beside him.

I took his hand. His fingers folded around mine, loose and warm.

"I'll be back before you even notice I'm gone."

"You shouldn't go alone," he murmured, but there was no weight behind it.

I gave him a look. "I'm planning to rob a few birds, not wage war."

"Don't be long," he said.

"I won't."

I stood, buckled on my sword, and took a wicker basket from the shelf. The water bucket waited near the door. I stooped to grab it, fingers closing around the smooth, worn handle.

At the threshold, my hand lingered on the latch.

A memory flickered, faded around the edges.

*An old gray horse.*

*Chickens and goats.*

*Me, years ago, slipping outside into the early light of dawn with a basket and a bucket just like these to gather eggs and draw water.*

*No sword.*

*No armor.*

*No world beyond the village.*

*Just a girl and her morning chores.*

My heart panged with the ache of realizing I had lost her, too.

"Something wrong?" Val said from the bed behind me.

"No," I said quietly. "Just… remembering. I'll tell you later."

He made a low sound—somewhere between acknowledgment and sleep—as he turned onto his side.

I stepped out.

The forest had begun to stir. Birds called overhead, leaves rustled in the wind, and the underbrush was alive. I paused, letting the sounds fold around me like a second skin. The air was warm already and thick with the scent of moss and morning dew.

Then I stepped forward, and the door closed softly at my back.

I found and followed a narrow trail toward the shoreline, basket in one hand, bucket in the other.

After finding a place to relieve myself, I turned my attention to the gulls. I'd seen them the day before, circling above the surf, nesting between tide-slick rocks. Loose clumps of grass and scattered feathers marked the nests, tucked just beyond the sea's reach.

The beach shimmered, gold and silver in the morning light. Waves rolled in slow and heavy, leaving ribbons of foam behind them.

I crouched low and moved carefully, boots near-silent on the damp sand. The gulls shrieked overhead, uneasy but not bold enough to dive. I worked fast—one egg from each of four nests. No more.

*Leave enough behind. Always.* Papa's voice.

On the way back, I veered toward a patch of brush and shaded undergrowth. Wild onions pushed through the soil in tight little clumps. I knelt, loosening the bulbs. I found a few young garlic shoots too, followed by a handful of pale-capped mushrooms near a rotted log.

Grandma's voice surfaced, clipped and certain. *Those are safe. Look at the stem.*

The ache was sudden. Deep. I blinked against it, then swallowed hard and let the air clear my chest.

This wasn't the place for longing.

At the pool, I rinsed everything clean. Cold water rushed over my hands, peeling away soil and memory alike. The scent of crushed onion clung to my skin. I splashed my face, ran wet fingers through my hair, blinked droplets from my lashes. No soap, but it would do.

By the time I turned back for the tower, the sun had climbed higher, scattering gold across the forest floor.

My stomach growled again. Time to eat.

I quickened my pace.

Inside, the hush met me like a held breath. Val still slept, one arm draped across the bed, the blankets tangled around his legs. He looked peaceful.

I set the basket down near the hearth and moved to the cupboard. I found a pan that was battered, but serviceable. Wiped it clean. Set it over the fire.

While I waited for the metal to warm, I reached for the dagger tucked in my boot—the one Val had given me in Asena's cave—and felt the surge of joy in my heart that I hadn't lost it to the sea.

He'd pressed it into my hands while fending off Asena's children, his sword a blur between me and the monsters. I'd broken the locks with this blade. Forced it into rusted hinges until they split and gave. When the chains fell, it wasn't magic that had saved me.

It was this.

Him.

It seemed like a lifetime ago.

I turned the blade once in my hand, then bent to the basket.

Wiping the dagger clean, I set to work slicing onions, garlic, mushrooms. The edge still held—each stroke clean. Measured. I let the motion carry me, then scraped the mix into the pan.

The eggs followed, one by one. I was careful not to waste a drop. They sizzled on contact, the scent rising quick and earthy.

Behind me, the bed creaked.

"What is that smell?" Val's voice came rough with sleep. "I think I'm dreaming."

"Breakfast," I said, letting warmth slip into my voice. "As promised."

I found two wooden bowls in the cupboard and a mismatched pair of spoons—one with a splintered handle, the other dark with age, worn smooth from years of use.

"*Testes di Anvallus,*" he muttered. "Did you let me sleep all day?"

"It's still early enough for breakfast," I said, mild as ever, wrapping a cloth around the pan's handle and lifting it from the fire.

Steam curled from the edges, fragrant and golden. I set it in the center of the table and reached for the bowls.

He swung his legs over the edge of the bed.

"I'll be right back," he said, running a hand through his hair again as he stood.

I nodded and watched him go. The door shut softly behind him.

I readied the table. Served the food. Poured water. Set it all in place.

When he stepped back inside, he looked more awake. His eyes found mine at once.

He crossed the space between us in a few steady strides, then reached for my elbow. His touch was gentle but sure, turning me to face him.

His arms came around my waist in the kind of embrace that expected nothing but offered everything.

I hesitated. Just a breath.

Then I lifted my hands and let them settle on his shoulders before sliding around his neck.

"I didn't know you could cook," he said, something warm flickering beneath the words.

"You must have forgotten how long you left me in the cook tent," I said, voice light. A faint smile tugged at my mouth.

I tilted my head just enough to meet his gaze.

Didn't say anything more.

He leaned in and kissed me.

Soft at first. Sure in a way that stole the breath from my lungs. His hands stayed at my back, steady and warm, while mine slipped into his hair, still tousled from sleep.

The taste of him, the feel of his mouth on mine—it sank into me like sunlight.

When we parted, I didn't let go. Neither did he.

"I wish every day was like this." My arms tightened around him.

"So do I," he said, and pressed a kiss to my forehead.

"We should eat before it gets cold," I said, stepping back.

We sat together at the small table and shared the simple meal I'd thrown together.

"I should've grabbed more eggs," I said, popping a bite into my mouth. "I forgot how much you eat."

"How much I eat?" Val raised a brow. "You ate as much as I did."

"I earned mine," I said. "You just rolled out of bed and sat down like nobility."

He shrugged, slow and unbothered. "Well. I am. Or I used to be."

I looked at him. A smile tugged at my mouth. "You could be again."

At first, I meant it lightly. Then realized I didn't.

He didn't smile back. Just watched me. "I'd have to petition the queen."

I looked away.

"I think the queen would grant it," I said, quieter now.

I felt Val's eyes searching my face.

"It's unwise to ask favors before one has earned them," he said.

I reached across the table and set my hand over his. Looked at him.

"If the title asks for more than what you already are," I said, "it's not worth having."

He turned his hand beneath mine, thumb brushing slowly over my knuckles. "I think we're talking about different titles."

I tilted my head. A flicker of heat stirred in my chest. "Are we?"

That stopped him.

He didn't pull away, but he stilled. His thumb paused. His gaze flicked to mine, then dropped to the table, like the thought had gone farther than he meant it to.

"I meant—" He cleared his throat. "The noble kind. Status. Standing."

I arched a brow but said nothing.

He shifted in his seat.

"But," he added quickly, "not that the other… I mean, *that* isn't—off the table."

Gods, I had flustered him. I lifted my cup to hide the smile pulling at my mouth. It was endearing and unexpected and far too satisfying.

"She'd take you in any way you'd offer," I said softly. "But she knows better than to overestimate her own worth."

He didn't flinch this time. Just met my eyes and didn't look away. "I think she's worth more than any crown I've ever bowed to."

It hit harder than he probably meant it to.

And I wanted—gods, I wanted so badly—to close the space between us with something that would make it real.

His thumb began to move again, slow and thoughtful, and his eyes stayed on mine, but the silence stretched.

I searched his face. Waiting—for what, I wasn't sure.

He looked down. Just briefly. And when he looked back up, whatever had flickered there was gone.

"I'll clean up," he said, gently drawing his hand away.

That was a sidestep.

The familiar ache opened in my chest.

The kind that settled in when I wasn't enough.

Not woman enough.

Not whole enough to be wanted without hesitation.

Good enough to fuck. Not enough to wed.

Maybe it was the scars. The dirt he couldn't see but surely felt. The places I'd been touched. Used.

Maybe he saw what I tried not to—that I was still stained from it. That some things didn't wash off, no matter how clean the water.

I reached for my cup. Took a slow sip.

Just to keep my hands busy.

Just to stop them from shaking.

"We shouldn't stay here longer than we have to," I said.

Val stared at me for a long moment.

Had he noticed? He usually did. Maybe he thought he'd said enough, done enough. And maybe he had.

But the ache hadn't gone. Not really.

Because part of it wasn't his to fix.

I would have to see my own worth, too. Not just in the way he looked at me, but in who I was, even when no one was looking. And that was a battle I'd have to fight on my own.

"Back to the beach?" I asked.

He nodded once. "If a ship's coming back for us, that's where they'll land."

We dressed quickly, the weight of the unknown pressing in around the tower walls. Whatever peace we'd found that morning, it was real.

But peace didn't linger. Not for people like us.

I strapped on my sword, helped Val collect a few supplies into some blankets, and without another word, we stepped out into the forest.

Together.

# CHAPTER ONE HUNDRED THREE
## *Another Life*

*"In every life I live, I will search for you."*
—The Song of the Stars, Cycle VIII: The Cycle of Mortals

Rudamos 86, 1231
*Aleaia*

As we stepped out of the tower, I reached for his hand and laced my fingers through his.

Val glanced down.

"Just in case the path gets steep," I said, unconvincing even to me.

His mouth twitched in that faint, almost-smile I'd come to know.

"You may hold my hand anytime you like," he said. "No need to make up an excuse."

We walked on, fingers twined.

"It'll be embarrassing when we're all together again," I said, eyes on the trail. My grip tightened slightly.

"Why?"

"The way I lost my temper. Before I fell off the ship. Which is also embarrassing."

"It was deserved. The temper, not the fall. I'll be the embarrassed one," he said.

"I drank all of Erik's mead," I muttered.

"Did you like it?"

"I think so. I don't remember."

He glanced at me sideways. "That usually means you liked it."

"Ale never betrayed me like that," I said.

"Betrayed you?" he asked.

"I fell off the ship."

He huffed a laugh. "The mead didn't push you."

I smiled as I bumped him with my shoulder.

"Not nearly as bad as this." He looked off the side of the trail. "Lucius wasn't lying when he said he tried to tell me. He threatened to go to you himself, and I… told him I'd break his jaw if I caught him near you again."

I glanced over at him, one brow lifted. That wasn't like Val. Not with Lucius.

"It wasn't my finest moment," he added, voice rougher now.

Something tugged behind my ribs.

"You don't have to be ashamed with me," I said, squeezing his hand.

We walked in silence for a while. My eyes searched the canopy above. I hadn't seen the raven in a while, but this was the kind of place and time I'd expect to find it.

"What were you remembering?" he asked.

"What?"

"This morning. When you left. You stopped at the door. I asked if something was wrong."

"Oh. That." I shook my head, a small smile tugging at the corner of my mouth. "Just remembering the last normal morning I had on my grandparents' farm. It's stupid."

"No it isn't. Tell me about it." He watched me, steady and quiet.

"I'd had the dream," I said. "So I woke early. Dressed in the dark. Went down to feed the chickens, milk the goats. I thought about taking Bran out—our old gelding. He wasn't fast, but he was calm. I wanted to ride to the edge of the southern field, let him stretch his legs. I carried water back for my family. Kissed my grandmother. Went hunting with Papa."

I exhaled.

"Simple things," I said. "Easy. Gone with that damn bird."

Val was quiet for a moment, then asked, "Is that the life you would've chosen, if no one had asked anything more of you?"

I looked at the trail.

"No," I said. "I loved that place. My family. But it was never meant for me. Even before everything… I think I knew. I wanted something more."

"More," he repeated. "Or different?"

"Both," I said softly.

He nodded but didn't speak, so I went on.

"If I'd stayed, my life would've belonged to the land. I'd have helped with the harvests, the animals. Married someone Papa approved of. Probably not someone I chose. Hopefully of my own age, but more likely, much older. Had a child every year until I couldn't. Or died trying."

Val glanced at me, but he didn't interrupt.

"And then, I'd have been buried in the village grounds. A marked grave if we had money. If not… just a memory."

A few heartbeats passed before he spoke again.

"I would've gone there," he said. "To Rhaelaith. I would've found you."

Something inside me stilled. I looked up at him.

"I wouldn't have known why. Not then. Just that we were meant to pass through Rhaelaith. I'd have seen you in the field, or at the market, or walking barefoot through the morning mist." He smiled a little. "And I'd have known. One look. That would've been it."

Had he begun to believe in things like destiny? Fate?

"And then what?" I asked. I couldn't resist.

He turned to me, gaze steady. "I'd have asked your name. Even if I had no right. Even if you told me to leave, I wouldn't have stopped looking back."

I watched him for a long moment, the path forgotten beneath our feet.

"If you'd asked my name, I'd have given it. Freely." I let out a breath. "And if you'd offered me your hand… I'd have gone with you. Wherever you asked."

No need for grand declarations. Just that. A truth I felt in my bones as certain as the feel of his fingers in mine.

"And I wouldn't have looked back," I added, softer now.

He lifted our joined hands and pressed a kiss to my knuckles.

Then, quiet as breath, he said, "I would find you in any life. And I would choose you. Every time."

I didn't answer. I couldn't.

So I held his hand tighter. And we kept walking.

The path wound down through the trees until the forest thinned and the sea opened before us once more. The beach looked exactly as it had the day we arrived—wide, pale, and empty, the waves hissing against the shore in steady rhythm.

I looked toward the horizon. Just water and sky.

"How long should we wait for Lucius to send help?" I asked, easing down onto a weathered log where the forest gave way to sand. The bark had long since been worn smooth by wind and salt.

Val stayed standing, eyes on the sea. "I hoped he'd reach Nuala, raise support, and return quickly," he said. "Or at least slip past the Calesians. But with no sails in sight and the sun already high…" He sighed. "We should prepare for another night here."

He sat beside me without a word, bracing his arms on his knees. For a while, he watched the tide roll in. He passed me his waterskin. I took it and tipped it back. The water was warm, but it helped.

"I keep thinking about Rasmus and Davena." His posture hadn't shifted, but something in it had drawn tight.

I didn't press. Just said, "I'm sorry, Val."

"As am I." He drew a slow breath. "When I was a boy, Rasmus taught me how to fish. I must've tangled every line he gave me, scared off half the river, and he never once raised his voice. Just laughed, as if my mistakes were worth smiling at.".

I didn't speak. Just sat up a little straighter and slipped my hand into his, our fingers lacing together. His thumb brushed mine.

"And Davena… she ran that house," he said. "When I was small, I used to sneak into the kitchen to steal sweets, thinking I was clever. She always caught me. Never scolded, just handed me a spoon and said, 'If you're going to eat the sweets, you'll learn to make them too.' She taught me everything I know of kindness. What I know of my mother, Davena gave me."

His hand tightened in mine. "They didn't live long enough for us to set them free. And there's no one left who remembers my mother alive. I don't know why that bothers me, because I never knew her either."

He said it plainly, but I heard what he didn't say—the guilt folded between the words. I looked at him, at the stillness in his face, the way he stared out at the water like it might absolve him.

I knew that kind of grief. The way it settles in your bones and pretends it was meant to live there.

"I don't know how you did it," he said. "Losing Jurian. Your grandparents. I don't know how to carry this."

I squeezed his hand tighter. "Just like… other burdens. You don't carry it alone."

He didn't answer. But he didn't let go.

"Heartache isn't something you fix or control," I said. "It's a storm you sail through. Sometimes you think you're past it, then something—some sound, or scent, or memory—brings it crashing back like you never left the wreckage."

I let the silence rest between us, just for a moment.

"But the people we lose—they're not just pain. They're light, too. Memory is a compass. It won't stop the storm, but it gives you something to steer by." I turned to him. "You protected them, Val. You gave them peace, even if you couldn't change the name the world called them. They were safe in Letia, for all the years they lived there. They were loved. That's not nothing."

He looked at me. His expression didn't shift, but the emptiness behind his eyes had eased.

"I'm here," I said. "You helped me carry mine. Let me help carry yours."

His hand gave mine a small, firm squeeze. No words. Just that. And in the stillness, something settled inside me.

The peace we'd found here wouldn't last.

I could already feel the wind shifting, the world pulling at our heels again.

My birthright.

The war.

Vengeance.

They weren't chains.

They were weapons.

And I would wield them.

# CHAPTER ONE HUNDRED FOUR
## *Veiled*

*"What the gods give in dreams, they rarely explain."*
—from the journals of Queen Eavan, written for Aleaia

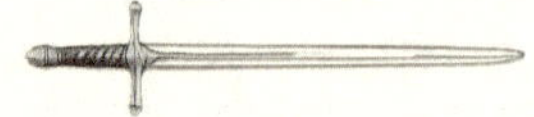

Rudamos 87, 1231
*Aleaia*

"Suppose we should start looking for our own way off the island." Val shook his head and stood.

"You don't think they're coming back?" I asked.

He glanced toward the mainland, gaze skimming the horizon. "Not that. Just… having a plan wouldn't hurt."

I knew what he wasn't saying—that Erik's ship might've been caught by the Calesians. It had been in poor shape. If it had gone down, or been intercepted—

I forced the thought away. I couldn't bear to imagine losing Mariana. Or Lucius. Or the children.

So I turned toward something useful. "We should leave a sign. In case they do come back."

Near the tree line, I found a few straight sticks and went to gather them. I broke one into three equal lengths, bound them into a triangle with a strip of vine, then lashed the shape to a sturdier branch, forming a crude arrow. Val drove it into the earth with a rock, pointing it toward the falls.

"Good enough. Hope it stays there," he said, brushing his palms clean. He slung our bundle of supplies over one shoulder.

I took the lead, guiding us back into the forest along a narrow game trail. We stopped at the falls to wash and refill the waterskin, then kept moving—south this time, down the path we hadn't yet dared to explore.

We pressed on for hours, winding through the trees.

Just after sundown, we found a village, hidden high in the mountains and long abandoned. The moon hung silver overhead. This place had been carved into the bones of the earth. Moss and lichen swallowed the stone houses, which had been built into the mountainside.

Val went first along the narrow footpath, pushing the heavy vines aside for me as we passed. I stepped close behind him, one hand lightly brushing his back to steady myself where the stone was hidden beneath the moss. Sometimes, he'd turn to offer me a hand in the slickest places.

I didn't need the help but I think it made him feel gallant, so I went along.

At the center of it all lay a wide clearing. A market once, maybe. A well sat in the middle, roof sagging, stones stained with age.

The terraced fields beyond had gone wild. Grasses rose shoulder-high, thorn-laced vines choking the old dry-stone walls. Whatever order once ruled this place had long since been overrun.

At the highest point of the village, a temple sat carved into the mountainside itself. I'd never seen one left untouched. The temples in Aeltyria had been stripped since before my birth—names scraped off lintels, reconsecrated in Anvallus's name.

This one still belonged to Aelan.

It stood dark and empty and in disrepair now, but whole. I felt drawn to it—drawn to this place that still honored my ancestor.

"Time spares nothing," Val said, eyes on the square. "Not even Aelan's house."

"Doesn't seem to," I said, gaze lingering on the temple.

He rubbed the back of his neck. "Where should we bed down?"

I nodded toward the nearest house. "There, if it's unoccupied."

The lock had long since rusted through, the wood hanging from one hinge like it couldn't be bothered to close. I stepped through first, senses sharp. No scurrying. No stink of rot. Just dust, and the hush of long abandonment.

Val followed. He dragged a battered table and two cracked chairs into place, wedging them against the door. It wouldn't hold much, but it would give us warning.

I spread our blankets on the floor. My knees ached just looking at it. There were beds upstairs, but the air up there reeked of straw gone to mold.

I'd slept in worse. So had Val. We'd manage.

When we settled between the blankets, he threw the thicker one over our shoulders and kept his voice low. "No fire. And stay dressed—just in case."

I tucked myself against his side, cheek to his shoulder. The stone still leached cold, but with his arm around me, I could almost pretend otherwise.

"I've noticed something about you," I murmured.

He kissed my forehead. "Should I be worried?"

"You state the obvious when you're nervous."

"Do I?" His hand slid slow down my back, fingers grazing just beneath the hem of my tunic. "Maybe."

I arched a brow against his collarbone. "Maybe? We've soldiered together long enough that I know you know I'm aware we shouldn't start a fire. And that we should sleep dressed. And you know what else?"

"I'm afraid to ask."

"You hate not being in control. And one more thing."

"Gods help me," he said, just at the edge of laughter.

*"You,"* I said, turning his face toward me with the tip of my finger, "*love* me."

"I do, amor mea." His hand stilled at the small of my back, holding me close. "So much more than I thought possible."

I let the silence settle between us, soft and full.

"Everything will be all right, you know," I said—partly for him, mostly for myself.

Val laid his hand across my brow. "No fever. Curious."

I blinked. "What?"

"You're unusually hopeful. I assumed illness."

I poked him in the ribs, right where I knew he was ticklish. He grunted, half-laughing, then caught my wrist and kissed the inside of it, then let it settle on his chest.

His voice came unguarded, softened by the dark. "I like it when you're warm like this."

"I'm always warm. You said so, before."

"You are. Like a coal in winter. But that's not the one I meant."

"Oh." I felt the pang of something painful deep in my belly, though I didn't know why. "You mean agreeable."

He shook his head. "No. I like you defiant, too. Most of the time."

A small smile tugged at my mouth. But something in me pulled back a fraction, quiet and wounded, as I realized what he meant.

I was a pain in the arse and he liked it when I wasn't. This wasn't the first time I'd been told I was too much. That I was better when I was less.

"I'm sorry I'm so difficult most of the time," I said softly. And I meant it.

His gaze held mine. "You're not difficult. You're alive. You fight because you care so much. That's not a flaw."

I looked at my fingers, playing at the neck of his tunic.

"Aleaia." He tipped my chin up. "I love you. You. Not just when you're one way or another. You."

I stared at him a long moment. Saw nothing but truth, and swallowed the tears that threatened. Again. Gods, my eyes were tired of crying.

I huffed a laugh. "You're lucky you have so many desirable qualities."

"Such as?"

"Well, I won't list them all. Your pride's already unbearable. But mostly your very large—"

He laughed as he silenced me with his lips on mine.

Then he tucked me close against his shoulder.

His hand found my hair and moved through it slowly, like he hadn't meant to but didn't want to stop. The steady rhythm of his heart anchored me.

This island had given us something we hadn't touched in a very long time, if ever: stillness.

No eyes. No judgment. No throne rooms or tribunals. No banners hanging behind us. No one asking for more than we had to give.

If we'd gone back to Aeldunon right away, we'd never have had these moments.

So maybe the fall—the drop—was worth it.

And as I fell asleep, I thought about how much I didn't want to let it go.

Not yet.

*I have to save him.*

The thought struck like a blade across my ribs—sharp as frost, old as bone. It echoed through me as I climbed, one hand clenched around the hilt of my sword, slick with blood. My knuckles had gone white. I couldn't feel my fingers.

The stairs spiraled upward, the stone wet with soot and ash. The air burned.

A door appeared ahead, half-open, bleeding light from the seam. My steps faltered.

No manacles.

I looked down. My wrists were bare.

I was free.

I stepped through.

Into war.

The chamber beyond was built of stone veined in gold. Pillars cracked and crumbled around me. Smoke choked the air.

And in the center of it all, he lay crumpled on the floor.

Val.

Pain bloomed behind my eyes—sudden, jagged, turning the world to pinpricks. Blood filled my mouth, thick and metallic. My vision blurred, but I kept moving. Step by step. Bone-sore. Wounded. Failing.

His blood spread beneath him, slick and dark. Too much. Far too much.

His limbs bent wrong, twisted like the gods had reached down and torn him apart by hand.

One arm lifted, shaking. Reaching for me.

Or warning me back.

Mist began to rise. Wet. Clinging. It curled around my ankles, my arms, up through my throat. It filled my mouth with silence.

I tried to fight it.

Tried to run.

But the floor stretched, lengthening with every step. The distance between us grew like a punishment.

Too slow.

Too late.

A blade flashed in the light—silver, clean, cruel.

It fell.

Then nothing.

Stillness.

Gone.

Pain cracked through my chest, splintering outward like frost through stone. I tried to scream, but the mist took it.

It swallowed him.

It swallowed me.

And the world fell with him—

into darkness.

I woke with a jolt, soaked in sweat, the blanket twisted tight around my legs.

"Val!"

My hand went for my sword. Half-blind, heart pounding, breath sharp in my throat. The stone floor was cold, unfamiliar, and for a breath I didn't know where I was.

His hand caught my wrist.

"I'm here," he said, calm but firm.

I blinked through the dark. He was already upright beside me, reaching, steady as ever. Whole.

Alive.

"Val," I whispered again, my voice breaking as I reached for him. *"Vedrānos, anarethos, carethos, am sceapin tó esin atrin!"*

He pulled me into his arms and held me there, one hand steady at the back of my neck. I felt his breath on my cheek. "Slow down, luce mea. You're going too fast for me. What happened?"

"I thought you were dead," I gasped.

"You're all right. So am I," he murmured. "It's just a dream."

But it wasn't. Not this time. My fingers clenched in his shirt. I could still see it. Him. The blood. The blade. His body convulsing under the strike. The stillness that followed.

"It was the same," I whispered. "The same, but worse."

His hand moved through my hair, meant to soothe. "You're safe. I'm here."

"I watched you die." I pressed my face into his shoulder. "I felt it. I could smell the blood."

"You've had this dream before," he said quietly. "We talked about this. You told me it started when you were little."

"I know." My voice cracked. "But it's different now. It's clearer. I saw the temple. I saw—"

I stopped. The words wouldn't come.

If I said it out loud, it would become real. And I couldn't bear that. Not yet.

But I knew.

Gods, I knew.

I'd come up from a stairwell. Blood on my hands. Wrists bare.

The manacles—

They were gone.

Something had happened in there.

Something that freed me.

And he was there.

Val.

Lying in the center of it all.

I saw the blade fall.

I saw the Vinculatore who struck him down.

I saw his body, broken and still.

And then I saw the one truth rooted so deep in me it hurt to breathe: I had to stop it.

I didn't know how.

But I would.

I had to.

Val's thumb brushed the edge of my jaw. "It's a dream," he said again, soft but sure. "That's all."

I nodded. Not because I believed him, but because I didn't want to argue. Not while his arms were still around me. Not while he was still warm.

I let him hold me. Let his breath calm mine.

But as the silence stretched between us, I lifted my head and met his eyes.

"Don't go anywhere without me," I said. "I mean it, Val. Not even for a moment. We stay together."

He didn't argue. Didn't try to soothe or smile. He just nodded.

"All right," he said. "Together."

And I clung to him like a promise, the image of his blood still vivid behind my eyes.

# CHAPTER ONE HUNDRED FIVE
*Legacy*

*"She did not ascend into godhood. She walked into the dark with open eyes
and paid the price the world demanded."*
—Caedmon of Aeltyria

Rudamos 87, 1231
*Aleaia*

Val had fallen asleep again long before I even closed my eyes. His breathing slowed beside me, steady and deep, but I stayed awake. Staring up at a ceiling lost in shadow, I tried to let the stillness soothe me. It didn't.

Because silence wasn't peace. It was tension, thin as thread, tugging at the edges of my thoughts.

The longer I lay there, the surer I became of two things.

First, that something in the temple could free me.

Second, that I had to keep Val close.

The dream—in every version—always ended the same. I arrived too late and found him nearly finished. But if I kept him with me, that would never happen.

I never went back to sleep. Dawn came eventually, bruising the horizon with faint color. Not long after, we packed and left the little house.

We took the path toward the temple, and with each step, something in me pulled tighter. Not fear. Not even dread. Just… readiness.

The stone steps had been worn smooth by passage. I felt their age beneath my boots, the way the mountain pressed back with every footfall.

At the summit, I stopped short, staring up at the temple doors. I felt Val's attention settle on me.

And then I felt something else watching us both.

I turned sharply.

There—tucked into the eaves above the doors, white against weathered stone—the raven perched, quiet and still.

"No," I said, already bending to scoop up a rock the size of my fist. "No. Absolutely not. Go on! Get out of here!"

I drew my arm back and hurled it.

The stone flew wide. The raven didn't so much as twitch.

I stooped again.

Val let out a slow breath.

"Aleaia, amor mea," he said carefully, "why are you yelling at the bird?"

"Because I am tired."

I threw the second rock, harder this time. Missed again.

"Tired of visions and birds and bad things happening to me."

He pinched the bridge of his nose. *"Deia mea…"*

The raven still hadn't moved.

I grabbed a third stone and flung it with everything I had left in me—anger, fear, refusal.

This time, the bird spread its wings.

White flashed against the sky, and then it was gone—lifting cleanly into the air and vanishing beyond the temple roof, as if it had never been there at all.

I dusted my hands off and turned back to Val.

"Finished?" he asked mildly. "Or shall we find some rabbits to torment next?"

He didn't understand. He couldn't.

"I'm finished," I said.

He studied my face for a moment, then nodded once. "You still want to go in?"

I didn't want to. But something was pulling me in. Just as the Fellglow Blade had done when we first found it.

"It's the only temple of Aelan I've ever seen," I said.

"So… yes," he said, moving toward the doors.

He braced his shoulder against it, and it gave with a low groan of wood against stone. Cold air spilled out, dry and stale, laced with dust and something older.

I stepped in first.

My eyes adjusted slowly. The dark inside wasn't just an absence of light—it was layered. Like the kind that lived beneath mountains, not behind doors.

Near the threshold, I found a brazier. I took the flint and steel from the pouch on my belt and struck until sparks caught, hissing in the dry air. It took a few muttered curses and a little coaxing, but flame bloomed at last.

The light spilled outward, pressing back the dark in flickers.

The atrium stretched wide, shadow-wrapped, carved straight from the bones of the mountain. Massive stone columns rose into the dark, their fluted shafts inlaid with gold that caught the firelight like veins of flame. Each was crowned with acanthus leaves, carved so finely they looked soft enough to stir with breath.

And along the walls, frescoes began to reveal themselves.

My lungs emptied all at once. This was the place.

*The place where he—*

Val approached with a torch and touched it to the brazier.

"Stay close to me," I said as I took his hand in mine.

The flame threw the fresco into harsh relief. The colors had endured. Not all, but enough. Time hadn't dimmed the intent behind the hands that carved them. This wasn't for decoration.

It was the memory of everything they'd tried to burn out of us.

At the center of the largest panel, a woman stood locked in battle with Drakaroth, the great crimson dragon. Her hair was black as pitch, and her deep indigo cloak coiled around her.

The dragon arched across the wall in a serpentine blaze, wings flared, scales gleaming in the brazier's firelight as if they moved.

The sorceress raised her hands, and from them poured a torrent of magic—light, fire, force—so alive on the stone I swore I could hear it. *Feel* it. She faced the beast as if she'd always known she would. As if it had been waiting for her.

Her eyes…

They were the color of pewter.

Just like mine.

It was Aelan.

And beside her was Caedmon. The first to bear the title First Sword. His armor shone silver struck with sun, sword lifted, light wreathing his blade.

The world around them was breaking—a battlefield carved from storm and fire. Jagged peaks tore across the horizon. Skies cleaved by lightning. The earth itself split by veins of flame and ash.

"Beautiful and terrifying," Val murmured.

I didn't answer. I kept walking, slow and careful, letting the torchlight sweep across the carved frescoes. The artist had known what they were doing. There was reverence in the detail.

"The artist even captured the constellations," I said, more to myself than to him.

Above the battle, five constellations shimmered in painted stone.

The Crimson Dragon arched over Drakaroth, a serpentine blaze with a blood-bright star at its center.

Over Aelan, the stars of the Broken Crown curved skyward, the cluster rendered in pale gold.

Caedmon knelt beneath the Eternal Knight, its stars forming the long line of a lowered blade.

And above them all, the Forged Heart blazed: two halves joined by one star so bright it had been etched in silver and inlaid with some kind of quartz.

Below it, the Fallen Star arced like a wound in the heavens, its tail trailing across the wall, ending in a radiant point.

Val stepped up beside me, brow furrowed as he studied the painted sky.

"Strange," he said. "You could never see all these in the sky at once. Not anywhere in the world."

"Indeed." My voice came out softer than I meant. I was staring at the Forged Heart, though I couldn't have said why. That constellation only appeared on Aelan's Day.

I didn't know the significance of it. Couldn't work it out.

I followed the curve of the dragon's tail, tracing it with my eyes. It coiled outward with theatrical flourish, its scales catching the light. But near the end, something caught. The pattern shifted—not in design, but in alignment. Subtle, but wrong.

"There's a seam here," I said, leading him toward the tail.

I pressed my hand to the stone, fingers moving over the surface, searching for a catch. One of the scales nudged slightly inward under my touch. I pressed harder.

It gave quickly, until pain lanced through my finger.

"Fuck." I yanked my hand back and stuck the finger in my mouth, tasting blood.

Val made a noise somewhere between amusement and exasperation. "A doorknob would've been too mundane, I suppose."

The wall groaned open in a rush of dust and grinding stone. A passage revealed itself—dark, narrow, stair-steeped.

Val stepped forward, peering inside. "The mage in the fresco bore a striking resemblance to you."

"It's a depiction of Aelan and Caedmon in the last battle," I said as we started down the stair.

"I know." He glanced over his shoulder. "I expected some resemblance, given the bloodline. But it was… uncanny."

I looked at him, measured. "Is that a bad thing?"

He shook his head. "No. Just… worth mention."

We descended together, the torch casting long, swaying shadows on the walls. The farther we went, the colder the air grew. I ran my hand along the stone, counting steps, trying not to think about how far down we were going.

"I've never heard of this place," I said. My voice echoed. Too loud.

"To my knowledge," he said, "this island doesn't even have a name. Every map I've seen marks it empty. But this village, this temple… they must be a thousand years old."

We reached the bottom.

The corridor opened wide, circular and cold, and I froze on the threshold.

Shelves carved from the mountain radiated outward like spokes on a wheel. They ran floor to ceiling, every surface packed with scrolls and tomes. Some were bound in leather so dry it looked ready to crack, others wrapped in waxed cloth, seals still intact. Dust lay thick over everything, but there was no decay. No rot.

This place hadn't been abandoned.

It had been preserved.

"It's like your mother's repository," Val said behind me, quiet, as if the room itself required reverence.

"Or maybe hers was modeled after this one."

He moved to light the wall sconces. One by one, flame flared to life, smoke curling up into the high air. The room shifted with it, the gloom peeling back to reveal more than just books. Worktables stood along the edges, cluttered with glass vials, delicate instruments, and sealed scrolls arranged in careful clusters.

I trailed my fingers along the edge of a shelf. The air was cool, dry, and laced with something. A thrum I couldn't name.

This was no mere archive.

It was a vault of what the world had tried to forget.

What my mother had sealed away.

What I'd unsealed.

Texts on elemental magic, divination, blood rituals, necromancy, alchemy—some in ancient Aeltyrian, others in scripts I didn't recognize at all. Entire disciplines outlawed by every crown that came after Aelan. And here they lay, untouched, hidden in the bowels of a nameless mountain.

I turned. Val stood motionless by a far shelf. His expression was open, full of wonder. The firelight gilded his face, soft and golden. Something about him in that moment—how reverent he looked—sent a strange warmth through me.

"Thank the gods my father never knew of this place," he breathed.

At the room's center stood a podium—white stone, polished smooth enough to reflect the torchlight. A single book rested atop it, open, its cover worn with age, the pages yellowed but legible.

I moved toward it slowly. As I reached the podium and read the title at the top of the exposed page, my breath caught.

"'The Defeat of Drakaroth'," I murmured.

The words drifted out like smoke.

# CHAPTER ONE HUNDRED SIX

*The Defeat of Drakaroth*

"Drakaroth—Anvallus's wrath made flesh—came down upon the world like a storm that never passed.

"Towns burned to their roots. Forests turned to ash. Men were not merely slain. Their souls were torn apart and devoured, leaving behind empty bodies that wandered and wept without sound. Where life had been, there was only bone and silence.

"Aelan and I swore we would end it.

"There was no one else. The gods did not answer her. Even the blood she carried could not summon them. Whatever hope remained fell to us alone.

"We followed the ruin.

"City after city. Hall after hall where the dead still sat upright at their tables, their mouths fixed in the last scream they had never finished. Rivers ran foul with rot. The skies bled soot. The wind carried no birds—only the low, endless moan of a dying world.

"I faltered more than once.

"She did not.

"Each mile hardened her resolve. Her power cut through the dark like a blade. When grief threatened to drag me under, she burned brighter.

"Beside her I found purpose. I was her sword. Her shield. Whatever strength I possessed was only the strength she gave it.

"On the final day we faced the beast.

"The sky itself seemed torn open above us. Fire fell like rain.

"Drakaroth rose from the ruin, vast beyond reason. His breath poisoned the air. The earth split beneath his weight. The sea boiled where his flame touched it.

"Aelan stepped forward to meet him.

"I have never seen anything like the light that came from her then. It poured from her as though the world itself had chosen her to carry its fury.

"We fought as one.

"And in the end, the dragon fell.

"His body struck the earth like the breaking of a mountain. Crimson scales burned black. The ground shook for miles.

"But victory was not the price the spell demanded.

"It demanded her.

"Aelan collapsed without warning. No cry. No farewell. One moment she stood beside me, and the next the strength had left her.

"I caught her before she touched the ground.

"Her eyes were already still.

"I called to her. I shouted until my voice failed. I prayed not to the gods who had abandoned us, but to her.

"She did not answer.

"Her body faded in my arms, returning to the world she had saved.

"The dragon was dead. The world endured.

"But the victory tasted like ash.

"I buried her.

"I raised our daughters.

"I watched kingdoms grow over the bones of what had been lost, and I kept silent while truth turned slowly into story.

"Now I am old, and silence has become a greater danger than memory.

"So I write this not for glory, and not for praise.

"I write it as a warning.

"Drakaroth must never rise again.

"And we must forget what it cost to bring him down.

"Aelan was no creature of prophecy. She was a woman who chose to fight when every sane voice would have turned away.

"She did not *ascend* into godhood. She walked into the dark with open eyes and paid the price the world demanded.

"Her bloodline remains. But blood alone does not carry her strength. Nor her will.

"The world has grown comfortable since those days. Histories softened into stories. Stories into myths. And the quiet that followed was mistaken for peace.

"I know better.

"I have heard the weeping of the soulless. I have walked through cities whose streets were paved with bone.

"There is no end to evil. Only the work of holding it back. Remember that.

"I have worn crowns. I have carried swords.

"None weighed as much as her absence.

"If these words endure, let them stand not as a song of triumph but as a lament.

"And a plea.

"Let no one wake the dragon.

"Let no one mistake survival for victory.

"And if the world forgets her, may these words burn the truth back into its memory."

# CHAPTER ONE HUNDRED SEVEN
## *Kindling*

*"It is poor form to court jealousy in a lady.*
*It is excellent form, however, to reassure her—firmly, and at length—*
*once she is already aflame."*
—On the Proper Bearing of a Gentleman

Rudamos 87, 1231
*Aleaia*

"The next pages speak of a ritual." I leaned closer, my fingertip grazing the faded script. "A guide. Something about preserving the heart. Or restoring it. It's ancient—the ink's almost gone. Gods. It's—"

Just at the edge of my sight, there was movement. A flicker.

Before I could react, steel hissed through the stillness.

Val had drawn the Fellglow Blade.

From my hip.

He had *disarmed* me.

The realization hit like a slap. Blood pounded hot in my ears. "The fuck do you think you're doing?"

He stepped in front of me, blade forward. "We don't know what's here. Stay behind me."

I followed him, every step pulling against something raw and furious in my chest.

"Give it back," I said, my voice tight with rage.

He didn't slow. "You asked me to be your First Sword," he said. "This is what that looks like."

Didn't that just twist the knife?

I bit down on the words burning in my mouth. Stepped into the aisle behind him instead, my eyes boring holes into his back.

Another hint of movement ahead—cloth vanishing behind one of the carved columns.

Val's voice rang out. "Who goes there? Show yourself!"

A figure emerged. Slight. Hooded. Obviously a woman.

She didn't speak—just drifted forward, slow and strange, before dropping to her knees on the stone. Slender hands pushed back her hood.

Red hair spilled out in waves. Bright as flame. Her face was pale and tear-streaked in the firelight. Her gray eyes were wide, lashes thick as crow feathers, lips parted like a prayer just waiting to be offered.

*Gods, look at her,* I thought. *All soft lines and ivory skin, like she's been carved to weep in someone's arms. A flick of wind would send her tumbling.*

I tensed. Tried not to shy away from the reflection she showed me.

I was filthy. Sword-callused. Tunic stained, boots still caked from the climb.

I looked like I'd fought my way here.

She looked like she'd been placed.

"Good sir," she purred, her voice lilting. "I beseech thee, bear me in thy company! Mine husband doth inflict upon me cruel blows, my kin offereth no succor, and I fear he shall bring about mine demise in the next onslaught—nay, of this I am certain. I care not whither thou leadest, only that I escape his wretched abode."

I stepped out from behind Val. She didn't even glance my way. Just fixed those dewy eyes on him like she'd already decided he was hers to fuck and forgive.

Val's voice was gentle. "I can hardly understand her, but she seems terrified. Poor thing."

"She speaks old Aeltyrian," I said, voice tight. "Says her husband beats her. Her family does nothing. She fears he'll kill her next time." I crossed my arms tight against my chest.

She still didn't look at me. Just rose and reached for his arm with dainty fingers.

"I might keep thy dwelling," she offered, soft and sweet. "Impart warmth to thy bed—"

"His bed is warm enough," I said, flat as a blade laid to skin.

She kept going, like I hadn't spoken. "—or tend thy wounds in times of strife."

I wanted to break her hand.

The thought startled me with its clarity.

"He has someone to tend his wounds," I snapped. "He's not looking to replace her."

"I possess modest skill in the kitchen," she said, so sweet it turned my stomach. "Though oft it drew mine husband's ire. I am willing to undertake any labor thou requirest, day or night."

Val peeled her fingers off his sleeve. Carefully. Like she was made of spun sugar.

"You don't need to offer anything like that," he said, voice softened at the edges. "You're safe now."

My jaw ticked.

"What is your name?" I asked. Polite in shape. Not in tone.

She folded her hands, eyes never leaving his face.

"I am Melicia. What is thy name?"

"I'm Aleaia. This is Valerius." Brisk. Efficient. "What are you doing in a place like this?"

"I am hiding from mine husband and mine father, and striving to thwart them both," she said, chin lifting a fraction. "Mine folk doth fear this place, so 'tis easy to remain concealed. I have dwelt here amid these strange symbols upon white leaves—though the leaves serve well for kindling. I shall ne'er run out."

My brow rose. "White leaves?"

"Yea, white leaves. Like these." She pulled two brittle pages from her robe, ripped clean from some ancient tome. "They are quite dry and ignite readily. Shall I show thee?"

*Oh, that got Val's attention.*

He snatched the pages from her hand. "No, gods, these are pages from an ancient manuscript!"

I looked between them.

Her, blinking prettily at him.

Him, frowning over the pages she'd almost burnt.

"They might be irreplaceable," he said.

Of course *they* were.

Melicia's lip trembled. "I—I thought them refuse, scattered and unwanted."

"They aren't," I cut in, before he could reassure her again. "They're valuable. Don't burn what you don't understand."

"I meant no slight," she crooned, her gaze flicking back to him.

He took a deep breath, ran a hand through his hair, then held out the pages toward me, without looking. An afterthought.

I took them without speaking. My fingers brushed his. He didn't notice. Didn't look. Not once.

And it stung. Not just anger. Not even jealousy, not really. Something deeper.

Dismissal.

Shunted aside. A handmaiden while my lord played gallant before a prettier guest.

I could play that game, too.

"Thank you," I said. Then, sharper, "*My lord.*"

Val stiffened. His head turned slow, as if unsure he'd heard me right. "What?"

I didn't answer. I was already walking down the aisle, pages clenched tight in my hand.

"Just… don't do it again," he said to her, softer, before following me. He lengthened his stride and stepped in front of me, blocking my path. His voice was tight. Controlled, but only just. "You want to tell me what that was supposed to mean?"

Where was that gentle tone now? The one he'd used just moments ago? Wasn't meant for me, evidently.

"I see you've a weakness for fair-faced girls with copper hair and trembling lips," I said coolly.

That stopped him cold. "Aleaia."

I still didn't look at him. "You haven't looked at me once since she showed up."

"That's not—" He dragged a hand down his face. "We can't just leave her here."

"No," I agreed, clipped. "She might burn the library down. Wouldn't want to lose anything *irreplaceable*."

He scoffed, astonished. "We can't send her back to get beaten to death."

"And she couldn't possibly manage on her own anywhere else on this entire island." I laughed, bitter and sharp. "Gods, what is wrong with you?"

He looked as if I'd struck him. "Me?"

"Forget it. Give my sword back." I held my hand out in expectation. "Please."

He looked down, like he'd only just realized it was still in his hand. "Oh. Right."

He flipped it, offered it hilt-first.

I took it, sheathed it, and stepped around him as if to leave.

"Aleaia," he said.

I turned. "What?"

"I don't know what I did," he said carefully, "but I know you. And I know when you're angry. So if you want to just tell me—"

"I already did," I snapped. "You just didn't like it."

His mouth opened, then closed again. He exhaled through his nose.

Footsteps came up behind him.

Melicia stood there, wringing her hands like she'd rehearsed the gesture in a looking glass. He turned.

"Sir, I cannot return home. I am despised there. Forsaken. Mine husband would surely kill me for mine flight, and mine father would permit it."

I looked at Val.

He was watching her. Brows knit. Eyes soft. Gods, he actually *believed* her.

"They'd kill you for leaving?" he asked, rubbing the back of his neck.

"Verily," she whispered, moving into his space like mist—sorrow-laced and scented with virtue. Beautiful. Broken. Begging to be saved.

That struck every chord in him at once, I was sure. Of course he looked stricken.

Melicia glanced between us, eyes landing on Val.

"May I come with thee?" she asked softly. "If thou art leaving this place, I would go also. I can be useful. I swear it."

"When the time comes," Val said, "you may leave here with us. First, though, we need to find a way off the island."

Something cold settled in my chest. That wasn't what we'd discussed. Not even close.

Melicia's face lit up. "Oh, thank thee! Thank thee most heartily! Might I be of assistance to thee? What doth bring thee to Velwyth?"

The rest blurred—her voice, his replies—drowned beneath the rush of blood in my ears.

I shifted, arms crossed so tightly they pressed into my ribs. I wanted to speak. To cut through it. To ask outright when I'd gone from his equal to his damned translator.

I didn't hear what either of them said next.

I barely heard his voice. "… fell overboard from a ship… washed ashore…"

Her giggling. "… dwelling upon the land? … far from the sea…"

I watched Val. Not that he noticed.

I clenched my fist until my fingers ached.

It wasn't just anger anymore. It was the ache of something I couldn't name.

Once, when I was a girl, the moon crossed the sun in the middle of the day. Grandma said not to look because the gods would take your sight for it, but this was how I'd always imagined it would be.

Something pale and wrong, between me and the sunlight.

A shadow cast over me.

I swallowed hard. Bit my tongue to school my expression away from the scowl forming. This wasn't like me. Why did I hate this girl so much?

She's only a girl, I told myself. Val isn't reciprocating.

"*I can set you free,*" whispered a voice.

Light. Feminine. Right beside my ear.

My skin prickled, a cold ripple chasing up my neck. I turned toward the sound.

Nothing.

"Did you hear that?" I said, eyes sweeping the shadows.

Val looked at me then, finally, brow knit. "Hear what?"

I ignored him, sweeping my gaze back to her. "Melicia. Have you found anything strange in this place? Anything unusual?"

Melicia shook her head, all wide-eyes and guileless innocence.

"Nay. Though…" She turned toward the back of the chamber, firelight threading through her hair. "There is a door. It refuseth mine every attempt. Mayhap thou wilt fare better. Come."

She swept away, cloak trailing behind her.

Val moved to follow.

I brushed past him, placing myself between the two of them. "Let's see where this door leads," I said.

The door was dark wood, carved in deep relief with runes I half recognized, faintly visible in the torchlight. They reminded me of the ones at the tower.

I leaned in, studying them. Their meanings tugged at memory's edge but refused to form.

Behind me, Val waited, Melicia at his side.

"How did you get into the library?" Val asked.

"Near the end of Drakaroth's tail, there is a… a needle," she said brightly. "I pressed it, and something did prick my finger. Then did the door open. There is no such mechanism here. I did examine. It is unlocked, but was merely too weighty for me to move alone."

Irritation spiked as I turned. "So you couldn't be bothered to push harder," I said slowly, "and you let me waste time looking for some way to open it?"

She tilted her head, eyes wide with polite confusion. "I thought it enchanted. Wouldst thou not have assumed the same?"

"No. I would not have thought the same were it unlocked."

*Fucking fool.*

My mouth tightened.

"Do you know what lies within?" Val asked.

"I believe it is the Soulforge," Melicia said, voice reverent. "I intend to make of myself a magus."

# CHAPTER ONE HUNDRED EIGHT
## *Say the Word*

*"Should a lady withdraw her consent, a gentleman does not question, coax, or delay.*
*He stops. Immediately. With dignity—and without complaint."*
—On the Proper Bearing of a Gentleman

Rudamos 87, 1231
*Aleaia*

"The what?" I stared at her. "You mean you're trying to gain magic?"

"Indeed, as all mine kin have done afore me," Melicia said, glancing between us with that doe-eyed innocence she wore like a veil. "Have I spoken something amiss?"

"How exactly does one do such a thing?" Val asked, brow tightening.

"Mine father knoweth more than I, as he is chieftain of our village," she replied, shaking her head. "I know a sacrifice must first be made—that was done last night, though it were meant for my sister—and then one must come hither and submit to the Soulforge. If one surviveth the ordeal, they become a magus."

I glanced at Val.

Everything I'd ever read about magic said mages were born, not made. But this island had already upended so many truths I'd trusted. First, there was the repository of lost knowledge, then a blood lock in my ancestor's sanctum that opened for someone else.

Maybe the library held answers, but we didn't have time.

"Shall we proceed, luce mea?" Val asked, voice soft but careful.

I nearly laughed in his face.

My gaze flicked to Melicia.

Melicia, who'd offered to warm his bed. Who'd clung to his arm like ivy. Who eyed him as though I were already dismissed.

And Val had let her. Said nothing. Handed me those pages like his godsdamned clerk.

Marcus's voice rose, unbidden—

*"He's had whores and noble girls both. But never one with dirt in her blood. Never one who smelled of sweat and smoke and the ruins of a dead country."*

Maybe that was it. Maybe that was the problem.

Just another truth I'd been wrong about.

I gave Val a tight nod.

He stepped toward the sealed door and shoved. It didn't budge. "Damn rusty—"

"On three?" I said.

I was useful, at least.

"On three," he said.

I counted. "One… two… three."

We slammed into it together. The frame groaned. The bottom scraped against the stone.

A second blow cracked it open a few more inches. Val wedged himself into the gap—back braced against the frame, hands on the door, arms flexing as he straightened them to force it wider.

Just enough space for Melicia to slip through before I could stop her.

"Thank thee, my lord," she said, breathlessly.

Her eyes dragged over him like she meant to unwrap him.

That was it.

I'd tried to let him address it. Tried to keep my composure.

I was out of patience.

I stepped through after her, let the chamber settle around me, then cut her off. Hard. I stood over her. Looked down my nose.

"He's not your lord," I said, voice sharp as flint.

Melicia blinked. "I—I meant no offense—"

I stepped closer. Close enough that she had to tilt her head back to meet my eyes.

"You mistake me," I said softly. "I'm not offended."

My hand drifted to the hilt at my hip. Not drawing. Just resting there.

"I am warning you to stop eyeing him like you mean to ride him straight into your godsdamned ritual."

Whatever color she had left drained from her face. She dipped her head, cloak swishing as she fled into the dark.

*Good riddance.*

Val sighed. "Aleaia—"

"Don't."

"Aleaia, listen—"

"Oh, I did listen. Listened as you let her flirt with you. Listened as she offered to warm your bed. While she draped herself all over you. Touched you. As you stood there and let it happen. Not once did I hear you say you were mine."

"I didn't take her seriously."

"No. You didn't take *me* seriously," I snapped. "Not when she spoke to you like I wasn't there. Or when you handed me those pages like a servant."

He shook his head, his face taut with restraint.

"You made me look small, Val. You."

"I didn't mean to hurt you."

"You did, though," I spat. "Again."

The silence that followed wasn't empty. It was weighted with heat and pride and possession.

His voice was strained, bruised. "That's… not fair, Aleaia."

It wasn't. But I wasn't about to admit that. Not with my temper up and my heart aching.

I stepped in close. Gripped his tunic in my fist. "You're mine."

Val met my eyes, unblinking. "Yes, I am yours. And you are mine."

His calm certainty usually steadied me, but just then, I found it infuriating.

I shoved him against the wall and kissed him—hard, full of fury and want and ache.

Val groaned into my mouth. His hands found my waist, then my hair, gripping like it was the only thing keeping him tethered.

I bit his lip as I pulled away, breath ragged. "No one else gets to look at you like that. Touch you like that. Not while I'm breathing."

"Oh, luce mea." His voice was frayed with heat. "I didn't know how much I'd love seeing you like this. Jealous. Fierce. Claiming me like anyone else stood a chance."

"I'm not jealous," I lied.

His lips—smiling, wicked—brushed mine again. "You are. Like anyone even compares to you. To what you do to me."

He was insufferable now.

I pressed into him, mouth at his ear. "I want you to fuck me. Now."

His smile sharpened. His hand curled tighter in my hair. "Say that again. I might not give you time to regret it."

My fingers traced the laces of his trousers as I leaned in and whispered, "Promises, promises."

His breath left him all at once—I felt it—and his restraint stretched tight as a drawn bowstring.

I had control. And I liked it.

And I knew exactly what I'd do with it.

"Actually, I think I'll make you wait," I said. Then I stepped back—slow, smug—and turned to walk away. Hips swaying, just enough to make damn sure he was watching. "And don't touch my sword again."

The curse behind me struck like flint to steel. "Fuck."

Then—

One hand caught my wrist, held it against the stone above my shoulder. The other slammed into the wall beside my head as he spun me to face him. His body pinned mine, solid, searing, everywhere at once. His thigh pressed between mine, holding me open for him.

I could've broken free if I wanted.

I didn't want to.

His breath came fast. He dipped, his mouth brushing the side of my throat. "You want to be claimed, is that it? Want me to fuck you right here—your thighs around me, your voice breaking from how much you need it?"

My fingers gripped his shoulder. Gods help me, I wanted that, even when I was furious with him.

"Because I want that too." He eased back just enough to see me. Let his hand slide from my wrist to lace his fingers with mine. "But not like this."

I met his eyes for a moment, then looked off somewhere behind him.

His voice dropped. Still thick with heat—but softer now. "Not like this, amor mea. Not when we haven't mended whatever's wrong."

I couldn't look at him. The breath caught behind my ribs.

"Look at me." His hand came to my jaw. Gripped. Tilted.

The words spilled—raw—before I could stop them. "I know… I don't have the right—"

He tensed, brow furrowing. "You have every right—"

I shook my head. That wasn't the point.

"Even if I did, I know I don't need to be jealous. But I was anyway." I swallowed hard. Took a breath. "I saw her touching you, and all I could think was—of course. Of course she would try. She's soft. And gentle. And sweet. Everything I'm not. She'd take one look at me and—"

My throat tightened. I couldn't even finish that thought.

"And worse yet, I've been sleeping beside you every night and I only ever asked to be with you once. In Letia." My voice dropped. "But after that… I didn't want to ask again. I didn't want to do the asking every time. I was hoping you'd ask me next."

For a moment, he looked like a man who'd been struck, not with anger, but with the weight of what he hadn't known.

I knew I wasn't being fair. We'd only had four days between that first time and the razing. But when we were together before Avitum, we never went that long between and I didn't know what it meant.

"I'm jealous because she touched you like you were hers. And all I could think was—what if you wanted *that*? What if…" The tears spilled, hot and sudden. Gods, I hated them. "What if you wanted someone like that? Someone I could never be? And what if you didn't ask… because I'm not?"

I let my head fall back against the wall. Breathed deep—ragged, wet.

"You think you're not soft?" His thumb grazed my cheek, wiping a tear. "Under my hands, you're softer than anything I've ever touched. Not sweet? Gods, amor mea. You forgave the unforgivable in me. That's sweetness."

My grip on his hand tightened.

"And gentle? The way you pull me back when I'm fraying, your touch when I need it most—that's gentle."

Then he kissed me, deep and aching, like he didn't know how to give gratitude in any language but this.

When he pulled back, he rested his forehead against mine.

"I've only ever thought of myself as strong," I said. "Strong enough to fight. Sharp enough to survive. Everything else just felt like pretending."

"Who says you can't be all of it?" His voice was rough velvet, threaded with heat. "Strong and soft. Sharp and sweet. Who says you have to choose?"

He leaned in, breath hot against my ear.

"You are all of those things. And you have no idea what that does to me." His mouth touched the side of my neck. "That you're strong enough to take me as I am, sweet enough to love me for it."

His hand slid to the small of my back, dragging me flush against him. The hard line of him pressed against me and I swallowed a sound I didn't mean to make. "That you fight for me like a war goddess and still melt when I kiss you. Like your whole body trusts I'd never break you."

His fingers threaded into my hair, gripping just the way I liked, tipping my head back until I met his gaze.

"I can't believe you thought I wanted someone else. That I wanted anyone but you." He took a ragged breath. "I've only ever wanted you."

I shook my head. "You had so many—"

"And I only ever wanted you. From the day we met, amor mea." His lips brushed mine. "If you don't believe me, give me the word. Say it, and I won't stop. I'll take you right here, right now, and leave no part of you untouched."

I looked up into his eyes and found the truth of it. And his gaze held more than hunger. It held grief. Quiet and raw enough to bleed.

He kissed me like he meant to brand me, like the taste might be the only thing keeping him tethered to the world. One hand stayed tangled in my hair. The other still held my hand to the wall, our fingers laced tight.

"You don't know how far gone I am, do you? Let me tell you," he said thickly. "Almost every night for a season, I came in silence beside you, praying you wouldn't wake. I'd lay there, when I was spent, shaking in the dark. Night after night, when I thought wanting you might split me open. It never helped. It only made it worse."

His mouth brushed mine, slow this time. When he drew back, his lashes were wet.

"Because it wasn't you. Because I didn't even try. Because I'd rather shame myself in the dark than touch you when you weren't ready." He took a deep, shuddering breath. "I thought I was giving you the choice. But the truth is that I was too afraid to even ask."

I reached for his face, for the ache breaking behind his eyes. But he turned slightly. Shook his head once.

"No," he said, voice tight. "Don't comfort me. Not yet."

His hand slipped from my hair and found the one I still had free. Guided it between us. Pressed my palm to the thick heat straining behind his trousers. Held it there. Ground against it.

"You need to feel this. You need to know you've never had cause to be jealous. Not of her. Not of anyone." He touched my cheek, thumb stroking once. "Say the word. I'll drop to my knees right now. Bury my mouth between your legs and stay there until you're writhing. Then I'll take my time. Slow. Deep. Mark you. With lips. With teeth. With everything I've got."

I kissed him hard. Messy. Desperate. My mouth moved against his like I could pour every unspoken word into him. When I pulled back, I didn't hide. I let him see all of it.

"I want to fall apart for you," I said, voice ragged. "With your mouth on my skin and your voice in my ear, guiding me."

His hand slipped beneath my tunic, touched the curve of my ribs, then higher, cupping my breast with a hunger that made me ache. Like he'd starved for the feel of me. Like he'd dreamt it.

His hand slid behind my thigh, pulling me tighter against him. My body rose to meet him before I could stop it. I hooked my leg around him, grinding, needing the pressure—needing him.

I was soaked. Undone. Already his. Always his.

"Val," I breathed. "I want days. I want to be taken. I want to be ruined. I want to erase every stolen moment with pleasure until all that's left is us."

He made a sound, low and reverent, and kissed me as though I were breath and salvation.

"I want to give you everything," I said, quieter now. "Not just my body. Not just once. Everything. You never have to hide from me, vedrānos. Not the wanting. Not the ache. Not the dark."

I wanted to strip him bare and crawl into his arms and never leave.

But not here. Not like this.

"But you're right about one thing," I whispered. "We can't do this here. Not like this. Not while we're dirty and tired and half-starved. I want time. A locked door. Your mouth on me. Hours."

His forehead dropped to mine.

"Then we'll wait," he said, hoarse. "But when we don't have to—gods, Aleaia, the stars themselves will burn for what I do with you."

"Then let them watch." I clung to him. "Please don't make me ask every time. I want all of it. All of you. The way you want me."

"And don't you dare think I want anyone but you," he said with a soft laugh.

When he let go of my hand, I wrapped my arms around him. Held him close. "I'm sorry. For what I said. About you hurting me again."

His arms closed around me without hesitation, pulling me in. "It was true, though. I'm sorry I hurt you. Sorry I didn't stand for us."

"I know you didn't mean to," I said. "I was already wounded. I just didn't know where else to aim it."

After a moment, I stepped back. Let my hands smooth the front of his tunic where I'd wrinkled it. Tugged the edges straight. He brushed his fingers through my hair, taming what he could.

He drew a long, slow breath and said, "Now. Back to… whatever we were doing before."

I laughed softly and turned to walk away before either of us cracked again. Melicia hadn't gone far. Not with her ritual unfinished.

His palm landed, hard, on my arse.

I gasped and looked over my shoulder, found him entirely unrepentant.

He looked composed, but his eyes had gone molten.

Like he was already planning my undoing.

"For later," he said.

My smile was slow. Shameless.

I kept walking.

Heat still clung to my skin. My lips were swollen. My thighs ached. And a low, pulsing throb had settled deep between my legs, echoing with every step.

My heart, though, was lighter even if it was full.

I didn't envy the girl. Not anymore. But I pitied her.

Just a little.

# CHAPTER ONE HUNDRED NINE
## *The Cost of Power*

*"There is no safe method to unbind a soul.*
*Only calculated risks—and the will to pay what they cost."*
—The Writings of Aelan

Rudamos 87, 1231
*Aleaia*

By the time we caught up to Melicia farther down the corridor, my blood had cooled just enough to let me think again.

She flinched when she saw me. She'd recovered quickly—I'd give her that—but not well.

Her gaze slid past me, clinging to Val like he might shield her. She reached for his arm. "Ah, there be ye at last, my lord."

Val shifted away before she could make contact.

Her brow furrowed. She tilted her head.

"Art ye wed?" she asked sweetly. "To one another, I mean."

His answer landed low in my chest. "Not yet."

And for the first time in a long while, I believed he wanted that. Us.

I said nothing. Just surged ahead, the echo of his footsteps trailing after mine. I forced myself to focus.

I didn't know what lay within this place. And I didn't like it—the whispers from nowhere, things that could make a person into a mage, strange birds that were often harbingers of the worst things that had ever happened to me.

And the dream. The one I'd always had. The more strange things happened here, the surer I became that this was the place it happened, too.

I had to keep Val near me.

The end of the hall opened into another circular chamber.

And there it was, looming in the center of the room. I'd have thought it an instrument of torment if I didn't know better.

Carved from gnarled ebony, the frame looked half-grown, half-formed, like something ripped from a cursed tree and crafted by desperate hands. Its base clawed at the stone floor with etched ancient sigils. Two tall pillars of some sort of crystal rose like gallows to either side, framing a flat obsidian slab stretched between them.

Near what I assumed to be the head of the contraption, a thick iron vice jutted up like a jaw, meant to lock someone's skull in place. To keep them from thrashing, most likely. At the foot stood a smaller pedestal, also obsidian, with a single, fist-sized bowl carved into its surface.

This was what she'd called the Soulforge. It could be nothing else.

"What is this thing?" Val asked, glancing first at me, then at Melicia as he gestured toward it. "Is this it?"

"This is the Soulforge," she said softly, placing her hand on the pedestal. "But it seemeth to lack the source of its power." Her fingers traced the rim of the crater. "Here are symbols, nonsensical to mine eye. Canst thou discern what might be placed here?"

I stepped forward and blew the dust away to read the words carved there.

"Where ancients' secret softly lies,
Return Aelan's Heart, let magic rise.
Within this cradle, secrets bide,
Unleash the power long denied."

I looked at Melicia.

She raised both hands. "Look not upon me. I know not what it signifieth."

"Hmm." I circled the forge slowly, scrutinizing each angle.

The Heart of Aelan. It couldn't mean her actual heart—Aelan's remains had never been found. They were dust on the wind, if the account we'd read was actually Caedmon's.

So what relic did it mean?

And if Melicia's people worshipped Drakaroth, what were they doing coming to the Temple of Aelan to *gain magic*, as she claimed?

Every question branched to another. I wondered why they weren't born with magic, as my people were. And if they'd been affected when my mother locked the magic away. How had she—

"That's probably it, then. Aleaia, come here," Val said, interrupting the endless string of questions. Thank the gods.

I returned to the pedestal.

He turned to Melicia, voice even but firm. "Tell her what you told me."

"Firstly," she began, wringing her hands as she spoke, "thou must understand that mine folk do not revere Aelan. As Drakaroth's people, they bear deep animosity toward her and her line. I do not share their sentiment—and that is but one of many reasons I departed from them."

She glanced at me, bracing, like I might strike her down for daring to breathe Aelan's name. I wouldn't but I'd be lying if I said I didn't like it, just a little.

"I know not of any relic called the Heart of Aelan," she continued, "but my father possesseth one called the Eye of Drakaroth. I have ne'er seen it, but I am familiar with the chest in which it is kept."

"And you want it?" I asked, voice cool.

"Aye. I believe the relic my father keepeth is the one needed to use the Soulforge," she said. "I must acquire it if I am to become a magus."

I was drawn to the Soulforge, and I had no idea why.

"Retrieve it, then. We'll remain here," Val said.

I almost laughed aloud, bit my cheek so I wouldn't.

"Certainly, I cannot enter the village," Melicia replied, as if the fact should have been obvious. "I would be slain on sight."

Val exhaled. "Then why didn't you take it before you left?"

"I fled swiftly. There was no time."

*It is the Heart. Use it. Free yourself.*

Then a quick flash of my hands placing a golden orb on the pedestal.

Another, my wrists suddenly bare.

The thoughts crawled cold and certain across the inside of my skull.

"Very well." I cut the conversation short. "Val and I will retrieve it."

He gave me a look, brow arched.

"Thou didst agree to aid in its retrieval with notable swiftness," Melicia said, eyes narrowing. "Why is that?"

"What else do we have to do while we await rescue?" I asked flatly. "Now, tell us about the village. Where is the artifact kept?"

She hesitated, as if still wondering about my sincerity. That was probably the first intelligent thing I had seen her do. She clasped her hands together.

"It will be within his residence. In his chamber. Thou shalt know it by sight. It is the longhouse, the chief dwelling at the village's heart." She took a breath. "The best time to procure it will be just after the evening repast, when mine father attendeth his council meeting in another wing. There may be a guard. They are steadfast in protecting the relic."

"How's the perimeter guarded?" Val asked.

"The what?" She asked.

"The area around the village," he said. "Are there walls, or a fence? If there are guards, how many? When do they change?"

"The walls are watched well, at all hours. The guards do relieve one another at morning and evening meals."

I folded my arms. "So how did you sneak out?"

Leaving without permission was a death sentence. If she'd made it out alive, she knew the weak points well enough to stake her life on them.

"The western wall is sorely in need of repair," she said. "There is a breach near its center. Folk oft stack barrels and crates before it to keep beasts at bay. I have used it frequently, when it pleaseth me." As she spoke, she doffed her rough spun cloak and held it out. "My lord is too tall to pass for one of our men. It is likely thou must enter alone. Take this. It is plain and shall not draw notice."

She handed the cloak to me.

Val gave a single nod. "And where might we acquire weapons? I don't plan to go unarmed."

Melicia shrugged. "I know not. Perchance the old smithy in Velwyth. There may yet be something fitting."

I fastened the cloak at my throat and met Val's gaze. He gave a slight nod.

"Right, then. We'll be on our way." I turned toward the corridor, then—without looking back—added, "No burning books while we're gone."

"Books?" Melicia blinked.

"The white leaves," I said. "They're sacred. Don't burn them."

Gods. Like I was warning a child not to lick a godsdamned knife.

"And if we're not back by dawn," I added, "assume we've failed and met our end."

"Very well. Safe travels, and with the Creator's blessing, mayst thou be successful," she said, bowing her head.

Our footsteps filled the silence as we left the chamber and made our way out of the temple. Once we were outside, with the door shut behind us and the mountain wind curling through the trees, Val didn't wait.

"You might have talked to me before committing us to this, Aleaia."

"Oh, really?" I stopped on the steps and turned. He halted just below me, eye to eye now, close enough that I felt the heat of him. "As you spoke with me before offering her asylum?"

Something in his face went still.

"Are there any circumstances under which you would've refused to come with me?" I asked.

"No," he said. Not with heat, just clipped, like he'd only just realized I'd done to him what he'd done to me. "That's beside the point."

On impulse—maybe a little smugly—I leaned forward and kissed his cheek. "Is it?"

"Don't try to distract me, woman." He pressed his lips together, clearly resisting a smile. "What are you thinking?"

"Come," I said. "Let's look for this smithy while we talk."

We descended the steps and wound through the village—dark, unnervingly still. The sun hung behind thick clouds, casting the whole place in shadow.

I was careful with my words.

"I have an idea," I said slowly. He was not going to like this at all.

"Go on."

I took a deep breath. "I think the contraption might free me from these bonds." I lifted my wrists. "The device is meant to increase magical conduction. If the manacles suppress it—like a dam holding back water—then maybe, if I place myself in it, the surge could... break them."

He stopped walking.

So did I.

His voice was hard. "No."

I blinked. "What?"

"You think it'll surge enough that it'll break the manacles. I think it might break *you*." His eyes were sharp. "You don't remember what happened after the Pass. I do. You hit the ground like your body just gave up. No warning. Just... gone."

His voice broke on the last words. He looked away. Swallowed hard.

"You were almost dead when I carried you into that healer's hut. Burning up. Your whole body shook so hard I thought your bones would break."

I opened my mouth, but he wasn't finished.

"So no. I don't want to hear ideas that risk your life. I don't want to hear 'maybe this time will be different.' I want to hear that you'll stay the fuck away from that thing."

"Val—"

"Don't ask me to stand there and watch it happen again," he said, voice tight. "Don't ask me to lose you again just because you're tired of waiting. There are no healers here. No help. Just me. And you. And I can't—"

He broke off. Shook his head. He blew out a slow breath. One hand dropped to his belt, gripping it like a tether.

He was afraid. And I didn't blame him for it.

The silence that followed pressed hard between us.

I swallowed. "I have to, Val. I can't live like this—shackled, half myself."

"You didn't need magic before," he snapped.

"I hate this feeling. You've never had to live with something inside you that's yours, but untouchable."

"Aleaia, please. Don't." His voice dropped—quieter now, but no less fierce. "I won't pretend this is safe just because you've convinced yourself it's necessary. I can't."

I stepped closer.

"What if that's the reason we're here?" I asked. "What if everything we've done—everything we've survived—led us here? To free me from this?"

"It would've been better if the gods had stopped us before Avitum," he said bitterly.

"Don't you think they tried?" I asked. "Look at everything we faced just getting there. Look how many times we should've failed."

He didn't answer.

I studied his face—tension braced through every line, grief and fear flickering behind his eyes. "I'm sorry I scared you, vedrānos. I never meant to."

He said nothing, but he didn't look away. I took his hand from his belt, held it gently between mine.

"I still have the medicine the healer gave me," I said. "I'll take it before I begin."

His brow furrowed. "I thought it was in your pack. When you fell from the ship—"

"I don't keep it in my pack." I gestured to the pouch at my hip. "It's here. Always. Right next to my sword."

He stared at the pouch for a long moment before glancing at me, then looking down at our hands. The breath he let out was long and tight—relief slipping through like a fracture in glass.

"Good," he said quietly. "That's good."

Then, finally, he nodded. Short. Grim.

"If anything goes wrong," he said, "I'll tear you off that slab. Do you understand me?"

"Yes," I said softly.

He exhaled hard. "Then let's go get your damn relic."

I didn't know what to say to that. So I stayed quiet.

I just kept hold of his hand in mine as we turned to walk through the lanes of the village. He curled his fingers around mine and held on tight.

"I wonder who used to live here," Val said eventually.

"People who valued knowledge, I think. Scholars, maybe."

He pointed toward a structure with a soot-blackened chimney rising taller than the rest. "That might be the smithy."

We angled toward it, boots crunching over gravel and brittle weeds.

After a moment, I asked, "You took the book burning personally. With Melicia."

He didn't answer right away.

"I don't think she knew what she was doing," I added. "But I could tell it hit you."

His gaze stayed ahead. Focused. Unreadable.

"I did," he said at last.

I studied his profile. The tension in his jaw. The way his hand tightened, just slightly, around mine.

A long pause stretched between us before he spoke again.

"When I was young, my mother's books were some of the only things I had left of her. They were beautiful. Illicit, according to the law. Dangerous, according to my uncle. The Vinculatores came one morning and took them all."

I stayed quiet. Let him give me part of the old burdens he carried.

"I remember the sound more than the fire—pages crackling, the ink melting. I didn't understand half of what they said. I just knew they were hers."

My breath caught. "Val..."

"She was already dead. Had been all my life. I never knew her. And they burned what little of her remained."

I squeezed his hand. That's why he collected forbidden books. Why the library mattered so much to him. He had been trying to protect things that never should have survived.

And Melicia had walked straight through one of the things he carried like a wound.

Still holding his hand, I leaned into him until our shoulders touched.

*One day,* I thought, *I'll build you a library of your own. A real one. With stone walls and shelves of sacred contraband. And a lock only you can open. You'll never have to burn what you love again.*

# CHAPTER ONE HUNDRED TEN
## *The Asking*

*"A man may fight for love, but he must never ask for it unless he can offer land, legacy, and lawful name. Anything less is dishonor."*
—Gavius Triarius, lecture to fosterlings of the noble class

Rudamos 87, 1231
*Aleaia*

The door hung crooked on its hinges, swaying open with a groan. Val ducked beneath the sagging frame, stepping through first. He stopped just inside, eyes sweeping the room with that quiet, lethal caution I'd come to know too well. Then he reached back with a hand, inviting me forward to take it.

I did, and immediately regretted how much I'd let myself hope.

The place was little more than a crypt. Dust hung in the still air, caught in pale shafts of sunlight slanting through gaps in the thatch. Everything was buried beneath centuries of grime, soot, and broken tools. Even the anvil was cracked.

There wasn't much to pick through. Half-finished blades. A galvarium ingot beside the anvil, its edges still sharp despite the years. Ore fragments glinting faintly beneath the dust. It had been real once. A place where beautiful things were made.

Now it was just ruin.

I let go of Val's hand to move through the forge. I wanted to find something. Anything. I had the Fellglow Blade. Val had nothing. This mission could kill him if he went into it unarmed.

Every weapon I picked up was rusted or warped.

"I think I let myself expect too much from this place." The disappointment slipped through before I could stop it.

Val was still rummaging, gods bless him. "I'm just waiting to stick my finger in the wrong place and get pricked."

He dropped a half-forged blade back into its barrel with a clatter.

"I know somewhere you can stick it that won't hurt," I said dryly.

He laughed. "Luce mea!"

I turned away, smiling.

That's when I saw it.

Near the far wall, half-hidden in the shadows, a circular pedestal rose from the stone floor. Waist-high and dark as slate, its surface was blanketed in dust. I crossed to it and wiped it clean with my sleeve.

At its center was a raised emblem—starbursts connected by thinner lines, forming the shape of a heart.

Recognition struck.

"This symbol…" I leaned closer. "We've seen it before."

Val came to stand beside me. "It was in the temple mural," he said. "Above Aelan."

"The Forged Heart," I breathed. "Her constellation."

Four copper rings encircled the emblem, each etched with different markings. I ran my hand over the innermost and felt it give under my touch, clicking softly as it turned.

"Look at these," I said. "They're not just symbols. They're all constellations. The Broken Crown. The Eternal Knight. The Crimson Dragon. The Fallen Star. All from the mural."

"Maybe you have to align them in a specific order," Val said.

"They weren't arranged like this in the fresco," I said.

He leaned back against a table behind me, arms folded. Watching. Letting me work.

"Just going to stand there while I do everything?" I asked, glancing up.

"You don't need me," he said with a smirk. "And I'm enjoying the view."

I followed his eyes—directly to the neck of my tunic, which had slipped slightly open while I leaned over the pedestal.

I narrowed my eyes at him. He shrugged.

I didn't fix it. Just turned back to the rings.

I arranged them in the order I remembered from the mural—Broken Crown, Eternal Knight, Fallen Star, Crimson Dragon.

Nothing.

"How annoying," I muttered.

"What's your reasoning?" he asked. "Sometimes it helps to say it aloud."

"I thought it might be proximity in the sky," I said, frowning. "But that's wrong."

My eyes dropped to the heart at the center. The Forged Heart. Then the others.

"It's not about distance. It's symbolic." I turned the innermost ring to the Eternal Knight. "Caedmon was closest to her heart."

It glowed.

Success.

Next, the Broken Crown.

"She didn't lose it," I said softly. "She offered it. She would've given anything to keep Aeltyria safe. Her crown. Her name. Her life."

It clicked into place beside the Knight. Its glow came softer. Like it didn't need to shine to be known.

I turned the third ring to the Crimson Dragon. Its light flared at once, hot and pulsing. "Her duty."

Last was the Fallen Star. I turned the outer ring. It clicked into place. "And herself. Furthest away."

The Forged Heart flared white, bright as a lightning strike. I shielded my eyes until it dimmed. A low hum rose from the pedestal. Beneath it, stone shifted—grinding, groaning—a deep rumbling that rolled through the forge like thunder.

A door opened in the stone, slow and steady.

I turned toward Val just as he came to stand next to me.

His smile broke slow and warm as he met my eyes. "Brilliant and beautiful. This is why you always beat me at Talon."

I lifted a brow. "We haven't played that in a while. Thought you forgot how."

"I enjoy the illusion of dignity."

Then he stepped forward—

And the stone in the threshold sank with a heavy *clunk* under his weight.

Torches inside the chamber flared to life, one by one, along the carved stone, their flames casting it in flickering gold.

Val eyed them warily. "Convenient." The corner of his mouth twitched.

"You're lucky it wasn't a trap."

The chamber stretched wide, the air crisp with the scent of oil and metal. Shelves lined the walls, packed with armor and weapons untouched by rust or wear. The dark metal shimmered with that strange, shifting sheen of black and violet and deep blue all at once.

Galvarium.

Each piece bore a constellation I recognized, though never like this. Not etched into a cuirass, not chasing along the blade of a war-knife.

Val moved forward, to a full suit of plate displayed on a carved wooden stand. He stopped before it.

"Gods," he said under his breath. "It's stunning."

It was. And it was Aeltyrian craft—art and war woven together. Forged for a warrior long dead.

He reached out, fingers brushing the breastplate. I knew that look. Longing.

I'd never heard him say he wanted anything just for himself. A fine horse and armor for me, or for Lucius. Freedom for my people. Proper care for the poor. But never anything for himself.

"You should take it," I said, already pulling a longsword from its sheath to test its balance. It was long enough to need both hands, balanced enough that he could free one if he had to. "The sword too. It looks like it was made for you."

He drew his hand back, as if burned. "No. I have no right to it. This is Aeltyrian. Aelan's legacy. I won't wear what my people tried to extinguish."

"And yet here you are," I said. "Fighting to restore it."

He didn't answer.

So I turned to face him fully. "If it belongs to Aeltyria, it is mine to give. You're my First Sword. And I won't have you walking into danger in worn leathers and a good attitude."

"Aleaia—"

"No." My voice cut sharper than I meant, but I didn't take it back. "You don't get to refuse. Not this time."

I stepped closer. The edge in my voice softened, but not the meaning beneath it.

"This isn't pride. It's survival. You told me once you'd take the blade rather than let it touch me." My hand found his. "I believe you. But if you mean to protect me, I need you alive to do it."

He held my gaze, that same war behind his eyes—between loyalty and guilt, between what he thought he deserved and what I knew he did.

"I'm not asking," I added. "Put it on."

Val didn't move at first.

Then, finally, grudging as a winter thaw, he gave a single nod and reached for the armor.

He lifted the breastplate, turned it over, and frowned. "Needs padding."

*Still trying to get out of it.*

I exhaled through my nose and glanced around the room again. A trunk sat nearly lost in shadow along the far wall. I crossed to it, knelt, and lifted the lid. Inside, quilted tunics lay folded in neat layers beneath a thin film of dust. I touched one. Dry. Whole. Preserved somehow, like the air had held its breath for centuries, waiting.

"Still intact." I didn't want to know how. There were mysteries enough on this island without trying to solve this one. I held one up, eyeing it. "You'll stretch the shoulders, but it should do."

Val took it.

I tried not to watch what he was doing. I failed.

Every layer he shed made the room feel warmer, closer. The tunic slid over his head, muscles shifting beneath his skin. I knew every scar. Especially the one along his ribs—the wound that should've taken him from me.

A breath escaped me.

He didn't look back. "Is something the matter?"

"No," I said. Too quickly.

He pulled the gambeson on at that same maddening pace, each fastening an act of restraint. Not for show. For control. And somehow, that was worse.

When he reached for the armor, I moved without thinking.

"Here," I said, quieter now.

I helped him with the breastplate, cinching the leather straps beneath his arms. I circled behind him and fitted the pauldrons to his shoulders. Bracers, greaves, each piece as precise as the last. He moved with me easily, trusting me to see it done.

The plates shimmered in the torchlight, oil-slick light dancing at the edges. Etched constellations ringed every surface. And across his chest, the Eternal Knight burned faint and certain.

It fit him too well.

I let out a breath I hadn't meant to.

He didn't speak. Just stood there—composed, silent. A figure carved in shadow and firelight.

And for one strange, unwelcome moment, I wondered what it would be like if he were mine—not just in secret, not just in stolen hours and whispered words.

What would we be then?

What would *I* be, standing beside him—not as a weapon, not as a symbol, but as his equal?

If I could wake beside him every morning and call him husband.

The thought hollowed me out and filled me all at once.

I forced myself to breathe.

"I love you, vedrānos," I said softly, taking his hand in mine while it was still bare of the gauntlets.

He stilled.

Then, just as softly, he said, "And I love you."

I picked up one of the gauntlets and slid it onto his hand. My fingers brushed his wrist, lingered longer than necessary, but he didn't pull away.

When I looked up, he was watching me.

He didn't speak. Just stood there, all the more dangerous for the quiet. A shadow-cut figure of war, made not just to fight but to endure.

And I—

I couldn't look away.

I couldn't imagine anyone else beside me. Not now. Not ever.

He caught my eye, searching my face.

"What is it?" he asked gently.

I pulled a shaky breath.

And then the words were out—bare, unpolished, unplanned.

"Marry me."

For a few heartbeats, he just stared—no smile, no teasing, only something raw and reverent in his eyes.

"Aleaia..." He stepped closer, voice low. "You have no idea how much I want to."

The air went cold in my lungs.

"But I can't," he said carefully.

Of course he wouldn't want me like this—sweat and desperation in the flickering torchlight. What had I expected?

My face didn't change. I wouldn't let it. Not even a flicker.

I forced a nod. "I understand. Come on. We have a relic to steal."

The words were steady. My feet moved before he could say anything else. Carried me forward as if nothing had cracked open inside me.

But gods, it had.

I walked. One step. Then another. And another.

*Don't be foolish. You knew better.*

My throat tightened. My vision blurred, and I blinked hard, refusing to let tears fall.

*You knew better, and still you asked. What did you think he'd say? That he'd marry you right here, in the ruins?*

It had been a mistake. One of weakness, not strength.

I hated that I'd made it.

I hated even more how much the answer hurt.

I swallowed hard. Bit the inside of my cheek. My breath came sharp through my nose.

"Aleaia."

I stopped. I wiped my eyes and turned, slow.

He stepped closer, firelight catching on the black metal across his chest. Then, without a word, he tugged off one gauntlet and let it rest in the crook of his arm. His hand lifted—gentle as a breeze—and touched my cheek.

I didn't move. I couldn't. Not with my face aflame and tears rising fast.

It was already too much—my heart pounding like a drum, my eyes stinging despite everything I told them. If I looked at him now, I'd shatter.

It wasn't his fault that it hurt, and I didn't want him to see it. Just because I'd asked didn't mean he had to say yes. I wanted to tell him that, but my voice had gone somewhere I couldn't reach.

"*I* will ask *you*," he said. "Not today. Not like this. Not while we're hunted. Not while I've nothing to offer you but a sword and a name half the world would curse. But I will."

My vision blurred again. I blinked furiously.

"I want to give you more than love whispered in the dark. I want to give you mornings. Years. A place to belong. Something you can hold that isn't just war and wanting. And when I can, I'll ask properly. On my knees, if that's what it takes."

I tried to master the treacherous swell of relief in my chest.

"And if you say no then, because I took too long," he added, tipping my chin up to look at him, "then I'll still thank the gods I ever got to love you at all."

That broke something. A small sound escaped me—a tearful laugh—and I offered an aching smile.

"You don't have to prove anything to me, you beautiful fool," I said, voice unsteady. "I would never say no."

Then, gently, he kissed me.

A kiss that asked for nothing, and promised me everything.

# CHAPTER ONE HUNDRED ELEVEN
## *The Breach*

*"Infiltration under darkness requires two things: silence and fire. The former conceals entry. The latter ensures no one watches it happen."*
—Standard Infiltration Protocols of the Imperial Legions

Rudamos 87, 1231
*Aleaia*

The sun had begun to drop below the tree line by the time Val and I finished laying our plans. Below, the village was uneasy. Likely sparked by Melicia's disappearance.

She was right about one thing. I had a better chance of passing among them than Val. Too tall. Too foreign. He struggled with the clipped cadence of their speech. Even I wouldn't speak unless pressed, but if orders came, I could follow them without drawing notice.

I would go in alone.

At the evening watch change—as long as we hadn't missed it—Val would make his move, setting a few buildings alight far from the longhouse.

The noise and confusion should draw off the sentries, giving me time to slip through a narrow breach in the palisade. From the ridge, we'd spotted a line of windows at the longhouse's rear, overlooking a shaded path seldom used. Once the villagers cleared out after the evening meal, I would move.

Retrieve the relic.

Burn the longhouse.

Vanish in the smoke.

As to the relic itself, such things gathered titles like rotten meat drew flies. Whether it was the Heart of Aelan, the Eye of Drakaroth, or something else, it didn't belong in their hands.

And if it was the thing that was needed to get the manacles off—to set me free, as the whisper had promised—then I didn't care what it was called, as long as it did what I needed it to do.

"When you see the fire, that's your signal," Val had said.

"Be careful, vedrānos."

"I will. If you do the same."

"I swear it."

He'd leaned in and kissed me—firm and without flourish. Not for comfort, but to bind us to caution.

Then he was gone, slipping down the slope and into the trees.

Alone again, I ducked behind the rock that had hidden us from view, eyes fixed on the distant flicker of torchlight below. The plan was thin. Risky. But we didn't have time for anything better.

*Valerius*

When I was young, I was given my first command, and the first mission I led was to push the people of the southern provinces off their land and into the sea. We'd used fire, sword, and fear to get it done.

I hated it. Partly because it was cruel, and partly because I was powerless to stop it.

So I'd told one woman—one with a baby on her hip—about the boats beyond the last row of huts, where the marsh thinned and the water rose just enough for them to hold weight. They were fishing skiffs, pulled high into the reeds. Crude things, half-hidden—the sort meant to vanish between tides.

Half that little village managed to escape that way.

It's less impressive than it sounds. Half the village was only forty or so people. But no children washed up on the shore, and none were among those we'd put to the sword, so I'd thought it a victory.

I hated razing places like that. Hated what it meant. What it stood for.

So I was surprised, then, that I felt so little guilt at the thought of burning this village. I acknowledged it, then moved on. The fire wasn't for vengeance or power—it was a tool. A distraction. If smoke and chaos gave Aleaia even a slim chance of slipping in and out unseen, so be it.

I'd burn the world to protect her. What's one part of one village?

I broke into a jog, boots pounding the slope. The galvarium armor fit well. As if it had been made for me. But I hadn't worn plate since Avitum, and it was heavier than anything I'd carried before.

Normally, I wouldn't wear plate unless I knew I was taking the field or riding. But she had insisted I take it, and wearing it was the most convenient way to transport it.

I kept going.

As the terrain flattened at the village's edge, buildings rose in uneven rows, slouched against one another like drunkards. The older stretch—abandoned docks, rotted timber—sat too close to the surf. The palisade was a joke. Sagging timbers. Gaps wide enough to ride a mule through.

Security here was pitiful. Two guards loitered by a crumbling well, neither watching their flanks. Half a patrol drifted in lazy circles.

The rest were likely still at the council hall, arguing over which gods demanded which blood.

Idiots. No wonder they hadn't seen us coming.

I ducked behind a slatted fence near the waterline, out of sight, and dropped the bundle I'd carried. Oil-soaked cloth. Flint. Steel. Torches I'd taken from the smithy.

My hands moved quickly. No wasted motion.

Shadows shifted beyond the fence. Voices carried, low and tense. Likely still talking about the girl. Not alarmed. That would change soon enough.

I struck steel to flint. On the third try, sparks flared and caught. The torch flamed to life.

I hurled it over the fence.

It landed with a clatter against the wall of the nearest house. For a heartbeat, silence. Then—the crackle of timbers catching. The dry wood went up fast, like it had been waiting for this. Heat surged through the night air.

I lit a second torch. The wind clawed at the flame, but I cupped it, shielding it with my hand as I moved toward the dock.

One boat sat tied there. Nothing worth stealing. Hull split in places, deck worn bare. A boat used often and cared for poorly. The mooring ropes looked ready to snap if the tide so much as turned. But it would burn.

I stepped to the edge of the dock, sighted, and threw.

The torch arced clean and wide. It struck near the center of the deck, rolled, then lodged somewhere. Smoke began to rise. First a thread. Then a twisting column.

The oil-slicked planks flared fast. Fire crawled over the vessel in crooked fingers. Within seconds, it was fully ablaze.

Perfect. Panic would spread fast.

I crouched again. Guards were shouting now, running toward the fire. Some pointed skyward. One drew a blade, though who he thought he'd fight, I couldn't imagine.

All she needed was a few minutes.

*Aleaia*

The plume rising from the docks was larger than I'd expected—thick and gray, curling skyward like a signal from the gods. The guards had turned toward it, shouting, distracted.

How big a fire did he set? I wondered.

I bolted down the hill, heading for the weak point in the western wall.

It wasn't hard to find. Up close, the palisade was even more pitiful than it had looked from the ridge. Boards split with rot. Crates stacked like afterthoughts.

I felt a pang of guilt for what Val was doing to them.

But there was no time for remorse.

I pressed my back to the crates, dug my heels into the earth, and shoved. The stack gave way suddenly, sending me sprawling backward onto the rough path inside the stockade.

I scrambled up, hand braced on my hilt in expectation. No one shouted. No one came running. I exhaled, put the crates back as best I could, pulled my hood up, and moved for the longhouse.

Crouching beneath the windows, I listened at each one in turn, letting the sounds inside guide me. The hall was quiet. I found one I thought was the chieftain's chamber, then hauled myself up over the sill.

Dim light met me. I stayed still, breath shallow, body low, until my eyes adjusted.

A bedchamber. Spacious. Austere.

Natural decor. Woven hangings suspended from tree branches. A carved eagle in the corner. The support beams—gods, they were beautiful. Each post engraved with runes in fine, spiraling patterns. Eerie, but beautiful.

The chest at the foot of the bed caught my attention.

It didn't match the rest of the room. Too plain, too foreign. That had to be it.

Satisfaction bloomed. I'd picked the right room.

I crossed to the chest and tried the lid. Locked. Of course. I drew my dagger, wedged it beneath the edge, braced my weight against the hilt.

As precious as this thing is, I can't believe they left a window open. Sloppy.

The lock groaned. Creaked.

I pushed harder. It gave with a crack—splintering wood, popping loud enough to wake the dead.

*Fuck.*

I froze. Listening.

No footsteps. No alarm.

I eased the lid open and looked inside. Light spilled out—warm and golden, bright enough to blind me for a breath. I blinked, shielding my eyes.

There it was: a glowing orb, the size of my palm. Swirling energy danced inside it, slow and hypnotic. It matched the socket near the Soulforge.

I sheathed my dagger and reached for it.

It was warm. Alive. It pulsed faintly in my hand.

*How could they think this was anything but Aelan's?*

The door swung open.

I didn't think. I moved.

Orb in hand, I sprinted for the window—but the guard was already on me. He caught the hood of my cloak, yanking me backward and slamming me to the floor, knocking the air from my lungs. The orb flew from my grip, skittering under the bed.

The axe came next, swinging for my skull.

I caught his wrist just in time, shoved his arm to the side. The blade buried itself in the floorboards, missing me by inches.

He snarled, yanking at the haft. I kicked out hard, throwing him off balance, then rolled and scrambled upright.

The orb flickered beneath the bed. I dove for it, just as he wrenched the axe free and turned.

He swung again.

I dropped flat, the wind of it slicing overhead.

On my belly, I stretched for the orb. My fingers found it. Clutched it tight.

He kicked me in the ribs before I could rise. Pain flared—deep—but I didn't let go. I couldn't.

He came again, axe raised high. I rolled, drew my dagger in one motion, and met him as he charged. Drove the blade up beneath his arm, punching through leather and flesh like wet cloth.

His eyes widened. He stumbled, choking on his breath.

I didn't wait. I ripped the dagger free and rose.

He collapsed, the axe clattering from his hand.

Groaning. Trying to rise.

I stood over him. I could leave him. Let the fire take him. But he'd only done his duty. He deserved better than that.

I sighed—and drove the dagger into the base of his skull.

His body went still.

Wiping the blood on his cloak, I slid the dagger back into the sheath at my boot.

The longhouse was a deathtrap waiting to happen. Dry wood. Dried herbs. Woven tapestries.

I grabbed the torch he'd dropped—he'd nearly lit the place himself—and touched it to the nearest wall hanging. The fabric caught instantly. Fire licked up the beams. Smoke rolled thick along the ceiling. I tossed the torch onto the bed and backed toward the window, shielding the orb beneath my cloak.

Outside, I turned to check my work. The longhouse was ablaze. Flames clawed upward, black smoke curling into the night sky.

I ran for the breach.

Voices shouted behind me—guards, villagers—but I didn't look back. I focused on the path ahead. Each step carried me closer to the trees. To escape.

To him.

*Let him see it. Please.*

We had only moments before they regrouped.

Before the forest was no longer enough.

# CHAPTER ONE HUNDRED TWELVE
## *What We Swear*

*"The weight of a vow is not in the words,*
*but in what you're willing to do when no one else can follow."*
—The Breath of the World

Rudamos 87, 1231
*Aleaia*

I shoved the crates aside and crawled through the breach—straight into Val's hand as he caught my arm, steadying me.

"Are you hurt?" he asked, eyes sweeping over me.

"Bruised. Nothing serious." I pushed off my knees. "We need to move."

We ran, fast and low.

My ribs throbbed where I'd taken the kick, but I didn't slow. Behind us, smoke curled into the trees, painting the canopy in shadow. Shouts rang out in the distance. Not far. Not far enough.

By the time we reached the temple, the last light had faded from the sky. Val grabbed the heavy doors and slammed them shut, then wedged a tall iron candelabra through the handles, jamming it crosswise.

Then he turned to me, took a deep breath in, and exhaled. "Glad that's done."

From the stairwell, Melicia emerged, eager for news and the thing she still believed was hers.

"Why dost thou barricade the door? Wert thou pursued?"

"Not that we know of," I said, brushing past her to descend the stairwell. Val followed me.

"Dost thou have the Eye?" she pressed, trailing after us. "Wert thou successful?"

Neither of us answered.

At the foot of the stairs, Val turned and stepped in front of her, barring the way. "You'll have it after Aleaia is done. There's something she needs to do first."

"What must she do?" she snapped, decidedly less sweet now that she wasn't getting her way. "What hath the artifact to do with her?"

I slipped away from them both. The Soulforge pulled at me like a tide. My feet moved faster than they should've, breath rising in short, shallow bursts.

Melicia's footsteps caught up quickly. "Thou canst not! Mine folk will return anon! I shall be defenseless!"

"I'll protect you," I said over my shoulder. "And once I'm finished, you can have your turn."

She surged in front of me, blocking the hall. "Why must thou go first? Thou wilt not be any more adept than I!"

I stopped short, body tense.

"Because I'm the Daughter of Aelan and I need to be free of these fucking things," I said, voice sharp, raising my hands to show the cuffs. "I've used magic before. Not long, but well enough. I need to be free of these manacles, and I believe this device can help."

She blinked. Once. Twice. "Thou art the heir? Truly?"

"I am." I stepped past her. "When I'm done, we'll explain the rest. We owe you that much."

I crossed the threshold into the Soulforge. Val followed at my heels.

My hands trembled as I reached beneath my cloak. The orb pulsed in my grip, its warmth steady and alive.

I placed it into the pedestal. It clicked home with a deep, satisfying *thunk*—and light exploded from the ring at its base. Thin strands of gold flared outward, racing down the carved channels in the floor, straight toward the Soulforge.

It was waking.

Val's voice was calm as he watched the light crawl up the rack.

"Are you sure about this?" he asked.

"I don't know," I said. "I don't have any better options."

He set his helmet down beside the Soulforge, then peeled off his gauntlets to lay them beside it. His hands, bare now, came to my shoulders. "I still don't like it."

"I know."

"If something goes wrong—"

"I'll come back to you."

His thumb traced a line across my cheek. "Promise me."

"I swear it."

The vision returned—him dead on the temple floor.

"Promise me you'll stay."

He didn't hesitate. "I swear it. I'll stay, luce mea. No matter what happens, I'm not leaving you."

He took my face in his hands, and I placed mine over his wrists.

Then he kissed me like he needed to memorize me—my taste, my shape, everything. In case this was the last time.

When we pulled apart, my palms rested on his cuirass, lingering for a breath before I forced myself to let go.

"I love you, you stubborn, stubborn woman," he said.

"And I love you, vedrānos," I said softly.

He lingered a moment more—then let me go. "You're not going in there without taking the leaf."

"I will. Once I get strapped in."

"No." His voice sharpened. "Now. Before. You promised you would."

"Val—"

"You gave me your word, Aleaia." His tone was still level. "If anything happens in there, while you're strapped to that thing—"

"I won't."

"You don't know that." His voice dropped, but it didn't soften. It turned cold with fear.

"I've seen what this power does to people. To you."

I swallowed. He was right, and no amount of pretending he wasn't would make him less so.

My pulse roared in my ears. With stiff fingers, I reached for the pouch at my belt. My hands shook. I tried not to show it. The leaf was small. Dry. Familiar. I pressed it under my tongue. The bitterness hit fast. "There. Done."

Then, without speaking, he crossed to the Soulforge.

He ran his hands over the stone, checking the fittings, the bands of iron that would hold me. He tested the clamps at the wrists, the one at the chest, the curved rest at the base. Then he turned to me. No hesitation. Only the efficiency of a man who had trained for precision.

I wasn't sure what he was looking for—what standard he judged by—but I let him do it, if it was what he needed to feel better.

When he was done, he waved me over, then patted the slab where I'd lay.

"Sit," he said.

I unbuckled my belt and set it aside. Then I climbed onto the stone.

The chill of it seeped into my bones. I lay back slowly, the cuffs on my wrists echoing faintly as they brushed against the iron grooves meant to receive them.

He bent over me, careful, methodical. Closed the cuffs one at a time.

The strap came across my chest, then my hips, then my ankles. He checked each one twice. Never rushed.

He reached for my blade next, sliding it from its sheath to place the hilt in my hand and close my fingers around it. This sword was never just a weapon. He knew that.

Our eyes met.

"I'll be right here," he said.

# CHAPTER ONE HUNDRED THIRTEEN
## *The Soulforge*

Rudamos 87, 1231
*Aleaia*

Val kissed my forehead. "I'll guard the door. But I'm never more than a few steps away."

Then he stepped back. I heard his boots on the stone, then his voice when he spoke to Melicia before the door shut.

Then silence.

I closed my eyes. I didn't want to see the ceiling. Didn't want to give myself a reason to hesitate.

I tried to look toward Val.

Couldn't. My head was strapped in.

My breath came faster. My mouth was dry, still bitter from the leaf.

I watched the light converge in the crystal above me.

Heard a hum.

Felt pressure rising in the air, in my chest.

Then warmth.

Then fear.

It wasn't too late. I could call out. He would come. He would get me off this thing before it began.

But I didn't.

Because this was my duty.

It could be no one else's, so I would bear it.

The warmth started as a tingle in my chest and spread fast. It surged, then spilled down through my limbs.

It burned.

Mana.

It flooded through me, carving new paths in me. I felt it tearing things open—things I hadn't known were closed.

The manacles seared my flesh.

I felt them resist—

One snapped, then the other. Metal shrieked as it split, fragments skittering across the stone.

My back arched.

My breath came shallow.

My fingers locked tighter around the hilt of my sword.

Light exploded behind my eyes. Color bloomed in my skull like flame.

And then—

Darkness.

# CHAPTER ONE HUNDRED FOURTEEN
## *The First Gate*

*"A soldier's task is not to win.*
*It is to hold the line until the one who can win arrives."*
—Principles of War, Calesian military doctrine

Rudamos 88, 1231
*Valerius*

I stood just inside the chamber, near the door, watching her.

She didn't make a sound.

Her body arched against the restraints, muscles pulled taut, the blade gripped tight in her right hand. Light bled from her skin in pulses—faint, then brighter—casting wild shapes along the stone.

Sparks.

Metal screaming.

The manacles split with a crack.

Then silence.

I wanted to cross the chamber. To tear the straps off, to pull her into my arms, to carry her far from this cursed place.

But I stayed where I was. Guarded the door.

My hands ached to move. My breath was tight in my chest. I had fought men and monsters, but this—this helplessness, this waiting—was worse.

I thought of the way she had looked up at me when she lay down.

The way she had trusted me to watch over her.

The way she'd traced the lines of my face with her eyes while I strapped her in, as if afraid she'd never open them again.

I wondered what she thought as she lay there, before she closed her eyes. Did she think again about how she'd asked me to marry her, and I hadn't said yes? Gods, I hoped not. I wanted her to think of something gentle. Something warm.

Maybe sitting under the olive tree in Letia. Or a night by the hearth—

Melicia's voice snapped me back to the present. "My lord!"

Her scream echoed off the corridor walls, high and sharp with panic.

I spun toward the door, already moving.

Something in me flinched. I looked back once. She was still breathing. Eyes closed. The sword still in her hand.

I'd be back soon. I hoped.

But what if she woke and I wasn't?

I crossed to her in two strides and unlatched the right wrist strap. Just in case.

Her hand fell free, limp.

I grabbed my helmet and gauntlets, turned, and ran.

Up the stairs. Toward the scream. Toward whatever waited above.

I reached the main chamber fast, heart hammering—but she wasn't under attack. Just standing there, hands trembling, eyes wide as she stared at the entry like it might explode inward.

"My lord!" she cried again, voice rising, breath wild. "They pound upon the door—they come! I know not how many!"

Boots. Voices. Scraping stone. Someone trying the door.

Not quite the attack her scream had promised.

"Seems your people have found us," I said.

"Mine husband is attuned to my mana," she stammered, clutching her skirts. "But he wouldst not have followed it here without effort, without pause." Her breath hitched. "Nay… tis likelier they followed the Eye, Creator preserve us."

I stared at her. "That might've been useful to know before we agreed to help you."

She turned toward me, still pale, but the honed edge of pride flickered through. "And how was I to know thou wert ignorant of my people's ways? I weened thou hadst some knowledge. Even among outlanders, mana-sense is not unknown."

"Why would I know anything about your people?" I snapped. "We don't share customs. We barely share a language."

"I assumed," she bit back, lifting her chin, "that I would perform the ritual and we would depart swiftly. But thou didst not obtain the Eye for me, didst thou? It was always for thy lady," she said. Her gaze flicked toward the Soulforge chamber.

No heat in it. Just cold certainty. That tone irritated me more than shouting would've.

She folded her arms, knuckles white. "In truth, I deem thou hast brought this upon thyself. They value the relic more than they value me."

I opened my mouth to answer—

But then came a voice. Muffled. Male. Too confident.

"Melicia! Thou shalt not be punished! Nay, thou shalt be rewarded for the capture of *Gena Aelané*! Open the door, mine own love!"

My hand found the hilt of my sword before I'd even thought about it.

"Let's not dwell on that now," I snapped, turning back to her. "I have one blade and no exit. Unless you've got a miracle stashed under your skirts, we should think about how to survive this."

The pounding resumed. Slow. Certain.

"How many of your kin wield magic?" I asked.

"None but mine father the Chieftain," she replied.

"Then how does your husband 'discern mana'?"

"Mana is the breath of the world," she said, as if quoting scripture. "It dwelleth in all flesh, even thine own. As blood windeth through thy veins, so doth mana bind thy soul to thy body. All mine kin are taught to sense it, that they might one day find Aelan's heir."

I closed my eyes for a moment. "*Merde.* They sense her."

She nodded slowly, then went quiet—eyes distant, gaze fixed somewhere beyond the stone.

"Ah… that is the signature I feel," Melicia whispered. "Not the Eye. Nay… 'tis her. Creator preserve us. She burneth like starlight."

I stared. "You couldn't feel that before?"

"She was veiled. Now… no longer."

The manacles. That was the difference. They'd shielded her.

I stepped closer, voice dropping to a warning edge. "She told you who she was. And you withheld it."

"I doubted her claim," she said, gaze slipping sideways. "I could not feel her. How was I to know?"

"You knew enough."

I pinched the bridge of my nose. I felt the throbbing starting there already.

Even if I got Aleaia out, they would follow. No matter where we ran. And she'd been strong before, but I had no idea what she'd become when this was over. What she might be capable of. Would it be enough to stand against a man who wielded magic with skill?

I wanted—needed—to pace. But I held still.

I turned toward the door, jaw set. "Will the Chieftain be among them?"

"I cannot say for certes," she said. "But if they feel Gena Aelani, he shall not tarry. If they breach this place, we are doomed."

Outside, the voice rose again—harder now. Colder. "Melicia! How couldst thou betray us thus? Come home."

I stepped forward, let my voice carry through the door. "You can't have her."

"Ah, the gilded butcher! Thou hast stolen much from us," the voice thundered. "The Eye of Drakaroth. My wife. And thou shelterest the Daughter of Aelan. Return her to us and thou mayst yet live. Deny us and thou shalt perish."

I drew my sword. "Not in this life."

Melicia straightened beside me, voice rising. "I disavow thee! This man is now my husband, and I am under his care!"

I shot her a look, sharp, incredulous. "I am no such thing. But I can't return her to you without endangering my queen."

Gods, if I thought I could hand Melicia over and keep Aleaia safe, I'd do it without blinking. But the moment that door opened, they'd come for her. And I would burn the world before I let them take her from me.

"She is a false prophet! A usurper! Thou owest her no allegiance nor promises kept!"

"I'm not opening the door," I said. "Further discussion is pointless."

Silence, for a long moment.

"Then thou leavest us no choice but to break it down and take all by force."

I slid my helmet on. The air narrowed. Steel pressed close at my jaw.

Melicia stepped near. "I am sorry… for burning the white leaves. The books. I thought them refuse and I was cold." Her voice had gone thin. "If they breach the door… prithee, do not let them take me. Grant me the mercy of thy blade instead."

I didn't look at her. Just tugged the gauntlets on. "Go."

"What?"

"We'll go into the stairwell and close the door behind us. Even if your father can breach it, like you did, it might buy us a few more minutes. Maybe by then she'll be out."

I gritted my teeth. I hated not having a more solid plan. Hated that I had to put so much on Aleaia's shoulders when she wasn't even awake to bear the burden.

Melicia turned and hurried into the stairwell, and I followed.

She moved to the etched stone at the side of the passage—the spot where she'd opened it before. Pressed her finger into it, winced when the mechanism pierced her skin.

"Close," she whispered. "Seal thyself. I beg thee."

Nothing.

No glow. No hum. The stone remained inert beneath her hand.

She tried again with a different finger, voice rising. "By blood and breath, I bind thee—close!"

Still nothing.

I took one step toward her. "What's wrong?"

Her hand fell. She turned, wild-eyed, and shook her head.

"It will not answer me," she said. "I have blood-locked this door twice—but now, naught. It doth not heed me."

I looked to the archway—still open. Still watching.

Of course it wouldn't close.

"She's on the Soulforge," I said. "The Temple knows, I think. It won't answer to anyone else now."

Melicia swallowed hard. "Aye. Aye, thou speakest true."

"You've done what you can," I said. "Go. Hide. Tell Aleaia what's happened, when she wakes."

I stepped back toward the main chamber.

She hesitated, then nodded, turned, and disappeared down the stair.

I waited until her footsteps began to spiral away, then turned toward the threshold.

The entrance was narrow. The perfect choke.

I braced in the archway, sword at the ready. If they came, they'd have to get through me first.

I'd fought long odds before. I'd lived through worse.

But not like this.

Not with her in the balance.

I shifted my stance. Tightened my grip.

Let them come.

# CHAPTER ONE HUNDRED FIFTEEN
## *Unbound*

*"The soul must be broken before the heart can be forged."*
—Inscription on the pedestal of the original Soulforge

*Aleaia*

The pain passed first. Then the pressure. Then everything else.

Heat dissolved into weightlessness, and the final tether slipped.

Something deep unfastened.

I drifted.

The dark around me wasn't empty. It was saturated with memory, or something older. Whispers moved through it, layered and ancient. They spoke no tongue I knew, but something in me answered anyway.

Grief.

Hope.

Judgment.

Names never spoken aloud.

And then—light.

A veil of stars parted above me, slow and reverent, revealing a realm of brilliance. Constellations in motion. Color like thought. Light moving with intent, every thread alive.

I didn't float. I hung suspended, caught in the breath between eternity and the beginning.

*Is this Astralis?* I wondered.

A current stretched before me. A ribbon of light, alive with celestial fire, flowing like a river that remembered every soul it had ever carried. The River of Time pulsed.

Far off, the horizon split and light was born. A sun. The first. Its fire screamed through the dark, scattering it like smoke. Stars blinked out, retreating to the edges of everything.

Light surged. The shadows fled.

Time began.

From that same dark, a sphere emerged, seething and unmade.

Molten.

Mad.

It spun with violence, splitting open as mountains clawed skyward, choking on fire. I knew its name as well as my own.

Veridion.

The plane on which I lived in flesh.

Then the sky broke. Rain fell in fury, slamming the flame-choked earth. Water fought fire. Steam rose. And in their war, shape came into being.

Mountains cooled. Valleys formed. Ash thickened into loam. Seas surged into place—vast, hungry.

The land exhaled.

I turned, and the moon revealed itself, silver and still.

A mirror to the light. A keeper of the dark.

Then came the frost.

Under Lithau's gaze, life began.

Forests surged from soil. Rivers carved their songs across the bones of the world. Creatures rose and for a time, the world sang with them.

Then, humans among them.

Shaped like Anvallus and Lithau.

But then—

Light.

Aelan.

Born of Lithau's love of a mortal man and left in the arms of two mortals. A child of fire and spirit. I watched her strength bloom. Her rise. How she drew scattered tribes from ruin and built something—a nation, unified under her banner.

Aeltyria, born of conviction and need, named by Caedmon in her honor.

Then the Cataclysm. I felt it break the world open.

Anvallus's hand swept over Veridion like judgment. Order fell upon the land—not peace, but stillness. Control. Beneath the mountains, fire cracked again and from ash, something worse was born.

Drakaroth.

A hatchling first. Then a storm. Flame coiled around him like wings. Every beat of them scorched the world raw. Forests turned to ash. Rivers boiled. The sky went still.

It was just as Caedmon described, but no words could've prepared me for the stillness that followed.

That was the true horror—

The earth, too stunned to scream.

Aelan rose in the dark.

Her radiance didn't burn. It restored. She came like dawn to a battlefield. Like memory pushing back oblivion.

Hope returned with her sacrifice.

Blood and will reshaping the world.

Hers. Always hers.

The River of Time surged.

The thread that was mine—bright with celestial fire—tightened. Glowed.

It slipped into the current, pulling toward the center, toward the present.

All other threads faded.

At first, the days of my youth. Barefoot. Wild. The river at my feet.

Then Val's thread, steady and soothing, braided into mine.

As I'd always known it would.

But as we neared the present—

His thread strained.

Faltered.

Then—

it snapped.

A jolt tore through the current, white-hot and final.

His light vanished.

"No."

I reached for where it had been.

Gone.

Not a possibility. Not a vision.

*Now.*

He was dying.

And without him—

my thread dimmed.

The brightness that had once lit my path flickered, weakened, faded.

It unraveled into the tapestry. Just another thread among thousands.

Aeltyria was never reborn. There was no war, no banner, no name remembered in firelight.

Only silence.

The Empire surged forward, unbroken. Unopposed.

And from the heart of its dominion, Drakaroth was summoned.

Not by chaos, but by command.

By order.

By those who ruled everything.

He rose like a second sun, not to destroy the world, but to possess it.

His wings blotted out the stars. His roar shattered the sky.

There was no battle. No collapse.

Only ownership.

And in that silence, the end of all things.

"What do I do?" I cried. The words tore free, raw and jagged. "How do I stop it?"

No answer.

Light bloomed.

Not the harsh blaze of prophecy. Something warmer. Older. A light that remembered.

A figure stepped forward.

Divine light and breath and memory shaped her form. Hair like sunlit grain. Skin as gold as the horizon before dawn. The heavens bent around her.

Every part of me knew her.

*Lithau.*

*Holy Mother.*

There was no ground, but I bowed anyway. I couldn't look at her—not at first.

"Aleaia," she said. My name was music and grief and home on her lips.

"Child of Veridion. Bearer of hope. Daughter of mine. The vision thou hast seen is not fixed, but is the path upon which thou walkest—the shape of what may yet be, wrought by the will of those who tread the living world."

I forced my head up.

"Even now," she said more softly, "there are those who read the end not as ruin, but as reward. They would yoke fire to empire and name it holy. They see not what it is they summon."

My voice broke. "But how? How do I change it? What do I do?"

"The fate of the world lieth in the balance of deeds done and paths chosen," she said. "Thou must forge alliances, awaken courage, and act with both resolve and compassion. The strength to turn the course of destiny dwelleth not in prophecy—but in thee, and in those who shall stand at thy side."

Her words wove through me like threads of light, stitching calm into my doubt. The fear didn't vanish. But it stopped shaking me.

She raised one hand.

The vision blurred. The horrors of the future dissolved like mist in sunlight. The cold faded. The stars stilled.

Warmth spilled from her gesture. It wrapped around me like a cloak that remembered who I was. Soaked into my skin, my soul.

"Remember," Lithau whispered, her form beginning to fade. "Thy deeds are threads within the tapestry of fate. Weave them with care."

"No!" I reached for her, arm outstretched into the void. "Wait! I don't understand!"

But Astralis was already breaking apart.

Light receded.

And then—nothing.

Darkness again.

Weight crept back into my limbs. My body returned, slow and aching.

The fire in my veins dulled to embers. My heart thundered. My breath came shallow.

I was falling back.

Back into flesh.

Back into the world.

# CHAPTER ONE HUNDRED SIXTEEN
## *The Quiet Hall*

*"You don't plan for death. You plan to survive it."*
—Gavius Triarius, Reflections on the Eastern Marches

Rudamos 88, 1231
*Valerius*

It felt wrong.

To hear the clash of blades, the grunts of men locked in battle, the thud of bodies striking stone, and not be part of it. Every instinct pulled me toward the door. My sword was drawn. Breath tight. All I had to do was open it.

I didn't know who had arrived to fight the men who threatened us, but they gave me what I needed most—time.

Aleaia was still below. If I opened the door, I risked bringing the fight to her. And that, I could not allow.

So I waited. Every muscle braced. Listening for her voice.

The din tapered off. Then fell silent.

"Val! Open the door!"

Lucius. Harsh. Alive.

I ripped the candelabra free and hauled the door open. He looked half-dead—exhausted, with blood streaked across his face—but he was upright. And behind him, legion cloaks. Shields.

I pulled my helmet off, tucking it under my arm. "Lucius! You made it."

He caught my forearm in a hard clasp. Solid. Like nothing had happened.

He exhaled. "Couldn't leave Aleaia behind. Not without answering to her uncle. You just happened to be in the same building."

"Again." I huffed through my nose. "Her uncle?"

I didn't think she had any family.

"Lord of Inveraria. Great pain in the arse. No love for you—or me, don't scowl like that—but very much looking forward to meeting his niece."

A soft place for her to fall, then, if it came to that. Someone to care for her if anything happened to me. That was good.

Lucius handed me a shield—plain, iron-rimmed. "Brought this, too. Figured you'd be light."

I tested the weight. Worn, but balanced. It would do. "You thought right."

His gaze tracked to the galvarium pauldrons on my shoulders, the gleam of the blade at my hip. "What's this, then? Find time for looting?"

"A gift."

His grin widened. "From her?"

I didn't answer.

Lucius gave a low whistle. "So that's the secret to getting galvarium plate, eh?"

"If you ever satisfied a woman, Lucius, maybe the gods would bless you too."

For a long moment we stared at each other.

Then he barked a laugh.

And I let myself smile. Just once. Brief.

"Where is she, anyway?" he asked.

"It's a long story. One moment." I turned toward the temple's interior. "Melicia! It's safe to come out now!"

She stepped from the shadows, wild-eyed, her gaze flicking between the soldiers and the bodies on the ground.

Lucius raised a brow. "Who's this?"

"Chieftain's daughter. She fled the village. I offered her safe haven in Aeltyria."

She didn't wait for introductions. Just pushed past us and dropped to her knees beside a body on the steps.

"Behold, mine husband," she cried, voice high and glassy. "Dead at last! I am free of him!"

Lucius gave me a sideways look.

"She helped us," I said, shrugging.

Melicia cackled, arms flung toward the sky. "Thank thee, great Almighty!"

I cleared my throat. "I gave her my word."

He snorted, watching her. "She's mad."

"Undoubtedly."

I gave Lucius the short version of what had happened on the island. The Eye—or Heart. The village. The Soulforge. The manacles.

When I finished, he let out a long breath. "Well, good news is we came to get you off this island. Bad news… there's a Calesian ship not far behind us. We couldn't shake them after the blockade."

Blockade? We'd have to talk about that later.

"How many?" I asked.

"I brought twenty, pulled from the Second. Looked like they had forty Vinculatores. You'll never guess who's in command."

I'd been awake too long to narrow it down. Could've been any prefect bloated on self-importance. I waited.

"Fucking Caius Varro," he said.

I sighed. Of course. "How long, do you think?"

"Couple hours. Maybe less. They weren't far behind."

"Come, then. Let's figure out how to hold this place."

We moved into the main chamber—high-ceilinged, columned. Now visible in the early morning light, I could see that the floor bore the wear of old battles, scuffed and gouged. I wondered if Caedmon had stood here once, as I did now, weighing how to hold it.

The others were already gathered. Some knelt beside the wounded.

A woman stood near the entrance to the stairwell, speaking quietly with Mariana. Tall. Lean. Armor marked with runes. Her braid hung like a whip down her back, a single silver streak running through it.

Lucius strode to them, his hand low at Mariana's back as he addressed the other woman. "Archmage, this is Valerius di Calesia. Val, Caitriona Lennan."

I'd have expected an archmage to be a cloistered mystic—some delicate thing hiding behind sigils and silk. I reached out to take her hand in greeting.

"Cait's fine," she said, clasping my forearm firmly.

Delicate thing she was not. "Well met," I replied.

Lucius pressed on. "We need a barrier at the entrance. Something to slow them."

"Fire rune. Anchored through the stone," she said. "Give me a few minutes."

He turned to Mariana. "Tend the wounded as they fall. If it gets close, get behind the line. We'll hold them there."

I crossed my arms, eyes fixed on the massive archway framing the temple doors. "We'll barricade the doors as best we can. They'll try to force it. Let the stone work for us."

Lucius nodded. "When they breach, fall back to the inner colonnade. Use the columns. Pinch them there. But no fallback beyond this hall."

"Agreed."

Melicia stepped forward again. Her voice was smaller now. "Where then shall I go?"

I gestured toward the dark mouth of the stairwell behind us. "Back downstairs. Hide. Just like before. Tell Aleaia what happened when she wakes."

She hesitated. I saw the fear in her eyes.

"And tell her… that I'm sorry I didn't stay down there," I said.

She nodded. "Aye. I shall do it."

"Can't close that doorway?" Lucius asked.

"No. Broken." No time for a better explanation.

A shout rang out from above. "Calesians approach!"

So much for a couple of hours.

"Archers, fire through the doorway. Make every shot count." Lucius turned to me. "They'll bring a ram. Locals did. Nearly cracked the doors. This one might finish the job."

I nodded toward the remnants of the ram, just beyond the threshold. "Then we use it."

With two others, Lucius and I hauled the broken log up the steps. We closed the temple doors, then wedged it beneath the iron rings, splintered ends biting into stone.

Cait raised her hands. The temperature dropped. Light curled around her fingers. Sparks sprang from the floor beneath the threshold as she began her incantation.

Lucius's voice cut through the hall. "Shields up! Hold formation. Tight ranks."

The soldiers around us moved without hesitation, falling into formation.

I took up position beside Lucius in the front rank. Helmet on, sword drawn, shield ready, and visible so the soldiers behind us could see I'd bleed for them, too.

And beneath it all, the weight I'd been carrying finally settled. Cold. Clear.

A young voice called from the rear—too eager. "We should strike first, lord!"

A few chuckles followed. Half nerves, half bravado. They were afraid. They should be.

Lucius didn't look back. "Let them wear themselves out on the door first."

The first blow landed like a thunderclap. The doors shook in their frame.

I rolled my shoulders. Lucius met my eyes. No words passed. We didn't need them.

Another crash—lower, heavier. The stone trembled.

Cait stepped back from the rune, sweat beading her brow. "Fire rune's locked in."

I set my stance. Tightened my grip.

The next blow echoed like a war drum beating out our names.

We would hold.

We had to.

# CHAPTER ONE HUNDRED SEVENTEEN
## *Hold the Line*

*"The cohort survives by holding formation. If it breaks, it dies.*
—Calesian War Manual, Section V: Siege Protocols

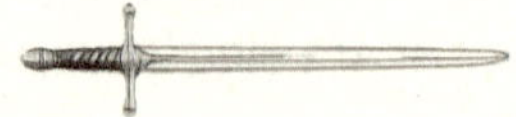

Rudamos 88, 1231
*Valerius*

"Ready!" Lucius shouted, his voice cutting clean through the silence between the battering ram's blows.

I looked back once. Cait stood just behind the third rank, eyes on the rune she'd anchored into the stone. The lines of fire she'd etched into the stone pulsed like veins beneath the surface.

Mariana stood beside her, speaking to a young man I didn't recognize. They both wore healers' gray tunics. An apprentice, maybe.

Another blow slammed into the doors. The oak groaned, cracking down the center. We heard it split.

The front rank shifted. Shields locked into place. Shoulders squared with practiced precision.

There were no chants. No desperate last words. Just the quiet weight of memory.

These were men who had trained with the ones now trying to kill them. Fought beside them. Shared their rations, their barracks, their blood. And now they stood across the line from them, branded traitors for doing what was right.

I felt it too. The pressure, tight and low in the chest.

Almost everyone I gave a damn about was under this roof. Aleaia, below. Lucius. Mariana.

If the line broke, none of them would walk away.

But tactics wouldn't hold this hall. Resolve would.

So I let these soldiers borrow some of mine.

"You've done a brave thing," I said, loud enough to carry. "Coming here. Standing with her. With me. Some of you are thinking of your homes. Your children. Wondering if the Emperor will strike back at them for what you've done."

I didn't turn. Just spoke to the stone in front of me, and let the weight carry behind.

"As long as I breathe, I'll do all I can to keep them safe. So cast off fear. Cast off doubt. And remember this. All each of you need do… is make two of them die for their Emperor."

It wasn't a cheer that followed. Not exactly. Just a laugh from one of the veterans, dry and sharp. Then another. Then more. Rough voices, cracking open the tension like ice breaking on a river.

I turned to Lucius.

"Don't die," he said. "I don't want to lie to your woman."

"Lie to her?"

"By telling her you fought bravely."

I huffed a laugh. Gods, it felt good to have him here. "It's good to stand beside you again, brother."

"Like old times," Lucius said, raising his shield.

I raised mine to match his. "Lucius… what happened in Letia, and on the ship—"

"You weren't yourself." He shrugged. Glanced toward the enemy beyond the doors. "But you are now."

That was as close to forgiveness as I'd ever get from Lucius.

"Buy me a drink if we live," he said.

The next blow split the door clean through. Hinges tore loose. The ram slammed inward, and the double doors burst apart in a hail of splinters. Dust surged in, and with it came the Vinculatores.

Not a charge. Just movement—cold, precise, surgical.

The rune flared when their first rank crossed the threshold.

Cait's ward unleashed itself in a flash of pure, blinding fire that howled through the breach like a living thing. The first to enter never made it two paces. One moment they were advancing, the next—they were gone. Not wounded. Not dying. Gone. Burned to ash. Armor twisted and glowing. Bones collapsing like charcoal across the stone.

Even through the galvarium, I felt it. The blast hit like a forge wind—heat that shimmered across the plates and crawled down my spine.

The breach smoked. Oak cracked and blackened. Flames licked the splintered edges.

First blood drawn.

Now came the real fight.

They regrouped outside the threshold—disciplined and efficient, even as the smoke thickened the air and the floor steamed beneath their boots. Hesitation would've been human. But Vinculatores weren't human. Not in the ways that mattered.

Five wide, maybe. That was all the breach could hold.

"Forward!" Lucius ordered. "On me! Step!"

One step, boots echoing in the chamber.

"Close ranks!" Lucius locked his shield to mine. "Step!"

He set a rapid pace up to the doorway—which is why we made it before the Vinculatores could regroup.

"Hold!" Lucius roared.

We braced—shields locked, boots dug in, jaws clenched. No chants. No glory. Just the silence of men with nothing left but each other.

They met us with shields tight. Blades low. No hesitation. No noise. Just the cold rhythm of trained killers doing what they were made for.

Then steel met steel.

The first clash was sudden and brutal. No charge. Just weight and impact. Shields cracked. Edges scraped. My shoulder jolted from the blow.

Then everything blurred—steel, noise, blood.

And I wished, for a moment, that I had a shorter sword. Long swords aren't meant for shield walls.

I fought beside Lucius, shoulder to shoulder. My world narrowed to the slit between his shield and mine. No room to maneuver. No space to think. Just the line—strike, brace, kill.

A blade came through the gap. I slammed my shield into it, hooked my sword under the rim, and drove the point up. It caught beneath a rib. I twisted. Yanked free. Heard him scream as he fell.

Another stepped in. Swinging high. I ducked, felt the blade hiss past my temple, and drove my blade up through his throat. Blood hit my faceplate. He gurgled as he dropped.

There was no thinking. No tactics. Just rhythm.

Thrust. Brace. Twist. Breathe.

Again.

The air thickened—smoke, sweat, blood. It clung to the back of my throat like ash. The floor turned slick. Bodies piled faster than we could push them aside. There was no room to fall, no space to breathe. Only the next man coming through the smoke.

We were holding. But only just.

Then I saw it.

A shape looming behind the haze.

The ram.

Same one that cracked the doors. Burned at the ends, but still heavy enough to shatter a line.

Smart. Exactly what I'd have done.

"The ram!" I shouted, voice raw.

Lucius saw it. Swore. Bellowed, "Shields tight! Brace!"

The front rank hunched low, shields overlapping like scales. The second line pushed in behind us, weight locked, boots grinding into blood-slick stone.

This was going to hurt.

Then—fire.

A bolt of it. Not wild. Not desperate.

Aimed. Controlled.

It tore through the smoke like a spear and struck one of the men bearing the ram square in the chest. He didn't stumble. He screamed.

Then he burned.

Flames curled up his body in seconds, then licked across the scorched wood. He dropped howling, limbs flailing.

The ram's resin caught instantly.

Fire roared across the shaft, hungry and high. One man let go, then another. They staggered back as the ram crashed to the ground and rolled once—smoking, spitting sparks—until it came to rest between the lines like a burning corpse.

Smoke poured upward. Thick. Choking. Shadows danced across blood-slick stone.

Then the fire shifted.

Outward, toward the Vinculatores, drawn off the wood in a sudden pull at Cait's raised hand. The flames arced toward the breach—leaping, twisting around the men still pushing forward.

Screams rang out.

One staggered as fire caught his cloak. Another flailed as flame climbed his arm like it chose him. They weren't just burning. They were being punished. Targeted. One dropped writhing. Another beat at the fire curling through the gaps in his armor.

The charred ram sagged, half-scorched and steaming.

Their line was weaker in its wake.

Lucius's order came quick. "Second rank—forward! Fill the gap!"

We surged. So did they.

Boots skidded on blood. Shields locked. We hit their weakened line like a hammer.

A spear jabbed low. I caught it on the rim of my shield, twisted, and drove my sword up beneath the bastard's jaw. Bone gave. The blade slid through and punched out the back of his neck. He dropped, gurgling.

Another slipped through the gap—faster. His blade skidded off my side. Pain jolted through my ribs. I caught his wrist, shoved him back, and slammed the pommel of my sword into his face. Something cracked. He went down groaning.

We held.

Barely.

Then I saw them coming.

Another ram, through the smoke, dragged by the second wave of Vinculatores. The wood still smoldered, embers trailing behind. Their formation parted to let it pass. They meant to finish us.

And Cait couldn't stop it. The breach was clogged with bodies now—too many of ours standing between her and a clear shot.

"Steady!" I shouted. "Hold the line! For your queen! For Aeltyria!"

Shields tightened. Men leaned into each other, braced like stonework.

Then it hit.

The ram crashed into the shield wall like Galdorin's fist. My boots skidded. My shield cracked. The man beside me screamed as his leg snapped like a twig. Another stumbled over him and went down, trampled in the crush.

The line twisted.

I twisted with it, dragged sideways. I staggered, but didn't fall.

The breach was opening.

"Close ranks!" Lucius shouted.

Too late.

The Vinculatores formed a wedge, shields high, blades raised. They punched through our center and the wall broke open. They came through like floodwater. The line was gone.

Then—chaos in its wake.

No orders. No formation. Just the crush of bodies. Screaming steel. Blood.

A sword flashed left. I turned it aside and countered, blade under the arm and deep into the collar. A scream, then dead weight. I pivoted, ducked another swing, slammed my shoulder into the next bastard and sent him staggering.

The floor was slick. Blood underfoot, warm and fresh. Smoke stung my eyes. My throat burned. Heat from the burning timber clung to my skin like oil.

We were losing ground.

Not in steps, but inches.

In blood.

I didn't think. Couldn't.

There was no time.

Just motion. Just survival.

Blade in.

Steel out.

Blood on stone.

Another breath.

The galvarium dragged now. Every swing cost me. My shoulders screamed. My back burned.

I couldn't stop moving.

Screams rose behind me—familiar, unfamiliar. Didn't matter. I couldn't turn.

The world narrowed to the shape in front of me. One man. One blade.

I met him. Broke him. Stepped past.

And still they came.

A body slammed into me, hard enough to stagger. I snarled, shoved back, shield-first, and felt the give of bone as the rim crunched into a face. The Vinculatore reeled, blood spraying from his shattered nose.

I didn't wait. Stepped in. Sword rising. Drove the blade up beneath his arm, past leather, past mail. It punched through tendon, caught bone, and stuck.

His weight sagged against me.

I shoved him off, yanked my weapon free, and surged back into the fight.

"Reform! Two lines!" Lucius's voice cut through the chaos like a whipcrack.

The Aeltyrians, bloodied and gasping, obeyed.

We pulled back a few paces. Just enough. Stretched across the chamber width, the line reformed. No walls to anchor our flanks now. Just open stone behind us, and imperial steel ahead.

Still, we locked shields.

I found myself shoulder to shoulder again, boots braced, shield high. The wall held—for now—but it was thinner. Frayed. Every charge stripped another man from it.

Steel rang on steel. Blades stabbed through the gaps.

It went on.

And on.

A grinding eternity of shield and blade. Thrust, block, counter. A dance that stank of blood and sounded like death. My arms ached. My legs shook.

It was inevitable that the line would break again.

And it did.

Too much pressure. Too few left.

Through the haze, I caught a glimpse of Cait near the rear, casting fire with deadly purpose.

Then something cut through the air. A flash of silver.

An incolumium bolt buried itself in beneath her ribs.

She staggered, fell backward with the force of it, swearing.

Mariana's apprentice threw himself over her, dragging Cait toward the rear, trying to shield her as more bolts hissed overhead.

"Hold the line!" Lucius bellowed. "Protect the heir!"

The words caught like fire.

They passed through the soldiers in a rush. It wasn't just a command, but a cause.

Every soldier understood what it meant.

We were buying time.

We were buying *her life*.

I braced. Took a blow on my shield. Returned one harder. My sword caught a Calesian across the jaw. Blood and teeth flew. Another stepped in.

Then I heard it.

A roar, rising through the din.

"Valerius di Calesia!"

# CHAPTER ONE HUNDRED EIGHTEEN
## *To the Last*

*"I'll be the shield that does not falter, the blade that does not bend. I'll give my life for you. My strength for our people. My soul for Aeltyria—*
*until death, until ruin, until the world ends."*
—Valerius di Calesia, First Sword of Aeltyria

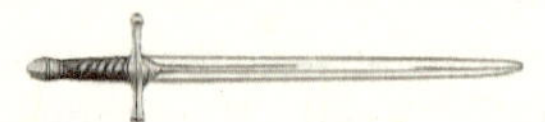

Rudamos 88, 1231
*Valerius*

I turned toward it on instinct, blade still raised.

At the far end of the chamber, just beyond the churn of men and death, stood Caius Varro. Wolf-headed helm.

Bastard was too clean. Too polished. He hadn't lifted a blade until now, content to let others bleed for him.

Disgusting.

"You've eluded me long enough," he snarled, pushing through the melee like it didn't matter. "Today, you pay for your insolence."

All around us, the battle raged. Swords crashed. Men screamed.

He stepped toward me, sword drawn, movements clean and sure.

"Where's your woman?" He raised his sword. "Huh. No mage. No heir. No matter. I'll find her."

My pulse thundered. My lungs burned. My whole body ached. Armor dragged at my shoulders like I bore stone on them.

But I raised my sword. Pointed it straight at him.

"Let's finish this," I said. "Just you and me."

He scoffed. "You offer me the Rite of the Blade?"

I said nothing.

"No," he spat. "No. Let your men die fighting. They chose wrong. That's what they deserve."

We circled. Blades up. Boots shifting in blood. I kept my stance square, weight forward.

He lunged—fast, sharp.

I stepped aside and let his momentum carry him past me. He recovered quickly, swinging down hard. I dodged and caught the follow-up on my blade, so hard it rattled me to the shoulder.

"Fight me properly, di Calesia!" he spat. "Or are you waiting for your whore to rescue you?"

My grip tightened. Fury flared.

I swallowed it. One mistake would get me killed.

I answered with a quick thrust, upward at his face. He jerked back, laughing.

"The way she moaned," he said, threaded with mocking. "Exquisite, really. Forgot we were in a dungeon. Almost forgot she's ashborn."

The words slid under my ribs like a blade.

"But the tears. The way she begged on your behalf." He mimicked her voice—taunting, cruel. "'I'll do anything, just leave him alone.' It was extraordinary."

My blood roared in my ears.

I brought my sword down in a savage arc.

He caught it. Used the flat and hilt, trapped my blade, grabbed my sword arm, and twisted. Tried to bring his pommel down into my face.

I caught his wrist. Snarled through my teeth, "Fuck you."

We grappled—armor grinding, boots slipping in blood. He leaned in, breath hot and rank, laughing. "Struck a nerve, have I?"

I slammed my helmet into his nose.

The crack echoed. He reeled. Blood sprayed. He stumbled back, shaking his head.

I didn't wait. Went in swinging.

He ducked—smart, fast—and hooked his blade behind my legs. Yanked.

I hit the stone hard. Breath gone. Sword skittering away.

Varro let his sword fall and drew the dagger at his belt in one smooth motion.

He came down like a hammer, straddling my chest. Dagger high.

I caught the blade with both hands. Twisted up. Drove my shoulder into his ribs. The move broke his balance.

I slammed his wrist against the floor—once, twice—until the dagger broke free and clattered across the stone into the fray.

We rolled, snarling, punching, boots kicking.

Both of us lunged for the nearest blades.

My hand closed on my sword just as he surged again.

I was up first. Blade raised. Breathing hard. Ready to end it.

Slammed steel into his chest hard enough to stagger him.

But he rolled fast and came up with the dagger.

A scream split the clash.

Sharp. Familiar.

*Mariana.*

I turned. Reflex.

One of his officers had her. Wrists locked in incolumium manacles.

Stupid, letting myself be distracted like that.

Varro struck.

He slammed into me, drove me down again. We hit the floor—tangled, brutal. He mounted fast, dagger raised.

I caught his wrists, arms shaking from the effort.

The blade hovered inches from my throat.

I pushed back, down, to the side. Tried, anyway.

Then—pain.

The dagger drove in.

Not my throat.

White-hot, just between the cuirass and pauldron. Deep. Clean.

Fire exploded through me. My left arm went numb. I couldn't hold him.

He leaned in close. "Still alive? Impressive. But not for long."

I roared through clenched teeth. Twisted—violently. Pulled his arm, rolled us across the blood-slick stone.

The blade tore free.

I shoved him off.

Grabbed my sword.

Staggered upright, legs trembling.

Blood poured down my side—hot, fast, terrifying. My shoulder pulsed with every beat of my heart.

He was already on his feet. Circling.

I tried to lift my sword.

Vision blurred.

Ground shifted.

I dropped.

To one knee. Then over, onto my back.

My sword didn't leave my hand.

I wouldn't let it.

I couldn't.

I rolled to my side, groaning. The stone was warm. Wet.

I moved. Hand. Knee. Elbow.

My left arm sagged useless at my side. I dragged it forward with the rest of me.

I reached for my sword again.

*Stand up.*

Varro's boot slammed into my shoulder.

Agony ripped through me. I screamed—couldn't stop it. The pain stole everything. Sight. Breath. Thought.

Varro turned away, calling out words that melted together in my hearing.

*Get up.*

One leg at a time.

Trembling.

I forced myself upright.

My vision swam.

I nearly fell again.

But I didn't.

I stood.

Once more.

For her.

# CHAPTER ONE HUNDRED NINETEEN
## *Slipping Through My Fingers*

*"I don't believe in premonitions. Or fate. Or destiny.
I believe in choices. In control. In fighting for what matters.
In fighting for you."*
—Valerius di Calesia, Succamos 21, 1231

Rudamos 88, 1231
*Aleaia*

I woke choking. Raw and rasping, like I'd swallowed fire.

My right hand ached, cramped around my blade. I forced it open, one at a time, shaking out the burn.

Then I realized—it was free.

Before I'd gone to… that other place, Val had strapped my limbs down.

And now I couldn't feel him nearby.

The iron band across my forehead bit into my skull. I unlatched it with trembling fingers and shoved it aside.

I couldn't see anything in the dim light of the Heart.

I sat up, the ashen remains of the manacles falling away from my skin. Pain flared down my back. My legs hit the floor—and buckled. I dropped hard to one knee, breath tight in my chest.

"Val?"

No answer.

"Val!"

Still nothing.

*Where is he? He promised he'd stay. He swore it.*

My heart thundered. The world felt wrong—off-balance. The Veil still clung to it like smoke.

I reached inward. Mana was there—but thin, flickering. Distant. Like a dying ember in a hearth long gone cold. I held onto it. Tried to coax it back to life.

My head pounded as I buckled on my sword belt, fingers clumsy in the dark. Sheathed my blade. Moved to the pedestal.

The Heart of Aelan sat waiting in its cradle. I took it in both hands. It pulsed faintly—dimmer. Still warm.

I went for the door, using the Heart to see.

Through the library. Black as pitch here, too. Something was wrong.

I drew my sword. It glowed faintly in my grip, casting silver light ahead. It wouldn't light for me—not yet. My mana was low.

Movement flickered between the shelves.

I almost struck the girl.

"Godsdamnit, Melicia! I nearly killed you!"

She raised her hands. "I waited down here, as my lord commanded," she whispered.

Then I heard the clash of steel. Distant. Above.

And I knew before I asked.

"Melicia, what happened? Where is Val?"

"In came men," she said softly. "They called them Vinculatores. They fight in the temple now."

My stomach turned. This was why I wanted him to stay with me.

I didn't wait to hear more.

I ran for the stairs.

Up them.

Through the doorway.

Into war.

Smoke hit me first. Bitter and thick, it curled from burning wood and scorched flesh. The scent of blood followed—iron-sharp, unmistakable. The temple's main chamber had become a battlefield.

*Where is he?*

I saw not Val but Lucius, to my right. His sword flashed. His face was set hard.

The Fellglow Blade snapped to life in my hand.

The hum of it crawled up my arm in a song of light and heat and blood. It pulsed with each heartbeat.

As if it, too, was waking.

As if it remembered me.

I tucked the Heart into the pouch on my belt and moved.

No armor. No time. I threw myself into the melee.

Steel clashed around me. I ducked under a swing, drove my blade into a man's gut. Another slashed across my left arm—deep. I gritted my teeth and pressed forward. Blood ran hot down to my fingers.

I didn't stop.

A glancing blow split my cheek. My vision blurred red. I kept going.

Soldiers in blue cloaks fought beside me, shielding where they could. But there was no room to fight clean.

A strike caught my ribs.

Another to the leg.

I faltered but stayed upright.

I reached for a shield spell.

Nothing.

Again—nothing.

The mana kept slipping through my fingers like water through cracked stone. I couldn't waste it.

Lucius saw me then. His eyes flared in alarm. He charged, cutting down two Vinculatores before reaching me. He shoved me down just as a blade carved air where my head had been.

He grabbed the collar of my tunic, dragged me behind a pillar. "The fuck are you doing?"

"Looking for Val. What happened?" I rasped.

"Later," he said, breathless. "Val's near the entrance. Fighting Varro, last I saw."

The blood in my veins froze.

*No.*

*No, no, no.*

*Not this.*

The dream. The vision.

It wasn't a warning.

It was happening.

He swore he'd stay.

He always kept his word.

He was out there. Dying.

Because I wasn't strong enough.

Because I wasn't fast enough.

Because he was trying to protect me.

I turned to run, then stopped.

The orb. The Heart.

I took it from my pouch. Pressed it into Lucius's hand. "Take this."

He looked down. "What is it?"

"The Heart of Aelan. And downstairs—Caedmon's writings. Black tome. Gilded pages. Center pedestal. If I don't come back, get them out. Both of them. Someone has to."

His eyes met mine. He understood.

"Protect them with your life," I said.

"I will," he promised, tucking it away. "You stay alive."

I nodded, though I wasn't sure I'd be able to keep my word.

My shoulder throbbed. My arm was useless. Blood trickled down my face. My leg screamed with every step.

But I didn't stop.

I forced myself back into the fray. Limping. Bloodied.

Unrelenting.

Val was ahead.

And I would not be too late.

# CHAPTER ONE HUNDRED TWENTY
*The Only Thing*

Rudamos 88, 1231
*Valerius*

And then I saw her.

Blood-streaked, sword glowing in her grip.

Radiant.

Fierce.

Unyielding.

Gods-touched and as achingly beautiful as the first time I ever laid eyes on her.

My heart surged at the sight of her wrists.

Bare. Unshackled.

Free.

Fighting her way to me.

Her gaze met mine.

Then shifted.

To Varro.

She was furious.

*If she's angry,* I thought, *she'll be fine.*

A faint smile tugged at my lips.

"What are you smiling at?" Varro snarled, his voice catching on the edge of unease.

My chest shook with a laugh—thin, ragged, wet with blood.

I staggered, leaning hard against my sword. The steel barely held me upright.

Every heartbeat felt further away.

Still, I laughed.

"What the fuck are you laughing at?" he snapped again.

I didn't answer at once. The breath caught in my chest like a blade. When I finally spoke, it scraped out low and raw.

"You're… going to wish… I'd killed you."

He shoved me.

I hit the floor hard, flat on my back.

There was no pain anymore. No fear.

Just silence.

Weightlessness.

The hush before the dark.

I turned my head. And I found her again.

Aleaia.

Luce mea.

Still fighting through the melee to reach me.

I smiled. I hadn't broken my vow.

Everything I was—every breath, every scar, every drop of blood—I spent it all to keep her safe.

And I would spend it again.

Gladly.

Without hesitation.

Without regret.

She was the only thing I'd ever truly believed in.

My beginning and my end.

The sword I chose.

The war I would never forsake.

*I love you.*

*Gods, I love you.*

*Fiercely.*

*Foolishly.*

*With all the reverence of a man who had no right to want more.*

*Like a man who touched starlight once—and would bleed himself dry just to hold the glow it left behind.*

*Like a man who knew the light was never his—yet gave everything to follow it.*

*You were always the reason.*

*From the first breath to the last.*

*The only thing I ever got right.*

Her figure blurred at the edges.

Light flared around her, silver and gold.

Vespera's hands brushed mine.

Gentle. Cold.

And in that last breath, all I could think was…

She was worth it.

# CHAPTER ONE HUNDRED TWENTY ONE

## *The Last Benediction*

*"Let the spark that once knew love rise again to the world that waits."*
—The Rite of the Last Benediction

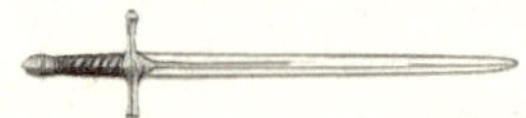

Rudamos 88, 1231
*Aleaia*

The blood pooled beneath him—spreading too wide, too far. My breath caught. Somewhere beneath the pain, beneath the bone-deep ache of everything I'd already lost, I knew—

*I have to save him.*

It beat inside me like a war drum.

I'd whispered it in dreams.

Screamed it.

Failed every time.

Pain bloomed behind my eyes, throbbing in rhythm with my heart. Blood filled my mouth, warm and metallic. Dripped from my temple, streaked my cheek. The scent of it—copper and ruin—was all I knew.

Every limb screamed. My fingers stuck to the hilt of my sword, tacky with dried blood.

Still, I fought.

One step.

Then another.

Then I saw the helm. Wolf-headed. Distinct.

*Varro.*

Standing over him like a carrion bird—sword raised, victorious.

*I have to save him.*

I raised my voice. "Varro!"

He turned.

Smiled between the cheek plates of his helm.

Turned back to Val.

His sword angled low—straight for the gap beneath the arm, where the plates parted.

*No. No no no—*

Val's hand twitched. Lifted. Reaching for me.

*Aelan, please, have mercy. Lithau, please—*

The blade drove in.

Blood surged. Dark and fast.

Val's mouth opened—not in a cry. Not in pain.

Just a sound. A gasp. Quiet. Shattered.

Crimson frothed between lips I had kissed.

His eyes never left mine.

Not until Vespera came.

And took him.

The noise of battle vanished. No steel. No screams. Only silence. Only my heart, breaking with each beat.

My sword hung limp at my side.

*I'm too late.*

The words etched themselves into the softest part of me.

*Too late.*

*Always too late.*

Tears fell. Hot. Unstoppable. I couldn't look away. Not even when Varro stepped toward me. "Ah, the reward I'll get for the head of the heretic princess herself."

I looked up.

Met his eyes.

There was no madness there.

Just rot. Ancient. Cultivated.

He was no man, but a monster.

My voice was stone. Splintered. Raw. "You killed him."

"Indeed I did," he said with a mock bow. "And it was far easier than I expected."

"He was the best of us," I ground out, breath quickening. "And you killed him."

"Spare me your grief." He raised his sword. "Put up a fight or don't. Either way, you die today, too."

I raised my blade just in time.

Instinct. Not thought.

Steel clashed—a brutal, jarring crash that shook my teeth. My feet slid on the blood-slick floor.

No footing. No give.

Then—

The memory hit.

*Val's voice.*

*"When you smile… it's like starlight. Bright. Beautiful."*

Varro crashed into me. Drove me down.

The floor slammed into my back. My lungs seized. Pain lit everywhere like fire through nerves.

I twisted. Rolled.

Found my feet.

I didn't think. Didn't plan.

And lunged with a cry.

I was rage.

I was grief.

I was every broken thing I'd ever tried to bury.

*"I love you, Aleaia. I love you because you never bow to the world. Because you fight for everyone but yourself. Because you're fierce, and reckless, and full of heart... Because you're everything I was too proud to reach for."*

His blade slammed across my temple. Flat edge. Heavy. White burst behind my eyes.

I dropped to one knee. Caught myself. Spat blood.

*Breathe. In. Out.*

If I stopped now, he died for nothing.

"Heard you were skilled with a blade," Varro sneered. "Suppose I heard wrong."

*"I'll be the shield that does not falter, the blade that does not bend. I'll give my life for you."*

The words broke something in me.

Or maybe they forged it.

Stronger.

Harder.

Sharper.

I rose.

I didn't remember moving.

I just did.

Mana surged—low, unstable—but I seized it. Drew it in like breath—

Varro raised his blade again.

*"I'll still thank the gods I ever got to love you at all."*

The shield bloomed from my hand without hesitation—not fire, but light. Gold and blinding. Sunlight pulled into form. A veil made iron by wrath.

His blade struck it with a thunderous crack.

The shield burst—because I let it.

The force hurled Varro backward. He slammed to the ground with a shout, his sword clattering from his grip. He clutched his wrist as he scrambled to his feet.

With a flick of my wrist, I cast the tether, the grip of it, sinking deep into his wellspring.

I tore it from him.

Lit the Fellglow Blade with it.

His body jerked. His limbs stiffened.

In two steps, I was on him.

My sword swept up.

I didn't strike with the edge but the pommel into his face.

Didn't feel it. Not the crack. Not the blood. Not the shudder of impact up my arm.

Nothing.

I felt nothing.

"Kneel," I growled.

He swayed—dazed.

So I struck again.

Harder.

And commanded him—

"I said *kneel*!"

He dropped. Both knees. Blood slicking his jaw.

Eyes wide.

Lips curled.

Not pain—fear.

I'd always thought rage burned hot.

But this wasn't fire.

This was ice.

Glacial. Absolute.

I reached out. Took his face in my hand.

"Do you remember the name he gave me, *Wolf of Calesia*?" I growled.

I remembered the words on Val's lips—

*"Dame Wolfsbane. Shield of Aeldunon. Sounds intimidating... You're simply Aleaia to me."*

"It irritated your master to no end." My fingers locked around the hilt of the Fellglow Blade like iron.

His eyes widened.

Mana surged in me—clean, bound, mine.

Still tethered to him, I willed him to burn.

No spell. No invocation.

Just breath. Cold against the air.

Fire along the mana paths inside him.

Along that which tethered his rotten soul to his flesh.

It bloomed *inside* his armor. Inside him.

Slow. Intentional. Spreading like vengeance.

His skin blistered.

He screamed—but I didn't flinch.

The heat roared up, white-hot and soul-fed. It cracked through steel. Melted metal. Blackened flesh. The stink of him hit my nose, sharp and sulfurous.

He had taken everything.

So I took him.

Still, I watched, until he collapsed.

A ruin of slag and char. Hissing. Smoking. Unmade.

Only then did I lower my hand.

My fingers trembled. I couldn't feel them.

My legs barely held me.

My nose bled. I felt the trickle slide over my lips, down my chin.

I was hollowed out. Drained—not just of mana, but of rage. Of fight. Of everything that had kept me upright.

I turned.

Shuffled to where he lay.

*Val.*

I fell to my knees beside him. The marble was slick with his blood. It soaked through my trousers, still warm.

I looked down at him.

There was nothing left to say.

Just silence.

And memory.

*"You're a storm. And I'd rather be struck by lightning than spend my life watching from a distance."*

He couldn't be gone.

Not him.

Not the man who walked through fire for me.

Who kissed me as if I were sacred.

Who held me as more than a weapon.

"Val." My voice cracked. "Vedrānos, wake up."

Nothing.

Maybe he couldn't hear me.

With shaking hands, I reached for his helmet.

Cradled his head as I pulled it free, tossed it aside.

His lips were parted. Blood there, dried where it had trickled from the corner.

His eyes—gods, his eyes—stared past me. Open. Empty.

No blink.

I bent closer.

"Val, please…" I reached for his cheek, a soft touch of my palm. "Please don't leave me. Not now. Not after everything."

I leaned over him, tried to will warmth into his skin. Wiped the blood from his mouth with my sleeve. Cradled his face. Pressed a kiss to his temple.

Then I laid my ear against his chest.

Listened.

Nothing.

No beat. No rhythm. No life.

Maybe I couldn't hear it because of the breastplate.

I tried to tether. Reached for him with every thread of mana I had left. But there was nothing.

No whisper. No trace.

Gone.

Well and truly.

"He's…" My throat locked. "He's dead."

Maybe I'd hit my head. Maybe I was dreaming again.

I looked around. Waiting for someone to tell me I was wrong. That he was just wounded or stunned.

"Lucius—" My voice shattered as I turned. "Lucius, what do I do?"

He knelt beside me. Pale. Stricken.

His arms came around me.

Real.

No dream.

"Aleaia…" His voice cracked. "I don't know. I don't know."

I shoved him off. "Where is Mariana? She can fix this. She *can fix him!"*

Lucius caught me again. His grip on my arms was firm, but he was trembling too. "She can't… she can't heal death."

Soft. Final. Like it hurt him to say it.

"He's gone, Aleaia." The word broke in his mouth. "He's gone."

Mariana knelt beside us, her face streaked with tears. Her hands moved over Val with healer's instinct—searching for life.

There was none.

She set a hand on my arm.

"Don't say it," I whispered. "Please, don't say it."

"He's right, Aleaia," Mariana said, barely audible. "I'm so sorry."

I collapsed onto Val's chest. Arms locking around him like I could will his soul back into his body.

I buried my face in his neck—and sobbed.

Raw. Primal. Ragged. Ripped out from the hollow he left behind.

From the pit of me.

From every wound I hadn't had time to bleed for.

Every promise we'd made. Every touch I'd never feel again.

I didn't care who heard.

Let them hear.

Let it break me.

Mariana's hand settled lightly on my back.

Her voice sounded far away as she talked to someone else. "… mad with grief… out of here."

I thought I might die from the pain.

And in that moment, I didn't care if I did.

Because if he was gone…

Then who was I?

*"Because you let me love you as myself. Because you're chaotic and wild, and you make me feel freer for it. I love you, Aleaia."*

*No.*

*No, no, no, no—*

"Gods…" I gasped. "The pain—I can't—bear it—I can't—"

My head bowed low. I lifted his hand, limp and bloodstained, and brought it to my mouth. I kissed his fingers. The knuckles. The back of his hand.

"Val…" I kissed his brow next. The spot between his eyes. His cheek. My breath stuttered. "I can't do this without you."

I pressed my forehead to his and closed my eyes, willing him back with every fragment of magic and memory I had left.

"You held my hand," I whispered. "You begged me to stay once. So I'm begging you now. Don't leave me in the dark."

No answer.

No breath.

"I love you," I whispered, cradling his face in my hands. "So gods-damned much I can't breathe without you."

I bent close, lips to his ear, my voice raw and shaking. "Please, Val. Come back. Please, please come back. I don't know how to do this without you."

Still nothing.

No flicker of breath. No warmth in his skin. No tether to reach for.

I kissed his palm. Pressed it to my cheek like he might remember the shape of me.

And when I had nothing left, I laid my hand against his cheek—holding his face to mine—and I broke, sobbing in gasping, heaving bursts that wouldn't stop. That couldn't. My shoulders shook and my lungs burned with it, but I didn't care.

I stayed there, clinging to his stillness, pouring every breath I had into the hollow where he should have been.

Until—

A voice.

Not mine. Not anyone's I knew.

*Calm, daughter. I will help you, that you might help the world.*

My throat burned.

"What do I..." I tried to swallow the splinters. "What do I do?"

I'd do anything. Anything it took.

*Take the orb from your guardsman.*

I turned, wild and breathless.

"Lucius," I rasped. "Give me—"

He froze.

"Give me the orb."

I saw the fear in his eyes—not of me, but of what I was about to do.

Still, his hand went to his belt. He reached inside the pouch.

And stepped forward to place the Heart of Aelan in my palm.

My trembling fingers closed around it.

It pulsed once. Bright.

And then—

*Now, repeat these words...*

And I did.

"Lithau, Maker of Breath and Bone, Flame of the First Dawn,
Mother of the Veil,
the blood has fallen. The price has been paid. The heir remains.

By the line of Aelan, by the sacrifice freely given,
Across shadow, across silence, across death,
I call him back.

Not by mercy. Not by theft. But by right.
Let the soul who chose me return to the flesh that bore his vow.
Let the spark that once knew love rise again to the world that waits.

So speaks your daughter.
So commands the blood of gods.
So demands the line of Aelan."

Warmth didn't flood me then.

It claimed me, pouring into every fracture.

Something ancient moved beneath my skin.

The tears stopped.

My spine straightened.
And my mouth opened.
Not mine anymore.
The voice that came was older. Deeper. Divine.
I looked at Lucius.
And said,
"Run."

# EPILOGUE
## *The Forged Heart*

Dēwamos 1, 1231
*Aleaia*

"'Fear not, dear child,' she softly spake,
Her tone as embers burning bright,
'For in my flames, the old is shed,
And from ash doth spring new light.'

Isor watched in silent wonder,
As Sulia transformed anew,
A phoenix rose, with nary a flaw,
From despair to light, she grew.

His heart was filled with hope's embrace,
His spirit raised by her bright flame,
He saw the truth within his heart,
That life reborn is ne'er the same."

My voice trailed off with the final verse. The words hung in the still air, weightless as a raven's wing.

I closed the book and laid it face-down on the table beside me, marking the page. Then I stood with a quiet groan, stretching legs folded too long.

My body ached from stillness. My soul from everything else.

I hadn't left his side since we made landfall on Signy.

Time blurred into tears and heartbeats and the sound of his breathing.

One memory stayed sharp, no matter how I tried to blunt it—the moment he died. It came to me every time I closed my eyes, vivid and cruel. I remembered the shade of his blood, the way he lay still and silent.

Like wind that suddenly stopped, all that followed was too still.

But everything after—Varro's face, my own scream, the fire—blurred. Like it had never belonged to me at all.

The others didn't speak of it. Not around me. They stepped gently through the space I left open, as if afraid to touch anything too heavy.

As if they, too, would be touched by Astralis if they touched me.

Maybe they were right.

I told Mariana first. Because she stayed. Because she saw.

But even she deferred to Cait.

Cait, who had taken a bolt meant for me.

Who had stood when others fled.

Who understood things I didn't know how to ask.

"The memory will return in pieces," she said softly. "Or it may not. The mind protects itself from what it cannot survive."

That made sense. Even if it didn't help.

What I knew came from Mariana.

"I've never seen anyone break like that," she whispered, tears in her eyes. "You collapsed. And then… you changed. You asked Lucius for the Heart of Aelan, and when you spoke, it wasn't your voice. You told us to run. Lucius grabbed Cait. Grabbed me. We ran. I looked back once. I saw the light."

A cord, she said, stretching from one Vinculatore to another, anchored into the earth. The entire island shimmered under that web of light. And then it began to die.

Everything on that island—every person, every animal, every tree and vine and blade of grass—I had tethered to me. And drawn.

Took all of the light and the life and the mana into myself.

And when they returned to the temple for me—

Val lived again.

The Heart of Aelan was gone.

I woke on the island, beside him.

On a bed that felt like a funeral bier.

Val hadn't stirred in the two days since.

Others had. They hid me away.

Afraid for me. Or of me. Or both.

And the gods said nothing.

Aelan had worn me like a cloak and cast me off, leaving only memories and ache.

Was I supposed to call this mercy?

Val's chest rose and fell. His body was warm. But he didn't wake. Cait and Mariana did what they could, but there was no answer to give no matter how many times I asked.

So I waited.

And I would wait—until the end of days, or until Val woke.

I washed his face. Held his hand until the bones beneath felt familiar again. Until my grief forgot how to scream and only whispered.

"Today is the first day of the summer festival," I told him. My voice sounded smaller than I meant it to. "The celebration starts at dusk. Firewalks, prayers, a toast to Sulia. You'd like the wine. I ordered three casks just for us."

If he were awake, he'd have said, "With what money, luce mea?"

I heard it so clearly, I laughed softly. "There has to be some advantage to being the Daughter of Aelan."

I realized I had answered nothing. Felt my cheeks warm. Reached behind his head to fluff the pillow.

"I'd walk barefoot across a thousand coals if it meant waking you."

I stood back and looked at him.

Peaceful. Too peaceful.

What had I brought back?

He looked like Val. He breathed like Val. But I had seen him die. And I did not know what the gods require in exchange.

There were no legends for this. No songs. No instructions passed down through the line of queens who died too soon.

Only silence.

I sat again. Reached for him. Ran my fingers through his hair, down his jaw. His stubble rasped against my palm, anchoring me.

*He's here. He's here. He has to be.*

But the thought didn't hold.

*If I'd only reached him in time.*

*If I'd only moved faster.*

I pulled my hand back.

The tears came fast.

First, quiet.

Then, not.

I bent into my hands and wept—ugly, broken, without grace or restraint.

I wasn't a warrior.

Or a queen.

I wasn't the daughter of anyone.

Just a woman who had lost her heart.

*If this was what it meant to carry a god inside me, perhaps I should have let her burn me hollow.*

The thought lanced through me.

And stayed.

I forced it back under its shroud. Clung to what was left.

His voice. His words. The sound of him in the dark.

He'd have said, "Don't cry, amor mea. I'm here. I promised I'd stay. Just a few steps away."

I raised my head. "I can't help it. You know I cry about everything."

I wiped my face with the back of my sleeve, then leaned in close, brushing my fingers once more across his brow.

"I love you," I whispered. "Gods, I love you so much it's killing me. It's tearing me apart from the inside—like there's nothing left under my skin but want and ash and the echo of your voice. I keep reaching for you in the dark like you might still be there, like maybe if I beg loud enough, if I break enough, you'll open your eyes."

My throat closed. I pressed my forehead to his, shaking.

"I'd give anything." My voice shook. "I'd trade every breath I've got left. I'd dig my own heart out if it meant putting it in your chest. If you needed my soul to wake, I'd lay it down without question. That's how I love you. That's what you are to me."

I rested my head on his chest.

Touched my mana to his, for the first time since we arrived.

This time it answered.

Maybe that would help.

So I stayed where I was.

Let myself be his light.

And breathed.

*Valerius*

I had walked the cobbled road to Letia a thousand times. And yet this time, something felt wrong.

The sky hung too still—sun caught behind clouds that didn't drift. The air was warm and unmoving. Soundless. Not peaceful. Empty.

I carried nothing but the sense that I'd come for a reason I couldn't name.

Where had I been, before?

I searched for the answer, but it slipped away like breath in cold air. Gone before I could grasp it.

Ahead, the villa came into view—whitewashed stone, red-tiled roof, the old fig tree outside the kitchen window. The path had been swept clean.

And they were waiting for me.

Rasmus and Davena.

Smiling.

Davena's hair was pinned up like always. Rasmus waved. The sight of them unraveled something inside me, and yet, I hadn't remembered their faces until I saw them.

A memory cut through the fog like broken glass.

They'd died.

For me.

And I had run.

I felt nothing.

"Rasmus," I asked, my voice dull in my own ears, "what is this place?"

"It's home," he said, smiling as if that answered everything. "Welcome."

Davena stepped forward and took my hands. Her touch was warm. Real.

"You have a visitor on the terrace," she said. "Best not to keep her waiting."

"I won't," I said, though I felt strange. Weightless. Untethered.

I moved through the halls of my childhood home. The doors I'd slammed as a boy. The hearth where Davena used to sing while the bread baked. All of it familiar but unreal.

The terrace should have opened over the sea.

It didn't.

Instead, I stepped into stars.

I pressed my hands to the marble railing. I forgot how to breathe.

Clouds and constellations stretched in every direction—silver, violet, green, blue. A thousand swirling ribbons of light shimmered like water caught in wind.

It was the most beautiful thing I'd ever seen.

No. That wasn't quite right.

Second most beautiful.

I tried to recall the first—it was her. I couldn't find her face.

I wanted to tell her.

The ache bloomed, urgent and sudden.

I couldn't remember her name. But I remembered *her.*

*Lavender.*

*Sunlight.*

*The silver of her eyes.*

*The way her laugh made the world tilt toward warmth.*

*Where is she?*

Then a voice came from behind me. Soft. Steady. "My beautiful boy."

I turned.

She stood just inside the archway. Pale hair. Green eyes. A face I knew only from a portrait. But that version had never done her justice.

"Mother?"

The word splintered something in my chest.

"I missed you," I said. "But how, when I never knew you?"

She opened her arms.

I walked into them like I had always meant to.

And I wept.

Openly. Without shame.

Tears I hadn't known I carried.

"There you are, my wonderful boy," she whispered. "I have always been with you, as I shall always be."

I closed my eyes.

"I can stay with you?"

"No, my darling," she said gently. Her hand moved along my back, light and sure. "This is Aetheria. You will come again, but not yet. There is still work for you in the mortal realm."

And before I could speak, the sky turned.

The warmth shifted.

And I was gone.

I heard the sea before I opened my eyes.

Waves. Slow. Heavy. Like the breath of something ancient.

The cry of seabirds was too loud. Each call echoed through me like a blade dragged over stone.

And somewhere past an open window, the hum of a town. Wheels turning. Wood creaking. Voices layered in dozens of threads I could almost—but not quite—untangle.

The scents came with weight. Bread baking. Sage. Rosemary.

Sunlight touched my face. And it burned.

Not with heat. With presence.

It felt alive, like the light itself knew I didn't belong here anymore. But it didn't feel real.

I kept still. My body felt too heavy. Every breath filled me wrong. Like wearing someone else's skin, or having taken mine back through a door that shouldn't have opened.

Memory, maybe. Grief. My throat tightened.

When I finally forced my eyes open, the room swam. Too bright. Too vivid.

Gray stone. Pale linen. A table in the corner scattered with herbs, bandages, books. I couldn't tell if I was dreaming, or remembering, or becoming again.

Then I saw her.

Luce mea.

And everything else fell away.

She lay asleep against me, her head on my chest, her arm draped across my ribs like she had refused to let go.

A book rested face-down at her side. The spine was worn. Pages soft with use.

*The Song of the Stars.*

I remembered the olive tree. The hush of summer afternoons. Her voice, low and lilting, weaving through verse like it was made for her mouth.

Her lashes were still damp. Eyes swollen. Nose red.

She'd been crying. And I knew—gods, I knew—it had been for me.

*I'm sorry to have hurt you. Never again.*

I moved slowly, like one wrong breath might shatter everything. My fingers found her hair—dark, matted in one place from sleep—and brushed it aside.

A cut on her cheek. Healing, but deep.

The sight of it sparked something in my chest. Protective. Possessive.

Then the memories hit like a wave breaking.

*The temple. Varro. The heat. The pain.*

*Her—radiant—walking through fire and ruin to reach me.*

*My death.*

I jerked the sheet down.

No wound. Just scars.

I was whole. Clean.

Wrong.

*Oh, Aleaia, what have you done?*

I let the sheet fall.

My breath came faster—not panic. Awe.

I had died. And she had brought me back.

But how? That kind of magic—that kind of love—didn't belong to mortals.

Not even in myth. Not even in the old songs.

Not even Aelan had—

No.

That wasn't true. She had brought Caedmon back.

But she was a goddess.

And Aleaia…

She was her descendant.

I looked at her again.

Her face was bruised. Cut. A split at her lip.

None of it had been healed.

She refused. She'd let it stay. Every wound. Every mark.

Punishing herself.

I didn't even think. My hand rose to her cheek. A golden glow sparked where my fingers met her skin, and the bruises vanished.

I stared at my hand. At the afterglow.

Not just power.

Something sacred.

Something I didn't understand.

Something that recognized her.

Recognized me, too.

I didn't know what I was anymore.

But I knew *who* I was.

My voice cracked as I whispered—raw, thick with wonder and fear and devotion.

"Aleaia, luce mea… please wake up."

# Pronunciation guide

| Name or Term | Pronunciation |
|---|---|
| Aelan | AY-lahn |
| Aeldunon | AYL-doo-non |
| Aeltyria | AYL-teer-ee-uh |
| Aetheria | ay-THEER-ee-uh |
| Alcaeus | al-KAY-us |
| Aleaia | ah-LEE-ah |
| Alvareti | al-vah-RAY-tee |
| Aneirin | ah-NYE-rin |
| Anvallus | ahn-VAH-lus |
| Ardhmor | ARDH-more |
| Asena | ah-SEE-nah |
| Astralis | uh-STRAH-lis |
| Attius | AH-tee-us |
| Avani | ah-VAH-nee |
| Avitum | ah-VEE-tum |
| Cadoc | KAY-doc |
| Caedmon | KAYD-mon |
| Caerlan | KARE-lahn |
| Caitriona | kah-TREE-nah |
| Caius | KYE-us |
| Calesia | cah-LEE-see-ah |
| Cassius | KASH-ee-us |
| Catan Row | KAH-tan row |
| Claudius | CLAW-dee-us |
| Cortueca | cor-TOO-eh-kah |
| Danwyn | DAN-win |
| Dēwamos | DAY-wah-mos |
| Dieter | DEE-ter |
| Drakaroth | DRAH-kah-roth |

| Name or Term | Pronunciation |
|---|---|
| Eavan | AY-vahn |
| Eira | AY-rah |
| Elisedd | EL-ih-sed |
| Emrys | EM-riss |
| Galdorin | gal-DORE-in |
| galvarium | gal-VAIR-ee-um |
| Gavius | GAY-vee-us |
| Gormlaith | GORM-lah |
| Inveraria | in-ver-AIR-ee-ah |
| Jurian | JUR-ee-an |
| Letia | LET-ee-ah |
| Lhannor | LAN-nor |
| Liora | lee-OR-ah |
| Lithau | LITH-ow |
| luce mea | LOO-chay MAY-ah |
| Lucius | LOO-see-us |
| mana | MAH-nah |
| Mariana | mah-ree-AH-nah |
| Melicia | meh-LEE-see-ah |
| Melicia | meh-LEE-see-ah |
| Mētanos | MAY-tah-nos |
| Orlaith | OR-lah |
| Pulcher | PULL-ker |
| Quiestra | kwee-ES-trah |
| Rhaelaith | RAY-lah |
| Riogal | REE-oh-gahl |
| Rudamos | ROO-dah-mos |
| Succamos | SOO-kah-mos |
| Sulia | SOO-lee-ah |
| Tauranis | tor-AH-nis |

| Name or Term | Pronunciation |
|---|---|
| Triarius | try-AIR-ee-us |
| Valerion | vah-LEER-ee-on |
| Valerius | vah-LEER-ee-us |
| Varro | VAH-roh |
| Vedrānos | veh-DRAH-nos |
| Velwyth | VELL-with |
| Vespera | VES-per-ah |
| Vinculatores | vin-coo-lah-TOR-ess |

# Author's Note

Thank you for reading The Forged Heart. Aleaia and Val's story continues in The Eternal Knight, the next book in the Veridion Saga.

If you enjoyed this book, I would be grateful if you shared your thoughts in a review on Goodreads or wherever you read. Reviews help other readers discover stories like this one.

You can follow me online for news, new releases, and updates from the world of Veridion:

Instagram: @hrvitale
TikTok: @h.r.vitale
Facebook: Author H. R. Vitale
Website: hrvitale.com

## About the Author

H. R. Vitale writes epic fantasy about fierce heroines, dangerous magic, and vows that refuse to break, even across death.

She lives with her family on the East Coast of the United States.

www.ingramcontent.com/pod-product-compliance
Lightning Source LLC
LaVergne TN
LVHW090543110826
845146LV00001B/5

* 9 7 9 8 9 9 5 1 1 4 0 0 0 *